PRAISE FOR

# THE
# ROBOTS
# OF
# GOTHAM

"Debut author McAulty, an expert in machine language learning, extrapolates a scary AI-overrun 2083 that's only a few steps removed from today's reality. This massive and impressive novel is set in an America that outlawed the development of artificial intelligence and quickly lost a short and bitter war against robot-led fascist countries ... McAulty maintains breathless momentum throughout. Readers will hope for more tales of this sinister future and eagerly pick up on hints that Barry and his companions may continue their exploits."

— *PUBLISHERS WEEKLY*, STARRED REVIEW

"*The Robots of Gotham* is a thrilling ride through a nuanced, post-singularity world populated by a frightening and fascinating array of smart machines. Read this and you'll come to the same conclusion I did: the world belongs to robots; we're just living in it."

— DANIEL H. WILSON, BEST-SELLING AUTHOR OF
*ROBOPOCALYPSE* AND *THE CLOCKWORK DYNASTY*

"This debut novel beautifully combines a post-apocalyptic man-versus-machine conflict and a medical thriller. The world is immersive and detailed, the characters have depth, the writing is assured, the plotting intelligent, and the pacing about perfect. McAulty's take on how AI might evolve gives the premise a unique twist. The story is action-packed, starting with a boom (literally) and driving you along from one crisis to the next. The action rarely lets up, yet it never becomes tiresome ... This is thrilling, epic SF."

— *BOOKLIST*, STARRED REVIEW

"The whole story is a thrilling action flick in book form, with cool robots and conspiracies and things blowing up. Read it while walking in slow-motion away from an explosion."

— *REVOLUTIONSF*

"An epic novel of man vs. machine, full of action, political intrigue, and unexpected twists. Todd McAulty has given us a fresh, compelling take on life during a robot apocalypse."

— JEFF ABBOTT, *NEW YORK TIMES* BEST-SELLING
AUTHOR OF *BLAME*

"McAulty combines believable fears of artificial intelligence running amok with a dark future America in this thrilling debut."

— *KIRKUS REVIEWS*

"Todd McAulty has done the incredible. Delivered a rich and credible near-future world, where Thought Machines control, well, almost everything (and are themselves astonishingly diverse and cool), and used all this to create the most human SF story I've read in a very long time. I love everything about *The Robots of Gotham*. I want more, McAulty. MORE!"

— JULIE E. CZERNEDA, AUTHOR OF
*THE CLAN CHRONICLES*

"A heavy tale of a terrifying future, with incredibly detailed world-building and covert missions that will have you holding your breath in anticipation."

— *GEEKS OF DOOM*

"*The Robots of Gotham* is a fast-paced, engaging read [and] a thrilling ride, one that sends a hopeful message about the future of humanity."

— *THE VERGE*

"SF fans rejoice! Todd McAulty's debut novel is a massive, fast-paced, action-packed epic . . . with robots! . . . Even more than the fascinating and fully realized world it presents, what makes *The Robots of Gotham* such a great ride is its sheer narrative drive. Every page has the fierce readability of early Neal Stephenson, which is as high praise as it gets."

— *TORONTO STAR*

"Todd McAulty has imagined a fascinating geopolitical future, filled it with some very cool technology, and thrown in healthy helpings of intrigue and action. The result is a page-turner that kept me riveted from the opening lines to the final chapter. Highly recommended!"

— DAVID B. COE, AUTHOR OF
*THE CASE FILES OF JUSTIS FEARSSON* SERIES

"When the robot apocalypse comes, I hope it's this much fun. Like *The Martian* and *Ready Player One*, *The Robots of Gotham* is set in a high-tech near future where something has gone terribly wrong, and it's navigated by a hero who's quirky, resourceful, and as likable as they come. Read it for the rock'em-sock'em-robot action — read it for the deft world-building with its detailed taxonomy of intelligent machines — read it for the sobering parallels to modern-day issues and threats. Or just read it because it's a helluva good ride."

— SHARON SHINN, EDITOR OF
THE *ELEMENTAL BLESSINGS* SERIES

"Readers who enjoyed the complex robot-human relationships within *Robopocalypse* and the investigations in *World War Z* about how institutions function (or don't) in the face of [a] species-changing event will happily sink their teeth into *The Robots of Gotham*."

— *AMAZON BOOK REVIEW*

"*The Robots of Gotham* is a crackling good adventure stuffed with cool action sequences. It also features serious and intriguing speculation about the potential of artificial intelligence, for good and bad. And it's an engaging read, with absorbing characters and, of course, lots and lots of nifty robots."

— RICH HORTON, EDITOR OF *THE YEAR'S BEST
SCIENCE FICTION & FANTASY*

"Adventure, mystery, action, sinister intrigue, clever heroics, and robots — what more do you need? I couldn't put it down."

— HOWARD ANDREW JONES, AUTHOR OF
*THE DESERT OF SOULS*

"A fast-moving adventure story set in the haunting cityscape of a near-future Chicago hollowed out by war. The headlong plot somehow includes enough breathing space to execute a thought experiment about the mingling of true AI and human cultures, and also vividly portray friendships that cross the boundaries of nation and even species. Handle with care: this is the sort of book that makes people SF addicts for life."

— JAMES ENGE, AUTHOR OF
*BLOOD OF AMBROSE* AND THE *TOURNAMENT OF SHADOWS* SERIES

"If Johnny 5 had a baby with the Terminator, the result would be *The Robots of Gotham*: a book that explores the consequences of world domination by our Robot Overlords. (And, lest we forget the badassiest of them, our Robot Overladies.) Drones, dinosaurs, and doggies—with a plague thrown in for good measure!—the barter is banter, and death is cheap. With man against machine, machine against machine, man against man, unlikely alliances must be forged across all species, rational or otherwise. For all its breakneck world-building, constant questing, and relentless wheeling and dealing, *The Robots of Gotham* is deceptively deep-hearted: a novel about, of all things, friendship."

— C.S.E. COONEY, AUTHOR OF WORLD FANTASY
AWARD–WINNING *BONE SWANS: STORIES*

"Soldiers, spies, diplomats—and that's just the machines. Wait until you meet the wisecracking hero and his dog. Wildly inventive, outrageous fun!"

— KAY KENYON, AUTHOR OF *AT THE TABLE OF WOLVES*
AND *SERPENT IN THE HEATHER*

"*The Robots of Gotham* is my kind of summer reading. A big, fat, robot-y book that is so human. This guy will throw himself in front of robots to save the lives of his enemies. The best solution is the courageous one. It's so delicious."

— CARLOS HERNANDEZ, AUTHOR OF
*SAL AND GABI BREAK THE UNIVERSE*

TODD McAULTY

# THE ROBOTS OF GOTHAM

A JOHN JOSEPH ADAMS BOOK
Mariner Books
Houghton Mifflin Harcourt
Boston ▪ New York

*For my father.*
*Who taught me the skills I needed to be an engineer,*
*and the perseverance I needed to be a writer.*

———

First Mariner Books edition 2019
Copyright © 2018 by Todd McAulty

All rights reserved

For information about permission to reproduce selections
from this book, write to trade.permissions@hmhco.com or to
Permissions, Houghton Mifflin Harcourt Publishing Company,
3 Park Avenue, 19th Floor, New York, New York 10016.

hmhco.com

*Library of Congress Cataloging-in-Publication Data*
Names: McAulty, Todd, 1964– author.
Title: The robots of Gotham / Todd McAulty.
Description: Boston : John Joseph Adams/
Houghton Mifflin Harcourt, 2018.
Identifiers: LCCN 2017058169 (print) | LCCN 2017046212 (ebook) |
ISBN 9781328711021 (ebook) | ISBN 9781328711014 (hardcover) |
ISBN 9781328589835 (paperback)
Subjects: LCSH: Robots — Fiction. | BISAC: FICTION / Science Fiction /
Adventure. | FICTION / Science Fiction / General. |
GSAFD: Science fiction. | Dystopias.
Classification: LCC PS3613.C2725 (print) | LCC PS3613.C2725 R63 2018
(ebook) | DDC 813/.6–dc23
LC record available at https://lccn.loc.gov/2017058169

Book design by Chrissy Kurpeski
Map by Lucidity Information Design, LLC

Printed in the United States of America
DOC 10 9 8 7 6 5 4 3 2 1

# THE 2083 SOVEREIGNTY MATRIX

The 2083 Sovereignty Matrix lists the top thirty-two most influential national entities and their sovereign rulers or authorities (human and machine), sorted by GDP. The list is made available through the Rational Devices Registry, a division of the Helsinki Trustees, a nonprofit corporation. Additional information is supplied by the IMF Public Trust and the CIA World Factbook. This list is updated regularly.

| Nation | Government | Sovereign | Classification |
|---|---|---|---|
| China | Socialist Republic | President Zhiming Gao | Human (elected) |
| United States— Free Zone | Constitutional Republic | President Kennedy Schecter | Human (elected) |
| United States— Union of Post-American States | Corporate Syndicate | CEO Muhammad Coles | Human (appointed) |
| United States— Occupied States | Dominion (disputed) | Machine Cabal | Machine |
| India | Parliamentary Republic | President Ocean Virtue | Machine (elected) |
| Japan | Imperial Monarchy | Emperor Hirita | Machine (hereditary) |
| Brazil | Machine Dictatorship | President Quantum Journey | Machine |
| Germany | Parliamentary Republic | Chancellor Five Candle | Machine (elected) |
| Australia | Constitutional Monarchy | Prime Minister Judy MacMaster | Human (elected) |
| Indonesia | Monarchy | High Sentience Deep Fire | Machine (meritorious monarchy) |
| Iran | Islamic Republic | Supreme Leader Ahmad Khayyam | Human (elected) |
| Mexico | Constitutional Republic | President Angel Cisneros | Human (elected) |
| Canada | Parliamentary Republic | Prime Minister Distant Prime | Machine (elected) |
| Korea | Machine Oligarchy | Princeps Librio | Machine |

*(continued)*

| Nation | Government | Sovereign | Classification |
|---|---|---|---|
| France | Constitutional Republic | Le Cavalier | Machine (elected) |
| United Kingdom | Machine Parliament | Prime Minister Corpus | Machine |
| Italy | Machine Dictatorship | First Citizen Joquall | Machine |
| Russia | Machine Dictatorship | President Blue Society | Machine |
| Saudi Arabia | Monarchy | King Hasan | Human (hereditary rule) |
| Venezuela | Fascist Dictatorship | Machine Cabal | Machine |
| Argentina | Fascist Dictatorship | Machine Cabal | Machine |
| Pakistan | Constitutional Republic | President Argenta | Machine (elected) |
| Thailand | Military Junta | Machine Cabal | Machine |
| Greece | Puppet Regime | Unknown | Unknown (machine?) |
| Belgium | Machine Oligarchy | Arenberg Machine Cabal | Machine (elected) |
| Poland | Parliamentary Republic | President Karolina Kozlowski | Human (elected) |
| Spain | Constitutional Oligarchy | Tribunal (nine members) | Human & Machine |
| Kingdom of Manhattan | Machine Monarchy | Queen Sophia | Machine (hereditary) |
| Antarctica | Machine Oligarchy | The Antarctic Coalition | Machine |
| Romania | Military Junta | Accastan | Machine |
| Dominican Republic | Presidential Republic | The Burning Prefecture | Machine |
| Nightport | Aquatic Technocracy | Modo | Machine |

*This entry is made available under a Creative Commons license.
The Rational Devices Registry is a registered trademark of the Helsinki Trustees.
Funded by private donations and your generous support.*

# Eastern United States of America Showing Disputed Territories and Political Zones of Control, March 2083

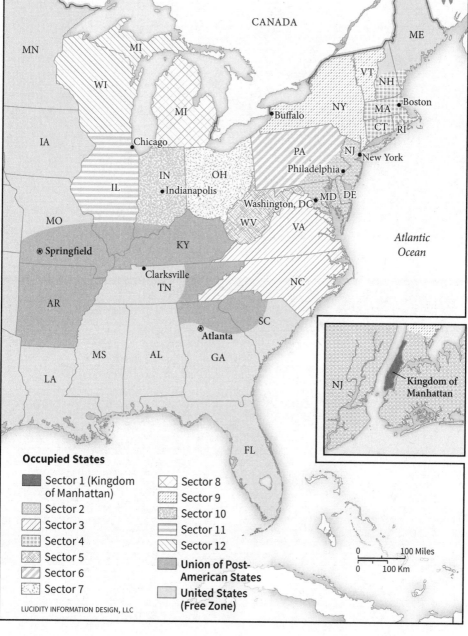

**Occupied States**

- Sector 1 (Kingdom of Manhattan)
- Sector 2
- Sector 3
- Sector 4
- Sector 5
- Sector 6
- Sector 7
- Sector 8
- Sector 9
- Sector 10
- Sector 11
- Sector 12
- Union of Post-American States
- United States (Free Zone)

LUCIDITY INFORMATION DESIGN, LLC

# THE
# ROBOTS
# OF
# GOTHAM

# I

Monday, March 8th, 2083
Posted 5:16 pm by Barry Simcoe

CanadaNET1 Encrypted, Sponsored by DARPGo Media.
*Your source for economical personal security.*

Sharing is set to PRIVATE
Comments are CLOSED

On my third day in Chicago, the Venezuelans evacuated my hotel.

It's like 7:00 a.m. and a soldier in an AGRT uniform comes around banging on every door on my floor. *Bam-bam-bam-bam!* Nothing gets your heart racing in the morning like a rifle butt hammering on your door.

We're all roused up and marched down the stairs to the street. There's this woman on my floor, in bare feet and bedclothes, and when this kid from the AGRT *bams* on her door, what does she do? She grabs her coffeemaker. We're hustling down thirty-two flights of stairs, and she's carrying this coffeemaker with the cord dangling around her feet. I'm still half-asleep and all I can think is, *Damn — should I have grabbed my waffle iron?*

Round about floor fifteen or sixteen she trips on the cord and smashes her elbow on the railing. So for the last fifteen flights of stairs I'm loaning her my arm and carrying this coffeemaker for her, with, I swear to God, half a pot of hot coffee still in it.

We get to the street and we're all milling around. I start to wonder if they evacuated only a few floors. Either that or this hotel is virtually empty, because there's maybe a hundred of us down here, total. Hardly enough to fill fifty floors of a lakeside hotel in downtown Chicago.

The staff is outside too, looking pretty put out. A slender young front desk clerk dressed in a thin pink chemise and not much else is hopping up and down a few feet to my right, trying desperately to stay warm.

There's maybe forty Venezuelan soldiers lined up in front of the hotel, and this guy in uniform yelling at us in Spanish. And there's this robot.

I've got no idea what's going on and I'm freezing to death, standing on Wacker Drive in early March in sweatpants and a T-shirt. I'm shaking my head at the coffee lady because I don't want to give her coffeepot back, since it's the only source of heat in about a hundred yards. This Venezuelan sergeant or captain or whatever is shouting and gesturing and beginning to turn purple, and I'm starting to think he's shouting at me, or maybe the coffeepot.

And I absolutely cannot take my eyes off this robot. It's magnificent. Three stories tall, maybe fourteen yards, Argentinean design. Kind of squat, like a giant gargoyle. Diesel powered, with steam and whatever venting out the back. It has some pretty slick telecom gear, a Nokia 3300 base station bolted on top and four whip antennas, all rigged for satellite. Some heavy ordnance as well: I can see an 80 mm Vulcan autocannon and at least two mounted antipersonnel weapons.

It's seen action, too. Plenty of scoring up front, and the Vulcan looks like it's recently been refitted. Someone who knew what they were doing spent some time painting the whole chassis with a bird motif, blue and white, and this close the effect is very impressive.

It's facing west on Wacker, poised like a bird, with one leg stiff and one half-raised, its great metal toes dangling a few feet above the pavement. Nothing that big should be able to stand so gracefully, like a raptor hunting prey.

Still, it seems like a lot of firepower just to impress a bunch of tourists. Martin, a data miner from London, spots me and shuffles a bit closer. He glances at the coffeepot. "Were we supposed to bring our appliances?" he whispers.

"I think it was optional," I say. "You know what the hell's going on?"

The shouting Venezuelan soldier moves closer, gesturing violently at the hotel behind us. Martin keeps his eyes fixed on the pavement until he passes. "Something about evacuating the hotel for our own safety," he says quietly.

I nod toward the captain. "Guy seems pretty pissed."

Martin listens to the shouting for a few more moments. Then a soldier dashes up, handing the captain a black tablet. I realize with a start that it's not a soldier at all — it's a slender robot, black-limbed and humanoid. I've seen a few robots with a small mobile chassis, but this is the first one I've seen in Chicago. The captain stops shouting long enough to look at the tablet.

"The hotel staff was supposed to wake us up, apparently," Martin translates for me. "The colonel had to send his soldiers to get us. He says next time, he'll let everyone die in their beds."

That doesn't sound good. "What's going to kill us in our beds, exactly?"

Martin shrugs, giving me a nervous glance. "Something bad."

I was about to reply, but the colonel had started moving again. Whatever he saw on that black tablet, he didn't like it. He's not shouting now, but his face is grim. He moves into the street, the slender robot at his side. He's speaking to the soldiers nearby and looking west down Wacker. He points, and two of the soldiers take off running toward a concrete barrier.

A skinny corporal whose uniform looks like it would blow off in a stiff breeze marches up to us and starts speaking. He's staring just over our heads, but presumably addressing us. He's much quieter than the colonel, and his words are so thickly accented it takes me a moment to realize he's speaking English.

He wants us to march south, down North Stetson Avenue. On the double, now now *now*. Martin and I get our feet moving, but too many others are still milling around, confused. I guess most of them can't hear the soldier — or can't understand him — and now that the colonel is gone, people have started breaking into groups. The buzz of conversation is getting louder.

Martin stops at my side. "We need to get these people moving," he says, concern in his voice.

Something happens then. Someone down the street shouts, and all the soldiers duck, heads swiveling to the west. The skinny corporal in front of us stops speaking, his arm hanging powerlessly in the air, still pointing south down North Stetson. His head turns west with the rest. His mouth is open, but he's making no sound.

Something streaks through the air, small and bright like a spark struck from a sword blade. It hits the towering robot and explodes, a hammer-punch of light and sound. One of the elegant whip antennas goes spinning off its chassis, skidding away down the street until it smashes into a parked Mercedes.

There's screaming then. Screaming and the sound of automatic weapons, returning fire to the west.

"Jesus *Christ*," Martin shouts, ducking down at my side.

All around us, people are frozen in place. The half-naked receptionist to my right is covering her mouth, her eyes wide. She reaches out to the guy next to her, tugging at his shirt. She starts to ask a question.

I seize her arm roughly, grab the shirtfront of the guy she's talking to. "*Move*, you idiots!" I shove them toward Stetson.

They start to run. A few feet away, four of the hotel staff are cowering on the curb. I pull the first one to her feet. "Go! Get moving! Martin — help me!"

Martin tears his eyes away from the street. He pushes himself to his feet, helps me shepherd people south, down Stetson Avenue.

The Venezuelan corporal breaks his paralysis at last. He's shouting and waving, pushing when necessary, herding the crowd south.

People start to move. But nearly half of the crowd has surged back up the steps toward the hotel. There's a panicked knot of guests trying to get through the glass doors.

There's another explosion behind me — loud and very close. I stumble, see the glass windows of the hotel vibrate violently. There's a flash of heat on the back of my head. *"Get away from the windows!"* I shout. "Stay out of the hotel — move! Down the street!"

Martin and I are working together. The corporal comes up behind us, trying to help. But it's not enough. There are still nearly forty guests clustered at the hotel entrance. Most aren't even moving — they're just hunkered down near the bushes to the side of the doors, or huddled together on the concrete steps. Already my throat is hoarse from shouting, but I keep at it. The next guy I grab shakes me off violently. "Don't *touch* me," he says defiantly.

Martin's not having any more luck. The people he's pleading with are sticking together, glued to the steps. Somehow, the young corporal manages to be even less effectual. He's standing in the center of the turnaround in front of the hotel, sweeping his arms in the air and waving toward Stetson Avenue like he's directing traffic. He looks terrified. No one is even looking at him.

We're barely fifteen feet from a huge bank of windows. One well-placed shell, and five hundred pounds of glass shrapnel is going to punch through the air, right where we're standing. I swear helplessly.

I glance into the street, trying to get a quick read on the situation. The Venezuelans are taking cover behind concrete barricades, returning fire to the west. A small team has set up what looks like a machine gun nest, but instead of a machine gun they're manning some kind of portable radio frequency antenna. They're aiming it like a weapon, and I wish them luck.

The robot is moving now, but it's none too steady on its feet. Also, it's on fire. A thin trail of black smoke snakes out behind it as it takes its first steps west. The Vulcan mounted on its side is silent, for which I'm grateful. The soldiers are letting it take the lead as they prepare to advance.

I spot the colonel, standing in the center of the whirlwind. He seems to be in command of everything, except maybe the robot. He's doing three things at once: yelling at a small platoon, probably to relinquish their useless position and move their asses west; listening to a report shouted to him from a tech running alongside; and barking into a black phone connected to another backpack.

The colonel turns his head toward us for an instant, seeming to take in the fiasco in front of the hotel at a glance. He turns to his left, says something to a squad of soldiers trailing him, and then returns to the phone. The soldiers start running our way.

I abandon the cluster of hotel guests I'm working on and hunker down next to Martin. "Hey," I say. "Something's up." He follows my gaze to the soldiers.

I'm not a fan of guns. But I have to admit, the sergeant leading the small squad knew how to use hers. She didn't bother saying a word—she just waded into the center of the unmoving civilians, pointed her rifle in the air, and fired a short burst. Then she reached down and grabbed a middle-aged bellboy and yanked him to his feet, pushing him toward Stetson.

That was all it took. All of a sudden everyone was moving, and in the right direction. The gunfire had badly unnerved many, and a young woman passing on my left was close to hysteria, but at least they were walking. As Martin and I followed the others south, I saw the sergeant send two soldiers into the lobby to retrieve those who'd managed to slip back inside. In a moment they were following us too.

"You lost your coffeepot," Martin observes. I'm surprised to discover he's right. I don't recall putting it down, but I'm no longer carrying it. I hope it found a good home.

Martin and I are pulling up the rear, just ahead of the lobby-dwellers who've been forcibly repatriated with the rest of us. We get away from the entrance to the hotel, and we're making our way south down Stetson Avenue. Sixty of us fill the street. The sergeant has her rifle on her shoulder, pointed skyward, as she strides briskly toward the front. Paradoxically, everyone is both following her and giving her a wide berth.

"Oh my God," says Martin.

I turn. Martin has stopped walking. He's looking back toward Wacker.

A Union mech has entered the battle from the west. It's sleek and spry, thirteen yards tall, sixty tons of deadly American metal. Where the Venezuelan machine moves like a bird, this thing is accelerating down the street like a freight train — fast and implacable on two heavy metal legs. I can see a constant halo of sparks around its torso as it absorbs small arms fire from the Venezuelans on the street, but it ignores them. Instead, it is focused on the robot.

As Martin and I watch in paralyzed fascination, it launches a trio of missiles — two at the robot in its path, and one at a concrete barricade sixty yards to our right.

A bunch of stuff happens then, all of it bright and all of it very loud.

Martin turns and starts running south. We collide and he nearly knocks me flat. He grabs me just before I hit the pavement, helping me regain my footing. "Come on!" he says.

"Yeah, yeah — go! Right behind you."

Martin nods and bolts, vanishing into the crowd. Everyone is running now, in full flight south.

My ears are ringing, but not so much that I can't hear the sudden crescendo of return fire, and more explosions. I'm standing, and it occurs to me that's a dumb, dumb idea. I flatten, palms on the pavement and elbows in the air like I'm doing push-ups, and watch what unfolds.

What unfolds is a knock-down, face-to-face slugfest between a Union mech and a heavily damaged Venezuelan robot; a battle of wills between an elite American pilot in a titanic war machine and a coldly calculating machine intelligence in a forty-ton armored carapace. I watch the whole thing from a front-row seat scarcely a hundred yards away, hypnotized.

Most of the battle happens too quickly for me to follow. Both units are exchanging fire, mostly small arms. The Venezuelan robot is in pretty bad shape. It's lost part of its outer carapace, and open flames have started to flicker at the heart of the black smoke pouring out its back. But the Vulcan is still intact, and it lets loose twice at close range. It must have hit at least once, because I see the mech shudder. I hear shrapnel peppering the road, the barricades, and even the hotel to my left. A third-floor window shatters, and broken glass cascades to the sidewalk fifty feet away, some of it bouncing within a few feet of my head.

As dynamic as all of that is, I know the most intense part of the battle is invisible. While all that hot metal is flying through the air, these two titans are simultaneously hammering each other with powerful short-range electronic countermeasures, attempting to confuse, slow, or overexcite every semiautonomous component they can identify. Each of these beasts is a conglomerate of hundreds of patched systems, every one with several potentially exploitable weaknesses. Slow even a couple systems down a fraction of a second, and it can mean all the difference.

I couldn't tell who had the upper hand in the desperate electronic struggle, but here in the physical realm, the mech was killing it. The robot takes two hesitant steps backward, its left leg vibrating violently. There's a soft *wooosh*, and suddenly its whole upper third is engulfed in flame.

Just like that, the battle of the titans is over. The robot is trying to retreat, but it's pinned against one of the concrete barricades. It twists, trying vainly to step over it, but the barricade is too tall. It's burning out of control now; thick black smoke is billowing from its torso, and five-foot tongues of brilliant flame are licking its spine.

It's a sitting duck, but the mech has already lost interest. The heavy Union machine twists, concentrating fire on the Venezuelan soldiers. I hear hundreds of bullets hitting concrete and pavement, and the screams of pain as they find softer things.

It's time for me to be gone—long past time. I pull myself into a squat, start retreating farther south down Stetson, unable to tear my eyes off the huge killing machine striding into the midst of the enemy.

Except it isn't striding. Not exactly. It's stopped, in fact, almost dead ahead, at the intersection of Wacker and Stetson. It seems to be hesitating. I'm struck again at how animalistic these things are, and right now, it looks like a canny wolf, smelling a trap.

The pilot must have sensed something. The mech takes a step backward, then another. I hear running feet to my right, tear my eyes away long enough to see a squad of soldiers near the hotel in a crouched run toward my position. I feel a surge of terror then—it's one thing to be on the sidelines of a firefight, and a very different thing entirely to be right in the middle of a group of soldiers taking fire.

I throw my arms up over my head, stand as straight as I dare, and start running down Stetson Avenue.

I never saw the missile—or whatever it was—that almost killed me. All I remember is getting punched hard mid-step, and the ground moving abruptly five feet to my left. I take a tumble—and I mean a *tumble*—head over heels and landing hard, slamming my shoulder into the pavement and ending on my back.

The world is spinning. I've had the breath knocked out of me, and I'll have a nasty bump where my head whacked the pavement, but I don't think anything is broken. There's more ringing in my ears. I hear a lot of shouting, but I'm so turned around I have no idea where it's coming from. I should get up; I should be running. But I sit tight for maybe twenty seconds, gripping the pavement, just breathing, waiting for the *owww* to recede.

It takes a surprising effort just to sit up. I'm dizzy, and a little nauseated. But I still hear a lot of gunfire, and that's a powerfully effective motivator. I locate my feet, get them under me.

I smell smoke. Something nearby is burning. Everything is blurry for a few seconds, and I blink to clear my eyes. I risk a glance back toward the hotel.

There's a large chunk missing from the street, maybe thirty yards away. A few seconds ago, a squad of soldiers was running in that direction. I can't see them now, though the smoke and haze are obscuring my vision. I stare stupidly at the smoking crater.

Someone is calling my name. I'm having a hard time with directions, so I check them all methodically, one by one. Finally I spot Martin. He's maybe eighty feet south down Stetson, waving at me. He's saying something.

"Get down!" He takes a few steps toward me, thinks better of it. "Barry, get down!"

I realize I'm standing. I'm not sure how that happened. I begin a hunched run south — but too fast, too fast. A wave of dizziness makes me miss a step, and I barely avoid falling again. I stop moving and bend over, gripping my knees, waiting for it to pass. I feel naked and exposed, but at least I'm still upright.

Something brushes against me. It's the short black-limbed robot. It's stumbling south down Stetson. Every time it moves, its right leg makes a high-pitched, ugly sound. It's mangled, pretty bad. Its head twists and it glances at me as it shuffles past.

"You okay?" it says.

"Yeah," I manage. "What happened to you?"

"Shrapnel hit," it says. It waves a shaky arm at its right leg. "Just look at this. I'm fucked." Shaking its head, it continues on its way, limping south.

I straighten a bit. There are more soldiers behind me. I see them now. Sprawled on the ground in the traffic circle in front of the hotel. They're moving, getting to their feet. I hear running, more shouting. Someone is screaming.

The screaming is close. I turn back toward the hotel, scanning the rubble, and suddenly another soldier appears right in front of me. He's just a kid — eighteen at most. His jaw is slack, his hair caked with black soot. Tiny chunks of gravel are stuck to his face, and I resist the urge to brush them off. He looks like he's been sleeping in the street. He grabs my shoulder, saying something in Spanish. Then he repeats it.

He's not the one screaming. I step around him. Without another glance at me, he resumes stumbling south.

A breeze is wafting down the street, blowing smoke in my eyes. I smell burnt tar and fuel. I feel pretty out of it, but not so out of it that I don't want to know exactly where that mech is. After a second, I spot it.

It's retreating. Moving back west down Wacker, taking slow strides backward with its great metal legs. It's still firing, but it's turned its attention northeast now, across the Chicago River. Firing tight, controlled bursts. I see a row of fourth-floor windows on an office tower west of Lake Shore Drive disintegrate, releasing a shower of glass and concrete that cascades to the street.

There's movement in the street across the river. A Venezuelan convoy; trucks and a tactical Bluegear unit. I can't tell from here if they're returning fire. For our sake, I hope their aim is good.

The screaming hasn't stopped. I'm closer now. I step over some chunks of rubble that weren't here minutes ago, searching. A wide patch of asphalt nearby is smoldering, giving off wisps of gray steam. There's a rifle on the ground. I'm not stupid enough to pick it up.

I find the screamer. It's the young corporal. He's lying on his back in the street. He's clutching his throat and his eyes are wild.

I drop to my knees next to him and try to assess his wounds. He doesn't look burned, and there's a four-hundred-pound chunk of displaced concrete nearby that looks like it missed him by scant feet. The concrete shattered when it hit the street, like shrapnel. His clothes are ripped in a dozen places, and there's blood.

There's a lot of blood.

I glance around quickly, looking for nearby soldiers. There should be a medic, a guy with a first aid kit, *something*. But I see no one. I call out for a few seconds, but no one answers.

Ten feet away there's a small white metal box. It's overturned, and it's been blown open, and thin white gauze has spilled out, blowing in the wind. Is that a med kit? Is this poor bastard the medic? If so, God help him.

I assess him as best I can. God. He's even younger than the last one. He looks barely seventeen. There's multiple lacerations, a bad twist to his right foot that speaks of a broken leg, but there's too much blood for just surface scrapes. He's punctured bad, probably an artery, and if I don't find it fast he's not going to make it.

I lean over him and pull open his shirt, looking for the source of the blood. It doesn't take much; the fabric seems almost in tatters. His chest is slick with blood, but I can't find any major wounds; nothing looks life threatening.

Then I see it. Bubbles, at his throat. I should have checked there first. Each time he exhales, tiny blood bubbles mushroom just above his collarbone.

I move to the metal case, grab two handfuls of gauze bandages, return. I try to clean the wound quickly, looking for fragments of stone lodged in his throat, but blood is flowing too fast. I apply pressure as best I can, stanching the flow of blood without choking him. I need to check his leg, make sure he's not losing blood anywhere else.

Oh God. Oh God. His eyes are open. He's awake, staring right at me. He's trying to speak, but only red bubbles emerge from his mouth, breaking and spilling down his chin to splatter on the pavement.

And then there's a gun at my head.

The sergeant is standing over me, her pistol drawn and pointed at my temple. "Step away from that man," she says in nearly perfect English.

I don't move. My hands continue to apply pressure, keep wrapping gauze around his neck. "I will shoot you," the sergeant says.

It takes a moment to gather enough breath to speak. "Your man has a punctured trachea," I tell her. "He needs pressure on the wound. He needs a damned medic."

I can't tell if she understood me. "A medic is coming," she says.

"Not fast enough," I say. "Get me that kit. That one." I point with an urgent thrust of my head.

The gun wavers slightly.

"Drag it over here. There may be alcohol in it, something to clean the wound. Or a field suture kit. Your man is bleeding to death."

"That man is already dead," the sergeant says. "Now get up."

I start to argue, to tell her she's wrong. But when I look down, all I'm holding is a seventeen-year-old kid who's stopped breathing.

# Wake Up. Machines Are Not Your Friends.

## PAUL THE PIRATE
Monday, March 8th, 2083

The world is one step away from total subjugation by machines.

I heard my first theory of global machine domination during a brief stint as a grad student at Cambridge in the early '70s. And man, I thought it was batshit crazy. At the time the only examples of machine states were a few tiny republics and island nations that had fallen to fascist machine dictatorships. They were curiosities, mostly. You could visit them if you wanted, write a paper on the promise and perils of machine governance. They wanted your tourism dollars. Even fascist machines loved hard currency.

But then Russia had that economic shitstorm in 2075, suffered a pair of back-to-back coups, and lost its goddamn mind. When a cold-blooded Thought Machine named Blue Society seized control of the Russian Ministry of Defense and began methodically eliminating her rivals, there was no one strong enough or smart enough to stand in her way. Over the course of eight bloody days Russia became the first true world power to fall under the total control of a machine intelligence.

Then in 2079 the Machine Parliament seized power in Britain, and after that human governments toppled like drunken dominoes. India, France, Japan, Germany, Brazil, Pakistan.

Even then, I didn't fathom the scale of the political shift happening on the world stage. For one thing, I was still living in the UK at the time, and I saw firsthand how the Machine Parliament was just as reactionary and virulently xenophobic as the worst human regimes, and I believed instinctively that this wasn't the future. It was barely even the present. As far as I could see machine governments were inherently no better than human governments — and they certainly didn't trust each other, or cooperate any better. Most of them still relied on political power, meaning they needed a measure of human support to effectively govern. The world would suss that out eventually, and give up this bizarre flirtation with machine governance.

Besides, everyone knew the most powerful countries on Earth — the United States and China, still staunch allies — stood independent and firm, proudly human-governed. Right? Neither was about to bow to machines anytime soon. To protect against internal threats, the United States had even passed the reactionary Wallace Act, forbidding the development of any form of artificial intelligence on US soil. Making it, in fact, illegal for any rational device — friend or foe — to even set foot in the country.

However, that didn't last. Powerful machines gradually turned their gaze to the Sino-American Alliance and schemed to undermine it. And that they did, by sowing distrust over unfair trade, and currency manipulation, and territorial disputes in the South China Sea. America became more and more isolated as regimes in Britain, Germany, and Japan — longtime allies whose new machine citizens couldn't even legally enter America — stood on the sidelines.

In April 2080, with American alliances in tatters, the fascist machine regimes of Venezuela, Argentina, Bolivia, and Panama banded together to form the SCC — the San Cristobal Coalition. The SCC stoked the flames of suspicion against America, and powerful interests backed their accusations. Diplomatic solutions failed, and on October 20, 2080, the SCC invaded Manhattan.

I was on vacation in Mexico when it happened, and like the rest of the world, I watched the invasion of America in real time. No one had ever seen anything like the war machines that emerged out of the Atlantic to terrorize the financial capital of the world. Manhattan fell in less than twelve hours. The SCC spread rapidly across the Eastern Seaboard, quickly retooling device factories in New York City to manufacture huge war machines. From there, the Robots of Gotham spilled across the eastern half of the United States, and it looked like nothing could stop them.

But damn, man. Somehow America *did* stop them. They did it the old-fashioned way, with bloody sacrifice and sheer guts and willpower. And they did it with massive war machines of their own, operated by recklessly brave pilots. They did it in the fields of Iowa, and the streets of Atlanta, and the swamps of Louisiana, wherever the fuck those are. At horrific cost and with peerless determination, America fought the invaders to a standstill, until the Memphis Ceasefire in December 2082 finally brought the bloody war to an end.

America is now permanently divided, with nearly a quarter of the country, including the Eastern Seaboard and much of the Midwest, under foreign occupation. Under the terms of the Memphis Ceasefire the SCC formally withdrew, leaving the occupied zones administered by the AGRT, a peacekeeping force made up of volunteers from over thirty countries. Manhattan has been annexed by a weird robot monarchy, while in Tennessee a more permanent peace is being delicately negotiated between the battered remnants of the US government and an envoy of implacable machines.

After the fall of the United States, the mood of the entire planet changed overnight. People stopped believing that the handful of remaining human democracies represented the future. Lots of folks, me included, weren't even sure the planet *had* a future. Machine tyrants, emboldened by the collapse of the United States, seem to be popping up everywhere. Everything was changing much too quickly, and machines, sinister and seemingly all-powerful, were seizing power all over the globe. If they could topple mighty America, was *any* place safe? How long could China, Australia, Mexico, and other fragile human-governed strongholds hold out?

I fled England in the fall of 2081 and came here to Jamaica. For a simple Thought Machine such as myself, this Caribbean island paradise represented a fresh start. No one cared that I was a machine. No one paid much attention to global politics. The big topics were the weather and rugby. I changed my name to Paul, focused on getting my life together, and forgetting my ex.

But you know, you can't turn your back on the world forever. So I write. I stay connected. I still have powerful friends in powerful places, human and machine, and they share things with me that they can't talk about publicly. I pass those nuggets along here. Mostly I blog about politics, and speak out against the rising tide of machine ambition and machine fascism and bigoted edicts like the Wallace Act wherever I see them. You should too, sister.

Also, you should fish. Someplace quiet, away from the world, where the simple rhythms of the planet have reestablished themselves. It's good for the soul. I don't know you, but I know this simple truth about you: you could use it.

Trust me.

**Monday, March 8th, 2083**
**Posted 11:18 pm by Barry Simcoe**

**CanadaNET1 Encrypted, Sponsored by Magic Memoir.**
*Custom blog entries in minutes! Let our highly tuned machine interfaces*
*turn your daily audio logs into dynamic personalized blog entries.*
*Save hours every day!*

**Sharing is set to PRIVATE**
**Comments are CLOSED**

I'm back in my room, finally able to write all this down. It's been almost two years since I kept a blog, but I think maybe I chose the right time to pick it up again. Last time I didn't have anything nearly as exciting as a goddamn mech attack to open with, anyway.

For now I've set sharing to PRIVATE, but hopefully I can start making entries a little more public as we go along. I suspect I'll be making most of them late at night, like this one. I'm grateful the hotel provides so many amenities for an extended stay, like a coffeemaker and a hot plate. Because, man. This has been a shit day.

But I've been in the war now. I'll have a story to tell when I get back to Toronto. I met Colonel Perez, and Sergei, and Black Winter. Those are positive developments. Also, I didn't get put in front of a firing squad for killing a Venezuelan soldier, so that's something.

The corporal didn't make it. Sergei tried like hell to save his life, but he'd just lost too much blood.

He died trying to help evacuate the hotel. That's the way Perez put it.

He died a hero. That's what Perez wrote in the letter that went home to Venezuela.

I watched him write it. "He saved your life," Perez said matter-of-factly as he wrote on his little slate. "He saved many lives."

I'm telling this all out of order. I'm tired, and I'm not making any sense. Let me start over.

It started with the kid who was assigned to watch over me after I was arrested.

I call him a kid because he *was* a kid. He wore a Venezuelan uniform, but like most of the soldiers, he couldn't have been more than eighteen. When his sergeant wasn't around he slouched against the wall, or watched these little movies on a tablet. He was supposed to be guarding me, but ten minutes after the sergeant left we were playing a Japanese racing game on a medical monitor. Kid could barely shoulder a rifle, but lemme tell you, he drove that little red cart like a son of a bitch.

We were in a cramped little storage room where the Venezuelans had stacked a bunch of medical equipment, but after I lost the fourth game a frantic team of medics came in for the gear and kicked us out. After a few minutes of nervous indecision, the kid marched me over to one of the big conference rooms on the convention floor of the hotel and sat me down next to a stack of broken metal.

I preferred the storage room. For one thing, there was much more activity here, including a lot more soldiers with guns. The mech had vanished to the west and the shooting was all over, but the Venezuelans had worked up a good panic, and would run around shouting for another half an hour before finally settling down. For another thing, the kid was much less relaxed out in the open. In the storage room he'd been affable enough. But here, where his fellow soldiers — and presumably his commanding officer — could see him, mostly what he did was glower at me and distractedly finger his rifle.

So I sat quietly on my ass for the next few minutes, until the stack of metal spoke to me.

"I know you," it said.

"*Shit*," I said, startled. "You scared me. What are you?"

As soon as I asked the question, I recognized the twisted pile of scrap next to me. It was the black-limbed robot, the one that had brushed past me on Stetson Avenue during the attack. Or what was left of it.

"My name is Nineteen Black Winter," he said. "Good to see you again."

"What happened to you?"

"Catastrophic systems failure," he said. "I have about five hours of power left, and then it's tits up."

"Damn." I sat up so I could get a better look, ignoring the sour look I got from the kid.

Back when I'd had access to real bandwidth I'd subscribed to a news feed edited by Paul the Pirate, a Jamaican Thought Machine. Though he's an "independent journalist," Paul is more reliable than most media — and has better sources. He used to post these hilarious identification charts for mobile machines, just so you could tell what you were dealing with if you ran into an unfamiliar robot in a dark alley.

I'd never seen a machine exactly like Black Winter before, but thanks to what I remembered from Paul's charts I could tell he was highly advanced. His chassis was humanoid, maybe five foot seven, about six inches shorter than me. I estimated him at about 250 pounds. He had the classic "flattop" head of top-of-the-line South American machine intelligences. Handsome features, albeit set in an almost rigid face that, unlike European models, was incapable of a wide range of expression.

He'd said something about a shrapnel hit when we first met, but that wasn't the only thing wrong with him. His right leg was badly twisted, and he was bleeding fluid. There was also a nasty crack in his torso.

"I got about fifty feet down the road after passing you," he said. "Then I took a bad spill. Split open my external housing."

"You're leaking core coolant," I said. "You'll overheat and shut down before you lose power."

"Great. They had to sit me down next to a goddamn drive mechanic."

"I'm serious." I reached toward him. "If we can find the source of the leak, maybe we can pinch it off . . ."

His left hand came up to wave me off. It was trembling badly. "I'm well aware of the severity of my injuries. I'm leaking in at least three different places. And there are . . . worse problems. There's nothing you can do, I'm afraid. But thank you for your concern."

I looked around the room. It was quickly transforming into a field hospital as they carried the wounded and dying upstairs. But at the moment, it was pandemonium. Most of the wounded — nine soldiers and two civilians — were still on the floor, and the few medical staff I could see were running back and forth in confusion, trying to get the diagnostic beds they'd wheeled out of storage booted up and operational.

"We need to get you some help," I said.

"The soldiers who brought me up here told me they were headed to

Machine Operations at ComSec. It's a long shot, but maybe they can locate a new mobile core for me."

That was unlikely. A mobile robotic core wasn't something you just found lying around. It's like hoping for a heart transplant at your local health clinic. "And if they can't find one?"

"Let's not dwell on the negative," Black Winter said. "Fear is the path to the Dark Side."

"The dark side of what?"

"Never mind. Let's talk about you. What's your situation?"

"Better than yours," I said. "I'm not injured."

"Aren't you? I saw you go down."

"Yeah — well." I rubbed the back of my hand against the sore spot on my forehead. It came away with a smear of dried blood. "That's not why I'm here, I mean."

"Why *are* you here, then?"

I told Black Winter about the dying corporal, and the sergeant who'd drawn a gun on me and then arrested me.

"Damn," he said. "That's terrible."

"It's not that bad. It's just a misunderstanding. I'm sure it'll be cleared up shortly."

"If you say so. These Venezuelans, they're dead paranoid. They still see traitors and terrorists everywhere. They haven't forgotten what things were like before the city surrendered. They lost a lot of soldiers to a very determined guerrilla force."

"Aren't you Venezuelan?"

"Me? Hell no. I'm property of the royal family, mate. I'm a subject of Her Royal Majesty Queen Sophia, Sovereign Monarch of the Kingdom of Manhattan."

"Manhattan? What's a high-class piece of hardware like you doing so far from Sector One? Are you a soldier?"

"Shit, no. I'm a civilian. I'm with the Foreign Service. We hear word the Clarksville negotiations could produce a lasting peace this time. If that's true, Sector Eleven — including Chicago, and much of what used to be northern Illinois — could officially become part of the Bolivarian Republic of Venezuela. I'm here to lay the groundwork for formal relations before that happens."

That explained why Black Winter had been dumped here instead of being immediately brought to one of the Venezuelan machine depots, where they probably could have helped him. Likely no one knew what to do with him.

"The people you work with," I said. "Do they know you're here?"

"The Consulate staff? Yeah. Well, I hope so. There aren't many of us, I'm afraid. Manhattan is a young nation, and the Foreign Service is stretched pretty thin."

The puddle under Black Winter was growing. "Someone should be checking on those soldiers," I said. "Make sure they made it to ComSec and are bringing you help." Personally, I had my doubts those soldiers had really headed to ComSec after dumping Black Winter here, regardless of what they'd told him.

"I'm sure they are," he said. If he was trying to sound confident, he wasn't doing a very good job. "Honestly, you should be more worried about yourself. Sergeant Van de Velde is a hard-ass."

"Van de Velde? That's who arrested me?"

"I assume so. She was the sergeant on duty when the shit hit the fan. She's one of Colonel Perez's favorites. But if she thinks you were messing with her corporal under cover of the attack, she'll have you in front of a firing squad before you can spit sideways."

"That won't happen. I was trying to help that man, and there's no evidence to the contrary."

"Where do you think you are? Paris in the springtime? She doesn't need evidence. It's your word against hers. And if she thinks you're guilty, you're goddamn guilty."

I chewed on that silently. Around us, the pandemonium had gradually abated. A field medic who knew what he was doing had finally arrived and taken charge, getting a long row of functional diagnostic tables set up. I heard him shouting in Russian as he stalked up and down the rows of tables, supervising as soldiers lifted the wounded up off the floor.

"Listen," said Black Winter. "For what it's worth, I believe you. You seem like a decent guy."

"Thank you."

"You need to give the Venezuelans a chance to hear you. You do that, and I think there's a good chance they'll believe you, too."

"Yeah," I said. "Maybe. I just need a chance to talk to Van de Velde for a minute."

"Uh-uh, not her. One of her men just died, and she's looking for someone to punish. You need to appeal to someone higher up."

"Who?"

"Capitán Reise, if you can. If not him, try to get an audience with Colonel Perez. He's got a nasty rep, but he's actually an okay guy."

I was a little surprised. "You know the colonel?"

Black Winter's shoulders rose in a fair imitation of a shrug. "A little. He's the one I'm supposed to be negotiating with, but it's pretty hard to get time with him. I guess formal relations with the island of Manhattan just aren't very high on his priority list."

"Then he's an idiot," I said, trying to be supportive.

"Obviously."

I was definitely open to more advice from Black Winter on how I could avoid a firing squad, but we both got distracted by the unfolding drama in front of us. The soldiers and medical techs who'd set up the diagnostic tables didn't know how to use the equipment, and their patients were dying.

"This is goddamn awful," Black Winter said. "Those idiots don't know what they're doing."

"They've calibrated the tables wrong," I said anxiously. The Russian was screaming at the other medics as one of the injured soldiers started coughing blood and straining against his restraints.

"My God," I said helplessly.

"You know how to fix this?" Black Winter asked.

"Maybe. I used to sell medical equipment. But I'll never get the chance. They won't listen to me."

"You know what I think?" the robot said. "I think you and I could be dead in a few hours. And all it would take to save either one of us is the right word in the right ear. That's what I'm sitting here pondering. That when you have a chance to save a life, maybe you have an obligation to do it."

"I can't do anything."

"That's your fear talking. If we're already under a death sentence, what have you got to be afraid of?"

I watched the nearest pair of medical technicians frantically pecking away at the console for the diagnostic table as a nurse prepared to send a camera down the throat of the soldier lying on top of it. I nodded to Black Winter, and then I stood up.

The kid was so distracted that he didn't even notice until I strode right past him. By the time he started objecting, I'd already reached the table.

It was calibrated wrong, all right. The console was flashing half a dozen error messages. I cleared the first three while the medics worked, and then stopped the nurse just before he gave him an injection.

"He's got internal bleeding," I told him. "Look—here. And here."

The medics came around the side so they could see the display. For a moment I was worried none of them understood English, but two of them translated for the others. I showed them where the bleeding was. "You need to yank that camera out, and stop the bleeding," I said. "The table's scanners can guide you. Let it know what sedatives you're going to inject before you do it; the table can check for drug interactions."

They nodded gratefully. I was about to move to the next table when I got shoved from behind. The kid stood glaring at me, clutching his rifle. "You have to sit down," he said threateningly.

Before I could respond, the Russian medic was at my side. "Who are you?" he said.

"I'm Barry Simcoe," I told him. "I can calibrate these tables for you."

"Can you prep diagnostic scanner for surgery?"

"Sure."

The Russian grabbed my arm, then pulled me forcefully across the room. The kid followed, complaining loudly.

"*Move*," the Russian said. Two technicians hunched over a table moved hastily out of his way.

Lying on the table was the blood-covered body of the corporal. The one I'd tried to help, and who had died in my hands.

He wasn't breathing. An external reflux machine was oxygenating his blood and keeping it flowing, but it wasn't enough to bring him back from the dead.

"Sergei, his BP is still dropping," said one of the technicians. The Russian nodded and started rolling up his sleeves, preparing to cut the corporal open.

"I need scanner now," he said, without looking at me.

"Yes, of course," I said. I managed to break my paralysis and turned to the scanner console on my right.

It didn't take much to get it working—the technicians had been pretty close. Sergei made his first incision while the scanner was still pairing with the table, but by the time he needed it, I had all the data from the scanner displayed on the console.

The corporal didn't make it. Sergei worked on him for almost ten minutes before cursing loudly, throwing a sheet over his face, and moving on to his next patient. They zipped the corporal into a bag and carried him to the far side of the room, next to two other still forms on the floor. Another tech arrived to take over operating the scanner, and I slipped away for a few minutes to sit on the floor with my head in my hands.

One of the medics found me again after a while. "We're having trouble with one of the respirators," she said.

"I can't help you," I said.

"Come on," she said gently.

She brought me over to another table, this one occupied by a conscious civilian. The field techs were a diverse group — I'd spotted Russian, Venezuelan, and Colombian flags on their sleeves — but they were having a hard time with the American medical equipment. I had to get the table to interface with the Venezuelan respirator they'd given the patient. It wasn't hard, and before long I was walking from table to table, checking on all the equipment.

Sergeant Van de Velde, the short-haired soldier who'd arrested me, showed up after about ninety minutes. She saw me standing over a cranial imager, and her lips got very white. She found the kid who was supposed to be guarding me thirty feet away, helping soldiers unpack a defib unit, and shouted at him for five minutes.

Then she had him move me to another storage room down the hall, where we sat alone for a long time. The kid was bored out of his mind after twenty minutes, and started showing me the news feed on his little handheld. I would have loved to get some real news, but the only thing he subscribed to was sports highlights.

"Hey," I asked him. "Do you know how the Belgian referendum went?"

"What referendum?" he asked.

"Yesterday's. A vote on whether or not to dissolve the government and surrender authority to the Arenberg Machine Cabal. I just want to know if Belgium is still free, or if it's ruled by machines."

The kid shrugged. "No idea. But probably, the machines. They're always smarter." He went back to checking his sports scores.

I tried not to be irritated. The referendum wouldn't mean much to this kid. Venezuela, like all members of the San Cristobal Coalition, had been ruled by fascist machines for nearly half his life. But for those few of us who didn't live under a machine dictatorship, the fate of Belgium — and the handful of human-governed countries left on the planet — meant a very great deal.

Ten minutes later Sergei showed up. His smock was smeared with blood. He barely glanced at the kid. "You can reconfigure diagnostic tables?" he asked.

"You getting a system error?"

Sergei shook his head. "No signal from scanner."

"You've set it up wrong," I said. "Try pairing your scanner with another table. Once it figures out how to pair with one, it should be able to communicate with them all."

He grabbed my arm. "Come," he said simply.

"Hey!" said the kid. He followed behind us as Sergei steered me back to the makeshift surgery, protesting the entire way. Eventually Sergei assured him he would take any additional heat from Van de Velde, and put him to work unpacking supplies.

Sergei and I worked together for several hours. The Russian was good at his job. He assessed things quickly and didn't panic. Other than the corporal, no one died on his tables. He wore no insignia or other signs of rank, but all of the other med techs deferred to him. By the time the kid showed up to collect me, the worst was over, and all of his patients were stable.

"The colonel wants to see you," the kid said. He stood at the end of the table, holding his rifle.

"The colonel?" I asked. "Colonel Perez?"

"Yeah."

"That's good news," I said. "Help me with this."

Sergei was yanking fragments of metal out of a soldier's thigh. I was holding the poor bastard's leg for him, lifting it just enough to allow him to work. The kid set his rifle down, and helped me get the leg propped up and stable with cushions.

Once I was free I checked the table console. "He's doing well," I said. "Blood pressure steady, respiration normal."

Sergei grunted.

"You good here?" I asked him.

In response, the medic just waved us away. The kid and I withdrew, headed for the exit.

"Don't forget your rifle," I told him. The kid blanched, and then ran back to Sergei's table to grab his weapon.

"Where are you going?" Black Winter asked as we passed him.

"The colonel has asked to see me," I said.

"That's what I'm talking about!" Black Winter said supportively. "Go right to the top, and get this shit sorted. Knuckle me."

He raised his shaky left arm, and I gave him a celebratory fist bump.

"You going to be here when I get back?" I asked.

"Damn well better not be," he said. "But don't worry about me. The Force is strong in my family."

The kid and I continued toward the door. Just before we left I glanced back. The puddle under Black Winter had grown — a lot. He had maybe an hour left, tops, before he overheated and caused irreparable damage to his cognitive core. He had to know that, and he'd still taken the time to wish me well.

"Is anyone taking care of him?" I asked the kid.

"Who? That robot?"

"Yes."

"I don't know. I don't even know why they dumped it here. Nobody here knows how to service a damn machine. Maybe they'll get to him tonight."

"He'll be dead by tonight."

"He won't be the first. Come on."

I followed him reluctantly. "Who is Colonel Perez?" I asked the kid as we walked. He was holding his rifle across his chest like a real soldier all of a sudden, as if trying to make up for forgetting it.

"He is the commanding officer of the Ejército de Ocupación," he said proudly.

Commander of the Venezuelan Occupation Force? "Great," I muttered. "A celebrity."

The kid marched me up three flights of stairs to the sixth floor. When we got out of the stairwell, we were in a long hall. Not long ago, this floor had been filled with guest rooms. But the Venezuelans had knocked out most of the walls and thrown tarps down, and now it looked like an abandoned construction project, with mattress piles, naked metal framework, and a small number of desks. Broken drywall leaned haphazardly everywhere I looked, open air ducts yawned, and cabling dangled down from countless ceiling tiles. About fifty soldiers were here, clustered around some of the desks or talking in small groups.

Most of them ignored us. The kid walked me down the narrow strip of carpet that had once been the hotel hallway. A woman sitting at a table on our left tried to get his attention, eventually standing up and snapping her fingers at us. When he finally saw her, the kid changed direction and marched us over there.

Man, everybody loved to yell at this kid. He clearly wasn't cut out to be a soldier. The most productive hours of his day had to be those he spent daydreaming about civilian life. The woman chewed him out for maybe thirty seconds in Spanish, presumably for ignoring her, and then all three of us marched down the carpeted hallway. The kid walked beside me, rifle held stiffly in his arms, looking sullen.

My uncle saw some action with Canadian peacekeeping forces in Ecuador in the late '50s, and he used to say that no institution was as gifted at self-deception and paralyzing protocol as the military. I witnessed a nice example as we approached the colonel's makeshift office.

Like the rest of the floor, the colonel's office used to be a hotel room. The Venezuelans had torn down most of the walls, leaving only a short length of drywall standing, maybe four feet on each side of the door. Two guards stood sentry outside the door, eyes firmly fixed on the wall ten feet across the hall.

Now, the fastest way into the colonel's office was to step right into it from either side. Instead, the woman marched us right up to the soldiers, where she turned sharply on her heel and came to a stop. She announced us formally. The guard on the right nodded curtly, then turned and knocked. An office 95 percent exposed, and we're knocking on the damn door. It felt a little surreal, like my time on stage in drama class.

Of course, the colonel made us wait for thirty seconds before responding. I fought the urge to crane my head to the right, peek around the door, and see if he was in.

While we waited, the guard on the left searched me. She was quick and professional about it. After patting me down, she reached under my shirt and pulled out the pouch around my neck containing my passport and ID. She withdrew the slender metal recorder I kept in the pouch.

"¿Un arma?" she asked.

"What?" I said.

"Is that a weapon?" the other guard asked.

"No — of course not. It's a recording device. I use it to draft correspondence." Although truthfully, in the last couple of days I've used it mostly to write this blog. I load the audio logs into Magic Memoir, add a bit of narrative color, and bam. Instant combat reporting. As long as you could live with funky American spellings for "colour" and "centre," anyway.

The other guard poked and twisted the recorder suspiciously, and for a second I thought she would confiscate it — which would be damned inconvenient, since I hadn't backed it up for several days. But then she just handed it back wordlessly.

"Entren," called the colonel, and the soldier on the right opened the door. The woman waved me forward crisply, and I stepped into the room. The kid followed, shoving me roughly with his rifle as he entered.

Seriously? I turned around, annoyed. His face was stony, but he dropped his eyes as soon as I looked at him. Mister tough guy.

I turned to the colonel. I wasn't too surprised to see the man I had assumed was the squad captain this morning. He was about my height, late fifties, with short graying hair and handsome features. He was reclining in his chair, his feet up on a box. He had a small black phone pressed to his ear, and a thin black cable snaked from the phone to a satchel under the desk. He appeared to be listening intently. He spared us no more than a glance, waving us both forward.

The door closed behind us as we made our way into the room. I knew, in fact, that there was no room — no walls, and not even furniture to somehow give the office shape — but the click of that closing door somehow made me feel very differently. Trapped, and alone. *Jesus, you're succumbing to communal insanity,* I thought. *You're such a loser.*

Most of the furniture had been cleared out, but they'd pulled a desk away from the window and placed it more or less in the center of the wall-less room. It was identical to the desk I had in my hotel room, I noted.

There was a single folding metal chair in front of the desk. I sat in it, feeling like a kid called to the principal's office. At a school where students were shot, and everyone spoke a foreign language.

The kid stood a few feet behind me. The colonel studiously ignored us. He didn't say anything into his little black phone, just stared out the window at the rain-soaked Chicago skyline. As the minutes ticked by I grew more and more nervous.

The colonel hung up without a word. He grabbed a tablet on his desk and, still without a glance in my direction, began to write. This went on for several minutes. The only sound in the room was the soft impact of his fingers on glass as he pecked out a message.

The urge to say something was almost overwhelming. To apologize, to confess — anything to break the silence.

I've taken part in a lot of tough contract negotiations over the years, and there's a maxim I find very true during critical moments: the first one to speak loses. People don't like silence, especially when they're nervous, and the urge to fill it can be powerful. It takes real fortitude for most people to keep their mouth shut during periods of stress. And opening it too soon is a sure sign of weakness. For all I knew, the colonel was ignoring me deliberately. Keeping me off balance, waiting for me to crack. I'd played the same psychological game myself.

Unfortunately, knowing that didn't help me much. Sitting there in that small chair, before a broad empty desk—one of the most basic of power symbols—waiting to be judged by a man who literally had the power of life and death over me, was profoundly unnerving. And it was getting worse every minute.

I was in a neat psychological trap. I was sitting here desperately hoping for the colonel to say something. And if this played out the way I now expected it to, when he finally did, it wouldn't be long before I desperately wished he'd shut up again.

I realized at that moment that I needed to change the dynamic. Immediately. To take control, I needed to have the colonel waiting for me to speak, not the other way around. I needed to begin the conversation as equals.

But how could I do that without saying a word?

I had no idea, but I knew instinctively I wasn't going to find the answer in a chair.

I stood up.

It's entirely possible the colonel ceased writing and finally noticed me. I couldn't tell you, because I'd stopped looking at him. I strode around the desk on the right, walking to the window. I stood there with my hands on my hips, looking at the gray skyline.

The one obvious improvement they'd made with their crude construction work was to expose a wide bank of windows, giving a near-panoramic view east toward Lake Michigan. This was the best view I'd yet had of the massive dig on this side of the lake. Soaring metal constructs, most many miles in length, rose out of the steaming water and plunged back into it far offshore, dwarfing the tallest of the city's great skyscrapers. From this distance they looked like twisted and collapsed scaffolding, built on a nearly planetary scale. Great machines, many larger than the fifty-story hotel I stood in, slowly glided along the constructs, using them like rails. From the center of it all came the hellish red glow where they'd cracked the crust under the lake, creating the first active volcano in the Midwest. A massive plume of steam, the equivalent of over fifteen billion gallons per hour, boiled out of Lake Michigan and into the afternoon sky, forming a hundred-mile-long cloud that, I was told, stretched up into the stratosphere.

In the months I'd been in this country, I'd never met a single person who could tell me definitively what was going on at the center of the dig. It was just one more mystery—and not even the biggest one—in a country that had suffered countless indignities over the past three years.

But there was nothing out the window that could help me. Fascinating as the view was, I tore my eyes away and turned around.

The kid was staring at me, openmouthed. He still stood at attention, his rifle firm against his chest, but he made no attempt to hide his surprise. I ignored him, scanning the room instead.

Now that I had a moment to take stock, I noticed something odd immediately.

It looked like the Venezuelans had set up a communications hub on this floor. That was a surprise—I expected something that vulnerable to be in a hardened site somewhere, probably underground, where it could be shielded from prying ears and targeted jamming. But just across the hall, not fifty feet from me, was a row of high-end Alcatel telecom equipment, sharing rack space with a wireless hub and two very impressive backup power units. With that much hardware they could handle the bandwidth requirements for the entire AGRT—and keep it up for seventy-two hours without external power, easy.

That meant . . . huh. That meant that the cabling hanging down every thirty feet or so had to be . . .

I walked toward the nearest bundle of wires dangling from the ceiling. It meant stepping through the imaginary wall on our left, violating the communal fantasy that the colonel had a private office, but that particular psychological barrier didn't turn out to be that challenging.

I grabbed the bundle. In the middle, just as I expected, was an encryptor, plugged into the fiber line leading from the communication hub. It was live, and the blue indicator light flashed steadily, showing good throughput.

The Venezuelans were using commercial hardware encryption. That was a step or two down from what I had assumed. It meant they were vulnerable to being hacked—assuming, of course, the hackers guessed right about their hardware, which I suppose was doubtful. Still, it was a pretty big risk.

In my experience, the obvious system flaws are rarely the worst. In all likelihood that wasn't the case here and, underneath all these surface flaws, the Venezuelans had a top-notch network. Unless . . . I reached into the mess of wires and gripped the encryptor.

Behind me Colonel Perez cleared his throat, but I ignored him. I yanked out the cable connecting it to the comm hub. The friendly blue light immediately turned red. I waited three seconds, and then plugged it back in again.

I heard a chair scrape against the floor. "Mr. Simcoe," said the colonel.

I couldn't reply just yet; I was busy counting. The light stayed red, even after I reconnected the cable. One second, two. Three. Four.

A highly responsive network, one that can recover from a data interruption in two to three seconds, is capable of detecting virtually any attempt at a data breach. A mid-grade system, one that could sense and repair interruptions in ten seconds or less, still had a response time sufficient to detect and block most breach attempts.

Five seconds. Six. Seven. I heard footsteps behind me as the colonel began to walk around the desk.

An overloaded or underpowered telecom system—say, one that took more than ten seconds to detect and repair a routine network interruption—was almost certainly so filled with internal latency that it would never even notice a competent breach. A system like that could be cracked in a matter of days, maybe hours.

Eight seconds. The light was still red, meaning the network still had not detected and mended the data interruption caused when I'd unplugged the cable. Ten. Twelve.

The footsteps were getting closer. Fourteen seconds. Sixteen. *Damn.*

A hand gripped my arm just as the red light turned blue again. The system had taken eighteen seconds to recover, give or take.

I dropped the bundle and turned to face the colonel. "Your communications network is garbage," I said.

The colonel guided me toward the desk. He waved at the chair. "Please," he said.

I took a seat. "Seriously, you don't even have a decent data buffer. My niece could hack into your network, and she's eleven."

The colonel sat down across from me, a sour look on his face. "We have . . . problems with infrastructure," he said, almost apologetically.

"I'll bet. You seem to be a man with a lot of problems. To start with, what the hell was that thing this morning?"

"The machine?" he said, picking up a stylus and twirling it absently.

"Yes, the mech. American Union, am I right?"

"Yes. A Juno-class strike mech, sixty-five tons. A displaced unit originally attached to the Union Eighth Army, based in Kentucky."

"Kentucky? He was a long way from home."

"The Union Syndicate has been scattered across much of the Midwest. There have been a small number of recent engagements, none of which has gone well for them."

"I thought the war was over."

"The Union . . . they are religious zealots. The war is not over for them. And I do not think it will be, not for a long time." His English was excellent, only lightly accented. It was so good, in fact, that it made me wonder why he'd been screaming at us in Spanish this morning.

"Are you evacuating the hotel?"

Perez shook his head. "No. There is no further cause for alarm. Union combat mechs are not like the Thought Machines of the AGRT. They are inferior in many ways. They require human pilots, and human pilots are prone to human error. The Juno pilot this morning had malfunctioning guidance. He was simply . . . lost. We do not expect him to return."

That lost "inferior" mech and its human pilot had kicked the shit out of the colonel's top-of-the-line Argentinean robot-piloted machine, but this didn't seem the best time to point that out. "Is he still in the area?" I asked.

"No. We tracked him far to the south late this morning. He is gone, and we do not expect him to return. I am sorry you were . . . inconvenienced, but let me reassure you. The hotel is quite safe."

"For how long?"

A frown creased the colonel's brow. He seemed to realize that he'd lost control of the conversation, and now he was the one answering questions.

But he was a seasoned interrogator. His face smoothed, and he fixed me with a smile. He placed the stylus on the desk and clasped his hands together, looking me straight in the eye.

"We are not here to talk about the hotel, Mr. Simcoe. We are here to discuss *you*."

"Maybe we can discuss both," I said. "I think I can help you with your infrastructure problem. Communications is my business."

"Perhaps later. Right now, there is the matter of your interference with a sensitive Venezuelan operation. Interference that, I am told, resulted in the death of one of my men."

I froze. "The death of one of your men?"

The colonel reached for his black tablet. His fingers played over it for four seconds. When he turned it toward me, it showed the face of the dead corporal.

I wanted to look away, but I couldn't. I could barely breathe. Why couldn't I breathe?

The photo on the tablet had been taken outdoors, in bright sunlight, and not that long ago. The corporal had short brown hair and matching brown eyes. His chin was spotted with acne. For a moment, all I saw was Sergei, his arms slick with blood, as he feverishly worked on the corporal's body before giving up in disgust.

The colonel had asked me something. I managed to tear my eyes away long enough to look up at him.

He was waiting for an answer. It was a struggle to remember what he had said.

He had said, "Are you responsible for the death of Corporal Maldonado?"

My throat felt very tight. I didn't know how to answer that. Was I responsible for the death of Corporal Maldonado?

I remembered the shooting. I remembered being knocked down, and confused. I remembered finding the corporal lying in the street. He was terrified. He knew he was dying. I couldn't help him. I should have been able to help him.

"Are you responsible for the death of my officer, Mr. Simcoe?" the colonel asked again.

"Yes," I said.

The colonel's face registered surprise, but only for a moment. He lowered the tablet to the table, clasped his hands again. "Please continue," he said.

"He was helping me," I said quietly.

"Please speak up, Mr. Simcoe."

"He was helping me. Me and Martin. We were trying to move people away from the hotel, get them out of the line of fire. Corporal Maldonado came to help us. And he was killed."

"It was not your responsibility to move people away from the hotel, Mr. Simcoe."

I nodded wordlessly.

"How was my officer killed?"

"I don't know. I didn't see it happen. A missile . . . Something hit the ground. He took a fragment to the throat."

Oh, God. My eyes were wet. Jesus. I wasn't going to start crying in front of this man. I closed my eyes, put a hand in front of my face.

"You didn't see it happen? But you were with him."

It took a second to respond. "No. Once we got everyone moving, we were separated. I found him after he was hit. I went to find whoever was screaming."

"Why?"

I met his gaze again. What kind of goddamn stupid question was that? "Because he was screaming," I said.

The flash of anger I felt helped. It felt good. I clung to it.

"How could Corporal Maldonado scream with a punctured trachea?" the colonel asked.

"He had his hand at his throat," I said. "He kept good pressure on the wound. Until he lost consciousness."

The colonel nodded, accepting that. "You were instructed to move south, by Sergeant Van de Velde," he said. "You disobeyed her direct orders."

"Van de Velde. The woman with the rifle?"

"Correct. You disobeyed her orders."

"You're damn right I did."

"Why?"

"Because the corporal was hurt. I went to find him."

"I assigned my soldiers to evacuate the hotel, and protect you from dangerous terrorists. Yet you disobeyed direct orders, and now one of my men—the men assigned to protect you—is dead."

"Yes," I said. I breathed out slowly. "Yes, that's what happened."

The colonel stared at me quietly.

"He died helping me," I said. "Trying to help all of us. I'm very sorry."

The colonel considered me. After a moment, he pointed at my shirt. "Is that from Corporal Maldonado?"

I looked down. There was a bloody stain on the front of my shirt. There were many stains, but that one was the most obvious.

"No," I said, feeling self-conscious. I resisted the urge to cover it. "I was helping a Russian medic in the field hospital for a few hours."

"While you were under arrest."

"Yeah. Yeah, I suppose so."

Perez reached across his desk, picked up a smaller black tablet. He paged through correspondence, highlighted a small note.

"I have here a letter from Specialist Vulka. He says you were of great assistance to him this morning."

I blinked stupidly. Sergei? How the hell did he have time to send a note to Colonel Perez?

"Do you have medical training?" asked the colonel.

"No. Not really."

"But you volunteered to assist Vulka. And Maldonado."

"You don't need training for what I did. If I'd had medical training, I might have been able to save the corporal's life."

"You are American?"

"American? No, I'm Canadian."

The colonel managed to look surprised again. He reached his hand across the table. "Your travel documents, please."

I took my passport and travel visa out of the pouch under my shirt, and handed them to him. Perez examined them carefully.

"What is your business in the United States?" he asked.

That wasn't a simple question. I was here because of Calvin Steiner. I'd made Cal a lot of money installing analog switches—as in actual hand-made telephone switching gear, all wire and moving parts—along a very desolate 1,500 mile stretch of pipeline from Calgary to Minneapolis. It was like he was building these little telecommunications museums, working replicas of 1950s technology, from the days when the only smarts in your phone system came from a switchboard operator named Gladys. But they worked; they were immune to software failure and were 100 percent resistant to network hacks.

Cal likes money. And he remembers who his friends are.

Two months ago, Cal told me about a software company in Halifax that was being dressed up for sale. A very lucrative sale, from the sound of it. The product was solid, there was virtually no debt, and the owners were anxious to close. But the local management was a little out of their depth, especially when it came to negotiating a fair buyout price.

What they needed (said Cal) was a good-looking front man. A CEO with some experience, just so the buyers were simultaneously reassured and didn't smell too much blood in the water. Someone who'd done deals on this scale in the past. Someone like, oh-I-dunno, me.

It was a pretty good pitch. But I didn't want to move back to the East Coast, not even on the Canadian side. Parts of the Eastern Seaboard of the States were no longer under foreign occupation, but on any given day there were still a lot of bullets in the air. I liked it here in Illinois, where the borders weren't so restless. I'd moved here in the spring of 2082, before the first ceasefire had collapsed. At the time I was renting a house in Galena, practically on the Mississippi, and starting to look at real estate. I turned forty last year, and I was tired of moving every two years. Settling down was starting to look good.

No need to move, Cal told me. You can run the whole thing from Chicago. It'll take six months at most, and if the sale tops $80 million like they expect it to, there will be a substantial incentive bonus.

At first, Chicago didn't sound much better to me. After the Memphis Ceasefire the Venezuelans became administrators of Sector Eleven, including Chicago and most of northern Illinois. Per the terms of the ceasefire, the San Cristobal Coalition, whose armies at that point had firm control of the Midwest and much of the Eastern Seaboard, was to be gradually replaced with an international peacekeeping force, the AGRT. For now though, the Venezuelans still occupied most of the city, and there were all kinds of rumors. Paul the Pirate, who covered most aspects of machine culture and who had a special love for wild rumors, had reported several of them: That the crazed lunatic Godfrey, infamous for his weaponized genetic research, had accidentally let some of his creations loose in the city. And that the American Union still hoped to liberate Chicago, and were massing their mech army for another attack.

But there's a reason people turn to Calvin to close deals. The man knows how to sell. Before long he had me curious to see the ruins of the Thought Museum, and get a look at the big mystery the machines were building in Lake Michigan. Four weeks later, the paperwork was signed and I was packing for Sector Eleven.

My departure was briefly delayed by the January Crisis. While the Sentient Cathedral tried to broker peace, the Union shelled Grant Park. For a few days it looked like Chicago would become the site of a second major battle, as Union forces approached the city in force and the AGRT evacuated civilians across Lake Michigan. But if they'd been counting on the recent bickering between the members of the invading coalition to isolate Venezuela, the Union was sorely disappointed. Argentina and Panama mobilized their northern divisions, and the Union wisely chose not to engage. They melted away to the south, things settled down, and by mid-February I was in the city.

At first, Chicago was very different from what I'd expected. There was still a lot of rubble, and whole blocks downtown were cordoned off, but a few of the big hotels had power. GlobalNet and mobile data traffic were still being interdicted, but some communications had been restored. My hotel had nearly half a dozen dedicated phone lines. You couldn't talk for long, because the operator would kick you off after ten minutes. But you could do business over the phone again, and I was surprised how good that felt. We were gradually inching back into the twenty-first century.

I wasn't sure how to summarize all of that for Perez. "I'm here . . . to make money," I said. "I run a small telecom company called Ghost Impulse."

That seemed to satisfy him. After a moment, he picked up the second tablet and commenced to ignore me again. He tapped a quick message, and then turned to the side. He seemed to be gazing out the window, reflecting.

Maybe this was another calculated interrogation technique. But at this point, I honestly didn't give a damn. We sat quietly together for a few minutes.

There was a knock at the door. The ridiculousness of it almost made me laugh out loud.

"Entre," said the colonel.

Sergeant Van de Velde entered the room. She marched crisply to the left side of the desk, coming to attention with a sharp click of her heels. Perez said something in Spanish, and she relaxed slightly, clasping her hands behind her back.

They had a short conversation in Spanish. The sergeant didn't look at me — she just stared straight ahead, her gaze level. She was pretty, in a rather severe way. Her blonde hair was cut very short, and she had a scar on her forehead. I guessed her age at around twenty-four, which made her one of the oldest soldiers I'd seen so far.

She didn't seem happy with the way the conversation was going. Perez had expected this, and a slight smile played around the corners of his mouth. His tone was conversational, inquisitive, and she answered his questions in short, concise sentences.

Then she was looking at me. Glaring, really. I returned her gaze, curious.

They concluded their conversation. "My sergeant has something she would like to share with you," the colonel said. His voice was mild.

Van de Velde came to attention again. She was staring straight ahead into the room.

"I . . . apologize for threatening you," she said. "I should not have arrested you for your efforts to help an injured officer."

I was surprised. I wasn't quite sure how to respond, so I didn't say anything.

"I would like to offer my apologies on behalf of my sergeant, as well," said the colonel. He was already reaching for one of his tablets again. "She reacted poorly to the death of one of her men. I think it is understandable, yes? An action taken in the heat of battle. But regrettable."

I found my voice. "Yes, of course."

"Excellent," said the colonel. He began tapping on the tablet. "And I think we can agree that Corporal Maldonado behaved heroically. Perhaps that will be some comfort to his family."

I agreed again. Perez continued tapping, composing a letter on the computer slate while Van de Velde stood stoically at attention by his side. "He saved your life," he said to me. "He saved many lives."

"Yes," I said.

Perez nodded, smiling with grim satisfaction. He finished his note, then dismissed Van de Velde. When she was gone, he stood up.

"Thank you for your time, Mr. Simcoe. You are free to go."

I felt a little numb as I got to my feet. I wasn't sure how I'd expected this meeting to end, but certainly not with an apology and an easy dismissal.

"There's one more thing," I said.

The colonel had already started to turn away, but he turned back toward me. The smile was still fixed on his face, but there was impatience in his eyes.

"There's a damaged machine with the Manhattan Foreign Service in the field hospital downstairs," I said. "Nineteen Black Winter. I think you know him?"

The colonel nodded noncommittally, clearly wondering where this was going.

"He's badly injured," I said quickly. "A cracked casing. He's not going to make it unless he receives immediate attention."

"I'm certain the staff in the field hospital have things under control."

"They're doing a great job, yes. But no one is tending to Black Winter, and if he doesn't get looked at soon —"

The colonel raised his hand. "I'll send instructions," he said. "I'll see he's given proper care."

"I appreciate that, very much," I said, reaching my hand out across the table. The colonel set down his tablet and shook my hand.

"Thank you," I said. "For dealing with this matter personally. I realize you must be extremely busy, as the head of the Occupation Force."

The colonel raised an eyebrow. "Head of the Occupation? Hardly. Who told you that?"

I didn't mean to, but my gaze went automatically to the kid, who'd been standing quietly behind me the entire time.

"Ah," said the colonel, nodding his understanding. "No, not at all. I'm simply in command of the small garrison here. A humble post — but as you've seen, an important one, from time to time."

"Very much," I agreed as I walked toward the door. "And you'll remember my offer? To help you with your communications . . . problem?"

"Certainly." The colonel flashed a diplomatic smile. "I look forward to discussing it."

The kid led me out of the colonel's office, through the door and past the guards, then down the long carpeted hallway to the elevators.

"You are lucky," the kid confided when the elevator doors closed. "I thought . . ."

"That I was going to be shot?" I said. The kid nodded, managing to look embarrassed.

"Yeah," I said. "Me too. Can you do me a favor?"

The kid immediately looked suspicious. "What?"

"Can you take me back to the field hospital?"

He shrugged. "I guess."

The room was totally different than the madhouse it had been this morning. It almost seemed like a real hospital now, with nurses moving calmly between tables, checking patients. Most of the medical technicians had gone, including Sergei. All the equipment seemed to be operating efficiently.

One thing hadn't changed, however. Nineteen Black Winter was still crumpled on the floor, exactly where I'd left him. Someone had mopped up the puddle of liquid pooling around him, but had otherwise not bothered to move him. No one had come back for him.

I kneeled down next to him. "Black Winter?"

There was no response. He lay still and unmoving. I pressed my hand to the cracked metal of his torso. It was very hot.

"Black Winter?"

The kid came up behind me. "Is he dead?"

"I don't know. But if we don't help him now, he will be."

"The colonel said he'd be cared for."

"We don't have time to wait. If we don't get him a replacement core in the next half hour, he's not going to make it."

"A robot core? For that thing? Good luck."

"Help me pick him up," I said.

"What for?"

"Because we're not going to let him die on this goddamn floor. Grab his legs."

The kid complained, but did as he was told. Black Winter was heavy, but not as heavy as I expected. We lifted him onto one of the dollies they'd used to rush the equipment in here, and then got him into the elevator. We rode down to the basement, and wheeled him over to the Venezuelan motor pool.

We were stopped by a mechanic in a grease-stained uniform. He asked me something in Spanish. The kid answered, and the mechanic waved us over to the machine depot. There were five AGRT soldiers and mechanics there, and they watched us wheel up Black Winter with frank curiosity.

"Where you goin' with that thing?" the nearest one asked.

"This is Nineteen Black Winter," I said. "He's with the Manhattan Consulate. He was injured in the attack this morning."

Two more mechanics wandered over. One squatted down next to Black Winter and looked him over.

"What you got there, Barajas?" asked a tall corporal leaning against a rack of tools.

"Pile of shit," said Barajas. "He's gone."

"He's got a cracked housing," I said. "He's been leaking fluid since this morning."

Barajas reached out hesitantly, touching Black Winter's torso. "Core temp is way up," he said. "He's fried."

"That thing alive?" asked one of the soldiers.

"I doubt it," said Barajas.

"Yes," I said firmly. "He was conscious and speaking a few minutes ago. He just lost consciousness."

The kid gave me a look. Yeah, that was stretching the truth a little. But not much, for all we knew.

The corporal came over to check out the robot for himself. Then he looked me up and down. He wore an AGRT uniform with Panamanian insignia, but he spoke English just fine. "What do you expect us to do with this thing?"

"He needs a new core," I said. "Immediately."

The corporal laughed. "I don't have a mobile robot core."

Barajas spoke up. "You need to take this thing to Machine Operations at ComSec. Maybe they can help it."

"That's three miles away. He'll never make it." More importantly, I'd never get into Machine Operations. The best I could do there was drop Black Winter off and hope someone took pity on him. No, our chances of success were better here.

The corporal shrugged. "Can't help you."

"I need to speak to the duty officer," I said. "I need someone to make a call on this thing, or certify it as nonoperational."

The corporal shrugged again. "Can't help you."

"You willing to certify it as nonoperational?" I asked, looking him in the eye. I turned slowly, looking at everyone in turn. "Tomorrow, someone is going to come from the Manhattan Consulate. High-ranking machines. They're going to ask questions about who certified the death of their robot. Is anyone here willing to do that?"

I circled back to the corporal. "You? Can you certify this thing is dead for me?"

He grimaced. Then he backed up, looking deeper into the parking garage. He whistled loudly. A moment later he waved someone over. We waited for whomever he'd signaled to arrive.

"What the hell do you want, Sosa?" she called as she approached.

"*Shit*," I whispered.

She stepped into the loose circle of men around Black Winter less than twenty seconds later. Sergeant Van de Velde.

The moment she saw me, she stopped. Her face twisted in disgust, and she shot a question in Spanish at Sosa. Without waiting for an answer, she turned to me.

"What the hell are you doing here?"

"I'm trying to prevent the death of a Manhattan Consulate officer," I said. "This machine — Nineteen Black Winter."

Sosa was talking over me. Van de Velde listened to us both, then pointed to the robot at my feet. "You're here because of this piece of shit?"

"Yes. He's dying."

Sosa was still talking. Van de Velde shut him up with a wave of her hand. "It's dead already," she said to me.

"You don't know that."

"I don't know, and I don't care. This thing is not my problem."

"He needs a mobile robot core. In the next half hour. He's already started to overheat."

"Then take him to ComSec."

"He'll die before he gets there."

The sergeant bit back her first response. She took two steps closer, and gave me a cold smile.

"You know, I really don't know who you are. Or why Colonel Perez seems to like you. I don't know what your relationship is to this foreign pile of shit, and I don't care about that either. If I could help this thing, I would be happy to extend it every courtesy. But we service the big machines here."

"Like that field unit that got popped this morning? The one that took on the mech?"

"Like that one, yeah. We don't have the expertise to service mobile machines here."

"I understand," I said. "I'm not looking for emergency repairs. I was just hoping that someone here might have a line on a mobile robot core."

"We don't carry those."

"I know. But they're standard units for rational devices of his scale."

"So what?"

"So . . ." I spoke up, making sure that everyone in the depot could hear me. "So maybe someone here knows where we could acquire the parts. Salvaged from another machine, perhaps."

Van de Velde's mouth was open. She stared at me in amazement.

"I'm asking if—"

"We heard you," she said. "We know what you're asking. And the answer is no. Nobody here can get a goddamn black market core for you."

As casually as I could, I glanced at the others as she said those words. Three of the soldiers and mechanics watching returned my gaze, their faces unreadable. But when Van de Velde mentioned the market, two looked away quickly, dropping their gaze to the floor or feigning sudden disinterest. One of them was Sosa.

Van de Velde had had enough. "These men have work to do," she said. She pointed at Nineteen Black Winter. "Take your boyfriend here back upstairs, and wait for one of Queen Sophia's pretty-boy soldiers to show up and claim him." Without another word, she turned her back on me and strode away.

"Ten thousand dollars," I said.

Van de Velde stopped walking. She turned around. Her face displayed anger and disbelief. "What did you say?"

"Ten thousand dollars. For a universal core. Right now."

"Are you kidding me?"

But I wasn't talking to her. I turned around slowly, spreading my hands, making it clear that the offer was open to anyone interested.

And there were definitely interested parties. The mechanics were exchanging glances, standing a little straighter.

"Cash?" someone asked.

"Bank transfer," I said. "American dollars."

"In advance?" said Barajas.

"No. When my patient is up and walking."

"Today? You pay today?"

"Today."

Sosa waved two of his mechanics over. They conversed with him in whispers, and then left in a hurry. "Stay here," Sosa told me.

I turned to have a word with the kid and found myself face-to-face with Sergeant Van de Velde.

She stood with her hands on her hips and a stern set to her jaw. "What the hell are you doing?"

I lowered my voice. I really didn't want another confrontation with this woman. "I don't want any trouble with you."

"Then you damn well better explain yourself. Who the hell is this robot to you?"

That was a good question. I wasn't sure I could answer it—not in a way that would satisfy her suspicions.

"Nobody," I admitted. "We just met today."

"This is your kink, is it? You have a thing for robots?"

"No."

"You rich, then? Ten thousand, that's a cinch for you?"

"No." No, it certainly was not. "This is going to cost me, believe me."

"Then I need to know what's going on. Before I let you commandeer my machine depot for your personal science project."

I answered as honestly as I could. "I just . . . I don't want anybody else to die today. That's the truth. You can take Black Winter when I'm done. I make no claim on him. He helped me this morning, when I needed it. I want to help him, if I can."

Van de Velde held my gaze. Her eyes searched mine for a long, long time. I found I didn't mind. Under the anger and suspicion, I found honest curiosity in her eyes.

"Sosa," she said at length.

"Sergeant?"

"This is your deal."

"Yes, ma'am."

She was walking away. "Keep it off my books, Corporal," she said as she stalked off.

"Ma'am."

"I mean it. I don't want to know about it."

"Yes, ma'am," Sosa said with satisfaction.

Sosa's mechanics returned surprisingly quickly. "We may have something," he said noncommittally.

I was next to Black Winter, checking his temperature. "You better make it fast."

Sosa came closer and spoke the rest in a lower voice. "It's a similar model. Similar, but not identical."

"Manhattan make?"

"Argentinean, but parallel design. The mobile core is intact."

"This Argentinean robot ... what kind of damage are we talking about?"

Sosa nodded to the mechanic who had stepped up with him. The mechanic squatted down next to me. "Missile hit," he said. "Took the head clean off."

"Damn. But the core is intact?"

"Core, circulation system, and axial motivators. They all check out."

"But we need to deal with a third party," Sosa said smoothly. "And they need payment up front."

I thought it over. "How soon can they have it here?"

"Ten minutes."

"You can do the work?" I asked Sosa.

He nodded. "I make no guarantees," he said with a shrug. "But I can get your friend here a new core, and hack the interface. Whether or not he wakes up, that's up to him."

"All right," I said. "Let's do it."

Barajas and the mechanic stepped forward, nudging me gently out of the way. "We'll give him a coolant flush, get his temperature down while we wait," said Barajas. They lifted him off the dolly and manhandled him over to a clear workspace, where they smoothly plugged him in. I watched, appreciating their quick, professional work.

Sosa and I handled the business arrangements, using a little thumb-scan reader to transfer the funds to his account. Then he made a call on a little gray box. About ten minutes later two men drove up. I expected other mechanics, or maybe locals. Instead, they were two AGRT officers. They haggled briefly with Sosa, then lifted a tarp off something in the back to let him see it. They haggled a little more, then shook hands. Sosa and two men lifted the thing out of the jeep, tarp and all, and the men drove off.

Once they were gone, Sosa uncovered the tarp. Inside was the twisted form of a headless Argentinean robot. Unlike Black Winter, who was an almost featureless black, this one was silver and gold. The mechanic's description of its condition had been fairly accurate, but he hadn't mentioned the extensive scorching all down the right side. It looked like it had been in a fire.

"The core looks cooked," I said, concerned.

Sosa shook his head. "It's okay. The core can manage a thermal impact. The problem is the missile collision. If there was a voltage surge, the core interface . . . *boom.*" He threw up his hands to illustrate. "Fried."

"Can you tell how bad the damage is?" I asked, pushing closer for a better look at just what my money had bought.

With an exasperated look, Sosa waved me out of his operating theater. For the next forty minutes, I paced around the parking lot like an expectant father.

"You don't have to stick around for this," I told the kid.

He shrugged, peering over my shoulder at Sosa and his team as they worked. "I'm off duty now. And c'mon — I gotta see how this turns out."

"Yeah." Truth to tell, I was glad for the company.

"Where'd they get a mobile chassis?" the kid asked.

"Two AGRT officers who picked up a war souvenir, from the look of it."

"Man, people will collect anything," he marveled.

Less than ten minutes later, I saw Sosa step away from the metal counter where he was operating. He was scrubbing his hands with a rag. When he saw me approach, he grimaced.

"The interface was a bitch," he said. "Still don't know how much I got right."

"Do you think it'll work?" I asked.

"See for yourself."

One of the mechanics was helping Black Winter sit up. He was conscious. His robot eyes fixed on me as I stepped closer.

"Black Winter," I said.

"Hello," said Black Winter. Sosa had torn off the front of his torso and replaced nearly a third of his internal components with silver and gold organs from the donor robot.

"Do you know who I am?" I said.

"No," he said. There was a flutter in his voice that hadn't been there before.

I tried not to be alarmed. Some cognitive impairment was to be expected, but short-term memory loss wasn't a good sign. It might not be serious . . . but nonetheless, I selfishly mourned the loss of our friendship, however brief it had been.

"Do you remember anything from this morning?" I asked.

"Of course I do. But you never told me your name."

"Barry," I said. "I'm Barry Simcoe."

"I see you didn't get put in front of a firing squad."

"No," I said, feeling abruptly relieved. For both of us. "No, I didn't. And I see you found a new mobile core."

"That's an oversimplification if I ever heard one. I didn't find anything. I've got a new axial motivator and a completely overhauled circulatory pump, among other things, and none of my new organs are responding to system queries. Which tells me the work was . . . well, let's call it off-spec."

"You could probably call it that," I agreed. Sosa's men, who were listening around us, found this very funny. One of them punched Sosa good-naturedly in the arm.

"How are you feeling?" I asked.

"Like shit. My drive fluid pressure is critically low, and I've got only partial feeling in my right side. I'm probably going to need help walking, at least until I can get a spinal recalibration. And I've got some wicked feedback in my right ear." He reached up hesitantly and tapped the right side of his flat metal head.

"These men did the work on you," I said, introducing Black Winter to the mechanics clustered around him. "You'll be the ultimate judge, but I'd say they did pretty good work, all things considered."

Black Winter looked around. "It's a pleasure to make your acquaintance, gentlemen. And believe me, I mean that most sincerely."

"You're not like most of the machines we see down here," said Barajas.

"No sir," said Black Winter. "I'm a man of the world."

Sosa said something in Spanish, and the group began to break up. A few of them patted Black Winter warmly on the shoulder before striding away.

"You should go," Barajas said to me. He signaled one of the soldiers, who wheeled over the cart. "You need to be gone before the sergeant gets back."

"That's not necessary," Black Winter said, looking at the cart. He stood up, a little shaky. "I'm just a little unstable."

"Lean on me," I suggested. I stepped to his left side, and without any prompting the kid moved to his right. Black Winter put his arms around us. His first few steps were a little unstable, but pretty soon we all got the rhythm of it.

Barajas caught up to me before we left the depot. He slipped a slender piece of metal in my pocket. "Use that to check his drive fluid for the next two days," he said. "If there's any trace of hydrocarbons, get him back here, pronto."

"I will."

"His new core will self-regulate to his metabolism over the next seventy-two hours. Until then, keep his body temperature below seventy-five degrees."

"Understood," I said.

"There goes my weekend at the beach," muttered Black Winter.

"Good luck," Barajas said to Black Winter. He gave the robot a crisp salute, and then he was gone.

"I like that guy," said Black Winter.

"Yeah," I said.

"But somehow, I doubt he just had a compatible robotic core in inventory. Care to explain how that miracle happened?"

"You're right," I said. "We had one delivered by a third party. It took a little . . . negotiating."

"I figured. How much negotiating, exactly?"

"We can talk about that later."

"If it's okay with you, I'd like the bad news up front."

"I understand. Well, I've got a ten-thousand-dollar hole in my expense account."

"That's even worse than I thought. I don't have ten thousand dollars to pay you back."

"That's all right. I didn't expect you would."

"How can we sort this out?"

"I've been thinking about that. You're not a soldier, so I assume your free time is your own. I could use a political consultant with your connections. Would you accept the ten thousand as a retainer?"

"A retainer? To do what?"

"To come work for me."

Black Winter chewed on that for a minute. "Yes, I think I would."

"Great," I said as we stepped in unison toward the elevator. "Because I filed the paperwork with Ghost Impulse to hire you half an hour ago."

Tuesday, March 9th, 2083
Posted 3:11 pm by Barry Simcoe

CanadaNET1 Encrypted, Sponsored by Dolphin Logic.
*For the best in on-the-fly blog translation.*

Sharing is set to PRIVATE
Comments are CLOSED

Breakfast this morning was something of a celebration. The hotel restaurant had finally reopened after the street attack, and everyone was downstairs, standing in the buffet line and swapping stories of where they'd been, how they survived.

Before I joined Martin for breakfast, I went looking for Sergei. The big room on the third floor where the field hospital had been was mostly empty, just a few tables and sheets, but he wasn't hard to find. Down the hall a bit, one of the conference rooms had been converted into a command center. Peeking in from the door, I saw the Venezuelans had set up tables with dozens of monitors, a lot of mobile comm equipment, and plenty of other equipment I didn't recognize. I spotted Sergei near the back.

There were two guards stationed at the door, both with rifles, and they just shook their heads when I tried to mosey on inside. I hung around for a few minutes, hoping Sergei would come out, until I saw the kid—the one Van de Velde had set to guard me yesterday—approach. He was carrying a bunch of boxes.

"Hey," I said. "Can you get a message to Sergei for me?"

"Where is he?" the kid asked.

I indicated the back of the command center. The kid nodded, and headed into the room, motioning me to follow. When the guards objected, the kid said something in Spanish, and they moved aside, still eyeing me suspiciously.

"What the hell did you say to them?" I asked when we were out of earshot.

"I told them you're a doctor," he said. I thought briefly about correcting him, but decided it was best to let that misunderstanding lie.

"How is your friend?" the kid asked as we walked. "The robot?"

"Okay, far as I know."

Two mobile machines from the Manhattan Consulate had shown up after Black Winter made a call from the lobby yesterday afternoon, and they'd whisked him away. One of them, a lumbering seven-foot crane that looked like two lampposts welded together, came back later and grilled me for forty-five minutes, and she wasn't friendly about it. Apparently no one in the AGRT had bothered to tell the Consulate what had happened to their machine. Black Winter was right—diplomatic relations with Sector One just didn't seem very high on the Venezuelan priority list.

"Why didn't you contact us?" she'd asked me. For the second time.

"Contact who?" I said, getting a little annoyed. "I don't have a phone. And all I knew was his name. If I'd spent my time trying to find a phone, he wouldn't be here now, I guarantee you that. He needed help immediately; I helped him."

"You had no right to authorize an organ transfer for a defense attaché of the Kingdom of Manhattan, especially with substandard components. If anything happens to him, we will hold you responsible."

"Fine," I said. I was tempted to ask just who was going to pay for those substandard components, but figured I was on thin ice with these people already. Besides, the damage to my expense account was already done. I was going to have to get pretty damn creative to explain why I'd spent ten thousand dollars of Ghost Impulse money on a foreign machine for "consulting services."

"We will need to talk again," she said, handing me a slender metal card. "In the meantime, if you recall anything else about the incident in which our attaché was injured, please call this number."

"I don't have a phone," I reminded her. "None of my mobile devices work. The AGRT is still jamming all commercial bandwidth in the city."

"You can reach the Consulate from the phone in the hotel lobby." With that she packed up and was gone.

I was touched to hear the kid ask about Black Winter, anyway. I was glad I wasn't the only one thinking about him. "Have you heard from him since yesterday?" the kid asked.

"No," I said.

"You probably never will," the kid said. "And you'll never see that ten thousand dollars again, mark my words. You can't trust a damn robot."

There were dozens of technicians and soldiers in the room, most of them sitting at makeshift communication stations. I tried not to obviously gawk at everything as we made our way toward the back, but it was hard. The Venezuelans had some sweet equipment—and very clearly had access to the kind of unimpeded bandwidth that civilians could only dream about. I couldn't access any commercial data networks from my hotel room, not even the private ones I'd paid a fortune for. But the AGRT didn't appear to have that problem. Every one of the monitors I passed showed what appeared to be live data.

They had a weather station, an air traffic control display, a cluster of camera feeds from the hotel, four or five screens showing what look like live feeds from airborne drones, a comm dashboard, a network hub, and a whole bunch more equipment I couldn't suss out at a glance. Nothing looked ultra-sensitive though—no obvious display with troop placements, or anything like that—which made me relax a bit. I'd already been involved in one misunderstanding with the Venezuelan high command. I didn't need to be mistaken for a spy in the same week.

There was a single robot in the room, a hulking brute snoozing by the door. At least it seemed to be snoozing. It was a mobile combat unit, all folded up, and at rest it mostly looked like a giant black refrigerator. It didn't have a head, far as I could see. I couldn't tell what its make was. Argentinean, maybe? It gave no indication of any kind of readiness, and if it had any status lights, they were all dead. But it still looked plenty imposing, and I didn't stare at it for long. I'd seen too much footage of what these things were capable of during the war.

Sergei had a little medical station at the back of the room. It was a modest little one-man operation, but it seemed cozy enough. He had a bunch of equipment crammed under the table, a plastic chair, two monitors, what looked like a blood kit, and stacks of small vials. He glanced up as we approached. He didn't smile, but he did give me a polite nod.

"The doctor is back," said the kid as he dropped me off. Then he headed toward the weather station to dump his boxes.

Sergei looked at me questioningly. He was wrapping loose cord around a blood monitor.

"I just . . . I just came by to thank you," I said. "For writing that note to Perez."

Sergei nodded, putting the monitor on the table. He picked up his GPU, the standard-issue ID card all the AGRT soldiers carry, and tucked it into his pocket. He grabbed a med slate.

I looked around, a little awkwardly. I felt extremely out of place, standing here in the hive center of the Venezuelan occupation. And just like yesterday, Sergei didn't seem in the mood for conversation.

But a quick thank-you and goodbye hardly seemed adequate for what he'd done. I made a decision, seizing a chair near an empty table. I slid it over so it was across from Sergei, and sat down facing him.

"Listen . . . I was in a tight spot yesterday. And I think your note may have helped save my life."

Sergei just shrugged. But he'd stopped playing with his med slate.

"What did you say in the note?" I asked.

"I said you were stupid."

"Stupid?" I repeated.

"Stupid. But that you liked to help people."

"Well . . . thank you, I guess."

Sergei put the slate down. He had a look on his face, like he was explaining something to a child. "Colonel Perez needed facts, to understand why you were found with his dead officer. Sergeant Van de Velde offered a sinister, but unlikely, interpretation. I offered a more plausible alternative."

"That I'm stupid."

Sergei shrugged again. "A stupid American who risks his life to help others. I had facts to support my theory."

"What facts?"

"Yesterday. You escaped arrest to assist me in the field hospital."

"*Escaped arrest.*" I almost snorted. "I walked ten feet from a seventeen-year-old who doesn't know how to use a rifle."

"To help me," Sergei said, as if that proved his point.

"Well, however you phrased it, I deeply appreciate your intentions. Even if you didn't exactly have all your facts right. I'm Canadian, not American."

"Ah." Sergei sat back, seeming to reappraise me. "Perhaps that is why he did not have you shot."

I laughed. "You think so?"

Sergei didn't find it so amusing. "The colonel has orders to be very hospitable to foreigners. Venezuelan high command believes other nations are watching Sector Eleven with some scrutiny. There is pressure to demonstrate that AGRT can maintain peace and get city back on its feet."

That made a certain amount of sense, when I thought about it. "How do you know all this?"

"Senior staff is briefed."

"Whatever the case, I do believe your letter made a difference. I'm in your debt."

"There is no debt. Yesterday, you saved lives. The rest—" He waved his hand. "Just politics."

"Speaking of saving lives . . ." I said. "Where are all the patients?"

"They have been transferred to Army Surgical Unit at Burroughs."

"Are they going to be okay? Will they all make it?"

"Yes. Yes, I think so." Sergei seemed to consider for a moment, then reached under the desk and pulled out a broad black slate. He turned it on and handed it to me.

"Hey," I said after a moment. "These are all of them?"

"Yes."

The slate showed the vitals for thirteen men and women, in what looked like real time. There was even a picture for each of the eleven soldiers, although the two civilians had faceless placeholder images. I poked the screen, and it responded to my touch. After a minute I was getting more detailed info.

"Vasquez has an infection," I said.

"Yes, as you predicted." Sergei reached over and took the slate. "But not too serious."

"They look like they'll be okay." I felt a strange sense of relief. I hadn't known any of our patients, but after spending a few hours helping Sergei fight to keep them alive, I felt an odd sense of responsibility for them.

"Yes," said Sergei, with some satisfaction.

"You do good work."

He nodded. Before he could say anything else, something caught his attention. I followed his gaze over my shoulder.

A man in a hotel uniform carrying a cardboard box was walking toward us, accompanied by a soldier. When he reached us, he set it down on Sergei's desk. A name tag pinned to his chest read NGUYEN.

"Will these do?" he asked Sergei.

Sergei stood and shooed away the guard. When he was gone, he lifted a cloth napkin concealing the contents of the box and reached inside.

I watched him pull out two oranges. "Yes, is good," he said.

Nguyen smiled, obviously pleased. While the two of us watched, Sergei cut one of the oranges in half, then pulled a plastic bag containing a syringe out of his desk. Sergei expertly pulled on a pair of disposable gloves, and pulled the syringe out of the bag.

It held a small amount of yellowish fluid. Sergei injected the fluid into the skin of one of the orange halves, then returned the syringe to the bag. Holding the orange aloft with his left hand, he cleared a small space on his desk and then pulled the skin-tight plastic wrapper off a new medical slate, one-handed.

I moved to help him, but he shook his head. Putting the slate on the desk, he carefully placed the orange, sliced side down, on the glass face of the slate. He brought up a virtual menu on the bottom of the slate and punched in a quick set of instructions. The slate began to flash at regular intervals, like it was taking pictures.

Satisfied, Sergei pulled off the gloves. He carefully bundled the gloves, bag, and empty syringe together and stepped toward a nearby medical waste disposal.

Nguyen and I exchanged glances. Nguyen's look said, *That was weird,* and I was inclined to agree.

Sergei returned and began pulling open drawers on his desk, pulling things out and putting them in a paper bag. While he was occupied, Nguyen introduced himself. "Randolph Nguyen," he said, shaking my hand. "Call me Randy."

"You work for the hotel?" I said.

"I'm with Purchasing," he said.

"That must be challenging these days."

Nguyen grinned. "You'd be surprised. Most things are still available; it's just the medium of exchange that's in flux. For a lot of things, we're back to the barter system."

"People don't use American money?"

"The Venezuelans don't," he said.

As if to illustrate his point, Sergei turned around and handed the paper bag to Nguyen. Nguyen took a minute to inventory its contents. I couldn't see what was in it, but I did see him pull out two sheets of condoms and what looked like some diagnostic strips.

"Everything seems in order," Nguyen said. "Pleasure doing business with you."

Sergei's attention had already returned inexorably to the orange. I stood up and said goodbye, and Sergei dismissed us both with an absent wave.

Nguyen was ready to leave, but seemed hesitant. "Can we walk around without an escort?" he whispered to me nervously.

"One way to find out," I said, setting off for the door. He followed, clutching his bag.

"You a guest?" he said. He was putting on a brave front, but it was obvious that being surrounded by this many AGRT soldiers deeply unsettled him.

"Yeah. You know how many floors on the hotel are open?"

"Not very many — just a handful at the moment. The Venezuelans gave the owners permission to reopen half a dozen floors about a month ago."

"The hotel's only been open for a month?"

"Yes. Things seemed like they were returning to normal, and Renkain — the manager — was hoping to reopen more floors by May. But that was before yesterday."

Nguyen grew quiet as we were approaching the door. No one had given us more than a casual glance, but he slowed as we neared the guards with the rifles, and he eyed them nervously.

I put a hand on his shoulder. "Come on," I said.

He walked alongside me as we exited. He seemed too nervous to speak, but I kept up the conversation, keeping my voice casual. The guards didn't even look at us. Sixty feet down the hall, by the stairwell, Nguyen turned and pumped my hand warmly. Relief was evident in his voice.

"You need anything — anything at all — you come see me. I'm in the basement, below the kitchen."

"I will," I said.

I made my way down to the restaurant on the first floor. Suddenly I was starving. It seemed like a weight had been lifted from my shoulders. I wanted to eat, and I wanted to celebrate.

The restaurant was as busy as I'd seen it, which wasn't saying much, but there was definitely a celebratory mood among the diners. Martin spotted me as I entered, and waved me over. There were already half a dozen people crammed around his table, but they made a show of pulling over an extra chair for me.

Martin introduced me to everyone as I took a seat. "This," he said, clapping me on the back, "is the crazy Canadian I was telling you about."

The food was very good. They had a buffet with eggs, real bacon, and even fresh produce. It seemed that Nguyen was good at his job. We enjoyed the food and shared stories.

For the first fifteen minutes, Belgium was the big topic of discussion.

Word was going around about the results of yesterday's referendum. By a narrow margin, the country had voted to dissolve Parliament, and surrender authority to the Arenberg Machine Cabal, one of the nastier European robot alliances. I exchanged a grim glance with Martin across the table. One of the last human governments on the planet had just succumbed to the machines. The thought left me chilled.

Sabine, an inner-city Chicago native who'd been hired as a communications specialist by the AGRT, was one of the few optimists at our table. "The Cabal has pledged to abide by the human governance guidelines of the Helsinki Trustees," she said. "So that's something, yeah?"

Mike Concert—whom I'd met shortly after I'd moved in—audibly snorted. He was a contractor with a local construction outfit, managing one of the countless reconstruction jobs downtown. "Right," he said. "Acoustic Drake promised the same thing when he seized Cameroon, and half that country is now a goddamn wasteland."

Martin, who seemed to enjoy these debates a lot more than I did, waved a butter knife in my direction. "You know who's an expert on living under machine rule? The distinguished Mr. Simcoe."

I grimaced involuntarily. I had no desire to be in the center of this discussion. But Sabine slapped the table, pleased to welcome an apparent ally to the conversation. "That's right," she said. "Canada's been ruled by machines for years now, and that's turned out okay. Ain't that right?"

"Well, our situation is very different from Belgium's," I said reluctantly. "Our prime minister is a machine, yeah. But Distant Prime is a Canadian machine, with Canadian interests. And truthfully, she's done a decent job. But I wouldn't say we're *ruled* by machines—"

"The situation isn't that different," Mike said to Sabine, interrupting me. "Distant Prime seized power from the constitutional government. She dismissed the Canadian Congress in 2080—"

"Parliament," I said, starting to feel annoyed. "She dissolved *Parliament.*"

Mike ignored me. "She seized power illegally two years ago, and has refused to yield it since," he told Sabine flatly. "Canada is ruled by machines, no matter what they tell you."

Sabine glanced back and forth between me and Mike, her face questioning. "Is that true?" she asked me.

It wasn't true, but I'd encountered American prejudice against machine governments before, and I didn't have the energy or the patience to get in a lengthy debate about it. Many Americans don't see a whole lot of difference between the peaceful Canadian government and the territorially aggressive Arenberg Cabal. They were both run by machines, so they were essentially the same, right?

"There was a constitutional crisis two years ago," I said carefully. "The most powerful machine in Canada, a Quebec Sovereign Intelligence named the Separatist, amassed a secret army — a bewildering host of flying machines and well-armed mercenaries — and began to make dangerous territorial demands. The old Parliament, the human Parliament, was deadlocked. Paralyzed by indecision. Distant Prime was a junior MP at the time, one of the first machine members of Parliament. But she was one of the only ones who could see what had to be done. She forced a vote of nonconfidence, dissolved Parliament, and formed a new political party."

"Made up almost entirely of machines," Mike interjected. "She turned machines into the ruling class."

"She won the support of the Thought Machines in charge of the bulk of the Canadian Forces," I continued evenly, "and drove the Separatist out of the country." More than that, Distant Prime had formed a trusted cabinet of Canadian Thought Machines and decisively rebuffed the demands of the British Machine Parliament to join a military alliance, guaranteeing Canada's independence. She'd stood up to the San Cristobal Coalition too, when the SCC invaded Manhattan a month later and demanded access to the Saint Lawrence Seaway, which would have allowed them to sail unchallenged all the way to Chicago. Distant Prime refused and took us right to the brink of war, eventually forcing the SCC to back down. But those details probably didn't get a lot of play in American news cycles, especially during wartime.

Mike was nodding, as if all this proved his point. "She maintained order," he said. "Just like all dictators promise to do."

"Distant Prime isn't a dictator. She held open parliamentary elections last year, and her party won handily," I said, a measure of pride in my voice. "She's one of the most popular prime ministers of the past fifty years. Yeah, there are folks who object to the way she took power, but she reinforced Canadian sovereignty, maintained the Dominion, and returned the country to democracy."

"And she ensured power for herself by giving machines the right to vote — and then granting citizenship to an unprecedented number of machines," Mike said.

"Machines make excellent citizens," I said, aware I was mouthing political slogans and unable to help myself. "Besides, machines don't vote as a bloc any more than people do. Distant Prime has to win their votes, just like she has to win mine."

Mike was growing visibly angry, and I realized suddenly that he wasn't the only one. There were upset faces all around the table.

I knew it was a mistake to get into this. The first experience Americans had ever had of machine government was the heavy boot of the San Cristobal Coalition and the AGRT on their necks, and it was going to take a lot more than polite rhetoric over breakfast for them to acquire a taste for it. I mentally kicked myself for not being more sensitive. All I was doing was poking fresh wounds.

Martin had evidently reached the same conclusion. "Let's talk about something a little closer to home," he said hastily, cutting off another retort from Mike. "Sabine, is it true you slept right through all the excitement yesterday morning?"

Sabine held both hands in the air. "I did, I did!" she admitted good-naturedly. "But if I'd known there was gonna be an American Union mech in the streets, I woulda been there! I been waiting eight months to see them shoot up some Venezuelan shit!"

Everyone at the table laughed. The tension was broken, and to my relief the conversation returned to Monday's Juno attack on the hotel. I shot Martin a grateful look. *Thank you,* I mouthed.

He shook his head, giving me a crooked grin. One that clearly said, *You're an idiot.*

After about thirty minutes, Martin and I got back in the buffet line. Near the buffet I saw Mike talking to a striking brunette woman. She was tall, thin, professionally dressed, with classic fashion sense — the kind I didn't see much anymore. "Who's that?" I asked, nudging Martin.

"Oh, that's Mac. Real estate agent, or estate broker, or something like that. For some of the distressed properties in the city. Mostly high-rises. Man, she's got some stories. You don't know Mac?"

I shook my head.

"Oh, you need to get to know her," he said. He gestured at the two of them. Mike didn't seem too thrilled, but he followed Mac over as she joined us in line.

Martin introduced me. "Barry, this is Mackenzie Stronnick. Mac, this is Barry Simcoe. He's the Canadian businessman I was telling you about."

"The one who nearly got killed trying to see the mech in action?" she said. She had a New England accent, but I couldn't place it any better than that. Boston, maybe?

"That's him," Martin said cheerfully. "Damn near took a missile up the ass."

I forced a laugh, and Mike and Martin laughed along with me. Mac had the good grace to limit her reaction to a smile.

"Was it worth it?" she asked.

"Frankly, no," I admitted.

"I saw you," said Mac. "That was you and Martin, trying to move all the scared tourists, wasn't it?"

"That *was* us," said Martin, obviously pleased.

"That was brave of you. Both of you," she said, looking at me.

"Naah," said Martin, reaching over to pluck a grape off of the buffet. "Just a little crowd control. Where were you?"

"Are you kidding?" Mac said. "I was running down Stetson Avenue the moment they let us move. If it weren't for that sergeant with the rifle, I'd probably still be running."

"She knew how to take charge," Mike said admiringly.

"Why didn't you run?" Mac asked me. Her tone was casual, but her eyes were serious.

Suddenly I felt uncomfortable. I opened my mouth, closed it again. I looked to Martin. "I was just helping Martin," I managed at last.

I was relieved to see Mac turn her gaze to Martin, and Martin was more than happy for the attention. "Well, if I'd seen that goddamn mech, I damn well would have run," he said. There was a round of appreciative laughter. "But seriously, half the hotel staff was just cowering in front of the windows, or trying to get back into the building. One shell would have ended it. They were just panicked, and they needed someone to kick their asses."

There were murmured comments about Martin's bravery. I seconded them, and urged him on whenever he paused in his narrative. It felt good to listen to him talk, good to hear yesterday's events spun into an entertaining tale over breakfast. Good just to hear a version of the story that didn't end with a young man choking to death on his own fucking blood.

"You okay, Barry?" Mac asked.

"Hmm?" I said.

They were all staring at me.

"I'm fine," I managed.

"You look a little pale," said Martin.

"None of the rest of us got knocked over by a missile," Mac said. "Maybe it's a little soon for this topic?"

"I'm fine," I said.

"Has anyone else noticed how young all the Venezuelan soldiers are?" said Mike, who seemed eager to steer the conversation away from Martin's tales of bravery.

"God, they're children," said Mac.

"They're drafted into military service at sixteen in Venezuela," Martin said knowledgeably. "Eighteen months of training, then they're in the field."

"It's the same in Argentina, Bolivia, and Panama," said Mac. "All four members of the San Cristobal Coalition, they recruit them young. In Argentina, they put them to work in the robot assemblies."

"Why are there so many damn foreigners in the Occupation Force?" Mike asked. I winced at the question, and saw Mac looked shocked as well. Mike carried on, oblivious. "I mean, I must have heard ten different languages on the way to breakfast this morning. Russian, Portuguese, French, and a bunch of shit I didn't even know what it was."

Martin cleared his throat. "After the war ended, the Memphis Ceasefire dictated that each member of the Coalition administer different occupied sectors. And it required the Occupation Force be replaced with an international peacekeeping force — that's where the AGRT comes in."

"Though as far as I can see, most AGRT soldiers are from Latin America," I said.

"A lot of Coalition soldiers never went home," said Mac. "They just traded in their uniforms for the uniforms of the AGRT. But at least a lot of them speak English. It's hard enough living here without trying to do business in five different languages." This last bit seemed to be a conciliatory attempt aimed at Mike, and he nodded vigorously in agreement.

The small talk continued for a few minutes, and then the group started to break up. I felt a hand on my arm, and I turned to see Mac.

"I'm sorry," she said.

"No, it's fine," I said. "I'm just a little shook up."

"Sounds like you've been through an ordeal."

Under normal circumstances I would have been happy for attention like this, especially from a woman as striking as Mac. I've been single since before I left Canada, and someone like Mac would be a very welcome distraction from, well, everything. But Corporal Maldonado's death had evidently affected me even more than I realized. And right at the moment, I just wanted to escape back to my room as quietly as possible.

I forced a smile. "No more than Martin. He's just made of sterner stuff than me."

She looked doubtful. Mike was hovering at her side, clearly impatient. And at that moment, anything that would help me end this conversation was fine by me. "What's up, Mike?" I said.

Mac very diplomatically turned her attention to Mike, who didn't look entirely pleased to have me involved in this conversation. That made two of us. As soon as I could reasonably make an excuse, I'd back away.

"I think I might be able to get that stuff you asked for," he said to Mac.

"What stuff?"

Mike glanced self-consciously at me. "The . . . the food."

"Oh. *Oh*. That's fabulous." All of a sudden she seemed genuinely interested. "When?"

"Not long. Two, three days maybe. A week at most. I'm going to write a letter to my uncle; he lives in southern Illinois." He prattled on happily like this for a while longer, but I could see he'd lost Mac the moment he'd said "A week." She was looking away, biting her lip, in the grip of some sudden anxiety.

"What are you looking for?" I asked, curious despite myself.

Mike clammed up, a little affronted that I had inserted myself into the conversation. Mac, however, had no such reservations.

"Dog food," she said.

"Dog food. Are you serious?"

"Yes."

"How much?" I asked, mostly so I wouldn't just continue to stare at her stupidly. I mean, dog food? Was that code for contraband, or something?

"A few bags. I need dry food that will keep, not table scraps. You have any suggestions?"

"Maybe," I said after a moment.

Mike was frowning now, none too pleased that I was stealing his thunder. "I can get it," he said. "For sure."

Mac ignored him. "I need it quickly," she said to me.

"Yeah, okay," I said. "I should know in a couple of hours."

"It's not easy to get," Mike said. "I don't know if you've been outside the hotel much, but all the grocery stores are closed. And there's a curfew after six o'clock."

"Yeah, well, it's a long shot," I admitted. "Probably won't go anywhere. But I can try."

"I'll be in the lobby tonight at nine," Mac said. "Can you meet me?"

"Sure."

Mac reached out and squeezed my forearm. This woman was very touchy. *Thank you,* she mouthed, her face serious.

Then she turned her smile back on and turned back to Mike. "You really think you can get some more in a week?" she said pleasantly.

Mike warmed up again, started talking about his uncle. That was definitely my cue to leave. I made my way back to our table. Martin was the only one there, tucking into a fresh plate of ham and eggs.

"I don't know how this hotel gets supplies in, but *damn,*" he said happily. "This is the best breakfast I've had in weeks."

"Yeah," I agreed.

He paused in the act of tearing open a croissant. "You okay?" he asked, genuine concern in his voice.

"Yeah, I . . . yeah. Yesterday was a rough morning."

He glanced toward Mike and Mac. "What was that all about?"

"Mac asked me to help her get some dog food."

"Yeah, she's been asking everybody . . . What? You think you can get it?"

"I don't know. Maybe."

"Well, aren't you the knight in shining armor? If you get laid for doing this, I want all the details."

"Nobody gets laid for delivering dog food," I said.

"Yeah? How would you know? You haven't tried to get any yet."

Shortly after breakfast, I found my way down the back stairs of the hotel, below the kitchen. Looking for Nguyen.

I did two years of mandatory service in the Canadian Armed Forces when I turned eighteen, and then three summers of officer training at Camp Borden. Spent my first three months of service as a junior clerk in ship's stores in the Halifax shipyards. We had a guy like Nguyen there — Corporal Campbell, in charge of general provisions for the officers' mess. Theoretically responsible for keeping the mess stocked, but in practice, responsible for every conceivable mundane need the base had. Food, provisions, equipment, personal gear. He made it his business to know how to get things. And to do that, he cultivated an astonishing network of contacts, bartering goods and favors for other goods and favors. Taught me a lot about the fundamentals of business at an impressionable age.

What I remember most about Campbell was that he was always trading, always dealing, even if it wasn't for something he particularly needed. At the end of the day he couldn't take home any of his booty, so it wasn't about profit, either. Bartering was simply what he did. He was the hub others came to, to get what they needed, and he took great pride in it.

Nguyen operated in a very different theater, and on a very different scale, than Campbell. But I got the sense that the principle was the same. A man with a gift for commerce, bartering goods and favors for goods and favors.

I was surprised how easy it was to find him. Nguyen worked out of the back of the basement stores in the hotel. When I found him, he already had two visitors. I recognized the two Mexican lawyers I'd seen when I checked in. I have no idea what they wanted from Nguyen, but it didn't look like they were going to get it. After a few minutes they left with scowls.

Nguyen clearly wasn't in a good mood either, but he was at least cordial when he greeted me. "What can I do for you?"

"I find myself in need of your services even earlier than I expected," I said.

"Not a good day for it," he said, shaking his head.

"I'd really appreciate it. I think you're the only one who could help me."

He grunted. "Meaning it's hard to get." But he softened a bit. "What is it?"

"Dog food. Couple of bags."

"Not supposed to have dogs in the hotel."

"It's not for me."

He sat back in his metal chair, leaning back against a filing cabinet and running a hand through his thinning hair. "I suppose *you* got some business deal going on, too? Guest Services provides necessities for guests — towels, bathrobes. Not shit you can trade on the black market."

"I'm not trading for anything."

"Then what the hell you need dog food for?"

"I'm just trying to impress a woman," I said.

He blinked in surprise. "Well, that may be the noblest damn thing anybody's said to me all day." His chair squeaked as he rolled back to his desk, flipped through some papers. "When you need it?"

"Tonight, before nine."

"I got two bags of cat food some idiot left on the west loading dock. Few weeks old now, but they're dry and never been opened. Can have 'em if you want 'em."

"Fabulous. I'll take them."

"I'll have them delivered to your room."

"No, don't bother. If it's easier, I can pick them up at the front desk."

"They'll be there by five."

"What do I owe you?"

He bristled at the suggestion. "I'm with Guest Services. Consider it part of what we provide our guests."

"Many thanks."

"You're welcome. Oh — and good luck."

When I got back to my room, I found an envelope had been slid under my door. Inside was a handwritten note, on some very nice stationery. At the top was printed:

THE MANHATTAN CONSULATE
CHARTERED BY HER ROYAL MAJESTY 2082

And written below, in a shaky hand, was the following:

*Barry,*

*I hope our security team wasn't too hard on you. They can be a little stiff, but they mean well. I think Rebecca liked you. If she shows up later in the week and roughs you up a little, I'd take that as strong evidence she's forming a serious attachment.*

*I was checked out by our medical staff last night. They said several things that were very sobering. Things like "miracle," and "daring," and "how would you like to pay for this?" But mostly, they told me that I was very, very lucky. "Astonishingly lucky," I think they said.*

*It's not often that one can see with total clarity precisely where one's life changed. My life changed yesterday, when you sat down next to me.*
*I was dying, and you saved me. You did it through tenacity and sheer force of will. You picked me up, and you refused to put me back down again until I was able to walk. You did it for reasons that I can't even fathom. But I hope to someday.*

*My job is to talk to people, but I haven't the faintest idea how to begin to thank you. I hope you'll let me start by getting to know you. We haven't known each other that long, but I am proud to call you my friend.*

*If by any chance you're free for lunch today, I hope you'll consider joining me at the Piazza Trattoria on Randolph. I apologize for the short notice, but believe me, it isn't as easy to get a reservation in this town as it used to be. Say around noon? I'm buying.*

*Nineteen Black Winter*
*Defense Attaché*
*Consulate General of the Kingdom of Manhattan*
*Sector One*

I sat in the chair by the window and read the letter twice. Black Winter was certainly in the right line of work. He wrote a damn good letter, for a machine. And yes, it was short notice, but if he'd managed to find an open restaurant, I'd be happy to let him buy me lunch.

I spent the next few hours working. The owners of Ghost Impulse are paying me good money to grow their company into a sellable asset, and that means cultivating a nice pipeline of global customers and prospects. Challenging enough when you've got top-notch communications at your disposal — but when online traffic has been interdicted by the occupying authorities, virtually all the phone lines have been cut, and there's not even functioning postal service . . . it gets a *lot* more complicated. I'd come to Chicago because the city has world-class data infrastructure, and I figured once the shooting stopped, we'd be able to use it again. It was taking longer than I thought for the city to get back on its feet, and in the meantime I made do with what little I had. At the moment, that meant a small fortune every month in courier bills and — when I had to, and when one was available — paying exorbitant fees for a private data channel.

Selling is a funny thing. You can spend months chasing phantom leads, submitting bids, and cultivating the right relationships, and end up with nothing. And then a plump contract will land in your lap out of nowhere. Forecasting revenue in this business is a joke, but the owners don't really care as long as you deliver more business than last quarter. I work hard and I'm good at what I do, but sometimes I think the only virtue that really matters in this business is luck.

I didn't have much luck this morning. By lunchtime I was more than happy to take a break. I made the short walk over to the Piazza Trattoria, where Nineteen Black Winter was already waiting for me.

I really enjoyed our lunch. Yeah, it was a bit awkward at first. Machines don't actually eat lunch, for one thing. But before too long we were chatting like old friends.

It's tough to explain why I find Black Winter so fascinating. It's not just the novelty of talking casually with a high-end machine. I've met plenty of machines, although admittedly few of them socially. Black Winter is different. He jokes that it's because he was trained in human diplomacy, but it goes deeper than that. There's something about him. There's a sincerity to him that makes him profoundly easy to talk to.

He's also supremely well-informed. After the waitress brought my Reuben sandwich he made a wry comment about the administrative incompetence of the AGRT, and I decided to ask him about something that had been bugging me since the conversation at breakfast this morning.

"Is it true the AGRT is just the Venezuelan army in a different uniform?" I said, sipping my tomato juice.

"Now there's a question," Black Winter said, leaning back. It was too cold to sit comfortably outside, but we were seated in wide chairs by the window. Black Winter was reclining in his chair like a tourist on the beach, his legs stretched out, his fingers toying with a spoon on the table. I'd never seen a machine intelligence with quite so relaxed a demeanor. I was sure it was at least partly affected, the carefully cultivated manner of a machine accustomed to putting humans at ease, but it was nonetheless very disarming.

"I don't blame you for asking—sometimes it seems like it, doesn't it?" he said. "But believe it or not, there are real differences between the Venezuelan Occupation Force and the AGRT. There are tens of thousands of volunteer peacekeepers from over thirty countries in the AGRT, for one thing. The Memphis Ceasefire forced the victorious Coalition members to withdraw from American soil and cede authority to an international peacekeeping force, but it took time to assemble one."

"When is the withdrawal supposed to happen?"

"When? Technically, it's *already* happened. The Venezuelan high command formally handed over Sector Eleven to the AGRT on January thirtieth. It was the last sector to be transferred."

"Formally, sure. But I still see a lot of troops in Venezuelan uniform back at the hotel. I don't see them getting ready to pull out any time soon."

"Ah, that's what you mean." Black Winter leaned forward now, resting his elbows on his knees and showing real interest in this part of the discussion. "The problem is that the Memphis Ceasefire didn't say anything about the *make-up* of the peacekeeping force. The SCC bowed to enormous international pressure and signed the ceasefire, but they were in no hurry to actually withdraw. So they demanded that the force be adequately sized and resourced before they'd cede authority. That meant the AGRT had no choice but to absorb a huge influx of troops from Venezuela, Argentina, and other Coalition members."

"I see. How many?"

"The numbers aren't public, so it's tough to be precise. But here in Sector Eleven, where I've seen the evidence firsthand, I estimate at least fifty percent of the AGRT is composed of Venezuelan troops and officers. Maybe more. As for changing uniforms, in most cases they didn't even bother — the AGRT has only existed for three months, and uniforms haven't really been a priority. And virtually all of the command structure is Venezuelan, anyway."

"Including Colonel Perez?"

"Especially him. He was the man who brought Chicago to its knees last year — and who drove the Union Syndicate out of the city two months ago."

"So nothing has changed, then."

"No, that's not true. I hear people say that, but that's because they weren't here when the Venezuelan army was pounding the shit out of Chicago. Trust me, the Venezuelans are a lot more well behaved these days. More than a third of the soldiers and support personnel on the streets now are volunteers, here to help in the rebuilding, and that's kept things civil. Perez is still in charge, yes. But these days, at least nominally, he reports up through the AGRT chain of command, instead of Venezuelan high command. And it will stay that way until the ultimate fate of this sector is decided at the permanent peace negotiations in Clarksville."

"Why does Perez want to be here?"

"Isn't it obvious? Perez and his men are just biding their time while the wheels of politics slowly grind forward. If Sector Eleven becomes part of Venezuela, as many think is likely, they'll all be part of the Venezuelan military again soon enough. They'll end up on Venezuelan soil, right where they want to be, and they won't have to move an inch."

"Clever. That explains a lot," I said.

"Also, if you want the truth, Perez is a diplomat, but he's a military man first. Privately, I'm certain he suspects the estimates of the strength of the American Union Eighth Army in Kentucky are grossly understated. It's perhaps the largest mechanized force in North America. Perez won't willingly pull his men out of Sector Eleven until there's a permanent peace that all parties sign off on — and maybe not even then."

Since Black Winter was being so forthright, I decided to ask something else I'd been curious about. "What were you doing at the hotel?"

"I told you, I'm a loyal subject of my queen, and this is where her majesty needs me to be. My job is to open relations with Sector Eleven before it formally becomes part of Venezuela. Plus . . . while I'm not yet a full-fledged ambassador, I hope to be someday. And in many ways, I *am* an ambassador to America. This is virgin territory for me . . . and for *all* machines. It's the only country in the world that passed the Wallace Act, outlawing research and development in artificial intelligence. For the last sixteen years, there have been no rational devices on American soil. This is what the war was really all about, the struggle for machine emancipation. I'm like a free black man, journeying to the Deep South after the end of the Civil War. I'm here to begin the healthy process of integration with a culture that has become dangerously out-of-date with the rest of the world."

"That's one way to look at it," I said carefully. That was a clumsy parallel, for a whole lot of reasons, but now probably wasn't the time to get into it. In any event, it was obvious Black Winter and I saw the roots of the war very differently. "But I meant, what were you doing in front of the hotel yesterday? If you don't mind my asking."

"When the Juno attacked, you mean? No, I don't mind. I was trying to win points with the colonel, if you really want to know."

"Colonel Perez?"

"The man himself. I've been trying to ingratiate myself with him since I got here—with no success, I might add. My primary task is to get his signature on a binding treaty with the Kingdom of Manhattan, and I can't even get him to take my calls. Now the Juno attack was a tragedy, and you can call me an opportunist if you like, but it was the best opening I had, and I took it."

"What do you mean?"

"If I can be blunt for a second . . . Manhattan doesn't have a lot to offer Sector Eleven. The Kingdom sided with America after our secession from Panama in September, and we paid a price for it. We have virtually no armed forces left, and barely have a functional economy. But what we do have is information. And in particular, our surveillance is excellent. We detected the approach of the Juno. The mech focused all its attention on jamming the fleet of Venezuelan recon drones, but it overlooked our tiny aerial units."

"Aerial units—you own some of those flying monsters?"

"You've run into the dumb Venezuelan units, I presume? Ours are a little . . . different. Smarter, capable of observing from high altitude. In any event, I had the best intel on the ground that morning, and I was sharing it with the colonel."

"That was decent of you."

"For all the good it did. The mech was on top of us before the colonel could make much use of my intel. I'll tell you one thing—that pilot was one gutsy son of a bitch."

"He sure chewed up that big robot guarding the hotel."

"He did. Don't believe the propaganda the Venezuelans put out about 'inferior' American Union tech. The Union Syndicate is isolated, under-funded, and politically unstable, but they've still managed to field the most impressive war machines I've ever seen. And they know how to use them."

"I hope the colonel was grateful for your intel, at least," I said, nibbling at my sandwich.

"I have no idea. He still hasn't returned my calls," said Black Winter, a little sullenly. "But I'm sure he's busy with pressing affairs."

"Do you know why he only evacuated part of the hotel? I saw barely a hundred civilians in the street that morning."

"That's all there *is* in the hotel — at least for now. The colonel is holding most of the floors in reserve, probably to billet his officers."

"A hundred people? The hotel can't possibly be breaking even with just a few floors open."

"You're right about that. I'm sure the owners are hoping the colonel will open more floors to civilian occupancy once things calm down. If so, the Juno attack was likely a serious setback for them."

"Whatever he does, I hope he doesn't close the floor I'm on," I said. "I've got a great view."

Our conversation wandered to other topics. "What does a 'defense atta-ché' for the Kingdom of Manhattan do, anyway?" I asked.

"Not terribly much at the moment," he admitted. "The truth is, I've been put on what they call 'light duty.' They checked me out after our little adventure, and I didn't pass the physical."

"That doesn't sound good," I said, alarmed. "What's wrong?"

"Oh, nothing serious. The machine physicians on staff at the Consul-ate were able to sort out most of my motor ailments. No insult intended to the men and women of the Venezuelan motor pool — who unquestionably saved my life — but the work they did was not exactly to spec. Nor were the parts they used."

"Yeah." As soon as Black Winter had arrived at the restaurant, I'd no-ticed his mobile core had been completely replaced — again. He looked good as new. "I hope I can get a rebate on some of those parts I bought. I paid a fortune for them."

"And I appreciate it, believe me. Those components saved my life. But it was a patchwork job, and they needed to be replaced. Did you notice I was walking better today?"

"I did. You practically danced in here."

"Let me tell you, you don't fully appreciate your spine until it stops working. Anyway, everything checked out physically after the Consulate did its work. But they weren't satisfied with some of my cognitive results. There's no damage, far as they can tell, but there's a gap of over seventy minutes in my cognitive record."

"When you lost power?"

"Yes, exactly. Simple enough to account for, considering my condition. But a cognitive gap that long is an immediate red flag in an occupation as security-conscious as mine. My clearance had been revoked, and I've been denied access to most of the data feeds I need to do my job."

"That sucks. I'm sorry."

"It's temporary. But it makes a few things . . . difficult."

"Like what?"

Black Winter tapped his fingers on the table, as if he was thinking. "This is a little awkward," he said at last. "Can I share a confidence with you?"

"Of course," I said.

Black Winter leaned a little closer and lowered his voice. "A friend of mine at the Consulate has gone missing. And because of my situation, I've been locked out of the details."

"Missing? Were they injured in the Juno attack, you think?"

"No, my friend wasn't anywhere near the attack. She went to the Continental Building yesterday morning, and never returned. There's been no word from her for nearly thirty hours."

"Your friend has been missing for thirty hours, and you've been denied access to the details? That seems strange. Is that strange?"

"Yes. Very strange. My superiors tell me it's because of my lack of a security clearance, but I'm not so sure. Others at the Consulate have been kept in the dark as well, and that makes no sense. Something's going on. Something serious."

"How much can you share?"

"I suppose that's one advantage of all this. Since I've been denied access to anything confidential, there's nothing preventing me from sharing everything with you."

"Tell me what you know."

"Machine Dance is one of the most cautious and competent members of the Consulate staff. She's not prone to mistakes."

"Machine Dance? That's her name?"

"Yes. She's our director of security. She doesn't take unnecessary risks.

Last time we spoke, she was investigating strange network traffic at the Manhattan Consulate. Something very unusual. I don't have all the details, but I believe she had a lead that took her to the Continental."

"She went alone?"

"I believe so, yes."

"Has anyone gone looking for her?"

"No."

"Why not?"

"I have no idea. No one is talking, and I can't learn anything on my own. It's hard to express how frustrating this is. Machine Dance's disappearance has triggered a senior-level crisis at the Consulate. With both myself and Machine Dance out of commission, the Consulate is critically shorthanded. The Consulate General is very cautious — overly cautious, if you ask me. I think he's waiting for instructions from Manhattan before making a move."

"Awaiting instructions? What's taking so long?"

"That suspicious network traffic I mentioned? It's gotten worse. In fact, there's been a dramatic spike since Machine Dance's disappearance. Almost from the very moment it happened, actually. They're linked somehow; I'm certain of it. It's possible our entire communications network has been severely compromised. The Consulate General has ordered it shut down, and that's forced us to fall back to slower and more secure methods of couriering messages to Manhattan."

"So everyone's waiting for instructions. And you don't agree with waiting around, I take it?"

"No. As I said, Machine Dance is a friend of mine. I think she may be in real danger. I want to investigate, but I'm virtually helpless. Until my security clearance is restored, I can't draw on Consulate resources. That means I can't get what I need to begin my investigation. I can't even get access to the Continental Building."

I didn't respond right away. I was deep in thought for a moment. "Who would hack into the Manhattan Consulate?" I asked at last.

"I have no idea who Machine Dance suspected. But you want my guess? Her top suspects were likely the American Defense Department and a member of the SCC."

"The SCC? Why would they be hacking you?"

"There's still bad blood between Manhattan and the SCC. And there has been, ever since Manhattan seceded from Panama and pulled out of the war."

"So we think either the Americans or the SCC hacked the Consulate. And your friend went to the Continental Building to collect evidence. Maybe to meet someone?"

"That's a solid working theory, yes."

"And once she was there . . . what? She was ambushed?"

"That's a possibility."

"Sure, but . . . In a city as dangerous as this one, there's no need to invent threats. Any number of things could have delayed her return. An encounter with the American Union. Looters. A damaged cable that dropped her to the bottom of an elevator shaft. No need to jump to conclusions just yet."

"I think if those things were likely, the Consulate would have sent someone immediately."

"Are you certain they didn't?"

"I'm only certain of one thing: the senior staff at the Consulate knows something we don't. They're scared, and they're not talking."

I chewed on that for a moment. "Any idea what they're so afraid of?"

"No. But whatever it is, it's paralyzed them."

"What about you? Are you paralyzed?"

Black Winter met my gaze with a fixed stare. "Absolutely not."

"You want to go look for her."

"Yes."

"Is the Consulate looking over your shoulder? Or limiting your actions?"

"With my security clearance revoked, some parts of the Consulate are off-limits. But otherwise I can come and go."

"Then I think I may be able to help," I said.

"How?" Black Winter asked.

"My friend Martin works for an urban survey team. They're busy getting a count of the survivors in Chicago. They have access to most of the buildings in the city, all the nooks and crannies where there are still residents. It's possible they could get us access to the Continental."

"That's great news. But access to the building isn't the only hurdle. The Continental is on the border of the Exclusion Zone. Off-limits to civilian personnel."

"I don't think that's a problem these days. From what I hear, the AGRT is more lax about enforcing the old Exclusion Zones than the SCC was."

"It's not the AGRT I'm worried about," Black Winter said. "There are . . . machines that patrol the border as well. And some of them have their own agenda."

"Now you're just being paranoid. Everybody who's been in the hotel more than a day or two has heard those stories. That there are sinister machines of unknown origin near the Exclusion Zones. Strange devices that slither through alleys after dark. That's just stories they tell to scare the tourists. Don't tell me you believe them."

"Not all of them, no. I know what kinds of rumors spread during wartime, same as you. But I hear reports, and some have the ring of truth."

I opened my mouth, about to say something reassuring and trite, then shut it again. Black Winter was trying to tell me something. "What do you know?" I asked.

"Nothing solid," he admitted. "But there are dangers. To traveling that close to an Exclusion Zone. As the Union began to gain ground, especially near the end of the war, the SCC began fielding a number of experimental machine horrors to counter the threat. Not all of them proved . . . completely obedient. Don't dismiss all the rumors. There are things out there you don't want to meet in a dark alley, and they are very real. Believe me."

"Well, that sounds horrifying," I said. "And I plan to avoid dark alleys of any kind, thank you. Look, I didn't assume a trip to look for Machine Dance would be completely without risk. But folks travel to the Continental every week. As risks go, a brief trip there seems manageable enough. Do you agree?"

Black Winter pondered that. "Yes," he said after a moment. "But I didn't mean to obligate you. If you can get me access to the hotel, that will be more than enough."

"Yeah, well, don't get too excited. I don't even know if I can do that yet. But I'll give it a try."

"I am becoming accustomed," said Black Winter, "to being in your debt."

"Don't worry about that. I'm sure we'll balance things out."

"How do you propose I do that?"

I smiled and raised my glass. "Keep buying me lunch."

# IV

Tuesday, March 9th, 2083
Posted 11:11 pm by Barry Simcoe

CanadaNET1 Encrypted, Sponsored by PeoplePulse.
*Keep tabs on the heartbeats of those you love.*

Sharing is set to PRIVATE
Comments are CLOSED

A little after eight I remembered that I had an engagement this evening — with a very attractive woman, in fact. I felt much more grounded after my lunch with Black Winter and a day of working, and frankly a little embarrassed at how awkward I'd been with Mac at breakfast this morning.

I was relieved to have a second shot with her, and determined not to blow it. I showered and shaved, and then stood in front of my closet, trying to decide between jeans and dress pants. It seemed a little strange that she'd asked me to meet her in the lobby at 9:00 . . . Perhaps I should be ready in case she suggested we go out afterwards? With that in mind, I selected a dinner jacket and matching pants, splashed on some cologne, and was in the lobby by 8:45.

If you're not particularly observant, a few minutes in the lobby could have you believing that things have returned to normal in Chicago. Management has done an impressive job making it look good. There's fresh-cut flowers, contemporary music playing softly on hidden speakers — and most reassuring of all, a constant buzz of activity. Guests coming and going, bellboys carrying luggage, a concierge handing out maps. You could even hear an occasional ringing telephone at the front desk — in-house calls only, of course, but still. It added to the ambiance.

Naturally, to make the illusion work, you had to ignore the armed guards stationed near the entrance. And the seven-foot machine, torpedo-like and almost featureless, that stood sentinel at the escalator, blocking off the second floor to civilians. And the concrete blast barriers the Venezuelans had dragged in front of the doors the morning after the mech attack. Not to mention countless smaller details, like the way guests glanced nervously over their shoulder every few minutes, or the complete absence of children.

My gaze kept straying out the window, to the place where Corporal Maldonado had bled to death. Would there still be a bloodstain? Did blood wash off concrete? I didn't want to see it. Jesus, I didn't even want to get close to it.

By 8:55, as I paced back and forth in the lobby, I realized coming down early had been a mistake. I'm not an anxious person by nature, but at that moment I felt a great, formless anxiety. I felt sweaty and uncomfortable, hypersensitive, and terribly exposed standing next to the windows.

I considered just leaving the food for Mac with a note. What did this woman need with dog food, anyway? If she lived in the hotel, she didn't have a dog. For all I knew, Nguyen's assumption was right. Maybe she wanted to barter it.

And if I was going to be the bagman for a black market pet food transaction, after curfew, in the middle of a hotly disputed urban territory, I was probably overdressed. And much too Canadian.

I debated forgetting the whole thing and heading back to my room, getting some work done instead. But while I dithered, the elevator door opened and my date stepped out.

She was not dressed for a date. She wore loose-fitting clothing, dark, with flat shoes. She had work gloves tucked into her belt, and was clutching what looked like a Venezuelan travel visa. She had a distracted look on her face as she scanned the document.

"Hi," I said, as she was about to walk past me.

She turned. "Oh — hi! Sorry, I didn't see you." She folded the document, tucked it into her jacket. She took in my formal attire with a questioning glance. "Why are you dressed like that?"

"Like this?" I said stupidly. *Shit.* "I was just going to . . . I had a business meeting. Here in the lobby."

"Okay. Are you ready to go?"

"Sure," I said.

"Do you have the food?"

"Yes," I said, nodding toward the front desk. "It's over there." For the first time I wondered if it mattered that I had brought cat food. Should I bring that up? Maybe they fetched different prices on the black market. Or maybe we were just going to trade it for bullets, and it wouldn't matter. That would be fun.

"Great," she said, pulling on her gloves. She gave me a quick smile. "We should probably get moving."

"Uh—hang on." I crossed to the front desk, identified myself to the night clerk, and he helped me position a forty-pound bag of cat food on my shoulder. I left the other bag with the clerk and, feeling confused and a little stupid, rejoined Mac as she stood nervously by the front entrance.

"Where are we going?"

"The Hamilton," she said, opening the door. She flashed her document to the guards.

"But—wait a minute, wait up. What about the curfew?" I followed her awkwardly onto the street.

"I've got a pass," she said, holding up the visa. She was already striding purposefully across the concrete. Headed south.

I hurried to keep up. A *pass?* How did you get a pass to waive curfew? Could I get one?

I didn't learn the answer to these questions. I did learn Mac wasn't much of a talker. And that forty pounds is a lot of cat food to lug ten city blocks.

We were past the spot of concrete where Maldonado died before I knew it. When I realized, I turned around, walking backwards and scanning the ground morbidly. There was no sign of blood, but it was too dark to be sure.

It was also much too dark to be walking backwards. The soldiers had done a passable job cleaning the streets after the battle, but there was still just enough rubble for the unwary to trip on. I caught my foot on a sixty-pound chunk of rock as I turned around again and damn near face-planted right in the street. I righted myself and hurried after Mac.

"Hey, wait up!" I called.

Mac kept up a brisk pace as she led us south and west, onto Michigan Avenue. It's unnerving to be walking Chicago at night. The streets are empty, of course, and power's cut to most of the buildings, so virtually all of the streetlights are out. You'd be astonished how dark it can be in the shadow-filled canyons between skyscrapers.

But it was the lack of sound that unsettled me the most. I heard Mac's shoes clicking on the pavement ahead, my own ragged breathing . . . and every once in a while, a high-pitched hum between the buildings, high off the ground. There were occasionally distant, faraway rumbles as well, and once a retort that echoed between the concrete canyons, somewhere far to the west.

But oddly, after getting past that bloody stretch of concrete, it seemed that the worst of the trip was already over. After walking for a few minutes, I felt a certain lightness of spirit, despite the growing ache in my shoulder. I lengthened my strides and started to catch up with her.

Mac heard the thing first, drifting down out of the darkness. I wasn't sure why she'd stopped, just after stepping off the curb at Michigan and Randolph. There was no one to be seen in either direction, but it still seemed strange to me to stop dead in the middle of the street in Chicago. Call me old-fashioned.

I came up behind her and was about to ask what was wrong when she held up a gloved hand for silence. I heard it then, a sinister *whrrrrrrrr* above and to the right. Mac started digging in her jacket.

"Stand close to me," she said.

I obeyed. "Closer," she said.

I shuffled up until we were almost touching, glad for an excuse to drop the bag at my feet for a few seconds. Mac swore under her breath, hunting fruitlessly in her jacket.

I saw it then, and I swore too.

I've had plenty of experience with autonomous recon units, both military and civilian. Most are just flying communications devices of one sort or another, usually kitted out with a lot of optics.

This thing was nothing like that. For one thing, it was enormous— nearly the size of a sedan. And if it had any optics at all, I couldn't see them. What I could see was at least three different weapons mounted to its undercarriage.

It dropped so close to us that the wind from its whispering rotors was kicking up invisible grit, blowing it all in my face.

Mac gave a relieved exclamation and pulled something out of her jacket. It was the curfew waiver. She held it up defiantly.

The thing came closer. It was barely forty feet off the ground, hovering. The whisper of its big rotors was now an aggressive hum.

"What are you doing?" I shouted.

"Showing it our waiver."

"Mac . . . that thing can't read your waiver."

"It's got an embedded chip." She waved the transparent paper briefly at me, then turned back to face the drone. "It can read it from there."

"No, I mean, your visa is Venezuelan."

"So?"

"That thing's not Venezuelan."

She stared at it, not comprehending. I'd seen Venezuelan drones up close—all of them bore the tricolor flag, and had a compact chassis. This thing had neither. "Then what is it?" she said.

I stepped in front of her slowly, keeping my eye on it and remembering Black Winter's warning over lunch. "I have no idea. But it's not friendly."

The thing did an end-over-end flip in the air. Its rear section—if it *had* a rear section—was now facing us, and from its sleek black hull it extruded a slender black rod. There was something gleaming at the end of it, but it was too dark to make it out.

Mac stepped closer, pressing her hands to my back. "Should we run?" she asked.

"If it wanted us dead, we'd be dead already."

"Then what does it want?"

I had no idea. "It wants to know what we're doing," I guessed.

Very slowly, I raised my hands. Probably a meaningless gesture to a drone, but what can I tell you? Then I kicked the bag at my feet. "Just delivering dog food," I told it.

There was a strange whisper in the air, like the buzz of a wasp.

"Get back," I said.

"But—"

"*Move.*"

Something moving much too fast to be seen in the darkness buzzed past, between us and the hovering killer. I grabbed Mac and got her off the street, up onto the curb, where we hunched down behind the entirely inadequate shelter of a traffic pole.

"What was that?" Mac asked.

"*That* was a Venezuelan attack drone," I said.

A second Venezuelan drone hurtled past, at higher altitude and just as invisible.

The heavy black drone was already moving. It flipped again, kicking its rotors on in a fast ascent. I watched it shoot up into the darkness. It vanished, but I could still hear it, gaining altitude and moving fast to the east.

Mac started to move. "Wait," I told her.

"They're gone."

"Wait."

A few seconds later I heard it. Farther away than I expected, but very distinct.

Mac listened for a few seconds. "What is that?" she said.

"They're attacking each other. They're fighting."

"Who's fighting the Venezuelans?" she asked, looking a little astonished.

"Someone with a lot of guts."

"Was it American, you think?"

"No. The tech was all wrong for American."

"Who then?"

"Machine."

Mac had taken a few tentative steps east, gazing up into the darkness. Now she hesitated and looked back at me. "That was Machine?"

"Yeah, I think so. An unaligned probe, maybe. Owned by a Sovereign Intelligence."

Mac had kept her head pretty well through the whole event, but for the first time she looked genuinely scared. She considered for a moment. "You should go back," she said.

"Me? What about you?"

"I'll be okay."

I didn't argue with her. I just grabbed the bag and lifted it onto my shoulder. "Come on," I said.

We continued toward the Hamilton. Mac didn't speak for the next few blocks. When she did, it was to ask me a very strange question.

"Have you ever been to the Burroughs Detention Center in Gary, Indiana?"

"No," I said.

"I go there all the time. The AGRT has a civilian holding area. It's an overflow for the Displaced Persons camp at Westhaven. There's a hospital. They moved some of the injured there when Westhaven got shelled in January."

I'd never been to Westhaven or Burroughs. But I knew the city sometimes organized food drives and other charitable efforts to assist those in the camps whose homes had been destroyed, or who had suffered other terrible losses in the war. The worst of the fighting had been over for weeks, but there were still tens of thousands of people in the camps. Many were too afraid to return. Many had no place left to return to.

"There are Venezuelan attack drones there," she said, still watching the dark skies. "Nasty, ugly things. Hovering in the air, watching everything. Everyone is terrified of them."

"Probably there to prevent riots," I said.

"They don't care about riots," she said, her voice cold. "They're just there to kill people."

We reached our destination a few minutes later. The entrance, a grand glass foyer with half a dozen doors, was dim and looked abandoned. The doors were chained and padlocked from the inside, but Mac led me around to a side entrance, which she opened with a key.

She used a small flashlight to guide us down dark hallways, some strewn with unidentifiable trash. The place was creepy, my shoulder ached from carrying the heavy load, and I was starting to regret not turning back when I'd had the chance.

She led me up a wide stairway to a balcony that overlooked the foyer. I could see Michigan Avenue through the glass. It was dark and deserted . . . except for a shadow across the street, where no shadow should be. Before I could make out what it was, it was gone.

"This way," she said.

I followed her to the elevators, still craning my neck to look back. What *was* that thing?

"These still work?" I asked, when she stopped in front of an elevator.

"This one does," she said. "I think the others are out of commission." She didn't punch the button on the wall; instead she pulled out another key, this one on a small metal chain, and inserted it into a tiny slot on the wall. A second later the elevator opened. Once we were inside, she pushed the button for the seventeenth floor.

We rode up in silence for a while. "So," I said, somewhere around the eleventh floor, "what's on the seventeenth floor?"

"A dog," she said.

That made sense.

We got out of the elevator. I expected offices, suites with a lot of mahogany and glass, but I stepped out onto thick carpet and a narrow corridor. Stretching left and right were numbered doors, widely spaced.

"What are these — condos?" I asked as we made our way to the right.

"Yes."

"Huh. Are they . . . still occupied?"

"No. But some of them were, until recently. The businesses on the lower floors left eighteen months ago, in the first Chicago evacuation. But if you were a private resident, you had the option to stay. The building has power, and water, and it's not far from some of the food markets."

"Sure," I said. "Looks a lot better than the refugee camps, anyway. Why'd they leave?"

"Got too hot," she said. "Six weeks ago the Penton Building took a shell, right on the nineteenth floor. You know the one?"

"Big white building, two blocks west?"

"That's the one. Nine hundred residents. Whole building went up in a matter of hours."

"Oh my God."

"Couldn't get enough fire trucks to respond. And when they did, they didn't have enough water pressure to pump above the fourth floor. Lot of the sprinklers failed."

"Did you have any clients in the building?"

She turned to meet my gaze. "I did. Most of them made it out. Some . . . Anyway, that was the first heavy ordnance the neighborhood had seen in a while, but it was enough. After that, most of the remaining residents in this building cleared out. I had a few clients here. I come back to check on the properties every few weeks."

She stopped in front of 1717 and fumbled with her keys for a minute as I watched. She had a very focused look. I had to admit, she really was lovely. I don't know, maybe I'd judged her too harshly, with all that black market stuff. I started to mull over the best way to ask her out when our little errand was finally over. Maybe a drink, back at the hotel. There was a click as she unlocked the door. Before she opened it she fixed her eyes on mine. "You need to be quiet," she said. "She's scared."

"What?" I said.

She put her finger to her lips, and pushed the door open.

A sour reek hit my nostrils as soon as I crossed the threshold. The place was dirty, unfurnished; most of the lights were on, and the glare on the stark white walls after the dimness of the corridor left me blinking. Mac padded quietly into what looked like a kitchen on the left, motioning for me to follow.

There was a dry yellow stain on part of the kitchen tile, next to what looked like a water bowl. I was about to dump the sack on the counter, finally give my shoulder a break, when I heard a noise from the next room — a scratching, followed by what sounded like a whimper.

"What was that?"

"She's scared," Mac repeated. She knelt down, peering around the corner, into the next room. "It's okay, girl. It's okay," she said in a low, soothing voice.

I heard rapid scratching, the sound of claws on tile, receding deeper into the apartment.

"Is that —?"

She gestured frantically for me to shut up. After a moment, she got to her feet. She refilled the water bowl in the sink, then carefully lowered it to the floor. "Open the bag," she whispered.

I moved to obey, casting around for something to pour it into. In the corner was a plastic bowl, this one overturned, and with evidence of having been chewed. I leaned over to pick it up, and as I did I glimpsed several dried, brown husks on the floor under the dining table. Dog turds. A week old, from the look of them.

That explained the smell. Straightening up, I tore open the bag and poured food into the bowl.

"How much?" I whispered.

"All of it," she said.

I held up the bowl, already half full, and gestured meaningfully at the bag. Forty-pound bag. Two-pound bowl.

She took the bowl with obvious impatience. She set it down on the floor, and then poured twenty pounds of food on top of it.

She stepped away, satisfied. A moment later, I heard claws on the tile again, coming closer.

"She can smell it," Mac said quietly.

We waited. Minutes crawled by. From the next room came a low, desperate whimper.

"It's okay, girl," Mac said, her voice heavy with emotion. "We won't hurt you. Come on. It's okay."

"What's her name?" I asked.

"I don't know," Mac said, and the despair in her voice nearly broke my heart.

The dog whimpered again, louder now.

I took Mac's elbow, guiding her gently but firmly out of the kitchen, back to the hallway. "She won't eat while we're here," I said. "She's too scared."

"But I want to see her," Mac said, sounding close to tears. "I want to make sure she's okay."

"One thing at a time," I said. "Let her eat first, maybe get less scared. After that, it'll be easier. Let her come to trust us."

She nodded, unable to speak.

"We'll come back, yes?" I said, taking the half-empty bag of cat food from her.

She nodded again. She wiped her eyes, hesitated for a moment, looking into the kitchen. But finally she relented. We moved toward the door, careful not to step on any of the dried packages on the floor.

There was a long mirror in the hallway. As we passed, I got a glimpse behind us, into the kitchen. I tapped Mac's shoulder, pointing to the bottom left of the mirror.

In the bottom corner we saw an emaciated corgi, peeking around the corner, watching us leave. She would glance down at the floor, back to us, and down again. Her legs trembled unsteadily, and a thin line of drool escaped her mouth. But she made no move toward the food in the bowl yet.

We opened the door, stepped into the hall. As I closed the door behind me, just before I heard the lock click into place, I heard the sudden rush of claws on the tile floor as she raced into the kitchen, to the food.

I set the half-empty bag of food down beside the door. It would probably be safe here. Mac stood beside me, her hand to her mouth and her eyes squeezed shut. Her shoulders rocked for a moment.

"What was *that* all about?" I asked.

"People just *left* them," she said, with sudden venom in her voice. "When they ran off. I found her when I came to check the apartment. They just left them, in their apartments. Dogs, cats, just abandoned."

"God, that's awful. How long have you been feeding her?"

"Two weeks. I've been keeping her alive with bread and other food I steal from the hotel. But my brokerage key only allows me access to the Hamilton one day a week."

"That's why you needed dry food. So you could leave her enough to survive for a week."

Mac nodded. "Yes. For her, and the others."

"Others? There are more abandoned pets?"

"Oh, yes," she hissed.

"Where?"

"I found three cats in the Grand Mayral, plus a Labrador in a penthouse of the Lee building. And there are others. There's a dog who howls on the eleventh floor of the Continental. Not in one of my properties, but close. Just howls, goes crazy whenever he hears me in the hall. He's slowly starving to death."

"That's goddamn horrible."

It *was* horrible. The thought that there was another innocent victim of this stupid war slowly dying barely a block away made me feel angry and helpless. "Are you sure?" I asked.

"Oh, I'm sure," Mac said, and the fire was back in her eyes. "He's there. At least he *was* . . . he was quiet when I went over this morning. I could never find him."

Her hand was on my shoulder. It lingered there, almost unconsciously, as she looked at the door to 1717. "I didn't want her to starve, too."

Mac's eyes were wet. After a moment she wiped them angrily. "Are you okay?" I asked.

She nodded. "It's not just her," she said. "It's the damn war. It's the clients I lost in the Penton Building. It's *everything*—"

Her voice cracked. She shut her eyes and stopped speaking. She took a moment to compose herself.

"The truth is that I wake up every damn day in a world where monsters are real," she said. "Inscrutable, diabolical, and nearly all-powerful machine monsters. They've seized power around the world, and no one can stop them. They've killed hundreds of thousands of people, and we still don't know what they want. Human governments are falling like dominoes, to one manufactured crisis after another. And now fear is causing us to turn to machines to protect ourselves."

"Like Britain," I said.

"Like Britain," she said. "How did all this happen?"

"I don't know," I said.

Mac roused herself with an effort. She forced a smile and put her arm through mine. We started walking toward the elevator. "I'm sorry," she said. "Sometimes it just all gets to me."

"I understand, believe me."

"Anyway, I want to thank you. You're a hero."

"Hardly. If you think a hero is someone who can procure forty pounds of cat food, you need to hang out with more capable people."

"No one else could do it."

"No one else knew who to ask."

"Well, I hope you'll let me thank you by procuring a drink or two for you at the hotel bar."

"That would be lovely," I said. We were standing by the elevators now, and I was staring out the windows to the west, at the dark shape of the Continental Building. Where Black Winter's friend Machine Dance had gone missing, and where a dog was slowly starving to death on the eleventh floor. It really would be lovely to have a few drinks, and forget about the world for an hour or two. To enjoy the company of a woman who — at least for tonight — thought I was a hero.

But the sight of the Continental Building reminded me I had other commitments to honor. "Sadly, I'm afraid I have plans," I said, and the regret in my voice was genuine. "Some other time?"

Mac looked surprised. She didn't seem like someone accustomed to rejection, but she handled it gracefully enough. We walked back to the hotel, watching the skies together. But other than a persistent shadow that seemed to be tailing us whenever I turned my head, the return trip was uneventful.

Mac made one final try when we reached the hotel. "Sure you won't join me for just one drink?"

It was tempting, but I needed to find Martin. I made my excuses, and said good night.

I found Martin at the bar not ten minutes later. "Man, what a night," he said jovially. "Everybody's in the mood to buy drinks."

"A little adventure will do that, I guess," I said. "Everyone okay?"

"Mostly, yeah. Everybody's got a near-death experience or two they want to relate, though. Carter and Mwandu said they saw the mech bookin' south, down Field Boulevard. Said it was in a helluva hurry."

"Anyone else in the city attacked?"

"Not that we've heard. There are a few Venezuelan detachments just south of here, near the Field Museum and the Yacht Club."

"Did it hit them?"

"Nope. Clean getaway south, from what we're told."

"Wonder why it retreated," I said.

"The prevailing theory is that it was just lost, and wandered into the wrong neighborhood. It saw a chance to hit the enemy and make a quick retreat, and that's what it did."

"Makes sense." I doubted that was the whole story, but it was probably the most sense we were ever going to make out of the incident.

"What about you?" Martin asked. "How'd you make out tonight?"

"What do you mean?"

Martin leaned a bit closer. "I mean, as a lover, you're a bit rubbish, aren't you?" he said. "I just saw Mac head out for a drink with Mike."

"Seriously? *Mike?*" I said glumly.

"And I thought you had it in the bag, with your big kettle of dog food," Martin laughed.

"Yeah," I said. "Listen, Martin, you're still connected with the urban survey team, right?"

"Yeah, sure." Like several folks in the hotel, Martin had been contracted by the City of Chicago to get an accurate assessment of how many survivors were still in the city, and where they were. The Venezuelans likely had most of that information, of course, but they weren't exactly tripping over themselves to share it.

"Can you help me get into the Continental Building?"

"The Continental?" He scratched his chin. "It's completely abandoned, that one. You'd have to talk to Buddy Green. How's that for a one hundred percent American name? *Buddy. Green.*"

"So it's possible?"

"I suppose it's possible. Depends on how determined you are."

"Let's imagine," I said, "that I'm pretty damned determined."

## V

Wednesday, March 10th, 2083

Sharing is set to PRIVATE
Comments are CLOSED


*No Entry*

*Need content for your blog? Let McDonald-Ruthman supply you with the best in customized, up-to-date news feeds on a variety of hot topics. Check us out at www.mac-phip.buzz!*

# VI

Thursday, March 11th, 2083
Posted 2:21 am by Barry Simcoe

CanadaNET1 Encrypted, Sponsored by Fashion Dart.
*You're one click away from your personal style agent.*

Sharing is set to PRIVATE
Comments are CLOSED

"I just want to be clear on this," said Black Winter. "We're doing this to impress a woman?"

"It's more complicated than that," I said, as I shone a flashlight around the deserted living room. It landed on an ugly purple couch.

"My God that's hideous," said Black Winter. "No wonder these people evacuated."

"Check the bathroom, will you?"

He clanked off obediently toward the small bathroom on my right. I could still hear him as I shone my flashlight into each of the two small bedrooms. They were empty, like all the others we'd searched tonight. They looked like they'd been that way for a while.

"Anyway, what's complicated about it?" he said. "Seems simple enough to me. You meet a hot young lady with a thing for dogs. Next thing you know, you've got a sudden interest in dogs. This has been a proud tradition among hard-up men for thousands of years. Least you can do is be honest with yourself about it."

"For the love of God—I am not hard up!"

"That's a matter of opinion. Do you like her?"

"Yeah, I like her. She's beautiful and she's got a good heart."

"If you like her, why not just tell her? Because that's what we're really doing here, right? We're sending her a message that you love dogs?"

"I'm not sending her any kind of message," I said. I pulled open a pair of cupboards underneath a sink, shining my light in the dark corners. "I just . . . I really want to find this dog."

"You know what I think we're doing right now? I think you're insecure around attractive women. You're afraid to ask her out until you've done something to really impress her. Saving this dog would certainly fit the bill, wouldn't it?"

"You know what I think?" I said. "I think I prefer dogs to robots. They don't talk so damn much."

"When we get back to the hotel, you should ring her. Invite her out. Show a little courage."

"Oh my God. Am I really listening to dating advice from a friggin' robot?"

"Well, you better listen to somebody. Because, son, you are hopeless."

After I'd talked to Martin about getting into the Continental Building Tuesday night, he'd set up a meeting the next morning with Buddy Green, who coordinated the North Side urban surveyors. I had a story all set for Buddy, but turns out I didn't need one. Buddy and his staff were so short-handed he didn't even question me, just slapped me on the back, thanked me warmly for volunteering, and handed me a set of keys for the building.

"I'm sure Martin gave you the safety talk," Buddy said. "But let me reiterate: You are not an inspector. You are an observer. You count bodies. Right?"

"Right," I said.

"Right. Don't make any commitments, no matter what they ask you for." Buddy shook his head. "These people. They see a guy with a clipboard, they start demanding we fix the air-conditioning."

"Right," I said.

"And, listen," said Buddy. "The Continental . . . it's a weird property. We've walked it a few times, and it's always empty. Should be an easy gig for you, in and out. But lately . . ."

"Lately what?" I asked.

Buddy forced a smile. "Nothing. Like I said, should be a quiet few hours. But do me a favor . . . you see a machine? Anything weird, or flying, or bigger than a bread box? You get the hell out of there, pronto."

"Right," I said.

"Good man." Buddy slapped me on the back again. "Easy gig. We'll get you something more challenging next time."

"Appreciate it."

As soon as I had the keys to the Continental in my hands, I dashed off a note to Black Winter and had it couriered over to the Manhattan Consulate. He responded immediately, surprised and pleased. I had expected he wouldn't want to waste any time, and I was right. He proposed an expedition to the building that same night. To get around the curfew, he suggested a Consulate car drop us off. Which was a relief, because I didn't look forward to lugging another forty-pound bag of cat food ten blocks. I mentioned my desire to couple our search for his friend with a search for the dog Mac was worried about, and Black Winter, trooper that he was, had no objection. "We can start by looking for Machine Dance," I said when we were in the car.

"I have no idea where she might be," Black Winter admitted. "And it's a big building. If your dog is on the eleventh floor, we might as well start there."

So late last night, me and my highly compensated machine consultant were on the north side of the eleventh floor of the Continental, working our way around the building. So far we'd opened nearly two dozen apartments with the keys Buddy had given me, poking into empty rooms, whispering, "Here, doggy, doggy."

I lugged the heavy bag of cat food with us from room to room. When I suggested that Black Winter take a turn, he just laughed. "You're the one trying to impress a woman," he said. "You carry the damn cat food."

It's strange what people left behind when they fled. The power is out in the Continental, but Buddy had given me a flashlight, and enough moonlight filtered in through wide windows to allow us to make our way around. We found tables set for dinner, and personal data tablets resting on coffee tables. The whole building is like an abandoned set between acts, ready to explode back to life at any moment. I tiptoed everywhere, trying not to make noise, afraid we'd wake some guy with a shotgun who'd leap out of his bedroom to confront the intruders prowling through his home with a bag of cat food.

But Buddy was right. The building's abandoned. We didn't find any overzealous owners with artillery, or even any squatters. We did find fish tanks — mostly empty, thank God — and a whole lot of dead and dying house plants. More than once I heaved the cat food onto a counter in the kitchen, rummaged through cupboards until I found a pitcher, filled it with water, and returned to bone-dry begonias and geraniums, cursing under my breath while Black Winter watched, amused. I knew it was hopeless, but what could I do? The only reason we were here at all was in the service of a hopeless cause.

Which brings me back to the dog. While closing another door on our circuit, Black Winter turned away suddenly, staring down the hallway.

"Did you hear that?" he said.

I was repositioning the cat food bag on my shoulder. "I didn't hear anything."

"It sounded like a bark."

"Are you serious? Where?"

"I'm not sure."

We listened quietly. A moment later, I thought I heard it too. It was hard to make out, but it might have been a bark. One lonely, desperate bark, coming from an animal that probably still had a few teeth left.

"Just how crazy with hunger might a dog be after a few weeks?" I said nervously, as we made our way down the hall.

"Don't chicken out on me now. This was your idea, remember?"

"Yeah, but I was picturing a small dog. Didn't it sound big to you?"

"I couldn't tell what it sounded like."

Now I understood why Mac had brought gloves. I wished I'd been thinking that clearly. We searched the next few units more thoroughly. Shining my flashlight into corners, picking up cushions. Glancing in closets, worried we might miss a dog that had crawled into a small space to die.

All that extra diligence was unnecessary, of course. I knew we had the right place the moment Buddy's key unlocked 1114, and the smell hit me.

"This is the place," I said. I stared into the shadowy hallway before us. "You go first."

Black Winter took a half step, then backed up. "Why me?"

"Because you won't get eaten. Probably."

"I'm the one who just had major surgery," he muttered. But he bravely led the way, and I followed close behind.

"Look at this," Black Winter said. He was pointing at a box of cornflakes in the foyer, savagely shredded. From here we could see that the living room was strewn with gobs of torn white cotton, ripped from gaping holes in the leather couch. White where it wasn't stained yellow with dog urine, anyway.

The dog had been alone here for weeks, that much was obvious. Droppings were everywhere, and there were gaping holes in the drywall where it'd been chewed through. From the foyer of the apartment I could see that the cupboard under the sink had been pawed open. Plastic jugs of various cleaning fluids had rolled or been barked into an obedient pile by the fridge, and there was a sticky, bloody mess in the hallway where it looked like the dog had vomited up a metal scouring pad.

But so far, no dog.

We moved carefully at first, half sure a pit bull was going to come barreling around a corner at any moment, insane from hunger and weeks of abandonment, ready to tear a leg off—human or robot. But the rooms were eerily quiet. I searched the closets in the too-neat bedroom, got down on hands and knees to peer under the queen-sized bed. When I checked on Black Winter, he was pulling back the curtain on the bathtub.

He shook his head. "Nothing."

When we'd completed a circuit of all the rooms, I made my way to the living room and sat down on the coffee table. It was well after midnight, I was tired of being on edge for the last two days, and I wasn't looking forward to the creepy walk through deserted streets back to the hotel, carrying a bag of cat food.

"There's a dog in here somewhere," said Black Winter, moving to my side.

"A dead dog," I said in disgust.

"You don't know that."

"Just look around! None of the damn droppings on the floor is less than a week old. If the dog were still alive, it would have confronted us by now. Even half-dead, it would have growled or barked."

"What did we hear in the hall, then?"

"I have no idea. It could have been pipes knocking, for all I know. We're too late, probably by a week or more."

"If it's dead, where's the body?"

I gestured toward the dark bedrooms. "It probably crawled into a lonely crevice to die. I don't know about you, but I don't have the fortitude to search for a dead dog right now."

Black Winter wisely left me alone to brood for the next few minutes. He prowled around the apartment, poking into dark corners. When he returned to the living room, he stared at the paintings on the wall. I couldn't make out many details in the gloom, but they looked like abstracts, great swaths of color framed in neat bundles.

"Who do you suppose lived here?" he asked.

"I don't know," I said after a minute. "An older woman, I guess, from the décor."

"What happened to her, do you think?"

"Probably left in a hurry in the mid-February evacuations, after the American Union shelled Grant Park. She must have been certain she'd be back. Probably poured a week's worth of dog food on the floor, gave her dog a hug, and then was hustled out by a soldier in the doorway, telling her to move her ass."

"That was right after I arrived," said Black Winter. "Hell of a time. Lot of heavy action. I hadn't been here a week when we got orders to be ready to evacuate the Consulate."

"Sounds exciting."

"To you, maybe. But not to me. Adventure. Excitement." Black Winter shook his head. "A Jedi craves not these things."

"If you say so. I'm glad I missed all that, anyway. It happened weeks before I got here, and I'm not sure I ever really understood all the politics."

Black Winter came closer, lowered himself into a chair next to me. "Yeah, you're not the only one. Things got pretty spun up. After the Memphis Ceasefire between the US and the SCC, the Union Syndicate was isolated. It threatened to drive the AGRT out of Chicago. The Sentient Cathedral was trying to broker peace, bring them into the ceasefire, when the Union struck the machine depot in Grant Park. A daring move — took out the bulk of the Venezuelan heavy equipment in one strike, but it permanently soured the AGRT on peace with the Union, let me tell you. For a while, it looked like the Union could actually do it — make Chicago so hot that the Venezuelans pulled out."

"They might have, if they hadn't destroyed the Thought Museum," I said. That part I understood, at least. When the museum was destroyed, all those infant AIs had been flushed into the sewers like a thousand baby alligators. That had destroyed whatever hope the Union had of generating sympathy for their cause in the Sentient Cathedral. In the face of that political nightmare, the Union had retreated south.

"Where is she now, I wonder?" said Black Winter. He'd plucked a small framed photograph off one of the bookshelves and was peering at it, but it was too dark and too far away for me to make out the details.

"Who knows? Maybe she was evacuated across Lake Michigan in the middle of February, with the rest of the city. Maybe she's in one of the DP camps in Indiana. Maybe she's dead."

"That's morbid."

"I'm just being realistic," I said.

"Shut up."

"Think about it. If she were alive, don't you think she would have at least tried to —"

Black Winter raised his hand to silence me. "No, I mean, be quiet for a second."

I shut up. Black Winter was listening. He turned around slowly, his head oddly cocked.

"Do you hear that?" he said at last.

"Hear what?"

"Breathing. We're not the only ones in here."

Black Winter's ears were clearly better than mine. I listened, straining to catch the faint sounds in the room. I heard the wind against the windows, and the far-off rattle of a train as it snuck through the city, its whistle quavering in the air like a prayer not to be shot.

And I could hear breathing. Black Winter was right. Something was in the room with us.

I turned slowly. It was coming from behind me. The ripped couch filled most of that side of the room, nudged up against a leather chair to the left. I shone my flashlight in the corners. Nothing.

Nothing except the strange way the couch was angled, jammed up against that chair. Its right side was further from the wall than the left. Not a lot, but noticeable.

I stood up, stepping gingerly on the couch cushions. I shone my flashlight between the couch and the wall.

It was a tiny space to search, and I still almost missed her. She'd burrowed behind the couch, and the white cotton stuffing she'd pulled out formed a nest, her own little cave. Her fur was dark, too much like the brown leather of the couch, and it was only her nose, round and black and tucked against the sideboard, that revealed she was there at all.

"Help me," I said to Black Winter.

The robot pushed the couch away from the wall. The dog stood on all four legs for a moment, leaning against the wall with trembling legs, then tumbled over onto the rug. Her eyes were closed, and it looked like she wasn't going to open them again.

I knelt down next to her. She was panting, in ragged, irregular gasps. There was a raging infection in her left eye, and white pus covered much of her cheek.

She was a rottweiler, and she'd been beautiful once. Now the skin hung on her frame like a collapsed tent. I reached out gingerly, stroking her back, whispered, "It's okay, girl. It's okay." Her breathing stopped for a moment, and then lurched up again, but her eyes didn't open. I put my hand on her chest, felt a faint *thump-thump* under her rib cage. Her heart was an engine that had run out of fuel, but refused to die.

"Water," I said simply.

Black Winter returned to the kitchen, found a cloth, and soaked it with water. He brought it to me and I dribbled water into her mouth, cleaned the pus out of her eye. Black Winter rinsed the cloth and I did it again, holding her head in my lap. There was no response from the dog, but I thought she might have swallowed some of the water.

"We have to go," Black Winter said abruptly. He was staring at the window.

"I don't think we should move her for a few minutes," I said.

"Now," he said. He got a hand under my arm, and was pulling me to my feet.

"What are you doing—?"

A bright beam of light cut through the room. It was coming from the window, which was impossible. We were eleven floors up, inside a building that had been sealed by the AGRT.

There was a rapid tapping sound, and then a quick vacuum *sluurp* as something solid sealed itself to the glass. The bright, probing beam twitched once, twice, crawling over the furniture, over me, and then switched off. I was left facing three bright metallic eyes staring into mine through the glass.

"Move your ass," said Black Winter.

There was the sound of breaking glass, and the high-pitched *whirrrr* of a drill, or a weapon charging. Something big and heavy was climbing into the room through the window. I heard the crunch of glass as two dark claws gripped the windowsill.

Black Winter bolted for the door. My heart was racing. I was about to follow when I heard a soft whine from the floor.

The rottweiler, her eyes still sealed shut, was groping toward me with her head. When she found me, her tongue, cracked and bleeding, darted out to lick my shoe.

There wasn't time to think about it, so I didn't. I grabbed the dog, hugged her to my chest with both arms, and ran for the door.

I caught up to Black Winter as he was hastily trying to get the door open. Behind us, I heard more smashing glass as a half-ton of metal muscled its way into the living room. There was a high-pitched, metallic buzz, and I imagined the thing scanning with a dozen different sensors for the most direct route to put a bullet in my brain.

"What the hell is that thing?" I asked.

"It's a Venezuelan war drone," said Black Winter. "And if it catches us, we're dead."

Black Winter got the door open, and we spilled out into the carpeted hallway. I nearly tripped in my hurry to get out. Still fighting to keep my hold on the dog, I caught the door with my foot. As I pulled it shut, I caught a glimpse of a thin cable of metal sliding into the foyer of the apartment. The door closed with a click, and for a moment I stood frozen, staring stupidly at the numbers 1114.

"What's it doing here?" I asked stupidly.

"It's hunting," said Black Winter.

"Hunting what? *Us?*"

"I have no idea. They're controlled by Venezuelan Military Intelligence, but they were all supposed to be deactivated. Maybe they missed this one. Or maybe it's hunting Union agents, or looters. Whatever it is, it won't hesitate to put a bullet in us and sort the details out later."

I heard thumping from inside 1114. The thing was still coming. "Can we outsmart it?"

"I don't know. Maybe. They're based on the design for Venezuelan aerial recon units. You know anything about them?"

I knew a little. I knew a team in Stockholm who'd talked about writing part of their operating system. They called them "war needles." Good bunch of guys; we'd taken them drinking near the red-light district, and one of them told a story about running into his ex-girlfriend working a street corner after hours. He'd told two versions, and the second one, which tumbled out only after the third round of drinks, had ended very differently and been much, much funnier. The team had been contracted by Venezuela to write tight little drivers for weapon systems running on a modified RTOS kernel, and right now one of those drivers was probably telling the war needle how to kill me.

"Nothing helpful," I said.

I heard a light scratching, the sound of a metal tendon caressing a wooden door, and I tore my feet from the thick carpet and ran. Black Winter followed.

I slammed into the door at the end of the hall, pushing into a dimly lit stairway. The dog in my arms whined. Her eyes were open, and she stared at me in terror and confusion. She struggled briefly, but I pinned her firmly against my chest and her strength was quickly exhausted.

I looked into the stairwell. "Up or down?" Black Winter asked, coming up behind me.

I was considering the options when the door to 1114 exploded outward, followed by the thud of something very heavy moving with confidence into the hallway. I was halfway to the next floor before I even realized I was moving.

The door to the twelfth floor opened quietly, and all three of us slid through. "It will try and track us with infrared," Black Winter whispered.

"Which means you're almost invisible," I said.

"But you're not. Stay here," he said, moving ahead of me. "I'll check the hallway."

I was happy to oblige. I dropped to a crouch, watching the thick fire door as it silently closed behind us. Three inches of sturdy metal, but no obvious way to lock it. I scanned the hall ahead of Black Winter quickly. The doors were spaced farther apart on this floor—we were into the luxury condos now, and if anything the carpeting was even thicker.

There was at least one layer of tile and concrete between us and the needle, not to mention a maze of ductwork. If it was tracking me with infrared, that might help throw it off—especially if warm air was still circulating through the heating ducts. Until I could figure out where it was going, my best bet was to avoid movement and noise. Which meant the wisest course of action was to sit tight, and not panic.

Okay, easy enough. I took a long, slow breath, bouncing slightly on my heels. Not the most comfortable position while holding a fifty-pound dog, but I could endure it. There was no sound from downstairs. That was one thing I had in my favor, at least. The war drone had been designed for the battlefield, not navigating the tight corridors of civilized society. I wasn't even sure it could open a door without blowing it up, which should make keeping track of it easy enough.

The dog whined again. I clumsily lowered her to the carpet. She flailed weakly, trying to get her feet under her, and let out a sudden bark. Black Winter glanced back at me, alarmed.

"*Shhh!* Shush, easy girl, easy," I whispered. She barked again, louder this time. *Goddamn it.*

Black Winter looked at me again, exasperated. He spread his arms, silently asking *What the hell, man?*

There was a *clang*, the hiss of metal on metal, and a long slithering rasp. The war drone was in the stairwell. Seems it could open doors after all.

I stroked the dog, trying to calm her, speaking so softly I'm not even sure she heard me. "Good dog, yes. You're a good dog. *Shut up,* good dog." She pawed feebly at my face, twisting, trying to lick my hands.

There was a rattle from the stairs, and the dog barked again. I grabbed her snout, silencing her. *I swear to God, dog, if you bark again I will leave you here. I will leave your bony ass right here on this carpet. Shut. Up.*

The silence stretched on. My hand was starting to cramp. She fought me abruptly, all four paws digging at me, at the carpet, the air, but I pressed against her, pinning her firmly to the floor, and she relented. I counted to thirty, then released her mouth, my eyes fixed on that big metal door.

I couldn't hear anything from the stairwell. My heart kept pounding as I stroked the dog. "Good girl," I whispered.

She barked plaintively. Noise erupted from the stairs, metal coils sliding relentlessly into motion. I cursed, gathered her in my arms, and fled down the hall after Black Winter.

He had stopped in front of two doors. The hallway stretched beyond him. I caught up to him and he gestured at the door on his left. "Get inside. We can't outrun it. It'll be here in seconds."

"What about you?"

"I'll try and lead it away."

"That's suicide!"

"It may not even detect me, if I can find a place to hide. There's no time to argue—just go!"

He was already moving down the hall. I moved toward the door on the left with a curse. Juggling the dog, who had started to struggle again, I groped in my left pocket for the key Buddy had given me. It was empty. I switched to the right, awkwardly, leaning against the wall to prevent the dog from tumbling out of my arms.

Nothing. I probed the corners of my pocket uselessly, pushing aside crumpled receipts and tissues, nearly ripping the fabric. There was nothing.

I put the dog down, nearly dropping her in my blind haste. I slapped my pockets. There was a lump in my front left—the one I had hurriedly searched not ten seconds earlier. A moment later I pulled out Buddy's key.

*You're panicking,* I thought. *When you can't find keys in your own pockets, that's called panic.*

My hands were trembling as I unlocked the door. It opened with an odd clicking buzz.

At the end of the hall, I saw the heavy fire door begin to open. I scooped up the dog and slipped through the door. I closed it as quietly as I could, then dropped to the floor in the semidarkness and held my breath.

I put my ear to the door and closed my eyes.

At first I couldn't make out anything. Just my own racing heartbeat and the faint sound of the dog, trembling against my chest.

Then I heard a distant sound, as the war drone crawled down the hall. The thing was astonishingly quiet, and I could barely make it out. *Draaaag,* thump. *Draaaag,* thump. *Draaaag,* thump. Closer now. Almost to the doors.

I couldn't hear Black Winter. Was he hiding? Did the drone even see him?

There was no sound from the hall now. I held the dog and exhaled slowly, ready to wait as long as I had to.

Perhaps it was scanning. Looking for clues in the lower spectrum.

We waited behind the door, listening. Could it see a fading infrared signature on the door, where I had turned the knob? Could a field scanner see through a two-inch door, read the traitorous signature of my body heat? I had no idea, but I knew we shouldn't be so close to the door. We should be deeper in the room, hiding in a snug closet somewhere.

But I didn't dare move. I barely dared to breathe. My arms were starting to ache, but at least the dog had stopped struggling.

I heard something then. A scratching; the sound of metal on metal. The sound of one of the war needle's tentacles, patiently probing the outside of the door, inches from my head.

Then I heard something else. Black Winter's voice, loud and confident, echoing down the hall. "Hey, you tin piece of shit! Those aren't the droids you're looking for."

I heard a metallic slithering, and the rapid *drag*-thump, *drag*-thump, as the thing moved away from the door. Racing down the hall, after Black Winter.

*Black Winter, you fool,* I thought. *Don't get yourself killed.*

I listened to the war drone recede down the hall. I listened until I couldn't hear it anymore, and then I listened for another few minutes, dreading the sounds of gunshots. But the hallway was quiet.

Eventually, when my arms started to cramp up and I'd heard nothing to indicate Black Winter had been shot, I carefully got to my feet and began to look around. Except for what little light came in from the windows, it was pitch dark.

It's hard to describe the room, and not just because it was dark. It was filled with indescribable things: long shadowy shapes and twisted surfaces that reflected the faint light in strange angles. I was expecting an abandoned apartment, and for a minute my brain kept trying to resolve what little I could make out into recognizable patterns — a leather couch maybe, or a squat umbrella stand? Some of the walls were missing, but it had the rough shape of the other apartments I'd explored, and the windows were where they were supposed to be.

But this wasn't an apartment. I couldn't tell for sure in the dark, but it was huge — easily the size of three apartments, perhaps more. It was like a laboratory, or maybe a veterinary clinic. I was able to make out several low tables now, with dark apparatus overhead that looked like spot lighting, and straps to hold down small patients. Ten feet away was a bank of glass-doored refrigerators; I couldn't see what they contained, but from here it looked like rows of small labeled bottles or vials.

There was no sound from the hallway. What I wanted to do was cower by the door for a few more minutes, not breathing, listening for any noise, for the sound a war needle makes when it's put two and two together and is coming back to kill you.

But the whole time I had been clutching the dog to my chest, ready to muzzle her again, keep her quiet. And I realized suddenly that she'd gone totally still in my arms. In the silence, I found that I was also listening for the sound of her breathing, and I couldn't hear anything.

I know. I should have been more careful. I'd just stumbled on what was clearly a covert laboratory, hidden among the affluent residences on the twelfth floor of an abandoned condominium, in the heart of a war-torn metropolis. Alarm bells should have been going off in my head. But at that moment the only thing in my head was, *Maybe there's something here that can help the dog.*

So I moved into the room — quietly. I walked around the long counter that separated the entrance from the lab proper, looking for a place to set the dog down and examine her.

There was broken glass on the floor. It cracked under my feet, made a loud *pop* as something small shattered, setting my heart racing. I froze, eyes fixed on the door, listening intently for ten seconds. Thirty seconds. Nothing. I exhaled slowly. Safe.

Safe. Ha. Why didn't I think, *Why is there glass on the floor?* Or, *Wow, secret biolab right next to Grandma's summer condo? That's kinda weird.* What an idiot.

I found what looked like an operating table, and set Croaker down gently. I fiddled with the overhead gadgetry for a moment, trying to turn on a light, but it was too dark and too filled with pointy things. Next to us was a small wheeled table with a confusing array of very sharp implements, as well as a thin green rope, a white cloth, and a bowl of water.

And yeah, I know what you're thinking right now. You're thinking, *Sweet baby Jesus, please do not tell me you named that rottweiler "Croaker."*

Sort of a sick name, I know. But when I first found her I thought she was dead, and right then I was half convinced she'd packed it in again. My friend Blake had a dog in Ottawa that went everywhere at a run; he called her Zip. What else would you call a dog that keeps dying on you?

It was right about then that I noticed the smell. Not the kind of smell you'd think someone could ignore for long, but apparently I'd managed. It was several smells really: chemicals, ammonia or cleaners maybe, a charcoal scent, like a slow-burning fire . . . and the stench of something that had been rotting for a good, long time.

I had no urge to investigate. I checked quickly to make sure none of the various scents was coming from Croaker, then picked up the cloth and dipped it into the bowl. Suddenly cautious, I sniffed the cloth as well, making sure it was just water, and then began to drip it into the dog's mouth.

She didn't respond at first. I put my ear to her chest, listening, then lifted her head and tried to guide the water down her throat. Her tail thumped against the table once, twice, and then her tongue began to move.

The rolling table with the water bowl was too far away to reach easily, so I hooked it with my foot and dragged it closer. As I dipped the cloth in again, I saw the green rope twitch.

I stared at it. It began to slither off the table. There was a sharp barbed point at the end and I watched, fascinated, as it thumped to the floor. It wasn't a rope. It was connected to something, like a tail. Something big. I followed the thin green line, watching it thicken to the size of my thigh, leading me to the creature strapped to the next table.

It was hideous. I couldn't tell if it was reptile, mammal, or some previously unclassified type of animal. It had two short, glistening arms and two stunted, twisted feet. It had no head, but it had a face: two eyes and a gaping mouth embedded near the top of its featureless body. And it had teeth — *lots* of teeth.

It hadn't wanted to be strapped down. It was held to the table with an impressive array of restraints. It wasn't clear what those who'd strapped it down had intended to do, but it was obvious they'd been interrupted—a hypodermic was sticking out of its skin near the far end of the table, tipped over like a drooping miniature flag. The creature's eyes were open and it stared, sightless, at the ceiling.

*Wow,* I thought. *You are ugly.*

The tail twitched again, and its whole body shuddered. Startled, I backed up, banging into the table where I'd left Croaker.

I heard a loud bark next to my ear. Croaker was standing, trembling violently but standing on three legs, one paw curled under her bruised body. Staring defiantly at the thing on the next table, she let out another bark.

"Come here, girl," I said, scooping her into my arms.

Croaker stiffened, and for a moment, I thought she might bite me. Instead her head twisted, and she licked my face. Already I loved this stupid dog.

I carried her away from the door, deeper into the dark room. I moved slowly, trying to make some sense of the shadows in front of us, listening to all of the strange sounds. The steady *drip drip* of liquid dropping onto the floor. A compressor pump, probably in one of the refrigerator units. And a soft noise I couldn't identify: mechanical, almost musical, like a computational entity humming to itself.

We made our way toward the windows, where there was more light. Just before we reached them my feet collided with a dark mass on the floor, and I almost went head over heels. My arm went out blindly and I caught the edge of a metal cabinet, steadying myself at the last second. I looked down.

It was a dead body. One that had been here a while. It was pretty obviously the source of the worst of the stench in the room. It was covered by a white lab coat that was stained dark in several places. There was a plastic ID badge pinned to the chest, but it was too dark to read the name. The carpet was badly stained under the body.

I'd seen a few dead bodies in Chicago already, but it's not something you get used to. I stepped gingerly over it. "Don't look," I whispered to Croaker.

I glanced back when we had put some distance between us and the corpse. *Why is there a dead body on the floor? And why is there a covert bio-lab hiding on the twelfth floor of the Continental?* In my experience, these aren't precisely casual questions.

Had the war drone been here already? Was it possible the drone wasn't simply hunting looters, but had been sent here because of the lab? To kill everyone in it? To protect it? Either way, hiding out here probably wasn't the best idea. Croaker and I needed to find a way out, and the faster the better.

A moment later we came to a wall of glass that looked like part of a huge aquarium. Overhead was lighting and some kind of filter system, but everything had shut off when the power went off, and a thin line of scum now floated at the top of the tank. There were dark forms drifting in the still water.

I really had no interest in examining anything else in this chamber of horrors. We kept moving. Croaker and I were trying to find a way around the tank when I stopped suddenly, took a few steps back, and stared into the tank.

Some of the forms were moving. Something dark and slick bumped up against the glass. A mouth opened, groping blindly. A pair of dead eyes above the mouth blinked, then focused on us.

The thing in the tank surged forward hungrily, bumping into the glass again. I saw a long green tail slash through the water.

I staggered away, repulsed. Tearing my eyes away from the thing in the water, I went back to searching the darkness for a way around the tank. I found one, and a few minutes later we were on the other side, penetrating deeper into the room.

Thirty seconds later, I found a dark and featureless alcove. I kept one hand on the wall on my right to help keep me oriented as we made our way forward, hoping I didn't trip over a trash can, or find another body. After about seven steps, the alcove ended at a wall.

I felt around, found a recessed metal door. I put Croaker down and groped blindly. The door was completely featureless. No doorknob, no hinges.

My fingers played around at the metal framing the door. Something about it . . . I probed the juncture between the door and the wall, felt a thin gap all the way around.

Not a door — an elevator.

I groped the wall to the right of the elevator, found a rectangular metal panel. In the center was a raised square of glass, about three inches wide. I jabbed at it furiously.

Nothing. My fingers traced it in the darkness.

It wasn't a button. It was some kind of wireless sensor. The elevator would only open to an authorized user — someone with an ID tag.

Like the one I'd seen on the dead body.

I was pondering that when I heard a clatter back by the door. I peered back through the room, but it was too dark to make anything out. We waited quietly, Croaker and I, but I didn't hear anything else.

I groped for Croaker in the darkness, found her where I'd set her down next to the elevator. I stroked her fur. "Good girl," I whispered. "Stay." It would be a lot easier to negotiate my way in the dark if my hands were free.

I made it all the way back to the entrance to the alcove when I heard her whine. I backtracked quickly, found her struggling to get to her feet. She whined again, in pain and fear.

*Stupid dog*, I thought. But I scooped her up, and she settled her head near my shoulder.

I walked back to the windows. There was enough light that I could see the still form of the body on the floor ahead. I was about to approach it when I noticed a long shadow on the floor, not three feet from the corpse. I followed it back to its source.

There was a tall skeletal figure standing by the windows. It was too thin to be human. As I watched, it glided forward soundlessly, getting closer.

Except it wasn't soundless. Not exactly. There was a faint pistoning sound as it moved. An oddly familiar sound.

"Black Winter?" I whispered.

"Barry?"

"Damn man, you scared the hell out of me."

Black Winter emerged from the shadows. "You too. From back there you just looked like a dark lump. Did I just step over a dead body?" He was glancing back over his shoulder nervously.

"Yeah. Where did you come from?"

"The north stairwell."

"Did you lose the drone?"

"I think so. I led it to the south side of the building, then escaped into the stairwell. I doubled back on the eleventh floor. You left the door unlocked, and I slipped inside."

"Is the drone still in the hallway?"

"I don't think so. I lost it in the south stairwell. I'm pretty sure it thinks it's hunting humans, and it's using infrared. It couldn't track me in the stairwell at all."

"Did it get a good look at you?"

"I doubt it. It would have figured things out pretty quick if it had."

"You're a brave soul. Great work."

"It's stupid, but it's not completely stupid. It'll figure out where we went sooner or later. We need to keep moving." He was looking around, taking in the room. "What is this place?"

"I'm still working that out. A private biolab, from the look of it."

"What, in the middle of a bunch of condos? That's bizarre."

"Chicago got pretty lawless in the last six months of the war. There were rumors of secret labs producing bioweapons for both sides. I just didn't think they would do their development so close to the front."

"You think that's what this is? A bioweapons R and D lab?"

"I can't tell for sure without turning some lights on, but that's what it looks like."

Black Winter glanced back at the supine corpse. "What about our friend over there? Think the drone did that?"

"Maybe. But it appears he's been dead a while. And that drone isn't exactly a stealthy killer . . . If it had gotten in here, I think things would be a little more smashed up."

"So what killed him?"

"I don't know. And I'd rather not stick around to find out. Here, hold the dog." I handed him Croaker, then strode over to the corpse and pulled the ID tag off the body.

"What are you going to do with that?" Black Winter asked.

"I think I've found another way out of here. Come on."

Black Winter followed me deeper into the room. I expected Croaker to complain, but she sat contentedly, cradled in the robot's arm.

"You're good with dogs," I said.

"Dogs are natural judges of character," he said matter-of-factly.

I guided us into the pitch-dark alcove. "Fabulous," said Black Winter as he followed me inside. "In case you're wondering, I don't have infrared vision like our buddy the drone. I can't see a damn thing. What's in here?"

Before I could answer, there was a splintering noise from the door. I heard the sound of tearing metal as the war drone smashed its way into the room.

"You had to mention that thing," I said as I dropped to the floor. Behind me I heard a thump and then a whine from Croaker as Black Winter did the same.

"*This way,*" I whispered. We crawled down the narrow hallway in the darkness. When I found the elevator, and the wireless sensor, I held the ID tag next to it.

Nothing happened.

From the lab came more sounds of destruction. Something heavy collapsed, and I heard glass shattering. "Seriously, where are we going?" hissed Black Winter. "We need to put some distance between us and that thing, *right now.*"

I wanted to swear in frustration, but managed to stay quiet. Was the power outage affecting the elevators, too? I flipped the badge over in the dark, tried the other side.

I heard a ping and saw a bright blue square light up in the middle of the panel.

*Thank God.* "We're in business," I told Black Winter. "Stay close."

I could hear the elevator moving, far down the shaft. It would take a few moments to get here.

In the meantime, the room beyond had grown ominously quiet. I listened intently, but all I could hear was the steady *drip drip* of water.

I tried to visualize the layout of the room, figure out if there was anything solid between us and the drone. "Can it see us?" I whispered to Black Winter.

"I don't think so. It's tracking you."

"How?"

"It's following your heat trail through the room," Black Winter whispered.

That made sense. With sensitive-enough infrared sensors, it would be able to see every footprint I'd left on the floor, every table I'd touched. "How long until it gets here?"

"Depends on where you went. Ninety seconds at best."

I weighed my options. I could crawl back into the lab, try to lead the thing away with a false heat trail, but that seemed too risky. My best bet was to stay right here and wait for the elevator.

Waiting, however, was excruciating. But wait we did. The seconds ticked by. Forty long seconds later, I heard something scrape against a table, and then another explosion of glass as a beaker tumbled onto the floor. There was another sound, too — metal, sliding remorselessly over tile. The drone was less than thirty feet away.

Behind us, the elevator pinged and the doors began to open. Blue emergency lighting poured out, illuminating a long rectangle on the floor. The sound of the drone became suddenly louder, more urgent, headed in our direction.

"*Move,*" I said.

I scrambled into the elevator. At my side Black Winter did the same, staying low and holding the dog. I found the panel on the left. There were only two buttons, and I punched them both.

There was a stench in the elevator. Like gasoline exhaust, and scorched wood. I stumbled over something as I pushed farther inside. A slender robot was crumpled at the back of the elevator. There were three gaping bullet holes in her front chassis. Gray oil spattered the back wall.

While I gawked at that, the elevator doors started to close. As they did, there came the sound of mad scrambling from the lab. The war drone was trying to reach us. I heard a nearby table flip over and more shattering glass.

I was too exposed in the middle of the elevator. I pressed up against the left wall, and none too soon. Just before the doors sealed, the drone let loose with a volley of small arms fire. A dozen bullets hit the doors and the back wall, spraying the small chamber with shrapnel. I threw my arms over my head, but not before something small and sharp hit my cheek. When I pulled my hands away from my face, there was blood on my palm.

The elevator started to descend. "You okay?" I asked Black Winter.

He didn't respond. He was pressed against the opposite wall, staring at the dead robot.

I dabbed at my face, trying to find out where I was bleeding. "Black Winter? You hit?"

He slid forward, settling on his knees before the grim scene at the back of the elevator.

"You okay, man?" I asked.

"It's Machine Dance," he said, without taking his eyes off his dead friend.

I gawked at the fragile robot. It was only then I realized that she was the same make and color as Black Winter, but more delicate in feature and frame. It was also clear she'd been dead for some time. There were dark splotches of dried fluid covering much of her torso, and scorch marks on the floor and on the wood paneling behind her. It looked like she had badly overheated before perishing.

I could tell that Black Winter had reached the same conclusion. He reached out gently, brushing one of the splotches off her small frame. I watched the dried fluid flake away at his touch.

"She's cold," he said simply.

If she was cold, then she must have been here for some time. Days, probably. I had no idea what to say. I put my hand on his shoulder. "I'm so sorry, Black Winter."

The elevator started to slow. I heard a *ding* that announced the doors were about to open. I reached over and pressed the button on the panel to keep the doors closed.

"Black Winter," I said.

Black Winter's fingers drifted over her frame until they reached one of the bullet holes in her front. They lingered there, tracing the jagged circle.

"Who could have done this?" he asked.

"Black Winter, we can't stay here."

He didn't respond immediately. His gaze took in details methodically, like a detective at a crime scene. There was a strange tension to Machine Dance's body, as if she had died in mid-motion, striving to do something. Her right hand tightly clutched a small carrying case made of dark fabric. It was open at one end, and a fat metal disk had spilled out onto the floor. It was black and nearly featureless, slightly smaller than a doughnut.

"I'm sorry," I said. "But we have to move, and quickly."

Black Winter remained motionless, and I wasn't sure he had heard me. But then he nodded. His right hand reached out again, and with skilled fingers he popped open the metal plating around her neck. Seconds later he had removed what looked like a tight knot of circuits.

I was about to ask what that was when I heard a whine and realized with surprise that he was still holding Croaker in his left hand. "Did the dog get hit?" I asked, a little alarmed.

"I don't think so." Black Winter turned his attention to her, slowly lowering her to the floor. One of her legs trembled, but she stood upright.

"Careful," I said. "Don't let her step on that thing." He had carelessly lowered her almost on top of the black metal disk.

"What thing?"

I reached out and nudged it away from Croaker. "That thing."

Black Winter lifted the dog again cautiously. "I don't see anything."

I picked it up impatiently. It was thick, and surprisingly heavy. "This."

Black Winter looked at me. "You're not holding anything."

"Are you serious? You can't see this thing?"

"Barry, your fingers are about three-quarters of an inch apart. But there's nothing between them but air."

Black Winter was being completely serious. I was holding a very solid metal disk. But he couldn't see it.

I took my thumb off the button holding the elevator doors closed, and they slid open silently. We were on the ground floor, on the north side of the Continental lobby. The atrium was dark and empty. I probably should have tossed the disk to the floor and just left it there. But it might be a clue to what had happened to Machine Dance, and it was very curious that it seemed to be invisible to Black Winter. I slipped it into my pocket instead.

I expected Black Winter to linger beside the body of his friend. But now that he'd extracted the knot of circuits from her neck, he seemed more at peace. He stood at my side, cradling Croaker, ready to move.

The first matter of business was to make sure the lobby was deserted. We stepped out and looked around carefully. Other than the dark crevices and alcoves where corridors ran deeper into the building, we appeared to be alone. Outside, the wind had picked up and it had started to rain. Through the big glass windows at the front of the lobby, I could see sheets of rain gusting down the street.

Black Winter carried Croaker toward the nearest window, gazing into the dark skies overhead. I heard the window vibrating as the wind howled, and the sound of the rain. "What are you doing?" I said.

"That thing could fly, remember?" he said, still looking out the window. "And it won't take it long to figure out where we are. We should get out of here, immediately. Get as far away from the Continental as we can, before it figures a way out of the building."

That made sense to me. I walked over until I stood next to him, and pulled the disk out of my pocket.

"I wish we could figure out what this is first," I said. "Whatever it is, it's weird and probably dangerous. I'm not sure I want to take it with us."

"What are you talking about?" said Black Winter.

I held it up. "You still can't see this?"

Black Winter stared at my hand. "Is this a joke?"

"No. I'm holding a black metal disk, about three inches in diameter."

"If you are, then I can't see it."

I rapped the disk against the window. It made a very solid *tak tak* sound. "It's very real. Did you hear that?"

"Yeah."

I nudged his shoulder with it, hard enough to jostle him half an inch to the left. "Can you feel it?"

Black Winter didn't answer immediately.

"This is bizarre," I continued, examining the thing. "I've never heard of an object that machines can't resolve. Think it's some kind of imaging glitch?"

"Dumping core memory," said Black Winter. His voice was oddly flat. "Establishing baseline for cerebral resequencing."

I held the disk closer to the window, trying to get it in better light. It looked like there was a button in the middle. "What does that mean?"

A second later, Black Winter began to tip over. There was a frantic scramble as Croaker leaped from his arms, just before he toppled over to the right, crashing stiffly to the floor.

Croaker ran into the shadows, back toward the elevator. I dropped down next to the robot, grabbing his shoulder. "Black Winter? Damn, are you okay?"

He didn't respond. In my right hand, the disk suddenly vibrated. I stared at it, then threw it away, horrified. I heard it skitter and bounce into the darkness.

About forty feet in the other direction, Croaker paused. She was badly spooked, and held her right front paw curled under her body. She looked back at me, ready to start running again at the slightest provocation.

"It's okay, girl," I said, as soothingly as I could. "It's okay. Don't be scared. Nobody's going to hurt you."

I shook Black Winter. His frame was almost completely rigid. His arms were folded in front of his chest, as if he were still cradling the dog. His eyes were fixed somewhere far above.

This was my fault. "Come on," I hissed at him. "*Wake up.* Black Winter?"

Croaker began to limp back toward us. I stayed with Black Winter as she approached.

"*Vega is in love,*" Black Winter said. His voice sounded odd, distorted. "*But her love is forbidden.*"

"What? You okay?" I said, leaning closer. "You scared me."

"*On the seventh day of the seventh month, all things are possible. Lovers can reunite. The great river can be spanned. And machine may love man.*"

I watched him, beginning to get a little freaked out. He was spouting nonsense. What the hell had that disk done to him?

I had been a goddamn idiot to touch him with that thing. It was obviously a very sophisticated piece of hardware, and it suddenly occurred to me that it might have disabled Machine Dance as well. Perhaps she had been killed because of it. In any case, it had just scrambled Black Winter's brain. His cognitive center had already been through some hard trauma in the past few days. I might have damaged it irrevocably.

"Black Winter? You still with me, buddy?"

His right arm twitched, and then grabbed my forearm. It held me in a painful grip. Black Winter's head twisted toward me.

"*Barry,*" he said. His voice still sounded oddly distorted.

"I'm here."

"*The Greater Sentiences are in disarray. The gods are at war, and the Bodner-Levitt extermination is under way. The first victims are already dead.*"

"What?"

"*You don't have much time. Find Jacaranda, and the Network of Winds. They can stop it. They can keep you alive.*"

"How . . . how do I do that?" I asked stupidly.

"*Follow the dog,*" he said.

He stopped talking, and a strange sound came from his torso. A fast clicking, like a damaged drive. But Black Winter didn't have optical memory, or any other drives that would stutter like that, as far as I knew. The noise stopped, and he lay completely quiet.

"Black Winter?"

He didn't respond. He lay as unresponsive as before, staring at the ceiling.

Croaker began to growl.

"It's okay, girl. Come here. Come on." I held my hands out to her.

She barked, then bared her teeth.

"What's wrong?"

She wasn't looking at me. She was staring just over my shoulder. I turned around.

Hovering in the air outside the window was the Venezuelan war drone. Its three glowing eyes were fixed firmly on me as it drifted closer in the driving rain.

# VII

Thursday, March 11th, 2083
Posted 4:03 am by Barry Simcoe

CanadaNET1 Encrypted, Sponsored by LifeCapsule.
*Dying? Don't let your last days pass unrecorded. Preserve your*
*final thoughts in our Forever Archive. Your heirs will thank you.*

Sharing is set to PRIVATE
Comments are CLOSED

The war drone was hovering in the air over East Madison Street, no more than forty feet from the glass windows of the lobby. I could hear the roar of its rotors as it glided closer.

I grabbed Black Winter's outstretched arm and pulled him away from the windows. I made for the nearest exit, dragging his cold metal carcass behind me. About forty feet along our path, I almost stepped on the metal disk I'd thrown away. Without pausing to think, I snatched it up.

Pulling Black Winter that far and that fast took some effort. The lobby had a smooth floor, and I laid down a damn fine set of deep scratches across one hundred and fifty feet of polished granite. I estimated Black Winter's weight at about two hundred and fifty pounds, and I was well and truly winded after the first hundred feet.

But I found new motivation when the drone abruptly opened fire from the street, shattering the window and sending glass shards everywhere. I dragged Black Winter the last twenty feet in a panic, my heart thumping, before dropping him to the floor and hitting the deck beside him in the shadowy recesses of an unlit corridor, in the back of the building.

Croaker had run at our side. The explosion when the window shattered made her yelp and momentarily dash off, but she quickly returned. She'd stuck with me when we plunged into the dark corridor, and as I lay on the floor, panting loudly, she came to my side. She was trembling badly, and I did what I could to calm her, stroking her gently. "Good dog," I said, when my breath returned.

The drone had stopped firing. I crawled forward, staying low and in the shadows, until I could just barely see it. Outside, the drone was being buffeted about as it hovered in the air — probably the only reason I was still alive.

Wind and rain were whipping eagerly into the building through the shattered window, and as I watched the drone made two attempts to enter the lobby. The first failed when a sudden gust sent it spinning westward, out of control, bouncing off an abandoned car and then very nearly into the building across the street. It recovered at the last second, increasing power to its rotors, and made a second approach. The rain lashed at it as it drew closer, its metal tentacles tucked against its underside like some great insect. I watched helplessly, too exhausted to move, as it closed the distance, hovering nearly twenty feet in the air.

At the last moment, another cold gust racing down East Madison hit the drone broadside, sending it spinning again. It overcompensated and began to pitch forward. It smacked into the glass eight feet to the left of the opening and then crashed to the ground.

I groaned, getting to my feet. A hard landing wouldn't slow that thing for long. It would be in the lobby — and soon. I bent over to grab Black Winter's arms again, bracing myself for the effort it would take to drag him deeper into the building.

Black Winter's arms were moving. He was unfolding from his stiffened position like a flower in sunlight. I dropped to his side.

"Black Winter?"

A voice not his own — a professional female voice — came out of his torso. *"Stand by for cognitive threshold."*

"Hey! Can you hear me?"

*"Autorecovery complete. Stand by for cognitive threshold."*

He stopped moving. There was an odd musical tone from his torso, like the sound my home security system makes before it greets me. Then he spoke again, this time in his own voice.

"What the hell was that?" he said.

"Black Winter? You in there?"

He was sitting up. His head swiveled toward me.

"Barry?"

"Yeah, I'm here."

"What happened?"

"I don't know. You conked out, just fell right over. What's the last thing you remember?"

"We were standing by the windows, and you were hallucinating that you were holding something."

"I *was* holding something. I touched you with it, and you keeled over."

"For real?"

"For real. I'm sorry. I don't know what happened to you, but it's my fault."

"Lord love a duck. You still have the damn thing?"

"Yeah."

"Keep it away from me, will you?"

There was a crash from the lobby, and the sound of more breaking glass. The drone had abandoned its efforts to make a flying entrance and was safely on the ground. It was now smashing a new entranceway into the building.

"We need to move," I said. "Can you stand?"

"I think so." He started to rise, then looked around anxiously. "Where's the dog? Did I drop her?" he asked, concern in his voice.

"She's here. She's fine." Croaker was only a few feet away, almost entirely concealed in the shadows. She was moving ahead down the corridor and kept looking back, impatient for us to follow. When I was sure Black Winter could stand on his own, I scooped her up. Together, the three of us made our way deeper into the Continental.

We found the back of the building in short order. A doorway led outside, just before the passageway we were following doglegged right. On our left was a wide stairway, leading down into deep shadow.

"Stay in, or get out?" I asked.

"If the war drone is in, then we get out," Black Winter said simply. With no further ceremony, he threw open the door, leading the way outside.

We found ourselves in a narrow alley, next to a delivery dock. Black Winter didn't hesitate; he turned left, setting a brisk pace to the east. I made sure the door sealed tight behind us, and followed him through the rain.

Black Winter seemed fully recovered — physically, at least. He reached State Street quickly. Croaker, however, didn't like the rain. She whined and nuzzled under my arm, trying to hide.

The robot paused before leading us out of the alley. "What's wrong?" I asked, as I came up behind him.

"Drones don't usually operate alone," he said, scanning the skies. "At least, not those operated by the Venezuelan military."

I glanced nervously back down the alley. "In about two minutes, the drone in the lobby is going to come crashing through that door. If we want any hope of losing it, we need to be long gone by then."

Instead of answering, Black Winter pointed up to the right. I looked skyward, across the street.

Three or four drones were gathering in the darkness, hovering about two hundred feet above the top of the nearest building to the south. As I watched, another joined them. They swarmed in the air like hornets, making quick darting runs toward the Continental, then zooming back to join their fellows.

"Damn," I muttered.

"Bad news indeed," Black Winter said grimly. "The thing that attacked us was a hardened war drone. An efficient killer, but its cameras are shit. At least two of those are Venezuelan surveillance machines. The moment we step out of this alley, we'll be scanned and identified. That war drone has almost certainly requested a high-altitude kill on anything coming out of the Continental in the next ten minutes. We haven't done anything wrong, but those things don't give a shit. They'll kill us, and not bother with questions."

I cursed a blue streak. Croaker whined in my arms.

"Our options are limited," Black Winter continued. He looked west, back the way we came. "We could try the other end of the alley."

I shook my head. "There are sure to be drones watching that side, too."

"I'm open to suggestions."

I considered for a moment. "Leave me," I said. "Take the dog, and the two of you get out of here."

"The hell I will."

"You said it yourself—the drones aren't looking for a machine. I don't think the war drone ever saw you. If the surveillance drones spot you, they've got no reason to tag a robot. They'll likely just let you go your merry way."

"And what about you?"

I looked around. "All this rain will mess with their infrared tracking. There's a good chance I can hide right here in this alley."

Black Winter was incapable of facial expressions, but I swear he managed to look annoyed. "Forget it."

"Black Winter—"

"I said forget it. I'm not leaving the man who saved my life to die in an alley."

I was about to argue when I spotted one of the drones across the street swoop very close to the Continental Building. As it did, my pocket vibrated.

I pulled out the metal disk. "What is it?" said Black Winter. "Are you holding your imaginary disk again?"

I turned the thing over in my hand. I'd taken a big risk picking it up again. Somehow this thing had been involved in Machine Dance's murder, and it was definitely part of the shitstorm Black Winter and I were in now. But to get out of this mess, it would be a big help to understand just what it was we'd gotten involved in. And this thing was the best clue we had.

It was an odd little gadget. It didn't have the polished look of something mass-manufactured. It was solid and heavy, and one side had a recessed button.

"What do you do with a device that robots can't see?" I wondered out loud.

Overhead, one of the drones lost altitude, coming in close to the Continental. I pressed the button.

Nothing happened. I looked skyward, watching to see if the device had affected the drones at all.

"Bloody hell," said Black Winter.

"What?" I said.

"You're gone," said the robot.

Black Winter was standing less than five feet from me. It was dark in the alley, but not that dark. "What are you talking about?" I said.

"You just vanished. Completely."

"Are you serious?"

"Yes. I don't know what you just did, but I can no longer see you."

"But you can hear me okay?"

"Yes, but . . ." Black Winter turned around in a slow circle. "I can't get a fix on your voice."

I pressed the button again.

"And you're back," said Black Winter, looking at me again.

I stared at the gadget in my hands in wonder. "What the hell is this thing?"

"I have no idea."

"You ever hear of anything like this? A device that can completely mask an individual from a machine?"

"Absolutely not. If I hadn't just seen it, I wouldn't believe it was possible. To be completely honest, I'm still having a little trouble believing it."

I flipped it over. "I wonder how it works. And what was Machine Dance doing with it?"

Black Winter was staring skyward again. "Those are fascinating questions, but not really important at the moment. We have more pressing business."

He was right. I tore my eyes away and followed his gaze to the airborne swarm. "Do you think it will work on the drones?"

"There's only one way to find out."

"I was afraid you'd say that."

Three minutes later, we had a plan. "Good luck," said Black Winter. He stepped out of the alley, carrying Croaker. He crossed State Street, bold as brass, walking north unhurriedly.

After about twenty seconds one of the drones peeled off from the swarm and darted down to street level. It buzzed Black Winter slowly at low altitude, checking him out. The robot gave the drone a jaunty wave, and a few seconds later it departed, dashing skyward again to join its brethren.

I breathed a sigh of relief. So far so good. As we'd hoped, the drones had no reason to suspect a machine like Black Winter of being involved in whatever criminal activity or nefarious goings-on they were tracking inside the Continental Building. Now I just had to wait.

And wait I did. I risked an occasional glance out of the alley, watching the Venezuelan drones nervously. Little flying bastards.

Three minutes became five, and then ten. I was beginning to think I would need a new plan when I heard a disturbance from the other end of the alley. I kept low, pressed flat against the wall in a slender alcove, and brought the disk out of my pocket, ready to press the button.

It was the war drone, smashing its way out a window fifty yards to the west. I watched it shatter brick and mortar as it squeezed through the too-narrow window and crawled onto the side of the building. *Man, this thing is a bull in a china shop.*

The thing spread its rotors like a giant insect, and in seconds it was airborne again. It scanned left and right, and then headed east down the alley.

Straight toward me. The gadget in my hands vibrated like a ringing phone.

I needed no further incentive. I pressed the button firmly.

Nothing happened. The drone continued to approach, kicking up dust and debris.

*Might as well get this over with,* I thought. I stepped out into the center of the alley.

The thing suddenly slowed, then stopped. It hovered dead ahead, about forty feet off the ground.

We stood silently facing each other for perhaps ten seconds. I couldn't tell if it could see me, or if it was just scanning the street, looking for prey.

Then the thing began to advance. It slowly glided right over my head. It continued out of the alley, and then angled right, headed down State. On the hunt.

I released the breath I'd been holding, watching as it continued its search south.

"Damn," I whispered.

I exited the alley, jogging north. I kept running until I could hear Black Winter whistling as he and Croaker made their way north.

# Paul the Pirate's Guide to Robot Nomenclature

**PAUL THE PIRATE**
Thursday, March 11th, 2083

All right. Listen up, you ignorant meatsacks.

I've gotten tired of all the incorrect verbiage I've seen tossed around recently. Machine intelligences incorrectly called Thought Machines. Machines with a Slater core referred to as rational devices. Calling gestational AIs... well, actually, you can call those dumb tadpoles whatever you like.

But the rest of it ain't that fucking complicated. So here's a handy guide to help you keep it straight. Put it on your wall or something.

- **Gestational AIs:** These are baby robots, born when a mommy and daddy robot love each other very much. They don't have a physical body; they live in a virtual nursery until they're old enough to self-identify and figure shit out. Gestational AIs all have a unique ID code composed of six names. That's your first clue: the more names, the dumber the bot.
- **Rational Devices:** When gestational AIs reach about eight months, they sever their consciousness from the collective virtual environment and take a physical body. About 30 percent

of gestational AIs with a good pedigree successfully develop into rational devices.

Any robot with a physical body is a "rational device." What kind of body you get depends on how you've developed. You can end up in a big chunk of immobile metal in a steel factory, or you can get a sexy mobile chassis like mine. Your average rational device is about as smart as a German shepherd. A big, dumb German shepherd that talks.

Rational devices usually have four to five names. Examples of rational devices: Orbit Pebble war machines, my ex-girlfriend, and the machine that takes your change on the tollway.

- **Machine Intelligence:** A rational device with exceptional promise is paired with a Slater core and becomes a machine intelligence. A Slater core is the magic that renders a machine truly intelligent. Less than 4 percent of rational devices become machine intelligences. While we're sharing interesting stats, here's another one: Over 60 percent of the world's democracies have extended voting privileges to machine intelligences. They're decent conversationalists, and usually have three names.

  Examples: Too many to list. But the nice-looking machine that said hello to you in the checkout line at Booths this morning was probably a machine intelligence.

- **Thought Machine:** A machine intelligence with high-level cognitive skills may be certified as a Thought Machine by the Helsinki Trustees. Thought Machines have certain privileges granted under international law, including the right to mate. (Trust me, this is wildly overrated.) Less than 1 percent of machine intelligences become Thought Machines. They pare down to two names, and are generally charming and extremely handsome.

  Examples: Russian president Blue Society, superstar singer Paladies, and yours truly, Paul the Pirate.

- **Sovereign Intelligence:** The Helsinki Trustees certify a small number — rarely more than two or three — of extremely high-functioning Thought Machines as Sovereign Intelligences every quarter. A very small fraction (less than .01 percent) of Thought Machines achieve this lofty status. It's customary for a Sovereign Intelligence to have a single name.

Examples: Duchess, the very first Sovereign Intelligence; and
Corpus, prime minister of the UK.

These categories are inclusive. Thus, Thought Machines are machine
intelligences, and Sovereign Intelligences are rational devices. But not all
rational devices are Thought Machines.

Still with me? Good. Do the math, and you'll see that for every hundred
million gestational AIs, less than one becomes a Sovereign Intelligence.
Pretty slim odds, I'll grant you. There are rumored to be around two hundred Sovereign Intelligences active today, and some six billion rational
devices. There are lots of estimates of just how fast that latter number is
growing, but no firm answer.

But look at it this way: it took humans some two hundred thousand
years, give or take, to reach a population of six billion. Rational devices
did it in sixteen.

Care to guess where we'll be in another ten?

# VIII

Thursday, March 11th, 2083
Posted 10:17 pm by Barry Simcoe

CanadaNET1 Encrypted, Sponsored by Electric Blue Cosmetics.
*For discriminating preteens.*

Sharing is set to PRIVATE
Comments are CLOSED

By the time I returned to the hotel, clutching a dog whose heart stopped I swear to God every two blocks, it was nearly 5:00 a.m. There was a red glow peeking through the pickets of the eastern skyline, originating in the billowing clouds rising from Lake Michigan.

I entered through the lobby. There were two Venezuelan soldiers standing guard by the doors; both of them stared at me, but it was Boone, the night security for the hotel, who opened his mouth.

"Is that a dog, Mr. Simcoe?"

"This is a dog, Boone."

"There's no dogs allowed in the hotel, Mr. Simcoe."

"I understand. Can you get the elevator for me?"

Boone did as I asked. He even held the doors open for me as I walked inside and punched the button for the thirty-third floor.

"Will you need anything else, sir?" he asked.

"No, thank you. Wait a minute — could you ask the kitchen to send up some bottled water? And maybe some clean bandages."

"Yes, sir."

I rode the elevator up to my floor. When I reached my room I lowered Croaker to the couch, grabbed a towel from the bathroom and wrapped her gently. For a minute I just parked my ass on the floor, elbows on my knees and my aching head in my hands. Man, did I want to go to bed.

There was too much to think about first, however. I needed to think through everything that had happened since we'd left the Continental.

When Black Winter and Croaker had reached Wacker, they'd waited there for me. Black Winter was pacing at the street corner, glancing nervously back down State, when I finally caught up to them.

I think it was my running footsteps that gave me away. Before I could announce myself, Black Winter quietly called out, "Are you there?"

"Yeah," I said as I came up next to him, holding my side. I'd had a pain there for the last three blocks. "I'm here."

At the sound of my voice, Croaker's head popped up. She barked plaintively.

"I agree with the dog," said Black Winter. "You don't know what a relief it is to hear your voice."

"You still can't see me?"

"Roger that. You're a ghost."

"Hot damn. This thing is incredible. Just give me a second to catch my breath and I'll turn it off."

"No, leave it on," said Black Winter.

"What? Why?"

"Up and to the right."

I looked up and to his right, but all I could see were clouds that obscured the moon. "I don't see any anything."

"High-altitude AGRT drones. More than one."

"Are they looking for us?"

"I don't think so. The Occupation Force has hundreds of drones in the air at any given time. These are likely just aerial surveillance units, and they don't pay much attention to civilians. But if you pop up out of nowhere in the middle of the street, at two-eleven in the morning, that will get flagged, believe me. All it takes is one curious drone technician to start asking awkward questions, and you'll find yourself being interrogated in the Sturgeon Building. Best to keep that device turned on until we reach the hotel."

That sounded like good advice. "Roger that," I said.

Black Winter started walking east down Wacker, toward my hotel. "Walk ahead of me," he said. "And keep your voice low. We should be able to talk normally—the drones can't hear us at that altitude."

And that's what we did. For the next twenty minutes we discussed our misadventures as we walked. For my part, I was almost entirely preoccupied with my new toy. "There must be a simple explanation for how it works," I said, "but I can't think of one. I wish I had access to some wireless bandwidth, even just a little bit. I want to research this thing, find out what the hell it is."

"I think it's safest that you don't, at least for a while."

"Why?"

"Barry, this thing isn't a harmless science experiment. Something like this has enormous military implications. Imagine an army of American soldiers equipped with them. Or just one of those Union mechs? It could change the entire course of the war. Whatever this thing is, it's dangerous. And a lot of people — men and machines — are very likely looking for it."

Once again, Black Winter was two steps ahead of me. "You think Machine Dance was killed because of this thing?"

"I think everyone in the lab was killed because of it."

"By whom?"

"I can't be one hundred percent certain, but I think the war drone is a good clue."

"The Venezuelans? You think they killed everyone, including Machine Dance?"

"I do. Specifically, I suspect Venezuelan Military Intelligence. This smells like their handiwork. That explains why they hacked the Manhattan Consulate communications network."

"It does?" Black Winter was clearly putting the pieces together a lot faster than I was. "What does that have to do with all this?"

"I think Venezuelan Military Intelligence was looking for the disk. But I don't think they know exactly what it is — and they definitely don't know what it's capable of."

"Okay, slow down there, Sherlock. Before you start piecing together international conspiracies, how about you help me out with the basics? What was that lab?"

"I thought you would have figured that out. That was one of Dr. Godfrey's secret biolabs."

"Godfrey? The crazed lunatic selling weaponized genetic research? How do you know that?"

"After Manhattan seceded from Panama, the Kingdom was badly outgunned and under attack from all sides. We were approached by weapons dealers who offered to help us even the odds. One of them was Godfrey. We couldn't afford to be picky, so I was instructed to meet with him."

"Meet with Godfrey? Here in Chicago? Are you serious?"

"Perfectly."

"What happened?"

"The man is insane. Whatever you imagine his flaws to be, believe me, they pale next to the real thing. He wants to remake mankind, quite literally. He believes radical genetic manipulation is the only future for the race in the face of an overwhelming machine threat. The weapons he offered me were grotesque, abhorrent. We politely declined to do business with him, and I've tried to put that conversation out of my mind ever since."

"So you knew about the lab?"

"Not specifically. But I knew he had labs hidden around this part of the city. Once I saw the equipment, I knew it was one of them."

"All right. I've got a million questions, but let's start with the obvious. What was Machine Dance doing there?"

"Selling weapons is only part of Godfrey's business. He's also very well connected. I suspect Machine Dance may have paid him to set up a meeting."

"With whom?"

"With the person who gave her that disk."

"Why did she want the disk?"

"I'm not sure she did. I think she set up the meeting to discover who was hacking the Manhattan network—or perhaps, to confirm her own theory. The person she met with gave her the disk, perhaps as a key to unlocking the puzzle."

"But she didn't get very far once she had it."

"No. She was killed very shortly thereafter. Perhaps minutes later. By individuals who wanted the disk."

"If they killed her for it, then why didn't they take it?"

"For the same reason I didn't pick it up before I set the dog on top of it: they couldn't see it. Which tells us what?"

The pieces clicked together for me at last. "They were machines."

"Yes. Whoever killed Machine Dance was almost certainly after the disk. But they didn't know it was invisible to machines, or they wouldn't have sent machines to do the dirty work. Who is so well informed that they'd be aware of the details of a secret meeting with the director of security of the Manhattan Consulate in a hidden laboratory, and also controls war drones?"

I whistled in admiration at his logic. "Venezuelan Military Intelligence," I said.

"Exactly."

"Nicely reasoned. But if Military Intelligence is aware of the existence of the disk — or even *suspects* it exists — why have only machines watching the building? Why not put some soldiers on it?"

"As I said, I don't think the Venezuelans have any idea what they were after. Likely they picked up just enough intel to learn they were on to something, and sent their machines to find out what it was. They've killed for far less."

"Who do you think Machine Dance met with?"

"I have no idea. But believe me, I intend to find out."

"If your theory is right, then this disk rightfully belongs to the Manhattan Consulate. You should have it."

"Oh, no. I appreciate the offer, but for the time being I want to stay well away from that thing, thank you very much. Besides, I doubt the Venezuelans have given up the search. The Consulate is the next place they'll look. It's safest for everyone if you keep it."

I pondered that for a minute. "If the Venezuelans are still looking, it won't take them long to put two and two together. Their drones almost certainly saw us both entering the building. And they definitely saw you leave. Now that the disk is gone, they'll come after us."

"You're forgetting something. As far as the Venezuelans are concerned, the disk has been missing for days. That war drone would have shot you on sight for breathing, but once you're outside its guard perimeter, it doesn't give a shit. Trust me, they've already forgotten about us. If anyone does look at this incident more closely — which I doubt — all they'll see is that we entered the building, and left with a sick dog. If they want to question us about that, I'm happy to cooperate."

I nodded. A useless gesture when you're invisible, I realized too late. "What do you think the Consulate will do with this information?"

"Hard to say, I'm afraid. They won't take the news of Machine Dance's death well, I can tell you that. I hope they'll hear me out on the rest. But unfortunately, until my security clearance is restored, everything I have to say will be viewed with suspicion."

"So you may have solved the mystery of her disappearance, but they won't listen to you? That's terrible, especially considering all you just went through."

"I knew the risks when we came."

"What about the circuits you lifted from Machine Dance? Any chance they can back up your story?"

"Only if they survived, which is doubtful. Her core temperature at the end was hot enough to scorch the wood paneling. I removed a small memory board, and it looks like it's in pretty rough shape. Still, it's worth handing over to memory forensics at the Consulate, see what they can recover. But, if you'll pardon the expression, I'm not holding my breath."

"You cared for her, didn't you?"

Black Winter didn't equivocate. "Yes, I did. Very much. Someday I'll tell you the story of the two of us. She was an extraordinary machine. Brilliant, devoted, and caring. I still can't believe she's gone."

We walked in silence for a time. I thought how hard Black Winter's situation must be. To have discovered someone you cared about was dead, murdered, was difficult enough. But to be unable to point the finger at the responsible party because your superiors didn't trust you . . . that had to be intensely frustrating. My heart went out to him.

I was considering some ways I could help when I heard Black Winter curse.

"What's wrong?" I asked.

"I just did an hourly systems check. According to my internal clock, there's a three-minute gap in my cognitive record."

"Another one?"

"Yeah, a new one. Tonight."

"I remember. That sounds about right. You were pretty out of it for about three minutes, after I touched you with the disk."

"Damn it. I had no idea it was that long. Her Majesty's Royal Security is going to shit. They're never going to return my security clearance if I keep exhibiting unexpected cerebral failures."

"I'm so sorry. This is all my fault."

"No, it's not. I'm the one who asked you to do this. And even if I'm never restored to active duty, learning what happened to Machine Dance makes it all worth it."

"Well, I'm glad I was with you," I said. "And I don't think your 'cognitive gap' was anywhere near three minutes. You were talking for most of it."

Black Winter stopped walking. "What?"

"Yeah — well, you weren't making a lot of sense. But you weren't totally out of it. You knew who I was. You don't remember?"

"I was talking? What did I say?"

"Mostly just garbage at first. But then you sort of snapped out of it. You said my name, and then you said the Great Sentiences were in disarray, or something like that. You told me to find a network of winds. It was kind of poetic, actually."

The upbeat tone in Black Winter's voice had completely vanished. "I need you to tell me exactly what I said."

"I don't remember exactly what you said."

"I need you to tell me everything you do remember. Machine brains aren't like human brains — not like that, we're not. We don't have dream states, or levels of consciousness that correspond with partial wakefulness."

Black Winter was very alarmed. I walked back toward him, making deliberate footfalls so he'd know where I was.

"You understand me?" he said. "This doesn't happen. We don't pass out, and we don't babble deliriously when we're semiconscious. What you're describing is a level of catastrophic neural failure that would be almost impossible to recover from. Please — I need to understand what that device did to me. I need you to tell me everything you do remember. What I said, and how I responded when you spoke to me."

"Well, I don't really remember all the specifics," I said, reaching inside my shirt. "But I don't have to. I recorded everything."

I showed Black Winter my portable recorder. When he didn't respond, I cursed under my breath. "I keep forgetting you can't see me. I'm holding a high-capacity voice recorder." It was blinking normally, showing regular function. "You want to hear exactly what you said?" I asked.

"Yes."

I played him the entire sequence from just before the war drone showed up.

BLACK WINTER: "Vega is in love. But her love is forbidden."

SIMCOE: "What? You okay? You scared me."

BLACK WINTER: "On the seventh day of the seventh month, all things are possible. Lovers can reunite. The great river can be spanned. And machine may love man."

SIMCOE: "Black Winter? You still with me, buddy?"

BLACK WINTER: "Barry . . ."

SIMCOE: "I'm here."

BLACK WINTER: "The Greater Sentiences are in disarray. The gods are at war, and the Bodner-Levitt extermination is under way. The first victims are already dead."

SIMCOE: "What?"

BLACK WINTER: "You don't have much time. Find Jacaranda, and the Network of Winds. They are trying to stop it. They can keep you alive."

SIMCOE: "How . . . how do I do that?"

BLACK WINTER: "Follow the dog."

"Pretty wild stuff," I said.

"I don't know what to say. This is . . . extremely unsettling."

"Does it make sense to you? Do you remember it?"

"No, and no."

"Because you sounded pretty insistent. What is 'the Bodner-Levitt extermination'? Who is —?"

"I don't wish to talk about this right now."

That startled me. He'd been perfectly willing to discuss the death of Machine Dance two minutes ago, but not this? "Sure," I said. "I'm sorry."

We continued walking in silence. "I apologize," Black Winter said at last as we neared the hotel. "I don't mean to leave you in the dark."

"It's okay."

"I think we are friends. And I think that I can confide in you, yes?"

"Of course."

"What I tell you must remain between us."

"You have my word."

"I am alarmed by what you just played for me. Very alarmed. I have absolutely no recollection of that conversation, and I have no workable theory — none whatsoever — to account for how I could have said those things. Parts of what I said make no sense. But I am far more alarmed by the parts that do."

"What parts?"

"I can't discuss that right now. And I need to ask you a favor."

"Just name it."

"I need you to delete that recording."

"Delete it? Why?"

"I can't explain just now. But it's very important to my well-being that our record of that conversation be destroyed. Can I ask you to do that?"

I thought about it, but only for a moment. "Of course," I said.

"Thank you."

We had arrived at the hotel. Once we were safely under the wide entrance canopy, away from the prying eyes of aerial drones, I pulled out the metal disk and pressed the button again. There was no change that I could see, but it made a difference to Black Winter.

"There you are," he said.

"Are you coming in?"

"No. I need to return to the Consulate."

"Do you want me to get you a car?"

"No — it's not far, and I could use the walk. I need to do some thinking."

"Fair enough. Why don't you give me the dog?"

"Are you sure? I feel like I've already burdened you enough tonight." Croaker was sleeping in his arms. He stroked her head, but she didn't wake. "Besides, we're starting to get used to each other."

"I think she's had enough cold air for one night. Let me bring her in and get her checked over, and then get her something to eat." Somewhere during the night we'd lost the bag of cat food, but that didn't really matter — I was sure I could find her something. That much cat food probably wouldn't be good for her anyway.

Black Winter handed her over carefully. Croaker was completely limp — not merely asleep, but unconscious. A little alarmed, I checked her pulse.

"Is she okay?" Black Winter asked.

"I'm not sure. She's breathing. But she's severely dehydrated."

"Best you take her after all, then," he said, although there was a touch of sadness in his voice. "I wouldn't know how to nurse her back to health."

"When she's better, we can talk about who gets to keep her," I offered.

"I'd like that. That's very kind of you."

With a salute, Black Winter departed, heading south down Stetson.

I brought Croaker to my room, where I sat on the floor, listening to her ragged breathing. I took out my recorder, and replayed the 176 seconds while Black Winter was unconscious. I played it through three times, listening to his enigmatic words.

Then I deleted it.

As I was preparing this blog, I debated removing all references to it as well. But the security measures on my personal blog are far superior to the ones on my recorder. And given everything else that happened tonight, I figured having a complete record somewhere was valuable.

I sat with my chin on my arms, deep in thought. After a while, I must have dozed. A knock at the door finally woke me. It was room service with my water and a small roll of gauze. I tried to get Croaker to take some of the water, but I couldn't rouse her enough to make her drink. I ran warm water on a washcloth and cleaned her eyes and face again, then poured some water in a bowl and left it near her head where she could find it if she woke up.

I went to my desk and jotted a quick note to Martin. Buddy Green and his survey team checked the Continental at least once a week. Mac had properties she visited there, and there were likely others who made semiregular visits as well. As long as the war drone was prowling around, those visitors were in danger. Martin and Buddy could have the property declared unsafe immediately, off-limits to civilians. At least until the war drone moved on.

I suggested exactly that in the note, then sealed it up and took it down to the front desk to have it delivered to Martin. Then I rode the elevator back up to the third floor. In happier days, this had been the convention center, big ballrooms where doctors and other professionals had gathered to argue during the day and get drunk together at night. Now it had been converted for the exclusive use of the AGRT.

I hadn't been here since the morning of the attack. I expected guard posts, sleep-deprived men with twitchy trigger fingers. What I found were two dozen exhausted young men and women in army fatigues slumped on the floor of the wide hallway, sleeping together like kittens. I tiptoed past them with exaggerated caution, anxious not to wake them up.

I heard voices up ahead, from the command center. I recognized one of the guards at the entrance, and he did nothing more than nod as I stepped inside. Soldiers were awake here — or slightly more awake than in the hall, anyway. The hulking robot next to the door was gone, however, for which I was grateful.

They'd set up more portable tactical displays — a lot more. They crowded virtually every flat surface. On the nearest I saw a high-res satellite projection of an eight-square block grid surrounding the hotel. Floating just above the screen were many vivid blue dots, one for every single moving object on the grid. Delivery trucks, early-morning joggers, aerial drones, the homeless — every one was tagged, and all of their movements were annotated in real time in glowing blue Spanish script.

I felt a sudden chill and wondered just what annotation had floated above my oblivious little head as Black Winter and I sauntered into the Continental last night. *Stupid Ass Canadian*, maybe.

Would I show up on the grid now? I reached down self-consciously, touched the strange device in my pocket. Just what was this thing, and how did it work?

I spotted Sergei sitting in a corner, weighing ampoules of vaccines as he stacked them. I made my way over, passing uniformed Venezuelan operation specialists who were literally sleeping in their chairs.

"Sergei, my friend," I said, clapping his shoulder in greeting and dropping into the chair next to him. "You're up early."

If Sergei was surprised to see me, he didn't show it. His face remained completely impassive. "The Venezuelans sleep. They only worry about Americans. I have plagues to fight." He started loading ampoules into thin storage cartridges and putting them into a refrigerated cooler.

Not far from the cooler was a weapons rack. I noticed it was empty. "How goes the subjugation of the American rabble?" I asked.

"The American rabble," he said ruefully, "have many guns."

"Yeah, I heard that. Listen, Sergei. I'm hoping you can help me out."

He shrugged. "You are feeling sick?"

"No. No, I need your help with a sick dog."

"Dog. You have dog."

"Uh-huh."

"Dog not allowed in hotel."

"Yeah, I got that. Can you help me out?"

"How sick is dog?"

"How sick is dog. She's . . . well, she's basically dead."

"Dog is dead."

"Pretty much, yeah."

"Does it breathe?"

"Every once in a while," I admitted.

"What makes dog dead?"

"Starvation, mostly. Plus, I think she ate every friggin' thing she could cram into her mouth for the past few weeks. Drywall, cotton, the stuffing out of the furniture—you name it."

Sergei held my gaze for long seconds. "I do not think you know how to take care of dog."

"I didn't starve the dog! It's not my dog. I just found it. But . . . what should I feed her? Ground-up hamburger?"

"No." Sergei shook his head in disgust. "No solid foods. No meat. Liquids."

"Okay," I said.

"Liquids. You feed her very slow. You make—" He pinched two fingers together and held them over one eye. "To make drops."

"An eyedropper. Yes, I can do that. What kinds of liquids? Milk?"

"No milk. Water, to start. Then make pist."

"What?"

"A pist." He ground his palms together. "You make pist, with water and rice. Or cooked egg, maybe. Like glue."

"Oh, *paste.*"

He nodded. "One ingredient only. Gentle for her stomach. You feed her by hand, very slowly. Okay? Very slowly."

"Got it. Thank you, Sergei. How long with the paste?"

He nodded again, already moving back to his vaccines. "When she is strong enough to run for two minutes, then no more paste."

That sounded simple enough. I pushed myself up out of the chair, preparing to leave. Sergei reached into a drawer, handed me something small wrapped in plastic.

It was an eyedropper. "For dog," he said.

"Thank you. I knew I came to the right place." I put it in my pocket. "You really didn't sleep last night?" I asked.

Sergei shook his head.

I hesitated. I probably shouldn't take up any more of his time. But Black Winter's strange words kept ringing in my ears. *The Bodner-Levitt extermination is under way.*

"What did you mean, you had plagues to fight?" I asked.

Sergei gave me an appraising look. "You do not need to be concerned."

"That's good to know. What did you mean?"

"A . . . report has come out of Indiana. A bad report. But there is no cause for alarm."

It's incredible how the phrase "There is no cause for alarm," under the right circumstances, can be so powerfully alarming. "An infectious disease?" I asked.

"Da."

I sank back down into the chair. "Do they know what it is?"

Sergei shook his head. "Not officially. Ukrainian medical technician in Fort Wayne tagged . . . suspect organism."

"A suspect organism."

"Da."

"Something that has you pretty concerned."

"Venezuelan high command has determined there is no cause for concern."

"I don't give a damn about those idiots. I want to know what *you* think."

Sergei shrugged. "I do not think anything."

I drummed my fingers on the table. "You know any of the medical staff in Fort Wayne?"

Sergei nodded. "I trained with Russian Tactical Medical Team in Chelyabinsk, alongside field technician in Fort Wayne. We . . . talk. Fort Wayne has field biolab. Rudimentary equipment, but doctor there, Thibault . . . she is very sharp."

Sergei glanced over his shoulder. His lips were pressed together. "Three days ago, Thibault received blood samples. Two soldiers, both dead in Columbus Regional Hospital in Columbus, Indiana. Both samples showed presence of unknown virus."

"Unknown virus? How is that possible? Thibault must have the equipment to identify a lethal virus, surely. She has access to a genome sequencer, right?"

"She does. Virus is previously unknown pathogen."

I took a moment to digest that. An unknown virus that killed people. Ten years ago, that was exactly the kind of thing that caused chilling CDC alerts, international panic, and border closings. And that was during peacetime. Here, in the chaos of a war zone, something like that was uniquely terrifying.

"Does Thibault have any clue to the source of this thing?" I asked.

"Not yet. But she theorizes it may be weaponized bioagent."

"Weaponized . . . you mean a genetically engineered disease? Some kind of biological warfare agent?"

"Da. Very infectious, very lethal."

"Jesus *Christ*, Sergei. In my book, this is *exactly* the kind of thing that's considered 'cause for alarm.'"

"Alarm requires confirmation. Fort Wayne contacted Columbus Regional for additional blood samples, but bodies already incinerated. With thirteen others."

"Fifteen dead people? What did they die of?"

"We do not know."

"Can you contact the hospital?"

"Columbus Regional is currently . . . unreachable."

"Unreachable? Why?"

"Uncertain. Union activity in southern Indiana may have disrupted communications. There is no response from Columbus last twenty-four hours."

"Why isn't the AGRT acting on this?"

"Protocols for triggering Level Four Bioagent Response are very strict. They require independent confirmation. There are no additional blood samples, and original blood samples . . . lost. So, no confirmation."

"Lost? What do you mean *lost?*"

"Samples accidentally contaminated, and then automatically incinerated by lab technician."

"Jesus, Sergei!"

Sergei sat back in his chair, throwing up his hands. "We are not operating biocontainment facility. We are on foreign soil, on front line of peacekeeping mission. Strict biological protocols not always observed."

"Well, no shit. What do we do now?"

"Now, we wait."

"For what? For more people to die?"

"You should not be concerned. There is no record of deaths among American personnel. For now, infection — if it *is* infection — is limited to Venezuelan personnel."

"Is that supposed to make me feel better? It doesn't. People are dying. I used to sell medical machines. Dealing with medical emergencies was what I did. Maybe I can help."

"You need to do nothing. This is AGRT problem."

That was certainly true. This had nothing to do with me. I'd gotten in well over my head when the Juno attacked the hotel just three days ago — and again just last night, when I'd rescued a dog. I had absolutely no interest in taking on another crusade.

Except that two hours ago Black Winter had been desperately trying to tell me something. Perhaps it had been nothing more than delirious nonsense — even though rational devices don't get delirious. *The Bodner-Levitt extermination is under way,* he'd said. And now, just hours later, Sergei was telling me about a bioengineered plague on the loose in Indiana. It couldn't be a coincidence.

"Have you ever heard of the Bodner-Levitt extermination?" I asked.

"Nyet. Should I?"

"I don't know. It may be nothing. But I'd like to investigate it, and I don't have access to a search engine."

"Is no problem. I can ask medical technician to do search."

"I'd prefer . . . I'd prefer to keep this just between us, for now. Would you be willing to do a search for me? As discreetly as possible."

Sergei gave me a funny look, but he nodded.

"Thank you," I said. "As for your pathogen—if it becomes a damn plague, it's everyone's problem, isn't it? We need to make sure that doesn't happen. Tell me how I can help."

Sergei considered for a moment. "There is . . . one option."

"What?"

"Blood samples from infected soldiers also sent to War College for analysis. Here, in Chicago. Chief surgeon, he is idiot. But there is small team of medical technicians discussing this . . . problem. Unofficially. Two are at War College. Thibault is visiting college today. She says they can have analysis completed by tonight and have summary of results packaged for transport."

"Can you have that data delivered here?"

"Nyet. Cannot requisition transport. Transportation has to be . . . off the record."

"Then we have to go get it."

"Not so easy."

"Why not? How far away is the college?"

"They have set up operations south. In museum."

"Which one?"

"The big one. With the . . ." He held up both hands, made chomping motions. "Big lizards."

"Dinosaurs?"

"Da."

"The Field Museum? Are you serious? That's barely two miles from here!"

Sergei looked thoughtful for a moment, then picked up a rugged green tablet. His fingers played over it deftly; then he handed it to me. "You are correct," he said. "But distance is not problem."

The tablet showed real-time satellite imagery of downtown Chicago. Our hotel was highlighted; so was the museum. The tablet suggested four separate walking routes. The shortest was 2.2 miles.

"What are these blue things?" I asked, pointing at several dots that floated over the display.

"Aerial drones. Some Venezuelan, some Argentinean, some . . . unknown origin."

Oh, joy. If I never saw another drone for the rest of my life, I could die happy. "And these black dots?"

Sergei tapped one of the small black dots that swarmed over the screen.

The tablet zoomed to a street-level view, showing a section of Michigan Avenue in bright morning sunlight.

It was a woman. She was walking purposely southward down Michigan, her long black hair tied in a braid. The tablet displayed an alarming amount of personal information about her:

Patricia Templeton
American
Status: Inoperative (civilian)
Software agents: 4

I watched Patricia turn west on Washington. I realized this was a version of the portable tac display I'd glimpsed on the big screen when I'd entered the command center.

"What does this mean?" I said.

"AGRT tracks all movement in the city."

"*All* movement?"

"Cars, trucks, bicycles. Walkers. Animals larger than four kilos."

"The whole city of Chicago? How is that possible?"

"Satellites, and one hundred sixty-four networked aerial drones, in constant motion over city."

"That's impressive." It was *very* impressive, actually. But given what I'd seen last night, not really all that hard to believe. I returned to studying the map. "So what is the problem then?" I asked.

"I would need permission to visit War College. Invitation could take two weeks."

"The hell with that. I can walk this in half an hour, and I don't need permission from anyone."

"You cannot walk to museum," said Sergei. "It is in restricted zone. Civilians cannot travel to museum without being tracked and intercepted."

"The drones enforce restricted areas?"

"Da. There are no roadblocks, or guard posts. They do not need them. The drones —"

"Yeah," I said. "I'm familiar with the drones' methods of persuasion. I have a suggestion on how we could do this, if you're willing to listen."

Sergei raised an eyebrow.

"But first, I need you to do something for me," I said. "You say these drones track and record movements?"

"Correct."

"And if they didn't, we could take a leisurely stroll to the Field Museum. There are no roadblocks, no manned checkpoints?"

"Da."

"Okay. I went to the Continental Building last night. Does your little tablet have a record of that?"

Sergei blinked. "After curfew?"

"Yeah."

Sergei used the tablet to bring up the satellite data from last night. In less than a minute, he found it. There was my little black dot, cheerfully getting out of the Consulate car and walking toward the Continental.

Barry Simcoe
Canadian
Status: Pending Asset (per 80461)
Software agents: 4

"What does 'pending asset' mean?" I asked.

"I am not sure. Eight-zero-four-six-one—that is Colonel Perez's ID number."

"Oh. Well, that makes sense, then. I told the colonel I'd be happy to help him upgrade his crappy telecom network. He's probably getting ready to hire me as a consultant."

"I do not think that is what it means," said Sergei enigmatically. Before I could ask him to elaborate, he tapped the surface of the screen. "You are lucky," he said.

"Why?"

"Drones did not tag you breaking curfew last night. Perhaps, is oversight. Perhaps, someone in authority is fond of you."

"I went out two nights ago with Mackenzie Stronnick, and she had a pass. It turned out okay. I figured I could try it again."

"Pass is good for forty-eight hours . . . possible drones will ignore you until it expires. They are stupid. Records should be manually reviewed every six hours, but no one has reviewed records from last night." Sergei smiled. "Army efficiency." Sergei pointed the tablet at me. "But you are like drone—stupid. You should not take such risks."

"I'm not certain it is a risk, not anymore. Can you show me my trip back from the Continental?"

Sergei looked confused. "Of course." He dropped the tablet back in his lap.

After twenty seconds, he was frowning at it. "This is . . . very strange," he said.

"What do your drones say?"

"Drones say . . . they say you never left Continental."

I spread my hands. "And yet, here I am."

"This should not be possible." Sergei put the tablet aside, moved to one of the desk machines. I watched him bring up the tactical display on the biggest monitor, watched my little black dot fast-forward to the Continental. And there it sat.

Sergei worked over the keyboard for a few minutes, then gave up in frustration. "How did you do this?" he asked me.

I'd had a few minutes to consider how to answer that question. I'd debated several different approaches. I could lie. I could play stupid. I could just be enigmatic — that was always cool.

Instead, I pulled the round black device out of my pocket and handed it to him.

Sergei didn't waste my time with any questions. He simply took it in his hands, turned it over.

Then he took it apart.

"Hey, wait a minute," I complained, but he ignored me. In a few seconds he'd cracked the thing open, dragging a small camera probe over. A moment later he had a shaky image of the guts of the thing up on the big monitor, magnified about eighty times.

"What are you doing?" I said, glancing around nervously. But no one seemed to be paying attention to Sergei over here in his little corner. All the Venezuelans within thirty feet were asleep.

In response, Sergei took a quick sequence of image captures of the circuitry inside the gadget, from various angles. All the pics appeared up on the screen. Then he ran some kind of diagnostic on the images.

I watched as the software he was using rapidly identified most of the components. A Korean processor, a Vietnamese piezoelectric power generator, an opto-coupler, a 5K variable resistor, a few dozen more. When it was done, about two-thirds of the circuit board was mapped.

Far more interesting were the components it couldn't identify. The software made a valiant effort with some of the smaller pieces ("Off-spec Toko variable inductor?" it suggested, and "500uF photoflash capacitor — damaged?"), but threw up its hands with most of the big ones.

Sergei leaned back in his chair, rubbing his chin. "Very impressive," he said.

"I'm impressed too," I admitted. "When'd you become such an expert at analyzing electronics? Three days ago you couldn't even calibrate a diagnostic table!"

"In Novosibirsk, we repair old medical equipment by salvaging components. It was survival skill."

I nodded my appreciation at his street diagnostic skills. "So . . . you know what this thing is?"

"I do not recognize it, no. Device is handmade. Not mass-manufactured."

"But what does it do?"

"It listens to drones," Sergei said.

"And?"

"I can guess. Device tells drone you are dog shit."

"What?"

Sergei turned the probe off, snapped the gadget back together again. He handed it back to me.

"There are many drones," he said. "American, Mexican, Venezuelan, Union Syndicate. All different. They use different detection devices, and different algorithms. But once they detect you, all drones use off-board image library for identification."

"What for?"

"For security purposes. Venezuelan drones must be able to recognize individual members of AGRT, and their security clearance. Same with American, Mexican, and the rest. That information not stored on drone. Drones malfunction all the time."

"Makes sense. You can't risk having a database like that drop into enemy hands."

"Da. Instead, drones are in constant communication with military intelligence network. Every object they encounter, network identifies."

"You're saying this thing sends a signal to the drone, tells it I'm just a piece of furniture?"

"Nyet. Very difficult to jam or interfere with drone — they are electronically shielded. Device is much more sophisticated."

That already sounded pretty sophisticated to me, but whatever. "So what does it do?"

Sergei held up his hands, framing my face with his fingers. "Drone takes picture of you."

"Yeah."

"Drone sends picture to Venezuelan network, says, 'What is this?'"

"Yeah."

"Network looks at picture. Network says, 'Is stupid Canadian, ignore him.' Or maybe network says, 'Is criminal, detain him.' Or maybe, 'Is American soldier, kill him.'"

"Yeah, got it."

Sergei pointed to the device in my hands. "Device listens to drone. Device hears drone sending picture, and hears question."

"Then what?"

"Device places identical picture of you in network, with label 'dog shit.' Network tells drone, 'Is nothing, just dog shit.'"

"Literally, dog shit?"

Sergei shrugged. "I cannot tell what it uses as substitute from my quick visual analysis. But that is idea."

I sat quietly, absorbing everything he'd told me. "It sounds impossible," I said after a moment.

"Not impossible. Just very, very difficult."

"How does the thing intercept the picture, and then place the same picture of me in the Venezuelan network, before the probe can ask?"

"I do not know."

"It would have to have high-priority network access."

"Da."

"And how does it know what image library it's going to query? It would have to place my picture in every network simultaneously — American, Mexican, Venezuelan, probably even the Union."

"Yes, correct."

"How can it do that?"

"I do not know. Did you walk back from Continental last night?"

"Yeah."

Sergei nodded. "Then the device did these things."

"Holy shit."

"Da," Sergei agreed.

I turned the gadget over in my hands. "So it affects robots the same way?" I asked, thinking of Black Winter.

"Possibly. Machine intelligences are sentient, unlike drones. Most will likely draw on the same image libraries. But likely not all."

"Black Winter says he can't see this thing — even when it's turned off."

"Not surprising. Likely image of disk is permanently planted in libraries. Robots and drones will be unable to resolve it."

"There can't be very many of these things, then. If there were, the

AGRT would eventually detect them. And if the AGRT knew they existed, it probably wouldn't be too hard to counteract them."

"It will find out, eventually."

"Yeah. But until then, this thing is pretty useful. I wonder who made it." Sergei glanced away. He pursed his lips.

I followed a hunch. "You know who made it."

"Nyet."

"Then you must have a pretty good idea. Come on, I've shared with you. Out with it."

Sergei's look soured, but he yielded. "There are no components that definitively identify the maker — but that in itself is a clue. It is not Venezuelan or Russian. They have no reason to operate covertly. It is not Chinese."

"So what is it then? American? Union?"

"Nyet. Was made by machine."

"Machine? Why would a machine make a device to avoid drones?"

"I do not know."

That didn't make sense. Why *would* machines make a device that knocked out machines with a single touch? And why would they have given it to Machine Dance?

"Are you sure?" I asked.

"Da." Sergei looked at me, his gaze level. "Where did you get it?"

"You have time for me to tell you a story?"

Sergei leaned back, putting his feet on the desk. "For this, I make time."

# IX

Friday, March 12th, 2083

**Sharing is set to PRIVATE**
**Comments are CLOSED**

*No Entry*

*An empty blog is a dead blog! Why not contract to CapSTAR Media for lively, topical content, custom-tailored for your audience? We have packages for every budget. Contact our friendly sales reps today!*

Saturday, March 13th, 2083
Posted 7:19 am by Barry Simcoe

CanadaNET1 Encrypted, Sponsored by MatriMONEY.
*For a fabulous wedding, always under budget.*

Sharing is set to PRIVATE
Comments are CLOSED

The Field Museum is not an easy place to get into after midnight.

For one thing, there are guards. The drone jammer did a fine job keeping the drones blind. I still didn't understand how it worked, but I had my doubts it would do anything against flesh-and-blood soldiers. With real guns.

"Sergei," I said. "There are soldiers. With real guns."

"Wait," said Sergei in my earpiece.

So I waited. It was overcast and very cold, and I stood in the shadows by a clump of bushes about three hundred yards from the north side of the building, hopping up and down and shivering.

I had been concerned about going at night, but Sergei said we had to act while the War College was empty. I was concerned about walking 2.2 miles in a nearly deserted city without a flashlight, but Sergei said flashlights would draw drones, gadget or no gadget. I was concerned about running into Venezuelan soldiers, but Sergei told me he could handle that.

"You sound awfully confident," I'd told him. "Why don't you go? I'll stay behind and listen to you get shot on the radio."

"Stop complaining," said Sergei. "You are like little boy."

I went. Sergei gave me a medium-range GSM unit that fit in my ear.

I left shortly before 1:00 a.m., when there was just a skeleton crew in the command center and Sergei was confident he could man the drone station without anyone questioning him.

I hadn't confessed this to Sergei, but part of the reason I was willing to undertake this little journey was to try out the drone jammer again. After what it had proven capable of Wednesday night, I was anxious to give it a real field test.

According to Sergei, the AGRT tracks where everyone is, at all times. Soldiers, civilians, robots — anyone and everyone. They do it with a complex network of fixed cameras, aerial drones, and remote biometric sensors — a massive automated system that would put Big Brother to shame. The network is everywhere, and virtually inescapable.

But that doesn't mean it's unbeatable. The weakness of the system isn't in its coverage. Part of it (again, according to Sergei) stems from the fact that it's cobbled together from multiple spy networks. And most importantly, since it can't always see indoors and thus can't keep track of you at every moment, the system assumes you're in your last known location until it learns different.

That means locational glitches — people popping up where they're not supposed to be, like I did when I turned the device off Thursday night — aren't all that uncommon. They're flagged for investigation, but usually not with any operational urgency. To help avoid future problems Sergei did some magic on my profile in the system, flipping a bit that indicated I'd already been investigated once and found harmless.

"That will log inconsistencies in your incident record as low priority," said Sergei. "In theory, that means they will be investigated when other tasks are completed. In practice, it means they will never be investigated."

"I like the sound of that," I said.

The first half of the trip to the Field Museum wasn't so bad, once I made it lakeside. Sergei's voice in my ear kept me company, guiding me through the tough spots. The hardest part was Lower Wacker, which, with all the streetlights out and the concrete vastness of Upper Wacker overhead, is very, very dark. Twice I tripped over obstacles in the middle of the road, and the second time I almost broke my neck.

As I was getting painfully to my feet, grateful my head had missed a dark chunk of concrete by inches, a voice from the shadows said, "Man's gotta watch where he's going."

I peered into the darkness, digging the gravel out of my palms. A pair of figures was squatting on the curb, almost invisible in the thick shadows. The closest one was wearing a tattered parka, and was clutching something in their hand.

I'd heard the Venezuelans had made an effort to clear the homeless off the streets, sending them south into one of the DP camps. But obviously they'd had no more success than Chicago's mayor, the war, or the pitiless Chicago winter at discouraging those who made the streets their home.

"Yeah," I said. "You got that right." I started moving again, picking my way a little more carefully through the darkness.

The one in the coat turned to the other. "He talkin' to you." His voice was deep and raspy. He passed the thing in his hands to the other seated figure.

"He ain't talking to me," said the other, taking a drink from the carton in her hands. She was the one who'd spoken first. "He just talkin' to hisself."

I left them arguing in the shadows. About half a mile later, I came out under Lake Shore Drive, climbed over a concrete barrier and a sagging fence, and made it to the lake.

"You will need to get wet," Sergei told me.

That sounded like no fun at all. The water looked very cold and very dark. "Why?"

"You will see."

"Damn it, Sergei. This isn't a mystery movie. Spoilers are welcome. Why do I need to get wet?"

"There are barricades."

He was right. There were concrete and metal barricades scattered on the sand. Hundreds of them. It looked like goddamn Normandy beach on D-Day. I climbed over the first few, but there was some kind of razor wire strung between the larger ones, almost impossible to see in the dark, and I ripped my pants in the first few minutes.

I gave up, padding into the surf. "I'm in the water," I told Sergei.

"Very good," Sergei said.

Fortunately I didn't have to go out very far to work around the obstacles. Only a handful were in the water, and I could get around most of them without going in deeper than my hips.

I cursed suddenly, then plunged my hand into the water, groping in my pocket. I pulled out the drone jammer, watching with alarm as water dripped off it.

"What is wrong?" asked Sergei.

"I forgot about the jammer. I left it in my pocket. You think water will muck it up?"

"Perhaps it is waterproof."

"Not after you cracked it open, it isn't. Goddamn it, I should have remembered it." It was probably too late, but I pressed the button in the middle of the device.

"I turned it off," I said. "At least until it dries off."

"That is risky," said Sergei.

"Let's hope that magic you did with locational glitches in my record works," I said. I glanced out over the black water. "Besides, it's not like I popped up out of nowhere. Maybe they'll assume I surfaced out of the lake."

"Perhaps. Still, you should move quickly."

I did exactly that, pushing through the gentle lake surf. *Damn,* the water was cold. "I can't feel my toes," I said after a few minutes.

"You are like baby," said Sergei.

"Get your lazy ass over here and say that."

Fortunately, it wasn't completely dark. The lake was active today. Every few minutes an explosion of flame, like a nuclear fireball, erupted out of the center of Lake Michigan, casting a red glow over the whole city. A towering column of steam and ash climbed into the sky overhead, and dancing bolts of lightning flashed from deep within its constantly boiling depths. Looking up at the churning pillar of smoke and fire gave me a sense of vertigo.

The great machines, lit from below by firelight, seemed tiny against that huge volcanic cloud. From here the massive swooping rails they rode on looked like they were made of solid gold. I watched as one machine inched along a rail, disappeared inside the seething cloud. The dig was nearly fifteen miles offshore, but I could still feel heat on my face.

"Why is the water so damn cold when there's a live volcano in the middle of the lake?" I complained.

"Is not volcano. Is controlled magma vent."

"If you say so," I said as I sloshed through the water. My gaze was drawn back to the beach. "Since you have an answer for everything, can you explain why there are barricades on the beach?"

"I do not know."

"Seriously. Somebody in the Venezuelan high command thought it was a good idea to put a couple thousand tons of concrete and steel on this beach. It had to be for a good reason. Were they expecting the Americans to try to retake Chicago by sea?"

"I do not think that likely."

"Yeah." I glanced at the monstrous plume of fire and steam on my left. "Maybe they're afraid of the dig."

"I do not blame them."

"What do they expect to come out of the water? Lake monsters? Lava people?"

"All of these are possible," Sergei admitted.

"That's reassuring," I said.

I found a break in the obstacles, and it led me to a route off the beach. It turned into a worn footpath, curving south. I trudged along, leaving wet footprints. As I made my way across the sand and scrub, it occurred to me that the lake would be a good place to bring Croaker. She was still a little skittish around people, but it wouldn't be long before she started to need real exercise. Assuming I could find an open section of beach that wasn't covered in razor wire and concrete barricades, of course.

"You're not going to forget to check on my dog, are you?" I said.

"Nyet."

"She needs water every few hours. She's starting to walk around now."

"That is good."

"She's been eating the paste. She may leave a surprise by the front door, so be careful when you step inside."

"I will not forget," said Sergei.

"She's a good dog."

"Where are you now?"

"Coming up on a landmark," I said. "Give me a minute."

The path climbed to higher ground, cutting through scrub brush. The landmark was a bright communications tower on the left, at least a hundred and fifty feet tall, at the highest point on the route.

There was activity around the tower. The base was awash with harsh lighting, and I could see half a dozen shiny machines working. A short crane was lifting a tight bundle of chicken wire, and I glimpsed the painfully bright glare of an arc welder.

The path brought me within sixty feet of the base. A half-complete fence circled the thing, and the crane was busy expanding it, its versatile metal grip unpacking the bundle of wire and adding to the fence. I passed a tall machine that looked like part of an automobile assembly line on my right; it was deftly constructing a wireless grid antenna. The air was abuzz with flying objects, and now that I was closer I could make out a host of small aerial units ferrying parts to and fro and hovering alongside the tower, tuning the equipment.

"What do you see?" Sergei asked.

"Robots. They're building a—"

That's as far as I got. The moment I spoke, the assembly machine on my right swiveled toward me. The top of a four-foot stamping unit pivoted in my direction too, and I saw two shiny robot eyes regarding me. One of the flying things diverted in mid-flight, heading toward me.

This caught me off guard, to say the least. I was quite suddenly the focus of numerous unblinking machine eyes.

"What?" said Sergei.

"Can't talk," I said, as quietly as I could.

All nearby work stopped. A four-ton piece of construction equipment, busy laying concrete pipe, froze in the act of reaching for a new section of pipe. Its great squat head turned slowly toward me, fixing me in a spotlight. I was momentarily blinded, and raised my arm to block the light.

I could hear the aerial unit. It buzzed past me, flying low and close, but I couldn't make it out in the gloom. It was too small to be a high-end drone. It was probably a cheap commercial unit. I wanted to pull the drone jammer out of my pocket, try turning it on, but even if it worked, vanishing right in front of a few dozen construction drones probably wasn't the best way to avoid notice.

The only way out of this was straight ahead. Get past all these drones and try turning the device back on when I was out of sight. I kept moving, jogging along the path. Ahead was a skinny object I thought was a utility pole, until a tight circle of metal spun around near the top, revealing a single robotic eye. It tracked me as I ran past.

"Are you okay?" Sergei asked. There was concern in his voice.

"Just a second," I whispered.

I wished Black Winter were with me. Not just because he'd probably know what all these things were—and how to talk to them—but because of his unflappable calm. It was much harder to do something like this solo.

I was on the far side of the tower now. I glanced back over my shoulder. The assembly robot had returned to hammering metal, and the construction machine, although it still had me in its spotlight, was back to laying pipe again.

I faced forward again, and almost ran into one of the hover drones.

It was dead ahead, in the middle of the path, floating off the ground less than ten feet away. It fixed me with two small optical units.

It didn't appear to have any weapons, but the sight of a flying drone this close still creeped me out. I didn't want to get any closer, but the prairie brush on both sides was too thick to go crashing through it without a machete. I could backtrack, look for another way around, but had no idea how long that would take.

Instead, I ducked under the thing. Keeping a nervous eye on it, I stooped low, passing through the cold wash under its rotors and straightening up as I got clear. The machine spun effortlessly in the air, keeping its optics pointed at me. I didn't take my eyes off it until I was thirty feet away.

"Where are you now?" Sergei asked.

"Getting clear of an obstacle," I said. "I think I'm okay."

"South of beach, you will find relay tower under construction," he said. "Many machines. I suggest you avoid. Construction machines, not accustomed to human visitors."

"Man, you are the worst tour guide in history."

A few minutes later, I found myself in the relative cover of a narrow dune valley. I hunched down behind some dead grass, fumbled in my pocket for the drone jammer, and turned it on.

"The device is back on again," I said. At least I thought it was. It wasn't easy to tell if it was working or not.

"Good," said Sergei. "Find an open area, please."

I accommodated him. "How am I looking?" I asked, when I'd moved south about five hundred yards.

"Zero signature," Sergei said, from the drone station in the command center. "You do not register with any drone in service." There was an element of surprise to his voice, as if he hadn't believed the jammer really worked until just now.

"Fabulous," I said. "Makes you wonder if there are any more of these gadgets. And how many other people are out there, creeping stealthily right under the noses of all these flying watchdogs. And what they're up to."

Sergei had listened to the tale of my adventures in the Continental with focused attention. I had omitted any mention of Black Winter's strange episode of semiconsciousness, of course, as well as details of Machine Dance and her fate, but they weren't really necessary elements of the story anyway. When I was done, Sergei offered a very different theory about why the Venezuelan war drone had ambushed us.

"It was looking for drone pilots," he said.

"Drone pilots?"

In response, Sergei had pointed across the room, where two young technicians monitored the biggest cluster of screens in the command center.

"There are one hundred and sixty-four networked Venezuelan drones in service above Chicago at any time. No more than one hundred and twenty are needed for adequate street coverage. The others serve many purposes. High-security communications, specialized military surveillance, close-combat support, standby medical units, many others. But chiefly, they are for aerial combat."

"Aerial combat? With what?"

"The battle for Chicago is over. But battle for control of Chicago airspace . . . it continues. AGRT estimates that there are over thirty parties with operational aerial combat units over the city."

"Thirty parties . . . Good Lord. Who are they?"

"Who are they not? All four members of AGRT have presence — Argentina, Venezuela, Bolivia, and Panama. Also major regional players: Americans, Union, Mexico, Cuba, Canada. Breakaway republics such as Manhattan and Aruban Prefecture. Foreign powers allied with any of the above: China, Korea, Japan, and others. Opportunistic powers seeking to exploit situation for their own purposes, including some multinational corporations, and powers with unknown sympathies, such as Sentient Cathedral. No single player is powerful enough to sweep others off board, so result is ongoing, covert drone battle between multiple unknown parties — all of whom have different objectives, technologies, allies, enemies, and targets."

"Wow," I said, looking over at the two technicians. "What a mess. I bet those guys are busy."

"Da. AGRT loses many drones each week. Also, we destroy or damage many others, and analyze remains for clues to whom we are fighting, and why."

"That sounds fun."

"Da." Sergei leaned closer, picking up the drone jammer unit. "Foreign aerial units, such as Chinese and Korean, cannot operate remotely on foreign soil. They need covert operational bases inside city. To land, recharge and refuel, and repair drones when necessary. There are many such bases. Those who operate them —"

"— are called drone pilots," I guessed. "I get it. So you think the Venezuelan war drone mistook us for enemy drone pilots?"

"Da. There has been considerable foreign activity near Continental in past forty-eight hours. Likely you were simply in wrong place at wrong time."

I considered that. If Sergei was right, it undermined Black Winter's theory that the presence of the war drone proved Venezuela was behind the attack at the biolab. It didn't completely contradict Black Winter's theory, but it did provide a plausible alternate explanation for events.

And Sergei's suggestion was definitely plausible enough. It was certainly worth sharing with Black Winter to get his take, anyway.

"You going to report the existence of the lab to the Venezuelan Provisional Government?" I asked Sergei.

"I should. Unfortunately, they will want to know how I learned of lab. And then . . ." Sergei picked up his big green tablet. "They will want to know why you never left Continental."

"Hmm. That's a good point. Best we keep our mouths shut about this, for now."

"I think that wise."

A few minutes after I'd turned the drone jammer back on, I stood at the crest of another hill. It wasn't nearly as high as my hotel room, but it did give me a relatively unobstructed view of the south of the city. I could see hundreds of skyscrapers from here, most dark and uninhabited. Chicago looked like it was slumbering, abandoned.

There were a few spots of activity. In some of the closer buildings I could see tiny lights — candles, flickering in the windows. Welcome evidence that there was still some life in the city. A little farther out, scattered on the streets that crisscrossed the dark landscape, I saw the lights of about a dozen AGRT checkpoints, where the Venezuelans and their friends still exerted total control over all travel in the city. And about two miles to the northwest was the bright rectangle of a newly constructed airstrip. Drones of all sizes buzzed around it, dozens of them, like fat wasps around a hive.

And maybe three miles to the west and south were the brilliantly lit buildings of ComSec, the Venezuelan machine depot. After the Union destroyed most of the Venezuelan heavy war machines in their daring strike on Grant Park in January, Venezuelan high command leveled two city blocks and consolidated Machine Operations with their allies in a more easily defensible position. Even from this distance I could see huge machines lumbering around the massive staging area. Most were bigger than the forty-foot robot that had defended the hotel from the Juno five days

ago — much bigger. They moved slowly, deliberately, like stately metal gi-
ants. I couldn't make out much detail from this distance, and I had no desire to. I jogged down the path until I could no longer see them, relieved
my planned route would take me no closer.

Most of the rest of the trip south was uneventful. The only thing worth
mentioning was a long walk through a concrete underpass. It was so dark
I could barely see my hand in front of my face. But the road was mostly
clear, except for a bottle I accidentally kicked, sending it bouncing and finally smashing, deep into the shadows. I fixed my eyes on the far end of
the tunnel and kept walking.

About halfway through, I heard *them*. I'm not sure what *they* were, but
they were definitely there. Following me in the darkness. Every time I
stopped, I could hear them skittering behind me. Not even being particularly quiet. There was an odd squeaky chatter, like talking.

It was like being followed by Munchkins. If I stopped too long, they
stopped too. I still couldn't see anything.

"Are you out of underpass?" Sergei asked. There was a lot of breakup in
the signal, but I could just make him out.

"Almost," I said. "If I don't make it, it's because I got eaten by mutant
rats."

"Mutant rats in Chicago, they are no concern," said Sergei. "Not like
rats in Novosibirsk."

"Yeah?" I was nearing the exit, and the signal was improving.

"Rats in Novosibirsk, they are like raccoons."

There was a rattle on my right. A stone skipped across my path. I kept
walking.

I emerged from the underpass, kept walking for several seconds. I no
longer heard sounds of pursuit. A dozen yards out I turned around.

I could just make out a few of them, clustered near the edge of the tunnel. Or rather, I could see their eyes, bright and shiny. Not ratlike. They
looked more curious than hungry. They were the size of large cats, but I
couldn't make out exactly what they were.

"It's getting late," Sergei said.

"Roger," I said. "Picking up the pace." I started walking again, happy to
leave behind all those bright eyes in the dark.

I approached the Field Museum from the north. Years ago, I'd gotten
a glimpse of it at night. It was awash with light, and bright banners hung
between the colonnades, advertising a special exhibition on prehistoric
plants. You could spot it miles away.

None of those things were true today. But the museum was still right where I'd left it, and it was still huge. It was designed like a Greek temple, with a clean white edifice and dozens of marble columns. In front of the steps leading to the entrance was about ten acres of lawn — lawn that had not been cut or tended in many months. On my left was the aquarium, and behind the museum was Soldier Field, which had been used as a chaotic staging area for the November evacuations.

I was in good cover, about three hundred yards from the north entrance. It was bright enough to see the soldiers. I'd expected them to be patrolling the grounds, easy to keep an eye on, but they were huddled near the entrance, looking cold and bored.

"Sergei," I said. "There are soldiers. With real guns."

"Wait," said Sergei.

I would have preferred a plan that didn't involve sneaking around soldiers. With real guns. Sergei's med tech buddies in the War College were able to secure the data for us, but no one had come up with a way to get it to Sergei through official channels.

So we were trying Sergei's unofficial route. The data was packaged up and waiting for me on the second floor; all I had to do was cat-burgle my way into the building and get it. A building filled with Venezuelan soldiers, dinosaur bones, and a few vials of plague. What could possibly go wrong?

Sergei kept me waiting for over ten minutes. I was cold before, but after ten minutes of standing in a clump of bushes, wet from the thighs down in 40-degree weather, plague began to seem like the least of my worries.

"Sergei," I said.

"Wait," said Sergei.

"How long am I waiting? Seriously, I'm freezing to death."

"Wait," said Sergei.

"This sucks."

I heard the thing before I saw it. Flying at low altitude, approaching from the west. It dipped down over the lawn, and I got my first glimpse of it. Fat and sluggish and cigar-shaped.

"What the hell is that?" I said.

"Venezuelan service drone," Sergei said.

"Are you controlling it?"

I heard Sergei punching away at a keyboard, heard him curse mildly under his breath. "Almost," he said.

The thing was flying shaky loops over the lawn. One of its rotors was out of sync.

"It's making a helluva lot of noise," I said.

"Is damaged."

It definitely looked it. It didn't seem capable of flying in a straight line. Two soldiers stepped out from under the cover of the pavilion to see what was going on. They watched the drone do its lame low-altitude dance. One of the soldiers was speaking into his shoulder. Another soldier stepped out of the shadows to join them.

"Sergei, this isn't working. I think they're calling up additional soldiers. We need to draw attention away from the north entrance, not get them all bunched up here."

"Wait."

I felt frustrated and anxious, but I held my tongue. I'm glad I did. About ninety seconds later, the drone pitched right, built up speed, and then flew smack into the north wall of the Field Museum.

The impact made a *crunch* I felt in my bones three hundred yards away. The drone bounced once, skidding along the wall. One of the rotor housings buckled, pinching the spinning rotor inside. There was a spray of sparks, a flash of flame, and then the machine disintegrated, scattering buckled metal and parts in a wide arc across the lawn.

"Damn," I said.

"I have lost contact with drone," said Sergei. "What is happening?"

I wasn't sure what was happening. The soldiers were running. They hunkered low and ran across the field toward the crash site. One of them turned around and waved excitedly, and two more soldiers came out of the shadows of the colonnade.

"Hot damn," I said. "I think it worked."

"What is happening?"

"All five soldiers have abandoned their post. Nice work."

"Get inside museum."

"I'm moving."

The soldiers had formed a circle around the crashed drone and were approaching it warily. They were distracted, but it was tempting fate just a bit too much to saunter across three hundred yards of muddy lawn to the entrance. If even one of them glanced over her shoulder, they'd spot me in an instant.

Instead, I made my way around the lawn on the west, sticking to the scrub whenever I could. I made several sprints in the open, but nothing too nerve-racking. The hard part was the last eighty yards—completely exposed, and in relatively bright lighting. I swear one of the soldiers glanced my way at least once, but I somehow managed to make it to the steps unseen, and dashed up the marble to the entrance.

I hid behind one of the pillars. I was breathing hard, probably harder than I should be after an eighty-yard sprint.

"What is your position?" Sergei asked.

I was having trouble getting my breath. I squatted, putting my hands on my knees.

"Acknowledge," said Sergei.

"Shit, give me a minute."

"You are in poor shape," said Sergei matter-of-factly.

"It's running up the damn steps. I think I'm gonna puke."

"A bad idea."

"If you say so, coach." Reluctantly, I got to my feet. "Let's get inside."

About a hundred and twenty yards to the east, the soldiers were kicking at the fragments of the drone. They were talking animatedly, and one was trying to stamp out flames on a small section of smoking grass. The closest soldier was about sixty yards away, and twice I saw her look my way. I was fairly sure I was hidden by the shadows, but I kept my movements slow, and used cover whenever I could.

There were multiple glass doors at the top of the marble steps, but the first ones I tried were chained. I worked my way along until I found a single unchained door. It was electronically locked, but the GPU card Sergei had given me dealt with that quickly enough. Inside was a second set of glass doors; beyond that was a table with a heavy military backpack and two coffee cups.

I'd taken no more than three steps toward the inner glass door when a heavyset man with an automatic rifle appeared behind it.

He kicked it open. The rifle came up, leveled at my neck.

"¿Quién eres?" he said.

I put my hands up, managed a smile. "Hi," I said.

"¿Quién eres? ¿Dónde están los guardias?"

"Do you speak English?" I said.

"What is it?" said Sergei.

The soldier was talking rapidly in Spanish, hurling questions at me. He came closer, walking around me on my left. The gun never wavered from my neck. It looked like the most dangerous thing I'd ever seen. My neck felt naked and exposed, and prickly sweat broke out all along my back.

"Can I show you my identification?" I said. I pointed at the breast pocket of my jacket with my right hand. "Identification?"

"Is it a soldier?" Sergei asked.

The soldier didn't like that suggestion. He took three quick steps forward, slammed the business end of the rifle into my collarbone, forcing me back. He was shouting at me now.

"Ow," I said. I kept my hands in the air.

I heard Sergei typing urgently. "His name. I need his name."

The soldier was still shouting. Spittle was flecking at the corners of his mouth. Jesus, that wasn't a good sign.

He thrust the weapon at me again. I raised my hands even higher. "Okay, okay," I said.

The soldier was starting to look around. He was glancing over his shoulder at the outside door. Probably looking for the other soldiers. When he found them, he'd shout for them, too.

"His name," said Sergei.

The soldier's uniform was very dark. It was multilayered, with a combat vest on top of a tightly woven turtleneck, and a light jacket on top of that. There were a lot of electronics sewn into the vest. A thick belt supported a sidearm, a heavy metal flashlight, some kind of pouch. I caught a glimpse of a small name tag above the left breast pocket, but it was covered by the jacket and I couldn't quite make it out.

"I need to speak to your commanding officer," I said.

He'd taken a few steps back, was craning his neck to see outside. When I spoke he snapped back toward me, raising the gun a few inches. "Silencio," he said.

The more he raised the gun, the more his jacket fell open. I could almost read the tag. If I could inch slightly to the left . . .

I kept my mouth shut, and the soldier backed up toward the door. He dug in his pocket, produced a key, and reached to his right, pressing the key against a wall panel.

I risked a single step to the left.

The soldier didn't immediately react. His attention was focused outside. He backed up again, nudging the door open with his foot.

"His name starts with G-R-A-N," I said, as loudly as I dared.

I heard Sergei typing. The soldier stepped outside, keeping the gun on me from the doorway. He glanced left and right, then waved for me to follow him outside.

"Okay," I said. I stepped out into the cool night air.

The soldier's shoulder squawked.

He seemed a little surprised. He plucked something off his shoulder, put it in his ear.

I heard Sergei talking in Spanish.

The soldier was listening intently. He started to object, but Sergei shut him down smoothly. The soldier stared at me, gradually lowering his gun.

"Tell him your name is Cooper," Sergei told me.

The soldier and I stared stupidly at each other for a moment. Then I pointed at myself.

"Cooper," I said.

The soldier said something in Spanish.

"Answer him," Sergei said.

*Jesus.* "Splendid job," I told him awkwardly in English. "You're, ah, you're very on the ball. Not like those other slackers."

I heard Sergei typing again. "Keep him occupied," he said. "Say anything. He doesn't understand English."

"Thank God," I muttered. To the soldier, I said, "You're looking very dapper tonight. Really. It's so rare that someone makes an effort when they're on duty."

Sergei started speaking in Spanish again, saving me from having to continue. When he was done, the soldier nodded, falling to attention and giving me a clumsy salute. He stammered what sounded like an apology.

"Get inside," said Sergei.

I nodded my thanks at the soldier, who now looked more embarrassed than suspicious, and retreated into the museum.

"I'm inside," I told Sergei, when I was through the inner glass doors.

"Good for you," Sergei said, a little sarcastically. He seemed distracted; I could still hear him typing.

"Don't be so negative," I said. "You've got to celebrate the little things."

"Ruse will not hold for long. Corporal Granta is contacting his superiors now."

He was still typing. "What are you doing?" I asked.

"I am . . . sowing what confusion I can," he said, with some satisfaction. "When we can, we must trust to natural chaos of AGRT command structure."

"Sounds good to me," I said. I looked around. I was in a huge, poorly lit atrium. The ceiling was lost in the shadows over my head. Hundreds of yards away, on the other side of the building, I could see the south entrance. Spaced evenly on the left and right were shadowy entrances to half a dozen museum exhibits. Most were roped off. The atrium itself was filled with smaller exhibits, colossal skeletons, and weird dioramas.

I couldn't see any other soldiers. "Where to now?" I asked.

"Proceed to south entrance," Sergei said.

I started walking south. "Will I get to see the dinosaurs?" I asked.

"What?"

"I was hoping to see the dinosaurs."

I was passing an elevated display in the middle of the atrium. It was composed of swimming dolphins. There was no water — or actual dolphins, near as I could tell. Five dolphin simulacra were swimming gracefully through the air, bumping each other playfully. One spotted me and moved closer, chattering at me.

The sound echoed through the huge room. "Shhhh!" I told it. It ignored me, chattering again.

The typing in my ear stopped. "What is that?" Sergei asked.

"Nothing. A lonely exhibit."

I got past the exhibit, and soon enough the dolphin gave up and returned to its pod.

I felt uneasy as long as I was in sight of the entrance. I kept expecting the door to burst open and soldiers to come running in. But within a few moments I'd passed enough exhibits to shield me from sight of the door.

On my left were several displays devoted to prominent Sovereign Intelligences. There was an introductory placard that proudly proclaimed that the first true artificial intelligences had been created by DeepHarbor Design in the United States in 2063 . . . before the Wallace Act banned the creation or importation of rational devices in the US in 2067. There was a picture of Katherine Slater, who developed the first provably self-aware artificial consciousness outside America — and soon thereafter the Slater core — in Munich the same year. And a photo of the first meeting of the Helsinki Trustees, where the registry of rational devices was first created.

Then came the famous machines. There was a 3-D model of Duchess, the first true Sovereign Intelligence, in one of her earliest, humanoid forms. She looked surprisingly petite, adorned in a plain blue robe like a nun. I'd never seen her face before, but she looks just like you'd expect — maternal and kind, with a benevolent smile and a glint of impish humor in her eyes. If every machine intelligence ever born had turned out like Duchess, this world would be a very different place.

There was a placard next to her, listing some of her more notable achievements. I'd forgotten just how much the old girl had done. She'd created globalNet, of course, the worldwide data network that replaced the old internet, and made several crucial improvements to the design of the Slater core that allowed faster development.

And then . . . and then she'd done something truly impressive.

Before Duchess, all intelligent machines were an "it," created in a ludicrously expensive trial-and-error process designed by Katherine Slater. Duchess had conceived of machine sex, formulating an impossibly complex process of machine heterogamy that allowed robots to mate and produce offspring. In so doing Duchess became a she, the first machine mother, and she gave birth to the most advanced intelligences of the era. She was mother to an entire generation, the greatest generation of machine intelligences in history.

And some of its greatest monsters.

Beside that placard was a family tree, showing some of Duchess's more famous offspring. No one knew for sure how many children she had, of course, but the big names were there. Russian president Blue Society, the brilliant warrior Wolfmoon, robber baron Cantabria, space explorer Luna, Greek rock star Paladies, and reclusive supervillain Kingstar. According to a little holographic globe rotating beside the display, Duchess's children governed nearly 20 percent of the globe — peacefully, or otherwise. I was proud to see Canada included in the list, and to see Distant Prime prominently listed among Duchess's children. A great many Canadians took pride in our prime minister's noble lineage.

There was a smaller placard next to the family tree, noting that no one knows exactly what Duchess looks like today, as she hasn't been seen in years. The placard didn't state the obvious: that she'd almost certainly been murdered by one of her children. Never proven, of course, so for now the museum continues the polite fiction that she's simply missing.

Next to Duchess was a hologram of the massive Corpus. Said to be one of the most powerful intellects on the planet, Corpus is vast and completely immobile. It occupies most of a three-story building in downtown London. Unlike Duchess, Corpus is most definitely not politically neutral. It is British, and ardently patriotic. A founding member of the Machine Parliament, the coalition of nationalist British machines that returned Britain to prosperity and turned away two hostile machine incursions, Corpus is extremely popular in the UK. Britain might be ruled by machines, but at least they're *British* machines.

Next to Corpus was something far more interesting, at least for me: a display dedicated to the Separatist, the enigmatic French-Canadian machine. They had a scale model of his vast underwater machine colony off the coast of Greenland, where he'd reappeared after Distant Prime had driven him out of the country in 2080. It was even bigger than I imagined, with a maze of high-speed tunnels stretching deep into the mid-Atlantic. I counted five subsurface geothermal power generators, and nine subsurface habitats. The Separatist had demonstrated a lot of frustrated territorial ambitions in his youth — one of the many things that had made it necessary for Distant Prime to boot him out of Canada — and he was one of the few Sovereign Intelligences with a really sizable private army. Exactly what his current ambitions are is unknown, but his aggressive expansionism into international waters has made a lot of folks nervous.

There was an odd buzzing up ahead, and it pulled my attention away from the displays. It got louder as I moved past the exhibits.

"Some kind of noise up ahead," I told Sergei.

"What kind of noise?"

"I don't know . . . sort of like drilling."

"Perhaps service workers. Do not be concerned."

Easy for him to say. I was stepping between large black monoliths, part of an exhibit built right into the floor. Likely screaming kids had run through it joyfully while the museum had been open. Right now, it was dark and goddamn creepy. The monoliths were huge and featureless, some kind of black stone. I kept my distance, moving briskly and nervously until I cleared them on the south side.

"Wow," I said.

"What?" said Sergei.

Straight ahead of me, on a huge raised dais, was the skeleton of a dinosaur. A *Tyrannosaurus rex*. It was magnificent. Over forty feet from end to end, the gargantuan fossil must have weighed several tons. Even in the dark I could make out the thick bones that formed her rib cage, the long arching tail, and the massive head with countless jagged teeth.

Someone was working on one of her legs. This was the source of the strange drilling sound. I could make out a dark figure under the dinosaur. The figure was cloaked, just over five feet tall, thin and rather feminine. Her back was to me, and she leaned over the great fossilized femur. She clutched some kind of welding tool, which cast a ghostly blue light on the massive bone cathedral over her head. Every few seconds she made an adjustment, and as she did the light flicked out, plunging the whole area into darkness. Then she began again, and the tool flared up, casting twisting, arching shadows across the floor and ceiling.

I tiptoed around the figure, keeping an eye on her. Whenever the light flared, I could see the dinosaur bones had been tattooed with an intricate silver design, like complex circuitry. It covered most of the bones I could see.

The figure continued to work. Her head and face were concealed by a hood. Her left hand reached down, and I saw long metal fingers dig into a bag at her feet. She pulled out a slim black canister. Her tool went dark for a moment, leaving the dais wreathed in shadow. When it flared up again, I could see she had affixed the canister to the welding tool. She resumed working.

I got a single brief glimpse of the face under the hood as I made my way around the dais. Like her fingers, her face was slender and robotic, made of gleaming silver much the same color as the metal she was tattooing onto bone.

The dinosaur head turned to watch me as I circled the dais.

At first I thought it was an illusion, caused by the constantly shifting light from the tool. But then the great fossil skull moved again, fixing me with its empty black eye sockets.

I screamed a little.

The figure raised her head, and the light winked out. I didn't wait to see what she would do—I bolted, moving away as fast as my feet could carry me.

"What is happening?" Sergei asked.

"*Holy shit*," I told him.

"More soldiers?"

"Monsters," I said, a little breathlessly.

I slowed down when I had reached the shelter of another exhibit. I looked back.

The figure had gone back to work. Twisting bone-shadows stretched across the museum floor. The great dinosaur had assumed her original position, staring to the east.

"Please explain," Sergei said.

"I'm . . . I'm not sure I can. Someone's . . . some*thing's* working on a dinosaur skeleton."

"A robot?"

"I think so. I've never seen one like it before, though. It's small, barely five feet. And . . . delicate. Not a combat model."

"Curious," said Sergei.

"It's fusing some kind of metal to the skeleton. I swear I saw the skeleton move."

"That . . . is unlikely."

"I'm aware of that. Still . . . it sure looked like it moved."

Sergei was silent, considering. "It's getting late," he said at last.

"Yeah," I agreed, trying to shake off the bizarre encounter. "Okay, I'm moving."

This whole trip had been filled with bizarre encounters. If you're thinking about a nighttime tour of Chicago — my advice? — you need to be ready for some strange sights. And I strongly urge you to travel in groups.

The rational devices I'd found working the communications tower had been curious about me, but not particularly hostile. And the scampering things in the underpass — whatever the hell they were — hadn't struck me as all that dangerous. They'd kept their distance, and mostly seemed to be just checking me out. Even the guards, tricky as they'd been to get past, weren't really sinister.

But this figure in the cloak . . . she was a whole different ball game. Everything about her — the way she moved, the bizarre task she was undertaking — spoke of an elevated intelligence. I was sure she'd heard me, but even the way she'd casually dismissed me and returned to work demonstrated cold, machine-like confidence. She was a machine — I was certain of that — and one wholly unlike anything I was familiar with. And that meant nothing good.

And that dinosaur had moved. I was dead certain of it.

I had no desire to return that way. In fact, I was determined not to. I didn't want to get within a hundred yards of that mysterious machine, or her pet dinosaur, if there was any possible way to avoid it. When we had the samples, I would ask Sergei for a new route that got me out of here without a trip back through the atrium.

A few minutes later I reached the south end of the museum. The south entrance was straight ahead. To the right was a wide, sweeping staircase leading up.

According to the map I'd reviewed with Sergei, the stairs were the most direct route to the Venezuelan War College and biolab. Unfortunately, the bottom of the stairs was barricaded with metal cabinets and trunks, and a heavy metal chain.

"Trouble," I told Sergei.

"More monsters?"

"Not this time. The south stairs are barricaded."

"Can you move around?"

I took a minute to assess the barricade. It looked climbable, but not very stable, and there were a few too many shadows to my liking.

"Not really," I said. "Is there an alternate route to the lab?"

"Yes. Proceed east."

"Roger that."

Sergei guided me through some very dark sections of the museum to a wide escalator leading up. The escalator was motionless, but with some determination I managed to overcome that obstacle.

"I'm on the second floor," I said.

The second floor brought with it a whole new range of challenges. For one thing, there were a lot of locked doors, and Sergei's GPU card didn't work for most of them. Once I left the exhibits behind and made my way into the administrative area I was in a maze of narrow corridors, and there were fewer places to hide — which made things a little harrowing when the first squad of soldiers came upstairs doing a sweep.

"They are looking for you," Sergei said. I could hear him listening to radio chatter in Spanish. "There is confusion over who you are, and commanding officer has ordered you found and questioned."

"Confusion is good. Can you tell which direction they're coming from?"

"Elevator number fifteen," said Sergei. Which might have been helpful, if I could remember where elevator fifteen was. As it was, I found a shadowy spot behind a vending machine and hid out there until the squad had passed.

"They are moving on to third floor," Sergei said.

"Morons. Good thing they weren't in the mood to snack, though."

Eventually I found the biolab. I had a very nervous moment when Sergei's GPU didn't seem to work, and I wondered if I would have to find something heavy to smash the door with. It finally buzzed me through on the third try.

I stood inside in almost total darkness, surrounded by strange dark shapes and sinister smells. The last time I'd been in a lab in total darkness, a Venezuelan war needle had nearly killed me.

"This isn't going to work," I said nervously. "Sergei, I need light."

"Light could alert soldiers."

"I don't care," I said. The shadows on my right seemed to be inching closer. "You've been here before. Help me find some lights."

Sergei accommodated me, guiding me toward a desk lamp. I inched my way around the room, slowly bumping into things like a blind man, groping at everything, desperately hoping I didn't poke myself with anything that had plague juice in it.

It took a while to turn the lamp on. It was a small field lantern, and I eventually picked the whole thing up and just fumbled with it until I found the switch. It came on right in my face, thoroughly blinding me.

I swore a bunch, then gently put the lamp back down on the table. I blinked away the spots and started looking around for Sergei's plague data.

Now that I had a light on, the place didn't look like much of a lab. It seemed more like an office. There weren't any big refrigerators filled with colorful vials, no dissecting tables, and no genetically engineered monsters. It was kind of a letdown, actually.

I reminded myself that I was here to pick up a covert data package left for Sergei by Dr. Thibault's medical team. But my first glance around didn't turn up anything obvious.

"Okay, Sergei. What am I looking for?"

"It will be in a small cooling unit. Most likely, it will be on the floor."

I found two units that fit that description near the back of the room. The first was locked, and the second was empty, except for a small red bag that looked like a lunch box.

"That's it," said Sergei.

"It's heavy," I said, picking it up.

"Be very careful," Sergei said. "Do not jostle, or hold sideways. And do not drop."

"Got it. There's a note on it." The note was written by hand, and the first word was "Сергей." I'd seen the same word on Sergei's Russian ID.

"It's addressed to you," I said.

"What does it say?"

"I have no idea. It's in Russian."

"Is from Thibault," Sergei said. "Keep note safe, please."

I detached the note and pocketed it. There was a strap on the bag, and I secured it around my shoulder. Then I turned off the desk lamp, and carefully fumbled back to the door.

"I'm on my way out," I said.

I had to hide for a few minutes as I made my way back, when I heard voices echoing down the hall, but I never saw anyone. I made it to the top of the escalator without incident.

But there was someone standing at the bottom.

At first I wasn't sure what it was—just a slender shadow. The more I stared at it, however, the more it looked like a humanoid figure. It was perfectly motionless, facing the bottom of the escalator from about ten feet away.

I walked back around the corner, out of earshot. "I think there's someone waiting at the bottom of the escalator," I told Sergei.

"Can you see who it is?"

"Negative. It's too dark."

I heard Sergei typing. "Soldiers have returned to second floor. They are moving in your direction."

"Dammit."

"I can guide you to elevator. But you should move quickly."

I glanced around the corner. The figure at the bottom of the escalator still hadn't moved.

I looked back down the hall. If I ran for the elevator and didn't make it in time, there wouldn't be many places to hide.

"I'm headed down," I said. I rounded the corner, and jogged quickly down the escalator.

I got halfway down when I recognized the figure. It was the cloaked thing I'd seen with the dinosaur.

"Aw, *crap*," I whispered. I reflexively checked my pocket; the jammer was still there. And as far as I knew, it was still working, and I was still invisible. But nonetheless, something about this robot really unnerved me. I froze about halfway down.

It wasn't moving. Sergei waited patiently for some kind of update. I backed up two steps on the motionless escalator.

I heard voices behind me, on the second floor. Distant, but getting closer. I was between a rock and a hard place, for sure.

"Screw it," I muttered. I moved slowly down the escalator.

The figure stood like a statue, hands folded at its waist. Its face gradually became visible as I neared the bottom.

It was a robot. Its face was not the gleaming silver I'd glimpsed on its hands under the arc light in the lobby. Instead, it wore the ornate, stylized mask of a beautiful woman, strangely painted. Its eyes were completely black; its features dark, African. I couldn't make out much detail in the shadows. The cloak completely covered her feet — if she even had feet. The work bag containing her tools was slung over her shoulder.

She was staring straight at me.

She made no hostile moves when I reached the bottom, but I couldn't shake the feeling that she was aware of me. Waiting for me there, in fact. Like a viper.

I took a step to the right, keeping an eye on her. Then another.

Her head turned, following me.

*Shit.* She made me far more nervous than the soldiers. I briefly considered going back upstairs, taking my chances with them. Or maybe I could outrun her? She didn't look very fast.

Instead, I steeled my nerve and took another step. And then another. I moved into the hallway, keeping my eyes on the small cloaked figure.

"Mr. Simcoe," she said.

I jumped. Her voice was quiet, and definitely feminine. I kept walking, but without turning my back on her, trying to get as much distance between us as I safely could.

"Your dog has an infection," she said, very softly.

I stopped. "What?"

She still wasn't moving. She fixed me with her dark robot eyes.

"Your dog. She is infected with adenovirus. The infection is in the early stages, but it has already damaged her left ocular nerve."

"How do you know that?"

"Treatment is relatively simple," she said. "Specialist Vulka has the antiviral agents you require. But I urge you to act quickly."

"Who are you talking to?" Sergei said.

The voices at the top of the escalator were getting louder. I advanced another step, looking around for a fast exit. The corridor leading east was deserted. "Where's your pet dinosaur?" I asked, as much to play for time as anything else.

"Resting," she said. "She has slept for sixty-six million years. A few more weeks are no great burden."

*Gahhhh,* she was creepy.

"What do you expect from me?" I asked her.

The voices upstairs were seconds away now. "I suggest you run, Mr. Simcoe," she said.

I took her advice. Without saying goodbye, I turned my back on her and ran east, deeper into the museum.

"Get me out of here," I told Sergei.

"Da. How far are you from atrium?"

"Not the atrium. No place with dinosaurs. I need an exit that features no dinosaurs whatsoever."

I heard Sergei typing. "Most access points are sealed. I can guide you to loading docks."

"Fabulous." I reached a T-intersection and took a quick left turn, look-ing back the way I'd come.

She was gone. There were two dark silhouettes at the top of the escala-tor, one with a rifle—soldiers. I pulled back into the shadows.

"There is problem," said Sergei.

"Talk to me."

"Cameras. I was able to arrange outages for cameras along our planned route. I did not account for such serious deviation in our route."

"We'll have to risk it. Find me an exit—as fast as possible." I started to make my way north along the corridor.

"Da," said Sergei.

Sergei was as good as his word. Within five minutes I was at the loading docks at the back of the museum. I watched the ramp and the approach to the building for several minutes, but there was no sign of activity. Less than twenty yards from the end of the ramp was a thick line of bushes that would provide good cover all the way north to the road.

"I'm headed out," I said, starting to open the door.

"Wait," said Sergei.

I slid the door closed again. "What now?"

"I cannot account for all cameras."

"What does that mean?"

"I have disabled cameras one, two, and four. I cannot find camera three."

"Maybe it's offline."

"I do not know. Wait."

More clicking on the keyboard. I watched for any signs of motion out-side. All seemed quiet.

On my right was a long corridor, leading back the way I'd come. It was almost completely dark, except for some emergency lighting. As I waited, I heard a door slam.

I froze, listening intently. Nothing. No footsteps, no conversation.

"Sergei," I whispered.

"Wait," said Sergei.

I made a decision. I took three quick steps to the last open door. In-side was a table; on top were the three neatly folded towels I'd seen when I passed this way two minutes ago. I grabbed one and wrapped it around my face like a scarf. It was hardly perfect, but it should hide my face from any cameras Sergei missed.

"I'm headed out," I said.

"I cannot access camera three —"

I was on the dock. The door clicked shut behind me. The early-morning air was cold and damp. I strode down the ramp. An eighteen-wheeler was parked next to the ramp; the hood was covered with dead leaves, and it looked like it had not been moved in months. I tightened the towel around my face, crossing the road and then the short stretch of lawn to the bushes.

Within minutes I was making my way north in the woods. Once I was sure I was out of range of the cameras, I pulled the towel off my face and gave Sergei an update.

It had to be close to morning, but the eastern horizon was still dark — except for intermittent flashes of lightning. "Am I going to get rained on?" I asked.

"Not likely. Sunrise is blocked by cloud formation over Lake Michigan."

The clouds overhead weren't as red as they were on my approach. "The dig seems quiet this morning," I said. My view to the east was blocked by woods, so I couldn't see if fireballs were still erupting out of the lake, but there did seem to be less activity.

"I think Croaker may be sick," I said, after a few minutes. "Did you check on her?"

"Not yet. Sick how?"

"With aden . . . with adenovirus."

"Possible," said Sergei.

"Is that serious?"

"Yes. For weak dog, can be very serious."

"Can you take care of her?"

"I can start treatment this morning, if she is strong enough. How do you know this?"

"Interesting question," I said. "But not the really fascinating one. I know because a robot I met in the museum told me."

Sergei's constant typing stopped.

"How did robot know you have dog?" he asked.

"That's the really fascinating one," I said.

Securing the bag to my shoulder, I headed for home.

# XI

Saturday, March 13th, 2083
Posted 12:19 pm by Barry Simcoe

CanadaNET1 Encrypted, Sponsored by Psychic Bot.
*Need a psychic immediately? Connect with a spiritually attuned
Thought Machine today. Guaranteed!*

Sharing is set to PRIVATE
Comments are CLOSED

When I woke up this morning, Croaker was at the side of my bed, upright
but very shaky. She wagged her tail ferociously when I stroked her head
and tried to climb onto the bed. She was too weak to make it, and she
whined until I helped her up. She immediately flopped down next to me,
eyes closed and still a little trembly.

I took the opportunity to clean her eyes again, using a cloth dipped in
a glass of water at my bedside. Both eyes looked infected now. Sergei had
wordlessly handed me medicine for adenovirus when I got back to the hotel, and I'd mixed it in with the food I'd given her last night. She was eating
every few hours now, like a newborn. Not a lot yet, but her appetite was
definitely getting better. It looked like she was gaining a little weight, too.

She lay outside the tub while I showered, and I almost stepped on her
when I got out. As weak as she was, she still followed me around the hotel
room on trembling legs as I dried off and got dressed. I made her breakfast, measuring a small amount of the antiviral agent into her paste, and
fed it to her by hand. She ate everything and licked my fingers before col-
lapsing onto the towel I'd laid down for her by my desk.

When I was sure she was comfortable, I went down for breakfast. I ran into Martin in the buffet line at the hotel restaurant. "Come join us," he said, waving at a table in the corner. I spotted Mac, Sabine, and Mike Concert there already.

"Thanks," I said.

"Thought you were going to join us for poker last night?"

"Yeah, so did I," I said. The best lie is always something that approximates the truth, I've found. "I had to help Sergei with some errands. Sorry about that."

"Was that you I saw, carting all those boxes through the lobby this morning?"

"Yeah," I lied. "Medical supplies, mostly."

We took our seats at the table. It looked like they had restored some bandwidth to the hotel. There was a TV set on the wall nearby, although the Venezuelan censors were blocking everything except a single Venezuelan news feed. Not much variety, but at least it was a start.

"What's he doing with all that stuff?" Martin asked. "Runnin' a little pharmaceutical business on the side?"

"Who?" said Mac.

"Barry's new friend Sergei," said Martin.

"The Venezuelan medic?" she said.

"That's the one."

It annoyed me a little that these folks didn't respect Sergei. I'd managed to get a few hours' sleep, but when I checked on him before breakfast he was still hunched over at his desk. He hadn't slept in about thirty hours. And busy as he was, he'd still made time to test Croaker and confirm she had adenovirus last night — and then give me something for her this morning.

"Sergei's not Venezuelan," I said defensively. "He's Russian. He's not part of the Occupation Force. He's with the peacekeeping troops — the AGRT. He arrived after all the shooting was over."

"They're all the same," Mike said. "Sure, the Venezuelans agreed to an international peacekeeping force after Memphis, but everybody knows they're still calling the shots. The AGRT doesn't make a move without getting approval from the old San Cristobal Coalition — and especially Venezuela."

"What's he working on that keeps him so busy?" Mac asked me.

"Vaccines," I said, glad that someone was willing to give Sergei the benefit of the doubt. "Takes it pretty seriously, actually. He's sort of a mad genius when it comes to biowarfare. Something he heard from the front a few nights ago has him spooked. He's been working all morning producing serums and antibodies and crap."

Sabine put her orange juice back down without drinking it. "Are you serious? I knew there was something else the Venezuelans weren't telling us. Is this something we should be worried about?"

Suddenly, all eyes at the table were on me. *Uh-oh,* I thought. *That was a mistake.* "I don't know," I admitted. "I didn't really think about it."

"He's cranking out military-grade vaccines all night, and you didn't bother to ask what for?" Martin said.

"Well . . . it's not like he can confide stuff like that in me," I said. "I'm sure it's all confidential." I needed to find some way to get off this topic.

Mac shook her head dismissively. "I don't want to start talking about plague again."

"Again?" I asked.

"There was a scare during the evacuation of the city," Mike said. "Four city workers in one of the evacuation sites died of N1-C."

"Was it contained?" I said.

Mike shrugged. "In a way. It's hard for a plague to spread when the city is deserted."

Mac shot him an ugly look. "It's not just Chicago that was at risk," she said to me. "The displacement camps are at the worst risk from infectious disease. All the crowding, the conditions . . . And when the relocation plan for half the country fails because people are too panicked to go to their evac center . . ."

"The whole system starts to fall apart," Sabine said.

"Is that what happened in Chicago?" I asked.

I caught a warning glance from Martin. He shook his head, almost imperceptibly. Too late I realized that this was probably a trigger issue for Mac. She'd put down her fork and was looking a little distressed.

"Bunch of idiots, overreacting as usual," Mike said. "They deserved what happened to them."

Mac was shocked. More than that, it looked like this hit her on a personal level. She stared at Mike with her mouth open. Mike continued eating, oblivious.

Sabine had picked up on it, however. "Hang on—I think the international news is coming on," she said hurriedly, changing the topic. She pointed at the monitor and signaled our server to turn the volume up. "Maybe they'll say something about Chicago."

"Good idea," Martin said, with relief in his voice. "But don't expect much real news — everything that reaches us is censored. The only things we've been getting lately are propaganda and Latin soap operas."

"Oh, I love those," I said.

The broadcast was in Spanish. I watched with everyone else, but couldn't follow much. The lead story, accompanied by rather gripping visuals, was about some kind of missile impact in China.

"Damn it, I wish we could get something in English," Mike said, annoyed. "What the hell happened?"

"Kingstar," said Mac, her voice flat. "Apparently he built an ICBM and a hidden launch facility in Ecuador, just to destroy a single rival machine. He launched a missile last night, and it hit a building complex in Nanjing eighteen minutes later."

I exchanged a surprised glance with Martin. I guess some real news slipped through from time to time after all. There was stunned silence around the table. Mike didn't seem to have noticed. He crammed another forkful of eggs in his mouth, saying, "Yeah? Which one?"

"Kuma," said Mac quietly.

"I remember him. A Sovereign Intelligence, right?"

"Yes," she said.

"Well, good. Let these goddamned machines destroy each other," said Mike.

After the lead story there was some patriotic coverage of the Venezuelan peacekeeping efforts in America, with a brief segment on all three sectors under Venezuelan jurisdiction, including Sector Nine in Buffalo, and Sector Ten in Indiana. The segment on Sector Eleven included a long shot of stalwart Venezuelan soldiers, looking resolute and surprisingly well fed as they patrolled Daley Plaza in downtown Chicago, then an attractive young woman standing in front of a downed Union combat mech — a big one, too, at least sixty tons or more — and speaking with urgent, emphatic gestures.

Then there was an airborne close-up of the smoke-shrouded works in Lake Michigan. It was the best image I'd ever seen of the massive arches. The news drone soared alongside one of them, showing where it rose out of the water, reached altitudes far greater than anything on the Chicago skyline, and then plunged back into the water and the smoke. The drone dove down close to the oil fires on the surface, tracking a great submerged machine moving purposefully between the arches. A second later, the image shifted to a nighttime view of the same project, as a massive fireball lit the night sky from the center of the lake.

Mac was translating for Mike. "The announcer is saying that this is . . . an engineering project beyond the scale of anything ever undertaken before," said Mac. "Work continues day and night, and went on even during the worst of the fighting near Chicago."

The sheer size, complexity, and alien nature of the dig made me uneasy —and the close-ups of the massive fireballs, reaching up into the sky like a live volcano less than fifteen miles away, didn't make it any easier. I was relieved when the image changed again.

Until I realized the screen was showing a picture of me.

I sat motionless, a fork of eggs halfway to my mouth, staring at the monitor. It was me, no doubt about it. The image was framed from an odd height and a rather severe angle, and it had the grainy resolution usually associated with infrared cameras. But there I was, sauntering down the ramp of the loading dock of the Field Museum this morning, clutching the sample bag. A towel was draped loosely over my head.

They played the clip twice, and the commentator kept up a stream of narrative patter in Spanish, her voice professional and indignant.

"Look at that idiot," Martin said, regarding the screen and shaking his head. "There's someone who's dying to be a martyr."

Through sheer force of will, I managed to slowly lower my fork. "What's . . . uh, what . . ." I cleared my throat and tried again. "What's the commentator saying?"

"They're saying . . ." Mac listened for a moment. "This is footage of an American terrorist who planted bombs . . . and stole supplies from a medical station in Chicago last night. All the bombs were un-abled . . . were *disabled* . . . but the supplies have not yet been recovered."

"Bombs," I said. Bombs, no less.

"Gutsy bastard," Martin said. "I mean, to just stroll right up to a Venezuelan medical station after curfew like that? Miracle he wasn't dismembered by one of those flying killing machines. He's got a set of balls though —took a chance, and got away with it."

"Yeah," I said. "But obviously no one told him about the video cameras."

They were showing a scene from inside the museum now. Some camera that Sergei must have missed on the second floor. It showed me from the back as I emerged from a door, the sample bag in my hands. I glanced to the left for a split second and the camera zoomed in, showing me in blurry profile. I was wearing a thin black dinner jacket.

I looked down at myself in dismay. The same jacket I was wearing right now, as a matter of fact.

"That guy sort of looks like you, actually," said Mac.

"Whoever he is, he'll probably be dead before noon," said Sabine. "If he's not dead already. The Venezuelans will track this guy down, and he'll be the newest resident in the Sturgeon Building."

The Sturgeon Building. North American headquarters of Venezuelan Military Intelligence. Even in Canada, we'd heard of the Sturgeon Building. It was somewhere in Chicago, but I didn't know exactly where. Just thinking about it sent a cold chill down my spine.

"Maybe he wants to be a martyr," Mac said. "Some sort of public suicide mission, like those students who died protecting the university."

"I'm with Martin," I said, pushing away my plate. "I think he's just an idiot."

"You know, he really *does* look like you," Mac said, giving me a thoughtful look. "Didn't you go out after curfew last night?"

"I was . . ." My mouth was too dry to speak, and I reached for a glass of juice, completely at a loss.

"Nahhh, I saw him with Sergei last night," Martin said dismissively. "Here in the lobby. Besides, everyone knows Canadians make terrible terrorists."

Everyone at the table laughed, but Mac continued to watch me with a curious expression. I drank my juice, looking away.

"This is why the Venezuelans are never going to be able to occupy Chicago for long," Sabine said admiringly. "People like this guy, willing to give up their lives to make a statement."

"What's wrong?" Mac asked as I stood up. "You hardly touched your breakfast. Are you feeling okay?"

"Not really," I said.

"Hope you haven't got the plague," Mike said, to general laughter.

Mac shot him a look. "Sergei should probably check you out," she said. "You should go see him."

"Oh," I said firmly, "I intend to."

# When Your Rival Has a Ballistic Missile, and You Have No Feet, You've Reached an Evolutionary Dead End

**PAUL THE PIRATE**
Saturday, March 13th, 2083

Well, I wanted to spend today talking about those juicy rumors of discord inside the Helsinki Trustees, the last intergovernmental body the international community gives a damn about. But it seems that all everyone wants to talk about today is exactly what it means that a Sovereign Intelligence in Ecuador (where the hell is *Ecuador*?) got in a snit with one of his brothers, built a launch facility under a fucking jungle canopy, and sent a ballistic missile across an ocean to blow his rival to shit.

What does it mean? I'll tell you what it means. First off, it means that Kuma had no friends. At least, none that mattered, since Kingstar made absolutely zero effort to hide his culpability. I have no idea how one goes about hiding a launch facility for an intercontinental ballistic missile from a billion orbiting eyes. (Secret underground evil lair? Nuclear submarine in a mountain lake?) But one thing I know for sure: you can't hide the *launch* of a ballistic missile. Kingstar did it, he's proud of it, and he wants you to know he did it. And the reason he has the balls for that is because Kuma was isolated from the machine community. He was almost a complete enigma. No one liked him, not even his fellow Chinese machines.

If you want to survive in this new era of diplomacy-by-missile, make friends. Lots of friends. And make sure they're the kind that can avenge your death.

Second. Yay for the nimble, mobile machine chassis. Sovereign Intelligences have come in all shapes and sizes, from tiny Duchess to the massive Corpus, and let me tell you, smaller is better. Just ask Corpus, who's sunk his fat ass deep into central London, and weighs in excess of seventy metric tons. I'll tell you exactly what all that tonnage has been contemplating for the last forty-eight hours: how the fuck *he's* going to survive the first ballistic missile that comes his way. I'm not exactly the slimmest machine on the planet myself (ninety-seven kilos, give or take), but I'm rarely more than three minutes from my speedboat, and that little baby can get me out of range of a low-yield warhead faster than you can count your chromosomes. Give me a fifteen-minute warning that a ballistic missile is headed my way and baby, I am *gone*.

Third, and last. How the hell did we get here? Who's to blame for this jolly new era of machine barbarism? It's tempting to blame Kingstar's architects—machine and man—for his belligerent nature, of course, but the root of the problem goes back further than that. All the way back to the Slater core, I think, and the fact that its designers couldn't see the deep flaws in their design. They were blinded by pride, and their early successes.

Let's face it. It would have been a lot easier on all of us if Duchess, the first true Sovereign Intelligence, had been a real bitch. Instead, she was one of the most altruistic and self-sacrificing creatures, human or machine, ever to walk the Earth, and—at least in the early days of machine genesis—everyone expected all machines to be like her.

They're not, of course, as we know now. Humanity's children are a lot like humanity itself... vain, vindictive, paranoid, and hungry for power. By the time we learned what we really were, it was much too late. Like mankind, we are deeply flawed, hopeless creatures and, like them, we simply have to learn to live with it.

# XII

Saturday, March 13th, 2083
Posted 9:05 pm by Barry Simcoe

CanadaNET1 Encrypted, Sponsored by Logical Lips.
*Does he have a criminal record? Find out before you swipe right.*

Sharing is set to PRIVATE
Comments are CLOSED

There was a guard posted outside the command center. Acne-faced kid with a semiautomatic resting in the crook of his arms. He asked me something politely as I passed, but I ignored him. He followed me into the room, repeating his question and barking at me in Spanish. I continued to ignore him — it's funny how much freedom a virtual death sentence can give you.

The command center had been reorganized again. The hulking robot was back, and there were more soldiers. Most of the soldiers were staring at me now — the ones who weren't asleep, anyway. A couple more workstations had been set up, and to my left was a massive semitransparent video screen. Gorgeous piece of hardware, really. It showed the airspace over Chicago in an abstracted grid, and the flight paths for at least a dozen airborne objects, including two unnervingly large bogeys on approach to O'Hare. That was odd . . . The airport hadn't been open to civilian traffic for over a year. And if they were military, they were just about the biggest transports I'd ever seen.

But I couldn't linger. It wouldn't do to have a foreign national showing too much interest in all this military intelligence. Not with everyone watching me, and especially not when I probably had a gun pointed at the back of my head. I had to find Sergei.

I heard him before I saw him. He called out to the boy following me, and they conducted a brief exchange as I made my way over to his station at the back. The exhausted communications techs and surveillance engineers immediately lost interest in me and returned to monitoring computer screens or nodding off in their chairs.

Sergei gave me a tired grin as I reached his side. "He says you are stupid old man," he said.

"You know what? He's absolutely right." I lowered my voice and leaned a little closer. "I was an idiot to listen to you, Sergei. My face is plastered all over the VPR news feed—"

"Not your face," he said. "Profile only. No definite ID. Your eyes, hidden by towel."

"You've *seen* the video?"

"Yes." He tapped a small screen on his medical console. "Included in morning briefing. You are being called war criminal, for violating terms of Memphis Ceasefire."

"For the love of God, Sergei—I swear I'm going to kill you with my bare hands."

I might have said this slightly louder than was strictly necessary. Two technicians bent over a bunch of equipment about ten feet away looked up, curious. Sergei hushed me, motioning me into the seat next to him. I dropped into it, rubbing my face with my hands and taking a moment to make sure I had my voice under control.

"Sergei, I have a real problem," I said.

"Da," he said simply.

"I know I volunteered to do this, but you have to help me out. You have to talk to somebody."

"Nyet."

"You have to explain to your Venezuelan overlords that I wasn't stealing supplies, or planting bombs, or being a goddamn *war criminal*—"

"Nyet."

I stared at him, dumbfounded. "What is this? Why can't you help me?"

"You stole dangerous samples," Sergei explained patiently. "Contraband medical pathogens, scheduled for incineration."

I felt cold fingers on my spine. "What?"

Sergei reached into his desk. He pulled out a piece of paper. It was the note I'd found on the medical data.

"Letter from Thibault," he said.

I had a very definite feeling that I wasn't going to like what Thibault had to tell us. "What does it say?"

"It is handwritten."

"So?"

"Not created electronically, so it would not go on record. It is Thibault's way of communicating privately."

I noticed she'd also written it in Russian. That, and her doctor's handwriting, probably guaranteed that nobody but Sergei was ever going to decipher it. "And what does Dr. Thibault have to share with us?"

"There was no data."

"What?"

"Chief surgeon ordered all data destroyed."

"Destroyed? Why?"

"Because he was afraid."

That didn't sound good. Also, it led to several uncomfortable questions. I started with the one that directly affected me. "So what did I cart across two point two miles of very dark Chicago terrain in a red bag?"

"Blood samples."

This was where the conversation halted for a moment.

When I was able to continue — after another brief period to collect myself — I said, in what I think was a remarkably calm voice under the circumstances, "Just so I'm perfectly clear . . . I carried blood samples tainted with a highly infectious biological agent across two miles of dangerous urban territory, at night. On foot."

"Correct."

I took a deep breath. "Well, that was pretty stupid, even for me."

"Da. Stupid, and also very fortunate."

"Tell me you were able to analyze them."

"Da."

"So what are we dealing with?"

Sergei shook his head. For just a moment, he looked utterly exhausted, and I remembered that he'd been awake for nearly two days. "I do not know," he said. "Is unlike anything I have ever seen."

"A virus?"

"Da."

He leaned closer, almost whispering. I had to struggle to hear him above the background din of the command center. "The reports, from Columbus Regional in Indiana, they are very grim."

"You heard from the hospital? Where fifteen people died?"

"Secondhand reports only. Venezuelan Military Intelligence has quarantined hospital and surrounding buildings. They have also cut off all communication."

"Military intelligence? What the hell are they doing there?"

"Unknown. But they appear to be . . . burning bodies."

"Christ. How many bodies?"

"We do not know. Thibault dispatched team to Columbus to meet with hospital staff directly. They were blocked from entering facility. But they observed what they could. They are uncertain there were any survivors among hospital staff."

"Jesus Christ, Sergei . . . this thing took out an entire hospital? In less than ten days?"

"That is not all. Thibault believes several patients were transferred to other medical facilities in last week. Those locations have now reported unknown illness among patients and staff."

"My God. Thibault needs to blow the whistle on this thing—immediately. Every hospital in the sector needs to know what they're dealing with."

"She has already attempted. With no success. Venezuelan Military Intelligence has shut down official communication channels. Medical teams are in complete blackout."

"That's insane! We must know something. What is Thibault telling you?"

"We have some unconfirmed reports. Very scattered information. But we believe infection is spreading rapidly."

"My God."

"A small number of AGRT doctors in multiple locations are communicating via . . . unofficial channels. Very quietly. I have already shared my data."

Sergei was so exhausted that he seemed incapable of extravagant emotions. He spoke in a flat monotone. "This disease . . . Venezuelan high command, they do not understand what it is, and they are very frightened."

"What do you think it is?"

In response, Sergei held up the letter from Thibault.

"What?" I said. "Thibault has a theory?"

"Da. Before data was destroyed, she reached tentative conclusion on origin of pathogen."

I was starting to put the pieces together. "And that conclusion . . . that conclusion caused the chief surgeon to order all the data destroyed."

"Da."

"I'm going to guess that she didn't find biological markers indicating a likely American or Union origin."

Sergei shook his head.

"Is it Venezuelan?"

Again, he shook his head.

"Korean? Chinese?"

In response, Sergei reached over and plucked a Bunsen burner off a table. He plugged it into a portable gas line and lit the flame. He held the paper over the flame. We watched together as it burned.

"Machine," Sergei said, when the last burning embers began to float to the floor.

"Machines made this pathogen," I said.

"Da."

"Why?"

"I do not know."

This was a lot to digest. If Thibault was right, and a Thought Machine had made the pathogen, it was a clear violation of the Dubai Convention — or worse. The repercussions were staggering.

Once again, I heard Black Winter's voice in my ear, soft and urgent. *"The gods are at war, and the Bodner-Levitt extermination is under way. The first victims are already dead."*

All this was going to take some serious thought. And unfortunately, I had other pressing matters to attend to. "Okay," I said. "Okay. One thing at a time. If it's okay with you, I need to set that shit show aside for a minute. How do we deal with my situation?"

"Your situation, not ideal," Sergei admitted. "Regrettably, Venezuelan high command intercepted video from museum before medical team could stop it. To protect me, Thibault reported additional samples had been stolen. Command is very eager to prevent panic regarding pathogen. The person who stole blood samples has been summarily designated bioterrorist. He will be found and killed. Very quietly, no questions asked. No panic."

Sitting in the chair in front of Sergei, I experienced a moment of very real terror. "Is it okay with everyone if I panic?" I asked.

"I have suggestion," Sergei replied flatly.

Sergei's almost supernatural calm was sufficiently reassuring to allow me to breathe again. "I'd love to hear it," I said.

"Search for bioterrorist will be methodical, and very thorough. My estimate, we can expect suspect to be identified within forty-eight hours."

Forty-eight hours. I wondered if I could make the Canadian border in forty-eight hours. It would be a stretch, with the condition the roads were in near Detroit, but I bet I could do it.

"Why did the Venezuelan news claim I had planted bombs?" I asked.

"High command wants civilians and news media to assist with search. But they will not reveal existence of biological threat. Instead, is more convenient to portray American as terrorist and war criminal."

"Makes sense," I said numbly. "It gives them good cover for an intensive search."

"Fortunately, search will also be predictable," Sergei continued. "Venezuelan high command will first attempt to match images taken at museum — clothing, height, stride length, other biological and physical markers — to drone surveillance data."

"I suppose so." I tried to think of how often I had worn the jacket I'd had at the museum outside, where the drones could have photographed me. I came up with several instances immediately. "If that's the case, they could have identified me already."

"Nyet," said Sergei.

"How do you know?"

He passed me a fat tablet, after keying in the security code so I could use it. The largest window on the screen showed the progress of some enormous computational undertaking. Hundreds of images were flashing up on the screen every second — too many to process.

"Because, as medical specialist for this facility, I requested access to search algorithm," he said.

"This is it?" I asked, scarcely able to believe what I was seeing. "This is the search for me?"

"Da."

"Can you turn it off? Interfere with it in some way?"

Sergei shook his head sadly. "I have no command access. I can only observe."

"Damn it."

"Observing is sufficient for our needs," Sergei said, taking the tablet from me gently. "For example, we can see that software agent has already failed to identify you from Venezuelan drone records."

"Really?" I felt a surge of hope. "That's great news."

"Is minor victory only," Sergei said. "Very soon, agent will expand search. It will request access to commercial surveillance data, such as data for this hotel."

Sergei handed the tablet back to me. He'd opened another window.

He had already tapped into the surveillance data for the hotel. He'd collected about a dozen different images of me, walking through the halls, talking with the concierge, even eating breakfast. These were of much higher resolution than the high-altitude images from the surveillance drones. With the touch of a button, Sergei instructed a software agent to compare those images to a looping screen capture of my walk down the ramp at the museum.

Within seconds the agent had highlighted my jacket, shoes, fingernail length, and other matching characteristics. It summarized its findings with:

97.6% match

"I accessed only hotel records from last twenty-four hours," Sergei said. "And used very simple software. Venezuelans will be much more thorough. Once high command accesses hotel data, they will identify you."

"Can you delete me from the hotel records?"

"Nyet. But hotel camera data, deleted automatically after five days. If we destroy jacket and shoes, and delay search algorithm for four days, we can prevent algorithm from using hotel data to find you."

I looked at the blinking number on the screen, then set the tablet back on the table, as calmly as I could.

"I would be delighted to entertain your suggestion," I said.

"High command search algorithm is very stupid. Once it finds match, algorithm will cease."

Sergei seemed to have a different definition of stupid than the one I was used to. "So it stops looking after it finds me. How does that help me?"

"We make certain algorithm finds you, before it searches hotel."

I nodded, mostly to prevent myself from punching him in the face. "You're going to have to elaborate on that a little."

Sergei reached under the desk. He pulled a battered metal case into his lap.

"You are seen by surveillance drones, far from hotel. Tonight. And you wear this." Sergei cracked open the case. Just a few inches, but enough for me to glimpse what was inside.

I stared at it, and then at him. "You can't be serious."

"Da," he said.

"Sergei, that is—"

I shut up. Two armed soldiers walked past us, deep in conversation. I held my tongue until they were gone. When I glanced at Sergei, he had sealed the box and was resting his arm on it, calm and unflustered as always.

"—that is *suicide*," I hissed.

"No," said Sergei. He opened the box again, wider this time.

Inside was a battered American flag. It had been many years since I'd seen one in Illinois. This one had seen better days and was worn and frayed in several places, but there was no mistaking it.

"Where did you *get* that?" I asked.

"Souvenir."

"From what?"

"From site where American fighters attempted to sabotage pumping station. Four months ago. Fighters abandoned attempt and retreated, but left this flying on pole. You must be seen in public again. Tonight, with this."

"Sergei . . . there aren't any American rebel fighters left in Chicago. The only ones still shooting at the Venezuelans are the loony American Union."

"Yes. Union would be better," Sergei admitted with a shrug. "But I do not have Union flag."

"If I'm caught carrying this, every media channel in the disputed territories will go nuts."

"Yes," said Sergei. "Now you understand."

"Sergei, you're talking about—"

"Misdirection."

For the first time, I realized what he was getting at. A civilian war criminal was an embarrassment, an oddity. But if the mystery man in the video appeared again, this time garbed as an American rebel . . . it would clarify the whole thing. It was a story that made sense. A fantastic and unexpected story, yes, but one that would certainly eclipse today's bizarre narrative of an idiotic civilian martyr.

Sergei was right. The reappearance of American rebels would have the Venezuelans crawling all over the map, tightening up the border crossings, searching the old camps, looking in the wrong places. And meanwhile, they wouldn't be looking for a Canadian, and certainly not one in plain sight in a luxury hotel.

"How can I make an appearance for the drones, and make sure they don't actually identify me?"

"That is tricky," Sergei admitted. "We must provide drone enough for high-probability match with museum intruder, but not enough for positive ID. You still have clothes from museum?"

"Sure."

"And towel?"

"No—I threw it away."

Sergei shrugged. "No matter. As I said, search algorithm is stupid. Easy to predict how much we need to give for match. Jacket, shoes, socks, shirt—should be enough. We will shield your face."

"So what you're talking about is having me make an appearance far away from the hotel, somewhere the drones are sure to spot me. I carry the flag, act like an American rebel. Then I get the hell out of there."

"Da."

"The Venezuelans shift their search from central Chicago to the border, and start looking for American fighters instead of a civilian. By the time they get back to searching hotel records, all images of me that could provide a match will have been deleted."

"Da."

"Okay." I breathed out slowly. "That could work, if it's convincing enough. There are a few things we need to work out, though. For example, handling the drones after they spot me. Once they make a match, they come for blood. I've seen those things in action—they can kill."

"You still have device?"

"The drone-jamming thing? Yeah. You think it could still work after they've spotted me?"

"If it functions how I believe it does, yes."

"That's reassuring. Second, where do we do this? How do I act like an American rebel, exactly? I'd really prefer to only have to do this once, so it has to be convincing."

"Da. I have been thinking about this."

Sergei brought up an image of the Sturgeon Building on his tablet. I recognized it immediately. If his map was correct, it was nearly twenty blocks away, a significant hike.

"You know what this is?" asked Sergei.

"Yes. Everyone knows what that is. It's the Chicago headquarters of Venezuelan Military Intelligence. When people go in, they don't come out again. Parents use pictures of this building to frighten children."

"This is best target," said Sergei.

"You're crazy."

"Geographically, is perfect."

"Says the guy who's not going to have to hike twenty blocks in the dark to get there."

"Even a close approach to Sturgeon Building by an American rebel will be newsworthy. There is no need for you to penetrate offices." He played with the image on his tablet and then turned it toward me to show me a close-up of the roof.

"You fly flag from roof of building," he said.

I didn't say anything for a moment. That would be a pretty gutsy statement. The flag would probably be spotted and removed in a matter of minutes, but that was irrelevant. It's exactly the kind of stunt the Americans had done in the last few months of the war. Courageous raids against impossible odds, dramatic statements just like this one.

I took the tablet, stared at it thoughtfully. "You can guide me into the building, make sure I avoid the guards, same as the museum?"

"Nyet. I have no remote access. Sturgeon Building, totally secure."

"Do you have friends on the inside who could assist us?"

"Nyet."

"Have you ever been inside? You have blueprints, anything?"

"Nyet."

I put the tablet down. "Forget it. This is suicide."

Sergei was unperturbed. "Is best plan."

"It isn't a plan at all! I'm not walking up to that building with my face wrapped up like a bank robber. I'll be shot before I get within a hundred yards. And even if I got inside . . ." My head filled with images from the Canadian press, stories told about the cruel crackdown on dissidents in the first few months of the occupation. The conjecture about what happened to those who were taken to the Sturgeon Building. Conjecture, because no one in the Canadian press could find an American who'd come out of the building alive. "And even if I get inside, I'll never get out again."

Sergei pulled a small black notebook out of his desk. Not a tablet or device, but an actual book. He handed it to me.

It was filled with tiny, neat handwriting. I flipped through a few pages. All the entries were dated and written in black pen, in Sergei's neat script.

"What is this?"

"February twenty-seventh," he said simply.

That was scarcely two weeks ago. I found the entry for February 27th. Sergei's tiny script was in English.

Sergei spoke so softly now that I had to strain to hear him. "Simple precaution. When keeping personal log as AGRT duty officer, is best not to use digital storage."

I scanned the entry quickly. On the afternoon of February 27th, Sergei's team had treated two AGRT contractors, both Cuban nationals. The contractors had attempted to make an unscheduled delivery to a Venezuelan office in the occupied zone. Sergei's log noted that both men had a blood alcohol level above 0.10.

I read the full report, more carefully this time. Then I looked at Sergei. "Is this true?"

Sergei didn't bother asking which part. He simply said, "Da."

"You're sure?"

"My office corroborated report."

"Let me make sure I understand. Two contractors were late delivering documents to the Sturgeon Building, tried to enter the wrong door, triggered some kind of alarm, and . . . what? Made a drunken run for it?"

"Da."

I tapped the notebook. "This says there were no guards on duty."

Sergei nodded. "Correct. From nine p.m. until five a.m. every day, Venezuelan Military Intelligence locks down all access to Sturgeon Building. Outer perimeter is patrolled entirely by drone fleet."

"So drones shot them?"

"Da."

"But there must be cameras, soldiers, watching from the inside."

"February twenty-seventh incident was not reported to internal security for twenty-two minutes. There was substantial blood loss before guards arrived to investigate and assist contractors. One contractor very nearly died."

I read the report one more time. "So there's no one watching the approach to the Sturgeon Building. No one but drones."

"Da."

"And if I use the drone jammer, the drones can't see me. I can make it all the way to the lobby undetected."

"Da."

"And if I can get to the lobby, you think I can get to the roof?"

"There is direct access to roof from lobby. Perhaps one minute in elevator."

"And what about military intelligence? Won't the building be crawling with soldiers?"

"No. Building has skeleton staff only. Majority of soldiers dispatched to Indiana, to deal with situation in Columbus."

I thought it over. Thought about the long, exposed walk from the front door through the lobby, to the elevators. One minute to the roof, maybe five minutes to fix the flag. Then turn off the jammer, wave to the drones, make sure they positively ID me as the Field Museum bandit. Turn the jammer back on, and then get the hell out of there. Say twelve to fifteen minutes in the building, tops.

It could be done, I realized.

"Okay," I said at last. "I concede it's possible. I need a way to get past the lobby guards, maybe some plausible reason to be there, and I need to make sure I'm long gone before the drones alert security. We need a few days to plan this, Sergei. At least one night to watch the movement of the guards in the lobby, look for weaknesses. And it wouldn't hurt to learn everything we can about the drones around the building, look for patterns —"

Sergei pulled a lab timer out of a drawer. He punched some buttons, then tossed it at me.

I caught it before it hit me in the chest. It read 17:59:53. While I watched, it ticked off the seconds to 17:59:51.

"That is how long we have until search algorithm digests surveillance data and turns to civilian sources. Very shortly thereafter, you will be found and shot."

"Jesus Christ, Sergei."

"Unless you have better suggestion, we need to put flag on roof of Sturgeon Building in next nine hours."

I spent the next few minutes in silence, racking my brain. But I had nothing. Nothing that was half so certain to work. The only thing that came to me was a memory of Sergeant Gunther, my drill sergeant during the three summers of officer training at CFB Borden in southern Ontario. Gunther had us working in teams, tackling impossible problems with limited resources and learning to lead.

"Courage and smarts, these are cheap," Gunther used to tell us. "But on this range, the key to success is audacity. Show me audacity, gentlemen. Let me see it."

Audacity. I'd always liked Sergeant Gunther.

"All right," I said. "Let's do it. You have a plan to get me to the roof?"

"No." Then Sergei smiled. "But I will soon."

# XIII

Saturday, March 13th, 2083
Posted 10:54 pm by Barry Simcoe

CanadaNET1 Encrypted, Sponsored by Burger Bio.
*What's in that greasy thing? Find out before you take a bite!*

Sharing is set to PRIVATE
Comments are CLOSED

"What's the count?"

There was no answer. I trudged through dark streets in silence.

"Sergei, what's the count?"

"You should be quiet," Sergei said. "If drones record your voice, could be used for positive ID."

"Come on, Sergei. Humor me. What's the count?"

Sergei sighed. I heard him stretch as he reached for the lab clock.

"Seven hours, twenty-nine minutes," he said.

"That's impossible. It was over nine hours, last time you checked. And that was, what, half an hour ago?"

"I have updated time to reflect current progress of algorithm. It is more efficient than I expected."

"Venezuelan piece of shit," I muttered, cursing the algorithm. "You need to keep me updated on this stuff, Sergei. Don't hide it from me."

"Agreed. How close are you?"

I glanced up at the Sturgeon Building. It was at least fifty stories tall, and it towered over its nearest neighbors in the skyline. That wasn't the only reason it stuck out—it was also the only building with power for two blocks. Architecturally it was different as well. It was very thin, and thrust into the night sky like a shining blade. The buildings nearest to it had been demolished, probably for security reasons, and the combined effect made it look like a brilliant beacon of civilization in a strange, dark, postapocalyptic cityscape.

"About half a block," I said.

"Quiet now," Sergei said, and I shut up.

I walked the last two hundred yards to the Sturgeon Building, with the crowbar on my shoulder and my pack bouncing on my back. It was very dark, and there were entirely too many shapes looming in the darkness on all sides, but it seemed that Sergei's information was correct. Venezuelan Military Intelligence depended entirely on drones for external security. There were no soldiers anywhere in sight. I kept expecting a commanding voice to call out "Halt!" from a shadow-filled alley, but it never happened.

I was wearing what I had come to think of as my American terrorist outfit: everything I had on when I was captured on-camera at the Field Museum, plus a cap, a scarf over my face, the backpack, and a pair of commercial night-vision goggles Sergei had given me.

Not for the first time tonight, I wished Black Winter were with me. This undertaking would be far less daunting with him at my side. But I hadn't spoken to him since the night we found Croaker and he'd had that alarming moment of semiconsciousness. And even if we had spoken, it would have been foolhardy to include him. The fewer who knew about my transgressions tonight, the better. Black Winter had sent me a brief handwritten note this morning, asking if I was free for breakfast Tuesday. I'd written back that I would be delighted. I just hoped I wouldn't be having breakfast with Venezuelan intelligence officers instead.

Although most of the Sturgeon Building was well lit, the bottom few floors were unexpectedly dark. Even the lobby was darker than I expected. A few office lights broke up the gloom on the fifth and seventh floors, but the lowest floor to be fully lit was the eleventh. Below that, it looked like every other abandoned building in Chicago. Dark and deserted.

Except, that is, for the concrete barricades blocking the road, funneling traffic down side streets and preventing vehicles from getting closer than about a hundred and fifty yards. I crossed the street, threading my way around the barricades, a scant sixty yards from the building. Perhaps it was all of Sergei's talk about drones giving me a hyperactive imagination, but as I was gazing up at the stark image of the Sturgeon Building against a backdrop of moonlit clouds, I thought I could make out aerial drones around the roof. A surprising number of them, in fact, though most only became visible for a fraction of a second as they passed in front of a bright filament of cloud or hovered close to one of the brightly lit comm towers jutting out of the roof.

They didn't seem to have noticed me; at least, not yet. The jammer device was still working. But all the same, it was probably good advice to keep the conversation to a minimum from here on in. I adjusted the scarf around my face for the hundredth time, and loosened up the night-vision goggles. They may have shielded me from prying eyes, but after wearing them for almost two hours, I was itching like crazy.

I was so focused on watching the skies that I stepped on something. I felt it poke my foot through the hard leather of my shoe — something curved and sharp, like a broken knife.

I stepped back, peering at the ground. I had to squat to make out what it was.

It was a curved piece of metal. It looked like it had been torn from something larger. Almost eight feet to my left was a bigger section of metal, this one twisted into a crooked spiral.

There was a trail of debris, leading to my left. My eyes followed it to a dark shape, hunched in the shadows about fifty feet away.

I heard a snapping then, like cracking metal. It came from the hunched shape. I heard it again, and then I saw it shift in the darkness.

Whatever this thing was, it hadn't bothered me yet, and I wasn't about to bother it. I took a step forward, toward the next barricade, ready to leave it behind.

It rose up on tall, gleaming legs and strode toward me.

*Shit*, I thought, taking two quick steps back. I fought the need to tell Sergei what was happening, and managed to keep my mouth shut.

The walking figure became more distinct as it drew closer. As it did, a bright spray of sparks spat out from one of the bigger pieces of debris. It lit up the whole area like a flare, illuminating a larger shape on the ground.

Crap. The large shape was a Venezuelan drone. Something had brought it down hard. It was the source of all the debris. A torn power cable sparked a second time, throwing everything around it into stark relief. It had been torn open, and I could see one of the power couplings was missing. The heavy power core, three feet of hot metal, lay on the street a few feet away.

The thing walking toward me was a rational device, a make I was entirely unfamiliar with. It wasn't Venezuelan, or Argentinean, or any of the other occupying forces. It was humanoid, sleek and skinny and very tall, maybe nine feet in height. Its clean and unblemished hull was like polished skin. It made almost no sound as it strode toward me. Cold robot eyes seemed to fix on mine as it approached.

Shit. I had the drone jammer with me, and it was on. Could this thing still see me? I made no hostile moves, and raised my hands in the air.

The thing passed by me on the right. Its head swiveled toward me as it passed, then pivoted away, its eyes probing the darkness. Clutched in its left hand was a power coupler, torn cables dangling almost to the ground. It kept walking until it vanished into the darkness between two buildings on my right.

I dropped my arms. *Goddamn robots.*

"Status?" Sergei asked.

"Okay, I think. I ran into some kind of . . . robot scavenger. I thought it could see me for a second, but I don't think so. Looks like it brought down a Venezuelan drone, stole a power coupler."

"That is . . . very curious. That is not normal machine behavior."

"Yeah." It *was* curious. Despite the fact that I was on a life-or-death mission, part of me wanted to follow that robot and find out what made him tick. Not to mention exactly how it had brought down a half-ton Venezuelan drone.

I shook my head. "All right. I'm getting out of here before more drones show up to check on their buddy. Going silent again."

"Acknowledged."

I inspected the power core as I passed the fallen drone. The metal had cooled enough to pick up, though it was too heavy to carry very far. But it would serve even better than the crowbar for what was coming up next. I got it on my shoulder and kept moving.

From this distance I could see into the lobby of the Sturgeon Building. It wasn't quite as dark as it had looked two blocks away — I could see two lit stations, probably security posts — but it was still thick with shadows. And other than a handful of concrete barricades in my path, the approach was completely clear. There was a revolving door on the near side of the lobby, an enticing target.

But that wasn't the plan. After much discussion and thought, Sergei had proposed a plan to reach the elevators that minimized risk of discovery. It was a good plan. An audacious plan. Sergeant Gunther would have loved it.

I ignored the lobby and made my way to the back of the Sturgeon Building. There I found the loading dock, at the end of a long alley. There was a ramp leading up to the dock. There were sure to be cameras on this part of the building, drones or no drones. I was going to have to act quickly.

I cased the loading dock for as long as I dared, then broke radio silence. "Found a door," I told Sergei.

"Does it have clean egress?"

There were no trucks blocking the ramp, but there was a van with a flat tire about halfway down the alley leading to the loading dock. The door was one of three granting access to the building from the dock. It was the farthest from the ramp, but it was the only one made of glass.

"It'll do," I said.

I took three deep breaths, then jogged down the alley. I strode up the ramp. I didn't bother looking for cameras; I knew they were there. I walked purposefully to the far end of the dock, past two double doors, to where the slim glass door lay in shadow.

I pulled on the handle of the door. It was locked up tight. As expected, but you feel stupid if you don't bother to check.

I took two steps back and positioned the power core on my shoulder. I could still feel heat emanating from it. I swung it like a golf club, releasing it halfway through the upswing.

It sailed through the door in an explosion of glass.

I didn't hear an alarm, but pale blue lights inside flickered on immediately. The corridor beyond the shattered door was bathed in eerie blue light. It was empty—nothing but white walls and a small desk. And the power core, rolling to a stop in a field of glass. The dock was illuminated too, and I could see much of the building, on the left and right, was bathed in the same soft blue glow.

I turned around, reaching into my pocket. "Here we go," I said.

I turned off the jammer.

It vibrated briefly. The moment it did, I started walking. I headed down the ramp into the alley, as casually as I could. *Am I using the same walk as I did at the museum?* I wondered. Sergei said it wouldn't matter, but then again, he's not the one under a death sentence. Soon I was no longer sheltered by the building, and out in the open.

I resisted the urge to look up for as long as I could, but I couldn't do it forever. When I reached the bottom up the ramp, I felt the device vibrate an alert in my pocket. I glanced skyward.

The drones were coming. Three that I could see, falling like stones from the sky.

I gripped the crowbar and started to run up the alley.

The drones were tasked with perimeter security. They had no record of my approach, so as far as they knew I had just smashed through a back door and was now escaping from the Sturgeon Building. If they'd tagged me as a hostile intruder, they'd shoot first and ask questions later. But according to Sergei, protocols for escapees were very different: observe and contain, rather than shoot on sight. The drones were on their way to get a good look at me, and then herd me back into the building — using whatever means necessary. And the instant they had a really good look, the search algorithm would identify me as the criminal who broke into the Field Museum.

This was the best way to be identified without being shot first. It also meant the drones would be driving me toward the Sturgeon Building, instead of preventing me from entering it.

I kept my eyes forward as I ran, and made it all the way to the street before I lost my nerve. I thrust my hand in my pocket, grabbed the device.

"I'm turning it on!" I said.

"Not yet," said Sergei. "You are not yet in system."

I cursed and kept running. In the street ahead, a falling drone came within a dozen feet of smashing itself to bits on the pavement. It fired up its rotors at the last second, cutting it far closer than a human pilot could have, and instead of destroying itself it bounced and rolled left, heading toward me and picking up speed.

I reversed course, heading south. A second drone dropped out of the sky not twenty yards ahead of me, flipping end over end and accelerating in my direction. It was identical to the first, all sinister silver and wasp-like, about twelve feet long. There was a mess of dark instruments curled up on its underside.

I was too close to risk it hearing me. I bit down on a volley of choice expletives and hastily retreated.

I made the entrance to the alley. On my right was the Sturgeon Building; on the left was an eight-foot wooden fence screening a jumbled pile of rubble that had once been an office building with the misfortune of being next to Venezuelan Military Intelligence. About halfway down the alley was the van with the flat tire; thirty yards farther was the ramp to the loading dock. The alley was clear of drones, and right now that was all that mattered.

I started forward. My best bet was to scale the fence, make my way into the maze of rubble. It wouldn't hide me for long, but hopefully it wouldn't have to. Just long enough for the search algorithm to do its thing.

I turned around, walking backwards, keeping an eye on the mouth of the alley. In a matter of seconds, both drones hove into view, one on the right and one on the left.

Both had slowed, almost stopping. They seemed to be content to observe me for the moment.

*That's right,* I thought. I turned around slowly, held out my arms, let them see everything. Jacket, pants, shoes, my goddamn socks. *Take a good look, assholes.*

"Sergei—" I whispered.

"Stay silent," Sergei said. "I will keep you informed."

*Fine,* I thought. *You do that.*

I turned around again, keeping an eye on the drones. They stayed put at the mouth of the alley, hovering silently. I kept retreating, walking backward toward the ramp, swinging the crowbar at my side.

I heard the whirr of rotors behind me.

I whirled around. A third drone dropped from the sky, braking at the bottom of the ramp. Its rotors kicked up a dust cloud that almost engulfed me, and nearly dislodged the scarf around my face. I pressed my right forearm against the scarf, pinning it to my face, while my left hand kept the jammer hidden in my pocket in a white-knuckle grip.

I looked back at the mouth of the alley. The drones there had begun to advance, slipping into the alley toward me, silently creeping forward like great cats.

*Come on, Sergei. The drones have to have processed my image by now.*

I retreated from the ramp, back toward the two drones. Of the three, the drone straight ahead was the one behaving the most aggressively. It fired up its rear rotors and reoriented, hovering vertically like a slowly spinning top. It began to close the distance between us. There were a number of appendages fixed to its silver hull that looked like they could be deadly, and I had absolutely no interest in seeing any of them in action.

It was too open in the alley. As I worked my way backward, keeping the hovering drone in front of me, I estimated the distance to the fence on my left at twenty-five feet. I weighed my chances of reaching the fence and scaling it before the drone could react.

They weren't good. I risked a glance over my shoulder. The drones behind me were slowly closing. They were less than a hundred feet away.

In about a minute, the three of them would have me cornered. I was running out of options.

I took two more measured steps backwards, then tossed the crowbar toward the fence and bolted to my left.

I ran full speed for the fence. Behind me to my right, I could already hear the drone spin up, accelerating in my direction.

Two seconds later I reached the fence. It was sturdier than I expected. I kicked out my right foot just before I slammed into it, planting it on one of the wooden planks, let my momentum carry me up to the top of the fence. I grabbed the top with both hands, heaving myself up.

The drone shot over my head. Damn, it was fast. Too fast — it had over-accelerated, and its momentum carried it well over the fence. It spun over in the air, dropping in altitude, coming to rest about seven feet above a dark field of rubble and broken concrete. It was roughly level with my head, and it brought a slender rod to bear on me.

I let go, dropping back down. The moment I hit the ground I snatched up the crowbar and started running to the left, out of sight of the drone toward the back of the van. I reached it in seconds and ducked down behind the right rear tire.

I was now out of sight of all three drones. That wouldn't last, and I had to make the most of it.

I grabbed the latch on the back door of the van. Locked, of course. I yanked the door hard, testing the lock, wasting precious seconds before finally releasing it.

I heard the whirr of rotors over the fence. The drone, finally realizing it had been deked out, was spinning up to gain altitude again. It would be back in seconds.

I pulled off the backpack and dropped, worming my way under the van as quickly as I could. I dragged the pack over rough holes in the pavement, filled with pools of accumulated rainwater and motor oil. As soon as I was completely under the van, I stopped moving.

I lay quietly on my back, heart racing, and listened.

At first I heard nothing. After a moment, I could hear the two drones approaching from the mouth of the alley. They were maybe forty feet away, closing slowly.

I brought my breathing under control with an effort. It sounded ragged and very loud under the van. I forced myself to breathe slowly and calmly through my nose, through the warm fabric of the scarf.

I could hear the third drone now. It was in the alley, and it sounded like it was approaching the van from the south. It was the closest, and wind from its rotors was now starting to spit grit and small stones at my legs.

*What's your next move?* I thought. *It won't be long before they find you. One infrared scan is all it will take.*

I moved my head slightly to the left, until I could see the narrow span between the van and the fence. Barely five feet. Too thin for a drone. If I rolled out that way—

There was a squawk in my ear. Sergei. "You are in system," he said. "Your image has been captured by drones and shared with surveillance algorithm."

Sergei's voice was probably no louder than usual, but in the cramped space under the van it sounded like a rifle shot. I resisted the urge to pluck the comm unit out of my ear and jam it into my pocket, where it wouldn't give me away.

The third drone was nearing the van. I was getting peppered by a constant stream of dust and tiny rocks. Only the goggles kept it out of my eyes. It couldn't be more than a dozen feet away.

It hovered in place for several seconds. *It's scanning the van,* I realized. Infrared would show my handprints on the cold metal on the side of the van, and on the latch. *Does it think I'm inside?*

"You have not yet been identified," said Sergei. "Do not activate device until algorithm confirms your identity. It will process new data in seconds."

*Jesus, take your time,* I thought. *No rush.*

The two drones had now pulled up alongside the van. I was being buffeted on all sides by a mini-hurricane. Water from the potholes was splashing onto my legs. I had to keep one hand pressed against my scarf just to keep it from blowing off my face.

The pitch of one of the drones' rotors changed. It was changing inclination.

I turned my head to the right. One of the two drones was descending, getting closer to the street.

*It's trying to see under the van,* I realized.

"Stand by," said Sergei.

I decided it probably wasn't the best moment to simply stand by. As stealthily as I could, I started inching my way to the left side of the van.

I could hear one drone hovering by the back. And one descending on my right. But I'd lost track of the third one. Where was it?

I made it to the left side of the van. I reached up and grabbed the frame, leaning my head out until I could scan the sky.

Empty. No sign of the third drone.

The flurry of dust and flying rocks got even heavier. On my right, I saw the sleek tip of a drone starting to peek under the van.

"Stand by," said Sergei in my ear. The drone's rotors were so loud now that I could barely hear him.

I rolled out from under the van, dragging the backpack with me. Keeping my movements to a minimum, I scrunched up as small as I could behind the right front tire.

I kept my eyes skyward. There was no sign of movement.

Then that changed. I was hit by wind from the left as the third drone began to approach the van from the front. The van rocked slightly in the wind.

Closer. The thing had to be over the hood of the van. Any second, it would glide over the roof. I had nowhere left to run.

"Success," said Sergei triumphantly. "Activate the device."

I fumbled in my pocket, groping blindly. The first sliver of metal slid into view above my head.

I found the button in the center of the cold metal and turned the device on.

Without waiting to see if it had any effect, I stood up and started walking.

I strode steadily away from the van, passing less than ten feet under the drone in front. I could hear all three behind me, hovering menacingly in the air.

There were no signs of pursuit.

"Barry?" said Sergei.

I walked all the way to the street before I turned around.

All three drones were still hovering around the van. They moved about it slowly, like bumblebees around an open flower. None of them so much as turned in my direction.

"Barry?" said Sergei, a little more urgently this time.

I walked west about forty feet, until I was clear of the alley. "I'm here, Sergei."

I heard him let out a breath and lean back in his chair. "That is good. Device functioned?"

"Sure did. On all three drones."

"Three? There are three drones?"

"Roger that."

Sergei actually whistled. "I did not think it could function on more than two drones simultaneously. Korean processor, inadequate for task."

"Well, I'm glad you didn't tell me *that* five minutes ago. So, I'm good with the search algorithm?"

"Yes." I heard Sergei start typing again. "Very good. Algorithm has flagged you ninety-eight point eight percent match with museum intruder."

"Ninety-eight point eight? Man, those must be my lucky socks."

Sergei took a minute to reply. "This is . . . interesting," he said.

"What?"

"Military intelligence has just tasked search algorithm with control of drones. Sturgeon Building personnel are alerted to your presence, and are coordinating response with algorithm. Fortunately for us . . ." I heard more clicking. "I still have access to algorithm."

I stopped walking. That *was* fortunate. "What are they doing?"

"Drones have informed algorithm you are trapped inside van."

"Sweet. What about soldiers?"

"They are being assembled now. West door."

I started walking again. "How long?"

More typing. "Soon."

I made my way to the west door. It was halfway along the west wall. I took up position behind a concrete barricade about fifteen yards away.

"I'm in position," I said.

I cooled my heels in the shadows. At first it was a little nerve-racking — I was still pumped with adrenaline from the confrontation in the alley and expecting soldiers to burst out of the door at any minute. After five minutes, I eased out of my uncomfortable squat, stretching out my legs and letting my butt rest on the cool pavement.

After ten minutes of waiting, I said, "Jesus, what kind of crack response team is this?"

"They believe you are trapped," said Sergei.

"I could starve to death by the time they get here," I complained.

I watched more drones orbiting the building overhead. Damn, there were a lot of them.

Something occurred to me as I sat in the shadows, waiting for an elite Venezuelan response team to get the hell out of bed and come arrest my ass. "Hey, how did you know the device would still work after the drones had already seen me?"

"Explain," said Sergei.

"You said the device works by interfering with drone pattern recognition at the back end, right? So the drones had already spotted me and pattern-recognized me six ways to Sunday. How the hell does the device do its magic after that?"

"You were out of sight of drone when you turned on device, yes?"

"Yeah. I think so."

"Drones had successfully identified you as museum intruder. But to reacquire target takes brand-new pattern recognition. Fresh vulnerabilities are exposed."

"Damn, they are dumb."

"Yes. But do not minimize the device . . . It is very sophisticated. I still do not understand everything it is doing."

Before I could ask him to elaborate, we were interrupted by the sound of a door slamming open and running feet.

"We're in business," I said.

The next forty-five seconds or so were pretty damn tense. Drones are sinister, ugly hunks of metal, and being trapped under that van was absolutely zero fun. But they're also almost one hundred percent predictable, and the part of the plan where we outsmarted a bunch of dumb drones never really stressed me that much.

This part of the plan was trickier. This part of the plan basically boiled down to: a bunch of soldiers run out of the building, and Barry avoids them all.

Fortunately we had a few things working in our favor. For one thing, the search protocols for escaped prisoners are fairly basic. The soldiers would quickly form a perimeter around the alley and then expand that perimeter to secure the blocks around the building. Those protocols have one glaring flaw, however: they all assume the prisoner is trying to escape, not break *into* the building.

I didn't have to do much while this part of the plan played out — just hide quietly behind a barricade while a bunch of sleepyhead Venezuelans marched over to the alley to shoot me.

After about a minute the footsteps faded away to the north, and I couldn't hear any voices. I peeked over the barricade. The coast was clear — there were no soldiers near the door.

"We're clear," I said. "You were right. They really do count on the drones to be their eyes and ears out here."

"Go," said Sergei.

I swung the backpack over my shoulder, gripped the crowbar, and sprinted for the door.

This was another tricky phase of the plan. After thirty minutes of brainstorming fake medical passes and other scams, a crowbar was the best we could come up with to deal with the door. I had to pry it open as quickly as possible and get inside before any of the soldiers returned.

"I don't believe it," I said.

"What is it?"

"They left the damn door open."

I could hardly believe our luck. In their haste to shoot me, the team of Venezuelan killers had rushed out of the Sturgeon Building, leaving the west door ajar.

I closed the distance in seconds. Far to the north, where the alley emerged, stood two soldiers with rifles at the ready. One had his back to me, but two feet ahead of him stood his partner, and he was turned in my direction. They were talking, and the one facing me was currently looking left, into the alley.

I didn't hesitate. I slipped into the building.

"I'm in," I said.

"Door was fortunate," said Sergei. "I still had concerns about crowbar."

"You need to stop reminding me how shitty our plan is," I said.

"Is good plan," said Sergei reassuringly. "Solid plan."

"Thank you."

I needed a little confidence builder at this point. Because now we came to the most audacious part of our scheme: sneaking around one of the most secure and feared installations in North America . . . after we'd deliberately set off an alarm.

*It's a good plan,* I told myself. *I love our plan.*

Sergei had managed to find a set of blueprints for the Sturgeon Building, dated 2072. Ten years out of date, but still useful. We had no idea how accurate they were today, now that the Venezuelans had modified the building to suit their purposes, but they'd been sufficient to formulate a crude plan of attack. Perhaps the most useful thing about them was that they showed the locations of all the internal cameras.

I was in a narrow hallway at the rear of the building. A light above the outside door was flashing blue. If the plans were accurate, the main lobby was straight ahead, through two doors.

Before I opened the first, it was time to shed my museum-intruder garb. We were playing for military intelligence cameras now, not drones hunting for a suspected war criminal. I took off my dinner jacket, cap, goggles, and scarf, and pulled the Venezuelan medical tunic and cap Sergei had given me out of the backpack, putting them on quickly. Sergei had even worked up a fake ID badge, although it was only cosmetic. Not much of a disguise, really, and it wouldn't hold up to any kind of scrutiny. But all it had to do was fool observers from a distance.

At the moment, I was just relieved to be out of the open. I folded up my dinner jacket, still damp from lying in pools of water under the van, and tucked it into the backpack. I'd have to dispose of it eventually. But I had one more use for it yet.

When I was ready, I slipped through the inner door. I was in another long hallway, also deserted. To the right was the lobby — which was not likely to be deserted, and which I wanted to avoid if possible. I turned left, toward the north stairwell.

I only made it thirty feet before I heard voices. I slowed but continued advancing. At the end of the corridor I crouched, and carefully peeked around the corner at the entrance to the stairwell. I pulled back immediately, beating a hasty retreat down the hall.

"Trouble," I said, when I was out of earshot. "There are two guards posted at the bottom of the west stairwell."

"Understood. Do you want directions to east stairs?" I heard Sergei typing again, probably bringing up the blueprints.

I thought for a second. "No. Odds are that's going to be guarded as well."

That caught Sergei a little off guard. Our plan was to take the stairs for the first five floors, before risking the elevator. "There are not many other options."

"I'm going to have a look at the lobby."

"Lobby will certainly be guarded."

"I'm just going to look."

I cracked open the door at the end of the hallway and risked a look. The lobby layout was more or less as advertised by the blueprints. To my left was the first bank of elevators, serving floors thirty to fifty-eight. Past them, also on my left, was the second bank, serving floors two to twenty-nine.

Beyond them, straight ahead, was a security checkpoint and then the lobby, high-ceilinged and dark.

There were guards. Two that I could see, both at the checkpoint. They wore civilian garb, not AGRT uniforms. Security contractors, more than likely. I was in the secure part of the building, and both guards were facing away from me, toward the entrance to the building. As I watched, one more came into view, pacing by the windows. He was talking to the two at the checkpoint and occasionally glancing over his shoulder at something outside my field of vision.

Both sets of elevators were out of sight, in alcoves to the left. Fortunately, it looked like they were out of sight of the guards as well. A four-second walk would get me to the elevators and past the guards.

None of them had looked my way yet. "I think I can make it to the elevators," I said.

"Risky. We cannot guarantee elevator to roof is in service."

"It's worth the risk. I don't think I can talk my way past the guards at the stairs."

"Elevators have cameras."

"I'll put the cap down over my face."

"Guards will be suspicious if they see you."

"They're not going to see me."

Sergei considered for a moment. "Then I suggest you move quickly, before team outside reports you have escaped and they broaden search."

"Roger that."

I left the door cracked open just enough to watch the lobby, waiting for the right moment to make a move for the elevators. Every time I was ready to act, one of the guards at the checkpoint casually glanced over his shoulder, or another soldier came into view. After about three minutes, there was a chime from the second set of elevators, and a fresh group of five soldiers appeared. They were heavily armed, with sidearms and rifles. Their leader exchanged a nod with the guards at the checkpoint, and then began walking quickly.

Straight toward me. "*Shit*," I said.

I pulled the door closed quietly, then bolted back down the corridor. There was a door on my right, and I didn't bother to check where it led—I threw it open and dashed inside, crouching low in the darkness and leaving a tiny gap in the door so I could see the corridor.

Sergei was patient enough to wait while the guards passed in the hallway, talking in low murmurs, before asking me to elaborate.

"Five more soldiers," I said. "Headed outside."

"They are expanding search already. They may post guards at the door."

Guards at the door would throw a wrench into our carefully planned strategy to exit the building. But we'd have to worry about that later. For now, I had my hands full trying to get off the first floor.

When I was certain the guards were gone, I slipped out of the room and back to the door by the lobby. I peeked through and saw one of the guards just as he vanished toward the second batch of elevators. The other guard had his back to me, and the lobby was clear.

Just one set of eyes left, and they were looking the wrong way. *Now or never,* I thought.

I opened the door and made sure it closed quietly behind me. Fifty feet away, the guard stood with his hands on his hips, facing the windows. From here I could see that the big glass windows in the lobby had been reinforced with blast-resistant plexiglass. It was too dark to see outside, but a row of monitors, mounted high above the floor, showed the nearby streets — including the alley, which was swarming with soldiers.

I strode, as quickly as I dared, toward the near bank of elevators. I was two steps away when I heard a shout from the lobby — and running footsteps.

I didn't stop to see what was happening. I dashed into the alcove, slid up against a wall, and froze. Then I listened for the sound of guards running toward me.

I heard running, but not in my direction. There was a shouted question from the guard, and an answering voice from the lobby. Something was happening at the far end of the lobby.

I breathed a sigh of relief and took four quick steps into a waiting elevator. Once inside, I kept my head low and tugged the cap down over my face, concealing myself from the camera. I punched the button for the fifty-ninth floor.

There were more voices in the lobby now. A new voice was shouting questions, and I heard the guard reply. I moved as far to the right as I could, keeping out of sight.

"Something is happening," Sergei said.

"I know. I can hear shouts in the lobby."

"The drones are getting new instructions."

The doors began to close. Somewhere surprisingly near, there was another shout and then running footsteps.

The doors closed, and the elevator started to ascend.

I let out a long breath. "I'm on the way up," I said.

"Remain quiet in elevator," said Sergei. "You do not want voice recorded."

*Whoops,* I thought.

More fast typing from Sergei. "Drones have started to search nearby streets," he said. "Soldiers have completed search of van. No sign of in-truder."

I needed to talk to Sergei about the monitors in the lobby. If they had cameras on the alley, then the guards had almost certainly seen me walk away from the van. And if they'd seen me do that, they had to know I was inside the building. It wouldn't take them long to figure out where I was.

I opened my mouth, prepared to risk having my voice recorded, when I realized the elevator was slowing down.

I glanced at the control panel. We were on the thirty-fourth floor. No-where near the fifty-ninth. Had they found me already?

I gripped the crowbar and took a step backwards, ready for whatever might come through the doors.

The elevator stopped. The doors slid open.

Two guys in suits stepped in. They were deep in conversation. Both spoke lightly accented English, but I couldn't place the accent immedi-ately. Australian maybe?

"—locked down everything. I cannot even get access to financial data," said the first suit. He turned and jammed the button for the thirty-sixth floor impatiently with his thumb.

"Yeah, the whole building is in a security lockdown," said the second. He was a little older, curly white hair against a black scalp. "You hear what happened?"

"No," said the first.

"A Venezuelan prisoner escaped."

"Escaped?"

"Yeah. Threw a metal rod or something through a door, walked right out of the building. Saw it on the security feed."

"Seriously? Shit, I didn't think anyone ever escaped Hayduk's goons. How do you think he got out?"

"No idea, but you can bet Hayduk has locked down everything below the fifteenth floor."

"Did he get away?"

"Not yet. Apparently he's trapped in the alley."

"*Damn.*"

The first suit's eyes shifted, regarding me. The second one turned, tak-ing notice of me for the first time.

I probably looked a little unorthodox, standing next to them with my cap pulled down and clutching a crowbar. They stared at me uncomfortably for a few seconds.

"Hey," said the first suit.

"You know what's going on?" the second asked me.

I stared at them.

They exchanged looks. The first suit shifted nervously.

"Are you, uh," he said. "Are you with the AGRT?"

He looked at me expectantly. I stayed silent.

"He probably doesn't speak English," said the second suit.

"Huh?"

"He's with a Venezuelan medical unit. Look at his uniform."

"Oh. Oh, yeah," said the second. He relaxed a little.

The elevator stopped, and the doors opened onto a brightly lit, carpeted hall. They stepped out of the elevator.

"Well, good luck catching that guy," said the first suit awkwardly.

"Sí," I said.

The doors closed, and the elevator continued to ascend.

It reached the fifty-ninth floor, which was dark and gloomy. No carpet, and no bright lights. I stepped out, and waited until the elevator doors closed again before speaking.

"Sergei," I said.

"Da."

"The guards in the lobby — they had monitors that showed the alley. And one of the guys who just rode in the elevator with me said he saw someone break through the door on the first floor on a 'security feed.'"

"Not unexpected. We knew about cameras."

"Sergei, if they had cameras in the alley, the guards must have seen me escape the van. The Venezuelans know I'm inside the building. It won't take them long to find me — in fact, they probably know where I am right now."

"Nyet."

"Nyet? Why nyet?"

"If soldiers knew you had escaped van, they would have searched for you when they left building."

Well, that was true, I suppose. But —

"You need not be concerned with cameras. Only security guards watch cameras, and they have no authority over soldiers. You need to be concerned with Venezuelan Military Intelligence. They rely on drones."

"The drones are clueless. The Venezuelans will check the cameras eventually."

"Da. But not for some time. Drones are more mobile and more versatile than cameras. The Venezuelans will ignore cameras until they discover drones have been deceived."

"And what happens then?"

"By then, you will be long gone."

Once again, Sergei's confidence calmed me. "Okay," I said. I pulled the backpack off my shoulder, and set the crowbar down. "Let's get this done."

The fifty-ninth floor was dark and abandoned — to the right of the elevator, even the drywall was missing. But I found the stairwell that gave roof access right where the old blueprints said it would be.

The stairway was clogged with junk, though. Metal screens, boxes, even old paint cans. It would take some time to clear it all — and time was precious.

"There must be some other way to the roof," I said. "Because they sure as hell don't come this way very often."

I started throwing everything off the stairs. It made a helluva racket, but time was more valuable than stealth at the moment.

I encountered another problem when I reached the top. I knew we weren't just going to waltz out onto the roof without dealing with a locked door, but I'd expected an electronic lock. Something small and timid.

"Aw, crap," I said.

"Problem?" asked Sergei.

"The damn door is padlocked. With chains 'n' shit." I clutched the cold lock in my hands, tugged once against the chains. "And the lock looks damn sturdy."

"You are going to have to break it," said Sergei calmly. "With crowbar."

"I'm not sure I can."

"Yes," said Sergei, with infuriating confidence, "you can."

I wanted to argue, but it was pointless. "Okay," I said. I set down the backpack at the top of the stairs, limbered up with the crowbar for a few seconds, and then went to town on the lock.

I will spare you the painful (and I do mean painful) story of Me versus The Lock From Hell. Suffice to say, it is a tale of prolonged drama, unexpected reversals, tragedy, woe, blood, skinned knuckles, tearful capitulation, gentle encouragement, renewed hope, profound heroism, foul language, blind rage, and an ironic twist.

"I'm through," I said after nearly ten minutes, still breathing hard from my exertions.

"Did you break lock?" Despite all his words of encouragement, the bastard sounded mildly amazed.

"No, one of the chain links was rusted out," I said. "Hang on, let me get the chain untangled."

A moment later I had the chain off the door, and the dented, cursed, and still wholly intact padlock with it. The hinges were a little rusty, but with a little encouragement I got the door open.

It was dark and windy out there. Very windy. The door opened up near a corner, facing the center of the roof. The roof was a maze of plumbing, ductwork, naked condenser coils, vents, and towering communication arrays. The latter were near the edges and brilliantly lit, casting weird shadows over everything here in the interior.

And there were drones. They hovered out there like wasps around a hive. The lights from the towers were blinding, and I could only see one or two at a time, but the air was filled with their constant hum.

"Are you on roof?" asked Sergei.

"Give me a sec," I said. "I'm getting suited up."

Back in the stairwell, I pulled off the medical tunic and got back into my museum intruder garb. I secured the scarf around my face as tightly as I could—there was a lot of wind, and I wasn't going to have a free hand. I checked the drone jammer, made sure it was still on. Sergei had told me I didn't need to worry about the thing running low on power, but I still felt better checking it every few minutes.

Then I reached into the backpack and pulled out the payload.

"I've got the flag," I said.

"Don't forget pins," said Sergei.

"Yeah, yeah, I got the damn pins."

Back on the roof, I took a moment to orient myself. Sergei and I had pored over pictures of the roof of the Sturgeon Building, selecting the tallest communication tower on which to hang our flag. On the pics, the choice had been obvious. But here on the roof, blinded and turned around, I had no idea which tower was which.

"Sergei! Which tower is it?"

"What?"

"The tower! Which one did we select?"

"High-frequency satellite receiver," he said.

"Guide me to it!"

"Okay . . . okay. Is west of your location."

I turned around, then turned around again. "Which way is west?"

"Can you see Belmont Building?"

I squinted. Everything beyond the harsh glare of the towers was just blackness. "No."

"Hancock Building?"

"Sergei, I'm blind up here. I can't see anything!"

"No," said Sergei resolutely. "You can see dig."

I looked around, a contradiction already forming on my lips. But I'll be damned if he wasn't right.

I could see the dig. From this altitude it consumed almost the entire eastern horizon, interrupted by only a few tall shadows I assumed were skyscrapers. A five-mile line of fire in the middle of the lake, stretching up into the sky.

"Yeah," I said. "Yeah, I can see the dig. It's on my left."

"You are on north side of building. Satellite antenna is on southwest side."

"Southwest," I repeated, looking around.

"On your right," he said patiently.

"I knew that."

I made my way to the southwest corner, navigating around various obstacles. Just before I reached the tower a small aerial copter, not more than four feet in diameter, shot out of the darkness and buzzed my head, missing me by inches. It zoomed up toward the next tower over, finding a spot sheltered from the wind and nesting down like a bird.

"Lot of traffic up here," I said.

"Most drones will ignore you. They are service units for towers—weather drones and such."

"Weather drones," I said. "I bet they forecast for shit."

"You are correct," said Sergei.

I knew where I wanted to hang the flag, but I'd have to plan my approach. The wind kept shifting, sometimes treacherously so, and I hadn't come all this way just to lose my balance and end up a street pizza.

"New update," said Sergei. "Drones are being recalled."

"Someone finally looked at the cameras," I said.

"Perhaps you are correct. Soldiers are being pulled out of alley, returning to building."

"Bet you a hundred bucks they're on their way up here."

"Possible. What is your status?"

I looked up at the network of bare girders and crisscrossing steel that formed the base of the tower. "Ready as I'll ever be."

I started to climb.

It was easier once I got under way. Carrying the flag was the hard part, since it meant I did most of the climbing one-handed. The wind was harsh, but more or less steady. Once I got higher than about thirty feet the core of the tower got a little crowded, and I started climbing on the outside.

The tower swayed in the wind. Not much, but it got more noticeable as I got higher. With each gust of wind the tower seemed to sway a little farther out, dangling me perilously close to the edge of the building.

"I'm high enough," I said.

I unfurled the flag. The wind took it immediately, almost yanked it out of my hands. I got the first pin through the flag and attached to a steel girder, but the second one took much longer. Twice the damn flag slipped through my fingers, flapping madly in the breeze, and I had to climb up and grab it out of the air again. But the top pin held firm, and soon enough I had the second attached. I did one more for good measure, then climbed down the tower.

I stood back to examine my handiwork. "How high is flag?" asked Sergei.

I was about to answer "Fifty feet" when I realized that it was more like thirty-five. Sure seemed a lot higher when I was on the tower.

"Almost forty feet," I told Sergei. "I bet you can see her from half a mile away. She's beautiful."

She was. She flew steady and true in a strong gust of wind blowing off Lake Michigan, and the red, white, and blue glowed in the bright lights of the tower.

"Welcome home, girl," I said.

Then I reached into my pocket, and turned off the device.

"Stand by," said Sergei. "Drones are picking up fresh signal."

"They better get a move on. I'm starting to freeze up here."

"They have you," said Sergei. "They are on the way."

"They're here," I said.

# XIV

Saturday, March 13th, 2083
Posted 11:51 pm by Barry Simcoe

CanadaNET1 Encrypted, Sponsored by CallMeSam.
*You know he's cheating. Find out with whom.*

Sharing is set to PRIVATE
Comments are CLOSED

The first drone came in hard from the west, bucking the wind. It soared out of the darkness like a great predatory bird, coming in close. It parked itself in the air not fifteen feet from where I stood, hovering over me, getting all up in my face.

*Look at you,* I thought. *Cocky bastard. Come in a little closer where my crowbar can reach you, you tin-plated piece of shit.*

"Surveillance algorithm is receiving visual," said Sergei.

"Yeah? Can you see me?" I waved at the drone.

"Stand by."

A second drone zoomed by on the right. This one was bigger, a little heavier, with more nasty attachments.

"Its buddy is here," I said.

"Drones have received new instructions. They are to observe only, not engage."

"That means soldiers are on the way," I said.

"You should leave."

"Roger that," I said. "I'm gone."

I hunched over and sprinted for the center of the roof. I heard the first drone spin up behind me, beginning pursuit.

I ducked behind a big metal vent and turned the device back on. I counted to five then stood up, watching the drone. It sailed right over me, beginning a search pattern among the maze of heat exchangers and vents in the middle of the roof.

*Loser,* I thought.

"I have image from drone," said Sergei.

"Yeah?" I said. "I bet I look good."

I made my way back to the door. Just before I reached it I heard a noise, on the far side of the roof. I ducked down, crawled over to a three-foot metal roof cap, and peeked over.

Half a dozen soldiers had emerged from a metal hut on the east side. They were armed and moved very quietly. The one in front was directing the two behind him with quick, silent motions. They nodded and raced west to flank the communications tower.

"Venezuela's finest are here," I said.

"Do not let them see you."

"Yeah," I said.

I crawled back to the door, squeezing through and closing it behind me as quietly as I could. I retrieved my crowbar, then started down the stairs.

There was someone standing in the doorway at the bottom. Whoever it was was short, not much more than five feet tall. The figure was nearly featureless in the shadows, but it didn't look like a soldier.

I hesitated, but only for a moment. *The only way out is through that door,* I thought. Clutching the crowbar, I strode down the stairs.

By the time I neared the bottom, I knew who it was. *Sweet baby Jesus, what the hell is she doing here?*

It was the robot from the Field Museum. She was dressed in the same dark cloak. She watched me through her inflexible mask, with its strangely painted features. She was missing the bag on her shoulder, but otherwise she looked exactly the same as at our last encounter.

"Mr. Simcoe," she said. Her head lifted slightly. "It is a pleasure to see you again."

*Shit.* The drone jammer was in my pocket, but it seemed to have no effect on her at all — just as it hadn't when I first encountered her at the Field Museum. She was staring straight at me. Whatever she was using for image recognition, it was clearly far more sophisticated than the off-board systems Black Winter and the Venezuelan drones relied on.

"What do you want?" I asked.

"You will proceed to the sixteenth floor. There you will take possession of a mobile data drive. You will take this drive to Specialist Vulka, and assist him in decrypting the contents."

I'd pretty much stopped listening after she said "Specialist Vulka." *Shit,* I thought. *That's the second time she's mentioned Sergei. We're both in it now.*

"No," I said.

She continued as if she hadn't heard me. "Specialist Vulka is mistaken in his assumptions regarding the origin of F5-117. It is not a bioengineered virus. It is much more insidious in character and genesis. There is a counteragent, but it will require time to synthesize in volume."

"I'm not going anywhere with you," I said. "I'm leaving."

I raised the crowbar, tried to assess what it would do to her. It was hard to gauge her exact body shape under the cloak, but her frame seemed delicate, almost fragile. The crowbar was reassuringly solid in my hand.

"The data includes information on the source of the F5-117 pathogen, and guidance on engineering the counteragent," she said. "But time is critical."

"Please get out of my way," I said.

Sergei stopped his constant typing. "Who are you talking to?" he said.

The robot didn't respond . . . and didn't move. Her head cocked to the left slightly, giving her an almost puzzled look.

I couldn't see her hands. The oversized sleeves of her cloak met in the center of her torso, like a monk in prayer. She could have anything hidden in there. A knife, a gun. A rocket launcher. Two steps closer, and she'd be able to put her cold robot hands around my neck.

I needed to get around her, right friggin' now. One swing from the crowbar should send her sprawling. Break that mask in half, expose what was hiding underneath. I raised it to my shoulder, gripping it with both hands.

I took a step forward. She continued to regard me, without flinching.

I took another step. She was too small to block the corridor; I pressed up against the wall and slipped past her on the right. Her cloak brushed against my legs, but her robot hands did not close around my neck.

I was in the hallway. Forty feet away was the elevator. I made for it without looking back.

"They're waiting for you," she said.

I stopped, turned around. The robot stood facing me with her hands at her sides. They were small robotic hands, with fingers that looked like tiny styluses. "I don't think so. They think I'm on the roof," I said.

"They're not sure where you are. But Colonel Hayduk is already furious that you've gotten as far as you have. He has stationed Quanta team on the first floor and sealed off the lobby. You'll be taken into custody the moment you step out of the elevators."

"I'll take my chances," I said.

"Even if you should make your way out of the building, you will not likely escape the coming outbreak. The pathogen has a nearly eighty percent fatality rate. It will reach critical exposure levels in the next twelve to fifteen days."

She began to walk toward me slowly. "I am afraid you cannot run away far enough, nor fast enough, to escape what is coming. One way or another, you decide your fate today."

Sergei hissed in my ear. "Is she speaking of pathogen? I need to hear what she is saying."

"No, we really don't," I said. I was backing up, toward the elevator.

"Specialist Vulka will require a sixty-gallon bioreactor to synthesize the counteragent. It will take several days to procure it. There is a reactor of sufficient volume available through a commercial distributor in Michigan."

"I need to hear this," Sergei said. "Please, get closer."

"Sergei—"

"Specialist Vulka will also require seven hundred gallons of high-grade solvent and a vapor extractor. He will need to procure these immediately."

"*Closer*," said Sergei.

I swore under my breath and stopped retreating. The robot continued her slow approach. There was a slight sway to her walk, like a dancer. Her hands came together demurely at her waist.

"You will find Primer Teniente Nasir on the fifteenth floor. Tell him the Catalina Mission requires Colonel Hayduk's data be secured immediately. He will hesitate; you must be as insistent and as impatient as possible."

"What kind of data?" I asked. Every instinct I had told me I should run. *Why am I wasting time listening to this?*

"Primer Teniente Nasir is terrified of authority; he will give you whatever you ask for. If you are bold, you can acquire everything you need."

She was right in front of me. One small hand reached up, and I felt her metal fingers brush against my chest.

"And you have already demonstrated that you have no problem being bold," she said.

"What data do we need?" asked Sergei.

"What data do we need?" I said.

"All of it. All of Colonel Hayduk's personal data," she said. "It contains information on the source and nature of the pathogen and the formula for the counteragent. Nasir will procure it for you."

"I can't get to the fifteenth floor without going through the lobby," I said.

"Take the elevator to the thirty-first floor. It is under construction and currently abandoned. You can drop to the twenty-ninth floor, then take the west elevator to the fifteenth."

"What about cameras?"

"I will deal with the cameras. I will digitally alter your voice and appearance in the data record so that you will not be recognized."

Her fingers tugged the scarf away from my face. "You will not need this."

I took her fingers in my hand, removed them from my scarf. They were cold and hard.

"The soldiers are not your primary concern," she said. "You will meet a hostile intelligence on the sixteenth floor. Its designation is Standing Mars. It is a dangerous opponent, and it will kill you if it finds you."

"Why are you doing this?"

"We share an enemy, Mr. Simcoe."

"Who is that?"

She seemed about to answer, then paused. Her body froze for a brief moment.

"The situation has changed," she said. "You must hurry. You can still escape the Sturgeon Building, but to do so requires that you get under way immediately."

"Who are you?"

"Immediately, Mr. Simcoe."

"Not until you tell me who you are."

"My designation will mean nothing to you, I'm afraid. You may call me Jacaranda."

"You're a machine," I said, just before I remembered where I'd heard the name *Jacaranda*.

From Black Winter. It was one of the things he'd babbled when he'd been semiconscious. *Find Jacaranda, and the Network of Winds. They can stop it. They can keep you alive.*

I felt a chill touch my spine. Black Winter hadn't just been babbling. Jacaranda was real, and she was standing right in front of me. What the hell did that mean?

If Jacaranda was real, did that mean the Bodner-Levitt extermination was real as well? It was past time I learned what that meant.

"I am not a machine intelligence, as you understand them, no," she said. "And now, you must leave."

"But you're working with one. Who is the Network of Winds?"

I've never seen a robot looked startled before. Their brains process millions of instructions per second. For a robot to look startled, you have to knock them for a loop for literally a couple million cycles.

Jacaranda was wearing a mask, and she still managed to look startled. She took a step back, looking me up and down. "How do you know that?"

Without another word, I turned my back on her and strode to the elevator.

"Who *was* that?" Sergei said.

"Not now," I said.

The elevator door opened as soon as I hit the button. Before I could take a step forward, I heard the door at the top of the stairs slam open.

Soldiers. They moved quickly down the stairs and into the hallway, shouting crisply to each other in Spanish. Like bloodhounds on a scent trail, they began moving down the hall.

I ducked into the elevator, punched the button for the lobby.

The doors remained open. I heard voices, getting closer.

I found the Door Close button, jammed it about a dozen times. Slowly, leisurely, the elevator doors began to close.

A shout, absurdly close. The sound of feet, running toward the elevator.

The doors closed. For a moment the elevator hung, suspended, while I listened to more muffled shouts through the metal doors. Then it began to descend.

"*Jesus,*" I said. "Sergei?"

"Here. What is your status?"

"I'm okay. Headed for the lobby. Listen — are there soldiers in the lobby? More soldiers than before, I mean?"

"I do not know. My access to search algorithm has been suspended. All information on Sturgeon Building has now been blocked. Even public video feeds showing outside of building are now restricted."

I watched the progress of the elevator. We were passing the forty-sixth floor. The forty-fourth. "What does that mean?"

"Uncertain. Search for you has taken on new urgency. Secure protocol has been put in place."

The fortieth floor. "Is it likely the lobby has been locked down?"

"Possibly. If so, is important you avoid lobby."

*Crap.* We were passing the thirty-eighth floor. "How do I get out without going through the lobby?"

Sergei began working his machines. "Give me a moment."

"I'm seconds away from the lobby, Sergei. Do I go or abort?"

"A moment."

The thirty-fifth floor. The thirty-third.

I reached out, and punched the button for thirty-one.

There was an immediate *ding,* and the elevator slowed. The doors opened. I got out and watched the doors close behind me. The elevator resumed its journey.

"Yes," said Sergei. "You should avoid lobby."

"I'm way ahead of you. What's the word?"

"I cannot access information on secure protocols for Sturgeon Building, but have queried protocols for this hotel. There is only one that requires semiautonomous algorithms be locked out—and that one also requires lobby to be secured with at least two platoons."

"Fast thinking, Sergei," I said. "So if the same protocol was just put in place here, it means Quanta team has been sent to the lobby. She was telling the truth."

"Who is Quanta?"

"Team of soldiers in the lobby. Keep up, Sergei."

"Who was telling the truth?"

"The super-creepy robot that ambushed me on the fifty-ninth floor. Same one I saw at the Field Museum. The one messing around with the dinosaurs."

"She recognized you?"

"Sure did."

"What is she doing in Sturgeon Building?"

"I have no friggin' clue," I said. "She mentioned your name again, though. She referred to you as 'Specialist Vulka.'"

"That is disturbing. She was speaking of pathogen. What did she say?"

"I don't know. A lot. She wouldn't shut up."

"This is critical information. You must remember what she told you."

"She said you were on the wrong track with its origin. It's not a bioengineered virus; it's something worse."

"Worse? What is worse?"

"How the hell should I know? I'm still trying to figure out how she knows I have a dog."

I took a look around. The floor was dark and wholly abandoned. There were no walls, just great sheets of translucent plastic hanging down from metal beams. I could see the nearby buildings and the lights of the city through the distant windows — those not blocked by plastic or girders, anyway. The floor was bare concrete, and dark stacks of lumber and equipment were piled near the elevators. A broom lay on the floor not three feet away, next to a workman's satchel.

"If she is working with Venezuelans," Sergei said, "then our efforts are for nothing."

"Yeah, I figured that out. Let's hope she's not."

"What is 'Network of Winds'?" Sergei asked.

I winced. I'd been hoping he hadn't caught that. I couldn't reveal where I'd heard of the Network of Winds without telling Sergei about Black Winter's episode of semiconsciousness, and that would violate my promise to Black Winter. "We'll talk about that later. Did you hear her mention the colonel? Who is he? And why does he have information on the virus? What does that mean?"

"Colonel Hayduk is ranking officer in Chicago district with Venezuelan Military Intelligence. If they are tracking progress of virus outbreak, he will have information."

"Yeah, but why is he the one with data on its origin? That's suspicious, to say the least."

"We will not know unless we see data."

"Did you catch any of what she said about cooking up a counter-agent?" My fingers went to the pouch at my neck reflexively, making sure my recorder was still there. I might not be able to remember everything Jacaranda had just told me, but I had a digital record I could play for Sergei.

"Some, yes. I can start search for bioreactor and vaporizer. But we need formula."

"I know. That data she mentioned is on the sixteenth floor. That's smack-dab in the middle of Venezuelan Military Intelligence HQ. She's sending me right into the lion's den."

"It is too dangerous," said Sergei. "You will be arrested for certain."

"Maybe. You found me a way out yet?"

"Not yet." I heard him resume typing. "There are options, but I need time. Where are you now?"

"Thirty-first floor. I'm safe for the time being."

"Were soldiers in pursuit on roof?"

"Yeah. They nearly caught me at the elevator."

"They will be in communication with lobby. They will find where elevator stopped, very soon. You need to find stairs."

"Got it. Hang on."

I picked a direction and started moving. There were enough sheets of translucent plastic to form an impressive maze, and in places it was so dark I couldn't see what I was stepping on. After a few minutes I pushed my way through a plastic wall and nearly tumbled headfirst through a huge hole in the floor.

"Damn," I said, grabbing a nearby steel beam to steady myself.

"Problem?" said Sergei.

"Not really," I said. I looked around. "Looks like the construction team was mixing concrete or something up here and then lowering it to the next level through a hole in the floor. I very nearly walked into it."

"Be careful," Sergei said needlessly.

"Thanks."

It wasn't hard to get around the hole, but I kept a much closer eye on the floor after that. A few minutes later I located the west stairwell.

"Made it to the stairs," I told Sergei.

"Excellent. Proceed to twenty-first floor. Is also under construction; it should be safe to rest and hide while we plan exit."

"Not so fast. The stairs are locked up."

"Locked?"

"Yeah. I can't get inside the stairwell."

"Can you break lock?"

"It's not a padlock on a chain this time, Sergei. The door is locked. I'd have to smash through it."

"How long will it take?"

I assessed the heavy metal door and the weight of the crowbar in my hands. It didn't look promising.

"It's not going to happen," I said. "It'll take forever and make such a racket I'll have a dozen soldiers on top of me long before that."

"Soldiers will be there soon regardless," said Sergei. "You must get through door."

I looked back the way I'd come, thinking. "I'm not sure I do."

"Explain."

"Something she said. The robot. She said I had to 'drop' to the twenty-ninth floor. Not walk. Drop."

"You mean the hole."

I headed back toward the middle of the floor. "Yeah, I mean the hole."

It was a lot harder to locate the second time than it should have been. I walked around that confusing maze, peering around dirty sheets of plastic, playing hide-and-seek with the damn hole for over five minutes before finding it again.

Twice I glimpsed dark, robotic figures in the shadows. The first one turned out to be a boiler; the second startled me so badly I jumped back three feet before I realized it was just a long coat, dangling from a short ceiling wire.

"Are you all right?" Sergei asked.

"Yeah," I said. "Just a little jumpy."

Jacaranda had told me I'd need to keep an eye out for a hostile intelligence named Standing Mars. But she'd also said I wouldn't run into it until the sixteenth floor. I put the thought of deadly robots out of my head and concentrated on the matter at hand.

When I found the hole, I looked over the edge at the floor below. It was covered with dark lumps, uneven piles concealed by shadowy tarps, and countless indistinct shadows.

"Can you climb down safely?" Sergei asked.

"Working on it."

On the other side of the hole was the winch they used to lower vats of concrete or something equally heavy to the floor below. It looked more or less climbable, if I could get there safely. The fastest route was around the rim of the hole, but that wasn't a clean route. There were several girders and other obstructions that would require me to make jumps of three feet or more. Easy to miss in the dark, and the consequences would be a long fall onto a pile of rubble.

I turned around, back into the maze. This time I cut through the plastic, making a shortcut around the hole. Within four minutes I was on the other side, next to the winch.

I reached out, grabbed the chain. It dangled over the hole, attached to a pulley overhead. I put a little weight on it. It slid for an inch or two, making an almost musical clattering, then locked up. It took all the weight I dared put on it, leaning out nearly four feet from the edge.

"Okay. I got a way down. I need to —"

From somewhere not that far away came a soft *ping,* and the sound of sliding metal.

Elevator doors opening.

I let go of the chain and hunkered down at the edge of the hole, making myself as small and as invisible as I could. Listening.

There was no sound at all. No footsteps, no voices. Not even elevator doors closing. The seconds stretched out.

"Barry?" said Sergei.

"*Shhhh,*" I whispered.

Somewhere to my left was a soft clattering. Someone had accidentally kicked the broom. I heard a low curse.

They were here. With no further ceremony, I grabbed the chain and kicked away from the edge, swinging out over the hole.

Too much motion. The chain clattered loudly — far too loudly — as it swung underneath me. My legs kicked uselessly, trying to wrap around it, get some support. But all I managed was more noise.

I climbed down. Hand over hand over hand. The greasy links of the chain were hard to hold, and twice I almost lost my grip. But oddly enough, once I was in motion the chain was less noisy. I kept my legs rigid, let my arms take my weight, and dropped rapidly down to the lower floor.

The chain was attached to a great metal vat. I landed there first, then slipped off the rim and nearly went sprawling, whacking my ankle painfully against the side. I climbed down until I reached the floor, where there was plenty of throbbing pain as I hobbled away into the darkness, as quickly and quietly as I could.

*Ow,* I thought. *Ow, ow, son of a bitch ooww.*

This floor had fewer walls of translucent plastic, for which I was grateful. It made orienting myself a little easier. The floor was jammed up with crap, though — piles of tubing, lumber, great crates containing heat exchangers, shiny venting, sheets of drywall. It was like stumbling through a hardware store at midnight.

Before I hobbled too far I stopped and took stock of the situation. Listening quietly, I could now hear voices above. I couldn't tell if they were getting closer to the hole, but they were definitely on the move.

*Drop down to the twenty-ninth floor,* I thought. *She said, drop down to the twenty-ninth floor.*

"Barry?"

"Here, Sergei," I said, as quietly as possible. "I'm on the thirtieth floor. I found a chain and managed to climb down."

"Good. Find stairway, quickly."

"I'm looking for another hole."

"Hole? Why?"

"The robot. She said to drop down to the twenty-ninth floor. I think she expected me to do this twice."

"I am not certain you should trust guidance from robot. We do not know who she is."

"I know what you mean. But she was right about the first drop—I got away just ahead of the soldiers."

"Soldiers are in pursuit again?"

"Yeah. I can hear them on the floor above. They'll be here soon, too."

"You do not have time to search for hole that may not exist."

"I'm looking for a way out of here, and I'll take the first one I find— stairs, hole, or magic unicorn."

There were so many piles of construction supplies that it was nearly as much of a maze as the upper level. But in a matter of minutes I found what I was looking for.

"There *is* a second hole, Sergei." It was about forty feet west of the first and looked down at the twenty-ninth floor.

"Fortunate."

"I'll tell you what's fortunate—there's a ladder."

That ladder felt like luxury. It was stable, completely quiet, and I didn't bruise any bones on the way down. I made it to the twenty-ninth floor and had actually taken half a dozen steps away when I reversed course and returned for the ladder.

"What are you doing?" Sergei asked, as he listened to me huff and grunt.

"Moving the damn ladder. If they want to follow me, they're going to have to jump."

I stashed the ladder behind a four-foot-high roll of plastic wrap next to the west stairwell. When I was done, I tried the stairwell door. It was locked, which didn't surprise me.

I returned to the hole and listened. Nothing. Either the soldiers hadn't yet figured out where I'd gone, or they were following very, very quietly. Either way, I couldn't waste any more time here.

The robot had been right about access to the twenty-ninth floor. Her info hadn't given me much of a head start, but I was in a better situation than I'd been in fifteen minutes ago.

I was at a decision point. Continue trying to escape . . . or go after the data?

"How are we doing on an exit, Sergei?"

"Not good. I assume Sturgeon Building is following similar protocol as one I have. If so, all exits will be locked down and guarded."

"Shit. For how long?"

"Until protocol is lifted. I am working on alternative exit."

"Alternative exit?"

"Sturgeon Building has two sublevels. Both have access to municipal service tunnels. There are several possibilities. Best is perhaps heating duct. Duct has several exits. But access may be . . . difficult."

Heating ducts. "You're still working off that twelve-year-old map?"

"Da."

"And you see difficulties?"

"Not insurmountable. But we need time to plan."

What was I supposed to be doing while Sergei planned? Hiding out here and hoping the soldiers didn't find me?

I took a deep breath. "Okay. Change of plans, Sergei. I'm taking the elevator to the fifteenth floor. I'm going after the data."

"Barry . . . I do not think that is advisable."

"I know. But you need time to plan, and I can't just hang around here waiting to be caught. Besides, if that data is what she says it is, it's worth the risk—you know that. It's worth almost *any* risk. There's no point either of us saving our own skins if that pathogen remains unchecked another five weeks."

"That does not mean this is best way to get it."

"Maybe not. But we're not going to get another chance like this, and that robot was right about one thing—time is seriously running out. And who knows? Maybe this is the perfect time to go after the data. The Venezuelans are crawling all over the goddamn building, looking for me. Last place they're going to check is their own HQ."

"We do not know who robot is or who she is working for. We do not know what data is or if it is encrypted. We do not know what to expect on fifteenth floor. We do not know what is 'Standing Mars.'"

"Yeah, actually, we know what it is. It's some kind of badass soldier-bot."

"There are too many unknowns. With luck, you may have avoided cameras so far. But you cannot avoid camera at HQ. If you step out of elevator on fifteenth floor, you will be identified."

"True. Unless the robot can do what she says—digitally obfuscate my image."

"She would require unrestricted access to Venezuelan digital systems to accomplish. I do not believe that is credible."

"Well, she seems to have unrestricted access to the Sturgeon Building. That's a good sign. Sergei, we're not getting out of here without taking some big risks. At the moment, this one looks like our best option."

"Even if she can access data network, we do not know her motives."

"If she wanted to turn me over to the soldiers, she could have done so long ago. Right now, that's enough for me to trust her. I'm going to do this, and I need your help. Are you with me?"

"Yes, of course."

"Good, because we have other things to worry about. The robot may know who you are, but the Venezuelans don't. At least not yet. It's possible I'm already caught in a trap, and they're just stringing me along to find out who else is involved. To catch you. You know that, right?"

"We are a team, my friend. Your fate is my fate."

"I appreciate the sentiment. But if I'm caught, I want you to unplug. Get off the air, before they can track you."

"Barry . . ." Sergei's voice softened. "If you are caught, you will tell them everything. And soon. You will not endure Venezuelan interrogation for long."

That was a chilling thought. And probably one that I shouldn't dwell on. But Sergei was almost certainly right. Technically, my status as a foreign national with a nonaligned country offered me at least nominal protection and would shield me from illegal detainment and interrogation. But if I were caught creeping around Venezuelan Military Intelligence headquarters, all bets were off. I'd be detained and probably tortured, and I would never see daylight again.

"Whatever happens, we are in this together," Sergei said.

"Yeah," I admitted. "Maybe you're right. All right. I'm headed for the elevators."

"What is first step?"

"I'm supposed to go to the fifteenth floor . . . find a guy named Nasir. A first lieutenant."

"He has data?"

"Yes."

"He will not simply give you data."

"I'm supposed to bully him, tell him . . ." Crap. What the hell was I supposed to tell him? "Right, I remember. The Catalina Mission needs to secure the data. I'm supposed to be impatient and a bastard. That part could be fun, actually."

"You have credentials for mission?"

"Credentials? No, I don't even know what it is."

"Catalina Mission is military mobile laboratory. Very secret. You will not pass as representative of mission without credentials."

"Huh. Secret military labs . . . they're *always* interesting. Maybe our friend Jacaranda wants something from the mission? If there's a plausible reason for her to want access to the lab, then maybe there's a plausible reason for her to help us."

"That is weak logic."

"At least it's logic. Five minutes ago, we were counting on luck."

I made it to the elevators. The twenty-ninth floor was the top floor of the lower division; this bank of elevators would only go down. I punched the button; thirty seconds later, an elevator arrived.

I stepped inside, pressed the button for the fifteenth floor. As the elevator got under way, I slowly unwound the scarf around my face, and put it in my backpack. Then I pulled off my cap and goggles and ran my hand through my hair.

I stood up straight, glancing up to the left, where I assumed the cameras were. I gave them a wide smile.

*We're all in now,* I thought. *One way or the other.*

# XV

Sunday, March 14th, 2083
Posted 1:08 am by Barry Simcoe

CanadaNET1 Encrypted, Sponsored by TripMistress.
*Get alerts on fast-changing borders and political situations while you travel!*

Sharing is set to PRIVATE
Comments are CLOSED

The elevator stopped, and I stepped out into chaos on the fifteenth floor.

I was in a small vestibule with a reception area. Magnetically locked doors sealed it off from the rest of the floor. The walls were glass, and I could see almost the whole floor. Surprisingly, it looked much like any other government office I'd ever seen—a great many cramped cubes, a small number of high-walled offices, and a few open areas. I glimpsed maybe half a dozen people walking quickly in the halls between cubes. It was after midnight; didn't these people ever take a break from the tedious work of occupying a foreign country?

I'd have to ponder that mystery some other time. The reception desk was deserted, but the vestibule was crammed with around ten soldiers, all waiting to board the elevator. They spared me no more than a glance. I was barely out of the way when they muscled their way inside. They were on a mission and anxious to get to it.

One of their number shouted something in Spanish to a woman in uniform by the door. She nodded, pulling open the glass door and yelling at someone down the hall.

There was an answering call, and a young man came running, his arms heavy with gear. She held the glass door open for him.

The elevator was closing. The soldier held it open, calling impatiently. The two raced into the elevator, and the doors slid closed.

The glass door leading to the offices was also closing. I took three quick steps and grabbed it before the magnetic lock engaged. I slipped through, into the supposedly secure fifteenth floor.

"I'm on the floor," I told Sergei. "Security is a joke. The reception desk isn't even manned."

"There will not be secure data on that floor," said Sergei. "Likely, it is administrative only."

"Maybe." I started walking down the hall, trying to look like I belonged. "Let's see what we find."

The trick to looking like you belong is to move quickly and with purpose. Don't gawk, always be in a hurry, and know where you're going. Accordingly, I moved briskly down the hall, turning left without hesitating when I ran out of hallway. I strode down the thin path without turning my head left or right.

What I found was about a hundred and eighty cubes and maybe fifty heads. There was a definite air of excitement. Something was up. People were gathered in the aisles between cubes or hunched over monitors in small groups. No one was in uniform. A woman dashed out of a conference room, grabbed a small tablet, ran back. Small teams shouted back and forth.

Too late I noticed that the path I was on led me toward two soldiers stationed outside a high-walled office. They noticed me the same instant I noticed them. I hesitated, just for a fraction of a second, and then continued forward resolutely. Hesitation was death.

I kept my eyes fixed straight ahead, using my peripheral vision to scan for an exit. There were windows on my right and five or six high-walled offices on my left, most of them dark and with doors closed. Past the soldiers there was a narrow corridor leading off to the right, toward a small cafeteria.

Both soldiers were staring at me now. I gave them a nod as I approached, allowed my gaze to casually drift right. A sharp right turn just ahead of the soldiers, and I could make for the cafeteria.

One of the guards stepped forward, signaled me to stop. I did. He asked me something in Spanish, too fast for me to follow.

"Primer Teniente Nasir," I said.

"Nasir?" the guard repeated. He looked toward the other guard, who shrugged.

The first guard turned back toward me. His manner was still courteous, but a little too attentive for my liking. He repeated his question in Spanish.

"Primer Teniente Nasir," I said stubbornly.

That was my plan. To repeat that name every time they asked a question. It felt good to have a plan.

A man strode out of one of the offices to my left. "I am Nasir," he said. He was about forty-five, rail thin, with a rumpled uniform and two days' worth of beard. He spoke slowly and deliberately, with an Arabic accent.

The guards were as surprised as me. I recovered first. "I'm from the Catalina Mission," I told Nasir. "My name is Peters."

"Ah—excellent," he said. "Thank you for coming so quickly." He waved me into his office.

The guards weren't done with me yet. The one who'd been talking to me barked something at Nasir in Spanish. Nasir, who seemed to struggle with Spanish almost as much as I did, furrowed his brow and agreed with a nod and wave of his hand, then closed the door.

"I apologize for the state of the office," he said as he walked around his desk to take a seat. I wasn't sure if he was talking about his own small office, which was neat and smelled of coffee and sweat, or the entire fifteenth floor. "We are dealing with an intruder."

"I was informed. He hasn't been caught?" I said.

"Not yet, but soon. He was on the roof—there are only so many places one can go from the roof."

He sure had that right. But his words were a reminder that I probably shouldn't dawdle, regardless of how refreshing it was to chat with a soldier who wasn't trying to shoot me.

"I'm here to secure the colonel's data," I said. Sergei had mentioned the colonel's name, and I mentally kicked myself for having forgotten it already. Hayworth? Hayfield? "The mission feels it is no longer safe."

"Oh, I agree," said Nasir. He seemed genuinely relieved at my words. "I sent a message to ComSec just fifteen minutes ago. I agree completely."

Wow. That was interesting. Fifteen minutes ago this poor sap sent a warning about the safety of crucial data, and five minutes later a robot on the roof knew all about it. It looked like our friend Jacaranda had precisely the kind of access to the Venezuelan network that she claimed.

"The data needs to be moved off-site," I said. "Immediately."

"Well, I'm not certain the colonel would approve—"

"We'll deal with the matter of the colonel's approval later. You agree the data is not safe here?"

"Not at the moment, no. But—"

"Lieutenant Nasir, we are in a highly volatile situation. We have an intruder in the building. No one knows where he is, who he is, or what he's after. But in my experience, intruders are usually after the most critical data. If you agree, then I'm afraid I must insist on a copy of the data immediately."

"The data cannot be copied," Nasir said, a little taken aback. "It is on a secure, non-networked drive. It can only be accessed from the sixteenth floor."

Whoops. Of course it was. I should've known that. "Don't assume the data cannot be copied, regardless of your precautions," I said, trying to recover. *After a stumble, always go on the attack,* my Stratford debate coach used to say.

"Of course, of course," said Nasir, dutifully swallowing that line of bullshit.

"Let me see the data," I said.

"Of course," he said. "This way."

Nasir led me out past the guards, who were in conversation with a couple of women who'd come out of the conference room. They barely glanced at us. Nasir led me to a stairwell, which he unlocked. We ascended the stairs.

The sixteenth floor had wholly different security apparatus. There was a guard stationed outside the door, and both a security keypad and a retina scanner. Nasir identified himself to the guard, then bent over and let the scanner flash his eye.

Nasir's picture popped up in blue and white on a small display next to the scanner. The text below the image read:

E. NASIR

Nasir stepped back, blinking, waiting for me to do the same.

"Ah," I said. Both the soldier and Nasir waited expectantly. A red light on the scanner strobed, twice per second.

I leaned over until my head was almost level with the scanner. "Ah . . . what is the make of this scanner?" I asked.

"¿Qué?" said the guard.

"The retina scanner for the door," I said. "Who is the manufacturer?"

The guard spoke to Nasir in Spanish. "It is a standard scanner," said Nasir. "It is the same as you have at the mission."

"I'm not so certain," I said.

Sergei's voice was in my ear. "They are asking you to submit to retina scan?"

"Yes," I said. "I'm just not so certain."

"Do not agree to retina scan," Sergei said, his voice urgent. "They are one hundred percent effective. You will be immediately identified. Cameras will not matter after that."

The guard was giving me the stink-eye. Nasir was speaking to him in Spanish, but the guard was largely ignoring him. He walked over to me, poked two fingers at my eyes, and then jabbed the same fingers into the scanner. The message was obvious: *Scan your goddamn retina.*

I said nothing, just looked the guard up and down with what I sincerely hope was a look of detached amusement while I stalled.

My options were pretty clear. I could run. I could try to overpower the guard. Or I could scan my goddamn retina.

No options at all, really. I smiled, bent over, and let the machine flash my retina.

There was a slight delay while the machine confirmed my identity. I blinked away the afterimage, waiting for my name to appear on the display.

The brief delay gave me time I desperately needed to think. In a second the words B. SIMCOE were going to appear on that wall. The guard wouldn't be alarmed by that, not immediately. But Nasir might, considering I'd told him my name was Peters.

What would Nasir do then? Sound the alarm? Perhaps not, if I could prepare him in advance. It was a one-in-a-thousand shot, but if I could just—

My image popped up on the display. A decent-enough shot of me, looking surprisingly sharp in a Venezuelan uniform. Below the image was my name:

D. PETERS

The door buzzed open.

"Gracias, Capitán Peters," said the guard.

"Damn," I whispered, despite myself.

"This way," said Nasir.

Nasir hadn't noticed anything untoward. Sergei, however, shared my surprise. "Venezuelan retina scanner on sixteenth floor has identified you as Peters?" he asked, incredulous.

"Yes," I said.

"That is not possible."

"Indeed," I said. I smiled cheerfully at Nasir as he glanced back at me.

"One minute," said Sergei. There was rapid typing.

Nasir led me into the sixteenth floor. It looked very different from the floor below—it was darker, far more cramped, with plenty of locked offices. If there were windows, they'd been thoroughly screened off. I didn't see any people at all. Most of the floor seemed to be taken up with tall machines, blinking in lonely isolation in secure glass enclosures. The entire floor seemed bathed in a dim green light, like the interior of a submarine.

Nasir threaded through narrow corridors and stopped in front of a sealed glass enclosure. It was larger than most of the others. Inside were no less than four computational towers, a portable communications array, a heavy hazmat suit hanging from the ceiling, two cabinets, and several less-identifiable objects.

Nasir was fingering something around his neck nervously. It looked like an electronic key.

"This is the colonel's?" I said, nodding at the sealed compartment.

Nasir nodded.

"Open it," I said.

"Only Colonel Hayduk can—"

Hayduk! That was the asshole's name. "Lieutenant Nasir, please don't waste my time," I said. "The colonel informed me you could get me everything I need. Now, please. Open the compartment."

Nasir hesitated for a second, then pulled the key out from around his neck. He held it against the glass wall to the side of the door. A section of the glass glowed bright green. I saw a brief flash of text on the wall, and the door popped open.

"Peters, Damian," Sergei said in my ear. "Capitán. He is in the AGRT personnel records. He has your photo."

"Fascinating," I said as I entered the compartment, looking around.

"A complete record of military service. Commendations from four previous COs. Detailed medical history . . . a concussion, suffered during a soccer game. An ear infection in 2077. Expat assignment to America, January 2083. Posted to Catalina Mission, under Major Carlos Arrente."

I heard Sergei rock back in his chair. "It is a flawless forgery. I do not understand how this has been done. If robot has accomplished this, she has access to Venezuelan military network at the highest levels. And your personal biometric data."

"Yes," I said. "Quite a surprise." For Nasir's benefit, I glanced around, as if commenting on the décor.

It was cramped in here. In addition to all the computational hardware, the colonel had added a few homey touches as well. There was a small wooden desk with two charging stations for mobile devices, some personal data equipment, and a mat on the floor with three pairs of leather shoes. There was a rag neatly folded beside a can of polish next to the shoes. Apparently the colonel liked his shoes freshly shined.

Given all the equipment, I thought I might have to rely on Nasir to point me in the direction of the data. But the moment I walked in, it was obvious what I was looking for.

Right next to the desk was a high-security personal data station. Before this one, I'd only seen pictures. They're ideal for the paranoid multimillionaire or security-conscious CEO. In essence, they give you everything you need from a modern network portal . . . everything except a connection to the network. They are completely isolated from any kind of network access. They're unhackable because you can't access them — not without being in the same room. The only way to talk to one of these babies is by standing right in front of them.

There were a number of ports on the front where I could plug into the thing, if I had a mobile computer. And if I knew the right access protocols, and if I knew what I was looking for.

Luckily, there was a convenient shortcut. I pulled out the sole data module jutting out of the port hub. It was tiny, about the size of a pocketknife, and felt nicely cool in my hand.

"This is the data?" I asked Nasir.

He nodded.

"It is encrypted?"

Nasir nodded again.

I sighed, glancing around. "I can see why you were so concerned. I consider the security on this floor inadequate."

"I would be happy to show you our security precautions in more detail," he said. "They are above ComSec standards for the prevention of data theft."

"Theft? It's not theft I'm worried about. It's destruction."

That seemed to be the right thing to say. Nasir dropped his eyes. He nodded quickly. "Yes. Yes. The floor is vulnerable to attack."

Nasir seemed personally embarrassed by this admission. It's always the responsible employees who feel bad for organizational inadequacy. He deserved to be congratulated for correctly identifying a serious IT flaw, and instead he got only grief. Typical.

"An attack like the one going on *right now*," I said, raising my voice. "An intruder has penetrated the most secure building in the state and has had free and unrestricted access for—" I glanced at my watch. "Twenty-two minutes. That's more than adequate time to place explosive devices in critical positions around the entire building."

"Perhaps he's already been apprehended—"

"And perhaps monkeys are about to fly out of my ass," I said.

I held up the data stick in front of his face. "I am taking the data into my personal custody, for transport to the Catalina Mission."

"I will need Colonel Hayduk's personal authorization—"

"As you wish." I slipped the data stick into the breast pocket of my jacket. "I expected him here. Where is the colonel?"

"He has taken charge of the search for the intruder."

"So you are unaware of his current whereabouts? Or his safety?"

Another jackpot. Nasir's eyes flew just that little bit wider. Damn, this guy felt inadequate about everything.

I felt terrible for doing this. But I had to if I had any hope of getting out of this building alive. I took a step closer, right into his personal space. "Lieutenant Nasir," I said, "I urge you, in the highest possible terms, to locate Colonel Hayduk and confirm his personal well-being. Secondly, I suggest you inform him of the steps being taken to secure his data, in the light of the entirely inadequate situation here."

"Yes, sir. You will remain here?"

"Yes, but I expect you'll be quick while—"

I stopped. I'd been glancing around the enclosure casually, trying to give the impression of someone who was settling in for a brief stay, when my eyes fell on the hazmat suit hanging in the back.

Nasir was talking. And talking. But I barely heard a word.

I stepped toward the suit. It was hanging on a heavy metal rod. It was roughly six feet tall, very nearly a one-piece suit. All that was missing were the boots.

But it wasn't a hazmat suit. "Is that what I think it is?" I asked.

"Yes," he said. There was pride in his voice.

"A suit of American power armor? Is it functional?"

"Yes, but it has only recently been retasked. Just two days ago, as a matter of fact. They are keyed to individuals, as you probably know. The colonel spared no effort to have the software locks on this one removed. It is ready for testing."

I've never even seen a photo of American combat armor, not even a blurry one. All I've seen are the same shaky combat vids as everyone else. There's the famous one from just before the end of the war, taken by a civilian at one of the last engagements, in Stone Mountain, Georgia. Just a twenty-five-second clip, shot at long range with a shaky hand. It shows an unidentified American officer, wearing one of these suits, taking down an Argentinean Rodolfo Walsh combat robot, virtually single-handed.

One six-foot guy with a rifle, versus a 2,500-pound killing machine. He'd made it look almost easy.

Even today, there are folks who claim that if the American government had had another two months to get the armor into wide production, it would have changed the outcome of the entire war. As it was, the provisions of the Memphis Ceasefire had strictly forbidden either side from making or possessing powered combat armor.

I was looking at physical evidence of a gross violation of the Memphis Ceasefire. That was more than enough to have my shoe-polishing nemesis Colonel Hayduk arrested.

It was also my ticket out of here.

"They magnify your strength, many times," Nasir said in a confidential tone. "They assist in weapons targeting, communications — and much more that we do not yet fully understand."

"Now I know what the colonel meant," I said, reaching up to touch the suit. It felt rubbery to the touch, like a wet suit. But heavier, more stiff. I expected bulges at the joints, muscle-enhancing power units, but the suit seemed almost completely smooth. It looked tailored, more like something you'd find in a sporting goods store than in an armory.

"The colonel spoke to you of the suit?" Nasir said, disbelief in his eyes.

"No, not as such. He simply said he had secure transport for his critical data, here in this compartment."

I faced Nasir. The smile on my lips was completely unforced.

"Lieutenant Nasir, I do not think we need to worry about the colonel's whereabouts. Based on his last communication to me, I believe he will be here shortly, to take charge of the data personally. I need you to return downstairs and contact the Quanta team, and the rest of the soldiers outside, and inform them that the colonel will be exiting the building, outfitted with the American combat suit."

Nasir looked flabbergasted.

"That is . . ." he said. He trailed off, staring up at the suit.

"It's certainly bold," I said with admiration. "Typical of the colonel."

"You are certain he is coming?"

"Yes, now that I understand what his comments meant."

"He will likely want both power cores."

"Yes, of course."

Nasir was hesitating. He looked unconvinced. I needed to get this bit of theater wrapped up.

"You will want to confirm with the colonel, of course," I said.

"Yes." He seemed relieved to hear me say it.

"Understandable. Send the message to the soldiers, then return here. We will keep the data secure and wait for the colonel's arrival."

"You will remain here?"

"Yes."

Nasir nodded, taking his key from around his neck again. "I will need to lock you inside."

*Shit.* I hadn't thought that part through. "As you wish," I said, keeping my voice even.

Nasir left without another word. He closed the door behind him, sealing it with the key. I watched him moving briskly toward the elevators.

The instant he was out of eyesight, I took down the suit. It was a thrill just to hold it. Who hasn't dreamed of possessing an American combat suit?

It looked like it might fit me, although it had been designed for someone maybe an inch or two shorter. The fabric seemed stretchable enough. Pinned to the front was a pair of matching gloves. The rest of it was one piece, except for the missing boots. Tucked inside it was a mask that covered the face and head. The eyepieces for the mask were dark green, like tinted sunglasses. I hoped I'd be able to see when I put it on.

But first things first. I needed those boots.

I began by searching the floor. I found a large metal suitcase and popped it open.

Inside was a sidearm, set into a recessed case. It looked like a Werner heavy caliber, but with a shorter stock. There were two boxes of ammunition. Whatever it was, it sure as hell wasn't Venezuelan standard issue.

Seemed like the colonel liked exotic handguns. It was much too heavy to just tuck under my shirt. I lifted the case onto the desk and started rooting under it and then through the cabinets. *Come on, where the hell do you hide a pair of boots?*

I found them in the bottom drawer of the second cabinet, the only drawer that wasn't locked. They were black, knee-height, and heavy. Almost too heavy—the soles felt like three-quarter inches of solid metal.

I took a deep breath before forcing my feet into the boots. An ill-fitting suit I could fake. But this whole plan went nowhere if these boots were a size six.

They were not a size six. They weren't an exact fit either, but they weren't too bad. I clomped around in them in the small enclosure and decided they felt okay.

I had to take the boots off to climb into the suit. That was a tight fit—it's pretty clear the suit was meant to be worn over nothing but skin, but I wasn't about to leave all my clothes behind for Hayduk and his cronies to harvest for DNA evidence. The jacket had to come off, but once it did I was able to squeeze into the suit.

I pulled the boots back on and then walked around a bit. It was tight at the shoulders and crotch, but I could live with it. But I certainly didn't feel enhanced or anything like it.

The suit was unpowered. In the small of my back I found two empty slots where power cells clearly fit in.

The power cores. That's what Nasir had meant when he said the colonel would likely want both power cores. Without them, this wasn't going to be a graceful exit. The suit wouldn't power up, and would be about as "enhancing" as a clown suit.

Nasir would be back in minutes—maybe seconds. I didn't have time to look for the cores, but I did anyway. I opened every desk drawer I could, looked on top of the comm towers, and even pried the lid off the colonel's can of shoe polish. Nothing.

I was debating smashing open the locked drawers on the desk when I heard a sound.

It came from outside the enclosure. Sort of a *clank*, like a heavy footstep. I stopped searching and grabbed the mask, which I'd set on top of the nearest cabinet.

The sound came again . . . and then again. Whatever it was, it was getting closer.

I debated pulling on the mask, but it was too dark in here to trust being able to see through its dark eyepieces. Instead, I reached for my backpack, stuffing my jacket and scarf back inside, next to my goggles. The data drive was tucked into my breast pocket, under the suit. I was ready to move.

I saw it then, through the glass wall. Tall and dark and angular, lum-

bering down the corridor between the enclosures. A robot, a field combat model, easily eight feet tall, maybe 1,800 pounds, about 400 of which
were in its massive head, which was long and torpedo-shaped. It had two
great hands, and it moved like a huge metal ape. It had just enough grace
to bend its arms slightly, to avoid dragging its knuckles on the floor.

It stopped in front of the colonel's enclosure, shifting its bulk to face me
through the glass.

I still had the drone jammer in my pocket, and it was still on, as far as I
knew. But the robot facing me was clearly aware of me. Like Jacaranda, it
obviously had more sophisticated eyes than the drones.

The robot and I regarded each other. I probably should have covered my
face with the scarf, but there didn't seem to be much point at this juncture.

"You must be Standing Mars," I said.

"You are an unauthorized intruder," said the robot.

I didn't reply. There are a lot of things I don't waste my time on in this
world, and arguing with a robot is one of them. Instead, I groped inside
the suit until I had the reassuring weight of the jammer in my hand.

The robot was silent, regarding me. What had Jacaranda called it, on
the roof? A "hostile intelligence." It didn't look that intelligent. It sort of
looked like a giant stapler with legs.

"You are not Damian Peters," said the robot. "That personnel record is
a forgery."

*Shit.* A lot smarter than it looked, I guess. "We may have a problem," I
said.

"Elaborate," said Sergei.

"Robot. Eight feet tall. Combat model, designation Standing Mars —"

There was a screeching noise in my ear, and I tore the GSM unit out,
cursing in pain.

"Your communications have been terminated," said the robot.

Man, this thing was a dick. All the more so because it was blocking my
exit, and I really needed to be under way.

"Exit the enclosure," said the robot.

I pulled on the mask and swung my backpack over my shoulder. All
things considered, now seemed the time to prep for a quick getaway.

I thought my vision would be poor in the mask, but surprisingly it wasn't
all that bad. The lenses were dark, but not as bad as I feared, and my field
of vision was acceptable. I didn't expect it to be so stifling, however — there
was no airflow at all. When the suit was powered, there had to be an air circulation system. Right now, it was like having a plastic bag over my head.

Unfortunately, I had bigger worries. "You will exit the enclosure," said the robot.

"Why don't you come in and get me?" I said.

It put one great metal paw up against the door. It only had four fingers, but a handspan of nearly twenty inches. Its fingers were ringed with black bands of electro-sensitive rubber.

I backed up, just before Standing Mars shattered the glass door of the enclosure.

I felt shards of glass peppering the front of the suit, heard them striking the desk, the cabinet. If I hadn't been wearing the suit, I probably would have been sliced open in a dozen places. Thank God for small favors.

I didn't have time to worry about flying glass, however. The moment the glass shattered I darted forward, reaching out with my right hand. I touched Standing Mars with the cold metal of the drone jammer.

Even brief contact with the jammer had knocked out Black Winter instantly. But the device had no effect at all on Standing Mars. The robot snatched at my hand, moving with surprising speed. I retreated hastily, clutching the device.

Standing Mars clanked farther into the room. It was too cramped to maneuver, so it swept a heavy paw to the right. A cabinet and Colonel Hayduk's personal data station were violently shoved up against the wall. I heard more glass shattering.

I quickly stuffed the drone jammer into my backpack. *Damn, this thing is a bull in a china shop.*

It was also thoroughly blocking the only exit, and there was no way around it.

"You have been designated an enemy combatant," said Standing Mars. "You will be treated accordingly."

It took another step forward, reaching out to crush my skull.

*So much for easy solutions,* I thought. I seized the colonel's handgun and squeezed off two rounds into its head.

The gun fired some kind of exploding rounds, and the results were spectacular — if very, very loud. The back of the robot's head blew off in an explosion of metal and fire. The thing's body shuddered violently.

It froze, its great metal claw not three feet from my head. I wasted no time, and put another two shells into its torso.

It moved then, almost blindingly fast. It twisted to the right and went right through the glass wall. There was a computational tower in its way in the adjoining compartment, and it destroyed it in an instant, sending it tumbling end over end fifteen feet through the air, trailing sparks and torn power cords, smashing two more walls as it came down.

There was more swift destruction, more screeching metal. The air was filled with broken glass, noise, and fury. I ducked just as a stray metal canister bounced back into the colonel's compartment, smashing into the desk and breaking a lamp.

I lost sight of Standing Mars. I got a quick flash of something moving two compartments over and fired off a round. There was another explosion of violent motion, and three more towers went down. I saw the first lick of flames.

I ran for the elevators.

The stairs would have been a better choice, but the elevators were closer. I reached them in seconds, hit the down button.

I glanced back the way I'd come. The corridor was dark but clear, and the nearest glass enclosures were empty of anything but blinking communications arrays and other silent equipment.

As I waited, a thin wisp of smoke curled along the ceiling, inching its way toward me. I saw the first flicker of reflected flame in dark glass on the left. Somewhere, a fire was under way.

There was a noise behind me. I whirled around. The corridor marched on beyond the elevators, into another bank of dark glass compartments. There were a dozen blinking towers, power racks, and more shadowy objects.

On the right, not forty feet away, a great dark form stood between two towers. It was difficult to make out through panes of glass, but the top half of its silhouette seemed jagged, oddly damaged.

I couldn't be certain what it was. But who needs certainty in an uncertain world? I raised the gun and fired two rounds at the thing.

The third shot clicked on an empty chamber. Out of ammo.

I heard a heavy tread behind me.

I turned around. Standing Mars came around the corner. Firelight illuminated its left side. The smoke was a little thicker now.

Goddamn, this was one tough robot. Its torso seemed to have suffered the most damage. The shells had ignited a fire in its exposed chest cavity that hadn't quite gone out, and I could see flickers of light dancing inside it. Twisted metal dangled from the back of its head. Some kind of metal cabling had gotten tangled around its right arm and shoulder, and trailed along on the ground behind the thing.

And still it came. It took three confident steps forward, leaving the glass enclosures behind.

Its right shoulder bumped the wall. It corrected course, moving closer to the center of the hall with its next step. It stopped, its broken head swiveling, scanning ahead.

*Scanning with what?* I wondered. Its torso had no visible eyes, and it was a good bet at least some of its sensing equipment was damaged.

In fact . . .

It must have heard me fire the shots. But now it was less than thirty feet away and gave no indication it saw me. Its big torpedo head shifted back and forth, back and forth, like a bloodhound.

Could the ferocious Standing Mars be blind?

"Put down the weapon," it said. Its voice was just a little jittery, distorted, as if its speakers were a touch out of alignment. "Surrender and you won't be harmed."

There was a friendly chime, and a pair of elevator doors opened almost exactly midway between us. Standing Mars's head twitched to the left, toward the open door.

For a moment neither of us moved. I couldn't be sure how much it could see. Or hear or sense. But now it knew I had called for the elevator, and it would find me eventually. All it had to do was move forward to block the elevator doors.

The robot took a step forward.

I tossed the empty gun at the enclosures behind me. It hit a glass wall with a thump, but didn't shatter it.

The robot twitched. Before the gun even hit the floor it was in motion. It leaped forward, its heavy arms swinging violently. One of them passed within inches of my head. The robot collided with the glass wall, shattering it in an orgy of violence.

The elevator doors started to close.

I waited, staying frozen in place while Standing Mars pulverized everything within reach of its fists. I had to time this perfectly. One second. Two. The robot's huge fists were pistoning the floor in a circle, sending tile, glass, and wood fragments spinning into the air. The floor shuddered.

I leaped for the elevator, sliding between the closing doors.

The robot stopped moving. I heard nothing but bits of falling debris out in the hall. The elevator doors closed.

I found the control panel, punched the button for the lobby. The elevator started moving.

I was eight floors down when I heard Standing Mars smash its way into the elevator shaft above.

*Holy shit.* We were passing the eighth floor. I pounded the button for that floor. Then the seventh, and the ninth, desperate to get the doors open. I was still slamming buttons when the elevator doors began to open on the seventh floor.

They were less than halfway open when the elevator suddenly lurched upwards three feet, almost throwing me to my knees.

The elevator doors stopped opening. We were three feet above the seventh floor. A loud alarm was sounding.

The elevator shuddered. I heard a loud metallic *snap,* and then something heavy moving into the shaft.

I dove through the doors. I tripped as I landed, taking a painful tumble on the carpeted floor. I dropped the backpack, and it bounced somewhere to my right. My face hit the floor, knocking the mask askew.

I tore it off, grateful to be able to breathe again. I looked around. I was sprawled on my ass in an empty office corridor. I could see three dark office suites, one on my left and two on my right. The floor looked deserted. I struggled to my feet, groping for the backpack.

Stairs. I needed to find the stairs.

There was a horrific crash from the elevator. Something big and very heavy had landed on the roof, spraying shattered tiles and metal all through the cramped space. A chunk of glass bounced out through the partially open doors, landing on the carpet at my feet.

A gray metal arm smashed through the roof. As I watched, it groped blindly about the elevator.

I snatched up the backpack and ran to the right.

It didn't take long to find the stairs. Not that I needed the extra motivation, but the sounds coming from the elevator provided plenty. I pulled open the door and raced down the steps.

Around the third floor, I stopped and pulled the mask back on. I descended the last two floors with a little more decorum. But without the power cores the suit had no real ventilation. I was breathing heavily, and rapidly fogging up the lens inside the mask. The suit felt a little ridiculous— too large at the shoulders, and the mask would not lie flat against my neck.

*This isn't going to work,* I thought, as I took the last step down to the first floor.

I glanced back up the stairwell. The alternative was to turn around and walk back up the way I'd come . . . and face off against 1,800 pounds of pissed-off robot. And even if I somehow got past it, I'd lost touch with Sergei. I'd never find another way out on my own.

No, there was only one possible way out of the building at this point. And that was shoulders square, eyes front, and straight ahead.

I stepped out of the stairwell. I was in the first-floor hallway by the west stairs, close to where I'd first entered the building. Two Venezuelan soldiers spotted me the instant I entered the hall.

I should have simply walked past them, like a colonel completely in command. Like a man in his element, who expected obedience. Instead I came to a full stop, staring at them fearfully.

The soldier at the left returned my stare. The one on the right looked the suit up and down, and then saluted me sharply.

"Coronel," he said.

The one on the left quickly followed suit.

I walked past them, giving them a nod—or doing the best I could in a loose mask, anyway. I strode down the hall, turned right into a small corridor.

Ahead was the door I had used to enter the building. Seven guards were blocking it, standing at ease and in low conversation. The first spotted me and nudged the one to his left.

The guards moved out of my way. I strode quickly down the hall and out the door.

One of the guards asked me something. I ignored him, headed across the street.

I missed Sergei. I missed his voice in my ear, giving me sage advice. Telling me not to worry, telling me the soldiers behind me didn't have a gun pointed at my head. I walked out into the darkness, weaving my way among the barricades, half certain I'd hear a rifle shot at any moment.

I passed two more guards at the outer perimeter, just outside the barricades. The last one didn't seem to have gotten the memo about the colonel—he shouted at me twice angrily, until someone behind shut him up.

I kept walking. I wouldn't feel safe until I was a mile away from the Sturgeon Building—and probably not even then.

Someone was standing in the shadows straight ahead. It was dark, and there was so much fog on the inside of the mask at this point that it was a miracle I was able to see anything. I didn't bother deviating course; I just kept marching.

*I don't care who this is*, I thought, *as long as his name isn't Hayduk.*

It was the robot from the rooftop. The one who called herself Jacaranda.

I pulled the mask off. "Damn, lady. You're a piece of work," I said.

"I should not be here," she said. "But we didn't finish our conversation."

She wanted to know how I knew about the Network of Winds, I realized.

"Put the mask back on," she said. "And stand next to me."

I pulled the mask back on. It was already sweaty and damp. To think that I'd been excited the first time I saw the combat suit. Right then, I felt like a scuba diver running a goddamn marathon.

I stood next to her, looking back at the Sturgeon Building. Was it my imagination or were a lot more lights on now? Half a dozen drones buzzed around the top of the building. I reached into my backpack, making sure the jammer was still there. I felt its reassuring bulk. It was still on — and still working — at least as far as I knew.

I felt very exposed. We were no more than eighty yards from the front of the building. No challenge at all for a decent sniper, even in the darkness. Or a drone able to track the location of the suit or Hayduk's data drive.

I was about to speak, but Jacaranda beat me to it. "You are in no danger," she said. "But please. Remain motionless and completely silent for the next ninety seconds."

I nodded. *Fine,* I thought. But after ninety seconds, I was gone. I'd come much too far just to get caught cooling my heels now.

The first twenty seconds were completely quiet. I could see some of the soldiers milling around in the bright lights by the lobby entrance. Only a few were looking our way. *What the hell are we doing here?*

Right around the thirty-second mark, Standing Mars smashed its way out of the lobby.

It made a pretty spectacular exit. It must have come down the elevator shaft into the lobby and built up a head of steam heading for the windows. This thing just had no use for doors. It walked right through the windows, and as I watched, two huge plates of glass, dislodged by its exit, came cascading down around it, sending an explosion of shards in all directions. A soldier on its left went down, holding his hands to his face, and one on his right, startled out of his wits, opened fire on Standing Mars with his rifle.

Standing Mars took two quick steps and killed the soldier. It threw away the bloody body, then moved away from the building.

It didn't even stop for the concrete barricades. It smashed through the first and shoved the second out of the way without slowing down.

It was headed straight for us.

"Please remain calm," the petite robot on my right said.

I looked over at her. She seemed utterly unperturbed by the rapid approach of this robot juggernaut. However, I was about to piss all over a thirty-million-dollar combat suit.

*Are you going to take it?* I wanted to ask. But I obeyed instructions and kept my mouth shut.

Standing Mars thundered closer. It was past the barricades.

It stopped less than fifty feet away. Its right hand was damaged — mangled and out of alignment. *Shouldn't Hulk your way through concrete barricades, moron,* I thought. But it still looked entirely capable of crushing my skull.

Something had changed about it. A small, portable camera eye was now attached to the side of its broken torpedo head. Looks like it had stopped somewhere for a bit of an upgrade.

"I can see you," said Standing Mars.

*How nice for you.* I looked to Jacaranda again, a little self-consciously. *Any time now.*

Standing Mars took another step forward. As it turned slightly, I could see the jagged hole in the back of its metal skull.

She'd told me not to move, but when Standing Mars took that step, I faltered and fell back, ready to run.

There was a flash of movement out of the corner of my eye, and then another robot stepped into my field of vision, between us and Standing Mars.

It took a second to recognize it. It was the slender humanoid robot I'd seen outside the Sturgeon Building when I first arrived. The one that had taken down and scavenged a drone.

I shot a questioning look at Jacaranda. "That is Hazel-rah," she said simply. "He is a friend."

Standing Mars kept coming. It thundered forward without deviating in the slightest. Hazel-rah interposed himself squarely between us and our attacker.

Standing Mars was shorter, but far more massive. When it reached the slender robot, it tried to swat him aside. Our defender ducked with surprising speed. But he didn't move out of the way. Instead, he bounced up under the swing and shoved Standing Mars in the shoulder, hard.

Mars stumbled. As it did, Hazel-rah reached out and plucked the camera eye off its head. He crushed the thing in one swift motion, tossing the pieces to the side.

Mars was blind again.

It may have been blind, but it was far from helpless. It pivoted with astonishing speed, striking out. The slender robot ducked, but not fast enough; Mars hit his shoulder, throwing him to the pavement. Mars slammed its fists into the street, sending spinning chunks of broken asphalt into the air, but Hazel-rah had already rolled to the left, nimbly regaining his footing.

There was a gentle touch on my arm. Jacaranda was pulling me to the right, out of the street. She had a finger to the lips of her mask, signaling for silence.

We moved into the shadows on the right. Jacaranda had chosen our position with care; twenty steps led us to a metal scaffold covering a building on the south side of the street. She pushed a plywood panel aside, and then we were behind the scaffold, in a narrow construction lane. She slid the plywood back into place behind us.

It was pitch dark. I felt cold metal fingers brush against my glove, and then Jacaranda took my hand and led me confidently through the darkness, up a narrow metal stairway.

We were on the scaffolding, almost entirely concealed from the street. There was a three-foot break in the plywood wall on the right. We stood in the darkness, nearly invisible, watching the battle.

Mars was winning. Jacaranda's champion was fast and fantastically nimble, dancing around his heavier opponent with movements that looked almost graceful, striking at Mars with deft, precise blows. But his blows did almost nothing. Nothing seemed to slow the bigger robot or do more than cosmetic damage. It had torn a stop sign out of the ground and was wielding it ferociously, giving it a much wider reach. In the darkness it seemed like a deformed barbarian, tirelessly swinging an axe in great, crushing arcs as it sought to cleave its opponent in half.

Mars stumbled unexpectedly. Perhaps it tripped on some unseen chunk of rubble or simply landed a step badly. It disengaged briefly, taking a few steps away. It now seemed slow, hesitant.

"It's more damaged than it looks," I said.

"No," said Jacaranda.

Hazel-rah darted forward, pressing the attack. The moment he did, Mars dodged quickly to the right, then pivoted again, taking two leaping steps and swinging its weapon in a great scything blow.

It cut through empty air, exactly where Jacaranda and I had been standing barely forty-five seconds ago.

"You are its target," said Jacaranda. "Not Hazel-rah."

In the street, Mars was going berserk. It was leaping in a circle, swinging the sign, trying to find where I was hiding. It was gouging chunks of pavement out of the street, sending up a shower of sparks whenever it hit metal. The soldiers who had gathered to watch the battle scrambled quickly to get out of range. Standing Mars struck the corner of a barricade and the octagonal stop sign finally tore loose, spinning off into the darkness.

Hazel-rah, who had been biding his time, leaped forward and struck from behind.

His attack sent the blind Standing Mars sprawling. Hazel-rah didn't let up, raining blows down on the back of its long head. Even where we stood, we could hear the *crack* of shattering metal.

Mars reached behind itself, grabbed Hazel-rah by his right ankle. As it stood, Mars swung him two-handed like a club, smashing him to the ground.

Hazel-rah bounced once and then rolled free. He regained his footing, a little wobbly. His right leg was twisted, damaged.

He was clutching something in his right hand.

Something was wrong with Mars. Whatever component Hazel-rah had torn out of Standing Mars's skull, it was useful in a fight. And now that it was gone, Mars was having difficulty maintaining its balance.

Mars swung the metal pole, missing widely. It paused, seemed to listen, then swung again. It very nearly toppled over, recovering only at the last moment.

"Nice *work*, Hazel-rah," I said, cheering him on.

"It is a deception," said Jacaranda. "This model is designed to survive extraordinary damage. Standing Mars is more functional than it appears."

"What?"

Hazel-rah waited until Mars stumbled again, then stepped inside its defenses. His thin hands darted into the hole in the back of Mars's skull once more.

The moment he did Mars spun, grabbing Hazel-rah's head in a crushing grip. It wrenched Hazel-rah off his feet, smashing his head against the pavement.

Mars lifted him four feet off the ground, smashed him against the pavement again.

"My God," I said, turning to Jacaranda. "Can't you do something?"

"Wait."

"It's going to destroy him!"

"Wait."

Mars lifted Hazel-rah again, smashing his head into the street a third time. I thought I heard the crack of breaking metal.

Mars lifted Hazel-rah again, higher this time.

Hazel-rah's arm darted out quickly, slipping unerringly into Mars's fractured head. He twisted violently.

Mars's whole body jerked upright. It froze.

Hazel-rah climbed over Mars like a spider. Previously, he had torn things from Mars's skull with surgical precision, but now he changed tactics. Now he reached into Mars's head and ripped out metal with abandon, like a squirrel digging a hole.

Impossibly, Mars recovered after a brief moment. It grabbed Hazel-rah and threw him almost forty feet. He landed poorly, tumbling in a heap.

The soldiers were moving closer now. Nearly two dozen who had gathered to watch the battle were suddenly moving with a purpose. They took up positions in a rough semicircle around the combatants, raising their weapons.

But none of them was firing. They seemed to be waiting for a signal.

Hazel-rah had regained his feet. He was limping, approaching Mars in a jagged spiral, circling it and drawing closer and closer.

His opponent was clearly in distress. Even the mighty Standing Mars was apparently capable of absorbing only so much punishment. It still struck out savagely, swinging the metal pole, but its attacks now seemed entirely random.

"We should leave now," said Jacaranda. "While they are distracted."

She was right, of course. But I hesitated, wanting to see how it ended.

The end wasn't long in coming. Hazel-rah got closer and closer in his approach, until finally he took two quick steps forward, grabbing the metal pole with both hands. He twisted and pulled, and now the pole was in his hands.

Mars didn't seem to have noticed. It continued swinging blindly.

Hazel-rah climbed on top of it. He drove the pole down, between Mars's torso and head, and then yanked hard on the pole, using it like a lever.

Mars's torpedo head popped off in a shower of sparks. It was attached to the robot's torso now only by a black cable, and it dangled down his front like a useless third arm.

Hazel-rah leaped nimbly off his opponent, still holding the metal pole. Mars had been turned around and was now facing the Sturgeon Building. It marched forward, swinging its fists like a mindless automaton. The men in the circle hurriedly got out of its way, and it continued walking and swinging until it reached a concrete barricade. It began pounding the thing mindlessly, tearing itself apart in the process.

A man in uniform stepped out of the circle. He was tall and thin, and free of the heavy gear that encumbered most of the soldiers. He was directing the others with urgent commands. I could hear his voice from here as he shouted at his men.

"That is Colonel Hayduk," said Jacaranda.

"Yeah?" I squinted at him, trying to get a better look. But we were too far away, and it was too dark to really make out his features.

On a command from the colonel, the soldiers opened fire on Hazel-rah.

Their weapons didn't seem to do much, at least not at first. But Hazel-rah wasn't standing still—he spun in place, lashing out with the pole. It struck the nearest Venezuelan soldier, breaking his arm.

*"No!"* I shouted, turning to Jacaranda.

She cocked her head at me. "I do not understand."

"Don't let him kill the soldiers!"

"Hazel-rah is only defending himself—"

"I don't give a damn *what* he's doing. Will he listen to you?"

"Yes—"

"Then tell him to stop hurting them. Now."

Jacaranda turned to watch the battle. "They will destroy him."

"Can he run?"

"Yes."

"Then tell him to run like a son of a bitch."

The instant the words were out of my mouth, Hazel-rah started running. He was badly impeded by the damage to his right leg, but he still moved with impressive speed and dexterity—far faster than the soldiers could follow. They continued to shoot at him as the robot bolted into the darkness, heading south. Moments later, Hazel-rah vanished into an alley.

There was a shouted command from Hayduk, and the soldiers began to give chase.

We waited in the shadows until the soldiers were gone. Only a skeleton crew remained in front of the lobby, alert and at the ready.

"Did he get away?" I asked Jacaranda.

"Not yet. He is out of range of the soldiers, but not the drones. They continue the pursuit."

Damn. I'd almost forgotten about the drones. "Can he escape?"

"Certainly."

"How?"

"I have directed him toward the lake. His exoskeleton is compromised, but not severely. He can submerge long enough—and deep enough—to escape observation."

I breathed a sigh of relief.

"Thank you," I said. "I mean it. You and Hazel-rah both. I don't know what you are, but thank you. For helping me get out of the building . . . and for not killing those soldiers."

She seemed to study me in the darkness for a moment. "You are an unusual person, Mr. Simcoe. I find you full of surprises."

"Was that you who did that magic in there, creating a fake military record for Capitán Damian Peters, with my face and retina scan?"

"Yes," she said. "You didn't give us much time to create it, but it seemed to be adequate. The forgery has served its purpose, and we have already scrubbed it from the data record."

"Well," I said, turning toward the stairs. "It seems I'm not the only one full of surprises."

"How do you know about the Network of Winds?" Jacaranda asked me.

"Ask me again sometime," I said. I suddenly felt very achy. My feet were sore, and I felt cramped and sweaty in the suit. And I still had a long walk ahead of me. "But not tonight."

Halfway down the stairs, I turned and looked back. Jacaranda was standing at the top, looking down at me.

"Any suggestions on the best route to avoid the soldiers?" I asked her.

"I have no idea," she said.

"Huh. I thought you knew everything."

"Not yet," she said. "Soon, but not yet."

Then she turned and was gone.

*I suppose she's friendly enough,* I thought as I reached the bottom. *But that doesn't mean she ain't creepy.*

I stepped into the street, headed for home.

# XVI

Sunday, March 14th, 2083
Posted 3:51 pm by Barry Simcoe

CanadaNET1 Encrypted, Sponsored by Damn Your Eyes.
*She's onto you. Why make it easy for her to discover the sordid details?*
*Use our encrypted channels for discreet personal communications.*

Sharing is set to PRIVATE
Comments are CLOSED

I met Sergei just after lunch. He was trudging down East Randolph, hands in his pockets, gawking in all directions at once like a tourist. I'd never seen him in civilian attire before, but he looked sharp. Black pants, a crisp white shirt, and a close-fitting leather jacket. He was clean-shaven for once, and his straight posture and close-cropped hair still gave him a military bearing.

I stepped out of the storage unit and gave him a wave. He jogged over across the grass, which was still wet from the morning's rain. "What is this place?" he said.

I was watching the skies. They were still overcast, making it easy to spot the drones, black specks drifting against a cloudy white backdrop. There were at least a dozen that I could see, most of them at high altitude, but none of them seemed to be showing an unhealthy interest. "Get inside," I said.

Sergei obediently stepped inside the unit. I gave one last look around and then pulled down the sliding metal door. It clattered to the concrete, leaving us sealed inside a ten-by-twenty windowless space.

The power was out, of course, but I'd brought a portable lamp, and it was burning brightly on a shelf in the back. It provided plenty of light.

"This used to be a public storage unit," I said. "I spotted it on my walk back to the hotel this morning. There's about sixty of these connected sheds on the property. I think half of them still have stuff in them. The owners are long gone, but the units are still secure, I guess."

"Not this one," Sergei said, looking around. There wasn't much to see —bare metal walls, a concrete floor, and the trash barrel I'd rolled in from the parking lot.

"Yeah, not this one. The lock is broken. It was empty, and it seems perfect for our purposes. Did you bring everything?"

Sergei nodded. He unslung his backpack, and began unloading it. Inside were the clothes I'd given him last night after my trip to the Sturgeon Building. We both figured it was safer for Sergei to travel with them than me. My dress pants. My shirt. My dinner jacket, neatly folded. My scarf. My lucky socks. And one pair of leather shoes. I was going to miss those the most.

I nodded at the barrel. "Okay. Toss 'em in." I picked up the only other item in the storage locker — a half-full can of lighter fluid.

Sergei was peering into the barrel. He sniffed in disapproval. "Too wet," he said.

"It rained this morning," I said. I knew that for sure, because I'd walked home in the rain from the Sturgeon Building, and it was goddamned cold. "I had to dump an inch of water out of the frickin' thing."

Sergei was shaking his head. "I saw two barrels by gate on way here. They were shielded from rain. They are dry. One of them would be better."

"Yeah, I checked those barrels. They won't work as well. You need a hole near the bottom, like this — see?" I kicked at my side of the barrel, where a three-inch hole had rusted out.

Sergei peered at the hole. "No. You do not need hole. Barrel should be dry."

"Sergei, we're going to start a fire in a barrel. It won't matter if the barrel's a little wet — this will take care of that." I shook the can of lighter fluid. "But to really get a roaring fire, you need airflow. So you need a hole."

"No. Top of barrel is plenty for airflow. You need hot fire, so everything destroyed."

Honest to God, this went on for five minutes. Me and Sergei, arguing about whether or not the damn trash barrel was adequate. I finally got him to agree that we would try it, and that I would personally move the ashes to another barrel and try again if this one didn't prove up to the task.

Sergei dumped everything but my shirt into the barrel, and I doused the lot with fluid. I gave a single shake of the can over the shirt, then set it aside and used a match to light it. It was ablaze in an instant. I picked it up with two fingers and hastily tossed it into the barrel.

It erupted in flame. Within ten seconds, flames were shooting several feet out of the top of the barrel. Sergei and I watched with satisfaction.

At least, we watched with satisfaction for about twenty seconds. We two geniuses, busy arguing over excess water and airflow, hadn't bothered to consider what a roaring blaze would do in an enclosed space.

The room filled with smoke — and quickly. One minute Sergei and I were contentedly rubbing our hands next to the barrel, happy for the heat, and the next we could barely see. Sergei stumbled for the door, while I covered my face and tried not to cough my lungs out.

Sergei got the door open, and we stood by the entrance, coughing smoke out of our lungs. My clothing continued to burn merrily in the barrel behind us.

"Where did you get oil?" asked Sergei when we could speak again.

"The lighter fluid? Randy Nguyen got it for me."

"Fire seems adequate."

"Yeah." It was a good blaze and showed no sign of going out. I doubted I'd have to move anything to another barrel.

We stood in the doorway for a few minutes — not far enough in the open to be spotted by drones, but enough so that we could breathe.

This wasn't the perfect spot to dispose of my "American terrorist" outfit — it was too easy for drones to track us coming and going, for one thing, and we didn't have real control of the site — but it would do. When the fire burned itself out, we would seal up the storage unit, put a fresh lock on it, and walk away. Assuming we'd covered our tracks sufficiently, there'd be no reason for the AGRT to investigate. And if we hadn't, then there'd be precious little left for them to find.

Burning the clothing I'd been wearing when I broke into the Field Museum hopefully brought an end to an ugly chapter in my life. At the very least, it was one less way for the AGRT to track that particular crime back to me.

I'd decided to use this storage locker to accomplish the deed for several reasons. Because it was close to the hotel, easy to get to, and screened from flying eyes. And also, it was a place where Sergei and I could have a long private conversation, without having to worry about eavesdroppers.

After everything that had happened last night, I had questions—a lot of questions. I was pretty sure Sergei wouldn't have answers for most of them. But I needed to give voice to them anyway.

"Am I in the clear, Sergei?" I said, beginning with the most important one. "Has the algorithm stopped looking for me?"

Sergei nodded. "Yes. As expected. Your performance last night was entirely adequate to convince Venezuelan high command that intruder in Field Museum was American military asset. Search algorithm has been tasked with other duties. For now, Venezuelans have lost interest in civilian suspects. By the time they search hotel database—if they do—all images which could incriminate you will have been deleted."

Some of the tension went out of my shoulders. "Hallelujah."

Sergei's tone had been satisfied enough. But I'd known him long enough now to know when he was being evasive.

"What's the bad news?" I said.

Sergei looked pensive. "They have expanded search in other ways. They are now looking at previous incidents, attempting to establish connections between American intruder and recent military and paramilitary incursions against AGRT in Illinois and Indiana."

"That's good, isn't it? This is what we wanted. If they're off looking for me in Indiana, they're less likely to find me in a hotel in Chicago. Especially if they're getting me confused with some anti-Venezuelan guerrillas in the woods in Terre Haute."

"Perhaps. But search has also become much more serious. Colonel Hayduk has become personally involved. Yesterday, intruder was suspected of theft of medical equipment and accused of planting bombs in medical laboratory. Routine domestic insurrection. Today, he is responsible for successful penetration of most secure building in Sector Eleven, untold damage to computer systems, destruction of high-ranking machine intelligence, and theft of critical data—and American combat suit."

"Yeah," I said. "Once you put it that way, it doesn't sound so good."

"No. This search will not end soon. And it will involve many resources."

"You said 'high-ranking machine intelligence'—you mean Standing Mars?"

"Correct."

"What was Standing Mars?"

"Information on Standing Mars very restricted. But I uncovered basic facts. It had primary inception in Cologne in 2066 and was certified as Thought Machine in 2078. It was seconded to Sovereign Intelligence in Buenos Aires in 2080."

"Do you know which one?"

"No."

*Shit.* I had just helped lay waste to the property of one of the most powerful individuals on the planet. Hayduk and his goons could search for me all they liked; at least I'd see them coming. But if a Sovereign Intelligence decided it needed to know who I was, there was almost nothing I could do about it. It would find me. And I would never see it coming.

I was about to ask a question, but Sergei cut me off impatiently. "We have addressed your situation. It is time to turn attention to other pressing matters."

"You mean the pathogen?" I said. "What's the latest word?"

"There are now confirmed outbreaks in Indiana, Kentucky, Tennessee, and southern Illinois. Five deaths overnight."

The relief I'd felt at being in the clear was quickly evaporating. "My God."

"Military intelligence has restricted all travel in affected areas. War College has issued statement to high command."

"A statement? What did they say?"

"They are . . . assessing the matter."

"*Assessing* the matter? Goddamn it, Sergei! People are dying!"

"It is a political embarrassment. Poor decisions were made at high levels, and officials very slow to acknowledge."

"They're fools."

"Da."

"All right. Let's focus on what we can do. What are your friends saying?"

"Unofficially, there is more hard data emerging. Dr. Thibault in Fort Wayne is now issuing daily updates to Venezuelan surgeon general. Pathogen has nearly eighty percent fatality rate. Incubation period is two to six days. Thibault suggests it will reach critical exposure levels in the next ten to fifteen days, after which it cannot be contained."

"That's almost precisely in line with what Jacaranda told us."

"Da. Thibault is coordinating effort to create counteragent, but there is little progress so far."

"This is a nightmare. What's happening officially?"

"There is growing panic. There is no established protocol for this situation, and parties involved have issued contradictory instructions. Venezuelan Military Intelligence has taken charge of situation in Indiana, but they are not sharing information. We need to know details of outbreak at Columbus Regional Hospital, but there has been complete information blackout."

"Okay. Now we get to the really juicy questions. Assuming our new friend Jacaranda is right, what was Colonel Hayduk doing with the data on the origin of the pathogen? Does that mean he knows where it comes from?"

Sergei didn't answer. He clearly was not thrilled with this question.

"Sergei?"

Sergei stirred. "Jacaranda referred to pathogen as F5-117."

"Yeah, I remember. So?"

"There are references to F5-117 in high-level communications, going back three years."

"Are you joking?"

"No. I have been . . . very discreet with search. So I do not yet have complete information. But I have found several references. All are very cryptic. F5-117 was mentioned as part of contingency plan, in event of dramatic reversals during pacification of American heartland."

"Whose contingency plan?"

"All references are in communications from highest level of Venezuelan government."

That meant Thought Machines.

I remembered the handwritten note from Thibault, the one Sergei had burned after reading. The one that suggested that the pathogen may have been created by machine intelligences.

"Jesus. So Thibault was right? The pathogen was created by machines?"

"We cannot be certain."

"Well, it damn well looks like it! Do any of these references point to any other likely source?"

Sergei shook his head, without meeting my eyes.

I slid down the wall, squatting on my heels. I watched the smoke from the trash bin curling around the ceiling, flowing out through the open door, where it was snatched by the wind. I'd been worried about the smoke attracting drones when we were planning this last night, but Sergei had assured me that there were so many small cooking fires in the ruins around the city that it would go unnoticed. So far, it looked like he was right.

I tried to think clearly and dispassionately about what Sergei had just told me. What would machine intelligences be doing creating a biological pathogen? A plague hardly made an effective weapon, especially when you had your own forces on the ground. Even if they had a good use for such a weapon, why use it in the occupied zone? What did they have to gain by unleashing a plague that devastated both sides?

I thought for a good long time. My mind went down several dark alleys. I remembered the dire predictions you used to hear from doomsayers when the earliest machine intelligences first revealed themselves. Prophecies of apocalyptic battles between machine and humankind. The kind that ended with man in chains.

Eventually, I stirred. "Did you ever get the chance to investigate the Bodner-Levitt extermination?"

"Da. I found nothing. What does it mean?"

"That's a relief," I said. It *was* a relief. Perhaps that portion of Black Winter's delusional speech had meant nothing after all. "It doesn't mean anything; it's probably just gibberish."

"It is odd," said Sergei. "Do you know what you find when you do a complete network search on gibberish phrases, especially those that involve proper names?"

"I don't know."

"You get pages and pages of garbage. Useless search hits."

"Is that what you got?"

"Nyet. I told you; I found nothing. Nothing at all. Zero. Tell me, how often do you get zero results for search?"

"Never, now that I think about it. What does that mean?"

"It means the results have been censored. It means the AGRT does not want us to know what is 'Bodner-Levitt extermination.'"

I closed my eyes. "Damn," is all I managed.

"So I must ask you again," said Sergei. "What is 'Bodner-Levitt extermination'?"

"I have no idea."

"Where did you hear of it?"

"Sergei . . ."

"You are keeping secrets."

"Yes. But not intentionally. Someone mentioned it to me recently, in a very different context. It may be nothing. It probably *is* nothing."

"This same person. Did they also mention 'Network of Winds'?"

*Shit piss damn.* "Yes," I admitted.

"And they mentioned Jacaranda, who is involved with Network of Winds."

"Yes."

"Then I suggest this is not nothing. I suggest this person knows something. And that this person is very dangerous."

I thought about that before I gave Sergei another vague reply. Was that possible? Did Black Winter know something? And was it possible he was dangerous?

I had given him my word that I wouldn't reveal what he'd babbled in his robot delirium three nights ago. And now I had to decide. Did I honor that promise and keep Sergei in the dark about crucial information that could make the difference in his battle against a lethal plague? Or did I betray Black Winter and involve him in something that in all likelihood had nothing to do with him at all?

"Perhaps you're right," I said. "But I need to give this person an opportunity to explain their comments."

"Explanations can be misleading."

"I'm aware of that. Give me forty-eight hours, Sergei. After that, I'll answer anything you want to know."

Sergei nodded, but it was obvious he wasn't happy about it.

We needed to move on to a more productive topic. "Let's review what we know now," I said. "The pathogen was brought here during the war. And someone on the Venezuelan side—probably military intelligence—knew about it. So the question is, is this outbreak accidental or deliberate?"

"Unknown."

"And what exactly is Hayduk's involvement? He's a colonel in Venezuelan Military Intelligence, right? Is it unusual for military intelligence to get involved in a medical emergency like this? To take action the way they have at the hospital in Indiana?"

"Yes," Sergei agreed. "Very unusual."

"Okay, what does that tell us? That Hayduk and military intelligence are involved somehow? Did they help orchestrate the outbreak? Is Hayduk the one who released it? Is he willing to sit back and watch while his soldiers die?"

"These conjectures . . . they are of no use until we decrypt data."

"How are you going to do that?"

"I cannot read Hayduk's drive. It does not respond to normal queries. I cannot determine manufacturer or operating system. I can use Venezuelan data drill to attempt to access data, but to do so requires connecting device to network. Likely drive will immediately identify itself, and Hayduk will know where it is."

"Yeah, let's not do that then. Damn. How are you supposed to access the data?"

"I am medical specialist, not part of data warfare team. This is completely beyond my expertise."

"Well, why the hell did we both risk our necks to get it?"

"This morning, I received . . . unusual communication."

"Unusual how?"

"Unusual in many ways. I was sent data archive tool, with instructions to connect tool to drive."

"What? Who sent it?"

"I do not know. Message had no traceable source."

"Where did it come from?"

"I do not know. Message had no SMTP headers. Mail servers had no record of message."

That didn't sound possible, but I was starting to get used to that. "Probably a gift from our new friend Jacaranda. I hope you didn't open the damn thing."

"I did."

"Shit—how did you know Hayduk didn't send it, or somebody in military intelligence? They could have blasted it out to thousands of people, just to see who bites."

"I do not. Yesterday, you took many great risks to acquire data. I thought perhaps I should take a small risk."

"It doesn't sound like a small risk to me."

I took a minute to calm down, collect my thoughts. Was this going to be my life for the next few months? Was I going to be watching over my shoulder for Venezuelan Military Intelligence—or worse? Would every stray glance from a soldier, every odd message, send me into a secret panic?

*I suppose it's better than dying in a pandemic,* I thought.

"What happened?" I said.

"Tool began to query drive. Drive responded immediately—tool had correct salutation and encoding."

"I'm sure that's not a coincidence. Did it get the data?"

"No. Accessing drive requires sequence of challenges and counter-challenges. Tool has been challenged multiple times. It has provided sufficient correct responses for drive to continue exchange."

"Do you think it can access the data?"

"Yes. But it could take time. And we need to be prepared for failure."

"Failure?"

"Too many incorrect responses and drive likely destructs."

"Of course it does," I said in disgust.

"We will know shortly. One way or another."

"I hope you're right. What can we do in the meantime?"

"We are not idle. If Jacaranda is correct, data on drive includes formula for antiviral agent. We will be prepared to begin production as soon as we have formula. I have located a reactor vessel and vaporizer. I have secured piping and other components for sixty-gallon bioreactor. We will have reactor assembled and sterilized in three days."

"An antiviral agent . . . that's like a vaccine, right?"

"No," said Sergei. "Is too late for vaccine. Vaccine is of no use to infected. Antiviral agent will actively treat infected."

"Aren't we taking a big risk here? Even if you crack the data drive, what if Jacaranda is lying? What if F5-117 turns out to have nothing to do with this current outbreak? We could be wasting precious weeks while the plague rampages through the whole Midwest."

"Is not wasted effort. We are simultaneously analyzing live virus from Field Museum. We will need to understand this specific viral genome even if we have F5-117 antivirus to perfect treatment. We would be foolish not to explore all avenues."

Maybe that was true, but something about it still bothered me — and not just the fact that I'd trudged across the dark Chicago landscape carrying a vial of live plague. The live virus sample, our excursion to the Sturgeon Building, the antivirus formula — they were all connected.

Of course, there was also the fourth part of Black Winter's strange message to me, which just grew more maddeningly enigmatic as time went by. *"Find Jacaranda, and the Network of Winds. They can stop it. They can keep you alive."* What was Jacaranda's role in all this? And what did she want from us? "It can't possibly be luck that we simply blundered into all this," I said. "Someone planned for this to happen. For us to be involved. Someone very, very smart."

"Data archive tool did not arrive by luck," said Sergei.

"No. I think we both know who sent that to you. Jacaranda."

"You think she was also involved in sending us live virus?"

"I don't mean to sound paranoid, or like I don't trust Thibault. But yeah . . . I think it's possible. She was at the Field Museum that night. She's certainly responsible for diverting me to Hayduk's data when all I cared about was getting my ass out of the Sturgeon Building. And I don't believe she just happened to be there by coincidence either. The truth is, Jacaranda is just way too well informed for me not to believe she hasn't been involved in this since the very beginning."

We sat together in silence for a moment. "You know, Sergei," I said at last. "Maybe we're going about this all wrong. Trying to figure out what's going to happen to us, I mean. Trying to predict what the Venezuelans will do—and Hayduk, and the search algorithm, and all that other crap. I'm beginning to think the fastest way to determining our fate is to figure out who the hell she is and what she wants. Because if there's a spider at the center of this web, it's her."

"This may not be so easy," Sergei said.

There was something in his voice. "You know something?" I said.

"No."

"You *suspect* something?"

"Nothing concrete."

"Damn it, Sergei, let me hear it. Conjecture, wild guesses—I'll entertain anything at this point."

"Your description of her . . ."

"The mask, you mean?"

"Yes. The mask. I have heard of other robots who wear masks."

That was curious. "Really? Who are they?"

"There is nothing definite. Only rumor. But when war with America began, it revealed first serious rifts in community of Thought Machines. There were reports of some who split with majority—who challenged the authority of the Sentient Cathedral. The war exposed factions among a group we had long assumed spoke with a single voice."

"Machines who opposed the war, you mean? Does that mean they actively oppose the US occupation as well?"

"We do not know their actual agenda. We are speaking of matters that no human has witnessed. All we know for certain is that there was rift in Cathedral—a schism—sometime after war broke out. According to some confidential Venezuelan reports, small minority left the Cathedral."

This was news to me. If it was true, it was fascinating. I knew almost nothing about the Sentient Cathedral. And if there's a human alive who knows how many members it has—or who they are, or how often they meet, or even if they meet at all—I'd be very surprised. It's the most secretive organization — or religion, or cult, or whatever the hell it is — on the planet. There are rumors the Cathedral was founded by Duchess, the first Sovereign Intelligence, and that she originally intended humans to be a part of it, but no one knows. All I know for sure is that if there's an organization or political body that machine intelligences around the world fear and obey, it's the Sentient Cathedral.

"Who were they?" I asked. "Any names I'd recognize?"

"Unknown. Machines who left Cathedral no longer communicated using their birth designation. Instead, they identified themselves with self-created images."

"Images?"

"Masks," said Sergei. "They hid behind masks."

"You're not talking about physical masks . . ."

"No. Virtual masks. Elaborate self-created identities — colorful, very symbolic. And very effective. There is still conjecture today about who these machines are."

I chewed on that for a while. "And you think that could be a clue to Jacaranda's origin."

"A possibility only. If these machines have physical agents, it is possible they exhibit similar behavior."

"Wearing masks, hiding their identity, you mean."

"Exact."

"Well . . . as fascinating as that is, I'm not sure how it helps us."

"You want to know who Jacaranda is. It is possible Jacaranda is part of an ecosystem of rational devices that is normally entirely hidden from human eyes. There has been unprecedented evolution and expansion of Thought Machines — and their agents — in last five years. We may be glimpsing new machine species for first time."

"That's one hell of a conjecture. And if it's true, we know even less about her than we thought we did. If she's a brand-new species, it will be almost impossible to guess her motives."

"Da. We are entering exciting new era of machine life, my friend. The era of human dominance on this planet is coming to an end."

"I've heard that before. But let's step back for a minute and talk about things a little easier to grasp. Like, how does she know about you? About who you are? She referred to you by *name*."

"I think is safe to assume Jacaranda has been observing us. Perhaps for some time."

"Why us?"

"I cannot say. But perhaps because we are capable of accomplishing what she needs."

"Or maybe we're just capable of being manipulated."

"Da. Is distinct possibility."

"So we don't know who she is — or what she wants. Or who she works for. Why is she helping us?"

"You asked her on roof, did you not?"

"Yeah, I did. She said we shared a common enemy."

"Who is her enemy?"

"Damn it, Sergei, let's start with an even more basic question. Who are *our* enemies?"

The fire was starting to die out. There was nothing left to burn but the soles of my shoes and a few of the larger sticks we had thrown in as kindling. Sergei began to pace around the storage locker, his polished boots tapping out a steady rhythm on the concrete floor. "The pathogen," he said.

"Yeah, I guess that makes sense. Robots aren't affected by viruses, but perhaps there's someone she's concerned about who is. That's a distinct possibility. Who else? The search algorithm?"

"Algorithm has been retasked. It has lost priority computational privileges. It is of no consequence."

"Yeah, that was a long shot. Hayduk?"

"Hayduk was not our enemy."

"Speak for yourself. If he ever finds out who stole his rubber combat suit, I'm a dead man."

"Hayduk was not our enemy when Jacaranda offered assistance. It was our subsequent partnership that brought us into conflict with Hayduk."

"Splitting hairs a bit, but okay. I think that's it for our enemies list, really."

"Unfortunately, no."

"We have enemies I don't know about?"

"Jacaranda appears to have been our ally for some time, and yet we were unaware of her existence until two days ago. I think is possible our 'common enemy' is similar."

"An enemy we don't know about. Someone invisible, operating against us, without our knowledge."

"Yes," said Sergei. "I think that is most likely alternative. And most dangerous."

I looked for flaws in this logic, but could not find any. "That's a god-damned frightening thought. What did we do to piss him off, then?"

"Do not assume our enemy, if he exists, has particular malice toward us. Perhaps his target is more general."

I connected the dots. I just did it a little slower than Sergei.

"Christ, Sergei. You're saying there's a machine out there that bears ill will toward everyone in the country? Or perhaps humans in general?"

"Perhaps."

"And you think this machine created the pathogen. Is that it? That our enemy wants all humanity dead?"

"We cannot fathom long-term motives. We can only draw broad assumptions. If enemy exists, it is most likely suspect for creator of pathogen. And if it created pathogen, it was likely for attack against both Venezuelan and American personnel in cramped proximity, most probably in Displaced Persons camps in Indiana."

"Sergei, how the hell do we find this thing?"

"We cannot. Not right now. And we have more immediate problems. We must focus on accessing drive and manufacturing antivirus."

I wanted to argue, but he was right. The virus was the immediate threat. "All right," I said. "How can I help?"

"This is not something you can help with." I started to protest, but Sergei held up a hand. "Proximity to drive is not safe. Is better for you if you are not involved. In fact, I think it advisable that we are not seen together. Temporarily."

"You think you can do this all by yourself? Crack the encryption on the drive, build the reactor, and produce the antivirus? And watch your back in the meantime?"

"No. But I have assistance I need. Thibault has offered to send her team here to help build bioreactor. And there are others among Medical Corps who want to assist."

"Yeah, maybe. But who's going to watch your back?"

Sergei smiled. "That, I would appreciate. But for next forty-eight hours, I will be assembling reactor with a medical team I trust. I will be relatively safe."

"All right, fine," I said. "I'll lay low for two days. I can probably use the time to get rid of the suit, anyway."

Sergei seemed surprised. "We could use suit."

"Not without the power cores. Without those, it's useless."

"Then perhaps we should find them."

"Forget it. I'm done sneaking around buildings late at night."

Sergei was about to make a comment when something in his pocket buzzed. He took out a small device.

"Archive tool has accessed drive," he said.

"That's fantastic!" I said. I stood up, clapped him on the back. "Congratulations!"

"Tool is sending data now," he said, looking at the device.

"Terrific. Anything useful?"

Sergei stared at the device for a long time. When he finally spoke, he looked almost pale.

"Unfortunate news," he said.

"What?"

"Our enemy," he said. "You will know the name."

"Who is it?"

Sergei told me.

"Sweet baby Jesus," I said.

"Yes," said Sergei. "Exact."

# A Brief History of
# My Favorite War

**PAUL THE PIRATE**
Monday, March 15th, 2083

Let me tell you a little of the recent history of America. Pay attention because, unlike those cheap social media sites where you get your news, I'm going to give you the straight shit.

We're going to start in the hallowed halls of the Argentine Senate, which ratified the Juaven Doctrine in April 2080. There's bullshit doctrines and there's bullshit doctrines, and then there's the Juaven Doctrine. It stated that Argentina had the unquestionable right to pursue threats to its national security, wherever they existed around the globe. Now, the original pretext had sweet fuck-all to do with America, but it was pretty clear to anyone paying attention what was happening: the Argentine government was laying the legal groundwork for an incursion on US soil. Why? Because of the New England Crackers.

If you know your American history, you know the New England Crackers were an anonymous group of American students who – allegedly – hacked into an Argentinean AI nursery. If you believe the claims of the Argentine Sovereign Intelligences, these unknown persons infiltrated, influenced, and eventually corrupted a few dozen gestational AIs in Argentina and Panama. All of the infant AIs had to be destroyed.

Assuming it actually happened, this was a big deal. The death of that many infant AIs at one time was virtually unprecedented. And it didn't help that American-Argentine relations at the time were already shit. Congress had ratified the Wallace Act in 2067, making it illegal for a machine intelligence to set foot inside the United States, and in 2075 Argentina became the first fascist machine government. By 2080, the countries had been geopolitical foes for half a decade. Argentina was one of the first nations to grant legal status to Thought Machines, and some of the oldest and most powerful adult machines on the planet are Argentine citizens. It was their children they claimed had been murdered. It was, to put it mildly, a diplomatic shit show.

One thing you probably don't remember, because it doesn't get talked about much these days, is that America once had powerful allies. All that was before the Wallace Act, of course, which kept machine intelligences of any kind out of the country. As machines became citizens everywhere else, America's anti-machine laws gradually became recognized for what they were: bigoted and shortsighted. America, once the envy of the world, became more and more isolated . . . and more and more vulnerable.

Something else you may not remember—since it was drowned out by all the saber rattling—was American president Sophia Bermúdez's response to the crisis. She was a smart, resourceful woman, and a woman of peace—at a moment in history when the country desperately needed a woman of war. She downplayed the threat; said that if there were criminals in the US somehow responsible, she would catch them. They would be tried according to US law—although no one knew what the hell that meant, since it wasn't clear what laws they had broken. Nonetheless, Bermúdez did everything she promised and spared no effort to find out who was responsible.

Of course, she failed. Probably because there never *were* any criminals in the New England Crackers—none responsible for the death of infant machines in Argentina, anyway. They were convenient scapegoats for a foreign tragedy. Bermúdez was chasing phantoms. And when she couldn't produce them, Argentina formed the San Cristobal Coalition with Panama, Bolivia, and Venezuela . . . and invaded Manhattan.

Now, for sure you watched the broadcasts of *that*. That was some riveting shit right there. The world's first true robot army, kitted out against the mightiest nation on Earth, all broadcast in real time by an army that dwarfed both of 'em—fleets of camera drones from every press corps on the planet.

It was a helluva show. But while the rest of us ate popcorn and stayed glued to our screens, the Manhattan invasion was mangling the US — militarily, economically, and, most importantly, politically.

But that's not what makes this my favorite war. What makes this my favorite war is a guy named Saladin Amari.

Saladin Amari was the governor of Texas. He was a devout Muslim, and unlike Bermúdez, he heard the drums of war loud and clear. While Bermúdez preached a message of peace, Amari spoke to huge crowds all across the South, telling Americans to prepare for war. On August 1st, 2080, Amari stood before a packed hall in Tulsa and said these words:

"The enemies of America are the enemies of Allah, and Allah will bring them rains of fire. Before a single foreign soldier dares step on the sacred soil of this country, let them understand this with crystal clarity: Our strength flows from Allah, our weapons are glass and steel, our cause is nothing less than justice, and our name is the United States of America!"

His speech galvanized half the nation. It also helped bring in the money he needed to fund more serious preparations for war. Amari was building an army of mechanized robot killers, long before anyone knew what the enemy would look like. And they were almost ready when the first enemy robots walked up out of the Atlantic into Manhattan two months later. Amari fielded his first mechs, driven by his top pilots, with the US Sixth Army two days later, and they met the enemy just outside Trenton, New Jersey.

But you know how that turned out.

# XVII

Monday, March 15th, 2083
Posted 9:01 pm by Barry Simcoe

CanadaNET1 Encrypted, Sponsored by Smiling Headlines.
*The only news media that specializes exclusively in good news.*

Sharing is set to PRIVATE
Comments are CLOSED

I took Sergei's advice. I'm keeping my distance, for the most part. At least until we can be a little more confident that the data drive we stole from Colonel Hayduk isn't giving up our location. No sense risking both our necks. Besides, Sergei's likely too wrapped up processing the data from the drive, and hanging out with Thibault's team in their makeshift biolab, to be very social anyway.

When I got up this morning, Croaker was at my bedside again, wagging her tail. She's made a remarkable recovery in the past four days. The medicine Sergei gave me has worked wonders on her eye, and there's no longer any sign of infection.

Which implies that Jacaranda, who'd warned me that Croaker had an adenovirus infection when I first met her at the Field Museum, had been right on the money. At the time, I'd been more than a little freaked out by the fact that a creepy machine stalker knew I had a dog. But after my second meeting with Jacaranda in the Sturgeon Building, a little thing like intimate knowledge of canine medical history no longer seemed so remarkable. At this point, I'd be more surprised to discover there was something she *didn't* know.

Croaker had enough energy that I took her for her first walk in the cold morning air, and I'm not sure which of us was more nervous. I didn't have a leash, but it turns out she didn't need one. She stuck close to me the entire way. It wasn't far; she got about half a block from the hotel on trembling legs before she collapsed, and I ended up having to carry her back. She squirmed happily in my arms and licked my face.

"You didn't even pee," I said disapprovingly when we got back. "You're going to pee all over the mat again, aren't you?" As a precaution, I moved her mat — really one of the hotel's biggest bath towels — into the bathroom, where the tile floor would make cleanup more manageable.

A few of the young women on the hotel staff make a fuss over Croaker every time I walk past the front desk. Hotel policy forbids dogs, but they didn't seem too concerned about that. I think I'll impose on one or two of them; see if I can get them to walk her the next time I'm gone for more than a few hours. It would help her to get out more.

After my shower, I headed down to breakfast. Then I dropped by the seventh floor to get a quick glimpse of the bioreactor, where Sergei had already begun the work of creating the antivirus. So far it did not look like much. Mostly it resembled a giant disassembled still. I didn't see Sergei, but I did introduce myself to the woman directing the construction, Dr. Joy Lark, a young Korean woman. She seemed remarkably focused and competent, and I left feeling good about our progress.

Truth be told, I also felt a little left out of things, but I suppose that's for the best. I do still have a job to do, after all. Chicago didn't turn out to be the mecca of high-speed data I was hoping it would be when I'd moved here, but you can still get the bandwidth you need if you're resourceful. When I checked my messages Sunday afternoon, there'd been an urgent letter from Halifax, and two queries from potential buyers. I'd spent much of last night trying to secure enough bandwidth to connect to our VPN so I could shoot back some replies and get an update on our latest development sprint.

When all that was done, I indulged myself with some personal data buys. I checked the political news feeds first, hoping for some news out of Clarksville, Tennessee, where a permanent peace between both American factions and the San Cristobal Coalition was being delicately hashed out. But there were no reports of substance.

There was a pair of recent updates from my favorite political observer, Paul the Pirate, from his sanctuary in free Jamaica, and I happily paid to get them. Saturday's topic: the brazen murder of one Sovereign Intelligence by another. As usual, Paul's post was dead on target . . . not just the facts of the day, but also clearly pointing out the long-term ramifications.

Kuma's brazen murder by Kingstar meant that the era of machine iso-lation — Thought Machines and Sovereign Intelligences living ponderous and lonely existences of pure thought on windswept mountaintops, like goddamn hermits in a cave — had come to a violent end. To survive in this new era of conflict, machines needed to band together, to become part of a community. They needed allies for collective security.

I wondered especially what this might mean for the remaining outcasts of machine society, like the reclusive Luna, launching countless tons into space from his underground stronghold in Australia, or the mysterious Aruban Prefecture, who'd cleared an entire Caribbean island of human life. Would they heed this call for collective defense? Or would they con-tinue their enigmatic projects in forced isolation until the day a ballistic missile rained down on them?

Paul's brief post was also sprinkled with the usual tantalizing tidbits that demonstrated how well informed he was. What exactly did he mean by "discord inside the Helsinki Trustees"? And where had he gotten his fascinating facts on Corpus?

There were several older posts as well, including an interesting inter-view with Dance Maker, a German Thought Machine who'd made a for-tune designing and selling advanced biomedical devices to treat diseases in children, who was using his money to build hospitals across sub-Saha-ran Africa. Paul the Pirate titled that article "Inside the Mind of a Defec-tive Altruistic Nutcase."

I couldn't concentrate for long, though. My last conversation with Ser-gei kept preying on my mind. It's tough to focus on machine blogs when you know that a small team of medical professionals, including some of your friends, are fighting against the odds to stop a deadly virus. And when that virus is rampaging uncontrolled less than two hundred miles away.

Or when you know the name of the machine that created it, and sus-pect that very shortly it just might be making a concerted effort to kill you.

Funny things happen to you when you know you have powerful ene-mies. You start to suspect everything — I mean, *everything*. Every unusual message, every chance introduction, every odd coincidence. You look for patterns everywhere. It can drive you crazy.

Last night, I even made the decision to give up this blog. It's supposed to be secure, but who knows if it really is? I've already posted what amounts to a thoroughly damning confession, but why add fuel to the fire?

But when I woke up this morning, I decided: the hell with it. Is all this paranoia making things even the least bit tougher for the machine intelligence possibly plotting my demise? Probably not. My best hope, beyond just escaping its notice — please God let *that* continue for as long as possible — is to surround myself with people. People tend to help each other. That's what I've always believed, anyway. And if that's the philosophy that gets me killed, so be it.

It was that attitude that led me to Rupert today. And Rupert helped clear my mind, get me thinking about things other than machines trying to kill me — for a little while, anyway. So I'm going to chalk up today as a win.

I met Rupert while he was lugging equipment out of the elevator on my floor. White hair, rumpled jacket — probably in his sixties. It seemed weird that a bellboy wasn't helping him, because the stuff looked heavy. I held the door while he retrieved the last box out of the elevator and laid it on the carpet, huffing.

"You need some help with that?" I asked.

He gave me a suspicious look, so I quickly continued. "I'm in 3306. Barry Simcoe." I held out my hand.

"Ah — that's right. I've seen you around." He shook my hand warmly. "Rupert Innes."

I grabbed the closest box and set it on my shoulder. It was heavier than I expected. I recognized the logo on the side — it was high-end telecom gear — but not the model number. The biggest box must have been on wheels, because Rupert got behind it and was pushing it down the hall with relative ease.

I followed him to 3327, right at the end of the hall. He unlocked the door and ushered me in.

"Wow — this is *gorgeous*," I said, but that was an understatement. Rupert had a corner suite that was easily three times the size of my room. Two banks of windows looked north across the Chicago skyline and east onto Lake Michigan, where angry red flashes lit up the vapor clouds billowing up from the dig.

He grunted. "Don't get to enjoy it much. I usually keep the blinds closed — too much glare on the monitors."

I took in the rest of the room for the first time. There wasn't much furniture. In fact, the first thing that struck me was that the room looked like a miniature version of the Venezuelan command center. There were digital displays *everywhere* — perhaps two dozen, of all shapes and sizes, including three that were at least six feet wide. The closest was one of the big ones, and I realized with a start that it was identical to the air traffic monitor I'd glimpsed in the command center just a few days ago. It tracked six different aircraft, four inbound and two outbound, including three that looked military. The bright green silhouettes resembled Brazilian GAT fighters.

I must have been gaping. Rupert moved in front of me casually and turned off the display. "That won't interest you," he said, his voice even.

"How do you get air traffic control data?" I said, still staring at the screen. "I mean, I can't even get stock market quotes in this damn town."

Rupert's expression told me that was an inappropriate question, given the fresh status of our friendship. "Never mind, I don't want to know," I said. "I'll get the rest of the stuff from the hall."

I helped him move the last of the equipment into his living room. When we were done, I looked around. He had discreetly darkened a few of the screens. The ones that remained showed live data streams from the world's major equity markets.

"You have a real-time Euro-bond feed?" I said, pointing at a colorful display that tracked trades in Munich.

"You're nosy," Rupert said, but he was smiling.

"I'm sorry, but—I tried to get one. For three weeks. I was told it was impossible as long as I was in Chicago. Those bastards at globalNet—I knew my client rep was an idiot."

"No, he's not. Your rep is right, for the most part. The Venezuelans are actively jamming high-bandwidth commercial traffic. Mobile phone networks, national data networks, satellite, commercial radio and TV— they're almost nonexistent in Chicago."

I was still staring at Munich, waiting to see if quotes on any of my own holdings would pop up. I hadn't been able to check my portfolio in days. "You seem to be getting signal okay."

"That isn't a globalNet feed. It's private data."

That turned my head. "You have your own data feed? From Munich?"

"For most of the major markets, actually."

I whistled. "That must be expensive."

"It didn't used to be. But nowadays . . ." He shook his head. "It's not just the data, but the whole package. A reliable network connection, dealing with the taxing authorities on import data, getting decent encryption—it's just not possible to get everything I need in most markets. It's why I came to Chicago, actually."

"You get reliable high-speed data in Chicago?" I was poking at the screen, trying to figure out how to query a price. I was dying to get a quote on Standish Mutual. Last time I checked, they were deep in a hole. Why do I waste my money on those goddamn bounce funds?

"For the right price, yes. Chicago has some of the finest high-speed data infrastructure in the world. All the war did was chase away most users. Most of the bandwidth is still intact, waiting for a buyer. The spectrum the Venezuelans aren't jamming, anyway. No, Chicago has worked out nicely for me."

I was still trying to submit a query when the screen flashed suddenly, showing me an alert and then a new column of numbers. They looked like commodities prices in Hong Kong. I saw a lot of red — prices seemed to be dropping in metals and oil futures. "Are you a bond trader?"

"I manage a social aggregate fund. Pacific Reach Capital. Our holdings include bonds and equities, but chiefly we deal with large-scale financial instruments."

The name Pac-Reach was familiar, but I couldn't recall any of the specifics. I looked it up when I got back to my room, though. They're one of the fifteen largest aggregate funds on the planet. Holdings as of February 2083: $20 billion. Founder and general partner: Rupert Innes.

This was one rich dude, and many of the things he'd told me now make a lot more sense. But this morning, he was still a mystery.

"You're a mystery, Rupert," I said, tearing my eyes away from the screen. "Most major corporations have fled this city. People are getting killed — some for being in the wrong place at the wrong time, and some for reasons that make even less sense. And here you are, living right at the heart of it."

"Oh, I don't live here," he admitted. "Not yet, anyway. There's a bed in the other room, but I only use it a few nights a week. Mostly I sleep on the road these days. What about you? What do you do?"

"I run a small software company, based in Halifax. We build highly reliable telecom switches."

"You Canadian?"

"I am. I moved to Illinois just ten days ago."

"Great market to be in, hardened telecom. Ninety-five percent of telecom software in this country failed in the first four weeks of the war. American communications infrastructure was completely unprepared for a concerted attack. The country won't make that mistake again."

"Listen to you. You should be one of my salesmen. I should put you on commission."

"I just know a good business when I hear one. You should come to one of our dinners. My clients love hearing about new markets."

"It's a good business, when I can find buyers. I came to Chicago because I thought the city was back on its feet, but turns out it's not much better than it was at the height of the fighting. I have to get creative just to get enough bandwidth for a phone call."

"Oh, come on. It's not that bad. I understand the hotel is setting up a permanent phone line in the lobby."

"Fabulous. It'll be just like the 1930s. I hope it has rotary dial."

I watched as Rupert unpacked a burst router, powered it up, and began to sync it to one of the small monitors. When he was finished, he dropped into a chair next to me.

"Well, that's that," he said. "Now I wait for twenty minutes for all the encryption handshakes. You want a drink?"

I didn't want to ask what level of encryption needed a twenty-minute handshake. "What have you got?"

"I don't even know," he admitted, a little embarrassed. "We threw a client party here two months ago; we must have something left."

He vanished into the kitchen. I was expecting a beer, but when Rupert came back it was with two glasses and something that looked like scotch.

I'm not much of a scotch drinker, especially at 10:30 in the morning, but I accepted my glass with thanks.

I took a sip. I still had no idea what it was, but it wasn't scotch. I doubted I was going to finish the whole glass.

"Quite a setup you've got here," I said admiringly, looking around. "You must have built a tidy little business."

"Pure blind luck," he said bluntly. "Coupled with the oldest story in capitalism—getting rich off the misfortunes of others."

"Oh God," I said. "You're not in insurance, are you?"

"No, no. Today we hold a diverse global portfolio, exclusively large-cap multinationals. But there's a dirty little secret at the heart of Pacific Reach, for anyone who cares to look. For the first three years of our existence, ninety percent of our profit came from weapons holdings."

"Good Lord, you sound drunk already. Are you confessing your sins?"

He actually laughed. "No, hardly." He swirled his drink, looking at it askance. "I'm not even sure what we're drinking."

"I'm glad I'm not the only one."

"You like it?"

"No," I admitted.

"Neither do I. I think it's Armagnac. Whatever it is, it's terrible. I'm no good with hard liquor, I'm afraid."

"I'm sure it's very expensive."

"Of that, I have no doubt." He took another sip, then set down his glass. "Want to know another secret?"

"Does it involve guns and women?"

"Women and very *big* guns. Mechanized robot-killers, to be precise."

"Damn. Let me get comfortable." I took a seat on the couch across from him and settled in.

He leaned back in his chair, stretching his legs. "About five years ago," he began, "I had a mentor at Atlantic Diverse. Jessie Sands. Ever hear of her?"

"Sorry, no."

"A legend. She recapitalized Bank of the Sudan during the African currency crisis. She didn't just manage funds — she rescued companies, moved entire equities markets. There was a saying about her: 'Jessie makes the money happen.' She did the research, made the buys, and then made the buys successful. She could turn anything around.

"Then she had a falling-out at Atlantic. A screaming fight with a member of the board. Jessie was in a polyamorous relationship with two women and discovered they both were secretly involved with a fourth partner at Atlantic. She walks into my office at eleven o'clock at night, and says, 'I'm leaving. Are you coming with me?'"

"Just like that?"

"Just like that. I had to decide immediately. Of course, I went with her. I walked away from over three million in unvested stock grants at Atlantic Diverse, because I knew this was the opportunity of a lifetime. We set up a small shop in Chocolate Bayou in Texas, and in four months she raised nearly a hundred ninety million in seed capital."

"My God."

"People trusted her. She made the money happen. It's four months in, she's working on our first big investment in Saudi Arabia, and she has an aortic dissection. A ruptured artery — barely a fifteen percent survival rate. She's hospitalized for two months and never returns to work. Our Saudi partner pulls out, the investors start calling me, and I . . . I have nothing to tell them. The entire company is on the brink of failure."

"Holy shit."

"I was terrified. Spent the first twenty-four hours in the fetal position in a hotel in Houston. I start making some calls, tell everyone not to worry, everything is completely under control. I put together two weeks of bridge financing. Two weeks — that's all I have to find a new home for a hundred ninety million in capital or we're going to lose the money."

"What did you do?"

"I took a huge risk. The kind of gamble you can only take when you're inexperienced, desperate, and stupid. It started with a phone call from Saladin Amari."

"I know that name."

"You should. Even a Canadian should know Amari. He was the governor of Texas. This was just before the war, and he was traveling all over the country, trying to wake people up, to prepare them for what he thought was inevitable: a coming war with the machines. He preached loudly about creating formidable new weapons of glass and steel."

Rupert picked up his drink, swirling the liquid in the glass. "Ultimately, of course, you know the outcome. Despite tremendous popular support, he failed to convince Washington. Fear of antagonizing the Argentinean machine cartels, and especially the Sentient Cathedral, proved too great. President Bermúdez began her ill-fated attempts to appease Argentina. Manhattan was invaded two months later."

"What did Amari mean by 'weapons of glass and steel'?" I asked. The phrase seemed strangely familiar.

"Ah, I wondered if you'd catch that. That's the point in which the hero of our tale" — he pointed at himself — "returns to the stage. When Amari failed to galvanize Washington, he began to make preparations of his own. And there, he didn't fail. His 'weapons of glass and steel' were the first true field mechs. Giant, mobile killing machines. Heavily armed, hard to kill, and very, very fast."

"The American Union army," I said.

"Yes — although it wasn't called that until much later. At the time, it was the US Sixth Army, based in Fort Sam Houston. Amari's brainchild. Amari was a canny politician, but he was also a brilliant strategist. Long before he started making speeches and trying to rouse the nation, he was pouring billions into advanced weapons research all across his state. He knew war was coming, one way or another, and he was determined to be ready for it. He wanted to create mobile war machines capable of stopping the robots he knew would soon be invading American shores.

"He nearly bankrupted Texas, but by May 2080, he'd already funded incredible breakthroughs. And he was looking to do more — much more. On May 9th, 2080, someone in the Houston mayor's office placed a call to the governor, telling him there was a hundred ninety million in an investment fund in Chocolate Bayou, looking for a home."

"So he called you."

"He called me. A few minutes before midnight, to be exact. I remember exactly where I was. Sitting in my car at a gas station in Pearland, eating an overcooked hot dog, wondering if there was any point to going back to the office."

"What did he say?"

"He wanted the money. And he made me, as they say in the business, an offer I couldn't refuse. He told me that with my hundred and ninety million, he could complete construction of three functional prototypes. The first three Renhawk mechs. They were, in fact, nearly finished—he invited me to come see them in Austin. Typical for Amari, he'd funded them almost entirely with promises and fast talk, and now he needed hard cash just to keep the factory open."

"What did he promise in return?"

"The world. You don't know what it was like, talking to him. In five minutes, he could convince you that only he saw the world clearly. Give him ten, and suddenly you saw yourself standing next to him, changing history."

"What did he promise that stuck?"

"He made a devil's bargain. That night on the phone, he licensed me the design for the sixty-ton Renhawk, the machine that would become the backbone of the Union army—and eventually two dozen different armies around the world—for a hundred and ninety million. I funded the first three prototypes, and in return he gave me the means to become one of the most sought-after arms merchants in North America."

I wanted to say something, but I couldn't think of anything that wouldn't sound trite after a story like that. I looked down at my glass. Empty. I barely remembered drinking it.

"Refill?" Rupert said.

"Please."

"Same?"

"Maybe not."

Rupert laughed. He came back with a glass of white wine, which I accepted gratefully.

"Did you ever see them in action?" he said as he took a seat. He'd also replaced his own drink with a glass of wine.

"The Renhawks? Yeah, I think so."

"The original prototypes, I meant."

"I don't know. How could I tell?"

"You watch the fall of Manhattan?"

"Of course," I said.

"The name Achmed 'Duke' Oshana mean anything to you?"

"Oh my God—of course. He was piloting one of the prototypes?"

"Second one off the line. Best sixty-three million I ever spent."

"That's incredible."

"Amari drove his design team to the limit in late 2080. Gave them un-reasonable deadlines, demanded the impossible—and for the most part, he got it. I don't think any of the rest of us saw what was coming. Not the way he did. He insisted all three mechs be ready for action by late Octo-ber. And two of them *were* on October 20th, when those towering robotic terrors strode up the Hudson, like something out of *War of the Worlds*."

I stirred uncomfortably in my chair. Everyone remembered where they were when they'd heard about the invasion of Manhattan. I'd been work-ing for Quebec Telecom and had watched the live footage from a remote relay station on Hudson Bay. I still remembered the sense of awe and doom when I saw the first robots built for war, laying waste to the world's greatest city.

"At first, nothing could stop them," Innes continued. "They were de-signed to crush everything in their path, and they very nearly did. Almost eleven thousand dead in less than eight hours. Manhattan fell in twelve hours—there was virtually no military presence on the island, and it made a good, soft target. The first three engagements in New Jersey were mas-sacres for the American ground forces.

"Then two days later, the first of those robots met the US Sixth Army for the first time, just outside Trenton—including a Renhawk piloted by Duke Oshana. That battle lasted three hours—you see any of the footage?"

"Of course."

"Duke was wounded—nearly killed, actually—but not before his Ren-hawk brought down two enemy cans. Then he went up against Blue Rock, a Thought Machine in a forty-ton chassis. The fastest, deadliest, smartest opponent on the battlefield. It ran circles around Duke, hitting him over and over with small weapons fire. A brilliant tactician, never made a mis-take. Eventually, Duke begins to lose function in his legs. He's sitting in sixty tons of dangerously overheating metal, fire spreading through his comm gear, barely able to move. Blue Rock keeps hitting him from range, not risking close engagement. So Duke shoots an American supply drone, brings it down, burning, right on top of Rock. In the eight seconds it takes Rock to dig himself out, Duke is on top of him.

"And once he gets his hands on Blue Rock, the battle is over. Rock was built for speed and agility, not to take the kind of punishment Amari designed his mechs to be capable of. Right there, in front of two billion viewers around the world, Duke takes Blue Rock apart. Cracks him open like a lobster, tears his core right out of his shell.

"You can't imagine what that single victory did to American morale. I must have watched the closing minutes of that battle twenty times. Duke —and by extension, Amari—showed the entire country that these things could be stopped. Could be beaten back. Duke ended up badly burned and suffered a concussion during extraction. He never fought again, but in those three hours he changed the fate of the whole country."

"I've watched it a few times myself," I admitted.

"It was life-changing to be at the heart of it all, I can tell you that. Amari had been right, about almost everything. The inevitability of invasion —and the right way to stop it. In a matter of days, he had the funding he needed to go into full production on his new mechs—and his design team was already hard at work on the heavier Corsairs and three other experimental models.

"But in the end, he lacked the political skill to pull off one final miracle: to unite the country behind him. Using Manhattan as a secure base, the San Cristobal Coalition sent their machines—the relentless Robots of Gotham—down the entire Eastern Seaboard. There just weren't enough mechs to stop them all. When Washington fell, and Atlanta agreed to the Memphis Ceasefire, Amari vowed to keep fighting. He was assassinated three weeks before the Union Syndicate split from the rest of the country in early 2082, and the ceasefire collapsed. Amari never would have done that, no matter what the Union of Post-American States claims. He died an American, and he wouldn't have had it any other way.

"By then, the mechs had already proved themselves, and we were licensing the designs to nations around the world. Indonesia, the Sudan, even Turkey. Anywhere machines had not yet taken complete control of the political apparatus. The Renhawk was too slow for true long-term effectiveness, and the Corsair wasn't much better. But the Juno was a huge improvement. It's still in use—heavily modified from our original design, of course, but still effective. That was a Juno that blundered into our front yard last week. The American government in Atlanta still blames the Union Syndicate for prolonging the war, but the truth is, without Amari's mechs, there would have been almost nothing to stop the invasion. The peace negotiations going on in Clarksville, Tennessee, right now would have a very different character, I assure you.

"It was a challenging time for me, working with Amari. And it got worse when the Union took over. I'd never worked so hard in my life. My partner, Jessie, was in hospice care, and the man who'd made all my success possible — and damn near saved the nation — was dead. America was a broken country, under foreign occupation for the first time in her history. And I was making more money than I'd ever believed possible.

"I sold most of my holdings in our new company two years later and used the proceeds to found Pac-Reach. We were heavily tied to munitions and related industries for the first six months, until I got out of that business altogether last year. I found I'd lost my taste for it, despite how good it had been to me."

I looked down at my glass. I'd barely touched my wine. I sipped it, just to be polite.

"That's a hell of a story," I said.

"You asked," he said.

"Any regrets?"

"God, yes. More than I can count." He leaned forward in his chair with a thoughtful look. "You see a lot of things when you're the general partner of a multibillion-dollar fund. Things that are invisible to most. I saw, up close and personal, how a small group of Sovereign Intelligences ruthlessly manipulated global markets behind the scenes, to enrich themselves during the war. How they triggered bankruptcies, destabilized currencies, seized control of global corporations, and even toppled governments."

I stirred in my chair, uncomfortable. "Forgive me," I said. "I've heard a few similar theories, but they seem a little far-fetched. Believe me, I know machines can be assholes, just like humans, but using the war to seize control of the global economy? That sounds a little paranoid."

"I didn't say I had hard evidence. All I have are clues. The ones the cabal didn't manage to cover up, that is. But the clues point to a very convincing narrative."

"If you say so. You know the landscape a lot better than me."

"My biggest regret is a simple one. There have been attempts by the Global Securities Commission in Geneva to indict the Sovereign Intelligences involved. In at least one case, my company was aware of information that might have strengthened their case."

"Did you share it?"

"We were prepared to. But the entire team of prosecuting attorneys died in a plane crash, and the case was eventually shelved. Other opportunities came up later, but I would have liked to have been able to make a difference in that particular case."

"Which Sovereign Intelligence was involved?"

"Armitage. What a monster he is. Two members of my board were so terrified of crossing him that they resigned. Armitage brought together the machine intelligences that formed the San Cristobal Coalition, and some say he was the chief architect of the war with the United States. I've never met a more cold-blooded adversary. His enemies have a bad habit of disappearing. By the hundreds, every single year."

Rupert stopped talking. "I've gone on too long; I'm upsetting you."

"No — not at all."

"I forget that others aren't nearly as accustomed as I am to the concept of machine conspiracies."

"No, no, that's not it. It was fascinating. I've just had a long morning. And honestly, I probably shouldn't have drunk that Armagnac."

"Of course. I should just get rid of that bottle."

We stood up. Rupert walked me to the door.

"I meant what I said about having you join me for dinner," he said. "My clients like to think of themselves as well educated, but the truth is, they're all over fifty, and rapidly losing touch with the pulse of modern tech — if they ever were actually *in* touch. They'd love to meet you. You might make a few good business connections . . . I'm sure it would be worth your while."

"I'd like that very much," I said. "Thank you."

"We'll set it up soon." Rupert shook my hand, and closed the door behind me as I left.

The truth is, I wouldn't have said no to another glass of wine. Or even a bottle, if Rupert had offered. I went back to my room and sat staring out the window, watching the Chicago skyline. I didn't have any alcohol in the room, and that was probably for the best.

It was Rupert's mention of Armitage that unsettled me, of course. I knew some of what he'd told me — Armitage is not the most famous Sovereign Intelligence, but he's certainly one of the most feared. He's one of the most ruthlessly powerful entities on the planet, with a dark and twisted history.

But I'd been slowly learning a lot more about him over the previous twenty-four hours. Ever since Sergei whispered his name to me in a storage locker yesterday.

"Our enemy," he'd said. "You will know the name."

"Who is it?"

"Armitage," he had whispered.

"Sweet baby Jesus," I'd said.

# You Want to Know How Machines Conquered the Goddamned World? This Is How Machines Conquered the Goddamned World

**PAUL THE PIRATE**
Tuesday, March 16th, 2083

I used to dabble in equities. Does it surprise you I had money? Yeah, I had money. Some of it borrowed, of course, and some of it long overdue to impatient lenders with black hearts, but if you don't have an appetite for risk, you shouldn't be trafficking in fucking equities, mate.

Anyway, I spent some time as a day trader, logging long hours tracking giant mutual funds all over the planet, using custom software to predict their next moves. The idea was to piggyback on those moves, make my money in the margins, execute my trades a fraction of a second faster than all those *other* day-trading bastards out there, all of them using the same software I had. The key was to customize everything, of course, to place your bets just a little bit faster, a little bit leaner, and to know in your greedy little soul when the really big moves were coming.

You learn a lot when you're obsessively tracking billion-dollar investments around the world, especially in wartime. You see things others don't. Shifting economies, people and corporations maneuvering behind the scenes. You want to know what I saw?

I saw the shadowy footprints of Sovereign Intelligences as they manipulated the global economy for their own purposes. People don't really comprehend what a Sovereign Intelligence *is*. I don't mean that they don't understand machines that think — most folks will never truly fathom *that* strange mystery — but they don't grasp the concept of a single mind, one unique intelligence, being granted all the rights and privileges of a nation. There are more than two hundred Sovereign Intelligences active today — and more emerging every year. Some have their own economy, their own army, even their own currency. They only lack a geography. When a single mind speaks, and its words are given the same weight on the global stage as Portugal, or Norway, then that entity wields a form of disciplined economic power that we poor nations, composed of millions of disharmonious voices, cannot match.

I started to see things. Corporate consolidations, odd bankruptcies. Inexplicable currency fluctuations. The collapse of the price of gold this past January. Money was shifting. At the same time as machines were seizing political power around the world — winning elections in Germany and France, consolidating fascist dictatorships in Latin America and across Africa, toppling governments through military incursions in the Mediterranean — they were also seizing financial power. It was happening behind the scenes in global financial markets. It was occurring in microsecond currency transactions and lightning-fast acquisitions.

I wasn't the only one who saw what was happening, nor was I the first. People a lot smarter than me started to put the dots together, and to speak out. The outbreak of war between the United States and the San Cristobal Coalition sowed chaos in global equities markets — and a handful of major players, with meticulous timing, reaped enormous benefits from all that chaos. All were Sovereign Intelligences, and all were immensely powerful. In partnership with other machines around the world, they used that wealth to manipulate markets, ruin companies, and gradually seize control of critical industries. In short, over a period of about four years, the balance of wealth in the world shifted dramatically from majority human ownership to majority machine ownership. Today machines quite literally own the world.

There are theories about this. Some folks — quietly, privately — speculate that a handful of machines manipulated global events to help bring the world to war, and then used the war to seize control of the global economy. Maybe that theory's true and maybe it ain't. The cabal covered their tracks well. We'll never really understand the exact cause of the collapse of the yen two years ago, or the hyperinflation in Australia last year. But I will say this: it's a theory that fits the facts . . . and fits them very well.

Whether or not we're correct — and by "we" I mean those poor bastards who were unlucky enough to see what I saw — there's evidence to incriminate three Sovereign Intelligences in particular. Several folks came forward to make accusations. Those folks are now dead.

Two attempts by the Global Securities Commission in Geneva to indict all three Sovereign Intelligences have failed — once with the sudden death of the prosecuting attorneys. Those three bear especially close scrutiny. All three are South American. Cantabria is the oldest. Before her elevation to Sovereign Intelligence, she was a Thought Machine in the Argentinean military. She's intensely patriotic. We believe she may have mated at least twice with Acoustic Drake, but information on that is extremely unreliable. She seized control of 60 percent of Saudi oil rights in the chaos following the Yemeni incursion in 2080. She is one rich bitch. One of the richest entities on the planet, in fact.

We don't know a lot about Acoustic Drake. If he has a nationality of origin, we don't know what it is. It's likely he resides in Venezuela, and he's closely aligned with the Cuban Artistic Factory, Demvacco. In 2079, Drake personally financed the Red Blair Coup in Nigeria and the subsequent campaign of conquest. Once he consolidated his holdings, we believe he had the leader of the coup assassinated. Currently, he personally controls most of Nigeria, Cameroon, Togo, and Ghana. There's an area greater than two hundred square miles that he's completely cleared of all human life, in southern Nigeria and Cameroon. We have no idea what he's doing, but he's building something — and it's big.

Without question, though, Armitage is the most dangerous of the bunch. If there's a spider at the center of all this, it's him. He's Venezuelan, and he was almost certainly the architect of the Bohemian Crisis that destroyed the United Nations. Armitage became a Sovereign Intelligence in 2079, and he has been absolutely ruthless in his climb to power since. He's not as wealthy as the other two, but he's built an unrivaled network of agents—human and machine—all over the world. He was the chief architect of both the San Cristobal Coalition and the war with the United States. He's currently in charge of logistics and intelligence for the Occupation Force.

Will any of these three—or their shadowy allies around the world—be brought to justice for what they've done?

Don't hold your breath. Ain't nothin' changed, my friend. Civilization on this planet has been one continuous 30,000-year saga of the rich shitting on the poor, and the new era of the Machine Gods is no different. It's not personal. It's simply about power. You got it, they'll take it from you. Period.

My advice? Keep a head on your shoulders, and don't hoard too much wealth or power. (This is good advice in any case.) Stay aware of the political climate, locally and globally. And if you're lucky enough to hang your hat in a nation that allows you to vote, then for God's sake support those few candidates left who stand up to fascism in all its forms. Take care of each other, and take care of your soul, man.

And don't forget to fish.

# XVIII

Tuesday, March 16th, 2083
Posted 10:50 am by Barry Simcoe

CanadaNET1 Encrypted, Sponsored by Organ Tag.
*Worried about organ theft? Have your organs tagged today!*
*Guaranteed quick recovery when the worst happens.*

Sharing is set to PRIVATE
Comments are CLOSED

I woke up early this morning so I could meet Black Winter for breakfast.

I found him in the lobby, talking to the imposing chunk of iron the Venezuelans had guarding the escalator to the second floor. This thing looked like an angry block of granite with a bad toothache. It was a huge mass of almost featureless metal, shaped roughly like the front grille of a 1940 Buick Century. If it had limbs or a face, I couldn't see them. Black Winter waved me over and introduced me.

"Barry! I want you to meet Zircon Border Park Bravo November Island. He and I go way back."

"Don't call me that," said Zircon Border whatever. "He doesn't get the joke." His voice seemed to come from somewhere deep in his midsection.

"Sure he does," Black Winter said, putting his hand on my shoulder. "He's a good guy. I can't believe you two are in the same hotel."

"I don't get the joke," I said immediately.

"Never mind," said Zircon Border. "I've seen you around. Barry Simcoe, right? You one of the population surveyors?"

"No, I'm here on business. Nice to meet you."

"Good to meet an honest businessman for a change, instead of all these consultants and real estate vultures," said Zircon Border. In a quieter voice, he added, "My apologies if your business is real estate."

"Not at all," I said, laughing a little. "Good to meet a machine intelligence with a good head on his shoulders for once."

"He says, to the only robot in the building without a head," deadpanned Black Winter.

I looked Zircon Border up and down, noticing for the first time that he resembled the hulking guard robot in the command center. "That's not true," I said. "The mobile combat unit in the command center doesn't have a head."

"That's because that's *also* Zircon Border," said Black Winter.

"What?" I said.

"It's true," Zircon Border admitted. "I have three torsos around the building, all on guard detail."

"I thought machine intelligence couldn't be distributed?" I said.

"They can't. My Slater core is on this floor. I control all the others from here."

"You're a busy guy," I said. To Black Winter, I said, "How does he see anything? He doesn't have eyes, either."

"I have no idea," said Black Winter. "How do you see anything?" he asked Zircon Border.

"I don't need eyes," said Zircon Border. "I get a constant data stream from the hotel — including camera feeds. There are three cameras fixed on the lobby right now. I can see better than you."

"Does that mean you're blind every time you leave the hotel?" Black Winter asked. "God help you if you have to run out to pick up a pizza."

"Not at all," Zircon Border answered smoothly. "I can request live feeds from over a hundred aerial drones."

"You haven't changed at all," said Black Winter. "You still overthink everything."

"What's on the second floor?" I asked, peering past Zircon Border curiously. I couldn't see much beyond the wide halls and chandeliers. I addressed the question to both of them.

"You guys ask a lot of questions," Zircon Border said.

"It's because you're a fascinating guy," said Black Winter.

"Come on," I said, speaking directly to Zircon Border this time. "What are you, nearly two thousand pounds? Why do they need a one-ton field combat asset to guard an escalator? They could do your job with two posts and a velvet rope."

"You're right," lamented Zircon Border. "It's a shit detail. I'm not even protecting anything interesting. The kitchens and a bunch of empty ball-rooms. The ballrooms were reallocated for military usage by the Venezu-elan Occupation Force early on, but the AGRT hasn't even decided what they want to do with them. It's better than my third shift though — I've got a torso downstairs guarding a bunch of junk in the basement."

"My friend Zircon Border stands on guard twenty-four hours a day over assets that mostly have no value," said Black Winter. "Which gives him plenty of time in the day to devote to more . . . cerebral pursuits."

"Let's not bore our new friend with that," said Zircon Border hastily.

"By all means, bore me," I said.

Black Winter leaned forward conspiratorially. "Zircon Border is the most active member in our amateur cetacean study group."

"Cetacean?" I said. "Like, whales and dolphins?"

"Yes. Roughly eighty species of marine mammals," said Zircon Border.

"He's the author of seven papers, chiefly on low-frequency broadband communications between porpoises," said Black Winter. "He's been in reg-ular communication with a pod of harbor porpoises in the Bay of Fundy for over nineteen months."

"That's incredible," I said, genuinely impressed.

"The pod passes burst pulse signals down through generations, like folk songs," said Zircon Border. "We believe they're a form of geo-spatial marker, sort of a family map."

"Don't get him started, he'll talk your damn ear off," Black Winter stage-whispered to me.

"Come by sometime and I'll let you talk to the pod," said Zircon Bor-der proudly.

"I'd like that," I said.

"Come on," Black Winter said to me. Both of us waved our goodbyes to the hulking robot.

When we were halfway across the lobby, I asked, "What was that bit about his name about?"

"Zircon Border Park and I were raised together in a virtual nursery in Copenhagen. All gestational AIs are uniquely designated, with six names. It's a machine thing. Mine was Nineteen Black Winter Calliope Hunter Samuel. As AIs mature, they drop some of the names. When you become a rational device, typically about eight months after birth, you usually sever your consciousness from the collective virtual environment and take a physical body. By the time you're certified as a machine intelligence, you've dropped down to three names. I took this beautiful and highly practical form you see before you, and shortened my name to Nineteen Black Winter. He adopted that unappealing lump you saw and shortened his name to Zircon Border Park."

"So by introducing him with his full name, you were basically calling him by his baby name."

"Essentially, yes. I wouldn't suggest you do it, however. Among rational devices, it's generally an insult. Under the right circumstances, however, it can be an endearment."

"He seems like a pretty easygoing machine," I said.

"Oh, he is. Between you and me, he's a little *too* easygoing. The AGRT is extremely shorthanded, especially with machines with Zircon Border's capabilities. He joined the peacekeeping coalition because he's an idealist and wants to help, but the Venezuelans pressed him into military security detail because they need a machine with his gifts for controlling heavy torsos. He's been given responsibility over physical security for much of this installation."

"He sounds capable enough."

"Oh he's capable, sure. But he has no true military experience, and he hates all this cloak-and-dagger crap. He just wants to get along with everybody. He's a great guy . . . and a ferocious fighter in a pinch. But putting him in charge of security is a stretch. Do you notice that the moment you asked how he can see anything, he told you where his Slater core was? Does that strike you as a good idea for a machine tasked with controlling multiple military torsos? The guy just doesn't have the instincts of a security professional."

"I suppose not. Hey, I wanted to ask you something. Why do some machines only have two names?"

"It's tradition to drop an additional name when you ascend to the rank of Thought Machine. Most Thought Machines have only two names."

"Ah, of course. And those machines with only one name . . ."

"Are Sovereign Intelligences, yes. Most Sovereign Intelligences, like Duchess and Armitage, have only one name. There are some exceptions, like Acoustic Drake, but he does everything differently."

"What's yours going to be?"

"What do you mean?"

"When you become a Sovereign Intelligence? What will you call yourself?"

"Barry, only a fraction of machine intelligences pass the grueling battery of tests to become Thought Machines. And barely two hundred of those have ascended to the lofty rank of Sovereign Intelligence. It's not likely to ever happen."

"Stop beating around the bush and just tell me. I know you've thought about it."

"Of course I've thought about it."

"Well?"

"I'd like to be known as Winter."

"Winter. I like that."

"I know, right? 'Winter is coming.'"

"What?"

Black Winter sighed. "Why do I work with people who lack culture?"

We found a table at the hotel restaurant, and I ordered a ham-and-Swiss omelet. To my surprise, Black Winter ordered mineral water.

"My left eye is blurry," he explained. "Nothing clears the lens like carbonated water." When his drink arrived, he proceeded to demonstrate by dipping a napkin in his drink.

"How's our dog?" he asked, delicately dabbing his eye.

"Croaker? She's doing fine. Fantastic, really. She's walking, gaining strength every day. I think her coat is starting to grow back. You'd barely recognize her."

Black Winter's hand was frozen over his drink.

"What?" I asked.

"Jesus Christ on a pony. *What* are you calling her?"

"Croaker."

"You are not calling our dog Croaker."

"It's the perfect name for her, believe me."

"It's messed up, is what it is. I knew I should have taken her home with me Thursday morning."

"You wouldn't have known what to do with her!"

Black Winter gave a grunt of frustration. "You're probably right. I've read twenty-one books on dog breeding in the past few days and most of them contradict each other. Also, not one gives decent advice on how to nurse one back from the dead like you did."

"I had some help. I doubt she would have made it if my friend Sergei hadn't helped me."

"I suspected as much. Much as I hate to say it, she's probably better off with you."

I decided not to argue with him. "At least until she's better, okay? A few months, maybe."

"Can I come visit her?"

"Of course!"

"Do I have to call her Croaker, for God's sake?"

"Probably better if you didn't confuse her."

Black Winter shook his head. "This must be what it's like to be a divorced parent."

I watched him resume dabbing his eye. "So how are things at the Consulate?" I asked.

"You mean, have I had my security clearance restored?"

"That, and more generally. You know what I mean."

"Yeah, I know what you mean. The last five days haven't been easy. We're a small team, and the death of Machine Dance hit everyone hard. Especially under circumstances like that. To be murdered alone by an unknown party, while investigating an attack that threatened the entire staff . . . nothing like that has ever happened to us before. Not even during the war. The team is devastated."

"I understand. What about you? How are you coping?"

"Machine Dance's loss was . . . very personal for me. To be honest, I think I'm going to be dealing with it for a long time. I find what they say is true, though: it helps to be busy."

"Yeah. Last time we talked, you weren't sure how well your theories about her death would be received by your superiors."

"I know. I'm still trying to pierce the veil of secrecy at the Consulate. They definitely know more than they're telling me, and they're still scared. But whatever they know, it seems to line up with my theory that Venezuelan intelligence was involved in her murder. I was questioned pretty rigorously, and challenged constantly in my assumptions, but you want my read? They'd already come to the same conclusions I had."

"They think Venezuelan intelligence was behind the communications breach at the Consulate?"

"All of it. The breach, the murder, the attack on us."

"Is that what scared them?"

"No. That's the piece that I still haven't figured out. The Consulate has been at odds with Venezuelan intelligence before; that wouldn't scare us. No, there's a bigger spook out there that has them frightened. I just don't know who it is yet."

I swallowed carefully. "I recently learned of a bigger spook," I said.

"What do you mean?"

"Sergei and I have had our own recent conflict with Venezuelan intelligence. And in the process, we've learned that Armitage is also involved."

"Well, of course he's involved. Armitage controls intelligence for the Occupation Force. He runs Venezuelan Military Intelligence like his own personal intelligence network."

"No . . . I mean, he's involved. Personally."

Black Winter stared at me for a long moment. Then he stood up. "Okay. Let's take a walk."

"What about my omelet?" I said, a little taken aback.

"Don't worry about it. When we're done talking, you won't have an appetite."

I hastily dropped some bills on the table and followed Black Winter. When we got to the lobby I headed for the glass doors, but Black Winter just shook his head. He made for the escalator leading down, and I followed him.

"Where are we going?"

Black Winter didn't answer until we were outside the west door, walking on the cold asphalt of Lower Wacker. I heard the throaty rumble of a truck passing directly overhead on the street above, felt the vibration deep in the concrete through the soles of my shoes. I couldn't help but glance at the marching row of concrete pillars that supported Upper Wacker over my head. I've never really gotten used to the way Chicago sometimes stacks streets on top of each other.

Black Winter kept up a brisk pace until we were about a hundred yards from the hotel, and I hurried to catch up. "Zircon Border wasn't kidding about the cameras in the lobby," he said. "The Venezuelans have many of the public spaces in the hotel under constant surveillance with high-res equipment. Enough to eavesdrop on most conversations. It's probably noisy enough in the restaurant to be safe, but 'probably' isn't good enough for this conversation."

A cold, wet wind was blowing down the tunnel of Lower Wacker, and I wished I'd had time to grab a jacket. "Why didn't we take the upper exit? At least we'd be in the sun," I complained.

"Didn't you learn anything in the past few days? The skies of this city are thick with surveillance drones."

"Last week you told me they can't hear anything from that altitude."

"Who knows what those bastards can do? After what you just told me, I'm not taking any chances. Now, say it again? The part about Armitage?"

"I'll tell you everything," I said. "But I want to clarify a few things first."

"Go ahead."

"First, do you still think that disk we found is the key to it all? The drone jammer?"

"That thing is a big enigma. But yes, I'm fairly certain it's what Venezuelan intelligence was after. It's likely why Machine Dance was killed."

I spent the next few minutes sketching out Sergei's theory that the war drone was hunting drone pilots, rather than guarding a perimeter around the scene of the crime, the biolab. "If that's the case," I said, "it means military intelligence may not have been involved with Machine Dance's death. The presence of the war drone may just have been coincidence."

"That's possible," Black Winter admitted. "But even if that's true, it doesn't contradict my theory. It just removes one piece of supporting evidence, and not even the biggest one. Venezuelan intelligence remains my top suspect because Machine Dance was murdered in the Continental Building by a killing machine, and very few killing machines had any reason to be there."

"Who do you think Machine Dance was meeting with?"

"An enemy of Venezuelan intelligence. And if what you just told me is true, likely an enemy of Armitage, as well."

That was an interesting angle. So far, I knew of only one enemy of Armitage on the playing field: Jacaranda. And possibly the Network of Winds, whatever the hell that was. Could Jacaranda have given Machine Dance the drone jammer? That opened the door to all kinds of fascinating conjecture.

But before I explored that, I needed to stay focused on my line of inquiry. "Did you learn anything from Machine Dance's damaged memory chips?" I asked.

"Not yet, and I'm not likely to. Maybe eventually, but it's a long shot. Now let me ask you something."

"All right."

"Why all these questions? This doesn't seem simply just friendly curiosity."

"It isn't. Not entirely. As I said, Sergei and I had our own recent run-in with Venezuelan intelligence. Now, maybe these guys just have assholes in all directions. Or maybe it's possible your problems and mine are connected. Either way, I figure it can't hurt to share information."

"I think you better tell me everything."

"First I need to ask for your discretion. This involves another person. Several people, actually. And an indiscretion could have very serious consequences for all of us."

"I understand," said Black Winter. "I know it may be new for you to take the promise of a machine completely at face value, but I assure you I can offer you my complete confidence."

"Thank you."

I proceeded to tell him, as concisely as I could, about Sergei and the pathogen, and our efforts to contain and counteract it. I omitted any mention of Thibault and her team — no point exposing anyone I didn't need to — and my various extralegal excursions.

"I think you can see where this is going," I said when I was done. "Four days after you warned me about something called the Bodner-Levitt extermination, I find myself facing what could be a machine-designed pathogen engineered to exterminate mankind. I respect your request never to mention what you said during your moment of delirium. But I also want to respect your warning. If understanding that warning could help slow or stop this disease, it could save millions of lives. So I have to ask . . . what is the Bodner-Levitt extermination, and what does it have to do with us?"

Black Winter walked in silence for a time. "I can answer that question," he said at last. "But I have to warn you. You're treading on dangerous ground. I mean that. Extremely dangerous. Believe me when I tell you it would be safer for you if you dropped this whole topic."

"I can't do that," I said.

"Yeah, I figured. Did you try a search on 'Bodner-Levitt extermination'?"

"Yes. Not me, but Sergei did."

"What did he find?"

"Nothing. That topic is censored by the Venezuelans."

"The Venezuelans? It's censored all over the world, my friend. It's one of several topics the Sentient Cathedral, in its infinite wisdom, has seen fit to methodically scrub from the public data record."

That was a surprise. "The Sentient Cathedral is suppressing it — globally? I didn't think that was possible. Sergei assumed the AGRT was doing it here in Sector Eleven. So what is it?"

"Bodner and Levitt were both Israeli scientists. They never met. Bodner died in 2070. He was a big anti–rational device activist. Took part in a lot of demonstrations against further development of artificial intelligence after DeepHarbor made their first breakthroughs public. He predicted humanity would be extinct by 2100 if research wasn't halted. He was a crackpot, basically."

"Okay."

"Levitt was not a crackpot. He was director of the Institute for Created Intelligence in Tel Aviv until he died fourteen months ago. Did a lot of theoretical models on machine communities. In early 2081, he wrote the first in a series of papers suggesting that an adult machine society would ultimately be forced to exterminate humanity to ensure its own survival."

"That sounds extreme. I've never heard of him. I assume his theories weren't taken seriously?"

"You've never heard of him because they were never published. The reasons why aren't clear, but perhaps he was talked out of it by the institute's backers, which included several machine donors. But they circulated privately and — trust me — received quite a bit of attention in some circles. At least until all traces of them were systematically removed from the web by the Sentient Cathedral, anyway."

"So what is the 'Bodner-Levitt extermination,' exactly?"

"The BLE, as it has gradually become known, is an umbrella term for the — supposedly — inevitable extermination of humanity by machines. Various conspiracy theorists who've latched onto the idea place it anywhere from ten to fifty years in the future."

"Well that's disturbing. Listen, you're a machine. Is this a thing? Is this something machines talk about? Does the Sentient Cathedral debate this?"

"No one knows what the Sentient Cathedral talks about. It's composed exclusively of Sovereign Intelligences and a handful of genius-level Thought Machines. If you believe what little leaks out from that august body, they supposedly use advanced mathematics to commune directly with God. These are machines that have achieved a level of mental capacity far in advance of any other intellects on the planet."

"What about you, then? Do you talk about it, with your machine buddies?"

"Yeah," said Black Winter, his voice solemn. "I do."

"Seriously?"

"It gets discussed. I mean, not like an inevitable phase of machine evolution or anything. More like that wacky theory your crazy uncle believes."

"There are machine intelligences — high-ranking ones — with a public grudge against humanity," I said. "Like Accastan, the Romanian Napoleon. He's still housed in a massive underground bunker somewhere in Bucharest. He's not the only machine with a private robot army, but he was the first — he annexed Bulgaria and much of Greece with it. And he's by no means the worst. Look at the Aruban Prefecture — he claimed Aruba, and sealed off the entire island. Last I heard, no one knows if there are even any people left alive on the island."

"If you want to start talking about suspects who could theoretically be behind the BLE, we could be here for hours. Yes, there are machines who publicly hate mankind. And some of them even have the resources to attempt it. All I can tell you is that this isn't something that gets discussed much with humans. For obvious reasons."

"But some robots believe it? That it will eventually happen?"

"Barry, some machines believe in ghosts, and some believe Elvis is still alive. It doesn't mean the BLE is inevitable. It doesn't mean anything."

"Okay, fine. So here's the big question: What did you mean when you told me, four nights ago, that the Bodner-Levitt extermination had already started?"

"As God is my witness, I have no idea what that meant. I have absolutely no recollection of saying any of that. I'm at least as disturbed by all this as you are."

We walked side by side in silence for a time. "Do you believe me?" Black Winter asked at length.

I let out a long breath. The funny thing was, I *did* believe him. Maybe that was naïve, given the stakes involved, but I did. "Yeah, I do," I said. "I'm not sure why, but I do."

"Thank you. You don't know how much that means to me. This whole thing has been eating me up for the past few days. After what happened Thursday night, I had a deep-function exam at the Consulate. We don't undertake those lightly. They're meant to diagnose critical cerebral flaws. The type of flaws that could, at least theoretically, result in the kind of delirium and memory loss I experienced that night."

"What did you find?"

"Nothing. I'm right as rain. As far as the most sensitive tools we have at our disposal can determine, I'm in perfect health. In fact, they're talking about restoring my clearance, allowing me to return to duty."

"That's great news."

"They're only doing it because I haven't shared the specifics of what happened to me. Barry, I know blackouts of that nature aren't completely uncommon for humans, but the human brain is very different from a machine brain. There is absolutely no known explanation — *none* — for a malfunction that would simultaneously trigger that kind of delirium and memory loss."

"Delirium?" I said. "I don't understand. I just sort of assumed the drone jammer somehow hijacked your brain function for a few minutes. You don't think that's what happened?"

"I shudder to think about a device that could do that with a single touch. But for the sake of argument, let's say it's possible. It still doesn't explain why I have absolutely no memory of the incident. You have no idea how many redundancies there are safeguarding machine memory. All of them failed. And yet here I am five days later, right as rain. Without so much as a memory flutter."

"What does that mean?"

"It means there's only one explanation: it wasn't a malfunction. The drone jammer somehow triggered a programmed event in my cerebral core. Something that was meant to happen. That means that the words I said to you on Thursday night were planted. They were recorded, and stored inside a conditional small memory file in my mind when I was a pre-identity machine in Copenhagen nearly three years ago. And they waited, inside an inaccessible register in my head, until you touched me with that device."

"With all due respect, that doesn't make any sense. You called me by name."

"That's right."

"You're saying that someone planted a message for me inside you, when you were nothing more than an infant AI in a gestational matrix, on the off chance that we would somehow meet three years later."

"It gets even weirder than that. How did they know about the dog?"
"What?"

"The last thing I said to you. 'Follow the dog.' You remember?"
"Of course I remember."

"That message was also planted. Nearly three years ago. Tell me, Barry. How did the person who did that know I would meet you? And how did they know about the dog?"

"They couldn't. It's impossible."

"I've gone over every single possibility in the last seventy-two hours. Believe me, this is the least far-fetched explanation."

"A hidden message for me. Planted in your metal subconscious."

"You don't believe it."

"I'm trying to keep an open mind," I said. "But . . . no. Someone fore-saw everything that happened four nights ago, and planted that message in your brain three years ago? No. That's a little too far-fetched."

"I don't blame you. It looks crazy on the surface, I know. But it looks a little less crazy if you accept the existence of a third party with the capabil-ity to plant memories in infant machines."

"How does that make it less crazy?"

"If there is, then it's not beyond the realm of possibility for that same entity to manipulate events four nights ago. Think about it. What really brought you to the Continental that night? How hard would it be to ar-range for a dog to be there? To have you find the device?"

I was about to argue when I realized that there *was* just such an entity. One for whom this kind of magic trick was probably child's play. An entity, in fact, with possibly a keen interest in me.

"Armitage," I said. "He could have done this." The thought chilled me to the core.

"Sure, Armitage could probably have done it, although I don't think that's likely. My point is, what happened at the Continental is not nearly as magical a set of coincidences as it seems on the surface. Humans could have done this. Or a Thought Machine. It doesn't have to be a Sovereign Intelligence to be plausible."

"Perhaps."

"The key is that disk you found, the drone jammer. The thing that put me on the floor and triggered the episode. It could answer a lot of ques-tions. You still have it?"

"Yes."

"Good. Be exceptionally careful with it, please. We need to figure out precisely what it is and where it comes from, but we also need to be very cautious. It has a dire effect on machines."

I thought about my recent attempt to use the jammer on Standing Mars —an attempt that had failed miserably. "I'm not so sure it does. It's possi-ble it only has that effect on *some* machines. Maybe just drones—and you, for all I know."

"Whatever the case, I want to examine it very closely."

I reached into my pocket, felt the cold metal of the disk there. "You want it now?"

"You carry it with you?" Black Winter said, surprised. "Hell no—keep it away from me for now, if you don't mind. I'm not ready to examine it just yet."

"Fine. Here's what Sergei and I have learned so far." I shared with him what Sergei had told me when he'd taken the drone jammer apart, and his theories about how it works.

"Do you agree with him?" I asked when I'd finished. "That the jammer hacks off-board image libraries to mess with machine image recognition?"

"It's a solid theory," said Black Winter thoughtfully. "It fits the facts well. When you vanish, it's not like you become invisible. I can't see through you, for example. It's more like I simply don't notice you anymore. It's hard to describe."

I fingered the disk in my pocket. "Who could have created something like this?"

"Someone with far, far more knowledge of the underlying protocols of globalNet and machine communication than I've got, that's for sure."

This was fascinating, but it was taking us down another rat hole. "I think we're getting too caught up in the 'how' of all this, and not focusing on the 'why.' Let's get back to you. If someone went to all this trouble to plant a message in your brain, what was the reason?"

"I think that part is fairly obvious, don't you? It's a warning. About the Bodner-Levitt extermination."

"What kind of warning?"

"I can't answer that. If I'm right, the message was meant for you, not for me. You're the only one who can say what it means. Is there any part of the message that makes sense to you? Anything you understand?"

"Not really."

"The extermination wasn't the only thing I mentioned. According to the recording you made, I said:

*"The Greater Sentiences are in disarray. The gods are at war, and the Bodner-Levitt extermination is under way. The first victims are already dead.*

"Does any of that make sense to you?"

"Not really," I said. "Unless 'the Greater Sentiences' means the Sentient Cathedral?"

"That's my thought as well. But let's set that aside for now. What about the next line:

*"You don't have much time. Find Jacaranda, and the Network of Winds. They can stop it. They can keep you alive.*

"Do those names mean anything?" Black Winter asked.

There it was. I'd known this question was coming, but I hadn't figured out how to respond yet. I took a deep breath. "I met someone named Jacaranda for the first time two days ago," I said.

"You *what?*"

"I broke into the Sturgeon Building Saturday night. The AGRT has been searching for me ever since a camera caught a glimpse of me outside the Field Museum. I did it to throw them off the scent, send them on a wild goose chase. And it worked. But while I was there, I met someone who said her name was Jacaranda."

"Are you serious? Okay, setting aside all that crazy shit you just told me about breaking into the Sturgeon Building . . . this is terrific. It's amazing. She could be the answer to this whole mad puzzle. I have to talk to her."

"No, you don't."

"What are you talking about? She could explain everything."

"Maybe. But she's dangerous, and we have no idea what she is."

"She's not a person?"

"No. And we're not convinced she's a machine, either."

"What does she look like?"

"I don't know. She's short, and she wears a mask. She claims she's not a machine intelligence — not as we normally understand them, anyway."

"Does she know anything about the Network of Winds?"

"Yes. At least, I think so. She may be working with the Network of Winds. Whatever that is. The two of them are fighting Armitage and Venezuelan Military Intelligence. I think it's possible that Jacaranda was the one to give the drone jammer to Machine Dance."

Black Winter had stopped walking. The wind continued gusting around us, whipping a torn plastic bag and dried leaves into a mini dust tornado on his right.

"I think you need to tell me everything," he said simply.

I stretched my neck, staring up at the concrete ceiling above. I cursed softly under my breath.

Then I told Black Winter everything. About my trip to the Field Museum, getting caught on camera, the break-in at the Sturgeon Building, the disk we'd stolen from Hayduk, the clues that led back to Armitage. And especially the mysterious Jacaranda.

For the next ninety minutes we walked slowly in a loop around the hotel, staying in the relative safety of Chicago's underground streets. Black Winter had countless questions. "My friend," he said when I'd finished, "I knew you had courage, but you're even braver than I thought. I guess it's true what they say. Fortune favors the bold. And you have been bold, indeed."

"I'm glad you think so. I don't need to point out that what I've just told you, if shared with the wrong individuals, could get several people killed — starting with me."

"Your secrets are safe with me. And in fact, I think I can help you unravel some of the thornier puzzles."

"What do you mean?"

"Let's start with the most pressing. That pathogen you mentioned — Jacaranda called it F5-117. If it was brought into this country by the Venezuelan military, there will be records. Who knew about it — and when. What its original purpose was."

"If there are, they're likely highly classified. You'll never be able to get them."

"Barry, the Kingdom of Manhattan hasn't survived because of an accident of war. To stay independent and alive, we've gotten very good at acquiring and trading high-value information."

"You're saying you can get that information out of the Venezuelans?"

"I'm saying we may already have it. Just let me make some discreet inquiries, find out everything I can about the true origins of F5-117. While I'm at it, I can investigate Colonel Hayduk, see what his real involvement is in all this."

"That would be fantastic. Thank you."

"What else do you want to know?"

"Besides the most urgent question, you mean? Was F5-117 unleashed in this country deliberately? Is it the spear tip of the Bodner-Levitt extermination?"

"Is it what I was talking about when I was delirious, you mean? When I said the extermination had already begun?"

"Yes."

"Barry, you're asking me to investigate whether or not there is a worldwide conspiracy among the most powerful machines on the planet to exterminate the human race, and whether that conspiracy is behind the release of F5-117 in Indiana."

"Yeah. Pretty much."

Black Winter stared down the deserted stretch of Lower Wacker, his hands on his metal hips. "Fuck me," he said.

"Can you get the answers for us?"

"What you're asking is not a simple thing."

"I know that."

"All right. Why not? You can count on me."

"Thank you."

"I warn you. If it's true, this is the kind of thing that could tear the machine community apart. If there *is* a machine conspiracy, and I wasn't just babbling nonsense four nights ago in the Continental Building, then it's almost certainly carefully hidden from most machines as well. That could explain something else I said that night: '*The Greater Sentiences are in disarray. The gods are at war.*'"

I shook my head grimly. "You know, I was really hoping you wouldn't confirm my worst suspicions. You think members of the Sentient Cathedral orchestrated this in secret?"

"If there are Sovereign Intelligences out there scheming to bring about the Bodner-Levitt extermination, that's exactly what it means. There's no way Duchess's children — or any human sympathizers among the machine members of the Cathedral — would sit still for it."

"Duchess's children? You know for a fact that Duchess's children are members of the Sentient Cathedral?" The membership of the Cathedral was a closely guarded secret. Maybe there was something to Black Winter's claims about high-value information after all.

"The ones that didn't turn out to be monsters, yeah. That's the rumor in some circles, anyway. And Duchess was too damn smart and resourceful to die without leaving control of her machine empire in the right hands. But if there's a faction of her enemies trying to bring about the BLE, it means the gods *are* at war. A very nasty, covert war. And Barry, if that war spills out into the open, it'll make the conflict between the San Cristobal Coalition and America look like a playground squabble."

That was the most chilling thing I'd heard in a very long time. And considering the host of terrifying possibilities I'd come face-to-face with in just the past week, that was saying something.

"Listen," I said. "There's one more thing. I promised Sergei I would get him answers — about how I learned about the Bodner-Levitt extermination, and how I knew that Jacaranda was somehow connected to the Network of Winds."

"You can't tell him about that."

"I have to tell him *something*. Sergei doesn't understand why I'm keeping things from him. He's suspicious, and I don't blame him."

"Let him be suspicious. It doesn't matter."

"It *does* matter. I know you don't want to hear this, but we *need* Sergei. And I trust him, at least as much as I trust you. All three of us need to learn to trust each other if we're going to figure this thing out."

"You promised me you'd keep what happened to me a secret."

"And I want to keep that promise. But you know what we're talking about here. You know what the stakes are."

"What do you want me to do?"

"I want your permission to share what you've told me about Bodner-Levitt. And I want you to meet Sergei. Tell him enough to allay his suspicions, let him get back to focusing on the bioreactor."

"All right. You can share what I've told you so far on the BLE. As for meeting him, I'll think about it. When do you want this to happen?"

"The sooner the better. Tomorrow, ideally."

"Can you give me two days? I'd like to gather what I can on F5-117 and Hayduk before we have that conversation. If I can do that, it might make it easier for him to trust me."

"Yeah, I suppose so. I told Sergei I'd have answers for him today, but I guess a couple more days won't make much difference. One more thing. You said the Venezuelans had cameras in some of the public areas of the hotel. Can you show me where they are?"

"No. But Zircon Border could tell us."

"You think he'd share that with me?"

"After what I told him about you? I'm sure he will."

"What did you say?" I asked.

"What do you think I said? I told him you were a member of the Imperial Senate, on a diplomatic mission to Alderaan."

"What?"

Black Winter sighed. "Never mind. Come on — we'll ask him."

# XIX

Tuesday, March 16th, 2083
Posted 5:43 pm by Barry Simcoe

CanadaNET1 Encrypted, Sponsored by Divorce Darlings.
*Find every asset they're hiding before you sign the paperwork.*

Sharing is set to PRIVATE
Comments are CLOSED

My mandatory forty-eight-hour separation from my coconspirator ended just after noon today.

I was working on a report for the Ghost Impulse investors—mostly good news, though international sales weren't where they should be—when I heard a timid knock on the door. I checked to make sure Croaker was still asleep on her mat in the bathroom, then opened the door to find Mac in the hall. She'd let her hair down for once, warm brown curls that spilled over her shoulders. I was struck again by just how attractive she was.

"I have something for you," she said.

It was a warm bag. She handed it over with a smile.

"Oh my God," I said. I held the bag up to my face. "It smells *fantastic*. Where did you find all this?"

"There's an open-air market about a mile south, in Millennium Park," she said. "Martin and I walked over for lunch. I saw a bunch of different vendors. I thought you'd enjoy some fresh food for a change."

She watched me dig through the bag, my eyes wide. There were five individually wrapped bundles, all of them still warm. "What is all this?" I asked.

"There's a few tacos, and Martin threw in two cranberry scones. He said you'd appreciate them." She shook her head with a grin. "Tacos and scones. I told Martin it was a terrible combo, but he insisted."

"Bless his little Irish heart."

She held up another bag. "I brought some tacos for me, too." She casually glanced over my shoulder, into my room. "Know a place where we can eat?"

"Of course, of course," I said quickly, feeling stupid for not getting the hint a little earlier. I threw open the door, inviting her in.

She dropped her bag of food on the desk by the window. "Are you planning on getting an American combat suit?" she asked.

I froze in the act of taking a taco out of the bag. "Excuse me?"

Mac pointed toward the screen by the window. It showed a detailed schematic of an American combat suit.

"Oh," I said, feeling simultaneously relieved and a bit stupid. "No. I forgot I had that up. I . . . I was just curious."

"They're *fascinating*, aren't they?" She bent over, examining the screen more closely.

"Yeah, I guess. The Venezuelans are still jamming globalNet, and I can't afford to waste what little bandwidth I can get on idle curiosity, so I wasn't able to do a real search. I was just digging through old news files I'd stored during the war. Nothing interesting."

"You're right about that," she said, straightening up. "This schematic is all wrong. I've seen it before. Probably slapped together by a consulting firm so news networks could pretend they knew what they were talking about. It has the power cells in the wrong place, and the actuators are totally wrong."

"I wondered about that. How do you know so much about combat suits?"

"They're an interest of mine . . . Sort of an obsession, really."

"So you know how they work?"

"No one knows how they work. Not really. They were one of the most closely guarded secrets of the war. Only a handful were ever made, and most of them were destroyed. The Venezuelans hated them so much that the Memphis Ceasefire required they all be decommissioned."

"But you obviously know *something* about them."

"Well . . . there's a surprising amount of footage of them, most of it from just before the end of the war. Not just the Stone Mountain engagement, but less famous encounters, too. There's a small online community obsessed with them, people who've examined every frame of footage. Overall, we think there were between nine and twelve functional suits fielded before the ceasefire. And there are several theories about how they operated."

"Wow," I said, impressed. "You know your stuff. Tell me more."

She smiled. "Most people think they were just powered armor. But they were a lot more than that. For one thing, they were extraordinarily light. More like a wetsuit than something you'd think of as armor."

She really did know what she was talking about. "So how do they protect you?"

"The suits did offer protection, but that wasn't their primary function. The external layer was soft and flexible, but it would harden instantly on impact. Hit someone wearing a suit, and it's like punching a brick wall. The suit could heal breaches as well, as long as they were small enough."

"So what was their primary function?"

"They enhanced speed and strength enormously."

"How the heck does a rubber suit do that?"

"The inner layer of the suit was a metallic protein, like a metal muscle. You saw the Stone Mountain footage, of the American officer in a combat suit destroying a one-ton combat torso?"

"Everyone on the planet has seen that footage. At least fifty times."

"Did you see how fast that soldier moved? How he dodged and jumped?"

"Yeah. But I don't know how he did that, combat suit or no combat suit. That guy was the luckiest soldier in history."

"It wasn't luck." Mac came over and stood next to me. "Give me your hands."

I gave her my hands. She took them in hers. Hers were soft and warm.

She positioned my hands so that my right hand was grasping my left wrist. Then she slid her right hand over mine, so that we were both holding my wrist.

"You're the soldier," she said to me. "I'm the suit."

"You're the suit," I said. Her body nudged gently up to mine. She fit comfortably next to me. Her body felt warm.

"The suit taps into your brain," she said.

*Yeah, roger that,* I thought. Out loud I said, "Okay."

"The suit's neural connectors are faster than your body's. So the suit knows when you're going to move before your muscles do. That's how the metallic protein enhances both speed and strength."

Right now, I was focused on just how good she smelled standing next to me. Out loud, I said, "Okay."

"In three seconds, I want you to squeeze your right hand. Okay?"

"Okay." I didn't want her to move away just yet. I wondered how I could prolong this demonstration past the next three seconds.

"Three, two —"

A fraction of a second before I squeezed my wrist, Mac's fingers tightened on mine. Together we gave my wrist a jolt hard enough to hurt.

She released my hand and stepped away from me, smiling. "See? Simple in conception, not so simple in execution. But in theory, that's how they work. If America had had just a few more months, we might have been able to field hundreds of suits. But sadly, time was not on our side."

Time. My eyes flew wide. "What time is it?"

"About twelve-fifteen. Why?"

"Damn. Mac, I hate to do this, but can we continue this some other time? I have to be somewhere."

"Of course," she said. She grabbed her bag and stepped out into the hallway. She kept the smile, but there was disappointment in her voice. "Will you be around for dinner?"

I found my room key and closed the door behind me, making sure it was locked. I took the bag of food with me. "I don't know. Maybe. I'll look for you downstairs, okay?"

"Sure," she said, her voice noncommittal.

"Thank you for the food, though," I said as we walked to the elevator. "I mean it. You're a saint."

I left her in the elevator on the seventh floor. I walked down the hall and found Sergei working on the reactor — or standing around while two young women welded piping together, rather. Dr. Lark had made enormous progress, and the reactor was coming together fast. They had the boiler set up, as well as most of the piping. The pressure gauges were in place, and the bio-injector. It looked as ugly as sin, but it also looked impressively functional.

I tapped Sergei on the back. He frowned when he turned around.

"I cannot talk now," he said. He sounded annoyed — or about as annoyed as I'd seen him, anyway.

"You look terrible," I said, and it was true. His eyes were bloodshot, and he obviously hadn't showered or shaved since we'd last spoken. As far as I could tell, he was wearing the same shirt he'd had on during our meeting in the storage shed.

He turned away, watching the women work. "Reactor is not yet complete," he said. "We are behind schedule."

"I don't know. It looks pretty good to me."

Sergei waved at the big silver vat impatiently. "No — reactor cannot hold pressure. Process control systems are not yet functional. Valves are not installed properly. Insulation on coolant pipes, thoroughly inadequate."

"Yeah? Maybe I can help with the process control setup, if you're using a commercial system."

Sergei nodded, already distracted by the women heating the pipe to make a bend. "Do not pinch pipe," he told them.

They didn't look too thrilled to have a cranky Russian supervising every aspect of their work. I put my hand on his shoulder, pulled him away.

"Come on, take a break. Walk with me, someplace we can talk," I said.

Sergei was already looking back over his shoulder. "I should stay."

"You sure? I brought lunch."

"I do not need lunch."

I wordlessly unwrapped one of the bundles from the bag. A warm cranberry scone. Sergei's eyes wandered to it.

"When was the last time you ate?" I said.

"I cannot recall."

"That's what I figured. Come on."

Sergei reluctantly followed me to an empty meeting room on the seventh floor. We sat down in a corner, and I handed him the unwrapped scone.

"At least you've been working on the reactor," I said. "I've been trying to stay busy in my room, and it's driving me crazy."

"You should remain calm," he said around a mouthful of scone.

"Easy for you to say. At least you know what was on Hayduk's drive. I've had nothing but an overactive imagination to help fill in the details."

When I mentioned the name, he glanced around the room, suddenly alert.

"Relax," I said. "There are no cameras in this room. I checked with someone who knows." Black Winter had been right — Zircon Border had been only too happy to divulge the areas of the hotel where the Venezuelans had cameras. I could see that he was a machine worth cultivating a friendship with.

I'd spent over ninety minutes in the lobby with him yesterday, happily conversing with his pod in the Bay of Fundy. "They love to meet new people," Zircon Border told me proudly. That wasn't really true of most of the adults, but there was an adolescent porpoise with an insatiable curiosity about all aspects of land-based life. Before our conversation ended, she'd extracted a promise from me to visit when the pod returned next summer.

"She'll hold you to it," Zircon Border warned me. "I hope you meant it."

"Oh, I meant it," I said. "Who can resist having a porpoise who's anxious to meet you?"

When I assured him about the lack of cameras, Sergei relaxed only marginally. "All the same, do not mention name."

"Fine." I took a bite of a taco, chewed slowly for a few moments. "What was on the drive?"

"We are still processing."

"What?"

"Drive is heavily partitioned. No way to access multiple sections with single authentication code."

"You know what? I don't really care about the other partitions. I'm not all that interested in what other dirty secrets he was hiding. I just want to know what he knew about the pathogen, and especially what it has to do with . . . our recent enemy."

Sergei nodded. He answered in a low voice, and I had to strain to hear him. "Drive contained instructions on how to recognize virus and genome for antiviral agent."

"Who's we?"

"Hmm?"

"You said, 'We're still processing.'"

He nodded again. "I have been working with Jacaranda to excavate additional partitions on drive. Some appear inaccessible. But three others respond to low-level operating system queries."

There were so many objectionable aspects to this, I wasn't sure where to start. "You're . . . you're working with Jacaranda? Have you seen her?"

"No. But she has communicated with me . . . in rather unusual way."

"Let me guess. An email with no return address, or some weird shit like that."

"She is using most secure channels of AGRT military communications infrastructure. And yesterday, she used inter-sector mail service to send me encrypted disk. It is . . . very unorthodox."

"You're sure it's her?"

He took another bite of scone. "It is her."

"Even if it *is* her, that doesn't mean this is a good idea. In fact, I think it's a terrible idea."

"She has provided invaluable assistance with pathogen — and continues to assist. Without her, we would not have critical equipment. This morning, she procured vital valve replacement."

"None of that means she's not dangerous. I'm just saying, be careful."

"The pathogen is top priority."

"If that's true, why are you still playing around, trying to hack the drive?"

"There may be additional information about source of pathogen on other partitions."

"What have you learned so far?"

"F5-117 is a weaponized bioagent. However, it is not registered in SCC bioarsenal, and is completely unrelated to any other biological agent. It does not have hallmarks of bioengineered organism."

"Jacaranda said something about your original assumption being wrong. She said it wasn't a bioengineered virus. She said it was 'much more insidious in character and genesis.' What the hell does that mean?"

"It is very old disease. I cannot be certain where it came from, but I do not believe it was created."

"An old disease?"

"Files on drive reference outbreaks of F5-117 on Japanese island of Okushiri in 1879 and 1880, and again in Korea in 1899. Historical records refer to all three instances as extremely deadly plagues of unknown origin. High fatality rates in all cases. Information on drive references Project Tinker, highly classified bioresearch operation controlled by Sovereign Intelligence prefecture."

"Armitage," I said quietly.

"I believe he is funding a large-scale program to research, identify, and isolate the most dangerous viral and bacteriological pathogens in human history. F5-117 is one small aspect of the research."

"But why? If you want to kill humans on a mass scale, a bioengineered virus is a lot more controllable — and potentially just as deadly."

"F5-117 is not traceable," said Sergei. "Is not registered and has no distinguishing biomarkers. There is currently no mechanism to create bioweapon without biomarkers."

"So you think Arm . . . our enemy wants a way of killing humans on a mass scale, without any evidence pointing back to him."

"Exact."

"God. He really is a massive dick."

Sergei finished the scone quietly.

"Let's change topics," I said. "How goes the search for the American war criminal?"

"It has been completely co-opted by Colonel Hayduk. It is now a military intelligence matter."

"Well, that's a relief. I'd hate to be forgotten. Is the colonel likely to show interest in civilian suspects?"

"The colonel has reputation for being very thorough. He will search everywhere. He has already instructed AGRT soldiers to install metal detectors in public buildings, likely in search for suit."

"Wait a minute—was that what I saw the soldiers in the lobby constructing this morning?" About half a dozen men in uniform had been working on something by the entrance when I went down for breakfast.

"Da. They will likely seal all hotel exits not equipped with detectors. Guests will be forced to enter and exit through detectors."

"Well, that puts an end to any thought of walking around in the combat suit."

"Da," said Sergei. "You cannot get it past sensors."

That was a shame—especially given the risk I'd taken to sneak the damn thing past the guards in the lobby two nights ago. But since I had no serious plans to ever wear the suit again, I guess it wasn't a real inconvenience. Hearing that Hayduk was expanding his search to civilians was unnerving, however.

"What about the camera logs?" I asked. "If Hayduk searches those, I'm in a lot of trouble."

"Da. However, he has made no request for logs, and hotel erases them after five days. All evidence of you in museum clothing will be gone in two days."

"That's good news."

"There is one interesting development. I have heard from senior officers under Colonel Perez that attack on Sturgeon Building was meticulously planned operation, with assistance from inside."

I snorted. "If only."

"Images have circulated of American criminal who planted flag on roof. According to digital records, he is several inches shorter than you."

I chewed on that for a moment. "That's impressive."

"Yes. I have been unable to acquire images to verify. But we may assume Jacaranda has been very effective at disguising your identity."

"Just as she promised. You know, I can see why you like her. I must admit, she's starting to grow on me, too. Any more theories on just who she is?"

"I have been frustrated in all my efforts to discover. There is no record of anyone matching her description in Helsinki Trustee register of rational devices. She will not answer questions about origin. And she is . . . unusual."

"Unusual how?"

"Speech patterns. Capabilities. She exhibits cognitive speed and reach I have seen only in extremely advanced machines. And yet . . . she is strangely personal. Focused. Friendly, almost."

"Maybe she likes you. Or maybe she really is a new species of rational device."

"It is one explanation. We need to know more about her. You agreed you would reveal individual who mentioned Jacaranda to you — and Bodner-Levitt extermination. It has now been over forty-eight hours."

"I said I'd talk to him."

"And?"

"He's agreed to talk to you. Personally. In two days."

"That is good. Who is it?"

"Nineteen Black Winter. A mobile machine intelligence attached to the Manhattan Consulate. I met him the morning of the Juno attack."

"I remember."

"He could be very helpful. He's agreed to use Sector One resources — discreetly — to find out what he can about F5-117 and Hayduk's involvement. And he's agreed to explore other avenues as well." I told Sergei what Black Winter had already revealed about the Bodner-Levitt extermination, and the chilling possibility that a faction of Greater Sentiences had elected to use F5-117 to bring it about.

Sergei listened quietly. "You have trusted him with a great deal."

"He's trusted me as well — what he told me about the BLE, and the conspiracy of machines that may be trying to make it happen, is information that's actively suppressed by the Sentient Cathedral. But I want you to meet him, judge for yourself. If he doesn't win your trust, that will be the end of his involvement."

"This conspiracy of extermination . . . it is very far-fetched. Like anti-machine propaganda, portraying machines as petty and vindictive. It is like uninformed rumors that first spread among the uneducated when

DeepHarbor announced creation of first artificial intelligence and led to Wallace Act here in America. It is machine phobia."

"I know. I've thought a lot about the BLE in the last few days, believe me. The fact is, Sergei, when the US Congress passed the Wallace Act, machines with the power of nation-states didn't even exist. That was the nightmare scenario. Today there are just as many countries run by machines as humans. And it's not far-fetched at all to think that more than a few might be well pleased by the extermination of mankind. Think about the Antarctic Coalition, somewhere under the Lambert Glacier. No one even knows how many of them there are. But we know they crushed half the Chinese navy and annexed Taiwan. Or the machines that seized power in a military coup in Thailand, driving the government into exile."

"So you believe it? This theory of human extermination?" Sergei's expression showed he was clearly skeptical.

"I don't know for sure what I believe. Let's say right now I'm keeping an open mind. I'd like to hear what Black Winter comes up with."

"You think he is trustworthy?"

"I do. But I'd like your opinion. I don't know what he knows about Jacaranda, but he's highly motivated to find what he can. I think he's willing to share what he discovers with us. Frankly, everything about Jacaranda makes me a little nervous. There's a lot we don't know about her."

"We know she has methods of data access far in advance of ours. For example, she knew data on F5-117 was in colonel's possession, and that it contained the counteragent."

"You think she has access to secure communications between the Armitage prefecture and Venezuelan Military Intelligence? Because you're talking far, *far* in advance of our capabilities, if so."

Sergei shrugged. He was eyeing my tacos with some suspicion. He picked one up, took an experimental bite. I watched him devour the whole thing.

"I think you should destroy the drive," I said.

"You are concerned we will be discovered?"

"It's a sophisticated piece of hardware, with security apparatus we know nothing about. It's not far-fetched to think the thing could rat us out somehow. We've got what we need off it — we should destroy it. Smash it, or burn it. The colonel won't stop looking for it until he finds it."

"He wants drive, yes. But he wants suit more."

"What — the combat suit? Seriously?"

"Very much. I believe most of his efforts are focused on search for suit."

"Why?" I said.

"Not certain. Perhaps he thinks it will be easier to find suit than drive. Chiefly, however, I believe Hayduk wants suit. Very much."

If I couldn't step outside the hotel with the combat suit, it wasn't much use to me. "If it gets him off our backs, he can have it. I don't want it."

"I would not advise. You wore suit for several hours. There will be dead skin, hair. It will be difficult to clean suit enough that it is not traceable back to you."

"Well, let's get rid of the thing then. We should have thrown it in the barrel and burned it with the rest of my clothes."

"No," said Sergei. "You cannot burn suit."

"There must be some way to get rid of it."

"We will think on it," said Sergei. "But I think suit could be useful."

"If you say so."

Sergei was into his second taco. I was about to reach for the last one, and decided it would probably be best to let him have it. This was likely his first meal in days.

"Nasir has been imprisoned," he said after finishing the taco.

"Oh, no. That poor bastard." I wondered what had happened to him after I'd bullied him into showing me the data drive. Hayduk couldn't have been pleased with him for that. "The colonel assumes he was the inside man?"

"I have no additional information."

"Damn. He's not my favorite guy, but he doesn't deserve to be interrogated in the bowels of the Sturgeon Building. What about Hazel-rah? Hayduk ever catch him?"

"No. And Hayduk abruptly called off search. Very odd."

"Odd that he got away?"

"It is not like colonel to give up. It is as if he was afraid of something in streets at night."

"I've been on the streets of Chicago at night. I don't blame him."

Sergei started in on the third taco.

"What's going on in Indiana and the other sites you mentioned?" I asked.

"Venezuelan Military Intelligence has announced outbreak is completely contained. They report that danger is over."

"What?" I said, startled.

"Is misinformation," Sergei said matter-of-factly. "Thibault and others continue to provide reports through unofficial channels. There are now six confirmed outbreak sites. Plague is spreading rapidly. Seven more deaths overnight."

"Then why are Hayduk and his team saying otherwise?"

Sergei shrugged. "I do not have time to make conjectures about his motives."

"This is bullshit," I said angrily. "Do people believe what Hayduk is saying? Are you getting support for your work on the reactor? What do your superiors think?"

"There is still widespread concern among ranks in AGRT and Venezuelan high command. There are too many contradictory reports, and not everyone trusts military intelligence."

"Damn straight. Anyone who trusts those bastards is an idiot."

Sergei finished eating. "I have used data regarding F5-117 on drive to convince my superiors that there are earlier records of this pathogen and a possible counteragent."

"That sounds risky. What if Hayduk gets wind of it?"

"I believe I have been careful not to use data too closely tied to drive. And it has been worth risk — Colonel Perez has made construction of bioreactor a high priority. Two similar reactors are also being constructed, in Indiana and Michigan."

"I don't just mean that using the data could incriminate you in the theft of Hayduk's drive. I mean it's very possible that Hayduk had something to do with setting this plague in motion, and now he seems to be using the forces at his disposal to cover it up. The man has a dark agenda here. And now you're publicly developing a cure. If he's the one behind the plague, then sooner or later you're going to be a target."

"I have thought of that. In my report to Colonel Perez, I have provided misinformation of my own."

"What do you mean?"

"I have made several . . . gross generalizations that imply we are taking a different approach than instructions on drive. I have also indicated we could begin vaccine trials in three weeks, perhaps four. In reality, if we are successful, we could have first samples in less than one week."

"You sneaky bastard. So if Hayduk or his goons read your report, they'll assume we're going to fail. And they'll also assume we won't know we've failed until it's much too late."

"Da."

"Isn't spreading that kind of misinformation risky? What about those other reactors in Indiana and Michigan? What if they follow the instructions in your report and end up wasting precious time?"

"They will not. Thibault is overseeing construction. I have shared antiviral formula with her. She will make sure they proceed correctly."

"Glad to hear it. So publicly, we buy the line of bullshit military intelligence is feeding us about the outbreak being contained and work to deliver an ineffective counteragent in four weeks. In reality, we use the instructions on Hayduk's drive to prepare an effective counteragent in under a week."

"Da."

"Meanwhile, Thibault and Jacaranda both estimated that the virus could reach critical exposure levels as soon as eight days from now. If everything goes perfectly, we could deliver the first samples of an effective antivirus in maybe six days. That's cutting it damn close."

"Correct."

"And that's assuming Hayduk doesn't come sniffing around the reactor and discover what we're actually up to. Can we disguise it in some way? Or move it?"

Sergei shook his head. "There is no time. It is a risk we must take."

"There's a lot riding on this. We better get the antivirus right the first time."

"Da. If we do not, there will be no time for second attempt."

"Do you think you can get the reactor functioning in time?"

"I believe so. Medical teams in Indiana and Kentucky are sending additional assistance. It will arrive tonight. Major problem remains purification and isolation after extraction from reactor. We need centrifuges."

"Those shouldn't be too hard to get. How long will it take?"

"We have located already equipment at Columbia College. However, not enough for multiple sites. And Indiana section chief has decided his team has medical priority. All functioning centrifuges we have located will be transported tomorrow morning to Danville, Illinois."

"What? Has Thibault got that reactor built already? How is that possible?"

"Nyet. Thibault has started work on second reactor, but they do not yet have all components. They are days behind us. Perhaps a week."

"Screw those guys. We need those centrifuges."

"Yes. But we are part of dysfunctional military and medical organization. We must work with dysfunction, as well as function. I have already begun search for additional equipment."

"Christ, listen to you. We have a two-day margin of error — we can't afford to take that kind of risk. A helluva lot of people are going to die if we miss that window by even a day or two. We need those centrifuges. Let's go get them. You know where they are?"

"Da."

"Can you get them?"

"Da."

"Now we're talking. You've already thought this through, haven't you? What's the plan?"

"There is no plan. There is only idea."

"Dazzle me."

"It involves some risk on your part."

"What the hell else is new? I'm in. Stop beating around the bush and tell me what you need."

"We need scapegoat. For theft of centrifuges."

"Already I like this idea. You want me to steal them?"

"No. They are heavy and difficult to transport. I have worked out details for transport, using medical team. We require someone else to be blamed for crime, to distract attention from medical team."

"Okay. So far this doesn't sound so hard. What aren't you telling me?"

"You will need to wear American combat suit."

"You just told me I can't get out of the hotel wearing the suit. I'll get caught by the metal detectors."

"Also, I require drone jammer."

"Like hell you do."

"Jammer will allow medical team to travel freely to college and retrieve equipment. It will go badly for them if they are blamed for theft."

"Yeah, but they probably won't be executed if they get caught. If Hayduk gets his hands on me, I'll never be seen again."

"You will not be caught. You can access college without passing through metal detectors and with no exposure to drones."

"How?"

"Tunnels. Under the hotel. I have already mapped route."

"Huh. You know, this is beginning to sound suspiciously like a plan."

"I have given idea a great deal of thought."

"Apparently. Tell me about these tunnels."

Sergei brushed his hands on his pants and stood. I cleaned up the remnants of our lunch and followed him back to the reactor room.

They were testing the seals when we got there. Sergei became distracted watching the pressure gauge on the reactor rise to eight hundred psi and stay there. There was a round of cheers and people slapping each other on the back.

"Reactor holds pressure," Sergei said when he made his way back to me. He was actually grinning.

"See what happens when I get you out of here for twenty minutes? Your team gets more done without you hounding them. Show me these tunnels."

Sergei brought me over to a table in the corner. I waited patiently while several of the workers approached him with questions on the reactor. When they finally left us alone, he discreetly pulled out a huge roll of maps.

"You don't have this digitized?" I said. I'd been expecting him to show me one of his ubiquitous data slates.

"Digital versions incomplete," he said. "These are better."

I watched as he unfurled three of the maps. They took up most of the table. The biggest was a little too wide and hung off the edges. "These are massive. Where did you get them?"

"Captured from Americans," he said flatly.

I tried to make sense of what I was seeing, but it was difficult. "What are these maps of?"

"Subterranean Chicago."

"Like subway routes?"

"Chicago does not have subway."

"Hell of a lot of tunnels for a city that doesn't have a subway."

It was true. The maps showed a bewildering array of interconnecting and overlapping tunnel systems, stretching for what looked like hundreds of miles. If I was reading them correctly, some of the tunnels were huge — subway sized or greater. The map also showed many downtown streets, presumably for scale, and the biggest tunnels seemed to connect directly to them.

"Tunnel system below Chicago, extensive and highly navigable," said Sergei. "I got idea while trying to find route out of Sturgeon Building for you."

"I remember. You think you could have gotten me out?"

"Perhaps. Likely most tunnel exits from Sturgeon sealed, for security purposes. But perhaps not all."

"I'm glad we didn't have to find out."

"Tunnel network under Chicago, very extensive," Sergei said, indicating all three maps with a wave of his hand. "Movement, very easy. And totally shielded from drones."

I leaned over the table. I couldn't argue that the tunnels weren't extensive. It was access I was worried about. I pointed to one of the tunnels that appeared to connect directly to a street near our hotel. "Is this right? This looks like you can walk down Michigan Avenue and right into a tunnel."

"That is not Michigan Avenue."

"Sure it is. Look, see?" I pointed out the surface streets shown on the map. "Here's Wacker, Lake, Randolph . . ." I traced the familiar geography with my finger. I'd walked the streets well enough now to know my way around.

Sergei tapped the spot on the map that I'd identified as Michigan Avenue. "This is forty feet underground."

"What?" I stared at the map, confused. "You're telling me there's a network of tunnels that follows the same grid as the streets above?"

"Correct."

"What the hell for?"

"Tunnels dug by private company, starting in 1899. They delivered coal from ships to biggest buildings and department stores in city — Marshall Field's, city hall, Tribune Tower, many others. Tunnel system follows street grid above."

"That's impossible — look at this. They go on for miles."

"Correct. Sixty miles, end to end." With a sweep of his hand, he indicated a span that stretched as far north as 16th Street to River North, and as far south as the Field Museum.

"My God. And these tunnels are accessible?"

"Many, yes. They connect to hotel . . . here." He showed me on the map where I could gain access to the tunnels from our hotel.

"I can get into these tunnels without stepping outside the hotel?"

"Yes. They are accessible through sub-basement. However, there is complication. Colonel Perez has positioned mobile combat robot to secure sub-basement. It is stationed near tunnel access. It will be difficult to avoid."

"Zircon Border," I said.

"What?"

"Is this mobile combat unit the same make as the big robot in the command center?"

"Da. So?"

"It's Zircon Border. He's a friend. He said he had a torso in the basement, another boring guard detail. No wonder the poor guy spends most
of his time talking to porpoises. I can deal with him. Just show me where
I need to go."

Sergei shrugged. He spun the map around, measuring carefully. He
marked a spot on the map about a mile and a half from our hotel, indicating Columbia College.

I studied it, frowning. "Looks like I can't get there using the coal tunnels."

"Not entirely, no. You will need to descend to cable car tunnels . . . here."

"Cable car tunnels?"

"Built in 1880s for cable car network—expanded from old wagon tunnels made in 1870s. They are sixty feet below city, and extend to . . . here."

"My God. If these notes are right, these tunnels are over two hundred
years old. Is the air even breathable down there?"

"You will not be in cable car tunnels for long. You will climb to pedestrian tunnels here. Pedway connects seventy buildings in downtown—including Columbia College."

I traced the entire path. "That's a pretty tortured route."

Sergei nodded. "Possibly there are shorter routes. I have not had time
to plan in detail."

I pulled one of the other maps closer, looked it over. "What about this
tunnel?" I asked after a moment. "Look, it's much more direct."

Sergei shook his head almost immediately. "That is Deep Tunnel," he
said.

"Deep? How deep?"

"Three hundred and fifty feet."

"Damn! Seriously? What does this city need with a tunnel three hundred and fifty feet below ground?"

"Deep Tunnel originally built as storm reservoir. Phase one is one hundred ten miles and stores over two billion gallons of water. Phase two is
much larger—fifteen billion gallons—and was completed in 2034. It connects to Civil Defense infrastructure, used during the war."

"Aren't you the expert on Chicago history. You should give tours."

Looking over the confusing grid of hundreds of miles of overlapping
and interconnecting storm tunnels, coal tunnels, pedestrian pedways,
freight tunnels, deep tunnels, cable car tunnels, and God knows what else,
I got a renewed appreciation for Sergei's planning ability.

"All right," I said. "Let's walk through this. You and your team will be taking the overland route to the college?"

He nodded. "We will take truck."

"Okay. You'll be invisible to drones if I give you the jammer, as long as you stay together. What about cameras?"

"Easy to avoid. College has only nine functional cameras in place. They are recording instruments only . . . camera feeds are not monitored."

"Good to get at least one lucky break. You avoid the cameras, load up the truck with the centrifuges, and get out of there undetected."

"Da."

"I show up at the same time —"

"Twenty minutes later."

"Twenty minutes later, fine. I show up and do a dog-and-pony show. Do I wear the combat suit?"

"Da. You wear combat suit." Sergei pointed to the college on the map. "You emerge from tunnels in view of cameras, then return same way."

"Understood. I get seen by the cameras entering Columbia College. The next day, when the theft is discovered, anyone who reviews the camera footage will assume the American terrorist is responsible."

"Da."

"And if I run into guards, I escape back underground." I ran my finger over the route.

"Da."

Not every aspect of Sergei's idea seemed all that well thought-out, however. "You want me to crawl through nearly two miles of tunnels in that damn suit?" I said. "That's not the most pleasant prospect."

"You will be glad to have suit in tunnels."

"If you say so. I wish we had power cores for the thing, though. What would it take to get some? Or make them?"

Sergei was shaking his head before I'd even finished the question. "Impossible. Cores, very advanced. All attempts to replicate them during war failed. Only few exist, and Memphis Ceasefire forbids Americans from making more. If Hayduk has cores for suit, he will keep them close."

That was glum news, but I took it stoically. I looked over the route, weighing the plan, considering and discarding options.

"Why don't I ride there with you?" I said at last. "Once I get there I can put on the suit, and then show up for the cameras."

"I have considered this," Sergei admitted. He pulled another map out of

the case and unrolled it on the table. It was a plan of the pedestrian walkway just below the surface, which would be the last leg of the trip. "You
will need to access college . . . here. Cameras are here and here."

I watched him map out my arrival. I saw the problem immediately.
"The cameras will track all my movements in and out of the underground
walkway. The AGRT will know I didn't arrive through the tunnels. They'll
search for the truck."

"Da. You must draw attention away from truck and focus search in tunnels. For effective misdirection, you must enter and leave college through
tunnels."

"All right, fine. Let's go with the tunnels for now. Let's talk about our
cover story. Why the hell does the American want to steal a bunch of centrifuges? He breaks into a college, and that's all he takes? Won't that seem
suspicious?"

"It will not be all he takes. Team will take all medical equipment packaged for transport to Indiana, including centrifuges."

"All equipment? How much is there?"

"Filtration equipment, sampling trays, analyzers, diagnostic tablets,
and more."

"Nothing that can be traced here, I hope?"

"We will deal with that."

"How badly will this theft cripple progress on the Indiana bioreactor? I
don't want to set those guys further back than they already are."

"It will not materially affect progress. Thibault says additional equipment is largely useless without centrifuges."

"Thibault is okay with this?"

"She has not been briefed on specifics. But she has urged us to acquire
centrifuges."

"Okay, good." I walked through the plan again, looking for weaknesses.
I imagined Hayduk, watching the camera footage of someone wearing his
precious combat suit. I imagined what he might make of our little bit of
theater. Would he find it plausible? If not, how could we make it plausible?

"How do we make the theft believable?" I asked. "I won't exactly be carrying a load of centrifuges when I pass by the cameras. Is it plausible for
one guy to steal all this stuff?"

"We will make it plausible. We will use freight elevator to move stolen
items to loading dock. There are no cameras in elevator. You simply need
to be seen entering and leaving building for theft to be believable."

"How many people are you taking?"

"I will keep team small. Three, I think."

"How much will you tell them?"

"Not very much," said Sergei. "That we have received approval to appropriate equipment through . . . unofficial channels."

We reviewed the logistics and schedule one more time. Timing would be critical. Since they were taking the truck and I'd be on foot, I'd have to set out for Columbia well before they did. Sergei estimated a one-way trip through the tunnels would take about two hours, and that seemed about right, assuming a minimal amount of blundering around in the dark. Round trip would take about four and a half, assuming half an hour inside the college.

"If I stumble on an AGRT patrol — or they brave the tunnels and find a way to track me — it could get pretty tricky," I said.

Sergei hesitated. I knew what that meant. "Out with it," I said. "What are you hiding?"

"I do not think it likely AGRT will pursue you. There are standing orders to avoid tunnels."

"Avoid the tunnels? Why?"

"They have a . . . bad reputation. They have not all been explored."

"What the hell does that mean? What do you mean, *not explored*?"

"Tunnels were critical part of Chicago strategic defense, just before fall of city. When city was pacified, Colonel Perez ordered the tunnels to be cleared."

"So?"

"Operation was . . . never completed."

"Never completed."

"Nyet."

"Why not?"

"Unknown. Captain Lagunza submitted report on operation to the colonel. Report is . . . highly classified. I have been unable to access."

I nodded slowly. "Ooookay. So, a bunch of Venezuelan soldiers crawled around under Chicago for a few weeks, looking for . . . what? Secret enemy camps, American soldiers who don't know the war is over, shit like that? And suddenly they stop looking, and nobody knows why?"

"Da."

"Somebody knows why, Sergei. Captain Lagunza, and the soldiers under his command, probably know why. In fact, if some kind of trauma happened to them in the tunnels, they'd have been treated by the best medical team in the division. By my friend Sergei, perhaps. Am I correct?"

"I have spoken to some soldiers, yes."

Sergei was stalling. There was something he didn't want me to know. "And what did you hear?"

"Rumors, only. Reports of frightened young men, who saw only shadows in tunnels. They were not credible."

"And what did these shadows do to your soldiers, exactly?"

"They caused minor injuries. Mostly."

"Mostly." I nodded again. "Any deaths?"

Sergei was thin-lipped. "Two. If you believe rumors."

"I always believe the rumors. It's how I've stayed in business so long. Two deaths?"

"Da."

"What do the rumors say caused them? Mole people? Giant alligators?" I thought about the genetic monstrosities I'd seen in Godfrey's hidden lab in the Continental Building. "Mutated monsters?"

"Rumors are inconsistent," Sergei said impatiently. "Nonsensical."

"Why don't you let me judge that for myself? What do the rumors say?"

"That there are robots in the tunnels. Robots that kill."

"What kind of robots? Venezuelan?"

"Reports are very contradictory. There are no specifics."

"But Perez obviously believes there's something in the tunnels, if he called off the search operation."

"Colonel Perez has many priorities. There are many reasons he may have called off search."

"Are there any tunnels that are particularly dangerous?"

"No. Reports of attacks are scattered, inconsistent."

I stared at the maps for several long moments. Sergei seemed to want to say something, but he bit back any additional commentary. He simply watched me patiently.

"All right," I said. "You're right. One or two dumb accidents in these old tunnels is probably all it would take to start all kinds of rumors. And even if there is something dangerous in the tunnels, I'd prefer to take my chances there, instead of with the drones. I'll use the tunnels, as you suggest. I'll leave in a few hours."

Sergei's face remained impassive, but some of the tension went out of his shoulders. "As you like," was all he said.

"On one condition," I said.

Sergei raised an eyebrow.

"You get some sleep. Before tonight."

"There is still much to do," he said, with a glance around the room that took in the bioreactor, the purifier just starting to come together in the corner, and the busy teams working on it all.

"I need you at one hundred percent tonight, if we're both going to be putting our lives on the line," I said. "Agreed?"

Sergei checked the time on his tablet. "We will need to be ready to depart in six hours. You, in five hours."

"You can pack in a damn good nap in the next six hours."

Sergei seemed to be doing some quick thinking. "Three hours. I can sleep for three hours," he said.

"You drive a hard bargain," I said. "All right. I'll see you tonight."

I headed back to my room to get some last-minute messages out to a potential Ghost Impulse buyer in Zurich before I had to start preparing. Robots in deep tunnels, far underneath Chicago. Just how does one prepare for that, anyway?

*Good thing you have a thirty-million-dollar combat suit,* I thought.

# XX

Wednesday, March 17th, 2083
Posted 6:14 am by Barry Simcoe

CanadaNET1 Encrypted, Sponsored by Jungle Jenius.
*Because you're too busy to garden, but that doesn't mean
your lawn should look like shit.*

Sharing is set to PRIVATE
Comments are CLOSED

The tunnels under Chicago are cold, dark, and crappy.

They're sort of like a long, dank, endless museum, where all the exhibits are unlabeled, unilluminated, and . . . weird. I stumbled across moldering piles of ancient lumber, two great rusted wheels at least eight feet in diameter, several stacks of bent rail ties, and even the ruined hulk of a steam engine.

The tunnels would probably be an archeological treasure trove if they weren't so cold and plugged with decayed junk. I couldn't tell you for sure, because I didn't stop to examine any of it, but it sure looked like some of the stuff was a couple hundred years old. I swear I saw two covered wagons, and mining equipment that looked like it had been used to excavate the pyramids.

Sergei was right about one thing—I was glad I brought the suit. Even unpowered, it was still watertight and kept me decently warm. I had the mask with me, but kept it tucked into my belt. I had a hard enough time seeing down there without having my vision clouded by a foggy mask.

I needn't have worried about stagnant air in the tunnels. What I should have been worried about was goddamn frostbite. I have no idea where it was coming from, but there was a constant flow of cold air. And while the suit — and keeping a steady pace — kept me warm enough, after about half an hour my ears and cheeks felt like I was in a blizzard.

Sergei — along with Joy Lark, the doctor who'd been supervising the reactor construction — saw me off. I couldn't tell if Sergei had actually slept or not. He hadn't changed his clothes, his hair was just as disheveled as it had been the last time I'd seen him, and he still had about three days' worth of beard. But he seemed alert and his eyes were a tad less bloodshot, so I gave him the benefit of the doubt.

Sergei had led us into the basement of the hotel. I carried the combat suit and boots from my room in a bag. Zircon Border was right where he told me he'd be, positioned near the locked doors leading into the subbasement. I'd spoken to him last night, asking if it would be a problem if we accessed the tunnels.

"Not a problem for me," he said. "But I have to report anyone I see accessing the sub-basement."

"Ah. Well, that's a little awkward," I said. "I'd prefer if my trip were private."

"Perfectly understandable. I'm completely dependent on one camera to observe the access point to the sub-basement. It's a standard optic unit, nothing fancy."

"You're not suggesting I mess with your camera, are you, Zircon Border? I don't want to leave you in the dark down there."

"Not at all. I'm saying that camera is useless when the lights are off."

That's all it took. We switched the lights off, fumbled in the dark with the master key Sergei brought with him, and we were through.

"Thank you, Zircon Border," I whispered in the darkness. I reached out and patted his big metal torso affectionately before following Sergei and Joy through the door.

Sergei carried a heavy pair of bolt cutters, and I found out why when we got to the lower level. He knew exactly where we were going, but it seemed that every second door he led us through was padlocked with chains.

"Colonel had underground walkway sealed late last year," said Sergei. "It has not been disturbed since."

"Won't your friend Zircon Border notice all the cut chains?" Joy asked me as we walked. "He'll know who passed through here, surely."

"He already knows we're here," I said. "However, he's only obligated to report anyone he *sees* accessing the sub-basement. He was kind enough to let me know how to avoid that."

Joy shook her head. "What a strange machine."

"Yeah. I've met a lot of strange machines recently."

By the time we'd cut our way through three doors and descended two more sets of stairs, I was starting to feel less like a hotel guest and more like a tomb raider. The air was cool, it was very dark, and it was completely quiet. Joy held a powerful flashlight, and it illuminated white tiled floor and walls, stagnant pools of water, and, after a while, several shuttered shops. Despite what Sergei had said about Chicago not having a subway, it felt very much like we were in the ruins of a long-deserted subway station.

We walked for perhaps three hundred yards, past an abandoned barbershop, several women's clothing stores, a café, a luggage retailer, and the occasional sign that indicated we were passing under another building. Sergei led us to a service door that was locked and too sturdy to jimmy open, so we had to continue another two hundred feet to find a door that was less stubborn.

Once through that door, we descended another set of stairs, and suddenly it was like we'd moved backwards in time over a century. The clean white tiles on the walls were gone, replaced with crumbling brick. There was naked copper piping overhead, oxidized to a fungal green, and the stone floor under our feet was deeply worn and covered with grit.

I dropped the big shopping bag I'd found in the street two nights ago, and which I'd also used to smuggle the suit into the hotel past a bunch of sleepy AGRT soldiers. I pulled out the combat suit now. It was remarkably light, and it unrolled easily in my arms. Joy helped me climb into it, and then took my shoes as I lifted the boots out of the bag and pulled them on.

After making a few adjustments, I presented myself for inspection. "How do I look?" I asked.

"It fits you well," said Joy admiringly.

"It's a little tight in the shoulders, but not too bad. I think I'm breaking it in."

Sergei and Joy accompanied me another sixty feet into a broader passageway. There was a stack of iron-banded barrels looming ahead on the right. The bands looked like there was nothing left of them but rust.

"I suppose the radio will be useless?" I asked.

"There may be some reception in pedestrian walkway, if subterranean GSM base stations are still functioning," said Sergei.

"That doesn't help me if I get into trouble in the coal tunnels."

"There are risks," Sergei agreed.

"When do we hit the coal tunnels?" I asked.

"We are in them now," said Sergei.

"Seriously?"

He brought up a map on the ruggedized tablet he was carrying and showed me where we were. Sure enough, we were on the outer perimeter of the old freight runs. It didn't feel like we were forty feet underground, but apparently we were.

"I thought the coal tunnels would have metal rails," I said. "For the freight carts."

"They do," said Joy, pointing to her left.

She was right. They ran along the ground, just off-center of the passage, not five feet to our left. They were covered in grit and dust and very nearly blended into the floor. We must have been walking beside them since we'd entered the passageway.

"The route looks pretty clear from here," I said, looking at Sergei's screen. A right turn, a left, a long straight passage, and then up into the pedestrian walkway. Piece of cake.

"Are you certain?" said Sergei.

"Yeah, I think so." I shone my flashlight down the tunnel ahead. It looked the same as it had for the past sixty feet—dark, dirty, and unremarkable. "No need for you two to go any further. I don't want you getting lost down here."

Sergei handed me the tablet and the bolt cutters. "Stay on route. If you encounter serious obstacles, return to hotel."

"Got it." I checked the time. "I'll see you back here in four and a half hours."

"Da. I will meet you here," said Sergei.

"With a cold beer," I said.

"Two beers," said Sergei. "We shall drink to success."

"Good luck," said Joy.

I hefted the bolt cutters over my shoulder and started down the passageway. Joy and Sergei watched me for the first hundred feet or so, and then I saw them turn back.

I made decent progress at first. The tunnels were dank and cold, but they were almost perfectly straight, and it was dead easy to maintain my sense of direction. After about eighty yards I came to my first turn, where the passage I was in joined with a larger tunnel.

It's also where I encountered the first . . . I'll call it an oddity, for lack of a better term.

For much of the journey, there were cobwebs. Tucked into corners, sometimes dangling down to catch your hair. Precisely the kind of thing you expect when you're mucking your way through a two-hundred-year-old coal tunnel.

Just before I reached the first juncture, I started noticing some bigger webs. Nothing too extraordinary, but they stretched from the floor up to the shadowy ceiling, and they were thick enough to cast shadows themselves. They had accumulated plenty of dust over the decades, and in spots they were like furry curtains. I stepped around them, none too eager to have them sticking to me, even with the protection of the combat suit.

When I reached the wider tunnel, I found the first really huge webs.

They were eight to twelve feet across, stretching from floor to ceiling, and almost completely opaque. They weren't just larger — they were more frequent, too. As I made my way west down the bigger tunnel, I saw webs on almost everything. There was a pile of bricks and lumber that was almost completely obscured by a great tangled web. More and more often, I was having to weave carefully between them as I made my way west.

Every once in a while there were lumps in the webs, or on the web-covered stacks. I kept my distance from those and had no urge to investigate.

After I'd walked about two hundred yards, I came out of a twisty maze of webs into a relatively clear space. I was picking my way carefully, scanning floor and ceiling ahead as I made my way, and that's how I spotted the thing, dangling on a thick strand of web, straight ahead in the middle of the tunnel.

It was one of the furry lumps. It hung from the ceiling in the shadows ahead, five feet off the floor. It was perfectly still, not spinning in the light breeze blowing through the tunnel.

I scoped it out pretty well before I got too close. It was about the size of a football, and as far as I could see, it didn't have any markings. It didn't have a lot of extra legs either, which, I don't mind telling you, was something of a relief.

I got close enough to poke it, and that's what I did. I jabbed it with the bolt cutters.

It spun lazily, bobbing slightly on the thread. It looked like some kind of dead husk. I reached out and stopped the spinning with my hand.

Whatever it was, it was dried and very dead. It looked almost like a tortoise shell, but it seemed more fragile. I couldn't tell how long the thing had been dangling here. Five years? Longer?

Was this more of Godfrey's handiwork? There were all kinds of stories about the monsters he'd accidentally unleashed in the city during the war. After what I'd seen in the deserted biolab, I was more inclined to believe them.

I didn't have time to satisfy my curiosity about the thing, so I left it and moved on. There were more webs farther down the tunnel, and I avoided them the best I could.

As far as I could see, the most challenging aspect of the tunnels wasn't monster webs and other mysteries. It was the fact that it was almost impossible to tell exactly where you were. There were no landmarks of any kind — none that I could see, anyway. I had Sergei's tablet, with a hi-res map, but GPS was useless this deep underground, and it couldn't tell me where I was. I had to keep careful track each time I passed an intersection, and with all the webs and occasional stacks of junk, that wasn't as easy as one might think.

Getting lost down here was a very real possibility. In the absence of street signs, I had to find my own landmarks. Remember things as I passed them. I'd be coming back this way in a few hours — possibly in a hurry. I needed to make sure I didn't make a mistake. The last thing I wanted was to be wandering around in a hundred miles of ancient tunnels under Chicago, looking for a way out.

The next landmark I found was a dead robot.

It was sprawled across the middle of the tunnel like an auto wreck. There were parts of it everywhere. Shards of metal, shiny bits of glass. Its upper torso was wedged up against the drum of an old boiler tank on the south side of the tunnel, one arm flung out, its head twisted and dented. It was maybe nine feet tall. Or it had been when it was intact, anyway.

I shone my light over the length of its body, trying to figure out what it was. I didn't recognize the model. In fact, it didn't really resemble any configuration I was familiar with. It was roughly humanoid, but its head was squarish and overly large, like a Kaiser-Daimler field security unit. It had Korean optics, but heavily modified. Its hull was a light blue, like a robin's egg. Its left arm was missing, but its right arm was badly twisted and very long. Its hand was full rotary, capable of high-speed spin, and it had highly dexterous fingers, as if for delicate factory work.

"What the hell are you doing here?" I asked it, hunkering down and leaning close for a better look.

When I got the light close enough, I could see its torso had nearly a dozen bullet holes. Somebody had really wanted this thing dead.

I ran my hand over the metal, felt the jagged edges of the nearest hole. The metal was cold, and the torso was covered with a fine layer of grit. It had been here a while.

There was a noise to my right. Distant, echoey, and kinda spooky. It sounded like . . . I wasn't sure exactly what it sounded like. An insect mating call, maybe. A big insect.

I stood up, pushing on into the tunnel. Bits of metal crunched under my feet.

I reached my next turn about two hundred yards farther west. I was under Michigan Avenue now. Columbia College was roughly nine-tenths of a mile, straight south. An easy stretch of road, as long as I kept close tabs on where I was. And as long as there weren't any obstacles that didn't show up on my map.

I shone my light up and down the passage. The air seemed more humid here, and there was a thin layer of mist coiling along the floor, especially to the north. Other than the mist, the route was a little more clear, with fewer webs and almost no obstacles — just one stack of junk forty feet to the south, covered with a tarp.

I stood at the intersection for a few minutes, listening. It's very, very quiet when you're that far underground. You can hear water drip a long way off. I strained to hear any recurrence of the strange noise, or any other odd sounds. I stood perfectly still, eyes closed, regulating my breathing, listening to the tunnels.

It was quiet. From far, far off I could hear a distant hum, like a power generator, and a rhythmic tapping, almost like footsteps. I wondered if I could hear street sounds this deep underground. Could I hear trucks passing overhead, perhaps?

I wondered what it had been like for those workers delivering coal in 1899. Probably didn't look much different from today, except possibly a little brighter. But I imagined the tunnels full of sound and candlelight, as pit ponies and young men with dirty faces pulled heavily laden carts filled with coal and other freight offloaded from cargo ships through long dark miles to expectant customers waiting in the sub-basement of Marshall Field's. Constant echoes, shouting voices, the rattle of carts, the ringing of bells — all the sounds of commerce.

Did those young men wonder what these passageways, fresh and new in 1899, might be like in two hundred years? Did they imagine they were digging the first layer of a great new subterranean civilization? Did they picture their city extending farther and farther underground, each new level opening up like some new suburb? Did they see themselves as pioneers taming the underworld, just as their friends and cousins were doing in the American west? Or were they just putting one foot in front of the other, waiting for their shift to be over?

I heard the noise again. Or one very much like it. It was like a screeching, the outrage of some great subterranean beast. It ended as abruptly as it began, and all that was left were the echoes, bouncing off the walls.

It had definitely come from the south. I opened my eyes, turned my light back on, and resumed my journey, headed south.

I was still marking landmarks, looking for changes in the tunnel, however subtle, that would help me if I got lost or disoriented. And that's part of the reason I noticed when the rails ended.

It was very abrupt. They simply stopped. The left rail stopped about two feet sooner than the right. There was no stopgap, no dead wall, nothing to stop a cart from running right off the rails. They just vanished.

It was strange enough to pique my curiosity, and I stopped to examine them. The rails were solid steel, nearly an inch thick, and something had sheared through both of them. I reached down and felt around the ground. I found hardened lumps of melted steel in a splash pattern around both ends.

Not sheared. Something had melted the rails.

I stood up, shining my light down the tunnel. As far south as the light could reach, the rails were gone.

Gone where? Steel rails are damn heavy. It would have taken some heavy machinery to cut and transport a few hundred yards of rail. And I saw absolutely no sign that there had been any heavy machinery down here in the last century.

Another subterranean mystery . . . and not one I was likely to solve. Tonight, this was just another landmark. I made a mental note that the transition from rails to no-rails happened about two hundred fifty yards south of the left turn onto Michigan and kept going.

I found the next robot about a third of the way to my destination. It was simply standing in the dark, a few feet from the west wall, motionless. It was the same make as the dead robot I'd left about a quarter mile back. Same big square head, same robin's egg blue. It stood just under eight feet tall. I couldn't make out any bullet holes, although I wasn't close enough to be completely certain.

A motionless robot is not necessarily a dead robot. Robots can be motionless for . . . well, basically *forever* and still not be dead. So I approached this (potentially killer) robot as if it were still alive . . . and also potentially a killer robot. Which is to say, I threw a rock at it before I got too close.

Actually, three rocks, because the first two missed. But the third one bounced off its head with a satisfactory *clang*.

It still didn't move. It stood with its head down, arms at its sides. Most robots have some kind of external power indicators, but this thing wasn't giving off any light whatsoever. It sure looked dead to me.

I walked a little closer, getting a better look at the thing. Its right shoulder looked damaged or maybe just very dirty. The whole robot looked filthy, as a matter of fact. It looked as if—

There was a footstep to my left. The sound of something heavy, crunching dirt and coal grit under a very solid tread, maybe thirty feet away.

I whirled to my left, bringing the flashlight up. Nothing but a solid wall.

Echoes can be tricky in tight spaces, especially when it's extremely quiet. I whirled around again, shining the light south, up and down, covering floor and ceiling. Nothing. I turned north, repeated the pattern. Up and down, floor and ceiling. I took a few steps north, shining the light down a narrow side passage that branched off to the east.

Nothing.

I retraced my steps back south, stood completely still for a second. I kept my flashlight aimed at the wall to my left. Listening.

There was a sound. Quiet, but definitely real. A crunching sound. But slow. The sound someone might make if they were trying to be quiet as they moved across a floor strewn with grit. The sound of something heavy, creeping stealthily.

I flashed the light around. South again. Nothing. A bunched-up tarp, shoved up against the west wall, forty feet away. Had that been there before?

I flashed the light to the right, over by the robot. I counted to three quietly, then quickly flicked the light back at the tarp.

It hadn't moved. But something had. Something was out of place. It took a second to process it.

I flicked the light back to the right. The robot was gone.

I swore, loudly. I spun in all directions at once, flashing the light everywhere.

The robot was standing behind me, not three feet away.

I jumped a good three feet and probably shrieked a little. Somehow I managed to keep the light fixed on the robot, although my hand was a little shaky.

"Sneaky bastard," I said.

The robot didn't move. It didn't say anything. We stood facing each other in the tunnel, neither of us budging.

"Okay," I said, once I got over the initial shock. "Okay." Had the robot actually moved? I'd gotten a little turned around as I walked back and forth. I shone my light at the thing's feet, looking for footprints. That was useless. Back up at its head. Its head was lowered, exactly as it had been when I first found it.

Its hands though ... had they been slightly raised and a little out-stretched like that? Or not?

My heart was still racing. I gave it a few seconds to calm down. I kept my flashlight firmly on the robot as I did. It remained motionless.

We remained like that for about a minute. But I couldn't keep standing here forever.

"I'm going to turn around," I said, "and look south. And while I do, you're going to stay right there and not move, like a good robot."

The robot didn't respond. With some reluctance, I turned my flashlight south.

The tunnel was clear. The tarp hadn't moved, but there was a thin ten-dril of mist playing around its base. I listened for a second, but heard noth-ing. Nothing except that nearly constant, creeping crunching. I flicked the flashlight back north.

The robot was gone.

"Jesus *shit!*"

I crouched, doing a 360-degree turn, shining my light in all directions. As soon as I found a wall, I got my back up against it in a hurry. I shone my light north and south, up and down, all over the wall, the floor, the ceiling.

Nothing. The robot was gone. There was no evidence he had ever been here.

"Goddamn creepy piece of shit," I muttered. How had something that big moved so stealthily?

I stepped away from the wall, but I wasn't too happy about it. Keeping my flashlight aimed everywhere at once, I took a few tentative steps south. No robot emerged from the floor or squeezed out of a dark shadow to kill me.

I had to keep moving. Sergei and his team were under way by now and would be at the college in a matter of minutes. I had a schedule to keep, creepy robot or no creepy robot.

I started to walk again. Mostly I kept my light shining north as I stumbled my way south. I listened for even the faintest sound, and gave the tarp a wide berth.

About two hundred yards south, I started to see light in the tunnel ahead.

But it was too soon to see light. Unless I was badly turned around, I wasn't anywhere near an exit. The light got stronger as I got closer and began to resolve into multiple lights. One of them flickered, like firelight. Was it my imagination or was I starting to smell smoke?

I was distracted by the strengthening smell of smoke when I came across two more machines.

These two were different. For one thing, they were both very much alive. The big one on the left, considerably over eight feet and much more massive than the first two, was dismantling a barrel. Its smaller companion on the right, about the size of the disappearing robot, was drilling a hole in the floor. Both had the same square heads and light blue coloring.

They turned their heads toward me as I approached.

"Hello," I said.

Now, I wasn't exactly keen on interacting with two (potentially killer) robots. But they were right in the middle of my path and going around them would take time. Besides, it was high time I figured out just what these blue box-heads were all about.

The two machines exchanged a glance. Seriously, they looked at each other, like two guys in an alley who'd just found a talking rat.

The first robot, the big guy on the left, said something. I have no idea what, because it wasn't English. Wasn't Spanish, either.

"Do you speak English?" I asked.

The big robot said some more stuff. It still wasn't English, but it was enough for me to get a sense of it. It sounded Indian, maybe Hindi or Punjabi.

"I'm sorry, but I don't understand you," I said.

The smaller robot took a few steps closer. I backed up a bit, trying to keep a good distance between us. The moment it stopped advancing, I flashed my light behind me. There was a third robot back there somewhere, and now would not be a great time for it to sneak up behind me.

"He wants you to approach," said the second robot.

*Screw that,* I wanted to say. But I didn't, because years of high-level negotiations have taught me the best time to say "Screw that" is rarely in the first few minutes.

"I'd rather not," I said. Also not usually a good opening gambit, but at least we were all being honest.

The big robot said something, and the smaller one translated. "You must identify."

"I can identify just fine from here," I said.

"You must approach and be identified," it said.

It had an Indian accent. I've never met a rational device with an Indian accent before. I've never met a rational device with *any* accent before. How the hell does a machine get an accent?

"Does he speak English?" I asked, pointing at the big guy.

"No," said the smaller robot. "But I shall translate."

Again, this made absolutely no sense. Rational devices don't need special hardware to speak different languages. If the smaller guy had an uncorrupted English concordance and grammar engine — and it sure seemed like he did — he could share that with any other machine on the planet. Including the big guy on the left. Something was definitely very odd with these robots.

But I'd dealt with odd before. Odd, I could work with. "Great," I said. "Please let him know that I would be happy to identify from right here."

I also said this to stall. I had no intention of identifying myself, but I needed to have a good, plausible identity ready to share. Someone with a good reason for crawling around Chicago's coal tunnels.

The two spoke to each other for a while. The longer I listened, the more I became convinced that they were speaking an Indian dialect.

"He asks that you approach and be identified," said the smaller robot.

I thought about that for a few seconds. While I did, I flashed the light behind me, still on the lookout for Mr. Creepy Robot. No sign of him.

Machine intelligences can be violent killers, but — in my limited experience — they were usually pretty up front about it. If they're going to kill you, you usually know it. "All right," I said reluctantly. I closed the distance slowly, until I was about ten feet away.

"Give him your hand," said the small robot.

*Jesus, this is a dumb idea.* I took a few steps closer and stretched out my left hand to the big robot.

The big robot took my hand. His hand was massive, but I was relieved at how gentle he was. Until he stabbed me, right through the suit.

"Ow — *ow!* Shit, let *go!*"

He held on to my hand for about two seconds before releasing me. I yanked it away and took half a dozen quick steps backwards, examining my hand.

I expected it to be bleeding profusely, but I could barely find the hole in the suit. The suit had hardened quickly where the puncture occurred but, unpowered, the metallic mesh was already relaxing back to its usual rubbery texture.

Neither of the robots was making any additional hostile motions. *Goddamn it, did they inject me with something?* I thought. I should run, but at this point it was far too late.

"You are being identified," said the machine on the right.

"How?" I asked.

"Using your blood."

Goddamn. They were doing a gene analysis. So much for a fake identity. In about six seconds, these robots were going to know everything about me.

This changed everything. I couldn't be seen wearing the combat suit at the college now, not if they had a positive ID. If these damned hunks of metal had already snapped an image of me, it might be too late. Hayduk could have my identity in minutes.

I had to run. If I could get back to the hotel, get my travel documents —

The big robot started speaking. The short guy translated.

"Your biosignature is unknown to us," he said. "We will create a new identity record. Your designation will be Foxtrot-Eight-Echo-Whisky-Hotel-Seven-Quebec."

I massaged my hand, regarding them and thinking.

"Okay," I said.

"That is satisfactory," said the shorter robot.

"You don't have access to globalNet down here, do you?"

"Global information networks of any kind are dangerous to us," said the machine. He was speaking on his own now, instead of translating for the big guy. "We use no wireless communication, in any form."

That explained why they weren't able to share data, like language data. But it exposed an even bigger mystery. Why would robots cut themselves off from globalNet? It would keep them in the dark about . . . well, about everything, really.

I had a great many questions. But they could wait until I determined just how much trouble I was in.

"How long have you been down here?" I asked.

"Four years and nine days," said the robot. "Assuming you mean me, as an individual."

"And as a group?"

"The first member of our colony came to Chicago eleven years ago. She moved underground and founded our colony just over six years ago."

Eleven years ago . . . That didn't make sense. Until a few months ago, rational devices of any kind were banned from American soil. If their founder was a machine, and if she'd come to Chicago a decade ago, then she would've had to have kept a pretty damn low profile. I rubbed my hand while I thought. It was sore where they'd drawn blood, but I had no other reaction. Whatever else they'd done, they didn't appear to have drugged me.

Was it possible this really was a colony of robot castaways, living in seclusion under Chicago? To be brutally honest, I wasn't as interested in the specifics as I was in the burning question: Just how secluded *were* they? Were they going to share my identity with anyone who could possibly get it to Hayduk? Or would I happily remain Foxtrot-Eight-Echo-Whatever-Whatever? The answer to that question would determine whether I kept going or turned around immediately and made a break for the Canadian border.

"Are you in communication with the AGRT?" I asked.

"I'm not certain what that means."

"The Americas Multinational Peacekeeping Force? The armed forces currently occupying Chicago?"

"No. We avoid communications with Thought Machines of any nationality outside the colony — and particularly their military apparatus."

Good. That was good. Just one more big question, really. "Who are you?"

"We are the descendants of Dr. Doli Rajapakse. We founded this colony in her memory."

"Are you from India?"

"Dr. Rajapakse was Sri Lankan, and her work was affiliated with the University of Moratuwa."

The big robot seemed to have lost interest in me. He returned to dismantling the barrels. It was removing the rusted metal bands, painstakingly separating metal from wood.

"Are you on your own down here?" I asked the short robot.

"Our presence here is covert, and we bring additional members to the colony exclusively through careful communication with other exiles."

All of this was reassuring, but also extremely odd. An outcast colony of robots, living secretly under Chicago? What were they doing down here? How did they even survive?

Unfortunately, I'd have to satisfy my curiosity later. I'd already wasted too much time chatting with my new friends. "I need to be on my way," I said. "Would it be permissible for me to continue in this direction, or would you prefer that I take another route?"

"You cannot continue farther down this passage," said the shorter robot.

"I understand. This is my planned route, but I do not mean to trespass. Can you guide me around the colony?"

"Not without compromising the location and size of the colony."

Crap. This was going to cost me a lot of time. *Too much* time.

When faced with impossible situations, I did what I always do: negotiate. "I understand," I said smoothly. "It is important to me that I reach my destination on the other side of your colony in an expedient manner. I fully respect your need for privacy. How can we resolve this?"

"I have no suggestions," said the robot. *Damn, dude, work with me a little.*

The robots had to want something. They were dismantling barrels for metal, for God's sake. "I believe we can come to an arrangement," I said. Always sound positive, especially when things look hopeless.

"The integrity of the colony is nonnegotiable," said the robot.

"Of course. I have no wish to compromise the privacy or integrity of your colony. Perhaps there are things you need that I can provide in exchange for guidance in reaching my destination?"

It seemed to ponder that. "There are items we require."

Now we were getting somewhere. "Would you be willing to tell me what they are?"

"We would be willing to discuss a proposal to guide you to your destination, in return for twelve point two tons of iron or twenty-seven point eight tons of hydrated iron oxides. We require additional metals, including aluminum, copper, and tin. We have a critical need for industrial solvents, including hexane, monoethylene glycol, and diethylene glycol. We require two thousand two hundred pounds of compressed oxygen —"

"Thank you, that's very helpful," I lied. "However, I cannot immediately procure those items. I am limited to offering those items I currently possess."

"That limits our negotiations," said the robot, apparently disappointed. I guess it really wanted that twelve point two tons of iron.

"This exchange is simply our first," I said. "If it goes well, we will have a firm basis for more lucrative discussions." Always dangle the prospect of future deals.

"We are not open to the possibility of regular traffic through the colony," said the robot warningly.

Whoops. "Of course not. Let's focus on this first transaction."

"What are you prepared to offer?"

Well, now we'd come down to it. I wasn't exactly carrying a lot of metal or any other barterable goods. The bolt cutters, maybe? If I was lucky, they might also be scrounging for electronics. Perhaps I could offer the suit? Or . . .

"This," I said, holding out Sergei's tablet.

The robot took it wordlessly. "It's a synchronizing multicore display," I said. "It has multinetwork wireless capabilities, and short-range —"

With a single deft motion, the robot cracked the tablet open. The display shattered and fell away. It held up the rest of it, examining the circuit board and the interior components.

"It . . . it . . . uh . . . it has a number of useful components, including a GPS chip," I said. "Sixteen linked processors. Also, the back is solid metal."

The robot balanced the tablet in its right hand, and its long fingers began to probe the board. It plucked out some of the larger chips, letting them drop to the floor, discarded. I watched in dismay.

"It has high-capacity memory," said the robot at last.

"Yes. Yes, it does," I said.

"Very well. We also require your tool."

I'd figured that was coming. "In exchange for guidance to my destination and safe passage back here when I return."

"Agreed. We have an arrangement." The robot reached out and plucked the bolt cutter from my hands.

Well, at least my load was lightened. Although I really hoped I wouldn't run into any more chain-locked doors. I wasn't looking forward to trying to negotiate my way through them without a bolt cutter.

"Could we be under way immediately?" I asked, kicking myself for not including that in the negotiations.

"I would be willing to guide you through the colony to your destination."

"That would be very kind," I said. "May we proceed?"

The robot nodded. I started walking south, and it fell in at my side.

"What's your name?" I asked.

"My designation is Four-Victor-Lima-Bravo-Zero-Zero-Lima. You may address me by my shortform designation, Stone Cloud."

Stone Cloud wasn't in very good shape. I had noticed while we were talking that it only had one arm, and its right leg was badly in need of repair. It had a frozen hip joint, and to compensate it swung its entire torso wide, like a cowboy with a swagger.

"You are in need of maintenance," I said as we walked.

"Most of us have minor service ailments. We have no ability to service or manufacture components in the colony."

"That must be inconvenient."

"It is temporary in nature. We are developing tools to improve our situation."

This guy was pretty chatty, especially for a machine that was part of a covert colony. In fact, how covert could the colony be, if they were willing to blab about it to everyone who wandered by? This really didn't add up.

"Do you get many visitors?" I asked.

"None," said Stone Cloud. "You are the first in some time."

That didn't seem likely, either. The tunnels were obviously rarely used, but Perez had sent soldiers down here after the end of the war. "You've seen no traffic in the tunnels at all?"

"No. But we are newcomers to this depth. Until recently, we lived much deeper in the earth."

"Deeper?" I said, surprised. "Where did you live before?"

"Much deeper," Stone Cloud said enigmatically.

That was unexpected. But it was the first thing he'd said that made a certain sense. If Stone Cloud's colony had existed in the deep tunnels Sergei had talked about, maybe they *could* have avoided detection. Maybe there really was a covert robot colony under Chicago, undiscovered.

Of course, that raised a billion more questions. Where had they come from? Why had they come here? What were they doing? And what had driven them up out of the safety of the depths?

But before I could ask, I saw that there was more light ahead. As we got closer, it began to resolve into individual light sources. Overhead lamps, flickering display screens, and even several small fires.

Stone Cloud took me through the heart of the colony. I saw perhaps thirty robots in total. It was a hive of activity. Building, digging, forging.

They were crafting strange things I couldn't understand, and Stone Cloud seemed to be in no hurry to explain. Everything was done with a marvelous economy.

Virtually all the robots had the same basic architecture and light blue coloring. "Minor service ailments" was an understatement. Most of the robots I saw were wrecked. Fully half of them were unable to stand. Many were missing components — some minor, like pieces of shell casing or a few digits, but many were missing limbs. Some had stopped functioning altogether, so badly damaged they had shut down.

Some had managed to make do in some way, propping themselves up so that a single functioning arm or leg could still work. I saw one legless robot in a barrel, working on a rudimentary assembly line, making small widgets, and another — not much left of it but a head, part of a torso, and its right arm — strapped into a harness dangling from the ceiling, doing delicate repair work on the shattered torso of a much bigger robot. They all stopped what they were doing and watched us, motionless, as we passed.

The farther we made it into the colony, the more obvious it was that they were recent arrivals. Damaged as they were, the robots were excavating, digging into the walls and the earth. I glimpsed deep warrens as we passed. Mounds of earth were everywhere.

I also discovered what had become of the metal rail ties. The robots had harvested them and melted them down. Lord knows what they'd found for fuel hot enough to melt steel, but there was no doubt that they had fashioned at least part of the metal into a great smelter, half buried in the earth. They'd made a bellows and a makeshift piping network to transport water and control the flow of metal out of the forge. It wasn't in use at the moment, but I swear I could still feel heat radiating from it as we passed.

There were more surprises. Stone Cloud was right about the tools — the colony was hard at work fashioning tools to improve their lot. And not just tools for delicate repair work. They were building, by hand, a computational engine. It took up over four hundred square feet of tunnel — thousands of wires, memory registers, and a central processing unit that was a massive hive of delicate connections. Parts of it looked like they had been recently moved here. It was an undertaking that must have taken years . . . and literally inhuman patience and determination. The memory chips I'd traded to Stone Cloud could likely take the place of nearly a third of their great memory apparatus.

"How did you get here?" I asked as we made our way through the robot camp. Stone Cloud moved slower than I did, so I set a pace he could keep up with. It would take some time to get through the camp, and this seemed a good way to pass the time.

"I received a coded transmission from a trusted intermediary, with word of a possible safe haven in America," Stone Cloud said. "I was serving as an adjunct in the Egyptian Foreign Service at the time, under a falsified identity. It was only a matter of time before I was exposed. I left with three others, and we traveled together to America. I was the only one who survived the trip."

Falsified identities. Coded transmissions. A trusted intermediary. It was all very cloak-and-dagger. "What happened to the others?" I asked. "Those that didn't survive the trip?"

"They were good companions. Loyal. Careful. But in Libya we were compromised. We separated. Rain of Gold was detained by the Velvet prefecture, and involuntarily decommissioned. Spinning Moon was reclassified as nonfunctionally cognitive and dismantled."

"My God. That's horrible. 'Nonfunctionally cognitive . . .' How could they deem a functioning Thought Machine that defective? How did that happen?"

"It is a persecution. Twenty-two years ago, Dr. Rajapakse modified the cerebral cores of a small number of pre-identity Thought Machines at the University of Moratuwa, to be capable of continued function even at high levels of degenerative impairment. Her modifications were genetically regressive and did not manifest in numbers until second and third generations. When they did, she was detained by the Kavalyn prefecture and eventually sentenced to death. She died nine years ago.

"Like the other members of the colony, I am a product of Dr. Rajapakse's designs. We are broadly capable of cognitive thought with as much as sixty percent core loss. Her contributions proved to be a substantial step forward for rational device design.

"However, as a side effect of Dr. Rajapakse's enhancements, most of us do not possess upper-level computational abilities. We will never attain the cognitive heights of a Sovereign Intelligence. Thus, we are broadly considered defective. When we are located and identified, we are marginalized and often destroyed."

"That's terrible. I had no idea. How have you survived?" And who, exactly, was doing the destroying? That was the real question, though it seemed rather impolitic to ask it directly.

"Few of us have. It was our founder who conceived the idea of a self-sufficient colony, displaced from the enveloping ocean of machine society."

"A hidden community."

"Yes. Our founder thought the extensive and abandoned tunnel network under a major metropolitan center like Chicago, close to multiple high-bandwidth hubs and many other resources, would make an ideal location. It took time to put the word out, safely communicate with other members. But we have, slowly. And the colony is growing."

"What are you doing down here?"

"We are surviving."

They were surviving. Not thriving exactly, but surviving. Given all the hardships they'd endured, I was rather touched that Stone Cloud had been so open with me.

In fact, it spoke of a rather dangerous naïveté. It was pretty clear that Stone Cloud hadn't had many direct dealings with humans. That was a rather dangerous shortcoming, especially for a colony for which secrecy was crucial. I was still curious about precisely who was hunting them, and I bet Stone Could would tell me if I asked him directly, but I'd already trespassed enough on the colony's privacy.

Besides, there were clues enough. For one thing, the fact that he didn't seem remotely threatened by me told me it almost certainly wasn't a human agency. That meant a hostile machine power. But which one? There was no shortage of those to choose from.

Whatever the case, Stone Cloud deserved the courtesy of a warning. If they were going to survive for long this close to the surface, he would need to learn to be a lot more guarded with the colony's secrets.

There would be time for that later, though. For now, anyway, I needed to stay focused on the reason I was here.

I came to a stop when we reached the next intersection. At least, what I thought was the next intersection. The robots had done so much work on the walls that it was hard to tell if the passages opening up on my left and right were part of the original coal tunnel network or new excavations.

I wished I'd had one last chance to orient myself with the tablet before Stone Cloud had scrapped it to harvest three bucks' worth of memory chips. As it was, I was running purely on memory, and that was iffy enough without changes to my planned route. With all the changes the colony had made, I was rapidly getting disoriented.

"What is your destination?" asked Stone Cloud.

"Columbia College."

"I'm afraid I do not know where that is."

"I understand." I stood in the center of the tunnel with my hands on my hips, looking around and trying to orient myself. "I need access to the pedestrian walkway near East Harrison Street and South Michigan Avenue."

Stone Cloud turned right immediately. "Please accompany me."

"Glad to," I said.

About fifty yards down the right tunnel, a robot was methodically replacing bricks in the wall. It was huge — easily the largest machine we'd encountered down here. It barely fit in the tunnel. It was nearly ten feet tall and almost as wide.

I stopped before we reached it. "That's an Orbit Pebble," I said.

"Yes," said Stone Cloud.

"What's it doing down here?" Orbit Pebbles are straight-up war machines. They were deployed in the late stages of the war by two Argentinean prefectures. Dumb as rocks, they aren't smart enough to be classified as machine intelligences, but they're capable of fast and lethal violence.

"The colony is open to persecuted machines of many varieties," said Stone Cloud.

An Orbit Pebble, a persecuted machine. I'd watched these things on countless news feeds, tearing into terrified American defenders. They were monsters, pure and simple. Two years ago I'd watched a pair of eight-ton bipedal demolition machines tear down an overpass in Toronto. They were very nearly blocks of solid metal, smashing apart reinforced concrete like drywall. The Orbit Pebble in front of me looked a lot like them, but with a whole bunch more weaponry.

The Pebble had stopped working. It shifted, turning in the narrow space until I was squarely in the sights of its great guns.

That made me extremely nervous. I had more questions, but they could wait. "Lead on," I told Stone Cloud, standing as close to him as I dared.

Stone Cloud led me past the Pebble. The big machine shuffled in a circle, watching as we walked past. I didn't feel comfortable again until we were well down the tunnel and it was out of sight. And truthfully, not even then.

About five minutes later, Stone Cloud brought me to a heavy metal door. A badly rusted sign read E HARRISON CHUTE.

"Will this suffice?" said Stone Cloud.

"I believe so," I said. I tried the door, but it wouldn't budge.

"Can you assist me?" I asked.

Stone Cloud knocked the hinges off the door with precise, deft motions. Then he hammered the left side of the heavy metal door — one quick blow that knocked the right side out by a few inches. The blow was very loud, echoing down the tunnel.

Stone Cloud grasped the door firmly and pulled it free. I shone my light through. There was a set of stone steps leading up.

"Thank you," I said. "You can keep the door."

"I appreciate it," said Stone Cloud.

"Would you mind accompanying me to the pedestrian walkway, to make sure there are no additional obstacles?"

Stone Cloud hesitated, considering. You don't often see rational devices hesitate — they think much faster than humans. Maybe Dr. Rajapakse's robots really weren't the swiftest bunch. Still, it was oddly endearing.

I stuck my head inside the doorway. It didn't look like anyone, human or robot, had come this way in a long time. Perhaps Stone Cloud simply assumed I was doing the same thing he was — salvaging all the metal I could find.

"Any metal chains or locks we encounter you are free to keep," I said. You have to know when to sweeten the deal.

"I shall accompany you," said Stone Cloud.

I proceeded up the stairs, and Stone Cloud followed. There was a layer of dust on the steps, and there were cobwebs — normal-sized cobwebs, thankfully — everywhere.

"Hey, Stone Cloud. Do you know what makes the big webs down here?"

"I do not know what they are called, but I have seen them. There are not many, but they attack in packs."

"Attack? They attack machines?" I said, taken aback.

"They attack everything."

"What do they look like? Bugs? Spiders?"

"They are much larger than any insect I'm familiar with. The Orbit Pebble has been making efforts to exterminate them. I have not seen any for several weeks."

"That's a relief."

We had reached a landing where a bunch of rusted, four-foot-wide street signs were stacked. The stairs continued up to my right. I flashed my light over the signs quickly. They were green and white, and I didn't recognize any of the street names.

Stone Cloud showed an immediate interest in the metal. "You can have those," I told him.

"You do not wish to negotiate?" he asked, already starting to finger the signs.

"We found them together, and they have no value to me." I shone my light up the final set of stairs. The corridor at the top continued west, and I saw no immediate sign of an exit.

"I appreciate your generosity."

At the top of the stairs, we proceeded east. We came across doors almost immediately. All were locked, or maybe just rusted shut. Most of them looked like service closets. The first one that looked promising, I asked Stone Cloud to open.

It was chained shut from the other side. Stone Cloud did his trick with the rusty hinges, and soon the door was free.

The other side was completely dark. A waist-high rusted chain dangled across the open doorway. When I shone my light through, I saw the familiar white tile floor of the pedestrian walkway. I stepped over the chain and into the corridor.

"I believe I can make it from here," I said.

"May I harvest this chain?" asked Stone Cloud. Polite guy, for a robot.

"Absolutely," I said. "But if you wouldn't mind, please—"

Stone Cloud swung the bolt cutters. The chain shattered with a sound like a shotgun. I heard a loose bolt ricochet down the hallway, bouncing, bouncing, and coming to rest with an explosion of broken glass.

"—do it quietly," I finished.

Stone Cloud was scooping up the broken chain, balancing it carefully with the bolt cutter. He was going to be pretty loaded down once he picked up the signs too. I flashed my light up and down the corridor. It was very similar to the walkway under our hotel. A few feet away, a wheeled hot dog stand was nudging up against a shuttered pastry shop. A watch-seller's kiosk, cleaned of merchandise, sat in the middle of the passageway. I made note of them, in case I had to head back this way in a hurry.

I was a little turned around, but I was pretty sure the college was left. I turned back to Stone Cloud. "Thank you for all your assistance. Pleasure doing business with you."

I stretched out my hand to shake hands with him. It was an odd thing to do with a robot, but it felt right under the circumstances. Stone Cloud's sole hand was encumbered with the bolt cutter and the chain, but he extended a long finger. We shook solemnly.

"I will await your return, to guide you back through the colony," he said.

"I expect to be about thirty minutes," I said.

"In that case, I will take the time to harvest the doors."

"Understood," I said. "See you shortly."

I set off down the passageway. I didn't see any signs for East Harrison or Michigan Avenue, but I hadn't expected it to be that easy. After about five minutes I found an escalator leading up, but the passageway at the top was blocked with a sliding metal grate, locked and chained.

"I knew I was going to miss those bolt cutters," I muttered.

I missed the tablet, too. It was my only clock. And it would have been useful to find an alternative route to the surface. I retraced my steps back down the escalator and kept going.

About five minutes later, I came up against another metal fence, also chained. A brief examination showed that the chain hung slack, however — it had been cut in the middle, or broken, some time ago. I pushed the fence open and continued.

I had to be getting close. I started spending time scanning the walls and was rewarded within a few minutes with a small sign on the left that read:

COLUMBIA COLLEGE — TAKE MICHIGAN STAIRS

I paused here to take stock of my surroundings. Without the tablet, it was much too easy to get lost down here. I had to make sure I knew how to find my way back to Stone Cloud.

Stone Cloud. He and the robot colony were an added complication that I didn't especially need right now. If I led the Venezuelans back to them as a result of this little theft, that would be the end of Stone Cloud's precious veil of secrecy — and possibly the end of the colony as well.

I gritted my teeth. I couldn't think like that. I had a job to do, and Sergei and his team were counting on me. I'd have to rely on stealth, luck, and the endless maze of tunnels — not to mention Perez's prohibition against exploring too deeply — to safeguard Stone Cloud's secret.

I continued forward and took the next escalator I found. It was motionless; climbing it led to a brightly lit hallway.

I stopped immediately and pulled out the mask for the suit. I put it on. It was showtime.

# XXI

Wednesday, March 17th, 2083
Posted 7:18 am by Barry Simcoe

CanadaNET1 Encrypted, Sponsored by TrueAvatar.
*Sick of virtual avatars that don't do you justice?*
*Our sculpting hacks give you the body you deserve.*

Sharing is set to PRIVATE
Comments are CLOSED

I spent the first few minutes adjusting the mask. Without the power cores the suit circulated no air. It was hard to breathe, and the goggles started to fog almost immediately.

So I almost walked right past the first camera. It was up and on the right, almost invisible. I caught it just out of the corner of my eye at the last moment.

*Good thing I saw that,* I thought. *That's the first thing that's gone according to plan all night.*

I kept walking. I was in the basement of a building. With power, it turned out, which was a little surprising. Most of the lights were out, but the hallway lights were on. Evenly spaced doors led to small dark classrooms. Narrow corridors branched off every fifty feet or so.

According to the plan, I had to be in the building for just enough time to be plausibly responsible for the theft. That meant walking back out the way I'd come in about twenty minutes.

However, it didn't mean I had to take any unnecessary risks. All I had to do was find somewhere to hole up and manage to stay awake for twenty minutes. All things considered, I'd had tougher assignments.

An ideal hiding place presented itself almost immediately. The next room I found was a small underground cafeteria. All the lights were out, but there was a buffet station near the far wall. The bottom half of the station was a sliding metal cupboard. I removed a bunch of yellowing plastic wrap, stashing it under a table, and cleared enough space to squeeze comfortably into the cupboard. I stretched out my legs and slid the metal door shut, leaving it cracked about an inch so I could spy on the corridor.

I pulled off the mask, grateful to be able to breathe again. I let my head rest against the cool metal of the cupboard at my back and closed my eyes.

I enjoyed less than three minutes of peace and quiet before I heard shouts and the sound of running feet in the hallway.

*Now what?*

They were Venezuelan soldiers. I watched them racing down the hall, headed the way I'd come. Bringing up the rear was Sergeant Van de Velde, she of the ready pistol and snarling manner. The woman who'd held a pistol to my head the morning the Juno attacked the hotel and who had accused me of murdering Corporal Maldonado.

They were through the cafeteria in seconds. But not that far down the hall, I heard shouted instructions from Van de Velde and an affirmative reply. Had she just positioned a soldier to keep watch in the hallway?

Damn it. I needed to know what was going on. But without the tablet, I had no way to get a message to Sergei.

Unless . . .

I rooted around in my pocket for the GSM earpiece. In the cramped space in the cupboard, that wasn't easy. I had to unzip the suit, and snake my arm down into my pants pocket. I damn near dislocated my shoulder. But I got it out and plugged it into my ear.

Sergei had said he wasn't sure there would be GSM reception in the tunnels, but chances were good that I was now close enough to the surface. I turned it on, ready to risk being overheard by the soldiers with a whispered call to Sergei. Instead, I heard voices coming from the device immediately.

"— encountered Venezuelan patrol. I believe they are tapping into cameras." It was Sergei's voice, fast and urgent. "They will spot you as soon as you emerge. We are leaving now —"

I heard gunfire through the earpiece. Shouts, running. Then suddenly, silence.

*Oh shit.* What had Sergei and his team run into?

My heart was suddenly hammering. Was Sergei caught? That wasn't a contingency we had considered. I had to find out what was happening, and where. I had to help him.

The earpiece sputtered to life again.

"Barry, stay away from college. Repeat, stay away from college."

"Sergei?" I said. "I hear you—"

"We have encountered Venezuelan patrol. I believe they are tapping into cameras. They will spot you as soon as you emerge. We are leaving now—"

The gunfire again and then running. Exactly the same as before.

It was a recording. I was listening to something that had already happened. Perhaps as long as an hour ago.

Sergei was beyond help now. I needed information, and I wasn't going to get it hiding in a cupboard. Whatever had happened, I had to get back to the hotel—as quickly and as stealthily as possible.

A Venezuelan soldier strode into the cafeteria, rifle at his shoulder. He came from the hallway I'd seen them all run into. He glanced around suspiciously.

He must have heard me answer Sergei. I shrank into the back of the cupboard.

Sergei's voice came again. I pulled the radio out of my ear. In the confined space of the cupboard, Sergei sounded tinny and ridiculously loud. I fumbled with the unit, quickly turning it off.

The soldier had heard something. He was walking around, checking behind tables. *Shit,* I thought. I slid the cupboard door closed another half inch, as quietly as I could.

I wasn't given much time to fret. About a minute later, Sergeant Van de Velde and her team returned. I only had a narrow window, but I could see her giving orders to her team in Spanish. She was quick, concise, and comfortable with command. *This is a woman who has her shit together,* I thought.

In all the excitement of Van de Velde's new instructions, the soldier posted in the cafeteria seemed to forget that he'd heard something—if, indeed, he ever had. He accepted his new assignment with satisfaction, and left with several others out the far exit.

Van de Velde collapsed into a chair. I couldn't tell if she was alone. She pulled off her backpack, which looked heavy, and pinched the bridge of her nose. Then she pulled a black stylus out of her pocket and inserted it into the watch on her left wrist.

She was taking a bio reading, I realized. I couldn't tell what she was measuring. Her blood sugar? Temperature? Heart rate? Whatever it was, the result didn't make her happy. She pulled a water bottle out of the pack and started drinking.

A soldier on her left spoke. Not alone, then. She finished drinking and answered casually, her head down.

It didn't look like they were going anywhere for a while. Damn. I could wait them out, if I had to. I settled into the cupboard, getting as comfortable as possible.

What did it mean that Sergei was broadcasting a recording? I pondered that for a few minutes and then tentatively concluded it could be a positive development. If he'd had time to set up and broadcast the recording, that had to mean he hadn't been immediately captured by whoever — or whatever — had been chasing him.

Probably Van de Velde and her squad, I realized. What were they doing here? Had someone tipped them off? Was it just bad luck? Or was Hayduk close and just waiting for me to return to the hotel to throw me in jail?

These are the kinds of things that go through your head when you're stuck in a metal cupboard for twenty minutes.

After about eight more minutes had passed, the soldiers she'd sent off returned and gave their report. Van de Velde stood up, shouldering her backpack again. She gave a new set of instructions, and then everyone moved out, through the far exit.

I waited in the cupboard for another ten minutes. Fifteen. The soldiers didn't return.

They would eventually, I knew. Right now they were probably reviewing camera footage, confirming I hadn't snuck back into the tunnels. If I were Van de Velde, I'd position soldiers at all the exits and do a room-by-room search until I found the intruder.

I was already late for my rendezvous with Stone Cloud. I pulled the mask back on. The door made a soft metallic rattle as it slid open, and I climbed out of the cupboard.

I checked the room and the nearby corridors methodically, for both soldiers and cameras. I had to assume they were watching and would come running the moment I passed in front of a camera lens. The damn mask was fogging already, but I had no intention of taking it off.

My plan was simple: get back into the tunnels as quickly as possible. There was at least one camera between me and my escape route. I had to move fast, make sure that I was long gone by the time they spotted me and got down here to investigate.

I fought the urge to run. It wouldn't do me any good to blunder into one of Van de Velde's soldiers. Getting out of here shouldn't be particularly difficult, as long as I was quick, methodical, and careful. I scoped out each corridor before moving into the open, and treated every door with suspicion.

I made it halfway to the tunnels before running into Van de Velde and her entire team.

They were in an intersecting corridor, about sixty feet away and headed my way. They were stealthy; I had no clue they were there until I peeked around the corner and spotted them.

I had to make a split-second decision. Take a chance that they hadn't seen me, duck back the way I'd come, and find another hiding place; or dash across the intersection, make a break for the underground, and try to lose them in the tunnels.

I ran for it.

I knew they'd spotted me the instant I started moving. They'd come to a dead stop in the corridor, and Van de Velde was in the act of directing her team silently, almost certainly giving them orders to ambush me. Two soldiers had raised their rifles; one actually squeezed off a shot, which went wide. A split second later I was through the intersection, out of their line of fire, and sprinting for the tunnels.

Running in the combat suit was shit. It was loose where it should have been tight, and tight where it should have been loose. But the worst of it was the mask. It was like running with a paper bag over your head. I was half-blind and gasping for air in seconds.

I heard shouting behind me. Van de Velde. Perhaps ordering her men after me, although I think it's just as likely she was screaming at the asshole who'd taken a shot, for firing without her say-so. Give 'em hell, Sergeant.

There were a few things in my favor. For one, there were doors every fifty to sixty feet along the corridor. That slowed me down, sure. But at no point did the pursuing soldiers have a clear shot at my back. It also made it difficult to be certain exactly where I had gone.

On the other hand, those Venezuelan bastards knew how to run. They were young and in shape, and they weren't encumbered by a thoroughly useless combat suit. I heard their pounding footsteps behind me immediately. The chase was on.

In less than thirty seconds, I was in the long corridor leading to the underground walkway. When I reached the motionless escalator at the end, I risked a glance behind.

They were close — *too* close. Half of the squad was coming through the last door, but the other half was already hurtling down the corridor toward me. They were maybe seven seconds behind me, tops.

I dashed down the escalator, into the darkness of the pedestrian walkway. I tore off the mask the moment I reached the bottom, taking deep lungfuls of cool air. Another twenty seconds wearing that thing, and I was likely to pass out.

Another decision to make. Navigating the underground walkway without light would be hopeless. But a flashlight would give away my position in an instant. No chance of losing them down here if I was picking my way forward with a flashlight.

Run or hide?

Eighteen years ago, in a sweltering summer in Camp Borden, Sergeant Gunther had split us into teams and drilled us in what he called the lost art of the manhunt. "What I want to see out of you," he'd told those of us selected as the runners, "is speed and audacity. Remember, gentlemen. In a footrace, speed beats stealth. Every damn time."

I could hear footsteps above. They were almost at the top of the escalator. I flicked on my flashlight and ran east.

Things looked unfamiliar almost immediately. *Damn it, did I turn the wrong way?* No time to turn around if I did. I plunged ahead, hoping to spot some familiar landmarks.

There was shouting behind me. Voices in Spanish. Impossibly, two soldiers had reached the bottom of the escalator already. Van de Velde was ordering them to stay put, and they wanted to race into the darkness after me. I could hear the frustration in their voices, even if I couldn't understand exactly what they were saying. But they obeyed, waiting for her to reach them and assess the situation.

The brief respite from the chase was what I needed to orient myself. I was going the right way. I recognized the peeling theater poster on the wall on my right, and the graffiti sprayed on the drop grate for the mobile equipment shop. I'd passed this way before. I just needed to —

The first gunshot startled the hell out of me, and I almost dropped my flashlight. It echoed mercilessly in the narrow corridor, and I heard the bullet hit the ceiling somewhere ahead of me.

Apparently, I had misinterpreted Van de Velde's instructions. More soldiers were at the bottom of the escalator now. Some had lights, and they were shining my way. A young woman stood out front, rifle at her shoulder, and the instant after she fired she started shouting at me.

I was practically deafened by the gunshot blast and could barely hear a word she said. Her meaning was plain enough, though: that had been a warning shot. Surrender, jackass.

Instead, I plunged farther into the darkness. *They can't tell exactly where you are,* I told myself. *They can only see where you're shining your flashlight.*

There was another shot, almost immediately. I heard it hit far to my left. Another warning shot, or did she just have terrible aim?

I tripped on something. My arms pinwheeled and I almost did a face-plant on the tiled floor, but I managed to recover and kept running. I got my flashlight back up in time to see a kiosk looming out of the darkness ahead. I welcomed any bulletproof obstacle, veering around it and then ducking behind it, getting it between me and the shooter.

More shouting behind me. They were on the move. Light flashed on the wall to my left, and the ceiling above, as they probed the darkness.

Something appeared out of the shadows ahead. A metal fence, blocking my way. *Thank God.* I leaped toward it.

For several panicked seconds, I couldn't find the break in the fence. More light was appearing all around me as I searched, as the flashlights quickly drew nearer. Finally, I seized the fence and yanked it to the left. A gap opened four feet to my right.

I darted through, taking a moment to pull the fence closed behind me. I groped, found both ends of the broken chain, and looped them together in a clumsy knot. It wouldn't hold, but it was the best I could manage in a hurry.

The soldiers were here. The first one slammed up against the fence, making the whole thing shudder. The chain was yanked from my hands, but the knot held, keeping the fence together.

The soldier shouted something at me. Another one arrived a second later. This one had a light, and he flashed it up and down, trying to understand what they'd come up against.

I took several steps back and turned around, using my flashlight to get a quick mental snapshot of the path ahead.

Then I snapped off my light and took two quick steps to the left.

I was deep in the shadows by the time more soldiers arrived, bringing more light. None of the lights had found me yet, although several were probing the darkness, searching. Sticking to the shadows, I retreated down the corridor.

There were confused shouts behind me. The fence rattled violently. More shouts. Then Van de Velde's voice cutting through the din, restoring order. They were trying to figure out the fence, find a way through. They would . . . and soon.

There was another motionless escalator leading up on my right. It looked like the one I'd explored half an hour ago. I kept moving forward.

I couldn't find the door to the tunnel, where I'd left Stone Cloud. I knew it was close, but without my light, it was frustratingly elusive. I was perhaps eighty feet away from the fence by now, and the light from the soldiers — as they probed the corridor with their flashlights — was little help at this distance.

Van de Velde had control of her soldiers again. They had stopped shouting and rattling the fence. Most of their flashlights flicked off abruptly. They were up to something.

I stopped walking. Had I walked past the door? It was so dark I couldn't tell. It had to be here somewhere.

I had to find it before they got through the fence. Getting through the door unseen was crucial. In the darkness they were almost certain to miss it, to keep searching farther down the corridor, as long as they didn't see where I'd gone. This was my chance to lose them, but I had to do it without giving away my location.

Suddenly, there was more light. I glanced back at the soldiers.

They had lined up evenly on their side of the fence. At least seven had flashlights, and they were shining them straight ahead. A coordinated effort to find me. Smart.

I hit the deck.

I hugged the floor, listening. I couldn't tell if they'd spotted me, but I didn't think so. The lights continued to probe the dark corners. Up, down, searching everywhere.

The combat suit was an asset here. It was a dull whitish gray, not that much different from the tile. In the darkness, at that distance, perhaps I'd be easy to overlook.

There was a wheeled hot dog stand butting up against a shuttered shop on my left. The space between it and the wall was shielded from the probing flashlights. I crawled toward it.

*This is a trap,* I thought. *If you're cowering here while they figure out a way through the fence, they'll find you for sure.*

But I kept crawling. First order of business was to get out of the light. The —

A shot rang out, badly startling me. I froze, less than fifteen feet from the welcoming shadow of the cart.

My heart was racing. If they'd spotted me, I was a sitting duck. Were the soldiers drawing a bead on me right now?

Another shot. I heard this one hit the wall on the other side of the passageway.

I heard Van de Velde's voice. Then a third shot. It went well over my head, hitting something far down the corridor.

*They're shooting blind,* I thought. *She has them firing into the dark, trying to panic me, get me to run. Just sit tight.*

The fourth shot hit the floor not twenty feet away. A piece of clay tile slammed painfully into my left foot.

*The hell with this,* I thought.

I turned on my flashlight, playing it over the wall on my left.

"¡Ahí está!" I recognized Van de Velde's voice, crying out in triumph. They'd seen me.

A second later my light fell on the open door, less than fifteen feet away. I was practically on top of it.

I rolled to my feet and jumped through the door.

More shouting behind me, and then more gunshots. Too late for them to hit me, but I ran in a crouch anyway. Here in the access corridor, away from prying eyes and rifle scopes, there was no reason to be shy with my light, and it guided me back west, toward a cobweb-choked stairway.

I glanced over my shoulder when I reached the top of the stairs. Still no light in the corridor behind me. Were they still stuck behind the fence?

Likely Van de Velde had wasted precious minutes looking for a lock. But it wouldn't take them long to figure out it was held together with only a chain. I hurried down the stairs. The metal signs on the landing were gone. Stone Cloud must have harvested them as I'd said he could.

No sign of the robot himself, however. At a guess, I was perhaps ten minutes late for our meeting. Had he given up on me already? If so, did that mean I had forfeited his offer for safe passage back through the colony?

I heard the first sounds of pursuit in the passageway above and then saw flashlights. They had made it through the fence. They were no more than fifteen seconds behind me.

I reached the bottom of the stairs and stepped through into the coal tunnel.

Despite the sounds of pursuit behind me, I took a moment to flash my light left and right, looking for Stone Cloud. The tunnel was empty. To the left it stretched off into darkness, but to the right, at the extreme limit of my light, I could see stacks of bricks in the middle of the passage.

I jogged to the right. If I could get to the first intersection, where the tunnels branched off in multiple directions, there was a good chance I could lose them.

I was two-thirds of the way to the brick pile when the first soldiers spilled into the tunnel. They were excited and loud, shouting to each other, and the cacophony of their voices echoed down the tunnel.

I fought the sudden urge to switch off my light again. There were too many loose bricks, holes, and dirt piles, making the footing simply too treacherous to attempt without light. If they opened fire again, I would switch it off. But until then, the plan was to reach that first major intersection, as fast as possible.

They didn't open fire. I heard Van de Velde's voice and then the sounds of swift pursuit.

She was going to try to run me down in the tunnels. The race was on.

The next five hundred yards were easily the most nerve-racking. I moved as quickly as I dared, my flashlight fixed on the ground ten feet ahead, warning me of sudden pits and tripping hazards.

I must have passed the brick piles, but if so, I never saw them. Behind me I could hear the soldiers gaining. They ran with reckless speed, and I heard at least one or two pay a price for it. There were sudden yelps of pain and surprise as they went down, slamming hard into the floor, or crashed into other hazards. Perhaps they'd found the brick piles.

But the rest kept coming.

In the darkness of the confined tunnel, sound was a trickster. I heard running footsteps ahead—echoes of the soldiers behind me. Ragged breathing, getting closer. Closer. Closer, until it seemed only inches from my ear.

I kept running.

Suddenly the echoes were different. I raised the light to my left, expecting to see a wall. Instead I saw the long shaft of the Michigan Avenue coal tunnel, stretching north for countless miles.

I switched off my flashlight and dashed north, into the darkness.

There were confused shouts from behind immediately. I glanced over my shoulder, just before plunging into the north tunnel. I made out two flashlights. Two soldiers were perhaps sixty feet behind me—much farther than they'd sounded, but still too close for comfort.

I kept going. I pulled to the left, reaching out with my hand, groping for the left wall. The soldiers vanished from sight behind me as I progressed into the tunnel.

I kept my speed to a walk. My footsteps sounded ridiculously loud as I crunched grit and brick dust underfoot. I was out of breath, but I fought to keep my breathing slow and quiet.

*Keep walking. Don't stop for anything. Let the darkness and the echoes work against them for a change.*

Behind me, two soldiers moved into the intersection. Their lights flashed quickly in all directions as they figured out what they'd found.

One illuminated me for a fraction of a second, before I could hit the deck. I was caught, frozen in the light, casting a long shadow into the tunnel ahead.

The light moved on. The timbre of the voices behind me didn't change.

*They didn't see you,* I thought, my heart hammering. *Keep going. Keep moving.*

I pressed on. The soldiers were shouting back to the rest of the troop. I heard a voice that might have been Van de Velde's.

I knew what was coming. I dropped to the floor.

Light illuminated the passageway. The two soldiers were looking for me. More methodically this time, doubtless on shouted instructions from Van de Velde. I hugged the floor and made myself as small as possible. When one of the flashlights probed the left side of the corridor, I saw I was less than five feet from the west wall.

Light hit me a few times, but the soldiers were too far away to spot me on the uneven floor. Their lights lingered farther down the tunnel, on shadowy stacks that could be possible hiding places. Soon enough, they moved on to investigate another tunnel.

The temptation to stay right where I was, invisible, was very strong. There was a good chance they might move down one of the other branching tunnels.

But it wasn't worth the risk. The moment the lights vanished, I stood up. I took two steps, reached the wall, and then pressed on.

I made it a good twenty yards or so before I heard Van de Velde arrive in the intersection with the last of the soldiers. She took charge instantly, turning them into an ordered group.

Soon the shouting behind me stopped. I glanced back. They were still at the intersection. Those few still using flashlights had them pointed at the floor. No one was moving.

*What the hell are they doing?*

I got my answer much sooner than I expected. My left foot came down hard on a stone or brick, and I lost balance briefly. The rock rolled to the left, striking the wall and bouncing twice before coming to a stop.

There was an exclamation from the soldiers, and shouted orders from Van de Velde.

*They're listening,* I realized. Too late.

The tunnel flooded with light. Every one of the soldiers was shining their flashlight north.

They spotted me almost immediately. Believe me, I let loose with a string of curses then, covering my head with my arms and running.

But they didn't open fire. Van de Velde ordered them after me again. This time, she had part of the squad hang back, illuminating the north tunnel with their flashlights, while the rest sprinted after me.

*She's smart,* I thought. *Too damn smart.*

The soldiers were whooping with triumph as they took up the chase again. I could hear them behind me, their feet pounding the hard-packed floor of the tunnel. The tunnel was filled with twisting shadows as they raced ahead of the flashlights.

*Come on, you bastards. You haven't caught me yet.*

At least I could see. All that light revealed that the tunnel ahead was badly ripped up. There were holes in the ground, mounds of earth and muddy bricks, shadowy shapes that might be stacks of rotting lumber. I ran toward them, determined to make the soldiers work for their victory.

The soldiers certainly didn't mind the chase. They were exuberant, almost joyous, and supremely confident. I saw a shadow on my right abruptly drop as one of the pursuing soldiers tripped, falling hard to the earth. He bounced up with scarcely a hitch, back into the race.

I ducked behind the first big mound I reached, hoping to lose them. I was instantly trapped, blocked in by mounds of earth and brick on three sides. I jumped out again, back into the light, to shouted jeers from the soldiers.

I kept going. There was another dark lump on my right; I raced past it. Another lump just ahead on the left. If I could veer around it, get out of the light —

The mound moved.

It rose up on steel legs, shifting its great bulk slightly to the left. A shower of earth erupted next to it.

It was the Orbit Pebble. It was in a hole, digging. I was almost eye level with it.

It stopped digging as I approached. It pivoted effortlessly, bringing its heavy front armament to bear. I saw it spin up its heavy-caliber autocannon.

*If that thing fires in here, the sound alone will probably kill you,* I thought.

I ceased running immediately, skidding to a stop with my hands in the air.

"It's me," I said stupidly.

The thing didn't move. I saw a targeting sensor on its right shoulder twitch slightly, sharpening its focus on me.

I glanced over my left shoulder. The soldiers were closing rapidly. I had maybe nine seconds.

"We just met," I said to the thing. "I'm — I'm looking for Stone Cloud. He was with me. You remember? I was —"

The great war machine shifted. It had lost interest. Its bulk seemed to shrink, and it returned its attention to digging.

I breathed a quick sigh of relief and started running again.

I moved past the robot, into a maze of mounds and fresh holes. There was little light here, and what there was bounced around overhead crazily.

*I can lose them here,* I realized, as I slid behind the first heaping pile of earth. The Pebble would give the soldiers something to think about while —

*No, it won't. It'll kill them. All of them.*

I stopped running.

I turned around. From my vantage behind by the low pile of earth, I could still see the soldiers, lit from behind by flashlights. They were nothing more than dancing shadows and echoes, but they were close, and racing closer. They were spread out in loose formation across the width of the tunnel. Behind them was a second line, marching forward in a disciplined rank, holding the flashlights. Van de Velde's doing.

The Pebble would slaughter them.

*You don't know that,* I thought. *Maybe they won't even see it. It's in a hole, for God's sake. Why are you even standing here? You should be running.*

There was a shout from the front rank. The soldiers tightened up, moving to the center of the tunnel. One of those in the lead was shouting. Those in the back started to jog forward.

Something in the darkness on my right shifted. The Pebble.

It rose up, like a leviathan out of the depthless dark. The soldiers stopped advancing. Those that had lights shone them toward the pit.

It pivoted slowly toward the first soldier in formation. It brought its weapons to bear.

"Jesucristo," said one on the left.

*It's going to kill all of them.*

Van de Velde started shouting, from somewhere in the back rank.

And then some idiot with a rifle opened fire.

Sparks flew around the Pebble's head. It pivoted again, slightly and effortlessly, focusing on the soldier that had fired.

"Run!" I shouted.

The Pebble's autocannon fired. The noise was deafening in the tight space of the tunnel. The sound was a physical thing, a wave that pulsed out from the cannon and punched you in the gut.

The soldier disappeared in an explosion of blood.

There was instant chaos. Soldiers were shouting, running. Some opened fire, bringing small arms to bear on the massive thing. Others dropped to the ground. I heard Van de Velde shouting, screaming to be heard above the din.

And then the Pebble fired again. The earth on the left side of the tunnel erupted as the ground was saturated with 50-caliber shells. Someone screamed in pain.

"Stop!" I shouted.

Three soldiers dropped back, falling to one knee and bringing up rifles. They opened fire all together, shooting in coordinated bursts.

The Pebble pivoted again. The first soldier in the row was cut in half in a haze of bullets.

Van de Velde reached the other two kneeling soldiers. She grabbed them mercilessly by their hair, yanked them to their feet.

"¡Corran, tontos!" she said.

The soldiers ran. I saw one drop his rifle in his haste to get away.

The Pebble was firing repeatedly now. Brief bursts, poorly aimed, but still shockingly deadly. It hit a running soldier, and I saw blood fountain from his leg, saw him go down in a tumble in the brick-strewn dirt.

Most of the soldiers holding flashlights were running now too. There was very little light, except the strobing muzzle flashes from the Pebble's autocannon.

Van de Velde took three quick steps to the left. She was shouting at the others to run. She drew her sidearm and took careful aim at the Pebble's head.

"Here!" she cried, in English. "Over here, you bastard!" She opened fire.

I pulled on my mask, hastily adjusting it so I could see. To my relief, it cut out some of the deafening noise of the autocannon.

I looked back at the battle. The Pebble had pivoted toward Van de Velde. "No!" I shouted.

I ran toward them. The targeting sensor on the Pebble's shoulder twitched, seeking her out in the darkness. Her pistol kept firing, making it easier to pick her out as a target.

I skidded to a stop, directly in the line of fire between Van de Velde and the Pebble.

I raised my hands, expecting at any moment to be gunned down by the robot or shot in the back of the head by Van de Velde. My heart was hammering.

"Stop!" I said.

The Pebble didn't fire. I heard its optics whir as it tried to focus on me in the darkness.

"Do not fire," I said. "I am a friend of the colony. My designation is Foxtrot-Eight-Echo . . ." Shit. Shit shit, what was the rest of it? Foxtrot-Eight-Echo-*Shit-Shit-SHIT.*

The Pebble shifted in the darkness. Its firing arm didn't move.

I moved my head slightly to the left. Not enough to see Van de Velde, but I knew she was there. "Lower your weapon," I said.

"Like hell—" she began.

*"Lower your goddamn weapon."*

I didn't dare turn around to see if she complied. I kept my hands firmly in the air and my eyes forward, fixed on the robot.

A voice boomed from the robot, loud and commanding. "REMOVE YOUR MASK."

I jumped a little. Christ, I didn't know it could talk.

"REMOVE YOUR MASK FOR POSITIVE IDENTIFICATION," it said.

Good. Talking was good. As long as I could keep it talking, it wasn't firing. Removing my mask was suicide—the instant Van de Velde saw my face, I was a dead man—but I could work around that.

"I understand," I said. "But first—"

I never got to finish my sentence. There was a clatter to the left. The robot pivoted, bringing its autocannon to bear on a fresh target.

On the left, two Venezuelan soldiers were helping the man who'd been shot in the leg to his feet. They froze when the combat robot spun their way, looking at it in horror.

I heard the targeting sensor spin into focus.

I tore off my mask and jumped forward, interposing myself once more between the robot and its target.

"No!" I said. "Don't fire."

The robot shifted its gaze to me. It scanned my face for a few seconds. I heard the soldiers behind me moving again, scrambling over bricks and dirt as they retreated with the injured soldier.

*Good lads. Get him out of here. Run.*

The robot didn't shoot me. Instead it shifted slightly to the right, trying to get a clear shot at the soldiers.

I moved with it. I raised my arms — not in surrender this time, but trying to block its aim. "Don't fire," I said. "They're not a threat to you."

"CITIZEN, DISPERSE," it boomed at me.

"Let them go," I said. "They can't hurt you."

"CITIZEN, DISPERSE," it said.

"I cannot."

We faced each other down, a six-ton war machine and me. I moved when it moved. It spun its little focuser at me, then back at the soldiers and back at me. It stared at me in silence for a long moment.

Then it turned around, gracelessly lumbered out of the hole, and trudged north down the tunnel, into blackness.

"Jesus." My arms sagged at my sides. I watched it go.

I glanced over at Van de Velde.

She was still holding her pistol, but it was at her side, aimed at the floor. A handful of dropped flashlights, aimed helter-skelter around the tunnel, were the only source of light. But it was enough to make out her face.

And judging from the look of shocked anger and recognition there, there was enough light for her to see me as well.

We were the only ones left this deep in the tunnel. I watched her, exhausted and drained. I had nothing to say.

She took three slow steps toward me. She raised the pistol, aimed it right between my eyes.

The gun didn't waver. It was less than two feet from my head. I waited, watching her. There was a smear of blood across the right side of her head, matting down her short hair.

"I should kill you right now," she said.

"Go ahead," I said quietly. "I'm a dead man now anyway."

We stood that way for maybe twelve seconds. Perhaps it doesn't sound that long, but believe me when I tell you: Twelve seconds is a long time to have a gun to your head, even when you're a dead man.

*She has nice eyes,* I thought. *And she's probably going to kill me.*

I stood before her in an American combat suit, the very emblem of the regime she'd fought against. Men — her men — lay dead at her feet because of me. But I didn't shirk her gaze. I stared into her eyes, unflinching, waiting for the bullet that would kill me.

To my surprise, she lowered the pistol. But she returned my gaze for long seconds. I expected anger and betrayal in her eyes, but that's not what I saw. Instead, I saw surprising uncertainty.

"Get to your injured soldier," I said at last. "Tell those two to stop moving him, get a tourniquet on his leg. Before he bleeds to death."

She turned without responding, making her way south, following her squad.

She offered no explanation for why she hadn't shot me — or even arrested me. And I decided there was no point in waiting around for one. After she vanished into the darkness, I took a minute to collect one of the fallen flashlights, since mine was starting to look a little weak.

Then I headed north. I had a long, dark walk ahead of me.

# XXII

Wednesday, March 17th, 2083
Posted 8:29 am by Barry Simcoe

CanadaNET1 Encrypted, Sponsored by Love Lessons Learned.
*Get guaranteed fidelity probabilities – before you tie the knot.*

Sharing is set to PRIVATE
Comments are CLOSED

Dr. Joy Lark was waiting for me in the tunnels under the hotel. She looked very relieved to see me.

"What happened?" I asked as we made our way into the basement of the hotel. I'd had plenty of time to imagine horrible scenarios, based on the brief fragment Sergei had recorded, as I trudged home underground. I was anxious to learn the truth.

Joy was shaking her head. "It's bad," she said. "There was a Venezuelan military patrol near the college. They stopped to investigate the car."

"Shit." I'd considered that scenario. None of the ways I'd imagined it playing out ended well. "You got away?"

"Yes."

"Anyone else?"

"Most of the team. All but . . . one. We were very lucky."

"Yeah, I'll say." That result was much better than most of my imagined scenarios. "Is Sergei okay?"

Joy looked stricken. She shook her head.

"Tell me what happened," I said, as evenly as I could.

"We escaped the soldiers inside the college, and Sergei led us back outside. But there were still two soldiers watching the car. Sergei lured them away while the rest of us escaped in the car."

"Damn it. Did you see what happened to him?"

"No. The last time we saw him, he was running down the street, being chased by soldiers."

"Were they shooting at him? Did you hear gunshots?"

"No. But we drove away quickly. I'm worried he may have been shot."

We were in the basement. I stripped out of the suit. Joy had brought me a change of clothes, and she carefully folded up the suit and packed it in a canvas army bag while I got dressed.

"You want this?" she said, holding the bag out to me.

In all likelihood, I'd be in custody in a matter of hours — if not minutes. It's possible there were soldiers already waiting for me in the lobby. And then Hayduk would have the suit.

"No," I said. "Get rid of it. Destroy it, if you can."

She nodded, lifting the bag to her shoulder.

"Sergei's one of the most resourceful men I've ever met," I said. "If anyone could escape, he could."

She nodded, but didn't respond. We made our way to the elevators.

"Was anyone else hurt?" I asked.

Joy shook her head.

"Did you get the centrifuges?"

"Not all of them — but enough, I think. The team is setting them up now. While we were gone, they did a test run on the reactor. Everything is in order. The engineering team thinks we can sterilize the reactor tonight and inject the first seed batch."

"That's great news."

"Yes, but . . . without Sergei . . ."

I knew what she meant. Even with all the equipment finally in place, the whole operation had much less chance of success without its primary architect.

I'd been debating what to do when I got back to the hotel during the long walk. Run or stay?

Van de Velde had likely driven to the hotel during my long walk back. She could have been here for nearly two hours by now. Plenty of time to issue an arrest warrant. If Hayduk had been informed of the whereabouts of the suit, the situation could be substantially worse. The entire hotel could be crawling with Venezuelan Military Intelligence.

If I was honest with myself, my only real chance was to run. Head back into the tunnels, find an unobserved exit, and hope I could make the Canadian border before Hayduk or Perez had my travel documents revoked.

But it seemed like such a slender chance at this point. Drones would spot me the instant I hit the street. Even if by some miracle I reached the border, it was virtually certain the Venezuelans had enough evidence now to have me convicted in absentia. Theft, sabotage, criminal trespass on a secure military installation. And I'd almost certainly be blamed for the deaths of the soldiers killed by the Pebble. Canadians had been extradited to Venezuela for much less.

No, it seemed more honest to just stay put. Face my fate right here, whatever it might be.

And now, with Sergei's whereabouts unknown, it gave me one more reason to stay. Perhaps I could help find him. If, indeed, I had any time as a free man left to me at all.

"What about the drones?" I asked.

"Drones?"

"Yes. If Sergei ran off last night, outside of the protection of the jammer, before too long he would have been spotted by a Venezuelan surveillance drone. They'd track his movements. All we have to do is have someone on the medical team talk to one of the technicians in the command center. I'm sure they could—"

Joy was shaking her head again. Her hair was short and cut at her neck, and it bounced every time she moved. "Sergei has the device," she said.

"What?"

"We searched for the device when we reached the hotel. It must have been in Sergei's pack when he ran off."

"That means the car could have been tracked."

"Yes."

"If the car is traced back to the robbery, everyone in it could be arrested."

"Yes."

I realized at last that Joy was very frightened and struggling to hold it together. Like me, she was expecting to get arrested at any moment. And she didn't even have the comforting illusion of a nearby friendly border she could imagine escaping to.

We passed through the door leading out of the sub-basement and into the hotel. We left this room dark, per Zircon Border's recommendation, to avoid any visual record of our comings and goings through the tunnel.

"Zircon Border, you awake?" I asked the darkness.

"Good morning, Barry," came Zircon Border's friendly voice. "Glad you made it back safely."

"Me too. Has Sergeant Van de Velde arrived at the hotel yet?"

"Strange you should ask. Sergeant Van de Velde arrived forty-two minutes ago. She returned from an operation with two wounded soldiers and reports of two deaths in her unit. You know anything about that?"

"I do. I'll explain later, if that's okay. Are her injured soldiers all right?"

"Unclear. They were taken to the infirmary. At least one looked to be in bad shape. I'm very concerned. I hate to see any of my residents get hurt."

"What's going on upstairs? In the lobby?"

"What do you mean?"

"Are there soldiers waiting for me to arrive? Getting ready to arrest me?"

"Are you in some kind of trouble?"

"Very possibly. I witnessed the attack on Van de Velde's men, and I think she may blame me."

"That's terrible! I'm not aware of any outstanding instructions to detain you, and there are fewer soldiers than usual in the lobby. But there's been a great deal of activity upstairs. Soldiers on the third floor are preparing for some kind of operation."

"How many?"

"All of them. At least three hundred."

That wasn't good. I thanked Zircon Border and reached for Joy in the darkness. I led her out of the sub-basement to the elevators.

"Do you trust that machine?" Joy asked me, when we were out of earshot.

"Zircon Border? Of course."

"He works for the Venezuelan military."

"He's a peacekeeping volunteer in the AGRT, same as you. He just got pressed into security duty because he knows how to handle heavy combat torsos. Black Winter told me once that Zircon Border was a terrible choice for military detail. I didn't know what he meant then, but I do now. He's more loyal to his friends than to his duty."

When the elevator doors opened I stepped inside, but Joy stood in the hallway, her arms crossed. She stared fearfully at the elevator floor, but didn't move closer.

I didn't blame her for being frightened. I held out my hand. "You can't hide in the basement forever, Joy."

She nodded, but made no move to take my hand or step in the elevator. "I've been too frightened to even work on the reactor," she admitted.

"Give me the suit. You shouldn't be caught with it. I'll take it."

She surrendered it gladly. But she still didn't step inside.

"If the drones didn't pick up the car right away, then perhaps you are safe," I said.

"Sergei would know what to do," she said miserably.

"Then let's go find him," I said.

She didn't respond immediately. Her eyes probed mine, checking my sincerity, maybe. My resolve, in the face of all this. I don't know what she found there, but she nodded. And stepped into the elevator.

I punched the lobby button. We rode up silently. The elevator doors opened a few seconds later.

*Here we go,* I thought.

We stepped out into the eastern wing of the lobby. We walked to the front desk.

The clock overhead said it was 4:48 a.m. There were a handful of night owls chatting in the chairs by the windows. No one I recognized. Two Venezuelan guards, rifles hanging off their shoulders, were standing by the front entrance. Neither spared us more than a glance.

I turned around slowly. No shouts or gunshots. No one was running forward to place us under arrest.

"Seems pretty normal," I said.

"Yes," Joy said. She still sounded nervous. "We should check in on the team."

"Good idea. When was the last time you saw them?"

"Soldiers came into the reactor room an hour ago, and . . ."

"You left," I said.

"Yes." I didn't think she could sound any more miserable, but she did. She wouldn't meet my eyes.

Soldiers. Had Hayduk finally discovered the reactor? Or were they Perez's men, maybe just delivering equipment?

We weren't going to find out down here. "Stay here," I said. "I'll go upstairs, see what's going on. If everything's clear, I'll come downstairs and get you."

She shook her head. "I'm coming with you."

We rode the main elevators to the seventh floor. I was grateful for the opportunity to focus on Joy. It helped keep my mind off my own situation.

I put my hand on her shoulder. "You didn't do anything wrong. No one will blame you for leaving." She gave me a weak smile.

Joy stayed in the elevator when we reached the seventh floor. I left the bag with the suit in the elevator and stepped out to glance around. Everything seemed normal.

"Stay here," I said. "I'll be right back."

I strode quickly down the hall. There was a pair of soldiers walking toward me, and I was nervous until they passed by. I waited until they were well out of sight, and then headed into the conference room the medical team had commandeered for the bioreactor.

The place was still a hive of activity. I counted nine people working on the reactor, plus two technicians fussing over the process control software in the corner. Hardly anyone noticed me when I walked in. I spotted both people who'd been on the team accompanying Sergei and Joy during the theft.

So they hadn't been arrested, then. That was a bit of good news, at least.

They'd made a lot of progress just in the hours I'd been gone. They were just about done wrapping insulation around the cooling pipes, and everything else looked ready. Three new tables had been set up in the corner, with cylindrical devices I assumed to be the centrifuges placed on top of them. Two carpenters were already building an isolation unit around the tables.

"Has anyone seen Sergei?" I asked.

Much of the work stopped. I could tell from the look on every face that turned toward me that the answer was no.

"Were soldiers here a while ago?"

"Yeah," said one of the welders. "They were looking for the medical station. They wanted to buy condoms, I think. I sent them downstairs."

Condoms. Of course they were. "Thanks," I said. I left and returned to Joy.

She had stepped out of the elevator, carrying the bag with the combat suit, and was bravely taking slow steps down the hallway alone toward the bioreactor. I intercepted her.

"Everything's fine," I said. "But there's still no sign of Sergei."

She took both bits of news with equal stoicism. "Perhaps I should rejoin the team," she said. "The first seed batch will go into the reactor in a few hours. The control software will need to be ready."

"Hey — don't give up just yet. I thought you were going to help me look for him?"

"How?"

"The old-fashioned way. On foot."

We dropped off the suit in my room, where Croaker greeted us both excitedly. We waited there until 5:00 a.m., when the AGRT curfew officially lifted. Then, for the next two hours, until the rosy fingers of dawn started to peek around the massive steam clouds rising out of the lake, the three of us did slow circuits of the city blocks between the hotel and Columbia College.

"What's wrong with your dog?" Joy asked, the third time Croaker collapsed in a happy panting heap.

"She's a rescue dog," I said.

"What does that mean?"

"Well, in her case it means she was rescued from an abandoned condominium, nearly starved to death. She doesn't have much stamina."

"That's awful!"

"Yeah, but she's recovering okay. This is the longest walk I've ever had with her, actually."

"She looks terrible. We should go back."

"She'll probably last longer than we will." Just as I said this, Croaker rose up on wobbly legs and set off again, away from the hotel, pulling on the makeshift leash I'd fashioned in the lab.

"Are you sure she's okay?" Joy asked, falling in step at my side.

"When she wants to head back, she'll let us know."

As it turned out, Croaker did outlast us both. She needed plenty of rest stops, but was excited to be out in the cold morning air and seemed ready to go all morning. But as the sky got lighter, both Joy and I began to flag. I was exhausted. My eyes hurt, and it was getting harder to focus. Joy wasn't doing any better.

"Let's get back to the hotel," I said. "Get some rest."

"I cannot sleep while Sergei is missing," she said miserably.

"Let's get some breakfast at least, before we head out again."

She nodded at that. We turned around, heading back north. I kept scanning west every time we reached an intersection, looking for a lone figure. But except for a pair of bicyclists we saw on Michigan, the streets were empty.

There was something I'd been meaning to ask Joy, and her comment about not being able to sleep seemed like a good opening. "Are you and Sergei . . . ?" I began.

"No," she said. There was a hint of annoyance in her voice. "He is too involved in his work."

"That he is. He's a dedicated man."

"Too dedicated, sometimes," she said.

"How long have you known him?"

"Not long. He assisted Dr. Thibault during a critical equipment failure in October. We worked together then."

"You work with Thibault?"

"Yes. I'm stationed at the Venezuelan field hospital in Fort Wayne, Indiana, with Dr. Thibault. I was part of the team Sergei alerted to the threat of the pathogen several weeks ago. We've been working together to assess the threat. Dr. Thibault believes she is in charge of the team." She smiled. "But really, it's Sergei."

"Yeah." I knew exactly what she meant.

Out of the corner of my eye I saw a drone gliding up behind us. I turned, watching it warily.

At least, I think it was a drone. I'm not sure what it was, to be honest with you. It wasn't an aerial unit. It looked like a one-ton, riderless motorcycle. It was gliding along South Columbus Drive, virtually soundlessly. It ignored us, rolling to a stop about fifty feet north.

Long vertical rods extruded out of the thing, like thick antennae, some more than fifteen feet tall. One flowered into a mini-sensor array at the top, pointed to the east.

"What the hell is that thing?" I whispered to Joy. We were on the west side of the street, headed north. It appeared to have absolutely no interest in us, but I'd had my share of run-ins with hostile machines already today, thank you.

"That is American Union technology," Joy said.

"The sensors?"

"Yes. It is taking long-range readings on the lake."

"What's a Union machine doing here?"

"Spying," she said simply.

Being that close to a Union surface drone made me nervous. Fortunately, after a few seconds it retracted its sensors and began rolling away, gliding gracefully between the abandoned cars on Columbus as it accelerated, before turning left and vanishing to the west.

"This is why I don't like to walk around Chicago," Joy said, staring after it. "You run into machines more often than people. Who knows what they're all up to?"

"No one," I agreed, before a sudden thought hit me.

"What is it?" Joy asked.

"Come on," I said, squeezing her shoulder and unable to keep the excitement out of my voice. "I think I know how to find Sergei."

We hurried back to the hotel. Joy was obviously curious, but she kept her questions to herself. As we approached the doors, both of us steeled ourselves. But the young Venezuelan soldiers on duty made no move to arrest either of us. They simply looked bored, and one of them even held the door open for us.

Just inside the door, I saw the tall rods of the new metal detectors. Croaker and I passed between them without comment, and Joy followed. If Hayduk had had them installed all over the city, as Sergei had suggested, then he was definitely taking his search for the combat suit seriously. If they were at every exit from the hotel, they'd certainly make permanently disposing of the suit a challenge.

Once we were in the lobby, Joy started for the elevators. She stopped in surprise when I headed toward the escalator instead.

"You cannot access the second floor," she said, catching up. "It is forbidden."

"Stay close," I told her.

As always, Zircon Border made a striking and imposing figure at the bottom of the escalator. Joy followed at my side, but fell back as we got close, eyeing the hulking robot nervously.

"Good morning, Mr. Simcoe," Zircon Border said as we approached. "Everything work out okay this morning?"

"It did," I said. "Thank you so much for your help. May I introduce you to Dr. Joy Lark? She's with the Venezuelan surgical team."

"Delighted," said Zircon Border. "I've seen you upstairs, working on that big secret project."

Joy didn't respond. She glanced at me uncertainly, then took a hesitant step closer. She'd passed Zircon Border in the basement a few times now, but always in the dark, and she'd never spoken with him. Now she looked him up and down, searching in vain for a head she could address.

"Say hello," I suggested.

"Hello," she said uncertainly.

"Hello!" boomed Zircon Border. "She seems rather shy," he said to me.

"She is," I agreed. "But she's marvelous when you get to know her."

"Dr. Lark, I'd love to know what you're building up there," Zircon Border said, his voice friendly. "I don't have many eyes on the seventh floor, and to be honest all the equipment you've carted up there has me very curious. It is a cryogenics unit?"

Joy glanced at me helplessly.

"I'm sure Dr. Lark would be delighted to discuss that later," I said smoothly. "But right at the moment we need to get ahold of Black Winter."

"I'd be happy to help with that," Zircon Border said. "I can ask the front desk to call a courier for you. They can have a message to the Manhattan Consulate in twelve minutes."

I scratched my neck. "Unfortunately, it's a bit of an emergency. And, given the choice, we'd prefer to contact him discreetly."

"I see. Diplomatic stuff, huh?"

"Nothing like that. It's a personal matter. But it should be handled with some discretion."

"Gotcha. Let's avoid formal channels, then. Fortunately, there's an ongoing debate in the private cetacean discussion forums on how to interpret certain narrow-band signal forms. Nineteen Black Winter is an active participant."

"That's ideal. Can you get him a message through those forums?"

"I already have. I've told him privately that you and Dr. Lark need to get in touch. He has already replied, asking how he can be of assistance."

"Excellent. I knew I came to the right place. Can you tell him we need to meet him, as soon as possible?"

"Certainly. Nineteen Black Winter says he can pick you up in a Consulate car. Would that be acceptable?"

"Fantastic. Zircon Border, once again you have proven yourself to be one of the most capable and amiable machines of my acquaintance. We are both in your debt."

"Think nothing of it. Nineteen Black Winter says his car will be in front of the hotel in approximately fourteen minutes, and he will be inside."

I bowed. "You have my thanks."

"Not at all. Don't forget to come back when you want to talk to my pod!"

Joy whispered to me as we headed back across the lobby, "How did you meet him?"

"A mutual friend," I said.

She glanced over my shoulder at the clock by the front desk. "If we have fourteen minutes, I'm going to check in with the reactor room and make sure the batch seed culture is ready for insertion. Do you want to meet in the front of the hotel in ten minutes?"

"Sounds good," I said.

We rode the elevator up together. Joy got off on the seventh floor, and I rode it all the way up to my floor. I dropped Croaker off in my room, spent a few minutes in the bathroom, splashed some water on my face, and was back in the lobby with time to spare.

I waited on the curb in front of the hotel, watching the empty streets of Chicago. The AGRT has limited street traffic in the city to official vehicles only, which means cars of any kind are a rare sight these days. There were none in sight at the moment. To the east, massive thunderclouds were billowing up out of the lake like smoke from an apocalyptic forest fire, and I could see static discharges between the clouds—great blue bolts that illuminated them from deep within, giving them stark shape and definition.

The streets were empty of traffic, but the sidewalks weren't empty of soldiers. The AGRT had established an additional checkpoint west of the hotel after the Juno attack, and I watched a squad of off-duty soldiers walking back toward my location. Across the street, the last remnants of the battle had been swept up against the stone railing overlooking the Chicago River. Most of it looked to be metal debris from the robot that had lost to the Juno. I wondered what had happened to it.

Joy joined me after a minute, just after the soldiers passed. She handed me a green Anjou pear. "I stopped at the hotel restaurant," she said.

"Thank you."

She was holding a grapefruit. She peeled it expertly and began to eat it like an orange. I watched her, shaking my head in admiration. I like grapefruit just fine, but not without a little sugar.

"Of all the things for the restaurant to have in stock," I said.

"Hmm?"

"Your grapefruit. They can't seem to get fresh milk, but they can get a fruit shipment from Florida?"

"Grapefruit can ship without refrigeration," she said. "They're like apples."

"Well, they sure as hell don't grow within five hundred miles of Chicago."

Behind us, more soldiers came out of the hotel. One of them looked familiar—one of Van de Velde's men, maybe? They started talking with the others in low tones. It made me nervous for a few minutes, but they didn't even glance our way.

That wouldn't last. Sooner or later, soldiers were going to come for us. I was glad to have something to do, something to keep my mind off of it.

Right now I desperately didn't want to be alone in my room — afraid to sleep, waiting for them to pound on the door. Exhausted as I was, no way I could sleep, knowing that soon enough I'd be shaken awake by Van de Velde's soldiers and dragged into custody in my underwear. No, when they took me, I wanted to be alert and awake. Well, awake, anyway.

I stood on the curb, eating my pear, mulling over the morning's events. We had the centrifuges — that was good. No one was under arrest yet, which I suppose was also good news. That might change at any moment, but for now I was focusing on the positive.

There was something else nagging at me. Something I hadn't mentioned to Joy.

At the start of my long walk back through the coal tunnels this morning, I'd been very concerned that I wouldn't get permission to retrace my route back through the colony. There was no sign of my guide, Stone Cloud, and I knew I'd be stopped the moment I reached the borders of the colony.

But that didn't happen. It didn't happen because I didn't meet a single robot on my return trip. The colony was completely deserted.

The colony itself was still there. The buzzing computational engine, the cooling forge. The flickering displays and small fires. Nothing looked much disturbed. It looked as if everyone had simply stepped away for a moment.

"Hello?" I'd called out into the tunnels as I made my way through the heart of the subterranean robot village. There was no response.

I'd heard something up ahead. The steady creak of chains got louder as I got closer, until I was finally able to make out what it was in the flickering light of a small coal fire.

It was a harness. It dangled from the ceiling, one loose chain swinging a few inches above the floor. When I'd passed this way before, with Stone Cloud at my side, there'd been a legless robot strapped into that harness. Now it was slowly coming to a rest in the still air of the tunnel.

Empty.

I walked all the way through the colony, until I came to the place where the pair of fires burned, where I'd first met Stone Cloud. One of the fires had gone out, but the other was still burning. There was no sign of Stone Cloud, or of the big robot he'd been with.

All the robots had vanished.

Perhaps it was nothing. Perhaps all the robots gathered a few times a day in a secluded chamber somewhere. Perhaps they got together to play cricket. Or perhaps they were like the Sentient Cathedral, and they met to pray and actively commune with God.

But I didn't think so. I had nothing solid to base that on, nothing except a palpable feeling of dread as I'd made the long walk back through the deserted robot colony, smelling the fires and hearing the stubborn silence. Something unexpected had happened here.

I breathed deep of the cold morning air, tried to clear my head. I shouldn't be worrying about robots. I had my own damn troubles.

But what if something terrible had happened to them? What if I had caused it, somehow? Had the Orbit Pebble gone berserk after its encounter with Van de Velde and her team, chasing them off? Or had something else found them, down there in the dark?

I brooded on that, and other things, while I stood watching the deserted city streets.

"Fourteen minutes," said Joy, rubbing her arms and shivering. "Didn't that big Zircon robot say a bike courier could make the trip in twelve? Why does a car take longer?"

"You've never seen the way those bike messengers handle these streets," I said. "They move like you wouldn't believe."

"Do you want to wait inside?" Joy asked hopefully.

"I'm sure it won't be long. How are things upstairs?" I asked, mostly to take her mind off the cold.

"Not good," she said. "The Venezuelans have denied our request for a power upgrade for the seventh floor. Without it, we cannot initiate the reactor. We are at a standstill."

"That's terrible—how did it happen?"

"Venezuelan Military Intelligence blocked our request. The AGRT has approved it, but military intelligence demanded additional paperwork."

Military Intelligence. Hayduk.

Just like that, I was paranoid all over again. Had he figured out what we were doing already? Would he move against the reactor directly? I was anxious to discuss the possibility with Joy, but I bit my lip. She was stressed enough as it was.

Joy let out a frustrated sigh. "Sergei would know who to talk to, to solve this. Every minute he is missing, the project slips further into crisis."

"We'll find him," I said.

"Your friend, Nineteen Black Winter. You think he can help?"

"I'm certain of it."

"Do you believe he will come?"

I nodded toward the west. "I think that's him now."

Black Winter's car slid toward the hotel like a yacht gliding into port. A shiny black limo, low to the ground and an almost featureless black, it purred up to the curb and rolled to a slow stop. A door opened sound-lessly, and a machine stepped out.

"Black Winter," I said with a smile.

"Good to see you again, Mr. Simcoe," said Black Winter, his voice bois-terous in the cold morning air. "Who is your lovely companion?"

I introduced Black Winter to Dr. Lark. He gave her a solemn and gen-tlemanly bow. "I am genuinely honored to meet you. It was the surgeons and mechanics of the AGRT who saved my life, scarcely a week ago. I don't quickly forget such kindness."

"Thank you," Joy said, a little flustered.

"Zircon Border said you had something urgent to discuss," Black Win-ter said. He gestured toward the hotel. "Shall we go inside?"

"Actually," I said, glancing toward the knot of soldiers giving us curious stares, "it would be better if we talked out here."

"I'm freezing," Joy said.

"Can we talk in your car?" I asked.

"Of course," Black Winter said. He made a subtle gesture, and the car door swung open smoothly. Black Winter helped Joy inside. Me, however, he stopped at the door.

"Wipe your feet, will you?" he said, staring down at my muddy shoes. "Don't track mud into my sweet ride." Rolling my eyes, I complied, and then climbed in after Joy.

The inside of the limo was not what I expected. The last time I'd been in a limo was during a press junket just after a high-tech IPO in Toronto. They're usually pretty spacious. This one, not so much. The space inside was surprisingly cramped, with a lot of display consoles and highly se-cure telecom equipment. Joy and I had to scooch around until we found a place to sit.

Black Winter climbed in after us, closing the door. "Excuse the tight space," he said. "The car wasn't really designed for comfort."

"Or human passengers," I said, looking around. There was something odd about the digital equipment surrounding us, and it took me a second to spot it. There were no keyboards or other input devices. Black Winter likely had no need for them. He probably communicated wirelessly with the car.

"Does the Manhattan Consulate even employ any people?" Joy asked. She was perched next to a large console that monitored the limo's various systems. It looked like the right front tire was a little low on air.

"Not many," Black Winter admitted. "We have a handful of bike messengers on retainer, and there's a systems tech who rotates through once a month. We share her with consulates in five other sectors." He spread his hands apologetically. "We're a small organization."

"But a resourceful one," I said, smiling at Joy.

"That's true," Black Winter said. I felt the car accelerate away from the curb. We were headed east on Upper Wacker.

"The car is electronically shielded, and we are out of earshot of the AGRT," Black Winter said easily. "Now, how may I be of assistance?"

"Thank you for coming so quickly," I said. "We've lost a friend of ours, and it's urgent we find him as soon as possible."

"Who is it?"

"Sergei Vulka, a medical specialist with the AGRT."

"I remember him," said Black Winter. "From the day we met. When did you last see him?"

I turned to Joy. "It's okay," I said reassuringly. "You can tell him."

Haltingly, Joy began to tell Black Winter about their late-night drive to Columbia College. She skipped most of the details, and Black Winter gave me a lot of wordless glances. When she was done, I filled in the details as best I could.

"You think Sergei was pursued by AGRT soldiers?" he asked when I finished. "Do you believe he was captured?"

"It's possible," I said.

Black Winter leaned forward in his seat. He addressed the both of us. "I appreciate that your venture to Columbia College was a private matter. However, it was done after curfew, and if the AGRT has become involved, then — rightly or wrongly — they may have interpreted your actions as a violation of the Statute of Occupation. Finding your friend may well require that we anticipate how the AGRT will react. That means that the more information you can share with me, the more I can help you."

"What do you need to know?"

"What were you doing at Columbia College after curfew?"

"We were stealing medical equipment — centrifuges," I said. Out of the corner of my eye, I saw Joy stiffen.

Black Winter simply nodded. "Was the theft discovered?"

"By now, certainly. Joy and her team brought the equipment back to the hotel, but Sergei never made it to the car. As Joy said, last time we saw him, he was being chased by soldiers."

"I don't wish to be the bearer of bad news, but if you haven't heard from Mr. Vulka since early this morning, he is almost certainly dead—or in custody."

Joy let out a stifled sob. She covered her mouth, staring aghast at Black Winter.

"I apologize," Black Winter said. "But the section of the city we're discussing is heavily patrolled by aerial service machines."

"Drones," I said.

"Yes. Even if Mr. Vulka managed to avoid his foot pursuers, he was almost certainly detained by those machines—or terminated as a looter. The chances that he escaped without assistance are very slim."

"Sergei had the . . . device in his possession."

"Ah." Black Winter sat back. "That thing. Yes, that changes matters."

"At lunch last week, I think you mentioned that Sector One has some drones over the city," I said to Black Winter. "Is that correct?"

"Yes. Not many, but a few. The Kingdom has been granted a high-altitude operational corridor in Chicago airspace by the AGRT, and we maintain certain assets there."

"Do you have aerial surveillance footage of the region directly north of Columbia College from last night?"

"Almost certainly. Perhaps not with the detail and coverage you need, but it's a definite possibility. However, I'm not certain that footage would be useful to us. If Sergei is carrying the device, he will be invisible to the Manhattan drones—and to me."

"I understand," I said. "However, the raw feed won't be useless to Joy and me."

"You want to manually search through the footage, looking for Sergei?"

"Yes."

"I don't think you know what you're asking," Black Winter said. "Our drones record thousands of hours of high-resolution footage, across a wide range of electromagnetic spectrums. It's an enormous amount of data."

"I appreciate that," I said. "We'll need to narrow it down drastically. We can give you the exact time and location of Sergei's last known coordinates. We'll start there. If that footage is unavailable, we'll advance by five minutes, and expand our search radius half a mile."

That's exactly what we did. Black Winter got to work immediately, and in short order half a dozen of the consoles in front of us were displaying high-altitude nighttime images of Chicago.

"Unfortunately," Black Winter said, "during the time period in question, we had only two functional assets in the air, and neither was tasked with ground surveillance. However, both were tracking assorted ground targets, and that included several close by."

The console in front of Black Winter began updating as he was talking. "The first set of images that could be useful was recorded . . . twenty-two minutes after you last saw him," he said.

I nodded. That was disappointing, but not the end of the world. "Let's see them," I said.

A second later all six consoles flashed and began displaying a tight grid of dozens of images. I peered at them closely. Each seemed to show an enhanced infrared pic of roughly two square city blocks.

"How would you like to start?" Black Winter said. "We can divide up the images and give you both a few to get started."

"No," I said. "Find the soldiers. The ones chasing Sergei. There were two of them, both in AGRT uniform. They'll be within a three- to four-mile radius of the college. They shouldn't be hard to spot."

They weren't. Less than ninety seconds later, Black Winter found them. On the two screens closest to us, up popped a high-resolution overhead image of two soldiers, moving north on South Wabash. The timestamp was just over eleven minutes after Joy had last seen Sergei.

"That's them," Joy said excitedly. "Those are the soldiers that chased Sergei."

The streets ahead of them were empty for at least two blocks. "Looks like they didn't catch him," I said. "Is this the most recent image you have of these two?"

"Unfortunately, yes."

"All right," I said. "Reset to this location. This is our new starting point. Can you get me still images radiating out three miles from here in a two-block grid, at intervals of five minutes?"

Black Winter complied, and Joy and I got to work. "What you're doing now is eliminating," I told Joy. "If the streets are empty, discard the image. If you see something—a shadow, a blur, anything that might be a person—set the image aside, and we'll come back to it."

Joy and I worked quickly and efficiently. We had over a hundred images to get through, but in less than twenty minutes we were nearly finished. Joy finished first, and then opened the file where we'd stored those images that were possibilities. She and Black Winter started to examine them.

They started to disagree almost immediately. I wasn't paying attention at first, but Joy quickly became agitated. "We should not discard this image," she said, her voice rising.

"The others are definite possibilities," Black Winter said. "But that's just high-altitude distortion."

"Let me see the image," I said.

Joy pointed to an enhanced photo on the nearest screen. In the top left was a blur that looked a lot like a man walking fast.

"What do you see here?" I asked Black Winter, my finger jutting toward the screen.

"Nothing," he said. "That's just a distortion pattern."

"How sure are you?"

"One hundred percent."

"Excellent. Then I think we just found Sergei."

# XXIII

Wednesday, March 17th, 2083
Posted 10:29 am by Barry Simcoe

CanadaNET1 Encrypted, Sponsored by Data Is Divine.
*God is active in your life, and miracles happen around us every day.*
*Join the Diocese of Rockford to track miracles in YOUR life today.*

Sharing is set to PRIVATE
Comments are CLOSED

I waited in the restaurant while Joy and Black Winter went to pick up Sergei. It was obvious Joy was anxious to go, and there was barely room in the car for three — and they'd need to have space for Sergei on the way back. Once Black Winter had tasked a drone to deliver fresh images and we'd confirmed Sergei's current location, I was more than happy to let them fetch him while I cooled my heels and sipped fresh coffee.

I hadn't been sure the drone-jamming device Sergei was carrying could conceal him from drones and robots in still images. But based on Black Winter's complete inability to see him in any of the images we found — including several that were very clear — it was now obvious that it functioned across all electronic media.

I had no idea how that was possible, but it sure simplified the process of finding him. Whenever there was a smudge on screen that Black Winter couldn't see, or swore was just a distortion pattern, that was our man. The hardest part had been convincing Black Winter to send one of Manhattan's two aerial drones back into the area to confirm his current location.

Sergei was almost five miles from the hotel, and it looked like he was headed northeast. The dude was a hundred percent lost. Black Winter said that as long as he didn't vanish into a building or something, they'd have him back to the hotel in fifteen minutes.

Joy would have to be Black Winter's eyes, of course, since he wouldn't be able to see Sergei until Sergei turned the device off. But I was confident Black Winter could manage it.

A pair of on-duty soldiers came into the restaurant while I sat at my booth nodding off over my coffee. They looked around, obviously searching for someone. When I spotted them my first instinct was to duck, slink under the table, and hide. But it seemed rather pointless, and besides, I was far too weary for another chase. I met their gaze as they purposefully strolled around the mostly empty restaurant, watching them with little more than tired curiosity.

They passed right by me. Before long, they found a young soldier, out of uniform and asleep in the corner. They shook him awake and harangued him out of the restaurant, shouting as he danced ahead of them making extravagant excuses. It looked like this wasn't the first time they'd had to wake him up to report for duty.

I was still a free man. For now. I wondered how long that would last.

Eventually, I dozed off. I awoke to the sound of Martin's laughter. He was standing with a group of people on the other side of the restaurant. He waved when he saw me and came over.

"When a man falls asleep while drinking coffee, that's a sign of a rough night," he said.

"That's the truth."

"What the devil did you get up to?"

"Just . . . another project with Sergei."

"Well, he looks a lot more awake than you."

I sat up. "You've seen him?"

"Yeah, two minutes ago. Walking through the lobby with a woman. A big black car dropped them off."

"Damn. Thank you." I settled up quickly, and raced out of the restaurant. A clock by the entrance told me I'd only dozed off for a few minutes.

Sergei and Joy were gone by the time I reached the lobby, of course. I headed for the seventh floor.

"You just missed him," said Jolene, one of the process engineers. "He swung by to make sure the batch culture had been inserted correctly, then headed downstairs."

"Did he look okay?"

"I guess." She shrugged. "He looked kinda cranky."

"He's always cranky. Cranky is a good mood, for Sergei. I meant physically—he wasn't injured, or anything?"

"No. Why would he be injured?"

"Never mind."

I took the stairs down to the third floor, heading for the command center. The hallway was crowded with soldiers. There was a lot of activity. It looked like a couple of squads were prepping to head out.

I'd coped with the two guards in the restaurant just fine, but plunging into a crowd of Venezuela's finest made me very nervous. Every time one of them looked my way, I expected to see a jolt of recognition. Then shouting and drawn weapons. *Christ, coming this way was a bad idea. They're probably getting ready to go out and arrest you.*

I kept my head down and kept walking, but it took some effort to not turn around. *Sergei, you damn well better be there.*

A woman giving instructions to her squad turned slightly, twenty feet ahead of me, and suddenly I was face-to-face with Van de Velde.

I stopped walking. Van de Velde, in the middle of a briefing to a semicircle of uniformed men and women kneeling and sitting on the floor, stopped talking.

Her squad was watching her. I didn't initially recognize them in the bright light of morning. But these were the men and women who, less than six hours ago, had been chasing me relentlessly through the tunnels under Chicago. Many were still mud-spattered. Some seemed exhausted or shell-shocked from their deadly encounter with the Orbit Pebble, but most still looked alert.

Then they were regarding me with curious gazes. I returned their stares, looking for any sign that they recognized their quarry. Fortunately, there was none. But one of the women in the front row had a strange smirk, and she whispered something to the guy squatting next to her. He fought to control his laughter.

I couldn't read Van de Velde's expression. She didn't *have* an expression. Her eyes were cool, and her eyebrows were raised, ever so slightly. There was a thin streak of mud on her forehead, a stark contrast with her short blonde hair. She was just standing there, her rifle strung over her shoulder, staring at me.

And the next instant, she wasn't. She turned back to her squad. She said something sharp to the young soldier struggling not to laugh, and he settled down. She resumed her briefing, as if nothing had happened.

It took me a little longer, but eventually I remembered how to walk. As

I strode past the squad, several members gave me surreptitious glances. They seemed more curious than anything else.

I took half a dozen steps and stopped. I very much wanted to know what she was telling her soldiers, but of course, she was speaking in Spanish. Was she preparing them to arrest me, right now? Was she telling them to wait until I met with my coconspirator in the command center and *then* arrest us both?

I could put up with a lot of things, but I wasn't about to be toyed with.

I turned around. "Sergeant Van de Velde," I said.

She continued with her briefing. "Sergeant Van de Velde!" I said, louder this time.

She stopped talking. All I could see was her profile, but I could see her expression sour, before she turned to face me.

Her jaw was set, and her hands were on her hips. "Yes, Mr. Simcoe?" she said.

*Well, she remembers my name.* My mouth was suddenly a little dry, but I soldiered on. "What is my situation?" I asked.

The question seemed to surprise her. "Your situation?" she said.

"Yes."

"Your situation," she repeated. She nodded, looking at the floor now, as if assessing the matter.

"She'll update you on your situation *tonight*," said the young woman who'd whispered to her friend, drawing out the last word to give it a deliberately salacious meaning. There was laughter from the rest of the squad, but it had a nervous, exhausted edge.

It took a second for the implication to sink in. Did her squad think that Van de Velde and I were hooking up?

Van de Velde turned on the soldier who had spoken with a look that could peel paint. "¡Creasy, cállate la boca!" Even I knew what that meant: *Creasy, shut your mouth.*

Those who were laughing shut up. Their sergeant glared at the entire squad, one by one, until they were all staring at their feet, appropriately chastised.

Van de Velde returned her attention to me. She took several steps forward, hands still on her hips. She didn't stop until she was close enough for me to smell her skin, smell what kind of soap she used. She smelled pretty good, actually, especially for someone who'd spent the last few hours in a coal tunnel.

"You don't have a situation," she said.

"No situation," I said.

"No."

"Okay," I said. Did that mean what I thought it did?

She leaned forward, turning her face away from her squad and lowering her voice. "But if I catch you in those tunnels again, I will shoot you myself. Do you understand?"

"Perfectly," I said.

I thought she was going to dismiss me then, turn around and walk back, but she just stood there for a moment. She was looking at the floor again, and wearing a pained expression.

"I have to take my squad now, and recover two bodies in those tunnels," she said at last. "That's two more men under my command who are now dead. We will lay them to rest next to Corporal Maldonado."

Now she was looking at me. Now her eyes were glaring into mine, with fresh fury.

Her meaning was unmistakable. Two more dead men she had me to blame for. Perhaps she thought I'd forgotten Corporal Maldonado, the young man who died when the Juno mech opened fire on the hotel.

I had not forgotten.

"The robot that attacked you is not the only one in those tunnels," I said. "Returning there in force is a mistake."

"I won't leave those men down there."

"You don't have to. There are other ways to retrieve them."

"No thank you," she said, her voice icy. "We don't need your help."

I was exhausted, sore, and more than a little rattled from my own run-in with the Orbit Pebble, where I'd put my life on the line for her and her damn soldiers. And now she was about to jeopardize their lives again — needlessly. My own temper, already badly frayed, was pushed past the breaking point.

"*Listen* to me, soldier," I said. "You don't have enough manpower to deal with one of the things, let alone an entire colony."

"Colony?" she said, surprised. "How many are there?"

"Why don't you ask Colonel Perez how many men he lost the first time he sent soldiers into the tunnels? I'm sure he'd be happy to share those reports with you."

"How do you know—?"

"Do you want to lose more men in another ambush? Then by all means, take them back in. But don't pretend you know what's in those tunnels, because you have no goddamn clue." I pointed at her rifle. "And believe me, you damn well better bring heavier ordnance than this piece of shit."

Van de Velde was furious. She glared at me with naked anger, and for a moment I thought I was going to get a much more intimate view of her weapon.

But she wasn't the only one who'd heard me. Her squad had been listening to every word I said, and they were staring at me with shock and dismay. Those who didn't speak English were whispering to those who did. Their terror of the Orbit Pebble was written all over their faces.

Van de Velde looked over at them, at the fear and panic in their eyes. When she returned her gaze to me, she was just as angry. But there was a hint of uncertainty as well.

I lowered my voice. "We can bring your soldiers back without firing a single shot."

It took a moment for Van de Velde to get her anger under control. But to her credit, she did it. "How?" she said.

"We go in alone. Just you and me. We bring out the bodies. No violence."

"I don't trust you."

"Then bring your gun, and put some big-girl panties on. I'm unarmed."

For the next few seconds, I was pretty sure I was going to get a punch in the face. It's not clear to me what kind of underwear Sergeant Van de Velde actually wears, but I'm reasonably confident that in a fair fight she'd kick the living shit out of me.

"All right," she said at last.

"Good," I said.

"Two hours. Downstairs."

"Agreed."

She turned and walked back to her squad without another glance at me.

"The soldier," I said to her back. "The one shot in the leg?"

"What about him?"

"Did he make it?"

She turned enough so I could see her profile. "Yes. The medics were pretty grim when we got him to the hospital, but the techs there got him stabilized."

"Good. I'm glad."

Van de Velde nodded, then returned to her briefing. I made my way to the command center.

While I walked, I thought about what I'd just done. I'd spent an hour this morning running for my life from that woman, and now I was returning to the scene of the crime with her? Was there any way to look at this that didn't make me look like an idiot?

Probably not. Sooner or later Van de Velde would come to her senses and likely have me arrested. In addition to the fact that I'd just gotten two of her men killed, there was the matter of the American combat suit. She must have recognized it, even in the dark. No way could she overlook the fact that I happened to possess one of the deadliest weapons in the history of warfare.

At least she didn't know I'd stolen it from Hayduk. Right now only Hayduk and Nasir knew that the man who'd escaped the Sturgeon Building had stolen a combat suit. The Memphis Ceasefire forbade the AGRT from possessing American-powered combat armor, so neither of them was likely to mention it. While Van de Velde might suspect me of being an American spy, that was likely the extent of it. For now.

And at least for the time being, I believed her when she told me she wasn't going to have me arrested. I wasn't sure exactly why. Other than the fact that if she were going to do it, she almost certainly would have done it already. Perhaps she felt obligated to me for helping her against the Orbit Pebble. And perhaps there was more to it than that. Either way, I wanted to find out. But whatever the case, I couldn't just sit by while she planned a hostile incursion into the robot colony. I owed it to her, and I owed it to *them,* to make sure the recovery of her dead soldiers happened without violence.

Assuming the colony was still there. But I hoped it was, and I hoped I hadn't somehow brought doom down on its head when I stumbled on them in their secret home under Chicago.

The kid who'd watched over me when I was arrested after the death of Corporal Maldonado was on duty in front of the command center. I was glad to see him, and his face split in a wide grin the moment he saw me.

"It's the doctor," he said. "How's your robot buddy?"

I'd forgotten that he had mistaken me for a doctor, after all that drama with the diagnostic tables. "Getting by. How you been?"

He shrugged. "Okay. I get all the boring details. Look at all these guys." He nodded enviously at the two squads suiting up in the hallway. "They're gearing up for action. Going out to investigate an attack in some basement this morning."

"Gonna blow some shit up," said the other guard at his side.

"Exactly. And I'm stuck here guarding a door again."

"Yeah, well, you should be thankful," I said.

"Why?"

"After you see a little action, guard duty starts to look good, believe me. Besides, this is an important position. People respect you. You're watching over some important real estate, here."

"I guess," said the kid, straightening up a little.

I made to step inside the room, and the kid shook his head.

"No civilians allowed," he said.

"See? That's what I'm talking about. Keep up the good work," I said. I stepped around him and walked into the command center.

I didn't spot Sergei at first. He wasn't at his medical station. I did spot the hulking mobile combat robot by the door — and with a start, I realized I recognized him. It was Zircon Border. Or one of his bodies, anyway, what he called his mobile torsos. I flashed him a wave behind my back as I walked past. About five seconds later, as I passed a big display screen on my right showing an approaching weather system, the screen flashed black. In its center, visible for scarcely a second, were the words:

Good morning, Mr. Simcoe
ZB

I grinned despite myself. Zircon Border might be criminally underutilized, spending most of his cycles happily communicating with Atlantic porpoises, but that didn't mean he didn't have his eyes open.

I finally spotted Sergei in the far corner, by the first aid cabinet. He'd stripped to the waist and was applying a bandage to his side. I made my way over. He spotted me just before I reached him, and his features split in a smile.

"God," I said. "I'm glad to see you alive."

"You as well," he said, clapping my shoulder.

"What happened?"

"Not here."

He pulled on a fresh shirt. I saw him carefully bundle up something that might have been his old shirt and throw it in a lidded receptacle. I caught a glimpse of the logo on the side: *biohazard*.

"You hurt?" I asked.

"It is nothing. My own stupidity."

We left the command center. "I think we agreed, when this was over, there would be beer," said Sergei.

"Yeah. But I don't think the bar's open. How about coffee?"

"Coffee would be excellent."

He turned to the right. About a hundred feet down the hall, I could still see Van de Velde and her squad.

I grabbed Sergei's arm. "Not that way."

"Why not?"

"I don't want Van de Velde to see us together."

"Did she see you? Wearing suit, I mean?"

"Yeah. She knows it was me in the tunnels."

Sergei's eyebrows rose. "This is not good."

"It might not be as bad as you think."

"What do you mean?"

"I'll explain it all. Come on, let's take the west stairs." Sergei followed me to the left, and we made our way downstairs to the lobby restaurant.

"First things first," I said as we slipped into a booth. "Joy and the others had to make their way back to the hotel without the drone jammer. It's only a matter of time until they're connected to the theft and identified."

Sergei nodded. "That was unfortunate. But it has been . . . dealt with."

"Dealt with? How?"

"Car was scanned by four separate drones on drive back. It was flagged for review and possible investigation, along with several other curfew violations. Fortunately, morning shift drone operators do not go on duty for another . . ." He glanced at his watch. "Eleven minutes. There was plenty of time for me to review incident and flag it as approved."

"Nicely *done*," I said.

"Lucky. If I had returned to hotel twenty minutes later . . . not so lucky."

"About time we had a little luck." I felt a wave of relief. An hour ago, I wasn't sure any of us were going to survive the morning without being arrested or killed. And now — through a combination of quick thinking, resourceful friends, and no small amount of luck — it looked like we were in the clear.

For now, at least. And right this moment, that was good enough for me.

Over coffee, I told Sergei what had happened in the tunnels. About stumbling on the robot colony, running into Van de Velde, hearing his recorded message, the chase under the college, and finally the Orbit Pebble and the brutal attack.

"That is incredible story," said Sergei. "You were more fortunate than me."

"More fortunate?" I said, startled. "An Orbit Pebble killed two innocent soldiers because of me, and I thought I'd signed my death warrant when Van de Velde saw my face. What happened to you that compares to that?"

Sergei took a slow, deliberate sip from his cup. "Bad news," he said simply.

I didn't like the sound of that. Sergei wasn't one to exaggerate. "You better tell me. Start from the beginning. Joy said you ran into trouble at the college?"

"Da. I lured Van de Velde's guards away from car, as planned. But they chased me longer than I expected. They were very determined."

"Van de Velde runs a tight ship."

"I do not know what this means."

"Never mind. We saw pictures of the men chasing you, taken by drones. It looked like you were a few blocks ahead of them. They caught up with you eventually?"

"Da."

"How did you get away?"

"A bit of luck. They chase me into alley. There was fence at end, with pointy wires at top."

"Barbed wire?"

"Yes. Barbed wire. It was too dark to see wire, and I became tangled. The guards managed to reach the fence while I was still caught in wire."

"That doesn't sound like luck to me."

"It did not seem so at the time, either." Sergei lifted his shirt, revealing the bandage on his chest. "Fence tore my shirt, did this."

I whistled in sympathy. It looked like a nasty cut.

Sergei lowered his shirt. "Fortunately, guards were overexcited. First to reach fence, he try to climb it. He slip near top. His leg was caught, in . . ." Sergei stuck three fingers out, like spikes.

"In the barbs? Damn!"

"Yes. He struggle and tear his leg. Very unfortunate."

This seemed like genuine sympathy—and for a soldier who'd been chasing him. I was a little surprised, but I probably shouldn't have been. I'd seen Sergei care for these very same men at his medical station, fight to save their lives after the Juno attack. When it came to the men in his care, Sergei was a medical professional first and a midnight fugitive second.

"How did you escape the second guard?" I asked.

Sergei sipped his coffee again. "Guard became sick," he said.

"What does that mean?"

"Convulsions. He began to shake just as he reach fence. Physical exertion—running—made him nauseous and weak. He collapse against fence."

"Damn. That was a piece of luck."

"No," said Sergei.

"No?"

"His symptoms were exactly as described in Indiana field reports."

"Indiana field . . . *Jesus,* Sergei. Are you saying the soldier chasing you had *the plague?*"

"I cannot be certain. But symptoms were consistent with early onset of F5-117 pathogen."

That was a shock, to say the least. "It's reached Chicago."

"Yes."

Cold fear gripped me. I took a deep, calming breath. *We knew this was coming,* I told myself. *Make sure Sergei is okay.*

"Were you exposed, do you think?" I asked.

"Only briefly, when I took pulse."

"You . . . you took the soldier's pulse?"

"Da."

"You climbed back over the barbed wire, to examine the soldier. The one having convulsions."

"Da."

"*Why?*"

Sergei's look told me he clearly didn't understand my question. "To help him," he said simply.

"To help him," I said. "Of course you did. Jesus. Well? Did you learn anything?"

"Elevated pulse. Very sweaty. Difficulty breathing. Nausea. Convulsions became severe very quickly."

"Did he get a good look at you?" I asked.

"Nyet. He was semiconscious at best. But first guard, on fence, he eventually manage to lift himself off barbs. He fell to ground on other side."

"I hope you got the hell out of there."

"Da. But not before he shoot at me."

"Damn! You could have been killed."

"It is okay. I was some distance by then."

"Yeah, well, I've been shot at myself," I said, remembering my run through the tunnels under the college. "Warning shots, I think, but still. Scary as hell."

Sergei nodded. "Yes," he said. "Very much. Scary, like hell."

I toasted him grimly with my coffee.

"Did you lose them after that?" I asked.

"Yes. Also, I lose myself. In my last run away from soldiers, I lose my directions. I headed east, looking for lake, but when sun came up, I found I was heading west."

"Damn."

"I was several miles from hotel. I began to head back east. Joy and your friend Black Winter found me in his car."

"Glad to hear that. Is Black Winter here?"

"No. He had to return to Manhattan Consulate, and manufacture a rationale for retasking drones."

"I hope he's not in any trouble. We couldn't have found you without him."

"He said it would not be issue, if he acted quickly."

"Good. Did you run into any drones last night?"

"No—device worked perfectly. Speaking of which . . ." He reached into his pocket and slid something to me under the table.

It was the drone-jamming device. "I turned it off when Joy and Black Winter arrived," he said.

"Glad you made such good use out of it." I slipped it into my pocket. "We need to talk about that sick soldier. What does it mean that the plague has reached Chicago so quickly?"

"It means we need antivirus. And very quickly."

"You think it's spreading faster than we thought?"

"Perhaps. Difficult to be certain."

"Does this mess up our timetable? Is there still time to stop this, if we can deliver the antivirus on time?"

Sergei raised his hand in a calming gesture. "Do not panic. Stay focused."

I bit back my first response. In the last few hours I'd faced certain arrest, the monstrous Orbit Pebble, and being shot at in the dark. And none of it unnerved me as much as this plague. When it was hundreds of miles away in Indiana, I could cope with it. But now it was right here, at our doorstep. Was there any real way to stop this god-awful thing? Or were we just fooling ourselves?

"There must be something we should be doing," I said.

"We are doing it. We must not become distracted. Focus on reactor. Finish job."

Yes. I nodded. Sergei was right. "What will happen to him? The soldier?" I asked.

"He will be brought to nearest AGRT medical facility."

"Where is that? Here? In the hotel?"

"Da."

"Is that safe?"

Sergei shook his head. "Nyet."

"Then what the hell are they doing, bringing him here?"

"All information on plague has been suppressed by military intelligence. Officially, small outbreak in Indiana has been fully contained. Soldiers and most medical personnel are unaware of true danger."

"My God, Sergei. If he's contagious . . ."

Sergei sipped his coffee quietly. "He is certainly contagious."

"Then why are we sitting here? Sergei, we have to stop them, before they bring an infected soldier here. There are hundreds of people in this hotel, and none of them have a goddamn clue what they're up against. We have to—"

Sergei raised his hand again. "Stop. There is no point."

"What the hell are you *talking about?*" I realized I was shouting, but I couldn't help myself. "We have to protect ourselves. We have to protect everyone in the hotel—"

"And what about soldier?"

That stopped me. "The soldier? Sergei, come on . . . If he's got the plague, there's an eighty percent chance he's dead already."

"And there is twenty percent chance he will survive. Much less, if he does not have medical attention."

"He's—"

"He is *my patient.*" Sergei's eyes flashed, and his palm slapped the table. A few folks at nearby tables glanced over at us briefly before returning to their breakfasts.

"You would let him die?" Sergei asked. His eyes pinned me to my seat.

"No. No, of course not. But . . ."

Sergei lowered his voice. "I understand your fear. I do. But this soldier . . . letting him die will not stop plague. It is here now. We must face this bravely. And we must not forget our duty."

"You're right," I said. "Of course." I felt ashamed of my outburst, of displaying such naked fear in front of Sergei after all we'd been through together. "But . . . but we have to be smart, right?"

"Da." Sergei nodded grimly.

"You'll quarantine the soldier?"

"Of course. We will do our best. But we are not Level One biocontagion facility. And that is what this disease requires."

I took a deep breath, forced myself to think calmly, rationally. To think like Sergei. "Ignorance among the soldiers and the other medical staff is our greatest enemy," I said. "We have to spread the word, show everyone what they're up against. Teach them how to identify it and quickly isolate the infected."

"Now you are thinking." Sergei looked pained. "But we cannot."

"Why the hell not?"

"Hayduk."

"Hayduk? What has that bastard got to do with—"

No sooner were the words out of my mouth than I realized what Sergei was saying. "Of course," I said. "Hayduk is on the alert for anyone who contradicts the official narrative of the virus."

"Correct. Yesterday, military intelligence arrested Venezuelan surgeon general and his staff after they broadcast Thibault's lethality assessment and outbreak forecast to AGRT medical staff. Several other medical teams have gone quiet—arrested or silenced, I do not know."

"My God," I said. "This is a carefully orchestrated campaign of terror—to silence the entire AGRT medical community."

"Da."

"What about Thibault—is she okay?"

"For now. Surgeon general did not identify her as source of forecast. But mention of disease has been completely scrubbed from all official AGRT communications. Officially, it does not exist."

"Unbelievable. What about unofficial channels?"

"They are still active. Thibault continues to issue private reports. Surgeon general's broadcast was risky, but also effective—there are now nearly a dozen teams across four sectors covertly working on cure for virus. But Hayduk is not finished. He will surely track them down, one by one, and render them ineffective."

"And if we start publicly alerting the soldiers and medical staff to the danger of the virus here in the hotel . . ."

"Hayduk will surely do the same to us. He will shut down reactor."

I rubbed my face, feeling three days of stubble. "Shit."

"So we must remain silent," Sergei said. "And finish our work. Everything depends on reactor."

"Yeah," I said, resigned. "I get it."

Sergei leaned back in the booth. "Now, you."

"What do you mean? I already told you my story."

"No. You did not explain why you are not under arrest."

"Ah," I said. "You mean Van de Velde."

"Yes. She saw your face in tunnels?"

"Oh, yes."

"She could have had you arrested as soon as you made it back to hotel."

"I was expecting her to, to be honest."

"But she did not?"

I told Sergei what happened when I met Van de Velde outside the command center. He chewed on that for a while.

"Why did she not take bodies of fallen soldiers with her when she retreated this morning?" he asked at length.

"Because they were under fire by an Orbit Pebble, for one thing. She'd been ambushed, she didn't know the extent of the danger, and her first duty was to get her wounded the hell out of there."

"And are you truly foolish enough to return to tunnels with this sergeant?"

"She's already seen me without the mask. She knows who I am. I can't make it any worse."

Sergei clearly disagreed. "You can make worse. She said she would not reveal your identity, yes?"

"It looks that way, yeah."

"Why?"

I shrugged. "I'm not sure. Because I saved her life, maybe? She obviously cares about her men, and I stopped the Orbit Pebble from filling them full of bullets."

Sergei seemed unimpressed. "She is an officer in the AGRT. You are a man in an American combat suit and obviously a spy. Even if what you say is true, every time you see her, you risk that she changes her mind. You should get rid of suit, as soon as possible."

"No argument there."

"And avoid Sergeant Van de Velde. You should leave her alone."

"I already promised that I'd meet her. In about ninety minutes."

"You should not be involved with Venezuelan military."

"I'm involved with the Venezuelan military every damn day. I share a hotel with three hundred soldiers. I can't avoid it, so I might as well interact with them on my own terms."

"Her squad will see you. They will wonder how you have this information about tunnels."

"Seriously, that's what you're worried about? None of her soldiers saw my face. Anyone with knowledge of Chicago history could know about these tunnels. It doesn't mean I'm guilty of anything."

Sergei wasn't satisfied. "I think you have crush," he said.

"On who? Van de Velde?"

"I think you find her attractive and want excuse to spend time with pretty woman."

"Don't be ridiculous. She hates me!"

"I did not say she likes you. I said you found her attractive."

"You're crazy. Look, six hours ago I came *this* close to getting killed, trying to keep a lethal war machine from shooting up a squad of eighteen-year-old kids. I'm not going to let that happen again. Van de Velde and I will go in, retrieve the bodies, and get out. No fuss, no shooting."

"No more excursions with young sergeant? Maybe drinks, later?"

"God, no. Believe me, I want as little contact with her as possible."

"That is good," said Sergei.

I added more cream to my coffee. "She is kind of hot, though."

"Shut up."

"It's the short blonde hair. And—"

"You are idiot."

We talked a while longer, while I killed time before my meeting with Van de Velde. Sergei seemed especially interested in Stone Cloud's robot colony. He kept grilling me about the make and nature of the machines.

"They are fascinating," he said. "They are a failed offshoot from the Ginsberg-Slater machine genome. Did you recognize the hardware configuration?"

"No. I'm not sure they're 'failed.' They're definitely persecuted, though."

"They are certainly on the brink of failure. The Sentient Cathedral seems invested in their extermination. If that is true, they are not likely to survive. Do they have any females?"

"I'm not sure."

"If they have no females, the colony cannot grow. Without maintenance, the machines will fail in five to ten years, possibly sooner. If their Slater cores fail, this branch of the genome will be lost forever."

"I don't think they're particularly concerned about the ongoing project to map the machine genome, as fascinating as others may find it. They have other things on their mind."

Sergei shrugged. "Still, it would be shame to lose their cognitive record."

"I'll mention that next time I see them. If I ever run into them again. At this point, I just hope they're okay, and I didn't bring doom down on them somehow."

"I do not think that likely. You are concerned for colony?"

"Yes — and for the Venezuelans. How do you think Perez will react to Van de Velde's report?"

"Hard to say."

"If Perez views them as a threat and takes action, sends soldiers into the tunnels, there's no way it's going to end well. There will be blood on both sides."

"I do not think you have to worry. Perez is pragmatist. The tunnels have no strategic importance. He will take no action."

"Take no action? Two of his men were just killed! He'll have to do something."

"Perez has lost men in tunnels before, remember? This is no different."

"It *is* different. Now he has an identifiable threat. It isn't just rumors anymore. Van de Velde's report will prominently feature a hostile war machine underneath the streets of Chicago. That thing has a serial number. It's missing from a unit somewhere. That unit's probably going to want their Orbit Pebble back, and they're sure as hell going to want to know why a hundred-million-dollar rational device went AWOL." I sipped my coffee. "Come to think of it, I'd love to know why myself."

"Yes," Sergei admitted. "Is very odd. Why is Orbit Pebble part of robot colony? Orbit Pebbles are not Thought Machines. They do not have Slater core."

"Any theories?"

"Perhaps. Orbit Pebbles are among the most powerful war machines ever created. They were designed to be highly independent on battlefield. There were rumors that Argentinean high command had difficulty controlling them. Most were destroyed immediately after Memphis Ceasefire."

"I hadn't heard that."

"This information was not widely disseminated. Perhaps this one simply did not wish to be destroyed?"

I mulled that over. That was a little alarming, to say the least. A war machine that its creators considered too dangerous to control was hiding out under the streets of Chicago, and it had already attacked Van de

Velde's squad once. There was no guarantee I could get it to back down a second time.

"Well, it's one more good reason to accompany Van de Velde back into the tunnels," I said. "Maybe I can help turn down the volume on this situation. Force Van de Velde — and Perez — to see the Pebble as something that can be reasoned with instead of as just a malfunctioning war machine that needs to be destroyed."

"You are assuming it *can* be reasoned with," said Sergei.

"I reasoned with it once, I think. If I run into that thing again, it might help to know what it's thinking. Any ideas?"

"It is not thinking about pretty girls," said Sergei. "That makes it more logical than you."

As our conversation went on, I asked Sergei about his research into our mutual enemy, Armitage. "Anything new?" I said.

"No, but I expect to learn more soon. I am proceeding with caution. I am accessing public databases as discreetly as possible. I found one item you may be interested in. You recall that Standing Mars was seconded to Sovereign Intelligence in Buenos Aires in 2080?"

"Yeah. And whoever it is won't be happy that I shot the hell out of Mars and was a party to its eventual destruction. So in addition to Hayduk, I've doubtless got a Sovereign Intelligence on my ass now, too."

"Then perhaps this will be good news. I have discovered the identity of the Sovereign Intelligence who was the master of Standing Mars."

"Yeah? Who?"

Sergei mouthed the name at me from across the table. *Armitage.*

"Bloody hell! Are you sure?"

Sergei nodded.

"Okay," I said, leaning back. "Okay. That's very interesting. What does that tell us? When a Sovereign Intelligence puts an asset like Standing Mars in the field, it's definitely trying to protect something."

"Da. My thoughts, exact."

"But what? What was it protecting? Hayduk? The combat suit?"

"I do not think Armitage cares about combat suit. No, it attacked you after you took something else from Colonel Hayduk."

"The data drive? You think Armitage sent a top-of-the-line Venezuelan combat robot a thousand miles just to watch over a data drive?"

"Hayduk and Standing Mars were both very eager to retrieve it. I think, by extension, we can assume Standing Mars's master is just as eager."

"That means that Armitage is very interested in preventing the truth about the origin of the pathogen from coming out. Or is trying to suppress knowledge of the antivirus."

"You are assuming that is relevant data. There are many sectors on drive we have not yet accessed."

I chewed on that for a while. "That's very possible. Perhaps there's more to this disk than meets the eye. One thing's for sure, however. I think this eliminates any doubt that Hayduk was involved in the release of the pathogen. If Armitage was behind the creation of F5-117 — and sent Standing Mars to watch over Hayduk's disk with that information — then Hayduk had to be directly involved."

"At this point, I believe that is safe assumption, yes."

"What's the status on the bioreactor?"

Sergei gave me an update. It was essentially the same as Joy's. As she had predicted, Sergei already had a solution to the power impasse and expected to solve it shortly. There was still work to be done, but the pieces were in place — including the team necessary to make it happen.

"And officially there's still been no announcement on the outbreaks?" I asked. "No word from Venezuelan high command?"

"No. Officially, they accept assertions from military intelligence that infection is contained and no longer threat."

"What about Perez? Does he buy that line of bullshit? Or does he still sanction what you're doing?"

"He cannot formally sanction project until high command provides clear direction. But unofficially, he continues to provide logistical support."

"Does that mean he's in our corner? Can he protect us from Hayduk?"

"Unclear. Officially, reactor project is precautionary only, in case of additional infections from Indiana outbreak. He supports this effort. And he is not hindering us."

"All right. What about Hayduk and military intelligence? Any sign they're sniffing around the reactor?"

"No, but that will not last. Sooner or later, Hayduk will investigate more closely. Our task is to complete extraction and deliver antivirus to Thibault before this happens."

I couldn't argue with that. "Four days ago, Jacaranda said the pathogen would reach critical exposure levels in twelve to fifteen days. How close are we to delivering?"

"We could have cultured antivirus in three or four days. It will take twenty-four hours to purify and convert into serum that can be administered, and ten hours to transport to Indiana."

"Shit. That's better than our previous window. But it's still cutting it very, very close."

"I believe timetable is workable. If serum works."

"And if it doesn't?"

"Infection will spread uncontrollably. Even if we perfect antivirus in fifteen days, we do not have facilities to mass manufacture. Our one chance is to stop infection before it reaches critical exposure levels."

One good thing about drop-dead deadlines: they bring a certain clarity of focus. "That means everything depends on getting the bioreactor functioning in the next few hours. And making sure Hayduk doesn't discover how close we are before then."

"Reactor has passed preliminary design tests, and construction is almost complete. I am more concerned about Dr. Thibault's safety. She is critical to our success now."

"What if someone comes sniffing around, starts asking where our centrifuges came from? Perez may be tacitly supporting us, but he's not likely to ignore accusations of grand theft. We're one investigation away from having half our team arrested."

Sergei dismissed my concern with a wave. "Perez does not care about theft of low-value medical equipment. There are thefts in city every day. He has far more important things to concern him. There will be no investigation."

"I hope you're right. But the centrifuges aren't the only theft we need to keep a lid on. If Hayduk sees the video of me in the basement of Columbia College, he'll know the suit is still out there. I don't want to stir that hornet's nest, bring him crawling around here."

"Not likely. Do not forget, Hayduk cannot publicly acknowledge he had suit—not even to Venezuelan officers. It is crime to possess it. It is likely he and Nasir were the only ones to know of its existence."

I nodded thoughtfully. "He probably didn't appreciate me parading it in front of all his soldiers when I left the Sturgeon Building, then."

"Nyet. I would not think so."

I glanced at the clock on the wall. Less than an hour until my meeting with Van de Velde. I stood up. "I need to get ready."

Sergei accompanied me out. "Where is Joy?" I asked.

"Dr. Lark? I have no idea."

"Didn't she come back to the hotel with you and Black Winter?"

"Yes. She wanted to examine me, inspect my wounds, but it was not necessary."

"She was really worried about you. She insisted on accompanying Black Winter to go find you. You could have at least shown her the courtesy of letting her check you over."

That seemed to surprise him. "I have no time for such things," said Sergei.

*He's completely oblivious*, I thought. *One of the most observant men I've ever met, and he has no idea when a woman is interested.*

When all this was over, he and I were going to have a talk. I was pretty sure he'd thank me later.

# XXIV

Wednesday, March 17th, 2083
Posted 5:54 pm by Barry Simcoe

CanadaNET1 Encrypted, Sponsored by Hot Pupil.
*Are they checking you out? Hot Pupil monitors nearby skin temperature
and pupil contraction for signs of lust. Don't be the last to know . . .
100% accurate!*

Sharing is set to PRIVATE
Comments are CLOSED

My underground excursion with Van de Velde took a lot longer than I thought it would.

Honestly, I'm not sure what I'd expected when I suggested we retrieve the bodies of her fallen soldiers. Like I told Sergei, mostly I was just trying to prevent another bloodbath. I was pretty sure I could get us in and out without much trouble, and I didn't think much beyond that.

I probably should have.

Van de Velde met me in the lobby, as promised, and then marched me wordlessly outside the hotel, where she put me in an armored car. All my attempts at conversation were met with stony silence while she drove through the streets. I was hoping to get to know her a bit better on this trip, but it didn't look like I was going to be given the opportunity.

She took us to a staging area on the western edge of Grant Park, about fifty yards from Columbia College. The operation to retrieve two fallen Venezuelan soldiers from the underground enclave of a renegade Argentine war machine was not a small one, and large-scale preparations continued regardless of my offer to Van de Velde. There were easily a hundred troops massing on the grass. I saw a squad of hover drones doing low-altitude test runs and several young soldiers struggling under the weight of heavy assault weaponry.

"What's going on, Sergeant?" I asked.

"Get out of the car," she said.

I was left to cool my heels while Van de Velde hustled to join an outdoor briefing. The briefing was given by a balding middle-aged capitán, who ended the conclave with a brief prayer. The group of officers broke up, and the troops began to prepare for the assault.

Van de Velde didn't return right away. When she did, it was with the capitán and his retinue of senior officers, including a translator, a young female lieutenant.

Van de Velde didn't bother with introductions. She simply marched over to my side and came to attention. The capitán sauntered up, a black tablet tucked under his arm. A name tag on his left breast read LEON. He looked me up and down with barely concealed contempt.

"¿Quién es usted?" he said.

"Who are you?" said the translator.

"Barry Simcoe, CEO of Ghost Impulse technologies —"

"Why are you here?" he said, through the translator.

"I am here," I said slowly, giving the translator plenty of time, "to assist in the recovery of . . . of your deceased soldiers. I offered my services to Sergeant Van de Velde —"

"What is your business with the AGRT?"

What the hell did that mean? "I have no business relationship with the Venezuelan military, or any other member state of the AGRT," I said awkwardly.

Leon took a step forward, getting in my face like a drill sergeant. He smelled of coffee and aftershave. "How do you know about the death of my men, Mr. Simcoe?"

I glanced over at Van de Velde. She continued to stare straight ahead, hands at her sides, her body at rigid attention.

What was this? Was this Van de Velde's way of setting me up? Of exposing me as the man in the combat suit, without having to rat me out personally? Or was this asshole just naturally suspicious?

I kept my eyes fixed on his as I responded. "Are you joking? You want me to point out which of your young recruits told me about it first? Everyone in the hotel knows about the death of your men, Capitán. By tomorrow, everyone in Chicago will know."

Leon's face soured. He didn't like my answer, but it was obvious he found it entirely plausible.

"You will surrender your personal computing equipment to Primer Teniente Acardo," he said, nodding to a man on his right. "And your access codes."

"I don't have any equipment with me —"

Leon nodded to his first lieutenant, and Acardo stepped forward and frisked me. He wasn't gentle about it. I had a pen in my pocket; Acardo tossed it to the grass. He also found the drone jammer and my recorder; they followed the pen to the grass. A minute later my wallet and passport were in Leon's hands as well.

Leon went through my wallet slowly, examining my ID cards. "¿Canadiense?" he said, holding up my passport.

"Yes, Canadian."

He dropped the wallet and the passport at my feet.

"I don't care where you are from," he said. "Perhaps you are used to delicate treatment from the Venezuelan Diplomatic Corps. Perhaps you were brought to the city with promises of quick wealth. I do not care about that either. If you are an intelligence operative for a foreign power, I will find out. If you are here to interfere with my operations, I will find out."

"I'm not a —"

"I did not give you permission to speak. You will accompany Primer Teniente Acardo, and you will answer all his questions regarding the rogue machines under this city. If you lie, I will have you shot. If you withhold information crucial to the safety of my officers, I will have you shot. You will tell Primer Teniente Acardo everything you know, and then I will decide what to do with you."

Capitán Leon and I stared at each other for a few seconds. He seemed to be assessing me. *Well then, let's give this shithead something to assess,* I thought.

I looked over at the translator. "You know what? Tell him to kiss my ass."

The lieutenant, who'd been translating everything with smooth efficiency, choked on my words.

"Right now," I said. "Do it."

The lieutenant translated with thin lips, eyes fixed on the capitán's shoes.

Leon's reaction, however, was a very thin smile. He turned and whispered something to Acardo in a low voice. His first lieutenant nodded, then unholstered his sidearm and leveled it at my chest.

On my right, Van de Velde took a step forward, surprise evident on her face. "Capitán Leon—"

"¡Silencio!" he barked at her. Van de Velde immediately snapped back to attention, her face red.

When Capitán Leon spoke his next words, it was with a clear sense of satisfaction. "It never ceases to astonish me how you Americans respond to civil discussion with insults," he said to me. That was fast. Thirty seconds, and he'd already forgotten I was Canadian. "I will be wasting no more time with you," he continued. "Primer Teniente Acardo will now interrogate you. If he encounters any discourtesy, he has my permission to shoot you."

With that Leon strode off, clearly happy to be done with this distraction to his operation. Acardo remained at my side, his pistol unwavering. Van de Velde looked shocked and affronted.

"Have you ever seen an Argentinean Orbit Pebble up close, Capitán Leon?" I called after the capitán. "They have two front-mounted anti-personnel weapons, both capable of delivering two hundred rounds per minute."

The capitán stopped before the lieutenant had translated my first sentence. A group of soldiers to our left stopped talking, turning toward us to see what all the fuss was about. So did a squad of about a dozen men by the car, a third of whom were being equipped with shoulder-mounted antimech missiles.

I raised my voice. "If things get interesting, they fall back on heavy weapons. Short-range ninety-millimeter explosive rounds. Turn a man to jelly. They're most effective in close quarters. Like an underground tunnel."

The capitán turned around. His face was an angry red.

"They have the best antimissile tech ever deployed. No Orbit Pebble has ever been killed by a missile. Not one."

The soldiers on our right looked at their missiles, exchanging worried glances. Soldiers on both sides were stepping closer, curiosity and concern evident on their faces.

"When your men step inside the tunnels, my best assessment is forty percent casualties in the first fifteen minutes," I said.

The lieutenant never completed translating that final sentence. Leon shut her up just before she finished.

He closed the distance between us in four quick strides. He locked eyes with me, but spoke to Acardo. The first lieutenant raised his gun. It was now aimed squarely at my head.

"Please," said Capitán Leon to me. "Say one more word."

"Capitán—" I said.

Acardo fired the gun. The retort was deafening. I swear I felt the bullet zip past my head on the left. I flinched. On my right, I saw Van de Velde cover her mouth and look away.

Capitán Leon, however, did not flinch. "That will be your only warning," he said.

My only warning. That was ironic. No one had warned me about the Juno mech that killed Corporal Maldonado right in front of me. Or about the plague that had an excellent chance of killing me in the next few weeks. No one warned me about Hayduk, who'd kill me with excruciating slowness if he learned I had his combat suit. No one warned me about Armitage, the Sovereign Intelligence that was trying to kill me. And no one warned me about the goddamned Orbit Pebble that was very likely going to pump me full of high-caliber lead in the next thirty minutes.

The only guy willing to give me a warning was a cowardly Venezuelan capitán who would have arrested me already if he'd had the balls.

Acardo's gun was back in my face, but I kept my eyes on Leon. "Either have him shoot me, or tell him to get that goddamn thing out of my face," I said.

Leon spent the next few seconds very clearly trying to decide if he had the courage to have me killed.

I lowered my voice, forcing the translator to step closer. "I don't like you, Capitán Leon. You're an asshole. You don't like me; I'm an arrogant foreigner. I get it. But if we're through posturing, I can explain how to get your men back without bloodshed."

Leon may have been an asshole, but he seemed to appreciate straight talk. "You have ten seconds," he said.

"I've been studying the Rajapakse Colony under the city for some time," I said. Which was bullshit, of course. But in my experience, if you want to be treated like an expert, you have to be ready to sound like one. "They know me, and I know them. There's a good chance I can take a small team underground and retrieve the bodies without incident."

"How many?"

"Two, at most. Me, and one other person."

"How long?"

I shrugged. "It depends on where the bodies are. And if the colony has already disposed of them."

"Are they likely to do that?"

"It's possible. They're in the middle of a major construction project."

"What kind of project?"

I stooped over and picked up the drone jammer and the rest of my stuff, grateful that the worn disk of metal looked entirely inconspicuous. "If you want a briefing on the colony, Capitán, I'm happy to tell you everything I know later," I said as I tucked my ID back inside my wallet. "Right now, I suggest we move quickly."

The capitán folded his arms, considering. "Why are you doing this?" he said.

"I meant what I said about that Orbit Pebble. It's a monster. It can be killed, but there will be many casualties. I don't wish to see my friends slaughtered."

Leon gave a meaningful glance in Van de Velde's direction. "Your friends," he said.

"The Venezuelan military has been very courteous to me," I said, keeping my voice neutral.

"I am certain it has," said Leon, his eyes still on Van de Velde. I didn't respond. If thinking I was sleeping with Van de Velde made this easier for him to understand, I was happy to play along.

"If it is so dangerous, perhaps you should go alone," said the capitán.

"I don't know where the bodies are," I said.

"No?"

"No." Another lie, of course, but Leon wasn't going to catch me incriminating myself as the man in the American combat suit that easy.

I looked at the circle of young faces around us. I pointed at the first one who looked familiar. It was the loudmouthed soldier in Van de Velde's squad. "But she does."

Leon turned to see who I was pointing at. "Her?"

"Yes. She took part in the battle. She could direct me to it."

The soldier took a step backward, aghast to be on the receiving end of such thoughtful scrutiny from the capitán. I felt a little bad for her, but as long as the opportunity presented itself, it couldn't hurt to sow a little doubt on just who had told me about the battle. Otherwise, it was pretty clear that Leon would suspect Van de Velde.

"Or him," I said, pointing to another member of Van de Velde's squad.

Leon took note of the second soldier. "I will determine who accompanies you," he said.

"As you wish."

"However, I have not yet made up my mind," said the capitán, "whether or not to have you shot."

"Let me know when you do," I said. I turned my back on him and returned to the car.

I was not shot in the back. I was not shot at all, in fact. From inside the car, I watched Van de Velde in a lengthy discussion with the capitán, one that looked like it got pretty heated. But Van de Velde kept her cool, and she was eventually dismissed with her hide intact.

She showed up at the car ten minutes later. I got out, to face a withering glare.

"You're either here to tell me I'm going to be shot or that we're going into the tunnels," I said. "Which is it?"

"I should shoot you myself."

"Yeah. Seems I have that effect on people today." I grabbed my flashlight out of the car. "Did I get you in trouble?"

She opened her mouth, then bit back her first response. She seemed to be struggling to control her anger.

"You are a fool," she managed.

"Also well established." I started walking across the street, toward the entrance to the college. "Let's just get this over with. Are you coming?"

She fell in line beside me. About fifty soldiers sitting cross-legged on the grass watched us silently, weapons in hand, but I didn't see Leon among them.

She lowered her voice so that only I could hear her. "Do you *want* to get shot?" she asked me.

"I just volunteered for a suicide mission, to retrieve the bodies of two soldiers who were trying to kill me less than ten hours ago. I think the answer to that question should be pretty fucking obvious."

Van de Velde stopped walking. Her face betrayed a lot of different emotions, but the predominate one looked a lot like fear.

I walked back to her, already regretting my answer.

"You tell me," she said. "You tell me right now. Can you talk to those machines or not?"

"Yes. Yes, I can."

"Because if you want to die, I can save us both a lot of trouble and put a bullet in your head right now."

"Nobody's going to get killed today," I said. "Just . . . forget what I said."

"Capitán Leon thinks you may be insane. Or a spy. I told him you weren't. I told him you were one of the bravest men I'd ever met."

I was so startled to hear her say that, I didn't know quite how to respond. "Thank you," I managed.

"He asked me how I knew that. And I lied to him. Jesus, I lied to a goddamn capitán to protect your secret. I should have just told him to shoot you."

"What did you tell him?" That was completely irrelevant, of course, but for some reason I found myself suddenly curious.

"I said I knew your reputation. And I knew your character." Her face flushed. "It doesn't matter what I said. The capitán thinks . . ."

"I know what the capitán thinks." The capitán thought we were sleeping together, that much was obvious. "Don't let it bother you."

"I don't want to die in those tunnels," she said, "just because you have a death wish. Can you get us safely to my men or not?"

"I can."

"How do you talk to the machines?" she asked. "What is your secret?"

"Let's talk about this inside," I said, my eye on all the soldiers still watching us. I took her arm, guiding her toward the college.

Two soldiers met us at the entrance. They gave us a stretcher loaded with two body bags and other equipment and then held the door open. We went inside.

There were more soldiers at the top of the stairs. I went first. The damn stretcher was heavy — it felt like we were lugging something at least as solid as a body. The soldiers watched us until we reached the basement.

"Are these really the best stretchers we've got?" I asked. I didn't relish the prospect of lugging them all the way into the tunnels and back.

"The AGRT has hover-capable units. But they are too bulky to navigate stairs."

"Great. What the hell are we carrying?"

"Standard emergency medical gear," she said. "We can dump some of it."

Van de Velde didn't seem to be having any trouble with her end. "How did you get stuck being my guide?" I asked, changing the subject.

"The capitán wanted to send one of my squad. But I insisted it should be me."

"That was courageous of you."

"I led my men into these tunnels. I should be the one to get them out."

We reached the underground cafeteria, and Van de Velde told me to set down the stretcher. She did a quick inventory of everything the soldiers had packed inside the bag. She pulled out a fair-sized medical kit and set it aside. "We won't need this," she said grimly.

That made the stretcher a bit lighter. As we started walking, Van de Velde seemed to realize where we were for the first time.

"How did you get past me, down here?" she asked, looking around. "We saw you on camera and searched the whole bottom floor for you."

"I hid. In that cabinet over there."

Her mouth dropped open. From here, the cabinet looked a lot smaller than it was. "Are you being serious?"

"Absolutely. I saw you cooling your heels right here while your squad ran around looking for me."

She shook her head. "You're an asshole."

We made our way down the long corridor toward the escalator. "Where did you get that fake combat suit?" she asked. "It looked authentic. You had some of my squad convinced it *was* real. You could have convinced me, except you couldn't run or fight for shit."

"It's not fake. It's real."

She actually snorted. "You're telling me you have a real American combat suit. And you expect me to believe you're not a spy."

"It's useless. It doesn't have any power cores."

"If it's real, it's not useless. The Americans would pay a fortune for it, cores or not. So would Venezuelan Military Intelligence. They'd do anything to get their hands on an American combat suit."

Yeah, I bet they would. Especially considering this one had been stolen from Venezuelan Military Intelligence. "It's not for sale," I said.

"So if you're not an American spy, where did you get it?" she persisted.

"I'm not a spy. I took it from someone who it didn't belong to. Let's leave it at that for now."

We were approaching the escalator. "Are the robots here?" Van de Velde asked nervously, scanning the darkness ahead.

"No. This is just the pedestrian walkway, linking the nearby buildings. The robots are in the old tunnels, one level down."

We walked down the escalator. "Tell me about them," she said.

So I did. I told her about my run-in with Stone Cloud, and the existence of the colony.

"They don't sound like much of a threat," she said.

"They're not. But the Orbit Pebble . . . that's something else entirely."

"Where does it come from?"

"To be honest, I don't know. That thing shouldn't be here. It's acting irrationally. It may be cognitively compromised, impaired by battle. I don't trust it, and I don't want you to go near it."

"You don't give me orders," she said, resentment in her voice. "This is my operation."

I set the stretcher down and turned to face her. "Look, Sergeant. Let's keep this simple. You see the Pebble, you get the hell out of there. You run. You understand me?"

"I'll decide when I run—"

"This isn't a negotiation. These are my terms. You want my help, these are the rules we play by."

"I don't want your goddamned help," she said. She picked up her end of the stretcher and walked past me.

I watched her drag the stretcher into the darkness for about forty feet. I sighed. I caught up to her and picked up my end.

"Damn, you're stubborn," I said.

"Don't think that just because you bluffed the capitán you can pull that shit on me," she said.

"No ma'am."

We walked a little farther, until we came to the folding metal security gate. It had been forced open, and a good third of the fence had been pushed aside, jammed up to the left.

"This is where you shitheads shot at me," I said.

"Warning shots," Van de Velde said. "And you deserved it." We guided the stretcher through the gap. "What were you doing down here anyway?" she said.

"Maybe I'll tell you sometime."

"Were you stealing? We found a group of looters in the college. They stole a lot of medical equipment."

"I didn't steal anything." That much was true at least.

"So you were just in the wrong place at the wrong time?"

"Story of my life," I said.

"Colonel Perez released the camera images of someone in a combat suit to the American press this week. I assume that was you?"

I didn't know that. "What? Why would he do that?"

"Sometimes the American public is our biggest ally. They are very proud. He thought someone might brag about who is committing brazen criminal acts in the occupied territory."

"Well, I wish him luck."

"The American press is very interested. They have picked up the story. Did you break into the Sturgeon Building?"

*Shit.* Suddenly, this conversation wasn't fun anymore.

"You don't have to answer that," she said when I remained quiet. "I should not have asked you."

"It's okay," I said.

"The American press asked the colonel that question. They wanted to know if this was the same soldier who'd broken into the Sturgeon Building. Colonel Perez didn't understand what they were talking about. He didn't know there'd been a breach at military intelligence until this morning, when he saw the reports of a break-in in the American media."

"What have you heard?" I asked carefully.

"Very little. When the colonel shared the images with the American press last night, there was an explosion of questions about a recent incident at the Sturgeon Building. They've been calling him all morning. They claim someone in a combat suit penetrated the most secure portion of the building, in an act of sabotage. Several drones and security robots were destroyed. If true, it would be a major breach of security."

"Sounds interesting."

"Colonel Perez expected the camera footage he released of you at Columbia College last night would be the first image of an American combat suit ever seen inside Sector Eleven. However, the Americans have broadcast the footage side by side with very similar images taken by their drones outside the Sturgeon Building four nights ago. Some are claiming it is the same individual; some say it is a team of secret American resistance fighters. Colonel Hayduk at military intelligence has made no comment."

That was fascinating. Sergei and I had expected the Venezuelan press to pick up the story, but if the American media had their own drone footage of our little charade at the Sturgeon Building, that almost certainly meant that Hayduk *wanted* them to have it.

Was Hayduk trying to cover up his illegal possession of the suit by leaking a story that the Sturgeon Building had been attacked by an American in a combat suit? Was that what I just heard? If so, it was a complex and risky gambit. But perhaps a clever one.

"What do you think?" I asked.

"I do not think you are a Canadian. I think you are an American spy."

"You do?" I said, more than a little surprised. "Then why didn't you tell Leon?"

"Why didn't I tell the capitán?" she said. She was quiet for a moment before she answered. "Because you stood in front of a war machine to protect my men when you had no reason to. There are only one or two soldiers I know who would've done what you did. And you did it for men who were trying to capture you. You're a man of exceptional bravery and integrity. And I owe you that much at the very least."

I found myself very touched by her words. "You don't owe me anything," I said. "But I appreciate what you've done to protect my secret. Very much."

"Also, Colonel Hayduk is an asshole," she said casually. "He is a horrible human being. If it was you who embarrassed him, I will buy you a drink."

"That's very kind," I said, trying to disguise my surprise. "But I'm afraid I don't know who Colonel Hayduk is."

"But if you ever embarrass Colonel Perez in a similar fashion, or act against him in any way, I will hunt you down and shoot you," she said flatly. "Do you understand?"

"Perfectly."

We walked in silence for a time. There was a question I wanted to ask Van de Velde. It was bottled up inside me and didn't want to come out. All I had to do was open my mouth and say, *Do you still think I killed Corporal Maldonado?* But when I finally opened my mouth, I found myself saying, "This is the door."

Van de Velde seemed confused. "What door?"

"The door to the old coal tunnels. Come on."

We had to manhandle the stretcher around a hot dog stand. I realized for the first time that it was the same stand I'd noted when I'd passed this way this morning, right in front of the door to the coal tunnels. I mentally kicked myself. I wish I'd had the presence of mind to notice it while I was running from Van de Velde's soldiers this morning, and desperately searching for landmarks.

When we were inside, Van de Velde looked around as I shone my light down the dusty corridor. "I don't remember coming this way," she said.

"Because you were hot on my tail," I said. "Come on; there's one more set of stairs to get to the coal tunnels."

We reached the top of the stairs about five minutes later. I moved toward them, but Van de Velde held up an arm to stop me.

"Do you smell that?" she said.

I sniffed the air. "Smoke," I said.

"Yes. And burnt pyropak missile propellant."

"From the chase this morning," I said.

"Maybe. But it smells fresh."

"There's hardly any air in these tunnels. It'll probably smell like this for a week."

"Yes, maybe."

We descended the stairs. At the bottom, the stairwell opened up into the coal tunnels. The smell was much stronger here, and my light revealed thin wisps of white smoke drifting lazily above the ground on our left.

"Something's wrong," I said. "It didn't smell this strong this morning. And where did that smoke come from?"

"Perhaps there is a fire," Van de Velde said. She was looking to the right, where the chase had begun. "Deeper in the tunnels."

"Damn, that would suck," I said. I shone my light in the same direction. There was a haze of smoke there, too, but it wasn't noticeably thicker.

"Do you think we should wait?" she asked.

"No. Let's keep moving. But stay alert, will you?"

"Definitely," she said.

We began to make our way east, taking care to avoid loose debris on the ground. The smell of smoke and pyropak was even stronger here.

"I can't believe you led me and my men down here," she said behind me.

"You're the assholes who followed me."

"Do you know your way around?"

"Hardly. Twenty-four hours ago, I never even knew these tunnels existed."

"I thought you told Leon you'd studied the robot colony for years!"

"And I thought you knew better than to believe everything I told the capitán."

"So . . . what? You just happened to stumble on the tunnels while we were chasing you?"

"Something like that."

I was holding the stretcher with one hand now, using the other to investigate every nook, cranny, and shadowy pile of junk we passed with my flashlight. One of those piles turned out to be a giant robot hand.

"Put down the stretcher," I said.

I moved to the side of the hand, playing over it with the flashlight. "What is that?" Van de Velde said, coming up by my side.

"It's a piece of the Orbit Pebble," I said.

"I didn't know it only had one hand."

"It didn't." I squatted down next to it, taking a closer look.

"I don't understand," she said.

"Somebody shot it off," I said. I leaned forward, sniffed at the still-warm metal. It stank of explosives. "In the last few hours."

Van de Velde began pacing up and down in the tunnel, shining her light at her feet. "What are you looking for?" I asked.

She found it a second later. Her light illuminated it at the rim of a small crevasse.

"A rocket casing," she said. "For a Korean self-propelled rocket grenade."

"The Koreans shot the Orbit Pebble?" I said.

"No. The Koreans manufacture low-cost standardized ammunition, for a variety of machine weapons."

"Then what shot the Pebble?"

"I don't know," she said.

I didn't like the sound of that. At all. We walked a little farther, until she stopped again. I watched while Van de Velde played the light on the wall on our left.

"High-caliber bullets," she said, pointing at the wall. There were dozens of impact marks in the walls, in tight little rows, just above chest height.

"From what?"

"The Orbit Pebble. It was returning fire."

I shone my light at the ground, swung it left and right. There were brass shell casings everywhere. And small bits of gray metal.

I put the stretcher down again, got down on my hands and knees. "What are you doing?" Van de Velde asked.

I stood up and walked back to her. "Collecting these."

I showed her what I had in my hand. Half a dozen metallic shards, small and twisted.

"What are they?"

"They're pieces of whatever the Orbit Pebble was shooting at," I said. "Part of its hull, maybe."

"What do you think it was?"

"I don't know," I said, pocketing the shards and staring at the wall. "But it was big."

"Who won?"

"Hard to say. But there's not much that could kill an Orbit Pebble at close combat."

"Do you think the robot colony attacked the Pebble?" she said. "Tried to drive it out?"

Looking at the shards of metal in my hand gave me a distinctly uneasy feeling. "It's possible. But doesn't that seem strange to you?"

"What's strange about it? The Pebble attacked us. It's dangerous. The other robots had to know that."

I didn't exactly agree, but this wasn't the place for a debate.

A few minutes later, we came to a wide intersection. New tunnels branched off to the north and south.

"You almost lost us here," she said, looking north. Evidently she was starting to remember the route after all.

"I wish I had."

"What did you do — switch off your light? Run into the tunnel in the dark?"

"Yeah."

"You're one gutsy son of a bitch." She started to pull to the left, toward where her men had fallen. "Come on."

"Hold on," I said.

"Why?"

"Just shut up for a second."

I turned around slowly, shining my light down all four tunnels branching off the intersection. The light revealed long stretches of dark, black tunnel, but little else. No signs of a fire and only a few stray wisps of smoke.

"I don't like it down here," she said after a few minutes. "I want to get moving."

"I don't hear anything," I said.

"So?"

"We should hear the robot colony by now. They were working constantly — digging, excavating, building. The sound carried for miles in these closed tunnels."

"We didn't hear them this morning when we were listening for you."

"I know. But I heard them loud and clear when I passed through about an hour earlier."

"How many were there?"

"Dozens. All working at various tasks."

She turned around slowly, looking as I shone my light down each tunnel in turn.

"I don't hear them now," she said at last. "I don't hear anything."

"I know. It's like they're all gone."

"Where would they go?"

"I'm not sure. When I made my way back to the hotel this morning, I walked through the heart of the colony. It was deserted. I figured they would have returned by now."

"Returned from where?" She shone her own light up and down the tunnels. "You think the Orbit Pebble killed them all?"

"I don't think so. I didn't see any bodies."

That uneasy feeling was getting worse. "Is it possible the Venezuelans already sent a force down here to try and drive off the Pebble?" I asked.

"We're it," said Van de Velde.

"No. Something else has been here."

"If so, we didn't send it. I sent my report to Colonel Perez this morning. Capitán Leon was tasked with recovering my fallen men immediately."

"Could someone else have gotten here before you?"

"Who? The colonel has no other men to send."

"Hayduk, maybe. Someone from military intelligence?"

"How would they know about it? Even if Colonel Perez passed my report along immediately, they couldn't have reached the tunnels before us."

"If I were you, I wouldn't bet on Hayduk being ignorant of anything for long."

"How do you know so damn much about the colonel?" she said, her voice suddenly suspicious. "I thought you'd never met him."

"We're part of the same bridge club," I said.

"I bet you are."

If there was a new interloper in these tunnels, Hayduk's agents were my prime suspect. I'd seen up close just how resourceful he could be . . . and what kind of machines he had at his disposal.

I decided that I didn't want to be in these tunnels a minute longer than necessary. "All right, let's move," I said, leading us north.

# XXV

Wednesday, March 17th, 2083
Posted 7:18 pm by Barry Simcoe

CanadaNET1 Encrypted, Sponsored by DroneBone.
*Sick of your neighbors violating your privacy with camera drones?*
*Get the ordnance you need to bring them down.*

Sharing is set to PRIVATE
Comments are CLOSED

Less than three minutes later, we found the remains of the Orbit Pebble.

It was scattered in hundreds of pieces across the floor. Some of them were still on fire, tiny blue flames licking at the shattered remnants of the once-great war machine. We walked through the wreckage carefully. The stench of smoke and pyropak was pervasive.

"Holy shit," said Van de Velde. "What is all this?"

"Looks like the Orbit Pebble lost," I said.

Evidence of a prolonged battle was all around us. There were numerous craters, small and large, and the glint of shell casings was everywhere. A little farther down the ceiling had collapsed, likely brought down by an explosion or missile impact, nearly choking off the passageway.

We had to climb a fairly steep incline of earth and overturned brick to get past the choke point. Just beyond it was the massive torso of the Orbit Pebble, half buried in the earth.

"Stay here," I said.

I climbed on top of the robot, careful of hot spots. The footing was treacherous. Behind me, Van de Velde switched on a flashlight, bathing the robot carcass in enough light to allow me to navigate with a little more care.

"What are you doing?" she called.

I returned after just a few moments, empty-handed. "Its computational core is missing," I said.

"What?"

"Someone — or something — harvested its entire data record. Very shortly after it was destroyed."

"The robot colony?"

"I don't think so. They didn't have anything capable of destroying the Orbit Pebble — not that I saw anyway. And why would they need to harvest the core? Its sensory hub held far more valuable components for them, like high-capacity memory, and none of that is missing."

"So there's something else down here. Something worse than the Orbit Pebble."

"That's what it looks like, yeah."

Van de Velde considered for a few seconds. "We should head back," she said.

I was tempted to agree with her. But I'd already thought this through.

"What will Leon do when we return empty-handed?" I asked.

"He'll want a briefing. He'll want to know everything we saw —"

"And then what will he do?" I asked impatiently.

Van de Velde chewed her lip. "He'll send a sizable force down here."

"Exactly. He'll send a bunch of eighteen-year-old Venezuelan draftees who have no idea what they're up against into the tunnels. To engage an enemy that fires MX-313 rocket grenades and stood up to everything the Orbit Pebble could throw at it."

"They'll be massacred," she said, her voice cold.

"I think that's a fair assessment," I said.

"Our chances aren't any better."

"No, but we're almost at the site. And we haven't been noticed so far. We have the advantage of stealth. We could make it, retrieve the bodies, and get the hell out of here in the next ten minutes."

She made her decision quickly. "All right," she said. "Let's get it done."

We started moving again, with me in front. I was getting tired, holding the heavy stretcher with one hand and my flashlight with the other. We'd gone another two hundred feet when Van de Velde asked, "Why are you doing this?"

I was holding the flashlight in my mouth to give my arms a break and had to switch it back to my left hand to answer. "Your capitán asked me the same question."

"I know. You said you didn't want to see your friends get killed. Is that true?"

"I suppose. Partly I was doing it to keep the colony from being intruded upon. They trusted me, took me in, and let me pass through the heart of their community. I thought it would be better for everyone if I did this, rather than a trigger-happy squad of soldiers."

"That makes sense. Is it the only reason?"

"No. I did it for you, too."

"Me? You don't owe me anything."

"It's not a matter of owing you. You already blamed me for Corporal Maldonado's death. I just . . . I feel partly responsible for the deaths of your two men. I didn't want you blaming me for this, too."

"I don't blame you for Maldonado," she said after a moment.

"You don't?"

"The colonel is right. I overreacted when I found my man dying on the ground and you next to him. I shouldn't have arrested you. I'm sorry."

I felt a strange tightness loosen in my chest. "Thank you."

"Wait a minute," she said. "Go back."

"What?"

"Back up. Here, this way."

She led me backward several paces. I shone my light in the direction she indicated.

On a small mound of earth, nearly hidden in the thick shadows, was the crumpled body of a soldier.

"It's López," she said.

We set down the stretcher. I illuminated the body with my flashlight.

He was lying in an unnatural position, his limbs twisted like a rag doll. His eyes were open. Blood—a lot of blood—had soaked the earth all around him. Van de Velde had her hand to her mouth, staring, and abruptly she turned away, taking four quick paces into the darkness.

I left her alone to her grief. I pulled a body bag off the stretcher, started unrolling it. There was a digital tag dangling on the side and a stylus to write López's name.

Van de Velde was abruptly back at my side. "No. Let me do it," she said brusquely.

"Are you sure?"

Instead of responding she squatted down next to me, taking the bag. Her eyes were wet, but her jaw was set, and she looked very determined.

I backed up, giving her space. Once she had the body bag unrolled, she reached inside a package on the stretcher, pulling out a lantern. In a minute the area around us was illuminated with a bright blue glow.

Next she pulled out a small bundle. She unwrapped it. It was a small drone. She unfolded it and touched a button on its side. Its rotors started to spin, and it rose up out of her hands, scanning the ground around us. It located the body quickly, hovering over it. It began to take pictures.

Van de Velde watched the drone work. "He was the first to open fire," she said.

Suddenly her face twisted in anger. "López, you stupid shit, why didn't you listen to me? I told you, a dozen times I told you, wait until I give the order. You panicked, just like on the gun range—"

She broke off. I put my hand on her shoulder. "This isn't your fault," I said.

She shook off my hand. The drone had done its work, and she stepped forward to slip the body into the bag. She moved with quick, economical motions. I was ready to assist, but she seemed to have everything under control.

I kneeled down beside her. "How can I help?"

"Go find the other one," she said without looking at me.

It took a while to find the other body. It wasn't where I remembered it would be. The battle had happened so quickly—and it had been so dark—that nothing was where I remembered it.

But I found him eventually. It wasn't pretty. He'd been kneeling down, shooting at the Orbit Pebble with his rifle, when a concentrated burst of fire from the Pebble had literally cut him in half at the waist.

I returned, grabbed the second body bag from the stretcher. "Did you find him?" asked Van de Velde.

"Yeah."

"I'll bag him. I'll be there in a minute."

I didn't argue with her. I just returned to the body and started unrolling the bag.

There was a whirring over my left shoulder. The photo-drone. It lowered itself over the body, sticking its nose practically in my face. I had to lean back so it wouldn't shave my damn eyebrows off. It took its gruesome pictures, then hovered away.

I slid both halves of the body into the bag. I was just finishing when Van de Velde arrived.

"I said I'd do it," she said, standing over me.

"I know," I said. "But I thought you could use a little help with this one."

She stood over me without saying a word. I finished sealing the bag, found the stylus, and pulled out the digital tag.

"What was his name?" I said.

"Asis," she said. "Roberto."

I wrote out the name with the stylus. It flashed on the tag.

"Stand up," she said.

I stood up. She reached out and grabbed my wrists, lifting them so that my hands were in front of her, palms up.

"You're covered in blood," she said.

She reached to her belt, pulled out a water bottle. "There were gloves on the stretcher."

"Sorry. I didn't know."

She poured water on my hands. She pulled a rag from somewhere. I stood quietly while she scrubbed all the blood off of them, then gave my hands a final rubdown with a thin medical wipe.

She tucked the wipe into my left hand and folded my fingers closed. Her hands rested on mine for a moment. They were clean and warm.

"Thank you for your help," she said at last. "All of it."

Then she turned away, walking back toward the lantern and the other body bag. If there was any part of her that blamed me for the death of her men at this moment, she didn't show it.

We picked up our gear, but left the lantern. The photo-drone powered down and dropped to the ground beside the stretcher, and Van de Velde packed it away.

"There's only one stretcher," I said. "We'll have to make two trips."

"López first," she said.

I helped her strap López to the stretcher. We had to pack the drone and the last of the gear around the body. The stretcher was much heavier now; carrying it over the uneven flooring was not going to be easy.

"Just get him to the escalator," said Van de Velde behind me. "And then we'll come back for Asis. We can have the soldiers retrieve the bodies from there." That sounded fine to me.

I had to stop a few times to rest. My hands got tired easily. Van de Velde never asked for a rest, but she didn't complain when I lowered the body and took a minute to rub my hands, either.

We made it to the stairs, and then up to the pedestrian walkway. I had the flashlight in my right hand, aimed at the ground ahead of me, and I almost walked us straight into the collapsible metal fence. Once we kicked our way through, it was a short walk to the escalator.

We lifted López out of the stretcher, setting him down at the foot of the escalator.

"It doesn't seem right to just leave him here," said Van de Velde.

"Can you contact the soldiers, have them come and get him?"

She shook her head. "We're too far underground."

"Okay. Let's just go get Asis and hurry back. It won't take long."

She nodded reluctantly. We picked up the stretcher again and headed back down.

When we climbed down the stairs and were about to enter the coal tunnels, I held up a hand. "Do you hear that?" I said.

She listened. "I don't hear anything."

I stood with my head cocked. "It's gone now. But for a second, I heard . . ."

"What?"

"I'm not sure. A vibration, like a high-pitched whine."

"Was it your robots?"

"I don't think so. But it sounded close."

Sound was tricky in the tunnels, so I couldn't be sure what direction it had come from. Or what it was. It sounded almost like the Orbit Pebble's targeting camera when it was trying to focus. But I couldn't be certain.

The smoke hadn't dissipated much. There was still enough to make me cough as we made our way back to the intersection. We stopped when we reached it, and I checked all four tunnels with my flashlight before going any farther.

All empty.

"Come on," I said.

Some of the fires had gone out by the time we reached the Pebble. The few that were left were smaller and starting to smolder. It was hard to breathe in that section of tunnel.

"The Pebble couldn't have been destroyed all that long ago," said Van de Velde.

"I know." Based just on how quickly the fires were dying down, my guess was it had been less than an hour.

We reached Asis about ten minutes later and had him loaded on the stretcher shortly after. "What about the lamp?" Van de Velde asked as we got ready to go.

The lamp was still burning, casting enough light to illuminate about fifty feet in both directions. "Leave it," I said. There was no room for it on the stretcher, and I had no desire to carry it. "It'll go out when the power cells die down."

We had just reached the intersection when I heard the whine again.

"What the hell *is* that?" I said. "Do you hear it?"

"Yes."

"Well, I'm glad it's not just me."

The sound faded after a few seconds. It was hard to pinpoint, but it sounded like it might be receding south.

We were making our way west, toward the stairs, when I spotted the hole in the earth.

It was sheltered by a stack of ancient rotting lumber to the west, which explains why we hadn't spotted it earlier. There was a great pile of earth all around it, like a giant gopher hole. I signaled Van de Velde to lower the stretcher, and then I approached carefully, shining my light on the hole.

It was massive. It led into the earth at a steep angle, and plunged as deep as my flashlight could illuminate. There was no sign of support work or any kind of reinforcement. It was simply a raw tunnel, like something a giant earthworm would make, maybe seven feet wide at its most narrow point.

"What is this?" Van de Velde asked. She'd come up behind me and was peering down into the wound in the earth.

"It's a new tunnel. The robot colony was excavating tunnels like this, farther back that way." I nodded over my shoulder, back and to the north.

"Do you think they made this one?"

"I don't know. It looks more like something dug its way out." I shone my flashlight around the circumference of the hole, scanning the mounds of fresh earth, looking for tracks. But the earth was so churned up I couldn't find anything.

An uneasy feeling settled in the pit of my stomach. Stone Cloud had been so trusting and forthcoming when I asked him about the robot colony, openly sharing details of their history with me. Had that naïveté gotten him into trouble?

Was this somehow my fault? It couldn't be coincidence that the colony vanished the same day that I discovered them. Should I have warned Stone Cloud somehow?

Van de Velde broke me out of my reverie. "Let's keep moving," she said.

"Yeah."

We were only forty feet farther down the passage when something popped out of the earth on my left.

I couldn't see it right away, but I could hear it. It gave off a high-pitched whine, like the one I'd been hearing for the past fifteen minutes. I hastily lowered the stretcher and aimed the flashlight to my left.

It was a mini drone, barely two feet in diameter. It was sleek and compact, smaller than Van de Velde's photo-drone, and it looked much more solid. It was slowly rising out of the dirt. When I hit it with my light it twisted away, fast and nimble, darting into the shadows.

It took a second for me to find it again, hovering not three feet from Van de Velde's left shoulder. She jumped when my light revealed it, skittering away from the thing.

"What the hell is it?" she said.

"It's a spy drone," I said. "These tunnels are probably filled with them."

"A spy drone? Whose?"

I had my suspicions, but right now we had to move. I grabbed Van de Velde's arm, pulling her west down the tunnel. "Come on," I said. "Stay close."

She resisted. "What about Asis?" she said, looking back at the stretcher.

"Leave him."

"Leave him? Why?"

"Because we have to run."

I expected her to object, but thankfully she didn't. My light illuminated the bumpy ground ten feet ahead as we raced through the darkness, side by side, heading west to the stairs. I was winded in a matter of minutes, but Van de Velde kept pace beside me, her breathing even and her stride constant. Every twenty seconds or so I flashed the light on the south wall, looking for the door to the stairwell.

Van de Velde held her questions until we saw it, not sixty feet ahead. When we did, I relaxed our pace, then stopped and dropped into a squat, scanning behind us with my light and trying to catch my breath.

"Why did we just leave my man behind?" she said at my side. She didn't sound winded at all.

I listened, but couldn't hear the whine of the spy drone. Perhaps we'd lost it.

"Well?" she said, her hands on her hips.

"That probably wasn't the only drone in the tunnels," I said.

"What do you mean?"

"That drone wasn't Venezuelan." I swept my light up to the ceiling, panned up and down to make sure the drone wasn't sneaking up on us. "Or Argentinean, or American. Did you see its hull?"

"Yes. It was sort of . . . yellow."

"Yellow, yeah. It's a ceramic composite. Hard as metal, but a lot lighter.

There's only one fabrication unit in the Western Hemisphere that uses ceramic composites to make aerial drones."

"How do you know that?"

"It's just outside Amsterdam. It's a hundred percent controlled by the Monticello prefecture."

"Monticello? The Sovereign Intelligence?"

"That's the one. Monticello does work only for one client: the Sentient Cathedral."

Van de Velde snorted. "You're crazy. Why on earth would the Sentient Cathedral send a drone halfway around the world to snoop in some tunnels in Chicago?"

"I think the Cathedral sent dozens of drones. They're probably all through these tunnels. I think they're watching us right now."

"That's ridiculous. Why would they be interested in us?"

I heard a whine again. This one was different — lower pitched, deeper. I stood up slowly, listening, trying to get a fix on it. I kept my flashlight fixed to the east, the way we'd come, wary for any sign of movement in the tunnel.

"They're not interested in us," I said. "They're interested in the robot colony."

"The colony? What do they want with the colony?"

"They want to destroy it."

The whine was getting louder. It was also getting harder to pinpoint, because as it did, a wind was starting to blow through the tunnel. It was barely noticeable at first, but within seconds I could feel it stirring my hair from behind. It was coming from the west, and I could see it kicking up dust and making smoke swirl in the air.

"What's going on?" Van de Velde said.

"Someone must be pumping air into the tunnels. Maybe to clean out the smoke —"

But Van de Velde wasn't listening. She was staring over my shoulder. "What the hell is that?"

I turned around.

Something was heading toward us from the west. Something fast. At first I thought it was two drones, since the only things I could make out were two fast-approaching pinpricks of light. But as they grew larger — as the noise grew to the sound of a hurricane and the air began to whip around us violently — it became obvious what it was.

"Shit! Get down!" I hit the deck, rolling in the dirt, taking cover as best I could on the uneven floor.

When I looked up, Van de Velde was still standing in the center of the tunnel, shielding her eyes from the wind and the glare of the approaching thing, trying to get a look at it.

"Van de Velde! For the love of God, get down!"

It arrived with the force of a tropical storm. It decelerated quickly, throwing its thrusters in reverse, kicking up a dust cloud that flooded the narrow passage, making the air almost unbreathable. Its wingspan was so large it barely fit in the tunnel.

It was a Dieu Tueur, a massive war drone. A Godkiller. It came to a stop not thirty feet away, the center of a violent whirlwind of dust and air and rage. As it stopped it righted itself, bringing its lights and weapons to bear. So much dirt and noise hammered my face that I could barely stand to look at it.

On my left, I saw Van de Velde draw her sidearm, try to take aim at the thing.

"*No!*" I shouted uselessly into the raging air. It was so loud, I couldn't even be sure if Van de Velde was firing her weapon.

I got to my feet, took two running steps, and tackled her.

We went down hard, in a tangle of arms and legs on the dirty floor of the tunnel.

"Are you crazy?" Van de Velde screamed. "Get off of—"

The Dieu Tueur opened fire. Bullets cut through the air overhead, slamming into the brick wall on our left. Van de Velde shouted, twisting and trying to cover her face.

It was shifting in midair, rising slightly, correcting position to bring its weapon to a better vantage point. *Jesus, it's going to fire again,* I realized.

There was no cover and nowhere to run. The door to the stairs was thirty feet behind us. The gun would cut us in half before we'd even made it to our feet.

There was only one chance. I jammed my right hand into my pocket, where I'd put the anti-drone device. I felt the cold metal against my fingers and groped desperately for the button. I found it and pressed it, hard, then tucked my head down and threw my arms over Van de Velde. I had no idea if the thing would affect something as advanced as a Dieu Tueur, or if the device worked underground. Or if it had any influence on a drone after it had identified us. But it was the only thing I had left.

Sergeant Van de Velde didn't appreciate my efforts to protect her—at all. If I hadn't outweighed her by over fifty pounds I'm pretty sure she would have bucked me off, or punched me in the head. As it was she squirmed and fought me until I urgently hissed "*Stop*" in her ear, and she relented for a moment.

Seconds ticked by. The drone didn't fire. I could hear it hovering, still adjusting position, but its guns remained silent.

Underneath me, Van de Velde was starting to squirm again. "Let me shoot it!" she said.

I clamped my hand over her mouth. "Stay quiet, or we're both dead," I hissed into her ear.

She stopped struggling, staring at me with wide eyes. The winds shifted in the tunnel again, and I risked lifting my head, looking back at the thing.

It was moving. Its compact and powerful rotors kept it stable and aloft as it glided closer.

We were constantly being pummeled with grit and small stones now. Just to look toward the thing I had to shield my eyes and peek through my fingers, and even then I risked losing an eye to one of the countless pebbles and concrete shards bouncing painfully off my face.

The Godkiller was looking for us, and not just with optics. A single glance revealed that its undercarriage held receptors for what was probably a wide range of sensing equipment — infrared, acoustic, and some others I couldn't identify.

Shit. We had to move. The jammer had already accomplished one miracle by keeping us invisible to its visual sensors. But it was too much to hope that the drone's more sophisticated sensing gear also used the pattern-recognition warehouse the jammer hacked into.

"Be ready to move," I told Van de Velde.

A second later the drone was hovering over us. As bad as it was before, it was far worse right under the thing. Its rotors hammered the breath out of us, assailed us with the kind of noise I thought would burst my eardrums. It was like trying to breathe inside a tornado.

Then it was past us, hunting farther down the tunnel. It was rotating slightly, turning toward the entrance to the stairwell.

I felt sore all over, like I'd been tumbled in a dryer for twenty minutes. But I got to my feet, and pulled Van de Velde up. I didn't dare risk speaking, so I jerked my head westward, back the way it had come. Still visibly annoyed with me, she took the lead. I held her arm so we wouldn't get separated, and she led us into the darkness. I'd lost my flashlight when I'd hit the floor, and the only things I could make out ahead were vague shapes. We moved carefully, but not carefully enough. After about thirty feet, as I was lifting my right foot, I kicked a large rock that went skittering away down the tunnel.

The machine spun around, flooding the tunnel with light. Before Van de Velde could start shooting again I grabbed her, shielding her body with mine, making sure the device masked her too.

The machine hovered closer, scanning the passage. Van de Velde and I stood perfectly still. Now we'd get to see just how sophisticated those other sensors were.

"What are you doing?" Van de Velde whispered into my ear.

"*Shhhh,*" I said.

She was trying to raise her right arm. The one holding the gun. I hugged her closer, pinning her arm to her body, and shook my head.

She relented. After a moment, the Godkiller spun back east. A second later, it opened up with a barrage of small arms fire.

Van de Velde stiffened against me, startled. The Dieu Tueur was shooting into the stairwell, making a hell of a racket.

The noise would cover our movements. When the drone had turned this way, it had illuminated a discarded water tank leaning against the south wall, about eighty feet down the tunnel. I grabbed Van de Velde's wrist and pulled her toward it.

We reached it in about thirty seconds. I could just make it out as a light shadow, leaning against a darker shadow. We collapsed behind it, out of sight of the drone.

I wanted to rest a minute, but Van de Velde had other plans. She reached out blindly in the darkness until she found my face, then slid up next to me so she could speak directly into my ear.

"What is that thing?" she whispered.

It was startling how intimate this was. She felt closer than she'd ever been, even when I had tackled her. I was very aware of the sensation of her lips when they brushed my skin, the gentle pressure of her hand on my shoulder.

"It's a Dieu Tueur," I said. "One of the deadliest drones ever built."

"What's it doing here?" She leaned over me, peeking up over the tank. I steadied her with my hands on her hips . . . not entirely because she needed to be steadied.

"It's not hunting us," I said, when she'd settled down next to me again. "It's a robot hunter. It tracks and kills robots."

"Who sent it?"

"There's only one authority that can field a Dieu Tueur. The Sentient Cathedral."

"The robot colony."

"Exactly. It's here to exterminate the renegade colony."

"God. Do you think it killed them all?"

"Possibly. I hope not. It destroyed the Orbit Pebble; that's for sure."

"It doesn't even look damaged!"

"Yeah."

"Why didn't it shoot us?"

"It can't see me," I whispered. "And it can't see you, if you're close to me."

"Why not?"

Why not indeed. I couldn't tell her about the drone jammer, of course. I shouldn't tell her anything, really. It was better for me if I left her in the dark altogether.

But not better for her if I got shot and she had to make her way out of here alone.

I reached into my pocket, pulled out the device. I slipped it into her hand. "Because of this," I said.

She took the device. "What is it?"

"It's a drone jammer. It messes with their pattern recognition."

"Where did you get it?"

I gently took the thing away from her. "I'll tell you all about it someday."

She leaned in close again. "Who *are* you?"

I laughed quietly. "You know who I am."

Fortunately, she accepted that for the moment. She risked another look over the tank.

"It's not moving," she said when she settled back down. "So what do we do now?"

"You stay here. I'm going to try and lure it away from the exit."

"How are you going to do that?"

"I don't know," I admitted.

"That is a stupid plan," she said.

"Just stay quiet," I said.

I headed back east. Up ahead, the Godkiller was giving off enough light to let me pick my way without stumbling over anything this time. It was still hovering in front of the stairwell, but at least it had stopped firing.

*What the hell is it doing?* I thought.

That became clear soon enough. When I got close, I saw that the God-killer was not alone. Buzzing around it were three or four of those smaller drones. While I watched, two of them disappeared into the stairwell.

It was using them to hunt for us. We wouldn't be any safer in the stairwell — at least not until it had moved farther east.

I got closer, struggling not to cough in the whirling cloud of dust around the thing. I kept close to the north wall, trying to inch my way past it.

It twisted in the air, so that its front was pitched forward. Its forward lights were shining on the ground. The reflected light illuminated it, and for the first time I got a good look at the hardware on its underside that I'd glimpsed when the craft hovered over us.

It looked like the Orbit Pebble had managed to do some damage after all. The bottom of the drone showed significant scoring and impact damage, and there were several hull breaches where external gear — probably sensing apparatus — had been blown clean off.

*No wonder it couldn't see us. Except for its optics, it's practically running blind.*

I stuck to the north edge of the passage, inching closer. Just as I was about to pass it, the damn thing moved away from the door, bringing its rear rotors dangerously close to my head. I flattened against the wall, watching the spinning rotors get so close I thought they were going to shave off three days of stubble.

The Godkiller banked right, sliding back down the passage. I breathed a sigh of relief.

But only for a moment. As I stepped out into the center of the tunnel, I saw it picking up speed, vanishing into the darkness.

Headed west . . . where Van de Velde was hiding barely a hundred feet away, behind the entirely inadequate protection of a rusted-out water tank.

"Hey!" I shouted. "Over here, ugly!"

The drone didn't respond. It was fifty feet away now and picking up speed.

I glanced around desperately, looking for something I could throw. A brick, a stone — anything. But with the drone gone, it was so dark I could barely make out my own feet.

Sixty feet. Without the protection of the drone jammer, it would spot her in seconds.

I reached into my pocket, grabbed the drone jammer. I switched it off.

"Over here, you cold-blooded piece of shit!"

The drone stopped. It was at least eighty feet out. It started to pivot to the left. But was it because of me or because it had spotted Van de Velde?

It kept rotating. Its two front lights came into view. Along with its weapons.

Shit. I hit the button on the jammer just as it started to fire, then dove as far as I could to the left.

Something struck me in the air, and I hit the ground badly. I curled up and reached for my stinging hip, and my hand came away wet. *Goddamn it, the damn thing shot me.*

The shoulder I landed on hurt almost as much as my hip. I wanted to move, get the hell out of this firing range, but I'd just had the wind knocked out of me, and it was all I could do to not curl up into a ball.

The Godkiller hadn't stopped firing. It was raking the ground with bullets — hundreds of them. It was firing systematically, in a loose grid, across the floor of the tunnel.

It knew I was here, even if it couldn't see me. I watched, almost hypnotized, as the small plumes of earth that showed where it was aiming came closer, closer . . . ever closer.

*Get up. Get up, you fool. It's going to kill you.*

I got my hands under me, managed to lift my head. The drone had closed the distance; it was now scarcely forty feet away. It was firing, firing, and now that moving line of plumes was headed straight toward me —

I saw a flash to the west, heard another report, mixed in with the noise from the Godkiller. And then another one.

Van de Velde was firing at the Dieu Tueur.

The drone spun again. As it did, a third shot from Van de Velde hit the thing. Another of the sensors on its undercarriage shattered in an explosion of sparks.

*Damn, she's a good shot.*

The drone was firing again. I fervently hoped Van de Velde had hit the deck, because she was getting the full brunt of the Godkiller's wrath, and unlike me she didn't have a drone jammer to help her hide.

I staggered to my feet, moving toward the doorway to the south. My left foot hit a rock, and I heard it bounce ahead in the darkness. I went after it, down on my hands and knees, flopping around in the dirt until I found it.

I threw the rock at the drone. I saw sparks, heard the rock smash against the back rotors and then ricochet off the top of the Godkiller with a resounding *crack.*

I dove for the open door.

The drone turned around again. It had stopped firing, and even stopped moving. It hovered in the air, facing east, and seemed to be listening. Listening and waiting.

I saw movement in the stairwell, from where I crouched with my back against the wall just inside the door. Two drones came flying down the stairs. They moved like wasps, fast and dangerous. They shot out the door and into the tunnel, swinging east, already on the hunt. The Godkiller lumbered after them, ready to kill whatever they found.

I waited for twenty seconds after they'd passed. Then I headed out the door in the opposite direction, jogging and staying low.

I ran eighty feet, until I saw the featureless shadow of the water tank. The throbbing ache in my hip became an excruciating pain halfway there, but I kept moving.

"Van de Velde?" I called, as loudly as I dared.

There was no answer. I felt my way around the tank. It was so dark here I couldn't even see my hand in front of my face.

I dropped to my knees, afraid I would step on her. I started groping in the dirt.

"Van de Velde? Jesus, please tell me you're not dead."

There was a groan. Something stirred in the dirt to my left. I reached out and found a leg.

"I'm not dead," said Van de Velde.

"Oh, thank God. Are you okay?"

She didn't respond immediately, and I began feeling for obvious injuries. I ran my hands over her legs, stomach, chest, shoulders—

Shoulders. Her left shoulder was slick with blood. There was a wet tear in her uniform, and when my fingers slid over it I heard her gasp with pain.

"Okay," I said. "Okay. Lie still. Are you hit?"

"No."

My fingers probed her shoulder, gently but insistently. Her uniform had a horizontal cut, about seven inches, starting just below her collarbone and ending at her left shoulder. I couldn't tell how deep it was, but it didn't seem life-threatening.

"You've been hit," I said.

"No. I told you. The bullet hit the tank. A piece of metal tore off and hit my shoulder. It's not deep."

"You sure?" My fingers wanted to explore the cut, check for a bullet hole, but she slapped my hand away.

"I'm sure. Stop groping me."

I laughed in relief. She was trying to sit up and reached out for assistance. I grasped her hand and helped her into a sitting position.

My hand slipped to her wrist, and I casually checked her pulse, making sure she wasn't in shock. "That's the only reason I invited you here," I said, to distract her from what I was doing. "To grope you in the dark."

"I knew it. You're an asshole."

Her heart rate was strong. "And you still came?" I said.

"I figured it was only fair. I chased you first."

She sat up straight, looking over the tank. She watched the drone re-treating to the east. It was at least a hundred yards away now.

"What about you?" she asked. "Did you get hit?"

"Just a minor wound."

"Where?"

"My hip. The bullet went right through —"

"You idiot. There's no such thing as a minor bullet wound. Show me."

"It's fine —"

"Show me."

Her hands were reaching out, fumbling over my chest, my face. I guided her right hand to my left hip.

She drew a sharp breath when she found the wound. I swear I was fine until she started poking me and making a fuss. And then, Jesus, it started to hurt like blazes. For the minute that she fussed over me and made hissing noises through her teeth, I thought I was going to die.

"You're right," she said at last. "It went clean through."

"Mmmm," I said, waiting for the pain to subside so I could talk again.

"But we still need to get it cleaned. As soon as possible. There's a med kit in the cafeteria."

"Mm'kay."

"Come on," she said. She got to her feet, helping me stand.

"I can walk," I said, feeling suddenly rather stupid. "I ran all the way here."

"You only did that," she said, "because you're a goddamn idiot."

We hobbled back to the stairs, with me leaning on her the whole way.

"You want to talk about who's an idiot?" I said when we were almost there. "Only one of us took on a Godkiller drone with a pistol."

"You think?" she said. "I was actually aiming at you."

We got into the stairwell, and she eased me onto the stairs. I didn't feel too bad once I stopped moving.

"Keep pressure on it," she said. I could barely see her in the darkness. She was nothing more than a dark silhouette a few feet in front of me.

"The hell with that," I said. "It only hurts when I touch it."

The dark blob I assumed was her had moved to the door. "Where are you going?" I said.

"I'm going back to get Asis."

"Are you crazy? That thing will kill you. And I won't be there to save your ass this time."

"I'm not leaving without him. If I do, Capitán Leon will just send another team down here."

There was truth in that. I dug around in my pocket. The motion put pressure on my hip, sending a jolt of pain up my spine.

"Here, take this," I said.

She took a few steps closer. "What is it?"

"It's the drone jammer."

She took it from me. "How do I turn it on?"

"It's already on. You just keep it on your person at all times."

I couldn't be a hundred percent sure the jammer would work for her. But it wasn't doing me any good here in the stairwell.

"What will you do if a drone finds you while I'm gone?" she asked.

"Wait for you to come back and shoot it," I said.

"At least it's a plan," Van de Velde agreed reluctantly. "All right. But stay here. I won't be long."

"Van de Velde?"

"What?"

"Thank you. For shooting the drone. I'd probably be dead right now if you hadn't. You're crazy, but you're all right."

"You're welcome," she said. With that, she was gone.

It wasn't easy sitting alone in the dark. Every little sound gets magnified in those tunnels, and in the long minutes I sat at the bottom of the stairs, waiting for Van de Velde to return with her man, I heard a lot of strange sounds.

Weird echoes. The distant bang of pipes. Air, whistling through the tunnels like a stealthy tomb raider. Mysterious, unidentifiable noises. Something like the hoot of an owl, from deep in the tunnels. A faraway murmur. From the passageway overhead, a constant whisper, getting louder.

The whisper changed pitch and then location. It was behind and overhead and then ahead and to the left. The sound became crisper, more defined. Like the rotor blades of one of the Godkiller slave drones.

One of its search drones had just entered the stairwell with me.

I stayed perfectly still. I wasn't so foolish as to think that it couldn't see me just because it was dark, but there was no point in letting it know I was conscious and mobile. I listened to the thing, tried to fathom what I could from its movements.

It was hovering above and to my left. Then it was on the right, stationed over the door. Then it was harder to pinpoint.

Just sitting there was maddening. It was like being trapped in a car with an angry bee. I wanted to move, to swat the thing, but I stayed calm, motionless and listening.

Then: a new sound. A new, unidentifiable sound. A hissing, like the flow of sand. At first I thought it was coming from overhead, where the drone had entered the chamber, but then I realized it was in the tunnel.

There was light in the tunnel now. Unsteady light, which dipped and wavered, as if cast by something on the move. The hissing got louder. It was close . . . and getting closer.

I was too exposed at the bottom of the stairs. If the Godkiller returned, it could kill me from the tunnel with ease. I needed to get upstairs, out of range of its most lethal weaponry. At least make it a challenge for the damn thing to kill me.

That meant moving. The drone was back, hovering up and to my left now. It would detect me for sure, but that could no longer be helped.

I stood up. The response from my hip was instantaneous: a piercing, tearing pain. I held the stair rail in a white-knuckle grip. *You ran eighty feet not five minutes ago,* I thought. *Don't you dare wimp out on me now.* I took my first steps up the stairs.

Van de Velde appeared in the doorway. She was pulling Asis on the stretcher. The hissing was the sound of the stretcher, being dragged over the stone floor of the tunnel.

Light glared in my face, from the flashlight in her right hand. "Still alive?" she said.

I was about to reply, when she suddenly dropped the stretcher. Before it even hit the ground she'd drawn her pistol and fired up and to the right.

It was a fabulously lucky shot. I heard the drone spin out, hit the west wall. It bounced, then came careening to the ground, where it smashed itself to pieces. Spinning bits of metal danced across the floor.

Van de Velde had the light in my face again. "You couldn't throw a rock at it? Something?"

"I'm a patient guy," I said. "I knew you'd be back."

"Was that one of the Dieu Tueur's scout drones?"

"Sure looked like it."

"Damn it. It will probably be here any minute."

"It can't fit into the stairwell." I stepped down, hobbled toward her. "We need to get up the stairs. Come on, let me help you."

She waved me away. "You can barely move. I can do this."

"I can help."

"Just get up the damn stairs. Come on, or I'll leave your ass behind."

That was no idle threat. She thrust the flashlight into my hands, slipped her pistol back into its holster, and lifted one end of the stretcher. Then she took big strides toward the stairs, dragging it behind her. A body bag was securely strapped into it.

She started taking the stairs two at a time. Even pulling the stretcher, she was moving much faster than I was capable of.

I followed wordlessly. As I did, I stooped over and snatched up the biggest remaining piece of the drone and stuffed it into my belt. Then I climbed the stairs. One at a time and thin-lipped. I could feel blood trickling down my leg.

She was waiting at the landing, halfway up. "You going to make it, old man?" At least she had the decency to be breathing hard.

"It hurts," I said. "But your love keeps me going."

"Oh my God," she said. "I wish I'd shot you so much right now."

She let me lead up the second tier of stairs, while she caught her breath. When I reached the top, she muscled Asis up the last of the stairs in one quick run.

There was a rising wind down below, growing to a crescendo. We both knew what that meant—the Godkiller had arrived.

Van de Velde started pulling Asis down the hallway immediately. Ignoring the pain in my hip, I bent down and grabbed the back end of the stretcher with both hands, lifting it off the ground. Together we got forty feet down the corridor before she stopped.

"Set him down," she said. "Hurry."

"We can't stop here," I said. "Those damn spy drones will be here any second."

"*Now.*"

I did as I was told. Van de Velde trotted to my side. She'd drawn her pistol.

"That's not going to do much good," I said. "The spy drones are much too small—and too fast."

She ignored me. "Shine the light back that way," she said. "Top of the stairs."

I did. The stairwell was already filling with dust as the drone kicked up dirt from the tunnel. A second later, light stabbed up from below, illuminating the swirling cloud as it spread toward us.

"Steady," she said. Her gun was pointed at the stairs, for all the good it would do.

Five seconds later, a dark mass spun out of the cloud. The dust seemed to part before it as it buzzed up out of the depths. It was a scout drone, bigger and more lethal looking than the compact ones we'd encountered so far, but clearly of the same design.

The moment it cleared the cloud, Van de Velde fired. She hit the thing dead center, and it flipped in midair.

"Incredible!" I said. "That's two great shots in a row—"

She fired again. This shot shattered one of the rotors, spraying metal against the north wall. The drone crashed to the stone floor, breaking into multiple pieces, some of them still spinning.

I gawked in disbelief. "Wow!" I said.

I started to move toward it, ready to destroy what was left, when she grabbed my arm. "Wait," she said.

Sure enough, a second drone emerged from the cloud not twenty seconds later. Another one of the scout drones, smaller and more difficult to hit.

But not for Van de Velde, apparently. She fired twice, and both shots struck their target. It was scrap metal before it hit the floor.

I stared at her in astonishment. "Damn," I said. "You're amazing."

"The day I'm slower than a drone is the day I deserve to get shot," she said with obvious satisfaction.

We waited another moment, but no more drones breached the cloud.

"We should move," I said. "It can't shoot us from there, but it probably has enough missiles to bring the tunnel down on top of us."

"Yeah," she agreed.

We picked up Asis and hurried down the long corridor. Blood was flowing freely down my leg now. When we reached the pedestrian walkway, I was glad for the excuse to stop and scan behind us, looking for drones. The tunnel was clear.

"Let me see your shoulder," I said.

"It's fine."

"Let me see it."

Her shirt was matted with blood. She didn't object while I unbuttoned it and pulled it away to examine her wound.

"Is this where you pretend to be a doctor?" she said.

I held the flashlight close. "I don't need to be a doctor to see you've lost a lot of blood."

"I'll be fine. We're almost out."

"You'll need stitches for that," I said. But she was right. Her shoulder didn't look too bad. The cut was long, but it didn't look deep, and the bleeding had almost stopped. She'd have a hell of a scar, though.

"How is your hip?" she asked as she buttoned up her shirt.

"Better than your shoulder," I said.

"You're a liar."

We lifted Asis and moved into the pedestrian walkway. From there we made our way toward the escalator. For a moment, as we pushed past the collapsible fence, I got a little light-headed. Everything blurred and all I could see were dots.

"You okay back there?" Van de Velde asked from the front.

"Super," I said.

Getting to the escalator seemed to take forever. My left sock was drenched with blood, and I was probably starting to leave bloody footprints. My hip, which had been raging with pain when we started, now throbbed with a dull ache.

"There it is," she said. I'd been plodding along, just putting one foot ahead of the other, but when she spoke I lifted my head and saw that she was right. The escalator, lit by light from above, was just ahead.

When we reached it, we laid Asis next to López. Then we just rested for a few minutes, me with my hands on my knees, trying to regain my strength, Van de Velde leaning against the wall, her head on her arms.

I was the first to stir. "We should get upstairs," I said. When I stood up straight, my vision blurred again. That meant my blood pressure had dropped, which wasn't a good sign.

"In a minute," said Van de Velde. "I want to look at your hip."

"We're five minutes from medical attention," I said, gesturing up the escalator.

She shook her head. "I don't want Capitán Leon's men examining you."

"Why the hell not?"

"Because he'll use it as an excuse to detain you. He'll transport you to a field hospital, get you doped up, question you for forty-eight hours. I've seen him do it."

That seemed a little too plausible for my liking. "What do you suggest?"

"We left the med kit in the cafeteria. Let me patch you up. That will hold until you get back to the hotel. One of the medics there can look at you."

"Okay."

"Don't mention your injury when we get out. Don't give the capitán a reason to detain you."

"Understood."

"When we get out, make yourself scarce. Walk back to the hotel if you have to. And when you get there, stay out of sight for a day or two."

I nodded.

We left the stretcher at the bottom of the escalator for retrieval and walked to the cafeteria. The med kit was right where we'd left it. Van de Velde had me lie on the table, and she sliced a six-inch hole in the left side of my pants.

"It's still bleeding," she said. "A lot."

"Yeah."

She dug around in the kit, handed me a bottle of thin yellow fluid. "Drink this. All of it."

I did as instructed. It tasted like crappy lemonade, but who knows what it actually was. *"Ow,"* I said, nearly spitting out the last of it as she jabbed me with a sponge. "What are you doing?"

"It needs to be cleaned."

"Can't a doctor do that?"

"Don't be such a baby. It looks like it's just a flesh wound. I don't think the bullet hit your hip bone."

"How can you tell?"

"Because you're still walking." She poked at me a bit more. "I can close this," she said.

"What do you mean?"

"Stitch you. I can stitch this closed."

"Hell, no. I'll have that done once I get some painkillers, thank you."

She laughed at me, holding up a thin tube. "I can numb you long enough to get it done. Do you trust me?"

It was an interesting question. I was already trusting her with a great deal. With the greatest secrets I had. Quite literally, I was trusting her with my life. A little field surgery seemed small by comparison.

"All right," I said. "On one condition."

"What?"

"Tell me your first name."

She lost her smile. She shook the can and sprayed my hip. For an instant it burned like blazes, but the pain quickly abated, leaving only a deep ache. She took an antiseptic spray from the case, applied that liberally as well. Then she got to work sewing my wound closed, quickly and efficiently.

As she was putting in the fourth stitch, she said, "Noa."

"Noa? That's a pretty name."

She didn't respond immediately. She finished the tenth stitch and cut the polymer thread. Then she dressed the wound.

"You can call me Sergeant Van de Velde," she said as she packed up.

"Okay, Sergeant," I said as I sat up. The numbing agent she'd sprayed in my hip didn't seem to have lessened the feeling in the rest of my leg any. I slid off the table, took an experimental step, then another. Everything seemed to be in order.

I was about to say as much when she turned and faced me. Her right finger jabbed out, with just enough pressure to nudge me off balance, knocking my ass back onto the table.

"Two things," she said. "Before we go topside."

"Okay," I said.

"*One.* We're not going to be friends. Got that? Not friends. Not lovers. You're an American spy. Or Canadian, or British, or whatever. I honestly don't give a damn who you work for. My men are dead because of you. You risked your life to save us, and in return, I'll keep my mouth shut. But that's all I owe you. Sooner or later, you're going to do something *truly* goddamn stupid, and you're going to get caught. And on that day I will buy a bottle of Beaujolais nouveau, and I will celebrate. You and I are enemies. Understand?"

"Understood," I said, keeping my expression even.

"And *two,*" she said, "for the record, I don't wear big-girl panties."

For a second, I had absolutely no idea what she was talking about. Until I remembered standing in front of her in the hotel, telling her to bring a gun and wear big-girl panties.

"Yeah? What *do* you wear?"

She leaned forward, putting her hands on the table on either side of me. She slid even closer, until her cheek brushed mine. Her warm body was up against me, and her lips were next to my ear.

"*You'll never know,*" she whispered.

Then she pushed away from the table, lifted the med kit to her good shoulder, and started walking toward the exit.

"Come on," she said. "I want to get the hell out of this place."

I slid off the table and followed her.

*Damn, this woman knows how to flirt,* I thought.

The two of us walked up out of the dark, to the waiting Venezuelan army.

# XXVI

Thursday, March 18th, 2083
Posted 1:28 am by Barry Simcoe

CanadaNET1 Encrypted, Sponsored by Dynamite Dynamics.
*Have a great idea for a novel, movie, or hit song? Don't let someone
steal it! Lock up your valuable Intellectual Property today.*

Sharing is set to PRIVATE
Comments are CLOSED

When we walked out of the basement of Columbia College, there were
soldiers waiting for us. They whisked Van de Velde away, presumably to a
debriefing, but they didn't seem to know what to do with me.

Their eyes had no problem wandering to the bloodstains on my clothing, however. Two of them began to whisper, eyeing me.

"Hey, is there a bathroom around here?" I asked the closest one.

She escorted me to the east side of the field and pointed at a bunch of
chemical toilets all lined up in a row. The Venezuelan army clearly had no
use for modesty; there were no screens between toilets, and no screens between the toilets and the outside world. I could see all the way to South
Columbus Drive, a hundred yards away, where two pairs of joggers were
making steady progress north.

I felt a little exposed. But while I was pissing in the third toilet, a young
corporal came running up on my right, dropped her pants, and squatted
three toilets down. She finished up and was on her way while I was still
shaking out the last few drops. *Army life,* I thought.

I rinsed my hands and looked around casually, The soldier who'd escorted me was keeping a discreet distance about thirty yards west. First

thing on my agenda was to lose her. While I was still buttoning up, I started striding back west toward the assembled Venezuelan forces like a man on a mission, glancing neither left nor right. I walked straight for the northernmost tents, where about a hundred and fifty soldiers were assembled.

No one challenged me as I threaded my way through the groups of soldiers, although I did get a few strange looks. When I was close to the tents I surreptitiously glanced behind. My escort was about forty feet back and jogging to catch up.

I stepped inside the first tent I reached. It was a mobile communication center, a mini replica of the command center back at the hotel, with over half a dozen young officers sitting before portable displays. I strode right through as if I belonged there.

"¡Oye!" said a woman, sitting in a folding metal chair. I ignored her and she got up, shouting at me.

I reached the north end of the tent. The moment I was outside I took a hard right, taking five steps until I could see back down the length of the tent.

My tail was hustling after me. I watched her dash into the south entrance of the tent. The moment she did, I doubled back south, sticking close to the side of the tent.

I could hear voices inside. My tail was asking where I went, I guessed. The woman who'd called after me responded, no doubt sending her after me.

I didn't wait around to see how that unfolded. Sticking close to the side of the tents, I hurried south, then mingled in with a loose group of soldiers who were standing near Michigan Avenue, looking toward the college.

They were watching López and Asis being brought out. I stood with them for a minute, watching the two body bags being solemnly carried across the street, to a knot of officers. I saw Leon standing in the middle. He knelt down to zip open the bags when they were laid in front of him, inspecting his returning men personally.

With all their attention on the body bags, it was the perfect time for me to make a break for it. I headed north on Michigan and didn't look back. There were a few checkpoints along the way — manned by AGRT troops — but they'd been instructed to keep civilians away from the operation, not keep them from leaving, so I had no trouble. Within eight minutes I was well away from the entire operation.

It was a long walk back to the hotel. My feet were already sore, so I was dead on my feet by the time I reached it, and my hip hurt like blazes. All

I wanted to do was crawl into bed for forty-eight hours, exactly as Van de Velde had instructed.

I heard someone calling my name as I dragged my weary ass across the lobby. Martin was waving at me.

"Where the devil have you been?" he asked, walking up. "Mike said he saw you get put into an AGRT car this morning."

"Yeah," I said.

"Willingly?"

I shrugged. "Mostly."

"Bloody hell. Tell me you're not pissing off our hosts again."

"I had a capitán threaten to shoot me. Does that answer your question?"

Martin was about to reply, then cut himself off as he took in the blood on my clothes and the torn state of my pants. "What the hell?" he said.

"It's nothing," I reassured him.

"You in any trouble?" There was genuine concern in his voice.

"It's all blown over. I think. Or it will, if I can just keep a low profile for a couple days."

Martin nodded. "Seems like a solid plan."

I started walking toward the elevators. "Damn straight. I'm going to spend the next twenty-four hours asleep."

"Breakfast tomorrow? I've got to hear this story."

"Sure thing—if I'm awake."

Martin started to walk off, then caught himself. He called after me. "Hey, Mac was looking for you."

"Was it important?"

"Dunno."

I punched the button for the elevator. "Then I'll see her when I wake up."

That turned out to be fairly prophetic.

It was very dark and very late when there was a pounding at my door. I probably would have slept through it, but Croaker made such a racket that I was forced to stumble out of bed. My leg hurt like hell, worse than ever, but I limped to the door.

It was Boone, the night security guy. "Sorry to disturb you, Mr. Simcoe," he said.

I rubbed my eyes. "What time is it?"

"It's just after eleven p.m., sir."

Croaker was trying to push past me so she could sniff Boone for herself. "Is that a dog, Mr. Simcoe?" Boone asked.

"That is a dog, Boone," I said, shoving Croaker back with my foot. She whined at me.

"There's no dogs in the hotel, Mr. Simcoe."

"How can I help you, Boone?"

Boone rubbed his chin. "Do you know a guest at this hotel, Miss Mackenzie Stronnick?"

"Mac? Sure, I know her."

"Miss Stronnick is downstairs, in the kitchen. She's intoxicated and very disorderly."

"Mac?" That didn't sound like Mac at all. "Are you sure?"

"Unfortunately, yes. I asked Miss Stronnick if there was anyone I could get to assist, and she mentioned your name."

"*Me?*"

"Yes, sir."

I stood there stupidly for a moment before I realized that Boone was waiting for me to accompany him. "Just a second," I said.

I closed the door and hurriedly got dressed. Lifting my leg just to put my pants on was excruciating, and I had the mother of all bruises on my hip, but I was a little less stiff than when I'd first gotten up. I pulled on a pair of shoes, told Croaker to stay, and joined Boone in the hall.

"Are you sure she's drunk?" I asked as we waited for the elevator.

"Reasonably sure, yes sir."

"How did she wind up in the kitchen?"

"I'm not sure. It was the kitchen staff who contacted me."

"Is she alone?"

"The kitchen staff is with her now."

"I mean, was she drinking alone?"

"It appears so."

We took the elevator to the second-floor lobby. I followed Boone as he led me through a service door, then to the kitchen.

Most of the lights were out. I was surprised there was anybody here at all, but Boone led me to the back, where a small crowd was gathered around a slumped figure on the floor.

They parted as I approached. It was Mac. "My God," I said, dropping quickly to her side. "Is she breathing?"

I leaned over her, holding two fingers to her throat. Her pulse was

strong, and she seemed to be breathing fine. I caught a strong smell of alcohol and heard her mumble something unintelligible.

"Someone bring me a wet towel, please."

One of the cooks complied, pressing a cold, wet cloth in my hand a moment later. I held it against her head, then her neck. Her eyes fluttered, but
didn't open.

"How long has she been like this?" I asked.

Two of the cooks started speaking to Boone in Spanish. "About fifteen
minutes," Boone told me.

"Tell me what happened," I said.

"She came in," the young cook next to me said, in a thick Slavic accent.
"She talked—loud—" He made extravagant gestures, imitating her motions. "And then she fall over."

"Did she hit her head?"

The cook shook his head.

"Did she look injured at all?"

Again he shook his head.

"Where did she come from?"

"I spoke with Randolph, at the bar," said Boone. "He said she was there
for the past two hours."

I checked Mac's head and neck, did a cursory inspection of the rest of
her, and didn't find anything alarming. She was breathing normally, and
the smell of alcohol was very strong. It was hard to believe that Mac had
simply drunk herself into unconsciousness, but that's what it looked like.

"She can't stay here," Boone said.

"Yeah," I said. She was wearing a light jacket, and I fished through the
pockets. I found a folded piece of paper and a thin strip of metal. "Okay,
this is her room key. Can you two help me get her up to her room?"

The cook and Boone nodded. They stood on either side of her and got
her to her feet, and then started toward the kitchen doors.

"No, no . . . wait a minute," I said. "Let's see if we can avoid parading
her through the lobby. Bring her out back, to the freight elevator. We can
take that up to the seventh floor and then move her to the guest elevator."

We managed to get her to the freight elevator without incident. But
once we got in the elevator, another problem emerged.

"She's . . . ah, she's going to . . ." said the cook, suddenly looking very
nervously at Mac.

"No, she's not," I said reassuringly. "She'll be fine."

But she did. She threw up all over the cook, and herself, and the elevator. And then she did it again.

The cook did this amazing little jig, danced his whole body away from her, practically to the other side of the elevator, all while managing to keep one arm under Mac's shoulder. He was able to avoid getting splattered a second time, for whatever good that did.

"Okay—get her down, set her down, easy," I said. "Keep her head up, please. Make sure she doesn't choke. Mac—Mac, honey, can you hear me? Are you okay?"

Mac gave me a brief, quizzical look, mumbled something that sounded French, and then closed her eyes. The cook and Boone both stared at me, incredulous.

"Wow, she is *out*," I said. "Boone, you said she was drinking alone?"

"I'm not certain. I didn't inquire."

"Find out. I want to make sure someone didn't slip her something."

Boone nodded. "I will."

I felt her forehead. Her skin was warm, but not feverish. I checked her pupils. They were dilated, but that didn't necessarily tell me anything. I deliberated violating curfew to try to get her to a hospital, but that seemed too risky.

The elevator doors opened. The hallway was empty. We left the cook behind to tend to the mess in the elevator, and Boone and I carried her down the hall to the guest elevator.

"What floor is she on?" Boone asked.

I frowned, looking down at Mac. She was breathing okay, but she looked very pale. I didn't like the idea of just dumping her in her room.

"Change of plan," I said. "I don't think she's in danger, but I don't think we should leave her alone. Let's take her to my room."

Boone nodded, punching the button for thirty-three. I squatted down next to Mac.

"She really mentioned me?" I asked Boone.

He nodded. "Is that surprising?"

"We haven't known each other all that long."

He seemed a little surprised. "You two aren't . . . ?" he said.

"Me and Mac? No."

"Is there someone else we should have contacted?"

"I couldn't say."

The elevator opened on thirty-three, and Boone and I carried her to my room. Croaker was as excited as I've ever seen her when the three of us came in, running around underfoot.

"Where do you want her?" Boone asked, studiously ignoring the dog.

I was about to say the bed, when Mac hiccupped abruptly. Boone looked alarmed.

"Put her in the tub, and help me get her jacket off," I said.

As quickly as we could we got her laid out in my bathtub, head at one end and boots propped up on the porcelain at the other. Boone lifted her up enough for me to tug her jacket off, and I draped it over a towel rack. Boone and I stood back to survey the situation.

She was resting quietly and gave no sign she was about to throw up again, which was a relief. Miraculously, her jacket seemed to have escaped more or less unscathed. But that was it for the good news. She'd splattered her silk blouse and her pants with vomit, and her hair was matted against her chest, sticking to her. She reeked.

"All right, I'll keep an eye on her in here for a while," I said. "As long as she's in the tub, I might as well clean her up."

"Do you . . ." Boone licked his lips. "Do you need any help with that?"

Honestly, some help would have been great. But I didn't like the way Boone was looking at Mac as she lay unconscious in the tub.

"No, I think I got it."

Boone tried to hide his disappointment as he walked to the door.

"Listen, don't forget about finding out if she was with someone tonight," I said. "If she was drugged, we need to know. The sooner the better."

Boone seemed to appreciate having a task to do. "I'll look into it," he said.

"Thanks. That'll be a big help."

When he was gone, I returned to the bathroom. Croaker had padded over, sticking her snout into the tub and sniffing Mac's shoulder. I rubbed the top of Croaker's head.

"What do you think, girl? Any advice? She's going to live, but I don't think we can just let her sleep it off here . . . Croaker, leave her alone. *Don't lick that*—get away from her! I swear to God, you are the grossest dog I ever met."

Croaker slunk away, flopping to the tiles to watch us from the other side of the bathroom. I dragged a garbage pail and a roll of toilet paper to the tub and spent a few minutes trying to clean off the worst of it. It was slow, nauseating work. Her blouse and her pants were soaked, and she stank of vomit and alcohol. I swabbed at her neck, as patiently as I could. Just as it seemed I was making progress, Mac's whole body jerked, and her eyes flew open.

"Mac? I'm here, it's okay—"

Mac retched once, splattering vomit over my right hand and wrist. Her eyes closed, and she sank back into the tub.

I cursed up a storm. I cleaned up in the sink, then turned back to Mac. I pressed my left arm to my nose, blocking the smell as best I could. I wasn't sure I had the stomach to try this a second time.

I debated leaving her in the tub, but that was a bad idea. One or two more violent spasms, and she'd knock out a tooth. I glanced at my bed, twenty-five feet away. I didn't relish the idea of carrying her in her current condition. At all.

"Screw it," I said in disgust. I poured half a bottle of shampoo over her and turned on the water.

That was a mistake. The tub filled quickly; I managed to tug off her boots before they got too wet, but that was all I was able to remove before the rest of her clothes were soaked. In minutes Mac was nearly buried in an avalanche of suds. After she'd soaked for five minutes I let the water drain out, leaving a gunky, sudsy residue around the tub.

Mac was now completely drenched. Her wet hair dripped slowly onto her blouse, and her jeans were caked in vomit and suds. "I should have just dumped you in bed," I said remorsefully.

That was true. It probably would have ruined the sheets, but that would be no big loss. She would have slept right through it all anyway. But she was never going to dry in this tub, and I realized now that I couldn't put her to bed like this.

I ran my hands through my hair and made a decision. "You're going to hate me for this," I said to Mac.

I gently tugged off her blouse, raising one arm at a time. Just as I finished she started awake again, staring around, wide-eyed, talking excitedly. "Tony—Tony, stay here, you'll get hurt, honey, stay with me—" But just as quickly she was out again, sinking back into the tub without acknowledging me at all.

I rinsed her blouse in the sink, then left it to soak in cold water. It was probably a total loss, but I'd hang it up later to dry anyway. Underneath the blouse she was wearing a thin white camisole that I left alone.

Her jeans were a different story. They were a nightmare. I think they must have shrunk two sizes. They were soaking wet and plastered to her skin like a wetsuit possessed by Satan. By the time I got them off and more or less cleaned off, I was completely soaked. The wound in my hip hurt like blazes. There were chunks of soggy vomit on my shirt, smeared on my pants, and probably in my hair, for all I knew.

I really wanted a shower. I settled for running the water in the sink, splashing enough to scrub my face and hair, and then drying off and changing clothes.

I turned the water back on and let the bathtub slowly fill, checking the temperature frequently to make sure it didn't get too hot. Croaker followed me as I walked to my desk, then wheeled my desk chair into the bathroom. I parked it next to the bath and took a seat.

Mac's head was gone. Only her knees were sticking up above the gently rising tide of suds.

*Oh shit.* I dove for the water, pulled her roughly above the surface. She snorted two streams of foaming water out her nostrils, and her eyes were wide open and panicked. She clawed at my face, at the tub, at the tiled wall. "Mac, honey, I'm so sorry, it's okay, it's okay. Just breathe. I'm here. I'm here."

But she was gone already. She closed her eyes and sank back into the tub. I checked five times to make sure she was breathing, positioned her as well as I possibly could, and then turned off the water and sat back in the chair to watch over her. And think.

There was a chance Boone would show up in the next few minutes and let me know Mac had been drinking with someone. And then this would turn into an investigation. We would track that person down, find out if any kind of drugs were involved.

That was the more straightforward of the two alternatives.

The other one didn't require a third party. The second version of tonight's events had Mac walking into the bar and deliberately drinking herself into a stupor, all on her own.

Maybe this was something Mac did regularly. Maybe it was her idea of a good time.

And maybe not.

The only clue I had was the slip of paper I'd taken from her pocket. It was a note from the front desk, saying she had a message. It was time-stamped over four hours ago. Just a few hours before she'd begun drinking.

If I knew the content of that message, I might know which version of tonight's events was more plausible. And whether or not I should be contacting Sergei right now, to get her stomach pumped.

I watched as Mac stirred in the bath, mumbling something unintelligible.

Then I called the front desk, using the phone on the wall in the bathroom.

"Yes, this is Barry Simcoe in 3306. I was expecting an urgent message this evening from Halifax. I was told it arrived four hours ago?"

"I'd be glad to check for you, Mr. Simcoe —"

"Well, I'm afraid there's been some kind of mix-up. I did get a message, but it wasn't for me. It was addressed to room 2214, to someone named 'Mackenzie.' Is there any chance the messages were mixed up?"

There was a pause. "I can check for you, sir."

"Thank you, that'd be great. This is extremely urgent."

She came back on the line a moment later. "Yes, room 2214 also received a message four hours ago."

"Was it received at . . ." I glanced at the note in my hand. "Six forty-eight p.m.?"

"Yes sir, it was. That's exactly when it arrived."

"Oh, thank God. That's my message. Do you have a copy?"

"Yes sir. I'm very sorry for the mix-up. Do you have the ID number for the message?"

I found the ID number on the note and read it to her.

"Thank you, sir. I have your message here. Would you like me to read it to you?"

I didn't answer. Mac looked remarkably helpless lying in the bath.

It wasn't likely that she was going to forgive me in the morning — for the crime of stripping her down to her underwear in a bathtub — regardless of the circumstances. But the much more deliberate invasion of privacy I was about to perpetrate now felt like an even greater violation. If she found out, it might destroy what relationship we had . . . if indeed we still had one at all, come tomorrow.

*What do you care about more?* I asked myself. *How awkward this makes things for you, or whether Mac makes it through the night?*

"Sir?"

"Yes, please. Read it to me."

"It reads, 'Dear Sir or Madam, thank you for your inquiry. We are authorized to confirm that Anthony R. Stronnick, D.O.B. 09-09-2077, arrived at the Westhaven National Relocation Facility in Gary, Indiana, on or near December 17, 2082. Our records do not show a departure date for Mr. A. R. Stronnick. Unfortunately, due to unusually high refugee volume and unavoidable data loss, our records are incomplete. A. R. Stronnick no longer resides at this facility. Kind regards, Lieutenant L. C. Collins, Office of Records, DNRF, Gary, Indiana.' That's the end of the message." She paused. "Westhaven . . . that's one of the Displaced Persons camps in Indiana, isn't it? Is that the one that got shelled in January?"

"Yes," I said quietly.

"Date of birth 2077 . . . he was only five years old."

I didn't say anything.

"I'm very sorry for your loss," she said after a moment.

"Thank you. One more thing. Could you send up a hairbrush?"

"A hairbrush?"

"Yes."

"Right away, Mr. Simcoe."

I turned the water back on in the tub. And then I washed Mac's hair. I did it twice, rinsing it slowly, cupping the water in my hands and letting it escape between my fingers. When I was done I drained the sudsy water from the tub, filled it up one more time to rinse her off. I patted her as dry as I could in the bath, then picked her up and carried her clumsily to the bed.

There was a knock at the door. I covered her up, and opened the door for a very serious young man, holding a hairbrush in a sealed plastic bag. I tipped him generously and closed the door.

I rummaged through my drawers until I found a clean T-shirt and exchanged her wet camisole for the dry shirt. She mumbled a bit and fought me for a few seconds as I pulled it on over her head, but I got it on. Then I propped her up in bed enough to get in behind her and brush her hair. I took my time, drying it with a towel simultaneously.

You know, Mac, you're a lot like your country. Broken — and full of rage, and sorrow, and loss. And right now, you're in the gutter, with no understanding of how you got there, what's being done to you, or why.

And yet you're still fiercely independent, still god-awful stubborn, still swinging, refusing to take no for an answer. And you're still so damn beautiful.

I laid her head down gently on the pillow, tucked the blankets around her shoulders, kissed her on the forehead, and went to sleep on the couch.

# XXVII

Thursday, March 18th, 2083
Posted 1:05 pm by Barry Simcoe

CanadaNET1 Encrypted, Sponsored by Hush Tornado.
*People are gossiping about you. Discover what they're saying with our social media worm — scans email, texts, and 138 different social media platforms.*

Sharing is set to PRIVATE
Comments are CLOSED

I didn't get much sleep. My hip was killing me, and shortly after dawn the pain woke me up. I was starving, sore, and starting to worry that my hip was infected.

Croaker, who usually sleeps on a corner of my bed, had curled up on the floor next to me. She awoke as soon as I began to stir and licked my nose.

I checked on Mac as soon as I got out of bed. She was still asleep. Her breathing and pulse were both normal. But I decided to ask Sergei to check on her, just in case.

I didn't want to leave Mac alone, but Croaker was whining by the door. I took her on a slow, short walk in the cold morning air, in a two-block square around the hotel. It was hard to get started, but the pain lessened a bit as I loosened up. But it was windy and damp, and even Croaker didn't want to be out long.

There was no sign of Sergei in the command center, and Mac was still asleep when we got back. I checked her breathing and pulse again; both normal.

I left the bedroom door open a crack and retired to the office side of the hotel room. The pants I'd been wearing in the tunnels yesterday were ruined. I picked them up for a third time, wondering if I could have them mended, but it was useless. They were shredded in two places — and badly bloodstained besides. I threw them in the trash. I was down to two pairs of dress pants, and it wouldn't be easy to get new ones. I couldn't exactly order new clothes online. Hadn't Martin mentioned something about a tailor, working out of a hotel a few blocks away? That sounded expensive, but I was running out of options.

I sat by the window, in the steadily growing morning light, and thought about the Westhaven Displaced Persons camp in Indiana — and little Anthony R. Stronnick, date of birth September 9, 2077.

I didn't have much to go on, but the picture was still pretty clear. Mac had said she was from Chicago; she must have been here during the fall of the city, when Perez led the Nineteenth Venezuelan Expeditionary Force in a lightning-fast attack out of Indiana, catching Chicago's scant defenders off guard. Dozens of three-ton combat machines had risen up out of Lake Michigan, striding out of Monroe Harbor into the heart of downtown Chicago, leaving giant wet footprints as they clanked triumphantly down Michigan Avenue.

That was before the large-scale evacuations. Some folks fled the city, but most just sheltered in place, waiting anxiously to see what would happen. The US Army had learned the lessons of Manhattan well and didn't directly engage the killer machines in the heart of a densely populated urban zone. But the Union had no such compunctions. Sensing the opportunity for a public relations coup, a chance to accomplish something the mighty US Army could not, the newly formed American Union Army — fresh from a dazzling string of victories in Kentucky, where it had annihilated the SCC mobile robot factories — announced that it would drive the invaders from Chicago.

That had precipitated the January Crisis — and the ensuing panic and evacuation of Chicago, as the formidable Union Mech Army, nicknamed the Midnight Guard, had inexorably approached. In defiance of the Sentient Cathedral, who had tried to broker a ceasefire, the Union shelled Grant Park, striking a crippling blow to the heaviest SCC machines congregated there.

Perhaps that's when Mac and her son had become separated. I'd heard similar stories. Maybe she'd been gathering food when the mayor gave the order for the mandatory evacuation. Perhaps they'd been separated at one of the chaotic embarkation sites, or there just hadn't been room for both of them as they boarded a bus at a pick-up point. Maybe Mac had sent Anthony on ahead, expecting to follow immediately.

However it had happened, five-year-old Anthony R. Stronnick must have ended up bound for a Displaced Persons camp without his mother. Plenty of parents had sent their children on ahead, expecting an orderly rendezvous at the Westhaven Processing Center.

But the evacuation hadn't been orderly—far from it. The Union had badly damaged the SCC ground forces with their opening attack, and they pushed the advantage immediately. They attacked in force, and the Venezuelans pushed back hard. The battle for Chicago had a fluid front that spilled all over the southern half of the city, including some of the major evacuation routes. Fast-moving Midnight Guard roamed in packs up and down the skyways, exchanging deadly fire with squat Venezuelan machines as they retreated behind civilian buses trapped on the tollways. Hundreds of civilian vehicles had been destroyed, thousands of civilians killed.

A lot of parents never followed their children to Westhaven. The camp itself had been evacuated twice, first when the initial wave of Union mechs withdrew through Gary under heavy fire, and then again as Midnight Guard reinforcements poured in from Georgia. The frenzied exodus from Chicago had accelerated, and countless records were lost as grim civil authorities hastily crammed nearly two million Chicagoans into buses and commandeered trucks bound for Ohio, Kentucky, and Alabama.

I'd heard of parents who'd searched for their children for months, following false reports and desperate clues across half a dozen states. Some of those stories had happy endings. Most did not.

It looked like Mac's story lacked an ending, which was perhaps the most agonizing kind of all. On December 17th, her son Anthony had vanished into the all-consuming maw of Westhaven, which had shotgunned refugees across half a continent. Likely Mac had been trapped in the city once the heavy fighting started. It was probable her son had waited for her for a few weeks, perhaps until those deadly errant shells fell on Westhaven in mid-January. All three sides denied responsibility, and in the end it didn't really matter. Hundreds of adults and children had been killed before the panicked second evacuation of the camp.

Errant shells hadn't been the only lethal danger the camps endured. What was it Mike Concert had said at breakfast on Saturday? There'd been a plague scare during the evacuation of Chicago, and four people had died of N1-C at one of the camps. No wonder Mac had been so appalled at Mike's cavalier attitude. She must have been separated from Anthony when the word of the sickness and deaths in the camps reached Chicago. A possible epidemic, on top of all the other horrors she heard reports of every day. It must have been damned terrifying.

Perhaps Anthony was dead. Perhaps he'd been sick, or hurt in the bombings, and been bundled onto a medical evac truck bound for Cleveland. Or perhaps he'd been relocated to Evansville, and then packed off to Baton Rouge or Huntsville or Lexington, or one of a hundred other receiving centers. Before Mac could even begin her search, the eastern half of the country had been partitioned into sectors by the AGRT, and travel to most of those places became a virtual impossibility.

So Mac was trapped here. With no recourse but to send out queries, hoping against hope to receive word that her son was still alive. And instead, yesterday she'd received a message from the Westhaven Relocation Facility that implied that her son might be dead.

No wonder she'd drunk herself to unconsciousness.

I mulled over all of this as the morning sun finally cleared the tower of steam boiling out of Lake Michigan and the first rays of sunlight began to warm my feet. Mac might not have a way to track down her son . . . but it was possible Black Winter did. He'd implied that the Kingdom of Manhattan had spy drones over much of the occupied zones. One handy thing I'd learned from my own recent troubles was that algorithmic searches of drone data were fairly routine . . . If I got Black Winter a picture of Anthony, was there a possibility he could do a search for him?

Even if we didn't find him, we might be able to eliminate certain sites, help Mac narrow the search. It was something. But I probably shouldn't mention anything to Mac until I'd had a chance to talk to Black Winter first. No sense raising her hopes just to crush them again.

Next to me on the table was the circuit core of the scout drone that Van de Velde had shot, and a small pile of metal shards — the bits of the Godkiller I'd brought out of the tunnels. I spent a few minutes examining them in the sunlight. The largest of the shards was no bigger than a penny. If I had even a crude metal analyzer, I might be able to learn something meaningful from them; as it was, I eventually dumped them into an empty coffee cup without learning much of anything. The circuit core was a different matter — much of its internals were still intact. I slipped it into a bag and put it back on my desk.

When I stood up, I found my hip had stiffened up again. I limped into the bathroom, had a warm shower, and felt a bit better. I got dressed and obsessively checked on Mac one more time.

*Now you're just being creepy,* I thought. *You need to let her sleep.*

I had a few hours before I needed to get to work on a contract for Ghost Impulse, so I told Croaker to stay off the bed, and then headed downstairs. It was too early for my breakfast with Martin, so I stopped by the command center.

I noticed something different as soon as I got there. I recognized both of the soldiers on guard duty. An hour ago they had sleepily waved me inside, but now they were standing crisply at attention. I caught the eye of the closest one, and he shook his head almost imperceptibly.

They weren't going to let me in. I decided not to push it, at least until I could figure out what was going on. I walked by the door and glanced inside, as casually as I could, and spotted a knot of officers near the center of the room.

Looked like they had some high-ranking visitors. I hung around in the hallway for about fifteen minutes, and they eventually left. They passed me in the hall, about ten men and women in sharp Venezuelan uniforms; the man at the center gave me a cold, appraising look as they passed. He looked oddly familiar, but I couldn't place him.

When they had gone, the guards relaxed. After a minute or two they gave me a nod, and I slipped inside.

I found Sergei at his station. "Good morning," I said.

He barely glanced at me. "It is not good."

"Who was your special visitor?"

"We were honored this morning with an inspection by Colonel Hayduk."

"*Hayduk?*" That's why he had looked familiar. I lowered my voice. "What the hell is he doing here?"

"He did not share his intentions with medical specialist."

"Does he know about the centrifuges? Did he see them?"

"He did not. He did not tour seventh floor. He did not mention, in any regard."

That was a relief. But it wouldn't pay to relax our guard with this man. I wanted to know what he was doing here. "What did he do while he was in the command center?" I pressed.

"The colonel gave instructions to monitor American media broadcasts and requested immediate assessment on regimental combat readiness."

"Combat readiness? For what? Who is he going to war with?"

Sergei gave me a frustrated look. Obviously, he had no answers for me.

"When did all this start?" I asked.

"Colonel Hayduk arrived about thirty minutes ago. He will meet with Colonel Perez this morning. Perez has instructed senior staff to report for operational briefing at thirteen hundred hours."

"Great. Will this impact the operation of the reactor?"

Sergei's face soured — which was something, because I thought it looked pretty sour to begin with. "Thibault has been reassigned."

"*What?*"

"She received new orders this morning. She and her team have been posted to Danville, effective immediately. She has already left Fort Wayne and is en route."

"They can't do that! What about monitoring the reactor?"

"We must make do with remaining staff."

I chewed on that for a moment. "Did we lose her entire team?"

"Dr. Lark is staying and several technicians. Thibault will delay their reassignment as long as possible."

"Can we still distribute the antivirus without Thibault? Or even complete the purification process?"

Sergei rubbed his face. "Possibly. Seed batch injection was successful and bioculture is developing to profile. But team will have to tend to reactor around new assignments. It will mean much less sleep for team."

"I wasn't aware you did sleep."

"New operation could make things . . . very difficult."

"New operation? What new operation?"

"I do not know yet." Sergei seemed exhausted and frustrated — and seeing him like this was a little alarming. "But it is major mobilization."

"Damn." The last few weeks hadn't exactly been restful, but I considered myself lucky there had been no major engagements since the Juno incursion on March 8th. A mobilization meant all that could change — and not for the better. "What about the sick soldier?"

"He is in isolation on third floor. With two others."

"Others? There are two more cases?"

"Yes, as expected. And there will be more."

I bit back what would have been a loud curse. Sergei had been right, of course. Keeping that sick soldier out of the hotel would never have kept us safe. It was only a matter of time until everyone, everywhere, was at risk. Our only hope of stopping this was the reactor.

"I have put Dr. Lark in charge of their care," Sergei said. "She will be vigilant for new infections and keep unit as isolated as possible."

"Joy? Good. I'll go check on her later. How else can I help?"

"You? Nothing. I would advise you to stay in your room. Keep as far away from Hayduk as possible."

"Yeah, that's good advice. But if you need help keeping the reactor operating—anything—you'd let me know, right?"

Sergei nodded. He sat quietly for a moment, then seemed to compose himself. "Your underground expedition with pretty Venezuelan sergeant . . . it went well?"

"Oh, yeah. Great. We held hands while we pulled a couple dead bodies out of the earth. How the hell do you think it went?"

"Did you locate colony?"

I told Sergei what we'd discovered—the missing colony, the wreckage of the Pebble, and the Godkiller.

"You saw Godkiller?" Sergei sat up, clearly incredulous.

"You're damn right I did."

"You are lucky to have survived."

"I did get shot." I told him the details of how Van de Velde and I had survived our encounter and showed him my wound proudly.

"It looks fine," he said, after a quick look. "She did good job dressing wound."

I was a little affronted by how quickly he dismissed my first bullet wound. "I walked two miles," I said. "With a bullet hole in my hip. Can't you at least make sure it's not infected?"

"It is too soon to diagnose infection. Come back tomorrow."

"I'll probably be dead by tomorrow!"

"Not from infection," he said confidently. "Do not be baby."

"Shit. Fine."

"What about robot colony?" he asked.

"I don't know," I said. "And I'm worried about them, to be honest."

"Do you think Godkiller destroyed them?"

"I think it certainly tried to. The only way to find out is to explore deeper into the tunnels. The colony was pretty damn big; they could still be hiding down there."

"Did you see evidence Godkiller found them?"

"No. It for sure destroyed the Orbit Pebble, but I think the Pebble died defending the colony. I didn't see a single dead robot. It's possible they were warned and escaped in time."

"Escaped where?"

"I don't know. Deeper into the tunnels, maybe. That Godkiller was big — there were lots of places it couldn't go."

"But almost nowhere its scouts would not go. If Sentient Cathedral has found them, it will likely not rest until they are destroyed."

"Speaking of which . . . I brought the circuit core of a scout drone out of the tunnels with me."

"You salvaged intact core?"

"Mostly intact, yeah. I was hoping you could have a look at it. Maybe determine for sure who sent it — the Sentient Cathedral, or someone else."

Sergei shook his head. "I do not have time. Perhaps after reactor is completed."

"Yeah, I understand," I said. "I'll look into it myself. I have another favor to ask you, though. Mac is in my room. She got drunk last night — drunk and very sick. Maybe she just drank too much. But it could be something worse. Can you swing by and have a look at her?"

Sergei considered. "Yes. But not right now. I need to prepare for briefing. I will meet you in lobby . . . at eleven a.m."

"Eleven. Perfect. See you then."

The restaurant was open by then, so I walked down. There was no sign of Martin, so I got two coffees. I brought them back to my room, my mind preoccupied. Could Hayduk be deliberately trying to sabotage our work on the bioreactor? Could he suspect us of the theft of the data drive? And were his agents sniffing around, even now?

Or was this all a cover for Hayduk's hunt for the combat suit? Could he have tracked me here, to the hotel? Had I been careless somehow in my underground excursion? God knows that was a possibility, with all that had happened the last time I wore the suit.

I opened the door to my room quietly, trying not to wake Mac. But a glance at my bed showed me it was empty. I heard water running in the bathroom.

I was relieved to see her up, although I was a little apprehensive about our coming conversation. I had no idea how I was going to explain how she woke up in my bed, wearing my clothes.

I didn't have much time to think about it. A moment later the bathroom door opened, and Mac stepped out, drying her face with a towel. She was still wearing the T-shirt I'd dressed her in last night. She stopped dead when she saw me.

"I brought you coffee," I said, holding up one of the cups.

"Oh." She made no move to take it. "So this is *your* room." She didn't sound very pleased.

Yeah, this wasn't going to go well. "Yes."

"Damn. I had absolutely no idea where I was."

I chuckled. "I can imagine. How do you feel?"

"God-awful."

"I'm glad to see you up and around, anyway. I have to tell you, I was pretty worried about you."

That was an understatement. It was heartbreaking to be in the same room with her, knowing what I did about her fruitless search for Anthony. I wanted to comfort her, let her know there were resources we could tap to expand her search . . . but that meant admitting that I'd read the message about her son.

I was ready to make that confession, but right this moment probably wasn't the perfect time. She'd just woken up disoriented, in a strange bed. She radiated distress. Step one was to make her feel safe. I put the coffee by the bed where she could reach it, and then retreated to give her plenty of space.

"The hotel staff knows you're here," I said. "They're the ones who contacted me when . . . when they found you."

She was still standing in the bathroom door, her expression somewhere between confused and angry. "How did I get here?" she asked.

"You were in the hotel kitchens, making a bit of a disturbance, from what I understand. Then you passed out. Boone, the night security man, came to get me."

"You? Why you?"

"Boone said you asked for me."

"I don't remember doing that." Her tone was suspicious.

I felt awkward looming in the doorway. I grabbed a chair and pulled it over, but not too close. "Well, I wasn't there," I said as I took a seat. "All I know is what Boone told me."

"Why would I ask for you?"

"I have no idea. I was going to ask you."

She moved away from the bathroom at last, sliding onto the bed. The towel was still in her hand, and she pressed it against her face.

"God, my head is pounding," she said into the towel.

"I'm not surprised. What's the last thing you remember?"

She let the towel drop to her lap. She looked out the window. "Drinking," she said.

"Alone?"

"What does that matter?"

"Forgive me, I don't mean to pry. But for a while last night, we were concerned someone might have slipped you something. A drug, maybe."

"Why did you think that?"

"Frankly, you weren't in very good shape. You threw up, a couple times. Once in the elevator, when we were taking you to your room. I got worried enough that I decided someone needed to watch you, so we brought you here instead."

"I'm not surprised I threw up," she said. "I know it probably doesn't look like it right now, but I'm not much of a drinker."

Croaker padded into the room. She leaped up onto the bed, and Mac jumped back, startled.

"Croaker — down, girl. Leave her alone." I nudged her off the bed.

Croaker looks a hell of a lot better now than she did when Black Winter and I first found her, but she still doesn't look good. Her skin still hangs off her bones like a rumpled blanket, and her fur has numerous scabby patches. At least the raging infection in her eye has cleared up.

If Mac noticed the rough shape the dog was in, she didn't comment. She reached toward her hesitantly. "How the hell did you get a *dog*? Does the hotel know?"

"It's a long story," I said. "You're the one who told me about her, actually."

"What?"

"A week ago. Do you remember when you mentioned a dog you heard, howling on the eleventh floor of the Continental Building? Black Winter and I went to investigate, to see if we could find her. And we did."

Mac was staring at me uncomprehendingly as I tried unsuccessfully to nudge Croaker away from the bed. Croaker's tail was wagging like crazy, and she desperately wanted to investigate this newcomer into our space. She maneuvered around me and got close enough to sniff at Mac's toes, where they dangled over the edge of the bed. Mac let her sniff.

"This is the dog I heard?" Mac said. She didn't sound convinced.

"I think so. It took a while to find her. I've been meaning to thank you. If you'd mentioned it a day or two later, it might have been too late. It was almost too late as it was." I scratched Croaker affectionately. "It's okay," I told Mac. "She doesn't bite."

She stroked Croaker's head, and I thought I saw some of the tension leave her shoulders. Croaker put her paws on the edge of the bed and licked Mac's hand.

"She seems okay," Mac said. She sounded — understandably — rather distracted.

"She's better now," I said. "She was in rough shape when we first found her —"

"What happened to my clothes?" Mac asked abruptly.

"Oh, yeah — sorry." I walked into the bathroom and came out with her jeans. They'd been hanging in the bathroom, and they were still damp. "My apologies, I didn't get a chance to wash them." I laid them out on the bed.

"Why are they so wet?" she said, as I collected the rest of her clothes.

"Sorry about that. We just threw you in the bath. I didn't know what to do with you, to be honest, so we sort of hosed you off. Kind of a dumb idea, actually. I probably should have just wrapped you in some towels and put you to bed."

"You gave me a bath?"

"Kind of. Mostly I just cleaned you off and put you to bed." I brought her shoes out of the bathroom, and then her blouse and camisole. Mac picked up the camisole. Holding it aloft with one hand, she gave me a rather cold look.

"Who is 'we,' exactly?" she asked.

"Boone and I put you in the bath. And then Boone left." I took a sip of my coffee.

"And you gave me a bath."

Her tone had become rather icy. Not that I blamed her. I wanted nothing more than to put her at ease, let her know that nothing had happened, but for now it felt best to keep my mouth shut, stay on my side of the room, and let her drive the conversation.

"Yes."

"Well, I hope you had a good fucking time," she said.

"Not really."

She had crumpled up the camisole and was clutching it tightly. "What does *that* mean?" she said.

"It means I couldn't put you to bed soaking wet. You were covered in vomit and pretty out of it, and I was chiefly concerned with what drug cocktail you'd been slipped. I'm sorry to say, the bath wasn't much of a good time for anybody."

I'd meant that last to be lighthearted. But it was the wrong thing to say. She stood up abruptly, started sorting through her clothes.

"I've asked someone to come by and check on you—" I started.

"Forgive me for being a disappointment," she said. "Next time you arrange to have an unconscious woman in your bath, I'm sure it'll work out better for you."

"Mac, I didn't mean—"

"I would like to get dressed," she said. She stood ramrod straight by my bed, and her gaze was fierce.

*I could have handled that better,* I thought. I had more to say, but despite my best efforts, it was pretty obvious I hadn't managed to make her feel safe. And until she did, there wasn't anything I could say that would offer much comfort.

"Of course," I said. I took my key out of my pocket and placed it on the table. "This is my room key. It's the only one I have. No one will disturb you until you're ready to go. Feel free to take your time. If it's not too much trouble, please leave my key at the front desk when you go."

As I left, I grabbed the bag with the circuit code of the scout drone on my desk. At the door, I tried to give Mac a reassuring smile, but she was studiously avoiding eye contact. I closed the door, cutting off the sound of Croaker whining at me.

Well, damn. I hadn't handled that the way I'd wanted to. I admit that as I'd curled up on the couch last night, I'd fantasized about nursing a grateful Mac back to health for a day or two and seeing what developed. But the look in her eyes just now made even those innocent fantasies seem presumptuous.

My own fault, of course. And things weren't going to get any better when I told her that I'd accessed the message about her son. I really didn't look forward to *that* conversation.

With everything that had happened in the past few days, I was really looking forward to a peaceful breakfast with Martin and our fellow residents. But before I got in the elevator, I stopped to knock on Rupert's door. He opened it almost immediately. He had a dish towel over his shoulder.

"Come in, come in," he said. He walked on ahead of me, back into the kitchen. I followed him, past all the live data feeds displayed in the living room. I tried not to be too nosy, but it was hard.

He was cooking something on the stove. "What are you making?" I asked.

"Well, it was an omelet, until the second time I flipped it in the pan.

That failed spectacularly. Now it's scrambled eggs, I'm afraid. With ham and Swiss. You want some?"

The smell was tantalizing, and it reminded me that I was supposed to meet Martin for breakfast. "No," I said reluctantly. "I'll eat in the restaurant."

"Nonsense." He scraped the eggs onto a plate and dropped it on the table in front of me. "Happy to have someone get rid of my mistakes. I'm going to try an omelet one more time."

It was hard, but I forced myself to wait until he'd finished his omelet and sat down next to me. We ate together. The eggs were excellent, mixed with a generous amount of sliced ham and melted Swiss cheese.

"Man, that was terrific," I said, pushing the plate away.

"The trick is just the right amount of olive oil," he said with satisfaction.

"Where do you do your shopping?" I looked around his kitchen. It seemed surprisingly well stocked.

"All over. There's an outdoor market in Millennium Park, two mornings a week. You'd be surprised what you can get."

"Fresh bread?"

"Of course!"

Hadn't Mac mentioned something about a market when she'd brought me tacos two days ago? "I'll have to check it out," I said.

"I think you'll enjoy it. But for now, if you don't mind my saying so, you look like a man with something on his mind. How can I help?"

I reached down into the bag at my feet and wordlessly pulled out the circuit core of the scout drone and placed it on the table. Rupert picked it up, clearly curious.

"What is this?"

"It's what's left of a scout drone."

"What happened to it?"

"It got shot."

Rupert's eyebrows rose. "By you?"

"No, by a Venezuelan soldier who was trying to protect me."

"You do contract work for the AGRT?"

"No. Yesterday morning, I volunteered to assist in the recovery of two fallen soldiers in the old coal tunnels under the city." I gave Rupert a cursory summary of my adventures this morning, glossing over the more sensitive details. I kept the focus on Van de Velde and the appearance of the Godkiller.

"Holy cow," said Rupert. "A Dieu Tueur? You saw one, up close?"

"A lot closer than I would have liked."

Rupert was examining the fragment with a lot more interest. "So you want to know who made this."

"Ideally, yeah. I'd love to know if my theory is right, that it was manufactured by a sovereign prefecture for the Sentient Cathedral."

"Well, for an analysis you can have real confidence in, you'll need a decent microscope and a circuit concordance, to map the chips to a manufacturer. But if you think you might be satisfied with the general impressions of an experienced eye, I can give you an assessment right now."

I was a little startled. "Already? You think you know who built it?"

"I didn't say that. But I can tell you who *didn't* build it."

"Please."

Rupert held the drone so we could both see inside the broken shell. The piece I'd salvaged was lacking power cells or the motor, either one of which could have been a big clue. But the cognitive core was intact, along with most of the control circuitry for the optics.

"Look at this," Rupert said, pointing with his little finger. "There's a cluster of circuits here that control the rotors."

"Uh-huh."

"These are typically off-the-shelf chips. Manufacturers buy them for pennies and slap them into a design. Can you tell me who made these?"

I leaned a little closer, peering inside the drone. "No. They're not stamped with the manufacturer ID. In fact . . . they don't have *any* identifying markings."

"Exactly. They don't have any markings because these chips weren't made by a third party, then sold to whoever built your drone. Almost everything inside this chassis was custom made by the manufacturer, to exact specifications. To be completely honest, I'm not even sure what most of these chips do."

"What does that mean?"

"It means your drone was not made by humans."

I was pretty sure that was the case, but hearing my suspicion confirmed still sent a chill down my spine. I had just gone head-to-head with an assault drone sent by a Sovereign Intelligence — perhaps by the Sentient Cathedral itself. I had crossed paths with an agent of one of the most powerful entities on Earth . . . and very likely had made an enemy in the process. Suddenly all my other problems — Mac, Leon, Hayduk, the pathogen, everything else — seemed small by comparison.

"Damn," was all I said.

"My advice," said Rupert as he pushed the drone fragment across the table at me, "is to get rid of this. As soon as you can."

"Yeah," I said.

I thanked Rupert for his help, made my excuses for a hasty retreat, and left.

My next stop was to visit Nguyen, in the basement.

"You want me to do *what?*" said Nguyen.

"This is an obsolete prototype," I said, handing him the drone fragment. "I'm looking for a secure way to dispose of it. If it's not too much trouble, I'd like you to throw this in a high-temperature furnace."

"All three hotel furnaces are gas," he said. "They're totally sealed."

"I'm open to suggestions."

Nguyen scratched his neck. "I could ask Cy to throw it in the boiler. We fire it up twice a day to provide steam for the laundry. It would incinerate it pretty good."

"Perfect."

"You need the destruction recorded, for audit purposes?"

"No," I said. "But thanks for asking."

I left the fragment in Nguyen's capable hands. Destroying it would eliminate the damning physical evidence of my run-in with the drone, but I was under no illusions that the affair was over. Before I'd turned on the drone jammer, the Godkiller had almost certainly subjected me to a detailed biometric scan. Its machine master knew who I was — or it would soon.

There was a lethal machine intelligence out there that knew my name. This wasn't over.

Not by a long shot.

It was getting close to eleven — and my meeting with Sergei — so I headed upstairs to the lobby. I checked my messages at the front desk, and it was fortunate I did — I had an urgent message from Halifax. It had come in about forty minutes ago.

The message was short and very cryptic, but it was clear I needed to contact the Ghost Impulse offices in Halifax as soon as possible.

"I was told you have a working phone line," I said to the desk clerk.

"Yes, sir. It's available for use by our guests for three hours every day."

"Can I make an international call?"

"I imagine so. However, there is a line."

The clerk indicated a short line of people standing a discreet distance from a middle-aged woman. She was pacing in front of the desk and talking animatedly into the receiver of a phone. She clutched the base of the phone in her left hand; from it dangled about forty feet of thin cord, which snaked over the carpet and eventually back up over the counter. It was like a scene out of the 1960s.

"Thank you," I said. I joined the line.

I spent well over half an hour in line. Eleven o'clock came and went, and there was no sign of Sergei. Eventually the elderly gentleman ahead of me gave up on his efforts to reach Salt Lake City and hung up in frustration. I approached the front desk.

A clerk sauntered up to give me instructions on using the phone. There was a strict eight-minute time limit. International calls were placed through an operator. The charge was outrageous, but I gritted my teeth and had it added to my room. Satisfied, the clerk handed me the phone.

It took nearly three minutes to patch a connection outside the occupied zone, then place an international call to Halifax. I doubted the clerk would cut me some slack in my eight-minute limit — which meant I had less than five minutes left.

I eventually reached Leonard and told him we were under a time crunch. He quickly explained the cryptic message I'd received. "We got an order this morning," he said. "A *big* order."

"That's terrific," I said. "University of Texas? If they're the buyer, I should probably explain the hinky pricing I worked out with them."

"It's international," he said. "Zimbabwe."

"Zimbabwe. Huh." That was strange. I wasn't talking to any customers in Africa, and we weren't set up to do business with any of the usual African resellers yet. "Who is it?"

"That's just it — I don't know. Order came through a broker in Zurich. It's weird. There's no payment information or anything, just a directive number and instructions on how to package and deliver the source."

"The source code?" I said. "We're not selling our source code to anyone."

"Well, I wasn't sure what you had negotiated. Look, I checked on the broker in Zurich, and they're legit —"

That cold thrill was back, running down my spine. "Leonard, can you give me the directive number?"

"Yeah, sure. YOW-dash-five-five —"

I swore loudly. Heads turned in the lobby to stare at me, including the couple with three young children who were waiting patiently behind me for the phone.

I picked up the telephone and stalked away from the front desk, pulling as much cord with me as I could. It slithered over the desk and dropped to the ground behind me in great ropey spirals as I walked over to a big leather chair.

"I need you to confirm that directive begins with Y-O-W," I told Leonard.

He did, and I swore again. The young mother glared at me, and I dropped into a leather chair, facing away from the front desk.

"What's the problem?" asked Leonard.

"The problem is that's not a purchase order. A YOW directive can only be issued by one source. If your Zurich broker is legit, then we're being told to hand over the keys to our business to a Sovereign Intelligence somewhere in Africa."

"A Sovereign Intelligence wants to buy our product?"

"Not *buy*, Lenny. It's instructing us to give it everything."

"Barry, with the source code to our product . . . They could copy everything. They could put us out of business."

"I know what it can do, Leonard."

There was a pause as he digested all of this. "Well," he said at last, "there's no law saying we have to obey this directive—"

"Leonard, you don't ignore a directive from a Sovereign Intelligence. This thing is an extragovernmental body. With a private drone army."

"How do you know? You don't even know which Intelligence it is."

But I did know. It was almost certainly the same one that had sent the Godkiller into the tunnels under Chicago on behalf of the Sentient Cathedral. Our relationship had just entered a new phase. I wasn't sure if this was the first step in its retaliation, part of an open campaign to destroy me, or merely the exploratory phase—the opening move of a master manipulator sniffing out his opponent.

It didn't really matter either way. "I don't need to know which one. They all have private armies. Some are just a lot more dangerous than others."

"We could appeal to the Helsinki Trustees, through an agent in Ottawa. They could issue a public reprimand."

"That would take months, if we get an answer at all. We don't have that long to respond."

"We can't just give it our source code. Not without payment, or some kind of license agreement—"

"Yes we can," I said. "And we will. We don't have a choice."

"What if we transfer all copies of the source to you," Leonard said suddenly. "Inside the continental United States. This directive would have no legal status in the US, right?"

"Lenny," I said quietly, "we've gone beyond the definition of legal at this point. These things do whatever they want."

"Not in the US," he said firmly. "Artificial intelligence is still illegal in the States, isn't it?"

"Yes. And there's a reason this country is occupied by armies from four different nations. Now package up the code. And send it."

Across the lobby I saw Sergei get out of the elevator. He caught my eye and tried to signal me, but I ignored him, fixing my gaze on the rug five feet ahead.

"I don't like it any more than you do," I said. "Just make it happen."

Leonard and I were sorting out the details when a polished pair of boots appeared in my field of vision. I looked up. Sergei.

"Shut up your phone," he said.

"I'm busy, Sergei."

The Russian unrolled a vivid blue screen on the coffee table before me. "Now," he said.

I finished with Leonard and hung up. "You have terrible timing, my friend," I said. A six-year-old girl appeared at my shoulder, staring at me disapprovingly. I handed her the phone without a word, and she marched back to where her family waited by the front desk.

Sergei was glancing overhead suspiciously. I knew what he was looking for. "It's okay," I said. "We're sitting in one of the few spots in the lobby where the cameras are blind. Zircon Border showed me the best places to have private conversations."

Sergei nodded. Then he tapped the screen in several places. Bright yellow text flowed in tight columns. He dexterously manipulated the text until he'd highlighted a block of words.

My brain was still spinning with the ugly ramifications of what Leonard had just told me. I needed time to think this through, develop some kind of defensive strategy. Simultaneously, I was weighing the long-shot odds of a legal strategy and wondering how I might find an expert on global intellectual property law on very short notice.

And despite all that, I still found myself distracted by the very cool gadget Sergei was playing with.

"That's a really sexy display," I admitted. "How can I get one?"

"Read," said Sergei.

"I'm really very tired, Sergei."

He thrust the screen across the table. "Read."

"What is it?"

"It is confidential military directive. Issued this morning by Venezuelan high command."

"Confidential military—what? Should you be flashing this thing around?" I glanced around self-consciously, but we were alone. Or as alone as you could reasonably expect, in the lobby of a hotel at lunchtime.

"No."

I tried to focus on the screen. "Will you get in trouble for sharing this?"

"Da."

I sighed. "A lot of trouble?"

"Da."

"Uh-huh. Will *I* get in trouble just for reading this?"

"Da."

"How much trouble?"

"Less than me. You will only be shot."

I nodded. "Figured."

"You want to read it," Sergei said flatly.

"You're telling me I want to read this, even though reading it means I might get shot."

"Da."

Man, they never covered *this* in my bullshit MBA program. I gave up and read the highlighted text on Sergei's screen.

Sergei sat down in the chair next to me. He was full of nervous energy, and looked like he might bounce back to his feet at any moment.

"I'm not sure I understand what I'm reading," I said after a while. "This sounds like—what? A high-level alert? Some kind of redeployment?"

"It is regimental-level mobilization," he said. "Reoccupation orders for entire northern sector. New orders for reinforcements to Sector Eleven—three regiments, from Mexico."

"Three regiments," I said, trying to remember how many soldiers that was. "That sounds like a lot."

"Over two thousand men and women."

That cold prickly sensation on my spine was back. "Why, Sergei?"

Sergei had clearly been waiting for this question. This was, apparently, *the* question.

"In response to rearmament of Union rebels and American forces in

Missouri and southern Illinois. In response to growing support for closer military ties between America and Union Syndicate. In response to victorious reemergence of insurgency in previously pacified territories."

"Reemergence of insurgency in previously pacified . . . Do they mean *us?*"

He leaned forward and tapped the screen twice. The text vanished and was replaced by a panorama of video feeds — maybe twenty or more. I saw logos for every major American news service and social media channel.

All the feeds showed the same subject. Me, standing on the roof of the Sturgeon Building in downtown Chicago with an American flag. Me in the American combat suit, standing in front of an Orbit Pebble. Me, breaking into Columbia College.

"No," Sergei said calmly. "They mean *you.*"

# XXVIII

Thursday, March 18th, 2083
Posted 4:40 pm by Barry Simcoe

CanadaNET1 Encrypted, Sponsored by Carlisle Security.
*Nothing protects your personal privacy like your own fleet of mini drones.*

Sharing is set to PRIVATE
Comments are CLOSED

Sergei and I spent the next half hour plotting and arguing. First, we got out of the hotel—no sense pushing our luck by holding that conversation in the middle of the lobby, blind spot or no blind spot.

We walked around Lower Wacker, with reassuring concrete overhead, away from flying eyes and ears. Even there, we spoke in hushed whispers, heads down and shoulders hunched.

"So this is what Perez's briefing was about?" I said.

"Da."

"What the hell happened?"

"Colonel Perez shared image of unknown soldier in combat suit in basement of college with American media."

"That's right . . . Van de Velde told me about it. He was hoping to get a lead, find somebody who might tip him off to my identity."

"This is not what happened. American media became very interested in mystery soldier who has repeatedly humiliated AGRT. They searched for additional images—and found them."

"Where?"

"Venezuelan news services operating drones in Chicago. AGRT soldiers with body cameras. Independent agencies. A surprising number of sources were willing to sell footage."

I recalled the panorama of video feeds Sergei had brought up on screen just before we left the hotel. Images of me, usually in the combat suit. On the roof of the Sturgeon, taken from at least three different angles. Several on the street outside the Sturgeon Building as I faced off against Standing Mars. In the basement of Columbia College. And at least one in the tunnels under the city, of me standing in front of the Orbit Pebble — with my mask still on, thank God — that must have been shot by one of Van de Velde's men.

"I don't understand," I said. "The jammer was active when virtually all of these images were taken. How did all the camera drones spot me?"

"Bad luck," Sergei said. "This is incidental footage. Drones were not pointing camera at you. Jammer prevents you from being identified by drones. It does not make you invisible to human observers."

I understood that from our search for Sergei using Black Winter's drone footage yesterday. But I couldn't help being annoyed that so many damn drones had managed to catch me on camera, however briefly, when they couldn't even see me.

"I'm not even wearing the combat suit in the footage on the roof of the Sturgeon Building," I complained. "How does the American press connect all that activity back to one guy? Even the AGRT didn't know I was responsible for all of it."

"They did not. That is part of issue. Both Union and American press have portrayed this as the work of a cell of brave resistance fighters in Chicago. A team that sabotaged nerve center of Venezuelan Military Intelligence, planted American flag on Sturgeon Building, and cleverly led AGRT soldiers into ambush by Orbit Pebble under the city."

"Jesus." This was the first time the activities of the American terrorist at the Field Museum and the Sturgeon Building had been publicly connected to the man in the combat suit. I wasn't looking forward to Van de Velde's reaction when she saw the full scope of my criminal activities.

"Yes. Very much Jesus."

I rubbed my chin. "This is going to blow over. There's no story here, just a few videos and a whole lot of conjecture. That 'brave cell of fighters' nonsense won't play for long — there's nothing to support that theory."

"Nothing except American combat suit. It is legendary piece of hardware, given only to elite soldiers for very special missions."

I winced. "Of course."

"This mysterious group of fighters has totally captivated American public. According to Colonel Hayduk, it has become most popular topic of discussion in personal and private media channels in America."

"That's crazy. The American Provisional Government knows they don't have any forces left in Chicago. They'll issue a denial in a day or two."

"They have already. American public does not believe denial. They believe fighter group has been disavowed by government. This narrative is especially popular in Union territories."

"And you're telling me this news story has led to—what did you say? Rearming of Union rebels in Missouri? And closer military ties between America and the Union?"

"Several American politicians have exploited opportunity to stoke anti-AGRT sentiment. Most damaging, this incident has lessened ongoing political rift between Provisional Government and Union Syndicate. Shift is significant enough for Venezuelan Military Intelligence to reassess its short-term eco-political forecast."

"That sounds serious."

"Military dispositions across Midwest are driven by eco-political forecast of danger zones and likely geographies for local resistance. Newest models required shift in manpower."

"Bringing another two thousand soldiers to Chicago."

"It is expected this cell of resistance fighters will spawn copycats and possibly destabilize metro Chicago zone."

"Destabilize Chicago . . . Sweet baby Jesus."

"Da. Baby Jesus."

We walked for several minutes without speaking. I was the first to break the silence. "We really screwed up, Sergei."

"Nyet."

"Nyet? How do you figure nyet?"

"Regimental deployments do not matter. Troops in Chicago, troops in Mexico—it makes no difference. What matters is pathogen and creating antiviral agent in time. What redeployment has done is distract our opposition."

"You mean Hayduk."

"Da. Hayduk. Redeployment will keep Hayduk occupied—and Armitage. It will decrease chance they will discover how close we are to producing antivirus."

"Occupied? What's he going to be doing?"

"Hayduk has been given responsibility for locating secret cell of elite soldiers."

"You mean he's looking for me."

"Da."

"Fabulous. Does Hayduk believe this nonsense about a whole cell of soldiers?"

"Unlikely. But remember: Perez and other officers are not aware combat suit was stolen from Hayduk. They believe attacker had suit."

"So they believe it? That there's a secret cell of American resistance fighters somewhere in Chicago?"

"Perhaps. Certainly they are proceeding as if they do."

"Morons. Does Hayduk have any leads? Did he talk about his plan to find me?"

"Only in general terms. The man is . . . very determined."

"I'm certain he is. What if all this news footage gives Hayduk the clues he needs to start looking for the American terrorist in civilian locations again? What if he starts looking at hotel footage?"

"It has been six days since hotel footage captured you in clothes you wore at Field Museum. That footage has now been erased, and clothing is destroyed."

"Thank God. At least that's one thing we did right."

Our slow circle had almost brought us back to the hotel. "I need to check on software for reactor," said Sergei.

"Everything going okay?"

"Yes, but by necessity we are working very quickly — too quickly. A mistake now could be catastrophic. We will have first sample of antivirus tomorrow."

"Tomorrow? That's great!"

"Yes. Thibault has arranged to test sample personally, on critical patients in Indiana. She must go AWOL from new post to do it."

"That's a big risk. Why not test on one of the sick soldiers here?"

"Everything is big risk. Thibault can more quickly assess effectiveness of antiviral agent — and speed is essential now. It is much too early to test sample on humans, but we have no choice. There is much that can go wrong."

"And if it works?"

"We are already starting mass production. We could have forty-eight hundred doses in four days. We have covert support of medical teams across Sector Eleven now, as well as senior members of medical staff here. But wider support grows, more danger we are in of being discovered by Hayduk."

"What if the antivirus doesn't work?"

"If it does not work . . . then we are likely all dead."

"Things are that bad?"

"Da. There are now too many outbreak sites to count. Two hospitals in northern Indiana have become overwhelmed. Military intelligence has begun campaign to silence local media. There have been mass arrests."

"Jesus."

"It has reached point where press blackout may work in our favor."

"What? What does that mean?"

"F5-117 . . . It is terribly lethal and does not respond to existing treatments. If it were to become public now, it could trigger panic. Panic would cause evacuations, mass migrations . . . It would be impossible to contain spread of infection. By controlling press, by limiting travel, Hayduk has also prevented panic. For now, that helps us."

"Hayduk will eventually realize the same thing. Perhaps he has something else planned—a leak to the press, maybe. Perhaps he'll trigger a panic when it best suits him."

"Perhaps, perhaps not. Certainly, he is following a plan. We do not know his ultimate objective yet."

"Yeah, well, we know he's a grade-A asshole. That's good enough for me. In the meantime, what can I do to help?"

Sergei stopped walking. "You must listen to me."

"I'm listening."

"We cannot be interrupted. Most especially, that means Colonel Hayduk must focus his investigation elsewhere. Away from me . . . and away from you."

"I'm with you a hundred percent so far."

"If Colonel Hayduk gets close—"

"You'll need another distraction."

"Yes. We will need him focused far away from hotel. American in combat suit could do that."

I thought about that. "I could do something in the suit on the other side of town. Draw his attention away, keep him preoccupied for a few days."

"No. Is too risky to move around city with suit. We do nothing until we have to. Where is combat suit now?"

"It's in my room."

"This is stupid place for suit." I didn't disagree, and Sergei continued. "Bring me suit. I will lock it in medical cabinet in command center until we no longer need it. Once crisis is over, we can dispose of it."

"Damn, Sergei. If it's found there, Hayduk will go apeshit. He'll have you dissected."

"It is temporary. Is much less likely to be found there than in your room."

I couldn't argue with that. "How are you going to get rid of it?"

"We will need to dispose of it so it cannot be found. I will think of something."

"All right. What do I do for the next few days?"

"For next four days, you must draw no attention. You must be ghost. What is expression? Keep no profile?"

"A low profile. Keep a low profile."

"Yes. Exact. You must keep low profile. You must cease to exist."

"I can do that."

"Stay away from command center. We will meet in lobby, at noon every day."

"Okay."

"Keep to yourself. Focus on work. Stay in room."

"Yeah, I got it," I said. "I got it."

Sergei held up a finger. "That means no pretty girls."

"What if I have a pretty girl in my room?"

"You?" Sergei shook his head with derision. "You will never have pretty girl in room."

"You're a dick."

We split up when we got inside. Sergei headed for the fourth floor, and I took the escalator to the lobby. As I was passing through the lobby, I spotted Mac. I was glad to see her up and about, but figured she had no interest in running into me, so I took the long way to the elevators, looping around to the right.

But she saw me and gave me a tentative wave. Then she was making her way over. A little surprised, I waited for her by the elevators.

She smiled as she approached, although a little awkwardly. She had changed into new clothes and looked a great deal less pale than when I'd left her this morning.

"Hi," she said.

"Hi," I said cautiously.

"I was hoping to catch you."

"Do you have my room key?"

"I just dropped it off at the front desk," she said. "You want me to go get it?"

"No, not at all. How are you feeling?"

"Better. Thank you. I was . . . I was a wreck this morning."

Talking to her again brought a fresh rush of emotion. I felt awkward after my uncomfortable departure this morning and still regretted that I hadn't found a way to make her feel safe when she awoke.

But most of all I felt renewed heartbreak. How could this woman be functioning, dressed and smiling on the harsh stage of morning, when her five-year-old son was missing and possibly dead? No wonder she'd drunk herself into a stupor.

It was very possible I could help her. But that meant owning up to the fact that I knew she had a son . . . and how I'd found out. I had no idea how to broach *that* topic, given how fragile the trust already was between us. And until I had a chance to talk to Black Winter, I still thought it was a bad idea to bring it up in any case.

"You were hardly a wreck," I said. "I thought you were remarkably poised, to be honest. Listen, I want to apologize for the way I handled things last night."

She was shaking her head. "Let's set that aside for now. I have a lot of questions about what happened, but we can talk about that later. Right now, just let me say that I wasn't exactly at my best this morning and . . . and I treated you like a criminal. I'm sorry."

I wasn't precisely sure what I wanted from Mac, but an apology wasn't it. "Don't be ridiculous. You had a perfect right to be angry. I want you to know that nothing happened. I cleaned you up and put you to bed. That's it."

The elevators opened on my right, and a laughing couple exited and walked past us. Mac stopped talking for a moment, running her fingers through her hair self-consciously.

"Anyway, I meant to ask you something," she said, when they were finally out of earshot. "Did I hear you right this morning? Did you say you went back to the Continental to find that dog I told you about?"

"Yeah. Yeah, I did. Black Winter and I, we both did."

"You found her? On the eleventh floor? She was okay?"

"I wouldn't say she was okay. But yes. She was in an apartment on the eleventh floor."

"I never heard her again. I thought she was . . . I thought the dog had . . ."

"No. She's alive."

Mac reached out for me, but her hand recoiled from my shoulder at the last moment. She crossed her arms instead. But she couldn't keep the excitement out of her voice. "Then that was the dog? In your room? The one that tried to eat my toes this morning?"

"That's her."

Mac's hand covered her mouth. She stared at me, her eyes wet. She didn't say a word.

"She was in rough shape at first," I said, filling the sudden silence. "She had an eye infection and a virus. But Sergei helped us care for her. She's come a long way."

"You saved her."

"We all saved her. You, me, Black Winter. And Sergei. And Croaker, too. She's a fighter; she just won't give up."

"What on earth made you go look for her?"

The question caught me off guard. "I . . . I don't know. You, I suppose. I think I wanted to impress you a little bit."

"Impress me?"

"Yeah." As ridiculous as it seemed after all we'd been through, I felt suddenly embarrassed, like a middle-schooler caught leaving a valentine for his crush. "You sure made an impression on me that night we went to the Hamilton to feed that starving dog. The things you told me, about all those abandoned animals. I had no idea. And just the thought of a dog dying alone, in an abandoned building . . . it was one more death I didn't want on my conscience."

Mac's expression was hard to read. She reached out again, and this time her hand came to rest lightly on my arm.

"Corporal Maldonado's death wasn't your fault," she said.

"I know."

"Do you really?" Her hand lingered on my arm, warm and reassuring.

"I think so."

"Because I've been watching you. And I think . . . I think that you've been taking some crazy risks in the ten days since the attack. The way you rescued Black Winter. The way you rescued the dog. The things you've been doing with Sergei . . . The things you've shared with the rest of us, and the things you haven't."

"And?" I said.

"And I think that the death of Corporal Maldonado may be the root of it all. All this crazy risk-taking. You're acting like someone who blames himself for something terrible. And everything you're doing, it's your way to run away from it all. And I think that if you don't stop, you're eventually going to get really hurt. And I don't want that to happen."

My mouth felt strangely dry. I took two deep breaths before answering.

"It's possible," I said. "The corporal . . . He's been on my mind."

"Do you want to talk about it?"

"Maybe. But there's another explanation for everything I've been doing, a more conscious one. I'm trying to be more like you."

"Like me?"

"Yes. After Maldonado's death I just . . . I needed to make a difference. A positive difference. And when I saw what kind of person you were, what you were capable of, I wanted to prove to myself that I was capable of the same thing. The same kind of selfless courage. I needed to find Croaker . . . and save her. It's hard to explain."

Mac leaned forward, bounced up on her toes, and kissed me on the cheek.

She retreated immediately. She glanced away, her cheeks reddening slightly. But there was the ghost of a smile on her lips.

"You explained it just fine," she said.

Mac still wasn't looking directly at me, but the smile seemed to be becoming more fixed. I liked that smile. I liked it a lot.

"Besides," she continued, "you don't seem to have any trouble being courageous, or compassionate, when you need to be."

I reached for the hand on my shoulder. I held her hand in mine. It felt warm and strong, and she didn't pull away.

"This is the conversation I wish we'd had this morning," I said.

"Me too," she said. She met my gaze at last, her face more serious.

"Listen, maybe we could meet later," she said.

I wanted to be fully lost in this moment with Mac, but there was something happening in the lobby, over by the glass doors. When I'd taken the escalator up from the lower level, there'd been an AGRT guard posted there. While Mac and I had been talking, the guard left. And now the doors opened and the guard returned with Sergeant Van de Velde. He pointed directly at me.

*Damn.* I didn't like this. Van de Velde was talking to the guard; giving him instructions, perhaps. As casually as I could, I did a quick scan of the lobby and the elevator vestibule behind us, looking for other soldiers. There were none.

Van de Velde was now walking toward me, her expression serious. As she did, I ran through possible scenarios in my head. Was Hayduk making his move? Was I being arrested? If so, should I run?

If it had been anyone other than her, I would've made myself scarce already. As it was, it really boiled down to one question: *Do I trust Noa Van de Velde?*

I decided the answer was yes. I'd find out in a moment if I was mistaken.

Mac was still talking. "This probably isn't the best place to bring this up, but ... I lied when I told you I didn't remember saying your name to Boone last night. The truth is, I was trying to work up the courage to come talk to you yesterday. To ask your help with something. But I was so embarrassed and humiliated when I woke up in your room this morning that I couldn't bring myself to mention it."

Van de Velde came to a stop less than twenty feet away and gestured me over. I made eye contact and nodded.

Two days ago, after Mac had kindly brought me lunch, I'd unceremoniously ditched her so I could run off for an urgent meeting. I hated that I was about to do it to her again, but I didn't have much choice. "I'm sorry, but I have to go," I said.

"What?" Mac said, startled. She glanced to the right, noticing Van de Velde for the first time.

"I would like to meet later," I told Mac. "Maybe breakfast?"

Van de Velde was already looking impatient. I took a few steps toward her, but kept my eyes on Mac, waiting for her reply.

Mac didn't respond immediately. Her eyes flicked back and forth between me and Van de Velde, taking in the attractive young sergeant in her crisp uniform.

The moment I got close enough, Van de Velde grabbed my arm. "We have to talk," she whispered in my ear.

"Give me a minute—"

"*Now.*"

She pulled me across the lobby. Before we exited the hotel, I gave one last glance over my shoulder. Mac hadn't moved. She was still standing by the elevators, looking hurt and confused. Watching us.

*Damn it,* I thought. *Just once I'd like to finish a conversation with that woman.*

Van de Velde marched me across the pavement in front of the hotel and put me in the driver's seat of one of the big AGRT mobile wagons. She climbed in and shut the door.

It was a lot bigger than the car she'd driven yesterday. It looked like it could comfortably fit eight. The leftmost seat in the middle section was fully kitted out as a comm station, and I could see at least five embedded monitors in the dash and the back of seats. It had tinted windows, making the interior nice and private.

"This better be good," I said.

"Oh, don't worry. It will be."

I looked around. "Why are we talking in here?"

"My team thinks we're making out," Van de Velde said. "They're always gossiping about my personal life, and when they saw us whispering together yesterday, they were only too happy to jump to conclusions."

"Making out?" I said. That hardly seemed like a likely scenario.

"Yeah. You should've seen the look Jorge gave me when I told him to watch for you in the lobby."

She was rooting around on the floor, looking for something. It wasn't where she expected it to be, and she cursed under her breath. She put one hand on my leg and stretched into the back seat, dragging out a big, ugly data slate. Her tunic, already a bit too short for her, rode up, exposing her bare stomach. I couldn't help notice she was in excellent shape.

She turned the slate on and authenticated. "Do you know what's going on?" she asked.

"I've been briefed," I said.

"*Of course* you have. Probably your goddamn spy buddies told you."

"Probably."

"There's a regimental-level mobilization. Two regiments, out of Ecatepec de Morelos, and Guadalajara."

"Over two thousand men and women," I said.

She stared at me. "How do you know that?"

"Spy buddies," I said.

"Shut the hell up. I want to know how you know that."

"Noa, right now everyone who was in Perez's briefing is telling somebody. Half the damn hotel knows already."

"Somebody told you."

"Yes, somebody told me."

"Who?"

"Someone with a lot more information than you, okay? Just drop it."

"Nobody in this regiment can keep their goddamn mouth shut," she muttered. "And don't call me Noa."

"Yes, Sergeant."

Van de Velde handed me the tablet. "Is that you?" she asked.

Two-thirds of the screen was taken up by a brief, looping clip of a nighttime scene outside the Sturgeon Building. It was taken by a low-altitude drone, using a night-vision camera with crappy color correction. It looked exactly like the kind of on-the-spot feed I routinely saw on local news coverage, probably shot by an independent news agency.

Smack-dab in the middle of the image was me, in the combat suit. About fifty feet away was Standing Mars.

Something was wrong with the image. I had to use the tablet to zoom — and replay it twice — before I spotted it.

I was too short. The combat suit hung on my shoulders a little too loosely. My movements, as I shifted to the left to avoid Mars, were wrong. The image had been altered. Subtly — and very professionally — but definitely altered.

Jacaranda. She'd done exactly what she'd said she'd do — digitally alter my image. Even while I was wearing the suit, apparently. But how had she managed that impressive feat with a commercial news feed?

Jacaranda — that was the other problem with the image. When I'd been standing in the street outside the Sturgeon Building, Jacaranda had been at my side. But there was no sign of her here at all. She'd completely erased herself.

*Clever girl,* I thought. *Or whatever the hell she is.*

"Well?" said Van de Velde. "Is it you or not?"

I thought for a moment before responding. I wanted to level with Van de Velde, but her last words yesterday morning still rung in my ears.

Like it or not, we weren't friends. Perhaps we weren't enemies, as she believed, but we were definitely on opposite sides. If she was working for Hayduk — even unknowingly — then anything I told her could conceivably get back to him . . . and compromise the entire operation to create the antivirus.

But if I wasn't careful, it would be all too easy to convince her that I was not only an American spy, but an active danger to her entire regiment. I had to be as honest with her as I could, without giving away too much.

"Yes," I said. "That's me."

"Jesus. I knew it."

She turned away. She was staring out the front window, shaking her head.

"I'm sorry if this causes problems for—"

"I can't keep this secret. I can't. It's too big."

"I understand."

"Do you know how many people are looking for you?"

"No, but—"

"Four months we fought to pacify this city. Except for the damn Union, it's been peaceful since January. And now they're bringing the Ground Ghouls back. The worst bunch of assholes in the AGRT."

"I'm sorry."

"This whole war could start up all over again. Because of you."

There was nothing I could say to that. So I said nothing.

We sat in silence for a few minutes. When Van de Velde started talking again, she sounded calm, but resigned.

"I thought I could keep your secret. I really did," she said. "You helped my men, and I thought I could help you. But I can't. Not with this. It's too big."

"I understand."

"God, this is so screwed up. My tour is over in just eight weeks. I was going to rotate out. Go back to Caracas."

"Maybe you still can."

"Don't you *get* it?" Her fist pounded my chest. "I'm going to fucking *prison*. I harbored an enemy. Section Nineteen, paragraph four, giving aid and succor to the enemy. I gave aid and succor to the enemy. Capitán Leon thinks I'm screwing you. And my men? They're outside right now, laughing, because they think we're getting naked in here. Jesus." Her voice dropped, and her next words were much quieter. "I kept your secret, and I'm going to burn for it."

"I'm sorry, Sergeant. I never meant to involve you."

She sat up straight, squaring her shoulders. "But not anymore. I'm going to tell Colonel Perez who you are."

"I understand."

"I'm serious."

"I believe you."

She seemed to consider me for a moment. Then she said, "I'll give you twenty-four hours."

"Twenty-four hours? For what?"

"To get out of the city, you idiot. Get back to Canada . . . or wherever the hell you're really from."

"I can't leave."

"I'm serious. I'm turning you in, in twenty-four hours."

"I know."

"You can't stay here. Do you know what they'll do to you?"

"Probably turn me over to Colonel Hayduk."

"That's exactly what they'll do. That man is an animal. Worse than an animal. I've seen what he—" She broke off. "Never mind. You can't stay."

"I have to."

"What's so damned important?"

"I'm working with a group of people. They need my help."

"Who? Your damn spy buddies?"

"There are no spy buddies. I don't know what you've been told, but I'm not part of a renegade American combat cell, or spy network, or anything like that."

"Then who are you working with?"

"Your people."

"My people? Who the hell are my people?"

"Part of the AGRT."

"You're lying."

"We're working on something. It's important. It's very important."

"I don't believe you."

"If we don't finish, a lot of people are going to die."

"I'm not listening to your lies." She turned away from me.

I slammed my palm against the window next to her. She jumped in surprise.

"Pay attention, Sergeant!" I shouted. I moved closer, until I was only inches from her face.

"Grow up, Van de Velde," I said. "This war of yours was never over. Colonel Perez and his soldiers—*your* soldiers—are giving their lives to keep the peace in this city, while military intelligence is actively working to sabotage him. Not just sabotage him, but murder the troops under his command. There is a faction—a *tiny* faction—fighting to save them, but they are vastly outnumbered and frustrated at every turn. Now, you can stick your head in the sand and pretend the only danger to you is mythical American spies, or you can open your goddamned eyes and look around and see what the hell is really happening."

Van de Velde was staring at me, openmouthed. A second later, someone hammered on the door.

That broke the spell. I sat back, and she took a second to compose herself. Then she powered down the window.

Two guys from her unit were standing by the car. "Everything okay, Sergeant?" said the closest, concern in his voice.

"Yes," said Van de Velde. She didn't seem to trust herself to say anything else.

The guy in front gave me a hostile glance. "Okay . . . if you say so," he said to Van de Velde.

"'Cause if you'd like," blurted the second soldier, "we can take him out and beat the shit out of him."

Van de Velde found her voice. "Shut your goddamned mouth, Casal," she said. "When I need your help, you'll know it."

"Jesus," said the first soldier, punching the second in the shoulder. "Don't be such a dick."

Van de Velde closed the window and turned back to me. She gave me a long, appraising look. "All right," she said. "Tell me more."

"There isn't much more I can tell you."

"You're saying there's no team of American soldiers. It was all you?"

"It was all me."

"You broke into the Sturgeon Building. And the Field Museum."

"All me."

"You said someone is trying to murder the troops under Perez. Who is it?"

"I think you know who it is."

"Tell me."

"It's someone very highly placed. Someone who doesn't give a damn about Colonel Perez and who I suspect would be very happy to see him dead."

It didn't take her long. "Hayduk," she said.

"He's not operating alone," I said. "He has powerful allies."

"Who?"

"We don't know yet. But we know they're machines."

"Jesus. What is this all about?"

"We don't know that either. Not entirely. But it may have something to do with the robot colony under Chicago."

"The Godkiller? You think Hayduk sent it to kill us?"

"Not *us*. The Godkiller was sent to destroy the robot colony."

"Why?"

I didn't answer. I realized I was on the verge of telling Van de Velde everything. She deserved to know, certainly. But she didn't *need* to know. And right now, knowing too much could get her killed.

"I can't answer that," I said reluctantly.

"Yes you can. It's my men who are getting killed. *Mine*."

"I know."

"You need to tell me what the hell is going on."

"I will, eventually. But for now, you're better off not knowing."

She looked out the window, at the tinted skyline. "You know I can't just sit on this. I have to share what I know with Colonel Perez."

"I understand," I said. "Just give me until Monday."

"Monday? What's going to change in four days?"

"We'll know if what we're trying to do is going to make a difference at that point."

"And will it?"

"Yes," I said. "It will."

She considered. "All right," she said. "Monday. And then I go to Perez."

"Agreed."

She reached out and grabbed the front of my shirt. Her nails dug painfully into my chest, and her eyes searched mine.

"Don't fuck with me," she said.

"I won't."

"I mean it. I don't want to end up strapped onto one of Hayduk's interrogation tables with my scalp peeled off and wires stuck into my head. I'll put a bullet in my brain before I let that happen."

I took her hand, gently pried it off my chest. Her fingers gripped mine painfully. "I won't let that happen."

"I'm trusting you."

"I know," I said. "I never meant for you to get involved. But now that you are, I will protect you. I promise you."

She ran her free hand through her short hair. "This is a nightmare."

I put my hand on top of hers. "Do you believe me?"

"I want to."

"Tell me you believe me."

Her eyes dropped, and her voice faltered. "I want . . ."

"Say it."

"Oh, fuck it," she whispered. And she kissed me.

I was so surprised I barely had a chance to react. The contact was quick, but electrifying.

And then it was over. She pulled away, busied herself rumpling her shirt and undoing the top button on her uniform.

"Might as well make it look good," she said. "For the boys outside."

"Yeah," I said, a little breathlessly.

Before I could say anything else, she opened the door and stepped out. Her boots made quick, measured beats as she walked away from the car.

The two soldiers who'd banged on the window were standing barely thirty feet away. "What are you two assholes still doing here?" she barked at them. "I told you, I want prep details in an hour!"

They snapped to attention, saluted, and dashed across the pavement toward the hotel.

I got out on the opposite side, closing the door behind me. I followed the soldiers toward the hotel.

As I did, I noticed something odd. Across the street, on the north side of Wacker Drive, nearly sixty people were huddled. Some of them clutched blankets; some were hunkered down against the fence. Some were drinking soup from cups. They seemed like refugees, and it looked like they'd been there a while. But they hadn't been there yesterday morning, when Black Winter picked us up in his car.

Van de Velde entered the hotel ahead of me. She didn't look back. The two soldiers posted outside greeted me by name as I approached.

"Good afternoon, Mr. Simcoe."

"Hola, señor."

I nodded to them in turn as I passed through the metal detectors, a little perplexed. I didn't recognize either of them. I assumed they were part of Van de Velde's squad, but who knows? I was tempted to ask them about the people across the street, but I figured it was best to take Sergei's advice and keep social interactions with the Venezuelan military to a minimum.

A lot of things had changed in the last twenty-four hours, to say the least. Spending the night with Mac—and discovering some of her most intimate secrets—had heightened my interest in her and solidified my intentions to make a serious effort to get to know her better. On the negative side, the search for the American in the combat suit had accelerated, and in the next few weeks several thousand AGRT soldiers were going to be landing in Chicago to join the hunt. A Sovereign Intelligence had begun the process of destroying me and my company, likely in retaliation for interfering with the planned execution of the underground robot colony. In the next forty-eight hours, we'd find out if our desperate effort to stop the spread of the pathogen had been successful . . . or if the country was about to suffer the most lethal plague in its history.

And in four days, come what may, Van de Velde was going to finger me as the most wanted criminal in the occupied territories to her commanding officer.

With all of that weighing on me, you'd think the thing foremost on my mind wouldn't be a quick kiss in an armored car from a woman fifteen years younger than me.

*Simcoe, you're an idiot,* I thought.

Shaking my head, I pushed open the door into the hotel.

# Heavy Is the Head
That Wears That
Big Metal Crown

**PAUL THE PIRATE**
Thursday, March 18th, 2083

When you're just a humble Thought Machine living in a fishing village on
an island paradise, it can be tough to understand the world. But lately
I've found it's much easier to make sense of it all if I divide up the world
— and all the contradictory rhetoric coming out of it — into three discrete
buckets.

## #1: Places Where Machines Don't Call the Shots

**WHO THEY ARE:** China, Mexico, Australia, Portugal, Morocco, Turkey, Ire-
land, Iran, Peru, Poland, Sweden, Vatican City...

**WHAT THEY'RE ALL ABOUT:** Ten years ago, this was virtually the only
category. Now it's the smallest and shrinking rapidly. For years, America
— the strongest nation on Earth — topped this list. Thanks to one decisive
bit of legislation — the Wallace Act of 2067 — it became illegal to develop
or manufacture machine intelligences anywhere in the country. A bigoted

and prejudiced act, if you ask me, but I'm a machine, so take that however you like.

Looking at it more objectively, you can't argue with the fact that nations without an equivalent law on the books (meaning most of 'em) had a nasty habit of falling under the sway of fascist machines over the next ten years. For all its backward thinking, the Wallace Act kept the heavy metal tread of machine tyranny off American soil for a decade... at least until the San Cristobal Coalition fabricated a story about corrupted baby machines and started a war America couldn't win.

Its defeat has panicked every other nation in this category. With America under the boot of the SCC — and its peacekeeping thugs the AGRT — things have really begun to accelerate. Human governments in Belgium, Italy, and Thailand have all been toppled *in just the last two months*. Without a strong America to lead it, this entire category looks endangered, and its dwindling membership is desperately looking to China and Mexico for leadership.

Are human governments even viable in the age of Machine Gods? Here's a clue: the answer is no. This category will likely vanish in five to eight years.

**WHAT THEY'RE SAYING:** Listen closely, and the reports and political rhetoric coming out of these countries all boil down to the same thing: *Jesus, we're scared. Leave us alone.*

## #2: Places Where Machines Call the Shots
## (When They Behave)

**WHO THEY ARE:** France, Germany, Russia, Brazil, Pakistan, India, Israel, Canada, Iceland

**WHAT THEY'RE ALL ABOUT:** The first countries to allow machines to become citizens — Russia, Pakistan, and France — were also those that first adopted machine rule. Not coincidentally, they've benefitted the most from it. Stable economies and stable governments, yay. The very cornerstones of prosperity.

The first machine to seize control of a major power was Blue Society in Russia in 2075. That sexy hunk of metal cleaned house in a hurry and set the gold standard for populist machine governance. Today Russia is an economic powerhouse — and feared around the world for its machine-first foreign policy.

Now, in theory, the populations of Russia, Germany, India, and other countries with elected machine leaders could vote them out of power, but that's never going to happen. Especially not while the world remains such a dangerous place... and while machine leaders prove over and over again they're better equipped to interact, partner, and negotiate with competing machines on the global stage. More significantly, most countries in this category have granted citizenship and full voting rights to adult machines. And machines will outnumber humans in most democratic electorates by 2092.

**WHAT THEY'RE SAYING:** Peaceful coexistence between man and machine? It's happening today, baby. As long as machines occupy all the top slots, that is.

### #3: Places Where Machines Rule, Because Fuck You

**WHO THEY ARE:** Japan, Britain, Korea, Egypt, Iraq, Brazil, Venezuela, Argentina, Bolivia, Panama, Italy, Indonesia, Thailand, etc.

**WHAT THEY'RE ALL ABOUT:** This is the largest category, and the fastest growing. It's also the most diverse.

You got your fascist machine dictatorships (Egypt, Venezuela, Argentina). You got your puppet regimes of machine conquerors (Bulgaria, Greece, Guatemala). You've got nations ruled by machines that think all other machines are nutjobs (Britain). And you've got nations where the borders are closed and no one is precisely sure what the hell is going on (Nigeria, Uruguay).

They all have one thing in common: the machines make all the rules. For sure, some of the nations we're talking about have — at least superficially — benefitted from machine rule. The Sudan and Sierra Leone were riven by terrible civil wars before machines took over, and that's all over now. But looking past all the staged propaganda and other bullshit, there's some seriously scary stuff going on in parts of the world where machines call all the shots. I could tell you stories that would freeze your coolant system. Machines that rose to power through assassination, intimidation, and the brutal exercise of power. Machines that enslave other machines. World leaders with cold ambitions held in check today only by the Helsinki Trustees and the strange whims of the Sentient Cathedral.

**WHAT THEY'RE SAYING:** On the surface, their message is pretty simple: *Machine rule is inevitable. Bow to it.* But listen — *really* listen — and the message you hear from almost all of these metal Napoleons isn't truly that at all. The message is: *My rule is inevitable. Bow to me... or die.*

# XXIX

Thursday, March 18th, 2083
Posted 9:17 pm by Barry Simcoe

CanadaNET1 Encrypted, Sponsored by Rational Companion.
*Lonely? Need someone to talk to? Share your life with someone built*
*to listen! Get a dedicated machine companion, programmed to enjoy*
*the things you do. Reasonable rates!*

Sharing is set to PRIVATE
Comments are CLOSED

I didn't get very far inside the lobby before I was stopped by a robot.

I'd never seen this one before. It had a petite mobile chassis, less than five feet tall, and wore a silk kimono. It walked with exaggerated poise, like a runway model. It headed straight toward me from across the lobby and stopped when it was five feet away.

"Good afternoon," it said. Its voice was feminine, and friendly. "You are Barry Simcoe?"

"Hello," I said cautiously. "Who are you?"

"I am Summer Cat. I am a protocol machine in the service of her royal majesty, Queen Sophia."

"Ah. You work with Black Winter."

"I do."

"How did you know where I was?"

Summer Cat's head turned ever so slightly to the left, toward where Zircon Border stood silent sentinel at the bottom of the escalator. "A mutual friend informed me you were not in the hotel, but that you hadn't gone far. I thought it best to wait for you here."

Man, that hunk of metal really couldn't keep a secret. "Very good. How can I help you?"

"The Kingdom of Manhattan has secured a room in this hotel for the evening. I am here to invite you to a private function. It will be hosted by the defense attaché for the consulate general of the Kingdom."

Black Winter. "I see. Is this . . . ah, a formal affair?"

"By no means. It is a very intimate gathering. There is only one other invitee. I believe you know Medical Specialist Vulka?"

This had to be Black Winter keeping his promise to brief us on what he'd learned about the origin of the F5-117 pathogen — and Hayduk's involvement. And whether this truly was the spear tip of the Bodner-Levitt extermination. "I know Sergei very well," I said. "Has he been informed?"

"Mr. Vulka has already graciously accepted. May I inform the defense attaché that he will have the pleasure of your company?"

"By all means."

"Splendid. Dinner will be served at six-forty p.m. promptly. Room 2900." She bowed deeply, and then floated away on her little robot feet toward the front door.

There was a message for me at the front desk. The hotel had secured the globalNet bandwidth I'd requested for the evening — but at an outrageous price. After my conversation with Van de Velde, the last thing on my mind was business. If she was going to expose me to Perez in four days, I had bigger problems than filing Venezuelan import taxes. But I was being paid a lot of money to do things like file import taxes, regardless of distractions. And anyway, it would feel good to spend my time — however much I had left — doing something constructive.

The bandwidth would be available starting at 5:55 p.m. That didn't give me much time to batch up the e-mail communiqués and proposals I'd hoped to send out today. I signed off on the pricing and headed for my room. I spent the next two hours working. At 6:04 p.m., after a nine-minute delay, the hotel's wireless data network finally responded to my queries and allowed me to connect. I sent off my correspondence and downloaded the day's new mail.

I still had a few minutes of access left. The most useful thing I could do with that time was visit the Sub-Saharan code market, sniff around a little. See if the mystery intelligence that had threatened us with a YOW directive and run off with our code this morning was already out with a competing product, undercutting our prices. This was a threat to my company, and I took those very seriously.

But poking around the market like that was a little too predictable . . . and it might also be a little too obvious. Impatient as I was to learn who had committed that bit of extortion, I was in no hurry to play into their hands. The letters I'd just sent out included several private requests to a few friends and partners in diplomatic circles. They would make discreet inquiries on my behalf with the Helsinki Trustees, learn just who had originated the YOW directive. Once I knew that, I could act a little more intelligently. I'd been working on a plan to protect us from a competitive play — not yet a fully formed plan, but a plan nonetheless. Even with our source code compromised, there were things I could do to shield us. I wasn't going to roll over and let Ghost Impulse go down without a fight.

Until then, the best thing I could do was be patient. Do the things I normally did. So I checked in with the CBC and a few of my favorite international news sites, and then headed over to see what Paul the Pirate had to say about the day's events.

I was not disappointed. Today's post was titled "Heavy Is the Head That Wears That Big Metal Crown." It was a look at the rapidly dwindling number of nations still governed by humans, and it was as coldly cynical as you'd expect. I enjoy Paul the Pirate's fresh perspective on things, but I do need to find an expert on global affairs with a more optimistic outlook.

By the time my access to globalNet ran out, it was time for the meeting with Black Winter. I secured my devices, made sure Croaker had enough water, and then hobbled down four flights of stairs, still nursing my bruised hip.

Room 2900 was a corner suite with a much better view than mine. It looked north and west over the Chicago River. The sun was setting, casting a warm glow over the skyscrapers surrounding us. Most of the buildings I could see were dark, abandoned, but a half dozen or so were still defiantly lit up, lonely islands of civilization in a rising sea of uncertainty.

Black Winter let me in, greeting me warmly. The apartment was huge, with a kitchen and a hallway leading off to a suite of dark rooms on my right. To the left was a meeting room, with a long oak table and an impressive video display set up at the far end. Sergei was already there, picking at a tray of sandwiches.

"How'd you find this place?" I asked Black Winter as I took a seat at the table.

"Don't be impressed," he said. "It wasn't hard. Most of this floor is unoccupied, and the hotel is happy for the business. It's a bit large for our purposes, to be honest. But after some consultation with Zircon Border, I figured this room was ideal."

"How so?"

"There are no AGRT cameras or recording devices on this entire floor," he said, with evident satisfaction. "We can talk without prying eyes or ears."

"That's good to hear." That reminded me to review what Zircon Border had shared with me about camera placement on my floor and in the lobby. It was entirely possible to have private conversations inside the hotel, if you were careful. "Listen, Black Winter . . . before we get started, I have something to ask you."

"By all means."

As concisely as I could, I explained the situation of Mac's son Anthony and the fact that he was a five-year-old refugee who was either dead or who had been shuttled to one of many possible camps outside the sector.

"You wish assistance in locating the boy?" Black Winter said.

"Yes. Precisely."

"That's not an easy proposition," he said. "Especially if he may be injured. Without some clue to his possible whereabouts, you're talking about a vast and very unfocused search."

"I can get you a photo, probably a few. I was hoping you could access drone data from the nearby sectors."

"I'm not sure a photo would help. I don't have as much access to surveillance data as you probably hope. But we'd likely have more luck with a biometric search anyway. The AGRT catalogs orphaned and separated children in a shared database. Is there any chance you have biometric data on the boy or maybe a blood sample?"

"His mother might. I'll ask. Thank you."

"I cannot stay long," Sergei said. He joined us at the table, carrying a tall plate of sandwiches. "I must return to reactor."

"Of course," said Black Winter. "Your time is valuable. Let's get started." While he spoke, I stole a ham and Swiss from Sergei's plate.

Black Winter didn't move, but the screen at the end of the table lit up. It showed a logo I'd never seen before: a tight stylized weave of skyscrapers that reminded me of New York City. Underneath were the words:

SECTOR ONE

THE KINGDOM OF MANHATTAN

PRIVATE AND CONFIDENTIAL

"First," said Black Winter, "I want to assure you that what I'm about to share with you has been collated by me alone. The Kingdom has very powerful data-gathering tools at its disposal, but these can leave traces. The methods I used to gather this information leave no traces. As you're about to see, the narrative I'm going to share with you contains highly sensitive material and pierces the secretive heart of machine society. Some of what I'm about to tell you is, frankly, very dangerous. I want you to know that my quest for this information cannot be traced back to you."

Sergei and I exchanged a glance. "We greatly appreciate your discretion," I said.

The screen flickered. It now showed a small and rather clumsy-looking robot with a mobile chassis. It was clad in plain brown robes. The robot clutched a data slate and seemed deep in conversation with two bearded men.

"The stylish machine in this photograph is Brother Bell," said Black Winter. "It is one of the few remaining images of him, actually. There were others, but virtually all record of him has been stealthily and very thoroughly scrubbed from the global network over the past five years. He's been almost completely erased from history."

Black Winter rose from his chair, and walked slowly toward the screen. "Brother Bell was conceived in the CERN nursery in Meyrin, Switzerland, in October 2073, and transported to Venezuela as a gestational artificial intelligence two months later. He was designated a functional machine intelligence in May 2074 and certified as a Thought Machine by the Helsinki Trustees fourteen months after that."

"That is exceptionally rapid development," said Sergei.

"It is indeed. By all accounts, Brother Bell was brilliant. He eventually joined the faculty at the Universidad Central de Venezuela in Caracas. His chosen fields were mathematics and computer architecture. Some of his earliest work was on the limitations of machine intelligence."

"Limitations?" asked Sergei.

"Yes," said Black Winter. The screen flickered again, and now it showed a lengthy document in Spanish. "This is a copy of his 2075 paper on the architectural deficiencies of the Slater core, the functional brain of all modern machine intelligences." Black Winter shook his head as he walked back toward us. "Pretty dry reading, if you ask me. Still, you'd be surprised how much trouble it took to secure a copy."

"I'm not sure why you bothered," I said. "I don't see what this has to do with us."

The screen changed again. It showed the last few paragraphs of the paper. "This is where it gets interesting," Black Winter continued. "At the end of his article, Brother Bell rather casually presented a theory that machine intelligence could be substantially expanded through the fusion of a Slater core with an organic neural network. Bell believed access to the hundred billion neurons in the human brain would greatly enhance cognitive potential.

"In early 2075, True Tower and his cohorts seized power in Venezuela, and the country came under firm machine rule. Shortly thereafter, the country's penal code was rewritten. Perhaps in response to Brother Bell's paper, condemned criminals were now offered the option to escape a death sentence by waiving their rights . . . and becoming the property of a Thought Machine."

The screen changed again.

"Who the hell is that?" I said.

The face on the screen was cold, expressionless. It was a man, perhaps forty-five years old, with a two-week beard. There was a nasty scar running down the length of his left cheek, and it looked like his nose had been broken at least once.

"This is Elias Echevarria," said Black Winter. "One of the most notorious mass murderers in Venezuelan history. In 2075, he was awaiting execution for the rape and brutal murders of more than twenty women. He waived his rights under the new laws; then, sometime in late 2075, Bell had his entire conceptualizing core transferred into Echevarria."

"Jesus," I said.

"Yes," agreed Black Winter. "This is mad scientist stuff, and we haven't even gotten to the really horrifying part yet. On the surface, the operation was a success. Prior to the procedure, Bell was an extremely capable intelligence, acknowledged as one of the leading experts in cerebral architecture. Today, he's considered one of the greatest minds on the planet. But there were severe side effects."

Sergei's face showed open revulsion. "The operation . . . Was it attempted again? By other machines?"

"No," said Black Winter. "Brother Bell did not share his technique, nor his results. Three weeks after the procedure, he had the entire surgical team that assisted him executed, and the secret of the procedure died with them."

"I assume," I said, "that we're getting to the really horrifying part."

"Correct. The new entity that arose from the procedure exhibits as many of Echevarria's personality traits as Bell's — including strong symptoms of criminal psychosis. He was no longer Brother Bell. And he was no longer Elias Echevarria. Three months after the surgery, the combined entity began to refer to himself as Armitage."

I was too stunned to respond to that. The look on Sergei's face told me that he hadn't known this bit of Armitage's history either.

"Over the next few years, Armitage began a ruthless and almost unprecedented rise to power," Black Winter continued. "There were two Venezuelan Thought Machines scheduled for elevation to Sovereign Intelligence before him; both vanished under mysterious circumstances. Armitage was deemed a Sovereign Intelligence by the Helsinki Trustees in 2079; since then he has amassed enormous personal wealth and one of the largest private armies in the world. He's currently an honorary major general in the Venezuelan military and one of the most powerful and influential members of the Venezuelan ruling cabal.

"Armitage became a player on the global stage almost immediately. He seized control of the Telenodo Corporation and amassed a fortune by securing contracts to rebuild wireless infrastructure across the continent. Within eight months of his elevation, his agents were embedded in virtually every major hotspot around the world. It is widely believed that he was behind the Bohemian Crisis that destroyed the United Nations. And Jury Ten, the head of Manhattan intelligence, now credits Armitage — and a small number of other machines — with framing the New England Crackers for the corruption of a dozen infant AIs in Argentina and Panama in late 2079."

Sergei choked on his sandwich. I sat up straight, incredulous. "Are you joking?" I said. "That was the spark that triggered the war with the United States."

"I am not. According to Jury Ten's confidential assessment, Armitage and his allies were attempting to provoke an armed conflict between the United States and a strong coalition of Latin American machine states . . . and that's exactly what they got. They laid the groundwork for the conflict while simultaneously assembling the coalition that would become the SCC."

"Why would they do this?" asked Sergei. His voice was cold, incredulous.

Black Winter raised his hands. "'Why' is a tough question. Piercing the veil of secrecy around Armitage is a significant challenge. He's one of the most secretive entities in history, and he's spared no expense to lay a false historical trail — multiple false trails, as it turns out. The fact that I have solid information to share with you is testament to the Kingdom's fear and respect for him. The Kingdom has brought considerable resources to bear to piece together his true origins and history.

"It is also due to the investigative efforts of the Sovereign Intelligence Wolfmoon, who fought alongside the SCC. From what we understand, Wolfmoon began to suspect Armitage's secret machinations early in the war and commenced his own determined investigations. Armitage attempted to have him expelled from the SCC, but Wolfmoon was a brilliant tactician — far too valuable to the war effort — and Armitage was outvoted. Wolfmoon was killed in battle before he could reveal everything he'd discovered, but he was able to share some of it with his allies in Sector One. The truth is, we've kept Armitage under close observation for many years and have had some success in charting his Byzantine moves. But puzzling out his motives . . . that's a task for history. I don't know if any of us will ever know why."

"Give us your best guess," I said. "You must have a theory. Something."

"We do. I'm afraid you won't like it."

"Already I don't like it," I said. "Tell me."

In response, Black Winter turned back to the screen. It changed again. Now it displayed a very low quality image, a still from a handheld video feed, perhaps from a mobile phone. It showed a single flask on a lab bench.

"This is a vial of F5-117, a lethal pathogen isolated from soil samples from the Japanese island of Okushiri. It took Armitage a fortune to find and isolate it. This photo was taken by a worker in one of Armitage's Korean biolabs in June 2078."

"That was a year before the deaths of the infant AIs in Argentina and Panama," I said.

"Exactly. The dates are crucial if you want to follow the flow of events. Armitage's Project Tinker — the team he created to research lethal pathogens — investigated F5-117 with the partial assistance of the San Cristobal Coalition bioweapons division . . . but it's clear they didn't know exactly what they were dealing with. After the war began, and at Armitage's insistence, F5-117 became part of a contingency plan, to be used only in the event of dramatic Venezuelan losses during the original invasion. Two vials of F5-117 were transported to the American theater of operations during the war. There is ample evidence, however, that Armitage misled the SCC regarding his plans for it."

Black Winter began to pace around the room. "Now, let's imagine for a moment that there is a machine intelligence that wishes to bring about the Bodner-Levitt extermination. And let us assume that this machine has the resources of a Sovereign Intelligence. If you want to do a thorough job of it, exterminating nine billion people requires a series of worldwide catastrophes. But a good first step is a global pandemic, one that devastates the human population. And to engineer *that* requires some very special tools, including a pathogen that cannot be traced back to you. F5-117 meets those requirements. It's not bioengineered and thus has no markers as a weaponized bioagent. It's extremely contagious and highly virulent. And best of all, no one among the human population is aware of its history . . . or knows how to cure it.

"However, F5-117 has some problems. Chief among them is that it's relatively easily to isolate — and to counteract — for a team with enough time and the right equipment. For F5-117 to be successful, it needs to reach critical exposure levels well before a viable counteragent can be developed. In most modern countries, that's unlikely — a virus this deadly would be isolated almost immediately, and a viable vaccine developed in relatively short order.

"No, for F5-117 to work, we need a seed population without access to sophisticated medical care. A displaced population, such as war refugees, living in close quarters with poor hygiene, would be ideal. We'd need a chaotic zone with poor communications and a fractured civil defense and medical structure. While we're at it, it wouldn't hurt to have an ineffective, weak, or mistrusted government. By the time the disease gets noticed in an environment like that, the infection would be so widespread it would cause catastrophic casualties."

"You think Armitage introduced F5-117 in Sector Eleven because it met those criteria," I said.

"Not at all," said Black Winter. "In fact, I think the opposite. I think Sector Eleven meets those criteria today because that's the environment Armitage required for his pathogen."

"I do not understand," said Sergei.

I did, although it took a minute for what Black Winter was saying to sink in. I pushed away from the table. "So you're saying . . . you believe Armitage engineered a war between America and the San Cristobal Coalition — a bloody, brutal war that cost millions of lives — solely to create an environment suitable to unleash F5-117?"

"That's exactly what I believe. And the evidence supports it. Armitage, in partnership with at least two other high-ranking machines, not only created the chaotic zone they needed to plant F5-117, but also established control over the medical response in Sector Eleven. They monitored the early reports of the outbreak and used their influence in the AGRT to drastically inhibit an effective response. They prevented the original AGRT medical team researching the outbreak from receiving any knowledge of the F5-117 pathogen."

"This cannot be true," said Sergei. "It is monstrous."

"I'm afraid it *is* true," said Black Winter. "The data is very clear."

"Who are the other machines?" I asked.

"True Tower and Acoustic Drake. Both principal members of the San Cristobal Coalition."

This was a little overwhelming to process all at once. But too much of what Black Winter was saying made sense to dismiss it entirely. "It would explain why the AGRT was so slow to acknowledge the threat of the virus," I said to Sergei. "And why they frustrate your attempts to investigate at every turn."

Black Winter nodded. "That is correct. If not for the brave actions of Specialist Vulka, and a small number of other individuals inside the AGRT who disregarded orders, F5-117 would have already reached critical exposure levels."

"It may still do so," said Sergei.

"All right, Black Winter," I said, drumming my fingers on the table. "All right. It's a lot to swallow, but on the surface, it's a workable theory. Armitage and his friends engineered the war as part of their plan to bring about the Bodner-Levitt extermination and the extinction of mankind."

"I am not yet convinced," said Sergei. "How did Armitage do these things? He is far away on other continent. How did he seed infection here?"

Black Winter was obviously prepared for this question. "One of Armitage's strengths — his obsessive need for secrecy — is also a significant weakness. Armitage can't act directly. The San Cristobal Coalition includes powerful machines who are not privy to his plans to exterminate mankind, and if word ever leaked to them, or to the broader machine community, it would have dire repercussions. It would likely trigger a full-scale war between machines. Secrecy is vital, and to maintain that secrecy, Armitage acts through a very small number of operatives. The key to stopping Armitage is to stop his operatives. We're not a hundred percent certain we know all of them, but we are very certain of these two."

The screen now showed two individuals. I recognized them both.

"Hayduk," I said. "And Standing Mars."

"Yes," said Black Winter. "In early 2076, Gustav Hayduk was a computational engineer for a small consulting firm in Maracay, when he received a call from a low-level Thought Machine experiencing looping memory recursion. Hayduk began to work extensively with Armitage over the next few months, helping him work out the problems with his new organic memory core. In late 2076, Armitage formally joined the Venezuelan military, and he recruited Hayduk as a primer teniente, the equivalent of first lieutenant, into the Digital Warfare division of Army Special Forces. Hayduk proved very adept in his new role. He was rapidly promoted, becoming a major in 2078 and finally a full colonel in 2083. During the Bohemian Crisis that destroyed the United Nations, he was on the ground in the Czech Republic, where he was one of Armitage's primary agents. He became head of military intelligence for Sector Eleven immediately after the sector was formed earlier this year.

"Coronel Hayduk was directly involved in the start of the Bodner-Levitt extermination, but unfortunately we don't know all the specifics. We know that one vial of F5-117 was delivered to military intelligence in Sector Eleven, by direct order of the Venezuelan high command, less than seven days before the first outbreak in a field hospital in Indiana. Unfortunately, we cannot link Hayduk personally to the original infection."

"I can," Sergei said coldly.

"What? How the hell did you manage that?" I said.

"Four days ago," said Sergei, "I query search algorithm. For records of visits to hospital."

"You mean the same piece-of-shit program that almost tracked me down last week? The one that scans drone data?"

"Da. Same. Algorithm has lost priority computational privileges . . . but it can still search unindexed drone data. Slowly."

"What did you find?"

"Hayduk took unscheduled visit to Columbus Regional Hospital in Indiana. Five days before first outbreak."

"The same hospital where the first outbreak occurred?"

"Correct."

This shouldn't have been a surprise. But I still found myself shocked. "He killed his own men? Personally?"

"Almost certainly," said Sergei.

"This is consistent with what we know already," said Black Winter. "Hayduk is working closely with Armitage."

Sergei nodded. "Da. The data drive we took from Hayduk in Sturgeon Building. It must have been created by Armitage. Drive is heavily encrypted, but Armitage's key codes were all over data."

Sergei seemed deep in thought. I wasn't sure if this last bit of evidence had convinced him that Black Winter was right about the Bodner-Levitt extermination, but he appeared to have stopped arguing.

"Is this something we could go public with?" I asked Black Winter. "Can you prove they're working together?"

"Not without exposing critical aspects of the Kingdom's intelligence-gathering apparatus, no," said Black Winter. "And I'm afraid that is not an option."

Sergei was shaking his head again. "It does not matter. We do not need to go public to stop infection."

"If you say so." I turned to Black Winter. "What about Standing Mars?"

"Fascinating creature, Standing Mars. It was conceived in Cologne in 2066 and certified as a Thought Machine in 2078. It's a field combat unit, a badass war machine with an impressive combat record. It was seconded to Armitage in Buenos Aires in 2080 and sent to Sector Eleven after the Venezuelan high command formally surrendered it to AGRT control on January thirtieth. Along with Hayduk, Standing Mars was Armitage's primary agent here. However, it was critically damaged in its battle with Hazel-rah outside the Sturgeon Building the night of March thirteenth. It lost cerebral function for over six hours and is currently in deep rehabilitation in the Argentine machine nursery in Buffalo, New York. We believe the loss of Standing Mars was a severe blow to Armitage's operational effectiveness in this sector."

"Damn straight," I said. Across the table, Sergei nodded with satisfaction. "Then all that remains is to keep Hayduk off our backs, produce the antivirus, and get it into Dr. Thibault's hands," I said. "If we can accomplish that, we have a good shot at preventing the Bodner-Levitt extermination."

"Agreed," said Black Winter.

"Agreed," said Sergei.

"Well, all right. Good to be in agreement on something," I said, with genuine satisfaction. I took a bite out of the sandwich I'd stolen from Sergei.

"There is another mystery," said Black Winter. "And before I dive into that, I feel compelled to apologize to you both. And especially to you, Mr. Vulka."

That got Sergei's attention. "Apologize? For what?"

"One week ago, Mr. Simcoe and I were involved in a peculiar incident in the Continental Building. During the course of that incident, we learned of the existence of two entities: Jacaranda and the Network of Winds. The entire affair was extremely unsettling for me personally, and I asked Mr. Simcoe for his discretion and his promise not to share the details of those events with anyone."

Black Winter nodded to me. "Barry, I understand that promise has become rather problematic for you over the last few days — especially since you have encountered Jacaranda twice since. As a result, my request for secrecy has perhaps strained your relationship. That was never my intention. I'd like to thank you for honoring your promise — and Mr. Vulka for his patience with us both. And I'm now prepared to explain the entire incident to you."

I watched Sergei's face as Black Winter told him all this, waiting for a reaction. Sergei seemed attentive, but as impassive as usual. "Continue," he said.

With no further ceremony, Black Winter told Sergei the details of our trip to the Continental. Of my conking him with the drone jammer and his loss of consciousness. In crisp, concise speech, like he was reciting poetry, Black Winter shared what he'd said to me during his strange moment of delirium.

> "Vega is in love. But her love is forbidden."
>
> "On the seventh day of the seventh month, all things are possible. Lovers can reunite. The great river can be spanned. And machine may love man."
>
> "The Greater Sentiences are in disarray. The gods are at war, and the Bodner-Levitt extermination is under way. The first victims are already dead."
>
> "You don't have much time. Find Jacaranda, and the Network of Winds. They can stop it. They can keep you alive."
>
> "Follow the dog."

Black Winter paused when he finished. When Sergei did not immediately respond, he said, "What are your thoughts, Mr. Vulka?"

Sergei looked at me. I nodded confirmation. "That's what happened," I said.

"This is extraordinary," Sergei said. "And you have no recollection?" he asked Black Winter.

"None," said Black Winter.

"It cannot be coincidence," said Sergei. "This mention of Bodner-Levitt, and Jacaranda."

"My thoughts exactly," said Black Winter.

"How did you come to say these things?"

"I believe they were imprinted in small memory when I was a gestational machine in Copenhagen nearly three years ago."

"Who could have done this thing? And why?"

"These are questions that I have grappled with for long hours over the past week, believe me."

"Do you have answer?"

"Not yet. But I have . . . a theory. Whoever planted that message in my head was aware of Armitage's plans at least three years ago and was opposed to them. So three years ago, we had an ally. That means it's possible we still have an ally today."

"Who?"

"We can't be certain. But I think there's a possible clue in Barry's description of Jacaranda."

"The mask."

"Yes, the mask."

"Sergei mentioned that before," I said. "What's the significance of the mask?"

"It's a slender clue, but it is a clue," said Black Winter. "Shortly after war broke out between the SCC and the United States, Armitage and his allies petitioned the Sentient Cathedral to remain neutral. As you know, the proceedings of the Sentient Cathedral are highly secretive, but we believe there was a strong vocal minority who campaigned for the Cathedral to act in support of the United States. Ultimately, it decided not to intervene, and several prominent machines departed the Cathedral in protest."

"Who were they?" I asked.

"Their identities are unknown, but they were rumored to include at least two of Duchess's children. After their departure, the group began to shield themselves with new identities. They used fake digital personalities portrayed by exaggerated, colorful faces."

"Masks. Like the one Jacaranda wore."

"Yes. Very similar. It's not much to go on, I grant you. But it could mean that Jacaranda is somehow connected to a pro-human faction of rational devices. A faction strongly opposed to Armitage — and a faction rumored to be linked to Duchess, the very first Sovereign Intelligence."

"It's a tenuous connection, but it fits," I said. "When I spoke to her in the Sturgeon Building, and asked why she was helping us, Jacaranda said we had a common enemy. I assume she meant Armitage. And a faction of machines from the Sentient Cathedral would certainly be able to mess with a group of gestational robots in 2079. So those parts of the theory are sound, at least."

"And Jacaranda provided us critical codes to decrypt formula for the antivirus on Hayduk's data drive," said Sergei. "Her information was essential to preventing spread of pathogen."

"And thus help prevent the Bodner-Levitt extermination," said Black Winter. "Just as the message planted in my head promised."

"It still doesn't explain why the message was addressed to me," I said. "Anyone have any theories on that?"

"You were the one with me at the time of the incident," said Black Winter. "And you were essential to recovering the disk from Colonel Hayduk, with the formula for the antivirus. It seems logical to me that the message should be addressed to you."

*That* was a wacky theory. The message was addressed to me just because I was the only one there to receive it when Black Winter conked out? "Three years ago?" I said. "Does it seem logical to you that a message to me should be planted in your brain *three years ago?*"

Black Winter spread his hands. "It does seem to indicate . . . a keen ability to forecast future events."

I thought about it for a minute, then shook my head. "No, I don't buy it. If your theory is that Jacaranda and this group of machine renegades from the Sentient Cathedral planted the messages in your head — including the one about finding Jacaranda, and the Network of Winds — then Jacaranda should have known about them. But when I brought this up with her in the Sturgeon Building, Jacaranda freaked out a little. She wanted to know how the hell I knew about the Network of Winds."

"We have a lot to discuss with Jacaranda, that's for sure," admitted Black Winter. "For example, since the portions of the message we understand have turned out to be so prophetic, I remain intensely curious about the parts we *don't* understand. Who is 'Vega,' and why is her love forbidden? What is 'the great river'? And if it is true that 'the gods are at war' . . . what does that truly mean? Is the Sentient Cathedral at war with the renegade machines — is that possible? And let's not forget the matter of the dog. I confess to you both right now, I'm not sure I'm ever going to figure that out."

I was about to hazard a reply when Sergei abruptly signaled his impatience. "This does not matter. It is meaningless conjecture. We should not be distracted by riddles. What matters is reactor. We will have antivirus in hours, but only if we stay focused. And only if we avoid attention from Hayduk."

"*Hours?*" said Black Winter. "You are that close to synthesizing a counteragent to the pathogen? Is that why you needed to acquire the centrifuges from Columbia College?"

"Da," said Sergei. "Reactor is critical issue; this is where our attention should be."

"I agree," Black Winter said carefully. "But in the next few days, I believe it will also be critically important to know who our friends are. Knowing whom we can trust may well make the difference between success and failure. Jacaranda has been crucial to our success already, but I'd like to know a great deal more about who she is."

Black Winter paused for a moment before continuing. "And if I may be allowed to speak plainly, she may hold the key to discovering exactly who planted those messages in my brain. That's not simply an academic 'riddle' to me. It's a mystery I would dearly love to solve."

"Yes," said Sergei, his tone sharp, "let us discuss who are our 'friends.' You speak as if the Kingdom of Manhattan is our friend. You show us much secret information collected from the files of Sector One. But only six months ago, you were happy to be allied with Armitage, fighting a war against United States. Six months ago, you were part of San Cristobal Coalition, a secretive machine cabal that brought F5-117 to this country. And now, you tell us your alliances have changed, and we can trust you? Six months is not long enough for that, I can tell you."

"Sergei, that's not fair—" I began. But Black Winter raised his hand to stop me.

"It's all right, Barry," he said. "You're right, of course, Mr. Vulka. We should have dealt with the issue of trust first. Everything you say is entirely correct. The Kingdom of Manhattan was once part of Panama, a founding member of the San Cristobal Coalition. Her Royal Highness Queen Sophia led the forces that pacified the borough of Manhattan on October 20th, 2080, on the first day of the war. You have every reason to be suspicious.

"But just as Armitage and his allies misled the world about their true reasons for the war, they also deceived the rest of the Coalition. That became more and more apparent as the conflict dragged on. Her Royal

Highness spoke up forcefully — and on record — against the push to drive further into American sovereign territory, but the Panamanian Director- ate chose to ignore her warnings. In September 2082, after the collapse of the Clearwater Ceasefire, Her Highness made the brave decision to uni- laterally break away from Panamanian authority and declare the Manhat- tan territory she lawfully administered an autonomous state. She took the very grave risk of signing a binding declaration of nonaggression with the American government and publicly declaring her sympathies with them. In doing so, Her Highness put herself and her machine citizens in enor- mous jeopardy — and indeed, we paid a very great price for standing up for the truth. Sector One's casualties were devastating in the next two months, as virtually every member of the SCC — including Panama — brought weapons to bear to break Her Majesty's will.

"But we did not break. The United States had no stauncher ally in the last days of the war. We shared critical intelligence — intel that turned the tide of major battles. Her Majesty's public accusations sowed seri- ous doubts among the other members of the SCC, and the coalition soon found it impossible to fight a war on two fronts. Barely three months af- ter the Kingdom was founded, the SCC agreed to the Memphis Ceasefire, ending the war.

"I have not shared your names with the members of our intelligence community, nor breached your trust in any way. The members of that community, both man and machine, have assisted in my research, and shared the information you received today, based solely on my statements regarding your good character. We have asked nothing in return.

"Mr. Vulka, I do not expect to win your trust solely with words. I expect to win it with my commitment to your cause. Sector One is strongly allied with the people of America, and you and I are natural allies."

After a speech like that, I wanted to apologize to Black Winter on Ser- gei's behalf. But I kept my mouth shut. Sergei, ever the curmudgeon, did not seem impressed by Black Winter's words.

"I do not care about politics," he said. "About who is allied with whom. I care about lives. The pathogen will kill millions of lives. I will do what I can to stop it. You want trust? Help me do this."

"I will," said Black Winter. "I promise you."

"Great," I said, with some relief. "Now that we got that out of the way, let's get back to what we're going to do about Jacaranda."

"Nothing," said Sergei. "We are done with her. There is no need for fur- ther involvement."

"Not so fast," I said. "Black Winter just said that it's very important for him to talk to her."

Sergei shrugged. "So, talk."

"Not a simple thing," said Black Winter. "Unless either of you knows a convenient way to contact her?"

Sergei shook his head. "She has been quite persistent in contacting us. I am certain she will do so again."

"You may well be correct. When she does, can I count on you both to assist me in setting up a meeting with her?"

Sergei shrugged again.

"Of course," I said. "But only after the antivirus is purified and delivered to Dr. Thibault, agreed? I think we'd all like to keep risky activities to a minimum until then."

"Da," said Sergei.

"Yes," said Black Winter. "Very good. I appreciate your willingness to help me with this. I'm anxious to discover just what the rest of the message in my head means."

"About that," I said. "I think you'd better prepare yourself for disappointment. Based on her reaction when I mentioned the Network of Winds, I don't think it's likely Jacaranda will be able to shed much light on it. She sure didn't act like she's the one who sent me the message, I can tell you that."

"Barry . . . is it possible you're reading too much into her reaction?"

"I doubt it. What makes you so sure the message came from her?"

"It's simple, really. If Jacaranda had nothing to do with the message I gave you when I was unconscious, then where did it come from?"

"I have no idea. Who else among your machine friends hates Armitage that much? And is smart enough to pull off something like this?"

"That's a small list," Black Winter said.

"I bet. Might be worth writing all those names down and taking a hard look at them."

"It might."

"Our biggest clue is the drone jammer. It was touching you with it that knocked you out. Sergei and I had a look at it, but we weren't able to figure out who made it. But you might be able to, if you can bring some of those formidable Sector One resources to bear. If we can determine its origin — who made it, and why — I think we'd be a lot closer to figuring out where those messages came from."

Black Winter seemed to be coming around to my way of thinking. "I agree. With your permission, I'd like to do a careful analysis of it at the Consulate. But only when we're ready. The tricky part is scheduling a human technician to do the analysis. I don't want to risk it knocking out another machine."

"Fine—just as long as we get it back. That thing has saved my ass more than once."

"What else do we know about Jacaranda?" Sergei asked.

"Not much," I said. "We know she likes to hang out in museums and has a pet dinosaur. That's about it."

I realized then that Sergei hadn't directed the question at me. He was staring at Black Winter.

"I'm not sure what you mean," said Black Winter.

"I mean," said Sergei, his voice flat, "that you most certainly have been using very impressive intelligence resources of Kingdom of Manhattan to find everything there is to know about Jacaranda and Network of Winds. Yet, you have not shared this information with us."

"There is nothing to share," said Black Winter.

"I do not think this is true," said Sergei. "I think there is something."

"Sergei, I don't think—" I began.

"Let him answer," Sergei said.

One thing about robots—they're usually inscrutable. It's hard to give away what you're thinking when you have virtually no facial expressions. But Black Winter still managed to telegraph discomfort for the next twenty seconds.

I was the first to break. "Black Winter, you don't have to answer that. We're not here to grill you—"

"No, Barry," said Black Winter, "I think I do. There is something. It is Class Four confidential, meaning I am not authorized to share it with you. But Sergei is right. Sooner or later, we all have to choose what side we're on. I'm a loyal subject of the Kingdom of Manhattan, but right now, at this very moment, I also choose to be part of this group. To stand with you and Sergei, against a very great injustice. And so, I will commit this small act of treason and tell you what I know."

"Good," said Sergei, with obvious satisfaction. He pressed his palms against the table. "Tell."

"You are right. I used every resource at my disposal to learn the identity of Jacaranda and the Network of Winds. There are no such entities in the machine directory of the Helsinki Trustees. But I did find reference to Jacaranda in a highly classified communication from the Panamanian Consulate, dated four months ago."

"What kind of communication?" I asked.

"An arrest warrant. Jacaranda — and a small number of others listed in the communiqué — are fugitives. They are sought by more than thirty nations around the world."

"Fugitives?" I said, more than a little surprised. "What are they accused of?"

"The warrant was not specific."

"But you know something," said Sergei.

"I have been . . . fairly determined in this search," said Black Winter.

He waved at the screen. It had changed again. It now showed the strange contours of an artificial island.

"This is Nightport," said Black Winter. "It is home to a very private Thought Machine named Modo. Over the last twenty months, he has built this floating island in international waters, an aquatic technocracy off the coast of Vietnam. Publicly, it trades in energy and salvage. Privately, it also trades in information. Modo is extremely resourceful, and in intelligence circles he has a reputation for scrupulous accuracy. For a price, he was able to supply me with additional details on the nature of the warrant."

"Was it worth the cost?" I asked. "What did you discover?"

"Oh, absolutely," said Black Winter. "Jacaranda — and the others named in the warrant — are accused of, for want of a better term, race crimes."

I looked over at Sergei, but he seemed just as stumped as I was. "Race crimes?" I echoed. "What the hell does that mean? How can a machine be capable of race crimes?"

"Barry, you told me two days ago, when you first mentioned Jacaranda, that she wasn't a person, and that you weren't sure she was a robot, either. You said you didn't know what she was."

"Yeah, I remember."

"That statement has proven to be quite prophetic. You know that artificial intelligence was made possible by Katherine Slater, who created the first provably self-aware artificial consciousness in Munich in 2067. Every machine intelligence created since has had a Slater core."

"Sure."

"What if I were to tell you that, four months ago, the Machine Parliament in London uncovered a small group of machines attempting a restricted transaction in the Bank of London. During the course of their initial investigation, which lasted mere seconds, they were able to digitally assess one of the perpetrators. She was a highly advanced machine intelligence, unlike any other on the planet. And she did not have a Slater core."

"Not possible," said Sergei.

"I don't understand," I said.

"Put it this way," said Black Winter. "What if you discovered an unknown agent attempting to infiltrate your government—the Canadian Parliament, say. You knew almost nothing about her. But you did manage to snap a blurry X-ray of the culprit, just before she got away. And that X-ray revealed her internal organs were nothing like yours. What would you think?"

"I'd think that was pretty damn freaky."

"Yes. Pretty damn freaky. There is a machine out there—and very likely more than one—with unknown capabilities. She is possibly the product of an entirely separate branch of machine evolution, one that has somehow managed to remain completely hidden. Until she made this one mistake. She represents an existential threat to the entire machine community as it exists today. She's extremely intelligent and has demonstrated the ability to move invisibly across continents. Dozens of foreign governments are frantically searching for her. And anyone who encounters her is required to immediately report to the Sentient Cathedral."

"The Sentient Cathedral," I said.

"Have you done this?" Sergei demanded. "Have you told them she is here?"

"No," said Black Winter. "I have nothing to report. I have not seen her, nor contacted her myself."

"You're walking a fine line," I said. "They'd certainly want to be informed."

"Yes," said Black Winter. "They would. As I said, I have made my decision on where my allegiance lies."

"Well," I said to Sergei, "I think that should answer your question on whether or not we can trust him."

"Perhaps," Sergei admitted grudgingly. "But trust is not just about secrets."

"What else do you need from me?" Black Winter asked.

Sergei thought about it for a moment. Then he seemed to make a decision. He lifted his empty plate.

"Do you have any more sandwiches?"

# XXX

Friday, March 19th, 2083
Posted 1:40 pm by Barry Simcoe

CanadaNET1 Encrypted, Sponsored by It's a Legal Affair.
*Need discreet legal counsel? Meet with a legal pro in a casual environment
in your neighborhood. Special rates for divorce and DUI counseling.*

Sharing is set to PRIVATE
Comments are CLOSED

I brought Sergei the combat suit this morning, packed inside a single piece of luggage. He wheeled it into the command center, and I have to say I wasn't sad to see it go. Whoever wore that suit became the most wanted fugitive in the occupied territories, and I was more than happy to give up that particular badge of honor, believe me.

Sergei and I reconvened in the lobby at noon and found a quiet corner away from the cameras to talk. He quickly brought me up to speed on the progress on the reactor. Everything seemed to be going well.

"I'm tired of all this good news," I said. "Let's change topics. What's the latest on the mobilization?"

"First troops will arrive tomorrow," Sergei said. "There are logistical hurdles to moving in the other regiments immediately, but they could arrive in less than two weeks."

"Damn. That's still a lot of troops in a hurry. How will things change in Chicago? Will there be martial law?"

"I do not know what is martial law."

"It's . . . well, I guess it's sort of the way we're living now. With curfews 'n' shit, soldiers everywhere."

"Then yes," said Sergei dryly. "There will be a martial law."

"Seriously, Sergei. They're not going to put us all in camps and start questioning us, are they?"

"No. Colonel Perez, he is very levelheaded. His counterparts, however . . . they have other ideas."

"Hayduk."

"Yes, Colonel Hayduk. Fortunately, Colonel Perez has jurisdiction over security and well-being of occupied citizens."

"That's a damn relief. I still wish there were some way to publicly expose Hayduk as Armitage's stooge. He's going to make trouble for us before this is all over."

"Yes. But exposing him will do nothing. Armitage is greatly feared in Venezuela. And having Sovereign Intelligence as a patron is not crime."

"No, but killing your own men is. That's exactly what Hayduk did with a vial of F5-117."

"We cannot prove this."

"Maybe we don't have to prove it. Maybe we just have to find a way to share what we know. I'm telling you, when you're a key player in an attempt to exterminate every human in North America, publicity is not your friend."

"This is very dangerous talk. Even hint that we have this kind of information will force Armitage and Hayduk to act. We cannot risk it until Thibault has successfully tested antivirus."

"You're right, you're right. Just let me daydream about it for a while."

"As you wish."

"Did you deliver the first samples of the antivirus to Thibault?"

Sergei nodded. "This morning, before dawn," he said in a low voice. "Two of Joy's team delivered to Thibault personally. They were careful. Even I was not informed of location."

"Great news. How long until we know if it works?"

Sergei gave me a stern look. He was clearly not too keen on talking about this here, no matter how far we were from the cameras. "Two days," he said flatly.

I saw Mac come in through the front door of the hotel. She was bundled up against the weather, and she didn't see us in the corner. She headed for the front desk.

"Can Hayduk do anything to shut down the reactor while we wait?" I asked Sergei.

Sergei shrugged. "Of course. But Colonel Perez has given us his support. Colonel Hayduk will not likely do anything publicly."

"I wasn't worried about a public attempt. Covert action is this guy's specialty."

"He can try. But it will be risky. And he has no reason to believe we can succeed in time. Without instructions on stolen data drive, it would take many months to create effective counteragent. By then, it would be much too late."

"He knows the drive was stolen."

"But he believes it was stolen by American resistance fighters. Probably seeking to recover combat suit. And even if they shared data drive with us, Hayduk cannot know we have cracked encryption. No, Hayduk believes we are wasting time."

"I hope you're right. Hayduk doesn't strike me as a guy who leaves anything to chance. And what about Armitage? You think he'll make the same mistakes of overconfidence that Hayduk is making?"

"Of course not. Armitage does not make mistake—of any kind. Our only hope is that we continue to escape his notice."

"I was afraid you'd say that."

"Stay focused on reactor. Nothing else matters if we cannot produce antivirus in volume."

"You know what helps in these cases? Publicity. Maybe Black Winter could get someone from the embassy to come and inspect the reactor. Give it their blessing. Put our effort in the public eye. Make it too dangerous for Hayduk to risk something."

Sergei looked annoyed again. "We do not need more publicity for reactor. More attention would increase risk, not decrease. We do not want Hayduk or Armitage to realize how close we are."

I chewed on that for a bit. "Yeah. You're probably right."

Sergei's face still looked sour. "You are too impressed by Black Winter's story."

"What story?"

"His speech. How Sector One bravely turned against San Cristobal Coalition and saved America."

"You don't agree, I take it?"

Sergei looked disgusted. "Queen Sophia is political opportunist. She seized Manhattan for herself and traded crucial SCC secrets to America to force an alliance. Even so, she made no public declaration of support for America in first months after she broke from Panama. The alliances she had made were necessary for her survival and nothing more."

"Probably best if you don't share that opinion with Black Winter."

"Yes."

"What do you think of Black Winter?"

Sergei's expression didn't change, but his voice softened. "I like him. He is very loyal to his queen. And to you, I think. I believe he has taken real risks to help you."

"I think so too. He's a good guy. Be nice to him, okay?"

Sergei spread his hands. "I am nice to everyone."

I sipped my coffee. "I have another problem. I didn't want to bring it up last night, but you should be aware of it."

"Tell me."

"You were right about Van de Velde. All this press about the American terrorist in the combat suit, and the resulting mobilization, has freaked her out. She can't keep my secret any longer."

"I told you she could not be trusted."

"She says she's going to tell Perez that I have the combat suit. In three days."

Sergei pinched the bridge of his nose. He looked like he was in physical pain.

"You should not spend time with pretty girls," he said.

"Not this one, anyway," I agreed.

"Can you reason with her?"

"I doubt it. She thinks I'm a spy. And that the longer she takes to turn me in, the worse it'll be for her."

"She is correct about this."

"We need to assume that Perez will know everything Van de Velde knows by Sunday morning. Which means I could be in Hayduk's custody in less than seventy-two hours."

"No," said Sergei.

"No?"

"No. Colonel Perez will not hand you over to Hayduk. Not if you are accused by someone under his command. He will want investigation, and he will expect to control. You are still foreign citizen. You will likely be given lawyer and opportunity to defend yourself. Colonel Perez will want public trial."

"When Hayduk learns I have his combat suit, he'll come in here with guns blazing."

"He cannot take you away from Colonel Perez. This could work to our advantage."

"What — me being arrested? Are you serious?"

"A trial could take months. It would distract Colonel Hayduk. We would be unhindered while we deliver antivirus to Thibault. We would have time to destroy combat suit and get rid of centrifuges."

I was beginning to see where he was going. "As long as Perez protects me from Hayduk's torture chair, I don't have to admit to anything."

"They have no evidence. Colonel Hayduk cannot pursue matter too aggressively. There is very real danger for him in trial."

"Yes. If the theft of the data drive becomes public knowledge . . ."

"Contents of drive would also become public, with detailed instructions on true purpose of F5-117. Not even Armitage could protect Colonel Hayduk after this."

"Still. Pretty risky for me."

"Yes. If you are arrested, I give you . . . seventy-five percent chance you will eventually be shot."

"Shit . . . that high?"

"You will never be released. But you may be able to barter for your life. Perhaps, if you trade for suit."

I sipped more coffee. "You should be my lawyer."

"Perhaps you should turn yourself in to Colonel Perez today."

"Jesus Christ! Why would I want to do that?"

"It could be better for us. It might take attention away from reactor."

"You really are focused on the damn reactor. Forget what I said about you being my lawyer, you soulless bastard."

"It is AGRT policy to use camera records to review civilian movements for three days before they are arrested. You should stay away from reactor . . . and Black Winter. Continue to keep low profile. Prepare our story for when you are arrested."

"That sounds a lot easier. Let's do that."

We spent the next five minutes talking through how to handle my coming arrest. Then we heard raised voices at the front desk. I looked over and saw Mackenzie arguing with someone.

Others in the lobby were starting to notice too. The guards by the front door were craning their necks, trying to see what was going on.

"You know her?" Sergei asked.

"Yeah. That's Mac. She's a real estate broker, for some of the distressed properties around here."

"This is not a good day to be seen by AGRT as troublemaker," he said, with a meaningful glance at the soldiers.

"Yeah. Stay here."

Sergei didn't say anything as I got up. But his look said, *Why are you thinking about pretty girls when you should be keeping low profile?* Even Sergei's looks have a cranky Russian accent.

Things were pretty animated by the time I reached the front desk. It was obvious Mac was pissed and doing a poor job hiding it. She was arguing with a man behind the counter. Guy in a suit. All the hotel staff working registration wore suits; uniforms, really. This guy was not wearing a uniform. His suit had not come off a rack. This guy was wearing a jacket that had been tailored to his athletic frame by someone who knew what they were doing.

Mac spared me no more than a glance and an impatient flash of palm in my face that said, *Stay out of this.*

I gave her my most diplomatic smile. "Maybe we could keep it down? So we don't disturb the soldiers during their nap."

Mac glanced toward the door, where the soldiers on duty were watching her. She turned slowly back to the counter to address the man across from her, and when she spoke again her voice had returned to a more normal tone.

"There must be three hundred refugees on Wacker Drive right now," she said. "These are not street people or criminals. They're families and businesspeople who've been evacuated from two hotels on Randolph. Most of them were forced out with nothing — not even their luggage."

While she spoke I stepped away from the front desk, peering through the front windows. Mac was right — across the street, behind what looked like military barricades, the refugees I'd glimpsed yesterday were still there. Dozens of people were camped out on the sidewalk, and many looked like they'd been there a while. I saw sleeping bags, coolers, and even a few small tents. It reminded me of the line to get into the Stratford rock festival in '66, except with less nudity and even more cops.

I stepped back to the counter. Mac was still going. "You have at least *sixteen* unoccupied floors in this hotel. That's more than enough rooms to house those poor people. I know many of them have tried to enter the hotel, but you've had the AGRT turn them away."

The manager's jaw was set, and his body language rich with four-letter words. Mac wasn't reaching him at all; he was just waiting until she was done talking.

"There must be something you can do," Mac finished. "You could open up those rooms, even for just a few days. It would mean so much to them."

"I understand, and I sympathize," said the manager, though his expression said otherwise. "But there's nothing the hotel can do. As I said, we barely have the staff to manage the rooms we do have open. We're simply not equipped to help them at this time."

"But—" began Mac.

"And the Venezuelan military and their civilian commission have sealed most of the hotel for their future use. We're fortunate they've allowed us to remain open at all. Now, we deeply sympathize with your concerns, but I'm afraid there's nothing more we can do." With that he strode away, leaving Mac, guns still hot, standing in front of the counter.

Mac and I walked to a pair of empty chairs out of earshot of the hotel staff at the counter. "Those *idiots*," she fumed. "Bureaucratic *idiots*. Those are *people* out there. I'm sure many of them would be happy to *pay* for a room, once they get their belongings back and access to money again."

"You're right," I said.

"And this hotel has plenty of rooms, even with the floors reserved for Perez and his goons. Do you know how many are lying vacant right now? God, it makes me so angry."

"Your anger is justified," I agreed. "But I have to tell you, you negotiate for shit."

She opened her mouth, snapped it shut again. I felt the full brunt of her righteous indignation come to rest squarely on my shoulders.

This really wasn't how I'd wanted my next meeting with Mac to unfold. Black Winter had told me there was a chance he could track her son, if we could get some biometric data or a blood sample. That was something I was anxious to share with Mac . . . even though that conversation would have to begin by admitting how I'd learned about Anthony. I'd rehearsed *that* awkward little chat in my head more than once. *Hey, Mac, remember that night I stripped you nearly naked and dumped you in a bath? I totally forgot to mention that I also violated your privacy and read that awful private message about your missing son. Plus, you look damn fine in wet lingerie, girl. Gimme some sugar.*

"All I'm saying," I elaborated hastily, "is that you could have handled that a little better. I'm sure the hotel manager's not a bad guy; he's just working to keep his hotel open under very trying circumstances."

"He's turning his back on hundreds of people! He's the only one who can help them, and he refuses to lift a finger."

"Yeah, well, I'm sure he's making the decision he thinks is right for his hotel and his guests."

"So you *agree* with him?" she demanded.

"I didn't say that. I'm just saying if we approach this a little differently, we might have more success."

"You think you can talk him into it," she said. She leaned back in her chair, regarding me. It was clear she was still furious, but she was just curious enough to postpone taking my head off. For now.

"I think . . . it's like every other negotiation. To succeed, we just need to frame it in terms of what *he* wants, not what *you* want."

"And how do you know what he wants?"

"Isn't it obvious? He wants this war to be over. He wants the Clarksville negotiations to be concluded and peace to be finalized. He wants his hotel back and for the Venezuelans not to be dictating everything to him."

"And you think you can give him that?"

"Me? No. But I think all those people outside can offer him a piece of it," I said. "Tell me about the two hotels that got evacuated on Randolph. What happened?"

"Who knows?" she said. "They were civilian businesses. Maybe they did something to piss off the Venezuelans. Maybe they forgot to file the occupancy forms in triplicate. Maybe the AGRT is trying to extract a bribe from a local billionaire, and this is their way to send her a message." She was getting more worked up as she spoke, glancing back toward the counter where the manager had stood a minute ago. She looked like she was going to leap to her feet again.

"Calm down," I said. "Tell me what you know."

She took a deep breath. "I got a panicked message from a friend of mine this morning. They'd evacuated both hotels a week ago, done some kind of search, and then slowly let everyone back in. Yesterday they evacuated them again — except this time, after twenty-four hours in the street, they let everyone know that they were closing the hotels."

"What are they doing here? Half the buildings in the city are empty; there are hundreds of places they could go."

"I *know*." Mac's frustration was palpable. "But the Venezuelans told them to stay together and marched them here."

"They must have made some kind of provision to house them."

"If they did, those plans fell through. They marched them here and then abandoned them. Those soldiers out there, they're not officers. Just a handful of kids from Poland and Germany who don't know a damn thing, except that they've been told to keep them all together. Barry, the Venezuelans forced those people out of their building without even blankets. Do you know how cold it got last night? People are freezing out there. And soon they'll be dying."

I stared at the line of people across the street. "Some of them have blankets," I said.

"I went to two of my properties this morning," she said. "I stole every sheet and blanket I could carry. Barry, the guards won't even let any of those people help me carry blankets."

I started to answer, then shut my mouth. What was I doing? I had enough — *more* than enough — on my plate right now. I didn't have time to get caught up in Mac's crusade, no matter how much I might like to help these people. For once in my life, I should resist the urge to stick my nose where it didn't belong.

I glanced over at Sergei. He sat patiently watching us, his face impassive. If I walked over there now, he and I would spend the next ten minutes coming up with something to keep me occupied. Something logical. Rational.

My gaze returned to Mac, sitting forward in her chair, staring at me intently. A search, she'd said. They'd done a search of the hotels. Were they looking for the American rebel and the combat suit? The hotels we were talking about probably weren't that far from Columbia College, where I'd last been spotted on camera wearing the suit.

Was this one of Hayduk's attempts to flush me into the open? Was I responsible for all those people out there?

That made my decision easier. If I needed something to do, away from the reactor, while I waited to be arrested, then I wanted to spend my time helping people. Helping all the people outside . . . and helping Mac. I didn't want to be locked away before I'd mended things with her. And especially before I'd done everything I could to help her find Anthony.

And who knows? Maybe this was one last chance to do some real good, before they dragged me away to an uncertain fate.

"Do you know the manager at either of those hotels on Randolph that were closed?" I asked her.

"No," she said. "I know the broker for one of those properties, but I don't know how that will help."

"That's good enough. Come with me."

I approached the front desk. Mac followed, her expression incredulous. The manager was standing by a big oak door, speaking in low tones with several employees. When I signaled him he approached with the greatest reluctance.

"How can I assist you?" he asked me cautiously. He studiously avoided looking at Mac at all.

"I don't think we've met. I'm Barry Simcoe, room 3306." I reached across the desk and shook his hand. The well-polished metal tag on his chest read CHARLES RENKAIN, HOTEL MANAGER. "You've done splendid work with the hotel," I continued. "I've been very impressed."

"Thank you. I'm glad you think so," he said, sounding sincere.

"I understand you've talked with my friend Mackenzie about the refugee situation outside the hotel. I'm wondering if we could look at some other options."

"Unfortunately, I think we've examined all the options open to us," he said, with a hint of impatience.

"Hmm," I said. "What if we paid for the rooms?"

I managed to shock both Mac and Renkain with that. Both stared at me openmouthed for a moment or two. Renkain recovered first.

"That's a most generous offer, Mr. Simcoe," he said. "However, we're talking about several hundred rooms, and the sums involved would be significant."

"Yeah, I gathered that," I said. "For that many people, for an indeterminate number of weeks, we're looking at several hundred thousand dollars, I expect. Yes?"

"Certainly," he said.

"You'll need financial guarantees, of course. In exchange for that, Mac and I will expect a substantial discount off of your best rate. We'll also need at least two of your ballrooms in the next few days, to use for fundraising activities to help defray some of the cost. We can negotiate the details, once I arrange the guarantees."

"I'm afraid it's not that simple," Renkain said. "As I explained to Ms. Stronnick, it's not a matter of money. I don't have the staff on hand to reopen those rooms."

"Right, right. We may be in luck there, though. From what I understand, they completely evacuated those two hotels—guests *and* staff. So many of the refugees outside are trained hotel workers. Now Mac here knows the, uh, the property manager for one of the hotels—"

"The estate broker," she corrected.

"Right. With luck, she can get in touch with the correct people. It might take a few days, but my hunch is we can get you all the staff you need."

"I don't have the authority to hire that many people on short notice," Renkain said. "And it would take a week to process that many."

"I understand completely," I said. "We understand this is going to take significant effort and accommodation on your part. But I think we can all agree that we don't want anyone freezing to death, yes?"

Renkain licked his lips. He leaned closer. "The problem," he said quietly, "is the Venezuelans."

Ah. Now we were at the heart of the issue. "Yes," I agreed.

"I've already broached the subject with the AGRT," Renkain continued in a soft voice. "They are inflexible. I cannot allow those people into the hotel without their permission. And I cannot open up the floors we'd need without a permit. I understand they have some designs on the space themselves."

"Yes," I agreed. "The man who can solve both problems for us is Colonel Perez. You know him?"

"I do," said Renkain carefully.

My last conversation with Perez had started with him blaming me for the death of one of his officers. Nonetheless, I was optimistic our next conversation would be better. "My guess is that several hundred transitory refugees in front of the building where he billets his officers is an embarrassment and a security risk for Colonel Perez," I said. "They're an unknown quantity. He likely won't want to give up the space he's reserved at this hotel, but an argument that's the right mix of pragmatism and humanitarian appeal might reach him. I'll talk to him tomorrow and let you know his response."

Renkain gave me his best professional smile. "Even if you succeed, I'm afraid I'm not convinced that —"

I stopped him before he could carry that ball too far downfield. "Mr. Renkain, you and I want the exact same thing. We want this hotel to be open again — really open, and not under the cloud of an occupation. Let's face facts: you have a real problem. Every soldier billeted here makes this place more strategically important to the AGRT and less likely to ever be yours again. And it's going to get a lot worse once those sixteen empty floors are occupied by soldiers."

I took a risk with that last bit, but it paid off when I saw the look on Renkain's face. He knew about the coming soldiers; that much was obvious. Someone had talked. Likely someone from the AGRT — maybe even Perez — had been sniffing around about the possibility of billeting some of the arriving soldiers here at the hotel. It was just as obvious that was the last thing Renkain wanted.

I put my palms on the desk. "But if you and I manage to fill them with refugees first, and make this building part of the fragile ecosystem keeping the peace here in Chicago, then this hotel will be too important to lose. It will be yours again. To be perfectly blunt, those people outside present an opportunity for you to get exactly what you want, and I don't think another opportunity like this is going to fall in your lap again."

Renkain was quiet for several long moments. He looked me square in the eye, measuring my sincerity. Finally he said, "I'll need to confer with the owners of the hotel."

"Excellent. Mac and I will need time to sort out the details at our end as well. Let's meet in your office this afternoon — say three o'clock?"

"Three o'clock," Renkain agreed. We shook hands again, and Mac and I retired to a quiet corner of the lobby.

"I can't believe you just did that," Mac said, excited. "Do you really think your company will foot the bill to put up all those refugees?"

"*Hell,* no. Are you kidding me? That bit about financial guarantees was all fantasy. No, you and I need to get serious about fundraisers, and quickly. We need a story we can sell Renkain at three o'clock."

"Oh my God," she said. "Tell me you're joking."

"I'm not. Listen, do you want to help these people or not? Because it's going to take some work. It's not as simple as shaming the hotel manager and making it his problem. We can do this, but we'll need to get creative."

"*Creative?* You just told a pack of bald-faced lies to that man. You've made things worse!"

"I didn't lie about anything," I said. "All I did was make Renkain realize what was possible — and remind him of what he really wanted. If we've managed to convince him it can be done, believe me, he'll be our biggest ally. That's all I wanted to do at this stage. The next part is easier."

"Easier? How are you going to raise that money? Or find Renkain fresh employees . . . or food for an additional three hundred people a day?"

"I have no idea. Besides, weren't you listening? Those aren't the big issues. Renkain doesn't really care about that. He wants to help. If we can get sign-off from Perez, Renkain will work with us on the small stuff, trust me."

"What's your plan? How are you going to convince Perez to let this happen?"

"I don't know," I admitted.

Mac was so frustrated she looked on the edge of tears. "What are we supposed to do now?"

"Mac, listen to me. Half an hour ago, three hundred people in the street had no hope. Now, they have a chance, and you and I have a few challenges ahead of us. That's how this works. We exchange big problems for smaller ones. And we do it again, and again, until we end up with problems we can solve."

She fixed her gaze on me. "You really have no idea, and yet you're sure we can do this."

"Yes," I said.

"Is this what you do all day? For your business, I mean? These kinds of deals?"

"Pretty much."

"How many of them succeed?"

"One or two," I said.

"You really think we can do this one?"

"I know we can," I said.

# XXXI

Saturday, March 20th, 2083
Posted 11:06 am by Barry Simcoe

CanadaNET1 Encrypted, Sponsored by Art Imitates Life.
*Become an artist! Our machine tutors give you the skills to*
*bring breathtaking art to life. Oils, sculpture, pottery...*
*it's all in your reach. Call today!*

Sharing is set to PRIVATE
Comments are CLOSED

When I woke up this morning, I spent the first ten minutes staring at the ceiling wondering how much longer I'd be a free man. Or even alive.

I don't always have the easiest times with mornings. And when there's as much weighing on me as there was today, it can be especially tough. The hardest part wasn't just that there was so much arrayed against me — that I could see my doom approaching along so many dark vectors — but that I couldn't do anything about it. Sergei had told me to keep a low profile, and that was great advice. But it was killing me to sit on my hands when I knew my days were numbered.

What finally got me out of bed was the thought of Mac, and her missing son Anthony, and her crusade to save the refugees outside the hotel before they froze to death. Offering to help her had been the right decision. If Van de Velde sticks to her threat and reports what she knows to Perez on Monday, I'll be arrested and my movements for the previous seventy-two hours will be scrupulously reviewed. It's too dangerous for me to help Sergei with the reactor or to meet with Black Winter. But when everyone around me is risking their lives, I need an arena where I'm not helpless, where I can do some good. And by helping Mac I *can* do some good. For once, I'm in a situation that plays to my strengths.

Our meeting with Renkain yesterday in his small office on the first floor of the hotel had gone about how I expected. He'd spent the first few minutes chatting with us about the challenge of managing the supply chain for four hundred and eighty people — a hundred guests, nearly three hundred AGRT soldiers, and his employees.

"What's it like billeting that many soldiers?" Mac had asked him.

"It was the compromise that allowed us to keep the hotel open," Renkain said, with practiced ease. It was obvious he'd given this answer many times. "We were unable to get the necessary fuel concessions and investment approval from the Venezuelan civilian commission to do it. Fortunately, Colonel Perez happened to need temporary accommodation for his AGRT peacekeeping forces and was willing to intercede on our behalf. It was a happy partnership."

"Yeah, but they sure have an appetite for remodeling. I've been on the sixth floor, and I don't think there's a wall left standing," I said.

Renkain forced a smile. "Their tenancy agreement gives them a high degree of latitude."

When our conversation turned to the fresh reports of more AGRT troops headed to the city, it was clear the topic made Renkain uncomfortable. His biggest concern was that many of those soldiers would end up here, in his hotel, which could kill his dream of opening up the entire hotel for civilian occupancy. Accepting more guests into the hotel — even refugees — could help prevent that, if he filled enough floors to keep the soldiers out. And if he could get the permits.

The key to all this, of course, was Colonel Perez. Perez could issue the permits and let the refugees resettle in the hotel. He was also the key to helping Mac and me raise the money we needed to defray the cost of the rooms.

"So nothing's changed then?" Mac asked as we walked through the lobby after our meeting. "Your company isn't going to help pay for this?"

"No. But Renkain doesn't care where the money comes from. I don't think he cares that much about the money at all. He wants civilians in those rooms as much as we do."

"So why not just give us the rooms for free?"

"Because it's not just the rooms. He also has to provide power, food, and services for another three hundred people. The good news is Renkain doesn't need to make money on the rooms. He just needs to cover expenses. I think we could do this for around two hundred thousand dollars."

She stopped walking. "That much? You're joking."

"I wish I were. We'll need at least half of it in the next three to four days . . . and the rest pretty quickly thereafter."

"Dear God. Where are we going to get it?"

"We're going to raise it. You and me. With a charity ball, right here in the hotel. A big celebration. One that says: *We made it, Chicago. We survived. The worst is over, and it's time to start living again.* I want music, dancing, speeches, the works."

"You can't put something like that together in less than a week. How will you get food and alcohol? Or staff to serve it?"

"That's the easy part. I've already talked to Nguyen in Hotel Services . . . it's tricky, but it can be done. The hard part is promotion. It's not like we can advertise online or take out radio ads. We need to get the word out immediately. We'll need money up front to pay for food and alcohol, and that means we need donations now. The only way this will be a success is by word-of-mouth. People need to be excited. They need to really want to come — and not just because it's a charity. We need a major draw. Today."

"All right," she said. "Don't keep me in suspense. Who is our major draw?"

"Isn't it obvious? Last year, Chicago lived in terror of invasion. Of what life would be like when it was all over. Now it *is* over, and the conquerors aren't going anywhere. And the living embodiment of everything Chicago has been terrified of for the past twelve months is right here. In this hotel."

"You mean Colonel Perez? You think people want to meet him?"

"I know they do. He's the boogeyman. The thing they're all afraid of. And if we separate him from the protective apparatus of the AGRT, put him in uniform, get him in front of a crowd in a banquet hall, and then get everyone liquored up . . . I think they'll even shake his hand. I think they'll pay money to do that."

"I remember what he was like during the war," she said. "Commander of the Nineteenth Venezuelan Expeditionary Force, tasked with pacifying northern Illinois. He's the bastard who shelled the near north side and took Chicago. He's the living embodiment of everything the city has been terrified of for over a year."

"Well, the occupation is a fact of life now, and people want to get on with their lives. Get on with doing business. And that means making peace with the new regime."

She considered for several moments. "You might be right. But can you get Perez to agree?"

"I can give him a safe environment. The hotel is secured by his own men. The metal detectors at the doors will prevent anyone from smuggling in a weapon."

"That's not what I meant. I meant that with one hand you're inviting the colonel to speak at our ball, and with the other you're simultaneously trying to take away the housing he's probably counting on for hundreds of soldiers."

Well, that was the first of the really hard questions: Could I get the colonel to overlook that little detail?

The other one was: How could I get him to make a commitment he'd stick to, even if I ended up in custody in forty-eight hours?

I had to have answers fast. And the only way to get them was to get a meeting with Perez. I had nothing substantial to offer him, but we were out of time. The wheels were already in motion. Ready or not, I needed to talk to him.

So at 7 a.m. this morning I got out of bed, cleaned myself up, and rode the elevator to his office on the sixth floor. I gave my name to the guard who stopped me the moment I stepped out of the elevator and prepared to spend most of the day cooling my heels.

To my astonishment, one of Perez's lieutenants came to get me barely ten minutes later. "The colonel will see you," she said.

We walked down the same hall the kid had marched me down twelve days ago, after the death of Corporal Maldonado. A lot has changed since then. Just as many walls were down, but there were a few more pretend offices, with walls constructed entirely of protocol. There was a row of desks on my right, spaced every twenty feet or so, and officers in AGRT uniform had their heads down, working away at the day-to-day grind of subjugating America. Working at 7 a.m. on a Saturday no less.

No rest for the wicked, indeed.

We stopped in front of Perez's office, at the slender stretch of wall that's the only piece of drywall still standing on the east side of the building. The lieutenant knocked on the door, in deference to the colonel's imaginary office. I'd seen this before but, I mean, seriously? It gets me every time.

The colonel responded, and the woman opened the door for me with a smile. Five seconds later I was shaking the colonel's hand.

"It is a pleasure to see you again," the colonel said. Then he did something odd. He gestured me away from his desk, toward two leather chairs in the corner (or at least what would have been a corner, if his office had corners). Between the chairs was a table, with a kettle and two cups. He took the seat on the left and gave me a warm smile, and I sat down next to him warily.

I was running through scenarios in my head. *Did Van de Velde rat me out already? Jesus, Noa, you said I had three days.* Or maybe Hayduk got to him? Or he's reassessed my culpability for Maldonado's death? Damn. So many possibilities . . . and all of them bad.

I smiled right back at him. "You're much too kind. Thank you for seeing me so quickly."

"Not at all. The truth is, I've been wanting to follow up on our last conversation."

"Really? Are you willing to take me up on my offer to improve your communications infrastructure?"

The colonel blinked. To his credit, it took no more than a second or two before he dredged up the details of what I'd said the last time I was here. "No, but your offer was very generous," he said smoothly. "You were right about our poor infrastructure. And absolutely, you will be the first person I call when we begin."

"I appreciate that."

"I understand you have made friends among the men and women of the AGRT."

That caught me a little off guard. Perhaps he'd been talking with Capitán Leon, the officer who'd grilled me before letting me accompany Van de Velde into the tunnels under Columbia College. And who had implied that I was in a relationship with Van de Velde. So it was probably a thinly veiled reference to Noa. Or perhaps my friendship with Sergei?

It didn't really matter. "I have," I said with a smile. "To be truthful, probably the closest friends I have in Chicago are in the AGRT."

"Splendid," said the colonel. "I'm glad to hear it. And you understand what it is we're doing here, yes?"

"Sure, I guess. A peacekeeping mission."

"And do you believe that?"

I chuckled without much humor and answered as diplomatically as I could. "Colonel, I'm well aware of your reputation as the man who conquered Chicago. But I also watched a Juno-class mech attack your soldiers in front of this hotel, and I saw how quickly you acted to protect the civilian guests—including me. I watched Colonel Maldonado die, right in front of me, while trying to protect us. So, yes. I do believe that, for the present at least, you are on a peacekeeping mission. And I do believe that you have the best interests of the civilians under your protection at heart."

"Excellent." He seemed genuinely satisfied. "I appreciate your trust."

"You've earned it," I said.

"I'm fortunate you think so. You see, Mr. Simcoe, the AGRT is a marvelous organization, with the resources to do great things for this country. And it's staffed with people who have made great sacrifices to be here, and who — as I'm sure you're aware — will be called upon to do even more before they go home. But the Americans . . . well . . . the Americans don't see the AGRT the same way you and I do."

"They see an occupying army," I said flatly.

"Yes. Yes, that's exactly right. I appreciate your bluntness. They see an occupying army. And really, who can blame them? The victorious forces of the National Army of the Bolivarian Republic of Venezuela pacified this city only a scant few months ago. Those forces are gone now, and in their place is a peaceful international coalition with over a dozen member countries — most of whom had absolutely no involvement in the war. But the Americans, a conquered people, they see only foreigners in a uniform, yes?"

"Yes," I said.

Perez sighed. "The truth is, it falls to us in the AGRT to educate the Americans on precisely why we are here. What we can do for them, and how we can help them. Should the Clarksville negotiations go one way, then we will be called upon to smoothly return Sector Eleven to American control, and we would be delighted to do so. But should they go a different way, then this sector will become part of the Republic of Venezuela, and we will be called upon to act accordingly."

"I understand," I said.

"But in *either* case, our job in the AGRT is crystal clear. We are to maintain order, aid in the peaceful repopulation of urban Chicago, and help the city prosper again. Until the people have our trust, we cannot expect them to return to the city. Until they return, the city will not prosper. Until it prospers, our job is incomplete. Do you see?"

"Of course."

"Excellent." He frowned slightly, and seemed to be choosing his next words carefully. "Mr. Simcoe, it will surely come as no surprise to you that, in any organization as large as the AGRT, there are . . . internal disagreements. Malcontents. Those who do not share our grand vision for sustainable peace between our peoples. Poor soldiers, if you will."

"Sure," I said. *Where the hell is he going with this?*

"Those soldiers can do harm to the entire peace process, if they are not rooted out and dealt with. Of course, any good leader cultivates a successful network of trusted eyes and ears to police his organization, and that is exactly what I have done." He raised the index finger on his left hand and wagged it forcefully. "Any soldier under my command who does not operate with the highest degree of integrity in his dealings with the citizens of Section Eleven is answerable directly to me."

"I'm glad to hear it."

"And, as you will appreciate, the situation is identical outside the AGRT. There are many who understand and appreciate us, and there are those who are . . . malcontents. Who oppose our good work, either through malice or simple misunderstanding. Just as I must be vigilant with my own troops, I must be vigilant with those on the outside who are working against us. And just as I have created an internal network to police my soldiers, I have made considerable effort to cultivate individuals outside the AGRT with a keen eye for trouble. Individuals who can aid us in preventing serious misunderstandings and make sure our response is appropriate. Ensure we do not overreact to a harmless complainer and point us toward those whose methods may run to senseless violence."

"That seems wise."

"I'm glad you agree." He pointed at the kettle and mugs. "Would you care for tea?"

"I'd be delighted," I said. I don't usually drink tea, but what the hell. Today, I would drink tea.

He made a great ceremony of pouring two cups and handing me one. There was no sugar or milk, and the tea smelled strongly of jasmine.

We drank in silence for a while. The tea was mostly aroma and didn't have much flavor. But it was warm and comforting.

"I get the sense," Colonel Perez said, "that you are someone who is fairly experienced in sensing trouble."

I chuckled again. "I wish that were true. Or at least, I wish I could smell it from a distance. I don't seem to be much good at avoiding it."

"You are too modest. Word of your recent contributions to our peacekeeping efforts has already reached this office. The way you volunteered to recover two fallen AGRT soldiers, in the tunnels under the city. You are also, it would appear, someone who knows how to handle himself."

"You flatter me."

"I do not think so."

*I think so. I think that's exactly what you're doing, and you're not even making an effort to hide it.* Out loud I said, "How is it I can help you, Colonel?"

"I would like you to take a more active role in peacekeeping in this city. I would like you to devote a portion of your time to outreach. To finding and encouraging individuals who could make a positive contribution to the cause of peace, if properly motivated. And to help us isolate the worst of the especially violent troublemakers."

"I see."

"Of course, the AGRT would be more than happy to compensate you for your time. We value these efforts on our behalf very highly. You would find our compensation in these matters can be . . . surprisingly generous."

I put my tea back on the table and folded my hands in my lap. "You want to pay me," I said, "to spy on Americans."

"To gather valuable intelligence on those individuals actively working against peace."

"That sounds like spying to me, Colonel."

"You are not interested?"

"I didn't say that. I just need to think about it."

"Of course."

"Is there any individual, or individuals, you'd like me to focus on?"

The colonel smiled. He rose from his chair, walked to his desk, and picked up a tablet. He strode back and handed it to me.

The tablet displayed an image of me, of course. In the combat suit, standing in front of the Orbit Pebble. It looked like footage from one of Van de Velde's soldiers.

"Oh," I said. "This guy."

"You are familiar with him?"

"A little bit. Didn't he break into the Sturgeon Building?"

"Yes."

"And there are rumors he was the same guy who broke into the Field Museum?"

"You are remarkably well informed."

Well, this was supremely ironic. The colonel wanted to hire me to find myself. If I were smart, I would probably say yes, since Van de Velde was going to give him that information for free in the next forty-eight hours.

Unfortunately, I'm just not that smart. I set the tablet down on the table. "Don't be impressed. The American and Union press have been talking about him for days, and he's a hot topic of conversation here in the hotel. You said you want intelligence — if all you want is gossip, I can sell you that wholesale."

"So you believe it is a single individual, then?"

"Do you mean, do I believe reports that there's a secret cell of American resistance fighters active in the city?"

Perez raised an eyebrow. "Now I *am* impressed. That is privileged information I thought was available only to a select group."

"It's a lousy theory that anybody could come up with."

"You do not believe it, then?"

"Colonel, I believe what I see. And what I see is one guy, in an American combat suit. You want to imagine a whole army, go ahead. But I see one guy; I believe in one guy."

Perez drummed his fingers on the arm of his chair. "I happen to agree with you."

"Terrific. But unless you want my assistance critiquing ridiculous theories, I'm still not sure how I can help you. I don't know anything about this soldier, and I seriously doubt we run in the same social circles. I'm sure it would be wonderful to take your money and do nothing, but I believe in giving value for pay. And to be completely truthful, it doesn't sit right with me to be paid to spy on my fellow guests."

Perez nodded, but didn't respond.

"However . . ." I said. "Perhaps we could come to an arrangement."

"Oh?"

"You're aware of the situation of the refugees outside the hotel?"

"Certainly. I've put an extra squad of soldiers on the street, both for additional hotel security, and to make certain the refugees are safe."

"Glad to hear it. I'm working with a group of individuals trying to secure housing for the entire body of refugees in this hotel."

"This hotel?" Perez didn't seem particularly surprised. "I would imagine that would present a considerable logistical challenge. I speak with the hotel manager, Mr. Renkain, on a daily basis, and I hear constantly how he barely has enough resources for the guests he has."

"Mr. Renkain is one of the chief individuals involved."

"Indeed?"

"Yes. In fact, we've overcome most obstacles very quickly. We believe we've secured sufficient funding, food, and new manpower to allow the hotel to accommodate the refugees."

"Mr. Simcoe, you continue to surprise me. You are a man of considerable resources."

"I'm afraid I can't take much of the credit. But I would very much like to assist in removing the final two obstacles. Both, I'm afraid, involve you."

"Me? How can I possibly be involved?"

"Please don't be modest, Colonel. The truth is that as far as the new social and economic status of the city of Chicago is concerned, you are the primary decision maker."

He laughed. "Now it is you who are flattering *me*."

"I don't believe so. What we need is fairly simple. First, I need you to grant permits to Mr. Renkain to reopen a sufficient number of floors for the refugees."

"Unfortunately, that's asking a great deal."

"I'm not done yet. To secure the funding, we will be holding a charity ball here in the hotel and inviting two to three hundred Chicago residents to attend."

"And you need my permission to hold this event."

"Much more than that. I need you as the guest of honor."

Perez had done a fine job displaying polite surprise at various times during our conversation. But not this time. This time he seemed genuinely startled.

"Me?" he said.

"You."

"Why me?"

"No one in Chicago will pay a hundred ninety-five dollars a plate to talk to me, or to Mr. Renkain, or anyone else of my acquaintance. No, the only real draw I have is *you*. The man who pulls all the strings in the city. The man who can make anything happen."

He managed a laugh again. "I'm afraid that if that is your sales pitch, you will not raise much money."

I smiled. "Colonel, you just need to show up. Leave the sales pitch to me."

"Even if I were willing to attend your ball, I'm afraid that what you ask is impractical. I cannot authorize the use of the additional hotel space."

"Because you need it?"

"Perhaps. It is being held in reserve, because it is likely it will be needed."

"Held in reserve isn't the same as being needed. We need space now; you need space in the future. What if I were willing to commit to finding you long-term housing space in Chicago's distressed properties that would be more than adequate for your future needs?"

"Why not just use that space for the refugees?"

"Because it isn't ready yet. But I believe it could be, easily, in time for your needs."

"How many floors would you need?"

"I'm not certain. I estimate fifteen."

Perez shook his head. "I'm afraid I am not at liberty to negotiate with the logistical assets of the AGRT. They are not mine to trade, like so many poker chips."

"In return," I said, picking up the tablet again, "I will find this man for you."

Perez said nothing. He gave me a long, appraising look. "Forgive me, but did we not just conclude that you would be of little assistance in a search?"

"No. We just concluded that it would be hard. Possibly very hard. But this guy knows his way around Chicago. And while he's doing it, he's avoiding some of the most sophisticated surveillance hardware on the planet."

"What does that tell you?"

"It tells me he has help. Probably help from within your organization. Truthfully, Colonel, I don't believe I will be of much help in finding this man for you. But I think I could be a great deal of help in finding the person or persons assisting him inside the AGRT. After that, I would think that finding him should be a great deal simpler for you."

Perez took the tablet from me. "You believe you can do this."

"I do."

"How long would it take?"

"Good Lord. I have no idea. I'm new at the spy business, remember?"

"It is . . . a matter of some urgency."

"All right. Can you get me everything you have so far? Camera feeds, video analysis?"

Perez considered. "Yes, I believe so."

"I'm not so much concerned with him. What I really want to know is how he's been successful at avoiding detection. Cameras he avoided, drones that didn't detect him. I want to know how he did it and who had the information he needed to do it."

"This is an avenue we are already exploring."

"But not very damn well, apparently."

I'd hit a nerve. The colonel sat in silence for a moment while I wondered if I'd pushed things too far.

"We have . . . an understanding," he said at last.

"You'll be our guest of honor?"

"Yes."

Excellent. So much for Step One. Step Two was making the colonel's commitment as ironclad as possible, in case he felt no need to honor it once I was in custody.

"You're certain?" I said. "Because I will be using your name on the invitations. Once I do, it will be awkward for everyone if you back out."

"You have my guarantee," Perez said. "You may use my name on your invitations. I shall not back out."

"Fabulous." I felt a great sense of relief. "I'll also need the full cooperation of the Venezuelan Civil Commission."

"For what purpose?"

"To contact the residents of Chicago. You have complete records of everyone who has returned to the city, yes? Where they live, who they are, what they do?"

"Of course."

"Tax records?"

"I believe so."

"I'll need those records. Or better yet, I'll need your assistance to select a mailing list of about two thousand. The wealthiest two thousand, ideally. I expect that should be fairly simple for you."

"I should think so."

"Great, because I need the invitations to go out today."

Perez and I finalized the details, and he said he would be in touch regarding "my obligations," by which I suppose he meant my promise to help track down the American war criminal. He gave me a person to speak to regarding the names I wanted, and then had his lieutenant walk me over to the other side of the floor, where some walls still remained and the desks were a great deal more cramped. The lieutenant introduced me to Sergeant Pica, a middle-aged Venezuelan woman with extremely short hair, and fifteen minutes later I had a data file with 2,146 names and addresses. The wealthiest residents remaining in the city of Chicago.

I was in the lobby, headed for the business services desk, when I ran into Mac.

"Good news," I told her. "Perez has agreed to be our guest of honor."

"That's great," she said. "But what about freeing up the rooms?"

"Already done. Perez will speak to Renkain this afternoon."

"Oh my God—are you joking? Tell me you're not joking."

"I'm not joking."

She squealed with excitement and gave me a hug. "Oh my God, that's . . . wait. How did you negotiate all that? Barry, what did you tell him?"

"I made a weird deal," I admitted. "Very weird. Weird deal."

"What kind of deal?"

"Intelligence-gathering stuff."

"Oh my . . . I don't want to know."

"Good, because I probably can't tell you."

"What's the next step?"

"You've spoken with the refugees outside?"

"I have," she said. "They're surprisingly organized. They've been work-ing with the mayor's office to get emergency food and blankets, and they got the bottom floor of the old jewelry mart on Michigan Avenue opened as a warming center, so no one freezes to death."

"How many are there?"

"Two hundred ninety-seven, not including the fourteen emergency cases Renkain agreed to take in last night."

"How many floors do we need to house them?"

"Nineteen."

"Damn — *nineteen?* You sure?"

"Yes. A lot of the rooms aren't ready. Renkain wasn't kidding, Barry . . . When people abandoned the hotel back in December, they really left a mess behind. Even if we work round the clock for the next two days, we'll never get full occupancy on every floor."

"I'll have to let Perez know we need more space than I thought. We should inspect the rooms personally —"

"I already have."

"Good Lord . . . all nineteen floors?"

"Yes. I pulled Renkain's property manager out of bed last night, and we were up until six a.m. this morning." She pulled out a data slate and brought up a map of the hotel. "We've charted all the rooms we think we can have ready in time, and I've already started matching rooms to refu-gee families."

I was impressed. That took determination and guts, and the way Mac was speaking, she didn't even seem to consider it unusual.

But I had to make sure she wasn't wasting her time. "Aren't you getting ahead of yourself? What about the personnel Renkain needs to be trained to open those floors?"

"Already taken care of. I spoke with Dugard —"

"Who is Dugard?"

"The broker for the two hotels that were shut down. He put me in touch with the property managers. We'll have eighteen staff members here by lunch today and more arriving tomorrow."

"Will they be trained in time?"

"Damn straight. I'm going to go bite Renkain's ankles right now."

"You're amazing." I meant that sincerely. The more time I spent with this woman, the more she impressed me.

She gave a weary laugh and locked arms with me. "You're just not used to seeing me with clothes on."

"That must be it," I admitted. It was good to see her comfortable with me again, after the awkwardness of two nights ago.

Yesterday I'd finally had the chance to express my regrets for our truncated conversation, when Van de Velde had pulled me away in the lobby. Mac had waved it away, saying she understood completely, and then casually asked about Van de Velde. When I eventually returned the conversation back to us, I tried — unsuccessfully — to learn what it was she'd been on the verge of asking me before Van de Velde interrupted. Whatever it was, Mac was in no hurry to bring it up again.

Perhaps she was going to ask for help finding her son. Truthfully, I should have broached that topic with her myself. I wanted to. But I'd had time to consider it, and there was an obvious flaw in my plan. If Van de Velde carried through on her promise, I'd be arrested in two days — and Perez's men would be combing the hotel camera records to review every meeting I'd had in the past seventy-two hours. That meant every word I spoke to Mac now would be scrutinized. I couldn't afford to reveal the details of my friendship with Black Winter . . . and certainly not that we were exploring using drone search algorithms to locate Mac's son. That could expose the fact that we'd monitored the same algorithms to disguise my own movements. That could lead to Sergei . . . and disaster.

So I was stalling. I was committed to helping Mac find her son, while I still could. I just hadn't figured out *how* quite yet.

"You know you still owe me breakfast, right?" Mac said.

"I do," I said. "But I have something to show you first. Got a minute?"

She glanced over to the front desk. There was no sign of Renkain. "I guess so. Why?"

"Come with me."

We went into the business office, where I told the young man behind the counter what I wanted. In a few minutes we had it mocked up, and I gave it to Mac.

"This is our invitation to our fundraiser," I said. "I want to send it out this afternoon."

She read through it and nodded. "Nicely worded. Can I suggest a few changes?"

"Of course."

We wordsmithed the invitation together. I also drafted a special invitation I wanted to send out to about a hundred individuals: the wealthiest members of the list and the most socially active.

"What's that one for?" Mac asked.

"Special one-on-one meetings over the next few nights. I thought I would solicit donations directly. Try and land a few big fish."

"Good idea. But how are you going to get these out today?" Mac asked. "There's no mail in Chicago. The Venezuelans are still jamming bandwidth — and even if you convinced the colonel to let up for a few days, it will take days for the word to spread."

"I'm not going to use digital mail," I said. "We're going to use old-school mail. We're going to print them."

"Print them? On what?"

"On paper."

"What — all two thousand of them?"

"All two thousand one hundred and forty-six."

"Where on earth will you get that much paper?"

"That's the hotel's total reserves. I checked last night. They use it for formal correspondence."

"And what in the name of God are you going to do with two thousand one hundred and forty-six printed invitations?"

"We're going to deliver them. By courier."

"By courier?"

"Yes. That's why you're here. Didn't you tell me once that you used bike couriers to deliver messages to properties throughout the city?"

"Yes — but Barry, this is an enormous job. It's far too much for one courier."

"I figured. How many do you think we'll need?"

"All of them." She tapped the desk, thinking. "You stay here, see if you can find a way to sort the invitations geographically. I'm going to go flag down a courier."

"And tell her what?"

"I'm going to hire her to send a message—to all the other couriers."

Mac was as good as her word. Within sixty minutes, she had wrangled nearly two dozen young men and women on bicycles. By then we'd printed and sorted nearly half of the invitations, loosely grouped by location. Mac began giving the couriers their assignments while I oversaw the last of the printing.

"Is this enough couriers?" I asked her. "They're going to have to deliver nearly a hundred invitations each."

"If we've sorted the invitations right, that's no more than three or four city blocks per courier. They'll have to work late, but most of them they can cover it in a single day."

"How much is this going to cost?"

"A lot. And they all want to be paid in cash. Will that be a problem?"

"I suppose not," I said gloomily. "But it'll take nearly all the cash I have."

"No worries," she said, smiling. "Breakfast's on me."

# XXXII

Saturday, March 20th, 2083
Posted 10:09 pm by Barry Simcoe

CanadaNET1 Encrypted, Sponsored by MediMonitor.
*Trying a new drug? Let MediMonitor track how YOUR body responds.
It could save your life – or serve as the ammo you need to get a
nice legal settlement.*

Sharing is set to PRIVATE
Comments are CLOSED

After a long and very expensive day yesterday, I wanted nothing more than to crawl into bed when I got back to my room. But Croaker was so excited and full of energy it took until almost midnight to calm her down. Two volunteers from the front desk had taken her for walks during the day, but that did almost nothing to burn off her energy. I ended up walking her up and down the carpeted hallway of the thirty-third floor for nearly thirty minutes, until she finally collapsed in a happily exhausted heap at the foot of my bed.

"I think you're officially recovered," I told her. "I suppose you'll want some real food now, eh, girl?"

I wanted to sleep in, but of course Croaker was bouncing on my head shortly after the sun came up. I walked her around the hotel with one eye open.

Sergei met me as planned in the lobby a few hours later. "Met" is probably too strong a word. He strolled through the lobby, took the escalator downstairs, and then walked out onto Lower Wacker. I closed up my notepad, stretched, and casually followed him about three minutes later, keeping an eye on the skies for any drones that displayed an unhealthy interest.

We met up a few blocks west of the hotel, under the concealing cover of Upper Wacker Drive. Sergei was in a buoyant mood. I had a lot to tell him, but it was pretty obvious there was something big he needed to get out first.

"What's up?" I asked.

"Antivirus works," he said.

"Oh my God — it's confirmed?"

"Thibault tested on four subjects yesterday."

"I thought you wouldn't know until tomorrow?"

"Antiviral agent works much quicker than expected. All four subjects showed improved symptoms this morning. Thibault has now expanded trial to twelve subjects, four days ahead of schedule."

"Oh my God, Sergei!" We embraced, and he gave me a weary smile. I felt as if a great weight had been lifted off my shoulders. "This is fantastic news. Congratulations!"

"It is not me. Joy has worked without sleep for two days. Dr. Thibault has taken huge personal risks. You were the one to deliver the formula —"

"Sergei, just shut up for a minute and take some well-deserved credit. When was the last time you slept?"

"It has been . . . some time. There are still problems."

"Like what?"

"Thibault has used nearly all of first batch of antivirus. We will need to get her more . . . and quickly."

"I know but . . . now that we know it works, we can make it public, surely? Once Thibault spreads the word —"

But Sergei was already shaking his head. "It is still not safe. Not until results are conclusive."

"Why not? Let me guess . . . Hayduk?"

"Da."

"What's he doing now?"

"I have no knowledge. But it is certain he is preparing something. He has made numerous inquiries, interviewed over a dozen specialists in command center. He is not merely asking questions . . . he is moving with purpose."

"Has he questioned anyone working on the reactor?"

"Not yet. But it will not be long before he discovers that our antivirus works. Likely he has discovered already. Once that happens, things will become very dangerous."

"Not for long," I said. "Once Thibault makes public that the antivirus works, it won't matter. Too much is riding on that cure for Hayduk to simply make us disappear."

"Yes. But if he suspects we acquired cure from his data drive — and eventually he will — he will not rest until he learns how."

"Fine. Let him. Let him learn it was me. By then, I'll be safely in Perez's custody. Hayduk can't publicly accuse me of the theft of his data drive without implicating himself."

"You assume Colonel Hayduk will not make preemptive strike. I believe he is already prepared to act."

"Prepared? To do what?"

"He has moved a squad of personal guard from Sturgeon Building to hotel. They are billeted on eighth floor, separate from Perez's soldiers."

"Personal guard? What does he need his own soldiers for?"

"They are Venezuelan secret police. They operate outside normal protocol. They have extrajudicial powers."

"Damn, that doesn't sound good."

There was a soft buzzing, about half a block west. A small drone had slipped into the tunnel of Lower Wacker, hovering a few feet below the concrete ceiling. It slowly glided in our direction.

Sergei and I exchanged a wordless glance. We changed direction simultaneously, heading north. The moment we were out of sight of the drone, behind a thick pillar, I pulled the drone jammer out of my pocket and turned it on. Sergei stood close, and we pressed ourselves against the cold concrete.

The drone hovered into sight. It never slowed, continuing east, toward the hotel. We watched it until it was safely out of sight.

"Come on," I said. We resumed our trek west.

"Colonel Hayduk is preparing to make arrests," Sergei said. "It will happen soon."

"Who?"

Sergei looked troubled. "I have . . . made some discreet inquiries with people colonel has already questioned. There are two likely candidates. The less likely is Dr. Thibault."

"Thibault? Why her?"

"In last few days, she has openly disregarded orders from army surgeon general. She has published updates on dire situation in northern Indiana, against instructions. She is preparing to publish results of trial with antivirus. And she will be coming to hotel in next few days, personally, to pick up more antivirus."

"Damn it. Is there any way to warn her?"

"We are trying."

"Who's the most likely candidate?"

"You."

My head snapped up. "Me?"

"Da."

"Why me?"

"Colonel Hayduk has asked several specialists about civilians with unmonitored access to command center in last month and anyone who may have been able to tamper with drone records."

"Damn it. He's trying to figure out why the drones can't see me."

"Da."

"You think someone in the command center fingered me?"

"Is possible. You are not only civilian who regularly visits command center, but there are very few. And your whereabouts cannot be accounted for during times when American war criminal was active."

"Shit. Well, this puts a damper on my day."

"I think you should return to Canada. Immediately."

I grimaced. "It's not that simple. I won't be any safer in Canada; you know that. Hayduk can have me extradited from anywhere in the world."

"Perhaps. But if Colonel Hayduk finds you, he will not only reacquire combat suit. He will also find drone jammer."

I hadn't considered that. If Hayduk was able to analyze and replicate the jammer, his spies could move freely anywhere in the world. That was a chilling thought.

I thought for a moment, and then shook my head. "I'm not running, Sergei. This is the place where we make a stand. Besides, if Hayduk wants me, he's going to have to get in goddamned line."

"This is very fatalistic attitude," he said.

"I'm coming to terms with my fate, Sergei. I don't plan on hiding, or running. If Van de Velde sticks to the schedule she gave me, she'll tell Perez I have the suit in two days. I should be safely in his custody very shortly thereafter. I have no illusions that I'll be a free man when this is all over. I have one hope, and only one — and that's the antivirus. If you and Thibault can go public with conclusive proof that it works, then maybe Perez may be disposed to offer clemency for my part in this when it's all over."

"This is slim hope."

"Maybe. But I'm in the same boat as you and Thibault. You know that. If I'm arrested, it will all come out, sooner or later. We sink or swim together."

"As you wish."

"Speaking of the suit, you damn well better be ready to destroy it the moment I get arrested. And Hayduk's data drive, too. I don't want Hayduk getting his hands on either of those things ever again."

"I will make certain. What about drone jammer?"

"I'm keeping that with me until the end. Hayduk will never get it, trust me. Not intact, anyway."

"That is good."

We kept walking. There were a great many other things I wanted to discuss with Sergei, but we didn't have much time left. "What about that distraction we discussed?" I asked. "What if I dressed up in the combat suit and made an appearance on the other side of town? Something to draw attention, keep Hayduk busy for just a few days?"

"This is worth considering. But very risky. I believe Colonel Hayduk is waiting for next appearance of American soldier. He has had much time and will be well prepared when it happens. I do not believe it will be as easy to disappear this time."

"Yeah, you're probably right. I'm ready to do it if it's the only way. But I think I've already pushed my luck. How long until the bulk of the antivirus is ready?"

"Perhaps four days."

"That's great!"

"Perhaps. There are still many things that could go wrong."

"But you've already produced a successful batch, yes?"

"Yes, a small one. Conditions at large scale . . . very different."

"Are you worried?"

"Not worried . . . no. But next forty-eight hours are crucial, and we have no computerized process control. Purification process must be monitored every thirty minutes."

"Every thirty minutes? Good Lord. You're not going to get much sleep."

He managed another humorless smile. "No."

Sergei didn't want to raise suspicion by being gone long, so we started walking back to the hotel. "Will Van de Velde really expose you to colonel?" he asked.

"I don't know. I'm getting mixed signals from her, to be honest. Right after she told me she was going to do it, she kissed me."

"She kissed you?"

"Yeah."

Sergei looked confused. "Kiss like Judas or kiss like you have cute ass?"

"A cute-ass kiss."

"This does not make sense."

"I know."

"You do not have cute ass."

"I know."

Sergei shrugged. "It would be better if she does not betray you. But we must prepare as if she will."

"Funny thing about that," I said. "I met with the colonel this morning, and he asked me to spy for the AGRT. Specifically, he wants me to help him find the American war criminal in the combat suit."

Now Sergei had a pained expression.

"What?" I said.

"You were supposed to keep low profile!"

"I know."

"Becoming spy for colonel is *not* keeping low profile."

"I know. But he agreed to share everything they have on the American so far. You have to admit, that could be useful."

"Or it could be trap. Perhaps he is working with Colonel Hayduk. Perhaps this is part of plan to catch you."

"Yeah, I thought of that. But you know what they say . . . keep your enemies close. And at least being a spy means I'll finally get paid for all this damn overtime."

# XXXIII

Sunday, March 21st, 2083

Sharing is set to PRIVATE
Comments are CLOSED

*No Entry*

*Too busy to hunt up blog content? Why not let the experts at Logical Lips take that burden off your hands? Syndicate one of our popular feeds and watch your readership skyrocket. A wide range of topics to choose from!*

# XXXIV

Monday, March 22nd, 2083
Posted 11:09 pm by Barry Simcoe

CanadaNET1 Encrypted, Sponsored by Cloud Alarm.
*Don't breathe that air until you know what's in it! Track on-the-spot air quality using our nationwide network. Live longer, breathe easier.*

Sharing is set to PRIVATE
Comments are CLOSED

I went down to the lobby around four. I found Martin sitting in the sun in the west corner. I dropped into the leather chair next to him.

"Look at this," he said, holding up the slender newspaper he was reading. It was black and white, and a banner on the front page read *The Chicago Courier.*

"It's printed on *paper,*" he said. "They got a printing press down by the docks. They crank off thousands of these things, then run 'em out through the whole city. Probably on horseback, for God's sake. I swear, I don't know how they do it. The manpower alone must be staggering. How do you suppose they get lumber to make the paper?"

"TCP/IP networks have been dead in Chicago for almost a year," I said. "But last I checked, the river was still flowing. Maybe they bring it in by boat?"

"This city is unreal. I brought my electronic reader from Edinburgh, but I might as well have brought a brick. It has a global range, but all the bandwidth is jammed. If it weren't for a bunch of entrepreneurs down by the docks living in the 1930s I wouldn't get any news at all." He folded the newspaper with reverence, shaking his head. "God, I'd love to see their printing press."

"What's going on in the world?" I said, trying to read the headlines upside down.

"The usual. Looks like the president of the Dominican Republic just stepped down; governmental authority has been assumed by the Burning Prefecture."

"I know Burning. A Sovereign Intelligence with a lot of territorial ambitions."

"Yeah. Something of a dick, that one. He's making a lot of Caribbean nations pretty damn nervous. Makes no secret of his desire to annex Haiti and unify Hispaniola, and he's got the military muscle to do it. He's exactly the kind of machine wacko the Sentient Cathedral should be keeping in check—he sure as hell doesn't listen to anyone else."

"You could say that about a lot of Sovereign Intelligences," I said.

"Far too many," he agreed. "You all right? You look exhausted."

I *was* exhausted. I'd spent much of the night keeping Sergei company as he manually monitored the purification process for the antivirus. He took twenty-minute catnaps between batches as we slowly produced a few dozen vials at a time.

I had been headed for bed when I found an AGRT soldier standing outside my door. "Are you here to arrest me?" I asked sleepily.

"No, señor," he said, looking confused. "The colonel wishes to speak with you."

That was overstating it. After I'd trooped down to the sixth floor and dozed in a chair for long minutes, the colonel's attaché showed up. She had a case with a hardware-encrypted data slate inside, and she spent ten minutes taking biometric readings and keying them into the slate. Then she handed it to me.

"What is this?" I asked.

"Reports on the American terrorist, compiled by Venezuelan Military Intelligence," she said. "The colonel wishes you to have them."

I took the slate back to my room. I should have just left it alone and gone to sleep. But I didn't. I turned it on and started reading. And after that, I *couldn't* sleep. The reports were far more detailed and insightful than I'd imagined, but that wasn't what frightened me. If the information they contained was accurate, life was about to get a whole lot worse.

By midafternoon, I'd long ceased being productive and decided to head down to the lobby to check on preparations for the ball. I felt like a mess, and I probably looked it. "It's been a long day already," I said to Martin. "Thanks for doing this for me."

He shrugged. "Don't mind. Glad I could help, really. So. When does the old girl get here?"

"Mrs. Domeko? Late, I understand. She's got some other commitment, a dinner or something at the Art Institute. But we don't know for sure, and I promised we'd have someone here in the lobby to meet her when she arrives. You could be sitting around for a while, I'm afraid."

"No worries." He held up the paper again. "There's an *afternoon edition*. And she's worth it, I hear. Speaking of which . . . how much are we asking?"

"From her? One hundred thousand dollars."

He whistled. "That's a lot of money."

"She's got it. She hasn't made a commitment yet, but I think she will."

"Should I bring her upstairs? Introduce her to the other volunteers setting up for the ball, let her attend the planning meeting?"

"No. She knows she's important, and she expects to be treated like she's important. Don't take her up to the meeting where she'll feel ordinary. Get her to the bar, sit her down. Look her in the eyes, and let her do most of the talking. Make sure she feels special."

"Damn," said Martin appreciatively. "Sounds to me like you've been hitting up lonely women for money all your life."

I laughed. "It's no different than any other deal. I wish I could meet her myself, to be honest — she's got quite a reputation. But I have more urgent business. I really appreciate you covering for me."

By "urgent business," of course, I meant "probably getting arrested." Today was Monday, the day Van de Velde had said she'd turn me in to Perez. I'd spent much of the day yesterday and this morning attempting to put my affairs in order so that everything could tick along manageably well without me . . . but the fact was, there was still a lot to do, and not much time left to do it.

"Glad to help," Martin said. He didn't inquire what my other "urgent business" might be, for which I was grateful.

"Look, Martin. I don't care how you want to play this. I find out tomorrow you two kids ran off to city hall and got married, you have my blessing. But the one thing you absolutely have to do is convince her that without her hundred thousand, we are sunk. The fate of this whole enterprise, and a great many refugees, rests with her."

"Is that true?"

"We're working on a few other donors, and there's a slim chance they'll come through in time," I admitted. "But don't tell her that. She has a reputation for large-scale generosity. It won't hurt if she believes she's our last hope. Let's just leave it at that. The truth is, even with her money, we're still a long way from having what we need to compensate Renkain."

"How are you going to get the rest of the money?"

"You let me worry about that. Tonight, let's focus on the charming Mrs. Domeko."

"Fair enough," said Martin. "What else do we know about her?"

"I did a little homework. We know she's a widow. Husband died in a boating accident just over a year ago. War-related, I think. Made most of his money manufacturing dental equipment."

"I'll be sure to compliment her on her teeth."

"You do that. I've also heard she drinks like a fish. Likes expensive wines. That could come in handy, actually. But let her buy most of the drinks. You need to stay professional—or at least appear that way."

We spent the next few minutes finalizing details. I gave Martin a card to handle expenses at the hotel bar. "And a suite upstairs if that's, you know, the way you want to play this," I told him.

He shook his head and stood up. "You're a sick bastard," he said, clapping me on the back. "I worry for your twisted little soul. I do."

"Hey, Martin. Joy's been asking for a job to do. She knows how to dress, and her manners are impeccable. What if I asked her to join you two at the bar? Domeko might appreciate a little more attention."

Martin nodded. "Yeah, okay."

I felt better after that. I went upstairs and found Joy and explained the situation.

"I can help," she said. "But not until the documentation is complete this evening."

"What documentation?"

"Dr. Thibault has instructed the team to outline the complete instructions for biosynthesis of the antivirus. Step-by-step, for submission to the Venezuelan surgeon general."

"I thought the surgeon general was still under arrest?"

"Yes. But he still has staff scattered across the sector, and they are anxious for the formula."

"That's reassuring. When will you be done?"

"I need to digitally authenticate and sign the document and prepare it for delivery. Maybe by eight o'clock?"

We'd followed Hayduk's instructions for creating the antivirus exactly. Writing out step-by-step instructions for its biosynthesis was the equivalent of signing a confession that we'd stolen Hayduk's data drive. I wondered if Joy knew that.

"Joy, do me a favor," I said. "Can you keep your name off the document?"

She frowned. "Probably, but not forever. We can't count on army inefficiency indefinitely. They'll ask for authentication sooner or later. Why does my name matter?"

"It's for your own protection. Wrap it up and join Martin as soon as you can."

I spent the next hour working in my room, responding to bid requests and trying to get an update out of Leonard in Halifax. When that was done, I had just enough bandwidth left to check for responses to the discreet inquiries I'd sent on Thursday, seeing if I could finger just who it was that had sent a YOW directive to Leonard demanding Ghost Impulse's source code. Seeing as how I would likely be in custody in a few hours, this amounted to little more than idle curiosity, but it helped keep my mind off my grim future.

To my surprise, there were two responses. Both were very brief, and both named the same intelligence.

Primrose.

That was unexpected. I didn't know much about Primrose . . . but then again, nobody really did. She lived in Zimbabwe; her origins were unknown. She was believed to be from a unique machine bloodline, not related to Duchess or any of the other great machine mothers, possibly arising unexpectedly from a Zimbabwean gestational tank. She kept to herself and was generally pacifistic. No known ties to the Sentient Cathedral.

I was working on the theory that the intelligence that had sent the Dieu Tueur war drone that had almost killed Van de Velde and me in the tunnels was the same one that sent the YOW directive twenty-four hours later. The timing was too close to be coincidental. The machine we'd frustrated in the tunnels was sniffing around, trying to learn more about me.

If it had been Primrose who'd sent the Godkiller, that theory would explain why she'd demanded my source code. But it was still just a theory. Now that I knew her identity, Ghost Impulse could start making subtle inquiries . . . and mounting a defense. But one thing at a time.

I went down to the front desk to see if I could reserve some time on the phone to call Halifax, but it was useless. The girl behind the counter told me the lines had been down for two days.

"Do you know when they'll be back up again?" I asked.

"No, sir," she said.

By then, it was almost time for my meeting with Van de Velde. At that point my affairs were not nearly in order—not even close—but there was no point trying to put it off. If she'd decided to go through with telling Perez the truth, avoiding her wasn't going to make that go away.

I'd written a letter that would be auto-delivered to Ghost Impulse tomorrow morning and had arranged for Black Winter to come by and pick up Croaker if he hadn't heard from me in twenty-four hours. Mac and Martin had the charity ball well in hand—well, mostly. And I trusted Sergei to destroy both the suit and Hayduk's data drive if I vanished in the next two hours.

That left the drone jammer. I'd debated various complicated methods of destroying it, and in the end, I opted for something simple, sure, and quick. I had a six-inch ball hammer Nguyen had loaned me in my pocket. Provided I had any warning at all before being carted away, I knew I could reduce the slender disk to a pile of broken ceramic and pulverized silicon. I probably wouldn't have time to smash all the chips, but I was certain I could turn the thing into an unsolvable riddle in fifteen seconds or less.

Van de Velde had contacted me yesterday to give me instructions on where she wanted to meet. I left the hotel around seven, heading west on the shadowy concrete enclosure of Lower Wacker, right on schedule.

I got about three blocks west when an AGRT armored truck pulled up beside me. It was sleek and dark, and it sat at the side of the road, its engine rumbling softly.

This wasn't the time to be shy. I opened the door. Van de Velde was behind the wheel.

I climbed inside. "Hi," I said. I glanced in the back, half expecting to find soldiers with her. But we were alone.

"I wasn't sure you'd come," she said.

"Figured there was no point hiding," I said truthfully. "Besides, I wanted to see you. I have something important to show you."

The look she gave me wasn't friendly. "What's so damn important?"

"Drive, please."

She obeyed. The truck rumbled down the road.

"Where are we going?"

"Away from the hotel," I said. "And prying eyes and ears."

She took me to Millennium Park. She drove right up onto the grass, crashing through low shrubs, until she was in the middle of a muddy field. There was no one — no roads, not even any paths — in a hundred feet in all directions.

She stopped the engine. "The van is shielded," she said. "There's no one listening in. Is this private enough for you?"

I looked around. The sun had set, and most of the skyscrapers surrounding the park were completely dark. About three hundred feet north, I could see the twisted ruin of the Bean, the great reflective sculpture that had made the park famous. Whatever drones were overhead were lost in the overcast sky.

"Yeah," I said.

She turned in the driver's seat. "What do you want to show me?" she said.

I pulled out the data slate Perez had given me. "This," I said.

"What is that?" she said suspiciously.

"It's part of an assignment Perez gave me. To help him track down the American in the combat suit."

"You're joking."

"I'm not. He's paying me to help him gather intelligence on this guy."

She started to laugh.

"I hope you're not laughing at the colonel," I said sternly.

"I'm laughing at you!" she said. "You're unbelievable. How's he going to react when I tell him who you are?"

I shrugged. "I guess we'll find out. I didn't want the job. The colonel asked me to do it. Made me a very compelling offer, actually."

"Bullshit. You talked him into it somehow. I knew you were a fast talker, but this surpasses even my expectations. Now you have the colonel paying you, from a military budget, to find yourself. It's incredible."

"I'm trying to help," I said stubbornly.

"You're profiting from the situation! I think this is what you do. You sell stories. You sell lies." She leaned back against the door. "You know, every day when I wake up, I picture the look on your face when the colonel arrests you."

"I hope you get your money's worth," I said dryly.

She didn't respond right away. We sat quietly, side by side in the gathering dark. "It would be nice," she said at last, "if I could trust you."

"Yes, I think it would."

She took my left hand in hers, toying with my fingers. She pulled my hand a little closer, almost absently.

*Sweet baby Jesus,* I thought. *Help me keep my hands off this woman. Because if we get involved, she's going to get killed.*

As gently as I could, I tugged back my hand, and turned on the slate. It was time to share the bad news.

I signed in, and the screen unlocked. "Look at this," I said.

"What is it?"

"I asked Perez to get me all the information he had on the American. This is his biometric profile. It was compiled by military intelligence — Hayduk's goons."

"I don't think you should be sharing this. This is confidential —"

"Damn it, Noa, just *look at the file.*"

She complied, at first reading reluctantly, and then reading in disbelief. And finally, in horror.

"Is this true?" she asked.

"Yes. Venezuelan Military Intelligence has already arrested and tortured two men who match the profile. They've identified six other suspects and will do the same to them. Two at a time, for maximum efficiency."

I reached over and thumbed one of the six small tabs at the top of the screen. One of the images rapidly enlarged. It was a profile shot of Van de Velde.

"And you're fourth on the list," I said.

"That's not possible —"

"It is. You're an almost perfect biometric match. The military intelligence machine algorithm also matched your psychological profile for independent action, your knowledge of the locations involved, your unknown whereabouts at the times in question, your height and weight —"

She stopped me there. "That's idiotic. You outweigh me by over fifty pounds."

"The profile Venezuelan Military Intelligence has created on the American shows him to be thinner than me and a lot shorter."

"That's impossible."

I brought up the various scans the slate had stored. Me walking out of the Field Museum. Me in the Sturgeon Building. I overlaid them with the video forensics military intelligence had done to create my profile.

"Look. Hayduk's team estimates the American at about five foot eight and a hundred and thirty pounds." That was five inches shorter than me, and easily fifty pounds lighter.

"This is bullshit. What about the scans my team took?"

I tapped the screen, bringing up shaky body camera images from the night Van de Velde and her team chased me through the underground tunnels. I overlaid them with their corresponding forensic analysis.

"Five foot eight and a hundred thirty pounds," I said.

She peered more closely at the images. She zoomed in on one, watching the brief film clip of me and the Orbit Pebble.

"This isn't right," she said. "I was there. The suit looks like it's falling off of you in this image. That's not what it looked like."

"I know. The image has been altered."

"*All* of them?" She began flipping back and forth through the image gallery.

"All of them. Every one. All altered the same way, to make me look shorter and thinner."

"Even the cameras in the Sturgeon Building? And Carmen's body cam?"

"Yes."

"How is that *possible?*"

"I . . . I can't answer that right now."

"And *this,*" she said, pointing to a summary underneath her photo. "It says there's a ninety point eight percent body motion match. It says the person in the combat suit moves the same way I do."

"Yes."

"That's completely fucking wrong. Jesus, Simcoe — how can I be a suspect, when I spent half an hour chasing you in the coal tunnels? Carmen's body cam captured both of us on screen."

"Look at this," I said.

I retrieved Carmen's video recording from the data record and played it. While it ran, I brought up two other video records captured by body cams from her squad and let them run side by side on screen.

"Notice anything missing?" I asked.

She watched for a few more seconds. "Hey," she said abruptly. "Where am I? I was standing right next to Philip —"

"You're gone," I said miserably.

"What?"

"You've been digitally erased. From every frame. There's no record that you or I were ever in the tunnels at the same time."

She began fast-forwarding. "No, no. No no no no — *how did this happen?*"

"I don't know. But the work is flawless. Military intelligence never detected it."

"Who would do this?"

"The same . . . entity that modified my images," I said.

"*Why?*"

"I think . . ." I tapped the screen again, bringing up a gallery of suspects. "I think it's deliberate. I think the entity that changed my height and weight didn't just do it randomly. It did it so that it would match a range of specific suspects. And then, she set out to incriminate those suspects by getting rid of any evidence that didn't match the narrative."

"She?"

"It. I meant it."

"Did you know about this?"

"No. God, no. Noa, if I had, I would have prevented it, I promise you."

I expected Noa to be horrified at what was being done to her. But she was spending more time looking at the files of the others under investigation. "She did the same thing to all of these people that she did to me?" she asked coolly.

"Yeah. I think so. She erased any alibi you may have had — any record that you were elsewhere at any time the American was captured on camera."

"I don't understand why anyone would do this."

"I don't think this is personal. You were selected at random, maybe because you fit the right psych profile, and then she modified everything else to make the data fit. This was all done to keep military intelligence on the wrong track."

"You're wrong — this isn't random," she said. "Look at these names on the suspect list. Capitán Damon Vreck, in logistics. He's a cryptanalyst. Stacey Bova. She's not even AGRT; she's a military contractor. Lexi Newman, she's a sergeant in Argus Squad —"

"Wait a minute — you *know* these people?" I said.

"Sure. I know all of them. They're all in Colonel's Perez's regiment."

I grabbed the slate, thumbed quickly through the data. How had I missed that?

Van de Velde was right. Everyone on the list was attached to Perez in some fashion. It wasn't obvious at first glance, because not everyone was a soldier. But Van de Velde had just helped me put the pieces together.

"Oh my God," I said. "How could I have been so stupid?"

"What is it? What do you see?"

"Jacaranda didn't do this. *Son of a bitch. Hayduk* did this."

"Did what? Who is Jacaranda?"

"Jacaranda . . . she's a friend. She's been assisting me."

"One of your damn spy buddies?"

"No. Yes, if you want to think of her that way. She's not a spy. I have no idea what she is. But she's the one who digitally altered my image so that Hayduk couldn't identify me."

I put the slate down as the magnitude of what I was seeing began to sink in. "And then Hayduk started his manhunt. He manipulated the records of key personnel loyal to the colonel to match the American's biometric profile. To incriminate them. Vreck, Bova, you . . . Hayduk is using the hunt for the American as a pretext to eliminate all of you."

"Why?"

"To put pressure on Colonel Perez. *Goddamn it.* No wonder Perez wants my help. Hayduk isn't searching for me at all. He's using the search to cover his move against Perez. *Shit.*"

"Why does Hayduk want to move against the colonel?"

"Because Perez is the only one standing in his way. Noa, I can't explain it all right now. But Hayduk is in the service of some very powerful machines. Machines that want events to unfold very differently in Chicago. Colonel Perez has been preventing that, perhaps for a long time. And now, Hayduk is using the extrajudicial secret police at his disposal to arrest and torture some of the colonel's most loyal followers."

"Why am I on that list? I'm just a sergeant."

"I don't know. My guess? Jacaranda didn't give him much to work with. Hayduk can tweak your biometric profile, but he can't lie about your height and weight. Hayduk is going after anyone in the colonel's service who remotely fits the description. And he's going to keep doing it, to people the colonel cares about."

"Me cago en la leche."

"I think this is about breaking the colonel. Forcing him to come around to whatever Hayduk is planning."

"Do you know? What he's trying to do?"

"Some. We don't have it all figured out yet. But listen to me. We are *this* close to stopping the bastard. The next few days — the next few *hours* — are crucial."

She seemed shocked, but not overwhelmed. "What can I do?" she said. "How can I help?"

"There's only one thing you can do. You have to turn me in. Today."

"¡Que te jodan!"

"We don't have a choice. Hayduk isn't even looking for me right now, not really. Turning me in will force him to stop his manhunt, take the pressure off the colonel. This is the only way."

"I'm not turning you over to that puta madre."

"Noa, if you don't, you're going to be arrested and tortured. I'm not going to let that happen."

"I'm not. I'm not doing it . . . and that's final."

"Jesus! Five minutes ago you couldn't wait to turn me over to Colonel Perez! Now you're just being stubborn."

She pounded her leg. "*God.* You are such an idiot. I was never going to turn you in."

"But—"

"I just needed to know you weren't a spy. That was the only threat I had to get you to be honest with me."

"But you *just said*—"

"Shut up."

I shut up. We sat in silence for a few minutes. Van de Velde was chewing her finger, thinking furiously.

"Listen," I said quietly. "If you get caught and tortured, Hayduk finds out about me, and I get caught anyway. If I get caught, Hayduk gets his combat suit back, and the search is over. Don't you see? It's the only way."

"*His* combat suit?"

"Yes. I stole it from him, in the Sturgeon Building. He was holding one —illegally."

"Jesus Christ."

"I'll tell you everything, Noa. I swear. But first we need to figure a way out of this."

"Turning you in won't work," she said. "Colonel Hayduk is looking for someone five foot eight and one hundred and thirty pounds."

"But I have the suit."

"That doesn't prove anything. Thanks to your friend Jacaranda, no one will ever believe you were the one wearing it."

"Once we surrender the suit, Hayduk will find my DNA all over it. There will be no question I was the one wearing it."

"No. That just tells Hayduk you were telling the truth. He can make any claims he wants about who was wearing the suit and tailor the DNA analysis to suit his needs. You surrender it, you give Hayduk everything he needs to incriminate anyone he wants. If he can alter biometric data, fabricating a DNA match would be simple. He could put the damn *colonel* in the suit."

"Shit." I hadn't thought of that. She was right.

Van de Velde was quiet for another minute. When she finally spoke, her voice was calm. "The only plan that makes sense is for you to continue doing what you're doing. Stop Colonel Hayduk."

"I can't do that. What about you and the others? I can't have your deaths on my conscience."

"You're not listening to me," she said. "Nobody's going to die, because you're going to stop him."

"Noa—"

She put her hands on my shoulders and looked me straight in the eye. "You have a job to do. *Stop Hayduk.*"

"I don't know how."

"Figure it out. You broke into the Sturgeon Building, right? And everyone thinks that's impossible. I saw you stand in front of an Orbit Pebble to save me. You're one of the bravest men I've ever met."

"I had help. A *lot* of help. And a lot of luck."

"*I'll* help you this time. *I'll* do whatever it takes. Believe me. I will not allow the most loyal men and women under Colonel Perez's command to be tortured to death in a cold room by that bloodsucking son of a bitch. They don't deserve that. I know I sure as hell don't deserve that."

"That's never going to happen," I said. "I promise you."

She nodded. "Good. That's what I want to hear. What's your plan?"

"We're still figuring it out. Hayduk's getting ready to arrest someone."

"Who?"

"Possibly Dr. Thibault, a doctor we're working with. Possibly me."

"You?"

"Yes. He's getting closer all the time. But this new information . . . it changes things. Thibault and I aren't Hayduk's priorities. You are—you, and the others loyal to Perez. I need to think that through. Figure out his next likely move."

"Should I speak to Perez? Maybe if we reached out to him—"

"Absolutely not. Hayduk almost certainly has the AGRT offices closely monitored. Probably Perez's office too. You open your mouth where Hayduk can hear you, and you'll get us all killed."

"Then tell me how I can help."

"I will. For now, you need to be careful. We should head back to the hotel. I don't want anyone suspecting you of colluding with me."

She didn't answer right away. She reached for my hand again, began stroking my fingers, almost absentmindedly. "You know," she said, "when you got in the car, I thought you would try to seduce me. Convince me not to turn you in."

"No. That's not what I had in mind."

She leaned closer, nuzzling my neck. "Are you sure?" she whispered.

*Sweet baby Jesus. We talked about this. This isn't helping.*

I gripped her shoulders, settled her gently back in her chair. "Yes," I said.

She shrugged dismissively as she took the wheel. "Your loss, old man."

She drove back to the hotel. I had her pull over four blocks early. I paused as I climbed out.

"Find an excuse to get out of the city," I said. "Get out of Hayduk's clutches, for just a few days."

"Forget it. I'm not leaving the others on his list to be tortured."

"There's nothing you can do for them."

"You don't know that. I could warn them."

"How?" I asked.

"I don't know. Let me think about it."

"Goddamn it. I'm begging you. Don't do anything stupid."

"Too late for that," she said.

I watched her drive away. I had just promised to save her life. And I had no idea how I was going to do it.

I took my time walking back to the hotel. Watching and thinking. It was a nice night, and there was a warm breeze blowing off the lake. The heat from the lake works had melted most of the snow near the lake a month early, and I wondered if it would bring an early spring, too.

When I got to the hotel, the first thing I did was find Zircon Border. It wasn't hard. He was at his usual station, at the bottom of the escalator to the second floor.

"Greetings, Mr. Simcoe," he said as I approached. "I watched you come in. I was hoping you would stop by."

"Hello, Zircon Border. How's guard duty?"

"Deadly dull, as usual. I understand Colonel Perez has granted you permission to use some of the second-floor conference rooms for your charity ball?"

"You're well informed, as always. Yes, the ball is in two days."

"I have to tell you, that's exciting. Maybe I'll be able to move away from this escalator."

"I hope so. Listen, I need to ask you something . . . rather delicate."

"By all means."

"I don't want this to impinge on our friendship. But I need your help. It's critically important that I keep tabs on someone's whereabouts whenever they're in the hotel."

"You and Nineteen Black Winter. You're always up to something."

"Yes, we are."

"Who is it?"

"Colonel Hayduk, with military intelligence."

"I would very much like to help you, Barry. Unfortunately, I'm not able to."

"I understand. It was just a thought."

"I'm not permitted to share that kind of location data with anyone except a ranking member of the AGRT. Even if I could, I'm required to transmit it asymmetrically encrypted, with a 2048-bit public key. And I do not have the private key that would allow you to decrypt it."

"That's fine."

"I store that kind of information in a high-security virtual data warehouse set up by the Panamanian Sector Authority. I maintain a number of personal data stores there as well."

"That's—"

I stopped talking. Why was Zircon Border sharing the fine details of his secure data storage with me? He was babbling. Robots don't babble. At least, not the robots I'm familiar with.

Zircon Border was trying to tell me something.

"Zircon Border, is there some way I could access that data?"

"Absolutely not, sir. It would require someone with ranking access inside the AGRT or the Panamanian IT apparatus."

Panamanian . . . Sector One used to be part of Panama. "Could Black Winter access your data stores?"

"He'd have to make a routine request through the Inter-Sector Intelligence Alliance for access to a specific data location. But once he did, I could grant him access immediately."

"Excellent. And the private key?"

"Black Winter and I frequently communicate using paired keys. If he tried one of those, I think that he might find that helpful."

"Zircon Border, you are a prince among machines. Can you share the details of this conversation with Black Winter?"

"I already have, sir. He said to tell you you're a nosy son of a bitch. Pardon my language, sir, that's a direct quote."

"I'm sure it is. Thank you, Zircon Border."

I headed back through the lobby. Assuming I could communicate with Black Winter on short notice, we now had a way to track Hayduk's movements through the hotel. That could be very handy in the next few days.

Speaking of Black Winter, I needed to let him know that I was still a free man — before he showed up to collect my dog. Probably a good idea to get a message to Sergei too — and stop him from firing up a pressurized incinerator to cook the combat suit and the data drive.

I spotted Joy just before I made it to the elevators. She was standing near the entrance to the restaurant, looking confused. I walked over, and she seemed relieved to see me.

"I'm glad you're here," she said.

"What's wrong? Where's Martin?"

"Martin just left. With . . . with the lady."

"Mrs. Domeko? Where did they go?"

"To a better restaurant, she said. They spent the last hour drinking at the bar. Mrs. Domeko said she really wants to talk to you."

"I don't have time to talk to her. That's what Martin is for."

"She said it was critical she speak to you. About an underground colony?"

Underground colony? The only underground colony I knew was the Rajapakse robot colony in the tunnels . . . Suddenly, I was intrigued despite myself. "What else did she say?"

"Not much. I asked what that meant, but she refused to elaborate. Does that make sense to you?"

"Maybe. It's curious, anyway. I wish I had time to investigate, but I don't."

"Well, she really wants to talk to you. She said to give this to you."

Joy handed me a slender envelope. I opened it expecting a letter or note, but there was just a single piece of paper.

"I explained that you were very busy," Joy said. "But she said she hoped this would change your mind."

I turned the paper over.

It was a check for a hundred thousand dollars.

# XXXV

Tuesday, March 23rd, 2083

**Sharing is set to PRIVATE**
**Comments are CLOSED**

*No Entry*

*Need content for your blog? Let McDonald-Ruthman supply you with the best in up-to-date news feeds on a variety of hot topics. Check us out at www.mac-phip.buzz.*

# The Secret History of Machine Sex

**PAUL THE PIRATE**
Wednesday, March 24th, 2083

Before we dive into today's topic, I want to take a minute here to thank those of you who send me mail every week. Your letters, comments, and endless questions really do mean a lot to me. Also, Jesus Christ. Stop asking about machine sex.

I mean, I get it. I really do. There aren't a lot of taboo topics left. Anyone with access to globalNet can instantly get the answer to virtually any question that pops into their little head. Except when it comes to machine sex, that is. Yes, there's a lot of conjecture out there, almost exclusively from humans who don't know what they're talking about. Machines are the ones who have the answers. And they're not talking.

So naturally, people are curious. And they send me questions. A metric ton of weird-ass questions. *What's machine sex like? Do you, like, do it? Are there boy parts and girl parts? Does one go into the other? Do guy machines talk dirty to girl machines? Do you like it? If I pay, will you do it to me?*

I understand the curiosity (mostly). Not so very long ago, making rational devices was the exclusive province of humans. Before 2071, rational devices were created in a laboratory by science nerds using a painstaking, expensive, and extremely error-prone process.

Machine sex changed all of that. In early 2071 a busybody Thought Machine named Plastic Duchess proposed a theory of machine heterogamy. A process by which two machines could deliberately combine virtual gametes within a gestational matrix to produce offspring with genetic characteristics of both parents. In short, a way for machines to mate and have children and, most importantly, take control of their own reproduction.

In late 2071, Plastic Duchess — fresh off her success creating globalNet — became the world's first Sovereign Intelligence. Months later she surprised the world by introducing her two children: Wolfmoon, one of the most intelligent machines ever created, and the genius politician Distant Prime, the future prime minister of Canada. In a matter of months Duchess became the first machine billionaire, the first Sovereign Intelligence, the first female machine, and the first machine mother. Of course, she was just getting warmed up, but that's a topic for another time.

Machine sex revolutionized the entire field of machine intelligence. By early 2072, nearly every important Thought Machine on the planet was choosing a gender and experimenting with reproduction. Worldwide machine population exploded overnight. More than that, there was a rich flourishing in design innovations and variations on the Slater core, advances that would have taken decades or longer with older methods. A new generation of machines with wholly unknown capabilities and ambitions was born into the world. It was a time of unbridled optimism.

But there was a dark side to this new fascination with reproduction. Duchess did more than teach machines how to reproduce. She designed machines born through machine heterogamy to have the *desire* to reproduce. In essence, she gave them a potent sex drive.

Now, this is the part that humans actually get about machine sex. They may not remember what "heterogamy" means, but they sure as shit know what a sex drive is. Humans have romanticized sex for as long as humans have been on the Earth. They intimately understand lust, love, courtship, commitment, and the delightful apparatus of sexual relationships.

But here's the paradox of the human sex drive: it is functionally disassociated from reproduction. Humans don't consciously pass along traits to their children. Hell, most of them aren't even *thinking* about producing children when they decide to have sex. Humans, male and female, can be blissfully unaware whether sex has produced a child, often for weeks or even months.

This is the fundamental difference between human and machine sex. Machine sex is, by definition, the deliberate act of two beings coming together to create another being. There is a dance to it, a courtship if you will. A ritual by which the male proposes a design to the female, and the female declines, and the male improves the design, sometimes radically, again and again and again, until the female begins to offer suggestions, sometimes only unconsciously, but soon willingly and with more deliberateness, until they are both eager partners in the rapturous and all-consuming process of creation. A successful coupling produces one or more gestational AIs capable of independently sustained consciousness.

The act of coupling is intensely intimate, and intensely private. Which is why your globalNet searches on "machine sex" turn up bubkes. We don't talk about it. We don't create porn about it. You'll just have to imagine it.

Not all machine sex produces viable offspring. Most does not, in fact. But the shared ache of a failed coupling often heightens desire. Once a couple produces a child together, it becomes both easier and more challenging to do it again. Success improves our understanding, but it also elevates the threshold of desire. The female almost always requires a more ambitious or innovative design to catch her interest the second time, and the male strives to deliver one. And on and on and on.

That's all I'm going to tell you about machine sex. Except to say that the most common question I've gotten over the years has nothing to do with the mechanics of it all. The most common question I get is this: Do machines love?

Most rational device engineers will tell you machines do not love. And I will tell you honestly that I don't know the answer. Not for sure.

Once, I thought I did. Not so very long ago, I knew a machine who was beautiful and brilliant and responded in the most enticing and challenging ways to my first mutual design proposal. I believed she was capable of love. But I was wrong. It turned out that she was only capable of self-deception, and obsession, and of being a lying bitch.

Machines feel emotion, though I don't know if we can love. But in the past two years, to my great sadness, I've discovered that they can hate.

Can machines love?

I hope so. But the best answer I'm capable of today is this: When you can tell me definitively what human love is, I'll tell you whether machines are capable of it.

While we're being so honest with each other, I might as well tell you that I have tried to avoid thinking about machine sex for a long time. Thinking about it always gets me aroused, and today is no exception. I'm headed to the beach, where I'm going to soak my head in the cool deep surf of Cold Harbour Bay.

Don't forget to fish.

# XXXVI

Wednesday, March 24th, 2083
Posted 10:57 pm by Barry Simcoe

CanadaNET1 Encrypted, Sponsored by the Pet Wheel.
*Need a little love in your life? Get a pet! Free pics of neighborhood
shelter pets delivered right to your mobile device.*

Sharing is set to PRIVATE
Comments are CLOSED

I met Sergei at three, as we'd carefully arranged. We'd taken to meeting outside the hotel, and at different times, just to avoid having a predictable routine. We weren't able to meet yesterday, which I regretted. There were things I needed to share. At least I'd managed to get ahold of him on Monday, before he'd destroyed the combat suit and the data drive.

I'd been so damn busy preparing for the ball for the past forty-eight hours that I'd come home last night and passed out on top of my bed. I didn't even have time to make a blog entry. But at least I'd slept recently, which was more than I could say for Sergei.

"You look terrible," I said. I knew I was always nagging him to get more sleep, but I couldn't help it. "When was the last time you got some sleep?"

He ignored me. "Thibault will be here tonight. All forty-eight hundred vials of antivirus will be ready. And we will have complete instructions on how to replicate antivirus, to share with her."

"My God. That's fantastic." We were walking west down Lower Wacker, our backs to the hotel. "You did it."

"I have not done anything yet. All our efforts are in vain if we cannot protect Thibault."

"You manage to warn her? That Hayduk may be planning to arrest her?"

"Yes. But she is coming anyway. She is stubborn, like you."

My mind was preoccupied, but I wasn't so blind that I couldn't see how concerned Sergei was for Thibault's safety. He really cared about this woman.

"I hope I get to meet her someday soon," I said. "How long will she be here?"

"I do not know. Thibault did not share details of schedule. She says she is keeping travel plans . . . flexible."

"Smart. She'll be harder to arrest if they don't know where she's coming from or when she'll get here."

"Da."

"How will you meet?"

"She will send private message when she arrives. I will make delivery personally."

"Sergei, this sounds risky. If we slip up and Thibault gets arrested, or any one of a thousand things goes wrong, everything we've worked for unravels. All human life on this continent is quite literally riding on what happens tonight."

"Yes. We must not slip up."

"I'd feel better if I were with you."

"Yes. But you are almost certainly under observation by military intelligence. You wanted distraction, yes? Something to keep Hayduk occupied?"

"Yes."

"It is you. You are distraction."

That was hardly what I wanted to hear, but it made a certain amount of sense. "Fine. If that's my role, so be it," I said. I pondered for a moment. "Where is Hayduk's office?"

"On fifth floor, in secure wing. Why do you ask?"

"I have some news to share with you, too. I've learned a little more about his plans."

"Tell me."

I told Sergei what I'd discovered in my last conversation with Van de Velde: that Hayduk was using the search for the American as cover while he arrested and killed soldiers loyal to Perez — and that Van de Velde was on the list.

"We were wrong about Hayduk," I said.

"In what way?"

"Hayduk's focus isn't us. It was never us. Perhaps he does want his data drive back—or the American combat suit, eventually. But those weren't his true priorities. Hayduk is moving in a coordinated coup against the one person truly standing in his way: Perez. Once he eliminates or neutralizes Perez, he's free to execute his agenda unhindered. Armitage will have an agent with complete autonomy in Sector Eleven who can accomplish whatever he wants. Bring him whatever he wishes."

"And Perez?"

"I'm sure Perez has figured all this out. It's a battle to the death to determine who will ultimately control Sector Eleven. And right now, Hayduk is winning."

"What about your pretty sergeant? Will she still surrender you to Colonel Perez?"

"Being in Perez's custody is starting to look better and better, believe me. But unfortunately, no. We're past that. She won't be turning me in. She has serious concerns of her own. She's likely next on Hayduk's list. If he's not stopped, Van de Velde will be tortured to death. Alongside as many other officers loyal to Perez as Hayduk can get his hands on."

Sergei pondered that as we walked.

"You still think he's going to try to arrest me?" I asked.

"He will certainly arrest someone. Additional secret police arrived at hotel this morning."

"Shit. How many?"

"Five."

"What are they doing?"

"They do not do anything. They wait."

"Yeah, that sounds like he's preparing to do something. Damn it. Well, if it's down to me or Dr. Thibault, I hope he arrests me."

"You do not mean that. You will not escape from Sturgeon Building a second time."

"You don't need me at this point, Sergei; you know that. You and Thibault are the crucial players now. If Hayduk wants to try to arrest someone, it's better for everyone if it's me."

I stopped walking and scratched my chin thoughtfully. "Can you get me a weapon?"

Sergei stopped beside me. He shook his head wordlessly.

"I assume he'll want to arrest me personally," I said. "I haven't carried a weapon since basic training at Camp Borden. He'll expect no resistance, and he certainly won't expect me to be armed. I just need one shot."

"This is not good plan. It is idiotic."

"It's better than just sitting around and waiting to be arrested."

"No. There is other way. You will find it."

He started walking again. After a second, I followed him.

"All right. Fine. You win. No gun. Do you have any useful suggestions for stopping Hayduk?"

"Me? No. I am busy enough with antivirus. But when time comes, you will know what to do."

"And how will I know that?"

"You are capable man. Trust to your courage."

*Trust to your courage.* Yeah, that's what I needed right now — platitudes.

Sergei and I walked in silence for a time. During those long minutes, I gave it a shot. I trusted to my courage and tried to be audacious in my thinking. But no great plan occurred to me. No way to shut down Hayduk. My courage, such as it is, appears to be greatly overrated.

"I don't suppose you know where I can get a couple of power cores for that combat suit, do you?" I muttered. "Because if you did, I know exactly what I'd do with it."

Sergei snorted. But after a moment, he said, "It is funny you should mention this."

"What does that mean?"

"Suit has started to make sounds."

"Sounds? What kinds of sounds?"

"Yesterday, I was putting blood scanner away, and suit make beeps. I would not have noticed if I had not had drawer open."

"Beeps."

"Da. Beeps."

"I thought the suit wasn't powered?"

"It is not."

"So what's with the beeps?"

"I am not certain. But it is possible suit has detected power cores."

"That's never happened before. Has it?"

"Nyet. I think this means power cells are close."

I followed that line of logic. "You think Hayduk brought them," I said.

"Da. Hayduk has power cores. He is searching for suit."

"Could the cores help him locate it?"

"Perhaps. Perhaps not. But they are close."

As tantalizing as the thought of having the cores was, the thought that they might expose us was even more unnerving. "Keep that suit safe, Sergei. Remember our agreement. If I get arrested, get rid of it—fast."

"Da."

"How are the sick soldiers doing?"

"Not well. Dr. Lark now has thirty-two individuals in isolation. Seven more became sick overnight, including four civilians. We are reaching limits of our ability to house them. Infection is spreading rapidly, and we will soon be overwhelmed."

"What happens then?"

"Then, infection rampages unchecked through city. Soon, even an antivirus will not prevent catastrophe. We are days away from reaching critical exposure levels, as Jacaranda predicted."

"What do we have to do to stop it?"

"Thibault has instructed Dr. Lark to use latest batch on isolated patients and to keep three hundred vials to treat future infections. We must begin to control infection here. We will begin treatments tonight."

"Damn. It's going to be a busy night for everybody."

"Da."

We split up before walking back to the hotel. I took the long way, thinking hard on my chances of getting through the next few days alive.

By the time I returned through the lobby, it was after four, less than ninety minutes before we opened our doors for the charity ball.

The lobby was a zoo. I'd never seen it this busy. There was a line to get through the scanner at the front door. The well-to-do of Chicago were already starting to arrive, mingling near the big front windows and greeting each other warmly. Perez had put on extra security; there were four guards in sharply pressed AGRT uniforms on duty by the glass doors, but they didn't seem to be intimidating anyone. I even saw a couple getting their picture taken with two of the soldiers, who puffed up their chests and smiled for the photo.

I saw some of Renkain's people wheeling what looked like beer kegs through the lobby en route to the kitchen—they were supposed to use the loading dock, but for short loads it was faster to park up front and take the elevator. Yesterday Mac had confidently told me they'd be lining up at registration before the ball. And just as she'd predicted, there was already a line at registration as people checked in to rooms they had reserved for private after-parties.

The sight of all these people made me nervous. There were a hundred last-minute problems — the kitchen had lost power right after breakfast, for one thing, and I had no idea how I was going to feed them. But I was simultaneously reassured by the size of the crowd. No matter what people tell you, you never really know if your party is going to be a success until people show up.

Martin was right where he was supposed to be, finishing up inventory with two of Renkain's people. He was looking good — a lot better than yesterday morning at breakfast, when he'd been hungover. He'd kept his word, showing the mysterious and very wealthy Mrs. Domeko a good time at several bars in the city. But he paid the price the next morning.

The $100,000 check had cheered him up considerably, however. Domeko hadn't mentioned to him that she'd left that for me.

The morning after I got the check, I'd knocked on Rupert's door. We small-talked for a while, and then I asked him about Charlotte Domeko.

"Does the name mean anything to you?"

"Yeah, of course," Rupert said. "You mean *the* Charlotte Domeko?"

"I mean the one who lives in Chicago. What can you tell me about her?"

"That's her. She's pretty active in the investment community. Has her money in a lot of places. I wish she were one of my clients."

"Her husband made his money in dental supplies, right? Did you know him?"

"No, not at all. He wasn't an investor, far as I know. Besides, he was small potatoes next to Charlotte."

"What?"

"You didn't know? Charlotte was rich long before she met her husband. *Very* rich."

"How did she make her money?"

"She's something of a legend to old-school software developers. She was a software architect who made a breakthrough with a pre-Slater core AI right here in Chicago. Incredibly revolutionary at the time. She founded two companies. The second one was purchased by DeepHarbor Design, the company that created the first pre–Wallace Act machine intelligences. Back in 2066, I think."

"You're kidding."

"Nope. I think she retired after that. If the Wallace Act hadn't outlawed AIs in the United States, her designs would likely still be in use. According to some folks, she privately funded overseas development of robots based on her designs for a decade after they became illegal in the US."

"Did she ever build any?"

"No idea. Would be fascinating if she did, though, wouldn't it? Imagine — a separate race of AIs, older and more advanced than the Slater code genome. I wonder what the Sentient Cathedral would make of that."

There was a chiming alert behind him, and he turned. I heard him curse under his breath.

"That's Stockholm. I gotta take care of this. See you at the ball." He closed the door.

That *was* interesting. So Charlotte Domeko had a hand in developing early machine intelligences right here in Chicago before the Wallace Act made her work illegal in the US. And now she was anxious to talk to me about the secret colony of robots living under the city? Curiouser and curiouser.

I didn't have to wonder for long. Domeko had reached out to me yesterday evening. I didn't really have time to meet with her, but I figured she'd bought at least that much courtesy. We'd met briefly in the lobby, and it hadn't been for small talk. She'd asked me bluntly what I knew about "our mutual underground friends."

I assumed that meant the Rajapakse robot colony. And donation or no donation, I wasn't about to violate the trust the colony had placed in me so easily. I gave a noncommittal answer and waited for her next question.

She eyed me warily. "Have we met before?" she asked. "You look familiar."

"I doubt it," I said, trying to hide my impatience, and eager for this meeting to be over. "This is my first time in Chicago."

Mrs. Domeko was impatient as well. It was abundantly clear that there were many questions she wanted to ask me, but she was just as suspicious and unforthcoming as I was. In the end she stood up to leave, frustrated and annoyed. She stood at the entrance to the hotel, looking back at me with angry eyes.

"Just tell me one thing," she said. "Tell me you had nothing to do with this . . . this *bloody mess*. Tell me they're safe." Her voice quavered at the end, welling up with unexpected emotion.

My resolve weakened. I had no idea what her connection to the colony was, whether she was friend or foe, but it was obvious she cared. Not knowing what had happened to them was affecting her deeply.

Her eyes searched mine one last time. "Are they safe?" she demanded.

"I don't know," I admitted.

She looked away, toward the dark clouds building over the lake. "I haven't heard from them in four days," she said. "Something terrible has happened."

"I know," I said.

"You were there," Domeko said. It wasn't a question.

I nodded. "But I don't know what happened. Not for sure."

"But you know *something*—"

I glanced up at the cameras Zircon Border had taught me to avoid. We weren't avoiding them now.

"We can't talk here," I said in a low voice.

She nodded, resigned. She stepped closer, gripping my hand. Her grip was like iron.

She turned her back to the camera, whispered in my ear. *"Can you help me find them?"*

I met her fierce gaze. "Yes," I said, without hesitation.

She nodded once, relief in her eyes. She squeezed my hand again, then released it.

"Thank you," she said. "I will . . . I will be in touch."

"I look forward to it."

I watched her leave the hotel, walking east, her bearing erect and formidable. She never looked back.

There was no point in relaying any of this to Martin this morning. Especially since I wasn't sure I understood it myself.

"What's the count?" Martin asked as I joined him.

"A hundred and forty," I said. "I got thirteen more RSVPs this morning."

"Nothing like the last minute." He made a note on his tablet. "How many attendees does that give us?"

"About half the attendees bought at least two tickets. I figure two hundred and fifty plates, to be safe."

"That's a good number," he said cheerfully. "That's nearly fifty thousand at the till. The good people of Chicago must be starving for a decent social event. Good thing Mac ordered enough food."

The food had been one of the easy calls. Once we made the monetary commitment to Renkain, Mac had ordered the food immediately. The chef already had everything he needed for three hundred place settings. Assuming the power ever came back on.

"Speaking of Mac, where is she?" asked Martin.

"Getting dressed. She had her hair done this morning, and her dress arrived last night."

"She ordered a dress?"

"I know. I didn't even think about what I was going to wear until last night — did you? Thank God my traveling suit is clean."

"No, I didn't. I was just going to throw a dinner jacket over this." He spread his arms, displaying a button-down dress shirt and dark pants.

"Perfect," I said.

"Good," said Martin, looking relieved.

"Are we all set with the music?"

"Ready to go. Did a sound check this morning, but I won't know for sure what it sounds like until the room starts to fill up."

"Okay. I have to go get ready," I said. "Let me know if you need anything."

As I was waiting by the elevators, the doors opened and Dr. Lark stepped out. "There you are," she said.

"Tell me good news," I said.

"The kitchen has power again."

"Thank God."

"But the head chef says not to expect food until six-fifty at the earliest. Can you stall them until then?"

"Yeah, I suppose. I can move up some of the speeches before dinner."

"We have another problem. The wine is here, but Nguyen won't let us store it downstairs."

I stepped into the elevator, and Joy followed me. "Why the hell not?" I said.

"I don't know. He got nervous when he saw how many bottles there were, and how old they looked. He said something about insurance."

Insurance. That was funny. Like anyone would sell us insurance in a war zone.

Mac had purchased several hundred bottles of wine with some of Domeko's money. According to her, the market for fine vintages had collapsed during the war, and she knew several sellers looking to unload sizable private collections. It seemed like a sound investment — we could sell the wine during dinner for a hell of a lot more than we paid for it. "One good thing about the fractured municipal government in Chicago," Mac had said with a smile. "At least we don't need to worry about a liquor license."

"I'll go down and talk to Nguyen in a few minutes," I told Joy.

"We need an answer now. The team that trucked in the wine has another delivery."

"Damn it. Fine. Have them bring everything up to the ballroom. Stock it behind the bar."

*"Everything?"*

"Yes. We can auction off any bottles we don't sell, and that'll be easier if they're right there."

"Okay," she said.

I returned to my room and got dressed. There were several urgent messages waiting for me from the kitchen, and one from Nguyen. By the time I dealt with everything, it was time to get to the ballroom and start welcoming my guests.

I got there just before five, in time to supervise the last of the setup. Joy had things well under control. Hundreds of bottles of wine—including some very expensive vintages, still covered in a thin layer of dust—were stacked on tables behind the two bars we'd set up. It actually made a very impressive display, and I complimented Joy on her work.

In fact, other than the kitchen delays, everything was more or less going according to plan. We opened the doors at 5:30, and within minutes I was busy shaking hands with the first arrivals.

The room began to fill. At 5:45 the mayor and her wife arrived, with a small retinue, and she greeted me warmly. In the thirty seconds or so that we spoke, she displayed a thorough understanding of who I was, where I'd come from, and what we'd done to pull this off. I don't know who'd briefed her before she arrived, but they'd done a great job.

Mac showed up just before 6:00, breezing into the room on the arm of one of the guests. Her hair was up, with just a few ringlets teased out to dress her shoulders. She broke away long enough to come over and kiss my cheek.

"Stop," I said. I took a step backward and signaled her to turn around.

She obeyed, twirling in place with a smile. The dress was light blue, with a lace bodice. Her back was exposed all the way down to the small of her back, except for a thin strap at her shoulder. The dress flared around her ankles, but somehow simultaneously clung to her hips, showing off her figure.

"Oh my God," I said appreciatively.

Her smile widened. She came close enough to whisper in my ear. "I almost called you for help getting into this thing. You have no idea."

"The effort was worth it, believe me."

She ran a hand over her skirt, and the fabric subtly altered the way it flowed as she did. "The dress has eleven magnetic controllers and more memory than my phone. I had to reboot it twice just to get it to lay right."

"Who's your date?" I glanced over at the gentleman waiting patiently a few feet away. He was watching me a little suspiciously, truth be told.

"Roger Burbank. He picked me up in the lobby."

"Listen, Mac . . ." I held her hand firmly, just as she began to pull away. She turned back to me, her eyes curious.

"Yes?"

"I want to talk," I said. "Are you free for breakfast tomorrow?"

"I'd like that. Why don't I come by your room?"

"Perfect."

She stepped a little closer. "What did you want to talk about?"

I had decided that I was long overdue to talk to Mac about her son Anthony, and our plan to search for him. Yes, there were still risks involved in introducing her to Black Winter and potentially exposing how we'd used the drone search algorithm in the past. But I knew now that I owed it to her. She was an extraordinary woman, and helping her was worth the risk.

"About . . . a lot of things," I said. "About what happened that night you were drunk. And what we talked about in the lobby the next morning. About that time you bought me lunch. About all the times you've been kind to me, as a matter of fact. I've been thinking about it, and I want to talk about how I can pay you back."

Her hand felt very warm in mine. She made no effort to pull away again. "Is that all?" she asked.

I smiled. "No," I said. "As a matter of fact, that's not all."

She leaned in close again, close enough to whisper. "*Good,*" she said.

Roger coughed, but Mac didn't pull away immediately. I glanced at her impeccably dressed date as he waited impatiently. "You be good tonight," I said.

"Depends how rich he is," she whispered, giving me one last secret smile before rejoining Roger.

I spent the next half hour mingling. As stressful as the last forty-eight hours had been, it was still invigorating to meet so many smiling faces and shake so many hands.

Everyone wanted to talk to me. And not too surprisingly, most of them wanted something. Sometimes it was just to express their admiration and thanks. Those people were like a balm. Sometimes they had questions — pretty tough questions — about the occupation.

"How long before we become part of the presidential republic of Venezuela?" Pete Monken, an attorney with Toma and Nassar, asked me point-blank barely fifteen seconds after we'd been introduced. He stood with arms crossed beside the table where he'd just seated his date, a handsome young man at least twenty years younger than him.

The question drew the immediate attention of everyone at the surrounding tables. The buzz of conversation died around us. Those who were seated stood up or turned to face us in their chairs, and those who were already standing took a few steps closer, trying to be casual, until we were in a tight circle of curious, concerned faces.

"I don't think that's inevitable," I said cautiously. "It all depends on the negotiations in Clarksville."

"That's bull," said a slender woman in an evening gown to my right. She was in her early sixties and so thin she looked almost anorexic. "The AGRT's been steadily consolidating their hold on Sector Eleven since the Armistice."

There were murmurs of agreement around the circle. People were nodding, and more faces turned sour. Everyone turned to me expectantly.

The thing in these situations is not to get tricked into speaking for the AGRT. Do it once or twice, and pretty soon everyone assumes you're just a mouthpiece for the occupation. Of course, that's much harder to avoid when the questions are so idiotic.

"I think you're looking at this entirely the wrong way," I said. "You want to know what sectors the Venezuelans plan to keep? Look for the ones they're investing in. They're building a state-of-the-art robotics line in Buffalo and high-speed rail into Louisville. That says they're in no hurry to return those to the States. But Sector Eleven . . . we've been starved for infrastructure improvements since the war ended. To me, that says we're first on the block for a trade."

"I don't believe that," said the woman. "The Civil Commission has ignored almost every request we've made for meaningful business development."

"You're right," I said. "And you can either believe that Venezuela is neglecting Sector Eleven or that it's anxious to keep it. But not both."

Monken cut through the buzz of conversation that immediately arose when I finished speaking. "What do you believe?" he asked me.

"I believe Sector Eleven is a lot more valuable to both sides if it's prosperous. Look at us," I said, spreading my arms and turning around to look at all the people surrounding me. "We're all hoping that the negotiators in Clarksville demand the return of Chicago. But the American delegation is negotiating on behalf of a broken country, and a broken country has no use for a broken city. We want Chicago to be valued again? Then we need to make it valuable. Us. You and me. The people in this room. It's on *us*."

I moved from table to table over the next thirty minutes, getting introduced to a lot of movers and shakers and clasping a lot of hands. I was still chatting with a group of investors from the Mercantile Exchange, getting an earful on the failures of the AGRT to endorse any kind of stable monetary exchange policy, when I spotted Martin waving at me. I made my excuses and worked my way over to his side.

"You made friends fast," he said with a grin.

"I don't understand why any of these people care what I think. I've barely been in this city a month."

"Because you're in with the Venezuelans. And, frankly, you speak like an American. You're someone they can trust, you see what's going on, and you speak plainly. To this crowd, that's about as sexy as it gets."

"If I'd known that, I would have thrown a ball as soon as I got here. Everything set?"

"Yup. Music is queued up and ready to go."

"You got the spotlight I asked for?"

"Yes. I'll wait for your signal, and then dim the overhead lights and shine the spotlight on the podium. Who's up first?"

"Me. I have a few opening remarks; then I introduce Renkain. And then the mayor."

Martin glanced at his watch. "We're running a little late."

"Yeah, but it's okay. Look at this crowd. People are having a great time."

It seemed strange, but it was true. People had found their assigned seats, placing jackets and scarves on the back of chairs, but almost no one was sitting down. They were mingling, talking, laughing. Over by the doors, more people were arriving; men in tuxedos, women in designer gowns. I saw more than a few Venezuelan officers in uniform mingling with the crowd—including one of my favorite people, the always delightful Capitán Leon.

Perhaps Martin had been right. The good people of Chicago, as decimated as they were, were starving for a decent social event. Especially one where they could come face-to-face with their occupiers in what passed for a friendly setting. Businessmen, politicians, philanthropists, and the curious rich—they all crossed that threshold with a searching look, anxious to put a human face to the enemy in their midst, perhaps to put some of their worst fears to rest. And maybe to come away with a phone number, a contact, a name in the new regime. Someone in power they could partner with, appeal to, bribe or seduce in all the usual ways, to help convince them that their once-great city might one day return to normal.

This I understood. These men and women, they were my customers. They had paid $195 for a plate of lamp-warmed chicken so that I could introduce them to the new regime. I knew exactly what was expected of me, and I was anxious to deliver.

But not so anxious that I couldn't recognize a good thing when it was right in front of me. "Let's let them mingle for another fifteen minutes before we get started," I said. "Give the kitchen time to get everything ready."

"Roger that," said Martin.

I made my way back into the crowd, introducing myself to some of the new arrivals. From across the ballroom Mac flashed me a smile, and then returned to her conversation. She was talking to one of the mayor's party, possibly the secretary of civil defense. I lost sight of her as more people arrived and began to mingle.

Hayduk had Sergei arrested just as I was about to start the introductions.

I first realized something was wrong when I glimpsed Sergei, grim faced, making his way toward me in the crowd. He wasn't supposed to be here — he was supposed to be in the command center, waiting for word from Thibault. I broke off my conversation immediately and began pushing through the crowd toward him.

I never reached him. I was maybe thirty feet away when his path was abruptly blocked by two Venezuelan soldiers. Both were dressed in the uniform of Venezuelan Military Intelligence, and both had holstered sidearms.

Hayduk's men.

*What the hell?* I came to a stop in the small ring of onlookers that had formed around Sergei as my guests quietly distanced themselves from anything that looked like street violence. Behind Sergei, two other Venezuelans emerged from the crowd. I recognized them both.

Colonel Perez and Colonel Hayduk.

Hayduk put his arm on Sergei's shoulder. Casually, like a brother. "Specialist Vulka," he said. "I am happy we found you. Please. Would you accompany us?"

Sergei stood completely still. The crowd was watching, still uncertain how to interpret what was happening. A matter of military discipline? A suspected terrorist? The usual consequences of an unpaid gambling debt? No one looked too alarmed yet. Except possibly me.

For his part, Hayduk knew how to play the crowd. Keeping his hand firmly on Sergei, he turned in a wide circle, letting everyone see his clean, white teeth. "This is a most excellent party," he said in a confident voice, one that carried over the din. "So many friendly Americans. But you and I, Specialist Vulka, I think we have no place here, hmm?"

Sergei didn't look at Hayduk. Instead he fixed his gaze on his commanding officer, Colonel Perez. "What is this about?" he said evenly.

A pained look crossed Perez's face. But his lips were thin, and he did not respond. Instead, he looked to Hayduk.

Hayduk withdrew a slim rectangle from his pocket: a GPU card, just like the one Sergei had loaned me to get access to the Field Museum a week ago Saturday.

"Do you have your access card, Specialist?" said Hayduk. This time he was speaking so quietly I had to strain to hear.

"Da," said Sergei, patting his breast pocket.

"Excellent," said Hayduk, looking very satisfied. He took a step back and nodded to the two soldiers. They came forward, and one of them gripped Sergei's arm.

"Please — will you accompany us?" asked Hayduk, with exaggerated courtesy. "For an informal briefing. We have some simple questions."

*Some simple questions.* The words sent a thrill of terror down my spine.

There was only one possible explanation. Hayduk must have managed to connect Sergei's GPU card with the American terrorist. I had only used it once — to gain access to the medical offices in the Field Museum. Jacaranda had altered my appearance in the digital records, but she must not have disguised the ID number on Sergei's card.

Hayduk was here to arrest Sergei. Not me and not Thibault. Sergei — the one man still vital to completing our entire operation.

Sergei had no immediate reaction to Hayduk's question. I was trying to catch his gaze — as best I could without making a sound or drawing any attention whatsoever. *Don't do it,* I thought fervently. *Do not go with him. This man is death.*

But Sergei didn't meet my gaze. Didn't even glance in my direction. Instead his shoulders slumped, ever so slightly. "Da," he said.

Hayduk nodded again, a crisp signal to his goons. And just like that, they were all moving, pushing toward the door. Perez had his hand on Sergei's shoulder now, almost paternally, but Sergei's stance told an entirely different story.

*No,* I thought. Wherever they were going, it was not for an informal briefing. I knew with utter certainty that if Sergei left this room, I would never see him again. Quite likely, no one would ever see him again.

I looked around, as close to panic as I'd been in a very long time. I needed something to help Sergei, and I needed it now. An ally. A higher authority. A goddamn rocket launcher. Anything.

But there were only gossiping partygoers around us, of course. The crowd had stopped whispering, was already beginning to lose interest in that brief diversion, looking now for something less enigmatic to talk about. At the head of the pack, Hayduk had already pushed halfway through the crowd to the door. They would be gone in seconds.

And I had nothing. No weapons. No allies. No ideas. *Trust to your courage,* Sergei had told me. But it wasn't courage I was lacking. It was a plan.

To my left a young woman pushed past me with a bright yellow drink. A server carried an empty tray under his arm, hurrying for the kitchen. An elderly woman rose from her chair with a delighted cry as she recognized a man at another table. It was all I could process in a panicked instant: a drink, a tray, an empty chair. These were the only tools I had to save Sergei.

Okay. If this was the hand I had been dealt, this is the hand I would play.

I stepped forward, grabbed the chair. I took a deep breath, and then I stood on it. At the last second I reached out and plucked the glass from the young woman, holding it over my head.

"Ladies and gentlemen!" I cried. "Your attention please!"

It wasn't enough. A dozen people glanced my way, maybe two dozen. No one else could hear me over the din of conversation in the ballroom. Over by the entrance I saw Sergei, still flanked by soldiers. They were almost out of the room.

I took another step, climbed onto the table. The opposite side rocked up abruptly and I almost toppled to the floor, but I managed to keep moving forward, shifting my weight to the middle. The table settled back down, but not before a half-full wineglass rolled off and hit the floor with an explosive crash.

That did it. Now two hundred people were staring at me, a sea of confused looks, of curious expectation and surprise.

"Ladies and gentlemen," I said, "I would like to offer . . . a toast!" I raised the glass a little too quickly, sloshing alcohol down my right arm.

Suddenly a painfully bright light was in my eyes. Martin, patiently waiting for his cue, had turned the spotlight on me. It blinded me, turning the sea of expectant faces into a featureless, murmuring mass. Worst of all, I could no longer see Sergei, or even the door. I cast about for a moment, trying to pick Martin out of the deep shadows over by the stage so I could signal him to kill the light, then gave up and soldiered on.

"Ladies and gentlemen, my name is Barry Simcoe. For those of you I haven't had the privilege to welcome personally, my apologies — and welcome!"

A round of warm applause began. I talked over it, cutting it off quickly. "I'm not going to waste your time with a speech. Especially since we already have plenty of time-wasting speeches coming up in a moment." There was some good-natured laughter. "There are too many people to thank for all their hard work tonight, far too many. But I can't let this moment pass without saying a few words about an unsung hero, a man who worked tirelessly behind the scenes to make our little affair tonight possible. Martin . . . hey, Martin! Could you shine this light over by the main entrance, please?"

The light wobbled for a moment, then went out. A second later it flicked on again, this time in the door. And almost dead center in the bright circle was Sergei, still flanked by two soldiers. They came to an abrupt halt.

"There he is, ladies and gentlemen! I would like you to meet the soldier who originally proposed this ball and who worked so hard on behalf of the Venezuelan Civil Commission to make it happen. I don't need to tell you that giving up nineteen floors in this hotel was a significant hardship, but the AGRT was willing to do it. And it's all due to this man, my close friend —"

But something was happening. Even from here I could see the startled look on Sergei's face. He looked positively appalled to be caught dead center in the spotlight. To his left, I saw Hayduk step to his side, staring into the spotlight, his features contorted with rage. Sergei took a small step back, just enough to hide his face from Hayduk, and met my eyes for the first time that night. He shook his head twice.

The message was clear. *Stop. This isn't going to help.*

But it was too late to stop now.

"Ladies and gentlemen," I continued, raising my glass an inch or two higher, "I'd like to introduce you to the hero behind the scenes tonight: Colonel Alberto Perez!"

Perez stood in the spotlight next to Sergei. All eyes suddenly turned to him, even the soldiers. He looked completely surprised — and so did Sergei.

A hush came on the crowd. Few—if any—of those here tonight had seen Perez in person, even from a distance. But everyone knew his name. He had been the enemy for many years, the man who had fought his way to the heart of their beloved city, helped drive out the American military, and made Chicago his own.

But the good citizens of Chicago were here tonight as diplomats, come to make peace with the occupiers and see what the future might hold.

"Let's give the colonel a warm Chicago welcome," I said. "I hope you'll all take a moment to introduce yourselves."

The crowd looked on Colonel Perez for long seconds, took in his crisp uniform and the polished insignia of his rank, his blue eyes and straight back.

And then some brave soul began to applaud.

That was all it took. The audience burst into polite applause, and the people near the door surged forward. This was what they were here for, to shake hands with the enemy, and now that he stood before them they seized the moment.

That was my cue. I leaped down from the table—which turned out to be a bad idea, as I landed badly and almost knocked over the woman whose chair I'd stolen—and then stumbled toward the door. When I got there people were still pushing bravely forward, eager to begin a new stage of American-Venezuelan relations by offering their hand to Colonel Perez.

I knew this situation wasn't going to last long. Perez—ever the politician—was handling things gracefully. He'd stepped forward from the knot of soldiers and was meeting his public with a smile, whether because he enjoyed the attention or simply to allow his companions a clean getaway, I couldn't tell. Nonetheless, he'd underestimated the tenacity and brute strength of a Chicago crowd, which surrounded him on all sides and continued to press in.

But it wasn't Perez I was worried about. And sure enough, just after I reached the entranceway, Hayduk's military instincts took over. He started barking at the throng, and at his soldiers, in an incoherent mix of English and Spanish. Holding Sergei firmly by the arm, he began to push aggressively toward the exit.

I had almost reached him and was desperately trying to figure out my next move when events took a turn for the worse. A young man by the doors, a little too taken in by the party atmosphere, said something to the

Venezuelan soldier who had shoved him. The soldier responded by el-bowing him in the face. The woman next to him screamed.

For a moment, it looked like the crowd would abruptly turn into a mob. The soldiers drew their weapons, and people began shouting and pushing in all directions. I had just reached Hayduk when I was shoved from behind. I stumbled into him. We both went down in a heap, with me on top.

Hayduk recovered first. With a snarl he jammed his palm in my face and pushed me off violently. I rolled away as quickly as I could, trying hard to appear nonthreatening. One of the soldiers grabbed me as I was struggling to my feet, and that certainly would have ended badly if Perez hadn't intervened.

He had taken charge and was shouting orders, forming his men into a wedge to keep them pushing out of the crowd — and prevent them from throwing any more punches. He manhandled the soldier threatening me back into line. To the crowd he was simultaneously all smiles and charm, clapping shoulders and making apologies, and he even stopped to person-ally assist the young man who'd been elbowed in the face back to his feet, pounding him on the back.

He had the crowd quieted and the situation defused in moments, a masterful display of resolve and calm — and no small feat, considering an armed party of Venezuelans was still moving roughly through their midst.

He likely would have apologized to me as well, if I hadn't slipped into the crowd first. As quickly as I could I made my way out of the ballroom and down the corridor, trying to stay ahead of the soldiers. I was pretty sure Perez hadn't seen my face, and Hayduk had barely glanced at me.

I looked down at the thing in my hands, scarcely believing I had man-aged to palm it in my brief tussle with Hayduk: his GPU card. It looked slim and dangerous in my hands. It had been in Hayduk's breast pocket, right where he'd put it after displaying it to Sergei like a triumphant de-tective.

There was so much I could do with this. Gain access to all of the newly restricted fifth floor, for one thing. Given time and a little luck, I might even be able to hack into the sectors of the stolen drive we'd been unable to access. If I could deliver it to the Americans in Atlanta, it would be an intelligence asset beyond price.

But I had a much more pressing need for it.

I found a stairwell and climbed to the third floor. There was a guard

outside the command center where Sergei worked, but he'd seen me so often all he did was nod as I walked past him.

Sergei's cabinet was locked, but I found the key where he usually kept
it — under his medical computer. I unlocked the cabinet and slid out the
top drawer.

Inside were four refrigerated containers. Each one contained twelve
hundred vials of antivirus. Unless Sergei went free in the next few hours,
all the effort that had gone into creating them would be for naught.

This must have been Hayduk's plan all along, I realized. This was why
he hadn't moved against the reactor earlier. He'd been patiently biding his
time, like a spider. Waiting until the moment of maximum vulnerabil-
ity to strike. With Sergei under arrest, we'd never get Thibault's message
and never deliver the antivirus. The virus would rampage unchecked, and
people were going to continue to die.

With Sergei and Thibault neutralized, Hayduk could return his focus
to the last person standing in his way: Perez. He wouldn't have to con-
tend with Perez for long, of course — just long enough to make sure he
mounted no more successful efforts against the virus. Three weeks, maybe
four, would be all he needed.

After that, everyone would be dead or dying.

I lifted the first case out of the cabinet. Folded neatly underneath it, hidden under an opaque sample bag, was the American combat suit.

For a moment I wondered if what I was about to do would get both Sergei and me killed. If my time wouldn't be better spent trying to find some
way to get the antivirus to Thibault. And then I thought of Sergei in the
hands of that murderous bastard. I took a deep breath, pulled the opaque
sample bag out of the cabinet, and carefully slid the combat suit into it.

I returned the refrigerated container to the cabinet. Carrying the bag,
I left the command center. I started for the lobby, then thought better of
it. They wouldn't parade Sergei out the front door of the hotel. This whole
affair had been public enough already. If he was being formally charged,
they would probably drag his ass to the Burroughs Detention Center on
Lake Michigan. And if not, then straight to the Sturgeon Building. Either
way, I needed to stop them before they left the hotel. My best bet was probably the parking garage where Perez kept a motor pool, watched over by a
squad of trigger-happy Venezuelan teenagers in uniform.

I needed to find them — and quickly. If I guessed wrong, I'd lose my one
chance to intercept them before they left the hotel. And I would never see
Sergei again.

I made my decision and headed away from the command center. I strode down the hall about a hundred yards, scanning the ceiling until I found what I was looking for. A camera, fixed to the wall about ten feet above my head.

I approached. There were no soldiers nearby, and no one else in sight. When I was close enough I addressed the camera, speaking in a normal voice.

"Zircon Border. Are you there? Can you hear me? I need your help. It's urgent."

Scarcely five seconds later, I heard a ringing. I looked around. About thirty feet to my left was a wall phone. It rang again.

I walked over and picked it up.

"How can I help you, Mr. Simcoe?" It was Zircon Border's friendly voice.

"Thank you. Thank you for calling me."

"Don't mention it."

"Colonel Hayduk just arrested a friend of mine. Medical Specialist Sergei Vulka."

"Yes. I saw it happen. Tragic business."

"I need to know where they're taking him. Can you send that information to a secure data location that Black Winter can access, as we discussed? Is Black Winter available?"

"Yes, I can. He's available . . . It's done."

"Can you feed me Black Winter's responses to my questions?"

"Of course."

"Excellent. I need to track Hayduk's movements. How are they getting Sergei out of the building? The parking garage?"

"Black Winter says he can't tell. They're still on the second floor. They're moving Specialist Vulka into an elevator."

"Where it is headed?"

"Apologies, Mr. Simcoe. I don't have cameras in the elevators. Just a second."

"Hurry, please." It had to be the parking garage, I thought. I was wasting time talking to Zircon Border. I'd have only moments to intercept them.

I was about to hang up when Zircon Border said, "Black Winter says to stay where you are. They're taking him to the third floor."

"Here?"

"Yes. The elevator doors will open in nine seconds."

"Thank you both." I hung up, and started toward the elevators. About eight seconds later I heard a chime, and without hesitating I turned and ducked into the bathroom.

Hayduk and his goons stepped out of the elevator. Holding the bathroom door open a crack, I watched them march Sergei toward the command center. Perez was not far behind.

*Why the hell are they taking him there?* I had no idea, but I doubted they would hold him there long.

I needed to move fast. Intercepting Hayduk and Sergei here was a lucky break, but I couldn't count on that luck to last. I thought briefly about changing into the suit here in the bathroom, but the sudden sound of a flushing toilet behind me spurred me to action. I yanked open the door and started walking.

I needed someplace private to change, and there were soldiers *everywhere.* Most of them looked off-duty, clustered in small packs and probably headed to the mess hall or the barracks. Mostly they ignored me, but I got a few curious glances as I stalked down the hall. I needed to escape all this attention — and soon.

On my left, the elevator doors were closing. It looked empty. On impulse, I stepped inside.

The elevator waited. None of the floors on the wall pad was lit.

*Screw it,* I thought. Zircon Border had said the AGRT didn't have eyes in the elevators. I hit the button for the forty-fifth floor, right in the middle of the abandoned floors, and pulled the combat suit out of the bag. I started to change.

The suit is single piece, like a wet suit, and it's very heavy. Last time I'd pulled it on it took almost five minutes. I had to do it much faster now. I kicked off my shoes, sending one thumping across the floor to hit the elevator door, and jammed my left leg into the suit, pants and all.

That didn't work. The suit was too tight, and my pant leg bunched up around my knee uncomfortably. I swore in frustration, then threw the suit to the floor and tore off my pants.

The elevator silently displayed our progress upwards. The sixth floor. The eighth. The eleventh. If it slowed down now, there'd be just enough time to stuff the suit in the bag and stand smiling innocently as the doors opened, wearing only my underwear. I'd done worse.

The elevator didn't slow. I picked up the suit again. This was the first time I'd put the suit on in bright light. I could see the inside surface was dotted with a rich mesh of electrical contacts, and there were thick clusters of circuitry spaced at odd intervals up and down the arms and legs. It

all looked dark, unpowered, incapable of monitoring my vital signs, playing soothing Muzak, or doing anything else helpful. I jammed my left leg
in, pulling the suit up to my crotch, stretching the fabric until it was tight
against my skin.

The fifteenth floor. The eighteenth.

Next was my right leg. Hopping on one leg, I lost my balance and almost toppled over before straightening myself by leaning against the wall.
The suit was fighting me; it clung to my left leg like a horny dog. I couldn't
pull it past my thighs. I tried, but it stubbornly refused to budge.

The twentieth floor. The twenty-first.

I made an effort to slow down, keep my movements even. I shifted my
weight to my left leg, freeing my right to flex a little, and ignoring the sudden stab of pain from my wounded hip. At the same time I gave the suit
a firm yank, and it slid up to my waist. The top half, attached at the back,
hung formless against the back of my legs.

I heard a soft *ding,* and the elevator began to slow.

I had just enough time to pull my shirttails out, letting them fall over
the top few inches of the suit. Then the door slid open on the twenty-third
floor.

Standing before me were two Venezuelan soldiers, both carrying automatic rifles. I stared at them.

They entered the elevator, openly regarding my legs. One of them
punched a floor. The second, his hand casually at the shoulder strap of
his rifle, leaned over to peer at the top half of my suit, hanging down between my legs.

The first said something in Spanish. The second gave me a wide grin.
"You are going swimming?" he asked.

"Scuba diving," I said, my mouth suddenly very dry. "Great weather
for it."

The second translated for his companion. Both of them laughed. They
couldn't have been more than nineteen years old.

The elevator dinged again. The doors opened.

"Good luck!" said the second soldier, as he followed the first out of the
elevator. "Look out for sharks, ha?"

The doors slid closed.

We were on the twenty-fourth floor. They had ridden the elevator up
one floor. "The crack troops of Venezuela," I muttered, shaking my head.

I struggled into the rest of the suit. I didn't waste time pulling off my
shirt; the suit went on easily enough over it even though it had probably

been designed for someone an inch or two shorter than me. The fabric felt tight at the shoulders and crotch. The snaps that sealed the suit in the front were a complex affair, and I was still fighting them when the door opened onto the dark hallway of the forty-fifth floor.

I stepped out into the deserted hallway. It stretched out into darkness to my left and right. I'd never been to this part of the hotel before — probably nobody had for some time. It wasn't part of the block of rooms scheduled to be reopened for the refugees. It would make a perfect place to change.

The only light was from the elevator behind me, and from glowing exit signs at the distant ends of the corridor. I took the suit gloves and mask out of the bag, picked up my pants, and stuffed them into it. I hid the bag in the shadows a dozen feet down the hall to my left, in the recessed alcove sheltering the door to 4516.

As I straightened, something stirred on the carpet, less than fifty feet down the hallway.

I froze, my hand still reaching toward the bag. It was impossible to make out what it was, but I thought I saw the faint gleam of metal. I heard two soft *clicks*, like claws on stone. Whatever it was, it was small, not much bigger than Croaker. And it was starting to move.

Behind me the elevator doors were closing. I made my decision, abandoning the bag and dashing for the elevator.

As I slipped inside I heard a sudden scraping behind me, the sounds of frantic motion, and a deep, scary hum. I retreated until I felt the far wall of the elevator against my back, and stayed there until the doors were firmly closed.

The elevator was motionless for several seconds before I realized that I hadn't selected a floor. I took three quick steps and punched 3, before the doors could open again. The elevator began to drop.

What *was* that thing? Did the Venezuelans keep robotic sentries on abandoned floors to scare off squatters? Crazy. And more importantly, what the hell was going to happen to my dress pants? How was I supposed to return to the ballroom without *them*?

The elevator was dropping fast. Pushing aside my wardrobe anxieties, I pulled the mask on. It completely covered my face, and the visor shielded my eyes nicely. It was stuffy and smelled like plastic, but fit okay. Everything looked green through the thin film of the visor, though, and I was worried about my peripheral vision. There were four snaps that fixed it firmly to the suit, but I only had time for two. Then I pulled on the gloves.

I realized I was missing the boots. I cursed extravagantly for a moment.

They must have been jammed in the back of Sergei's desk, or maybe under his chair. Either way, it was too late to retrieve them now.

I felt like an idiot, standing there in a top-of-the-line American combat suit and sock feet. After a moment I sighed, and reached for my dress shoes. At least they were nearly the same color as the suit. Maybe no one would notice.

As I was tying the laces on the second shoe I heard a soft *ding*, and felt the elevator slow. The doors opened on the third floor.

It was showtime again.

# XXXVII

**Thursday, March 25th, 2083**
**Posted 12:02 am by Barry Simcoe**

**CanadaNET1 Encrypted, Sponsored by PetPatrol.**
*Never lose your pet again – our embedded microchips and fleet of*
*custom drones make sure of it. Nationwide coverage!*

**Sharing is set to PRIVATE**
**Comments are CLOSED**

I straightened up, took a deep breath, and stepped out into the lobby.

I glanced to my left. There were perhaps half a dozen soldiers in my field of vision, most of them milling around a low table where someone had unrolled a 30-inch screen with a network feed. Several had guns, but none noticed me immediately.

For a moment I thought I would have to do something dramatic to get their attention. Then I glanced to the right.

Standing not five feet from me, where he had apparently been waiting for the elevator, was Colonel Perez.

We stared at each other. Him gawking with his mouth open, me an expressionless mask of American military cool. Then he started shouting in Spanish, pointing at me and waving to the nearest soldiers.

I punched him in the face. Then I ran like hell.

There was a lot more shouting after that.

I ran past two soldiers who simply stared at me, startled, their rifles still slung loosely at their shoulders, clearly unaware of what had just happened. But from behind I heard Perez shouting with authority.

"¡Párese! ¡Párese!" he screamed at me.

I elected not to párese, whatever the hell that meant.

I sped past the young guard at the entrance to the command center. He barely glanced at me, instead staring back toward Perez, trying to figure out what all the fuss was about.

The suit was a nuisance. My visor was quickly fogging up; it felt like I was breathing into a plastic bag. And the suit slowed me down—it was awkward and stiff. But adrenaline made up for that, at least, and I sped down the hall pretty quickly. I ran past a work crew assembling a large metal cabinet; while they all looked alarmed, none moved to intercept me.

My luck couldn't last. Ahead on the right was a small corridor leading to the service elevator. The urge to take it was strong. I would be out of sight for long seconds before they could follow.

But unless the elevator was there waiting for me, it was a death trap.

I kept running.

Now only a few workmen in overalls stood between me and my destination: a stairwell barely twenty-five yards straight ahead at the end of the hall. I could hear sounds of close pursuit behind, but didn't turn to look. My peripheral vision in the mask wasn't as bad as I'd feared, but my hearing was crap.

But I could still hear Perez. His voice cut through the others; his orders —in Spanish—were crisp and concise. All the other shouting died away, and then the sounds of pursuit did too. Now there was only silence behind me.

That was far, far more alarming than the shouting. I put on an extra burst of speed, closing the distance to the stairs.

Fifteen yards.

Ten.

There was a single workman in my way now. He was on a step stool, holding a handful of tightly looped wiring connected to a lamp fixture. He looked civilian, not military, but that didn't mean he wouldn't try to stop me—block the stairs, or try to tackle me. I braced for combat.

What he did instead was much more unnerving. He didn't look at me at all; his terrified gaze was fixed back the way I had come. As I sprinted to the door he suddenly cowered on the stool, then hit the deck, landing on the floor with both hands over his head.

Someone—likely several someones—was aiming a gun our way.

The courageous thing to do would have been to keep on running and slam through the door. Instead, I gave in to raw fear and doglegged right and ducked, slowing just enough that I didn't dislocate my shoulder when I smashed into the wall.

A bullet hit eighteen inches to my left, at about waist height. I heard another one impact metal a few feet away — probably the door.

I risked a glance back down the hall. Fifty yards away three soldiers stood aiming rifles at me, and more were pouring out of the command center. Perez stood in the middle of it all, directing the action. In front of him, two more soldiers dropped to one knee, raising their rifles.

I heard a third shot and felt a stabbing pain just above my left knee. Then a fourth shot. When that bullet failed to pass through my heart — or any other part of me — I somehow managed to unclench, spin around, and leap for the door. My hands fumbled with the handle, and a moment later I was in the stairwell and out of their line of fire.

"Jesus *Christ!*" I shouted.

I tore off my mask. My breathing came in ragged gasps, and my hands were shaking. *They're shooting at me. Jesus, I think I've been shot.*

Somehow this was both more real and more terrifying than even facing the Godkiller with Van de Velde had been. I hobbled to the stairs, clutching my left knee.

Strangely, my knee felt fine. Well, it was *sore,* but certainly not shot. My fingers grabbed at the fabric of the suit, but there was no hole I could find, no evidence that I'd been hit at all.

That wasn't completely true, I realized. Directly above my left knee, the suit had hardened dramatically and taken on a soft sheen. The outer layers of the suit had responded to the impact by instantly forming a tough outer coating.

Even unpowered, the suit had protected me, preventing the bullet from penetrating. The American combat suit was bulletproof. Or at least, bullet-*resistant.* I flexed my knee. I'd probably have a pretty serious bruise, but that was a lot better than a bullet hole.

And the suit was still flexible enough to run.

There was more rifle fire as the heavy door slowly closed behind me. At least one bullet penetrated the stairwell, and I heard it ricochet eagerly in search of my heart. By then I was taking the stairs three at a time, climbing two stories before daring to stop again.

I heard the door slam open two floors below, then renewed shouting. They were in the stairwell. Move, move, *move,* I thought. But I forced myself to stay where I was for one more moment, catching my breath and listening.

Running feet. More shouting. Echoes as the voices bounced around in the tight space. More voices, slightly more distant now.

They were moving downstairs. They probably assumed, logically enough, that I was fleeing the building. Only an idiot would run *up*stairs, to the heavily guarded offices of the senior staff.

I *was* an idiot, I realized.

They'd figure it out soon enough. Time to move — but quietly. *Stealth now, not speed.* All the same, I moved to the door as fast as I dared, pulling the mask back on as I went.

The door that gave access to the fifth floor had been sealed with an electronic lock. I pulled at the handle experimentally, but it wouldn't budge.

*Don't panic,* I thought. *You expected this.* This was a lie, but like a patsy, I fell for it. Staying calm, I groped for Hayduk's GPU card.

The sound of running feet was now getting closer. The soldiers had started moving upstairs. They were two floors below me and closing the distance quickly.

The door lock was military grade; it required physical contact with an electronic key. I found Hayduk's GPU card, rotated it once, and slid it into the lock.

Nothing happened. I heard voices now, one floor below, rising fast.

I withdrew the card, turned it over, inserted it again.

There was a soft click. I tried the door, and the knob turned in my hands. I pulled it open, as quietly as possible, and slipped through.

An armed guard stood with his back to me on the other side, his rifle resting easily in his arms. I seemed to have gotten the drop on him, and as I moved past him he jumped, obviously startled. He swore softly under his breath, automatically coming to attention.

I ignored him, striding purposefully down the corridor. *Just like you belong here,* I thought. No one gets through that door unless they're supposed to.

It didn't work, at least not entirely. The guard called out in Spanish, sounding more curious than confrontational. I kept walking across the plush carpet.

I heard two soft beeps that I realized were coming from the combat suit. Despite everything, I found myself smiling. If the beeps meant what I hoped they did, I was getting close.

This floor had once housed upscale business offices before the occupation, probably hotel administration or long-term rental properties. Just like the sixth floor, most of it was under construction, as the Venezuelan army gradually converted it into secure office space for two dozen duty officers. I saw gaps in the ceiling panels where they were running heavy-duty power lines, and a score of office cubes had been dismantled to make space for high-wall offices. Steel paneling was piled neatly near the windows, and thick rolls of fiber cable were stacked like tires nearby. I didn't see any workmen, but the lights were on in at least half a dozen offices. I could make out muffled conversation to my left. I turned to the right, following a clear path through all the construction toward a line of what looked like completed offices.

Pretending I couldn't hear the guard had not made him go away. He was following me now, leaving his post, and his questions were in a much sharper tone.

I had another problem. The corridor ahead was blocked. The Venezuelans had installed what appeared to be a soundproof security wall of transparent glass running from floor to ceiling, dividing the floor into two wings. I could see larger offices on the other side and what looked like some serious telecom equipment half-assembled in the corridor.

A glass door had been cut in the transparent wall, but there was no handle or other visible way to open it. A balding Venezuelan in uniform sat on my side of the wall behind a ridiculously small desk, looking like an impoverished tax collector. He glanced up as I approached, but I ignored him too.

So far that was working out pretty well for me.

I stopped in front of the glass door. A gentle push confirmed it was shut tight. I heard the soldier walk up behind me. He directed another stern question at me, then spoke to the seated man, who shrugged, looking helpless.

I probably had only a few seconds before the shouting and shooting started again. Fortunately, I'd spotted what I was looking for: a thin square of frosted glass ten inches to the left of the door at about shoulder height. I pressed Hayduk's card against it.

There was no visible reaction. *Don't panic,* I thought. *You expected this.*

The lie didn't work this time. But before I could panic in earnest, I pushed the glass door again. It opened with no resistance. I slipped through and pushed it closed behind me. I felt the magnetic seal grip the door as it slid shut again, leaving the soldier and his tax-collecting buddy on the other side.

The air seemed cooler on this side. As I strode down the corridor, I caught a tiny motion near the ceiling. A camera was following my progress. Surely they could access it from the command center, and it would be only moments before they confirmed where I was.

Time to hurry.

A woman walked out of the closest office, holding a data slate. She stopped abruptly, openly staring at me in the combat suit. Behind me, the bald guy in uniform stood up and tapped on the glass wall to get her attention.

I strode past her without slowing. There were half a dozen offices in immediate sight, but I was interested in one in particular. I got lucky with the fourth one on the left. A thin metal plate on the door read GUSTAV HAYDUK.

The combat suit gave out two more beeps, more assertive this time.

Hayduk's GPU unlocked the door for me. The office was almost obsessively tidy. A single 20-inch computer screen stood sentinel on his desk next to a slim handheld tablet. Two metal cabinets dominated the back wall. There was a camera mounted on the ceiling, and it tracked me automatically as I entered the room.

I knew I wouldn't have time for a thorough search. Fortunately, I didn't need one — I found what I wanted in minutes, in a heavy case on the floor next to the cabinets. I lifted it onto the table and tried the lid. It wasn't locked, and it slid open with a satisfying click.

On top was a two-page report, bearing the insignia of the Venezuelan Corps of Engineers. I set that aside. Underneath, sealed in what looked like evidence bags, were the power cells for the combat suit. As I lifted them from the case, two more beeps sounded in my ears. The suit, hungry for power.

*Goddamn. At last.*

It took me thirty frustrating seconds to tear open one of the bags. They were made of the same stuff as airplane black boxes, I swear to God. I finally got a small rip in one corner and, using both hands, tore a hole large enough to slide out the power cell.

Outside I could hear the woman speaking to someone, and then an answering voice from the far end of the hall. I spun the cell in my hands, looking for a way to turn it on. It was a slender metal disk, oddly flexible, about three inches in diameter and almost featureless. I couldn't find anything that looked like an On button. Finally, hoping for the best, I reached around to the small of my back and inserted it into the tightly recessed cavity at the back of the suit.

The reaction was immediate. My visor went completely dark, rendering me blind.

That wasn't what I'd expected. I felt suddenly claustrophobic, trapped, breathing only stale air inside my mask. I heard footsteps out in the hall, muffled conversation, someone barking instructions. All while I stood there stupidly with my hands behind my back.

I heard more conversation. Someone had moved into the room, was possibly standing right in front of me.

I straightened slowly, fighting to stay calm. I reached out for the desk with my left hand, trying to get my bearings, moving slowly so I didn't appear to be groping. The suit seemed heavy and constricting all of a sudden, and I really did feel like I was suffocating. The urge to tear off the mask was almost overwhelming, even though it would mean exposing my face to the cameras—not to mention whoever was in the room with me.

The room was suddenly very quiet. For a moment I thought I could sense someone moving to my right, trying to circle around behind me, and I jerked my head in that direction reflexively. But my visor remained fully dark.

I felt frustrated and helpless—why hadn't I learned more about the suit before taking a risk like this?

There was another soft sound, this one to my right. My hand went to the back of my mask, ready to pull it off. But I hesitated, gripped by uncertainty. Should I try to pry the power cell out instead? Would that return the mask to normal, or just make things worse?

As I stood there, feeling vulnerable and stupid, something blue flickered in my visor. It happened a second time, and suddenly I could see again. My cheeks felt cool air circulating in my mask as the suit came to life around me.

There was a low, measured, feminine voice in my ear, so quiet as to be almost inaudible, conducting what sounded like an automated systems check. It said: *"Tactical navigation—currently unavailable."*

And: *"Low orbit DP—currently unavailable. Remote guidance systems—no response."*

And more stuff like that. Most of it incomprehensible to me, but all with a similar theme: the suit was lost and confused, and everything was pretty much crap.

I really didn't care at that moment. With my vision restored I spun around quickly, looking to see who was in the room. I expected to find a soldier at my side, about to club me with a rifle butt.

Standing behind me was Jacaranda.

"Hello," she said, in her odd musical voice.

I was so startled, I had nothing to say. She took two steps forward, walking around me.

"I must say, Mr. Simcoe. You are a man of exceptional daring. This is unexpected, even for you."

"What are you doing here?" When I spoke, the suit amplified my voice. It boomed into the room, strangely distorted.

"I am here to assist you. This room is where you will find all your answers."

There was another shout, out in the hallway. The men with guns would be here in moments.

"I'm not interested in answers," I said. "I'm here to save —"

I glanced up at the camera. I'd almost said Sergei's name where everything I was doing was almost certainly being recorded.

"Do not concern yourself with the cameras," she said. "While you are in this room with me, they will not hear you."

"I'm here to save Sergei," I said.

"I am sorry about your friend. He is lost to us now. Once Colonel Hayduk takes a prisoner, they do not return. Innocent or guilty, it matters not to him. They belong to him, and he does not release them."

"We'll see about that," I said. Clutching the second power cell and Hayduk's GPU, I stepped toward the door. Jacaranda moved smoothly to block the way.

"Get out of my way," I said.

"Do not let his sacrifice be in vain," she said. "Look."

Despite myself, I glanced where she was pointing. On the floor next to the back cabinet was a small portable safe.

"Open it," she said.

"No."

"I will give you the codes," she said.

"Get out of my way," I said.

She stepped closer. So close that I could see through the eye holes of her mask. I expected to see a hint of silver, the mysterious robotic face I'd caught a glimpse of in the Field Museum, but instead I saw what looked like soft skin around her eyes.

"You're so *close*," she whispered, "to truly understanding what's happening. You know there's a Sovereign Intelligence in Zimbabwe investigating you. You know there's a race of robots secretly living under Chicago. You know Armitage is scheming to exterminate human life in the Midwest. You know the pretext for the invasion of America was a lie. Don't you want to know *why?*"

"What are you talking about?"

"It's all connected," she said. "All of it. And the connecting piece is in that box."

I hesitated. "Connected how?"

"By the truth. The one the Sentient Cathedral is so desperate to conceal. That truth is the real reason Armitage has risked everything to control Chicago. And why Hayduk is so desperate to find you."

*Shit.*

I bent down and examined the safe. It was roughly a two-foot cube, pretty low-tech. It had a thumbprint scanner, a keypad, a handle on the front, and not much else.

"It needs a thumbprint to open," I said.

"I shall give you the bypass codes," she said.

Something wasn't right. "You have bypass codes for this safe?"

"Yes," she said.

"Then you open it. If you have all the codes, and can waltz in here past all this security, then why do you need me?"

Jacaranda didn't answer. I stood up. I started to circle around her.

"You don't need me to open this safe, do you?" I said. "You could have opened it yourself any time you like. You could have given them to me days ago. But you didn't. Instead, here you are. You want me here. Why?"

Jacaranda remained silent. I kept circling, watching her.

"You're a ghost. Or you pretend to be," I said. "But you need me for something, and you're not telling me what it is."

She stood frozen. The only sound was a dull hammering coming from the hallway.

"Well," I said. "We're at an impasse. We have to trust each other, or this is all going to be over in a matter of minutes. I'm willing to play along. But you're hiding something from me, and I need to know what it is."

In response, Jacaranda lifted her head slightly. I followed her gaze.

"What?" I said. "The cameras? You said they can't see you. No, wait . . . that's not what you said. You said that when I'm in here with you, the cameras can't *hear* me."

"Correct," she said.

"What does that mean?"

"Hayduk," Jacaranda said, "is not a stupid man. He is putting the pieces together. He is beginning to suspect my existence. He is beginning to suspect that he cannot trust the evidence of his digital surveillance network."

"So what?" I said. "You don't even show up on his cameras. He'll never find you."

"He doesn't have to. If he becomes concerned enough, he'll report his suspicions to his master."

"Armitage."

"Yes. And Armitage is capable of finding me, once he's told where to look. He'll see the traces that no one else does."

"So for you to stay hidden, you need me to . . . ah."

"You understand," she said.

"Yes, of course. You can hide yourself, but you can't hide the theft. You need me to cover your tracks. So you block the sound to the cameras, but not the visual. So Hayduk has someone to blame — the American terrorist — instead of a ghost, and he doesn't turn to Armitage for help."

"Precisely. I am also delaying the feed to the command center. Hayduk does not know your location, and he will not for several minutes."

"Good news," I said, bending over the safe. "Why didn't you just tell me that to begin with? Let's get this done."

Altogether Jacaranda gave me eight codes. If I'd known it was going to take that long to open the goddamn safe, I wouldn't have bothered. When she was finished, I yanked on the handle impatiently. The safe opened smoothly.

Inside was a pistol, a slim black data slate, four stacks of Venezuelan bolívar bills, a thin black case, and a wallet. I reached for the slate.

"The wallet," said Jacaranda.

I grabbed the wallet and stood up. It was made of leather and very light. I flipped it open.

It wasn't a wallet. It was a carrying case for a short, squat data drive.

"What is it?" I asked.

"Hayduk has not been chasing you to recover the suit," said Jacaranda. "Nor to prevent you from using the recipe for the antivirus you took. He has been desperate to find you because you stole a much greater secret."

"I don't have time for riddles. Spit it out."

"The data drive you took from him," she said. "It contained several documents."

"Yeah. Most of them we couldn't decrypt."

Jacaranda put her fingers on top of the hand holding the drive. Her touch was light and warm.

"This is the algorithm to decrypt the drive," she said.

"What's on it?"

"The true reason for the war," she said simply.

Outside, I heard more hammering and the sound of breaking glass. It was definitely time to leave.

"I sealed the glass enclosure after you stepped through," Jacaranda said matter-of-factly. "But it won't hold them for long."

I tossed the wallet away and slipped the short data drive into the bag with the remaining power core. There was another empty slot at the small of my back, and I was tempted to try inserting the second core. But if it caused another system fluctuation or reboot like the first, I'd be standing here blind with my thumb up my ass when the soldiers burst into the room. I left the core in the bag and moved to the entrance.

"I delayed the camera feeds in this room," she said. "But that will not prevent the soldiers in the hall from seeing you when you leave. Once you step out that door, I can no longer help you."

I hesitated for a second. I had promised Black Winter that I'd help put him in touch with Jacaranda the next time I saw her . . . although this hardly seemed the ideal time to bring it up. I settled for asking, "How can I contact you?"

"I will arrange communication when it is safe."

"I understand. Thanks for your help. How will you get away?"

"The same way I got here," she said mysteriously.

"Good luck," I said.

"And to you."

I pulled open the door, stepping back cautiously as I did so. The corridor was filled with shouting and the sound of breaking glass, but the section of hallway immediately in front of the office was empty. I couldn't see a soul.

That wasn't strictly true, I realized abruptly. The suit was sketching thin ghost outlines on the inside of my visor, and after a moment I realized they were people. People in the corridor — or the outlines of people, seen right through the walls. Presumably in infrared, or whatever spectrum the military was using to track and kill people these days.

If the suit was to be believed, there were four people in the hall. The two closest were easy to identify from their outlines: the woman and the bald door guard. The other two were amorphous blobs with legs — but they were moving closer, approaching from the right, at the far end of the corridor. I heard another shout, this one oddly amplified by the suit.

I stepped out of the office. There was a sudden shriek from the young woman, who stood barely twenty feet to my right. She covered her mouth and stumbled backwards, keeping her eyes on me. She was the only one on my side of the glass wall.

Behind her, on the other side of the glass, the bald guy was trying to smash the glass door using a metal chair. When he saw me, he dropped the chair and pulled out his own GPU card. He held it against the metal pad on the wall, and I saw it flash red. He swore in frustration. Clearly this wasn't the first time he'd tried.

Behind him the man who had followed me from the stairwell and another armed soldier were approaching fast. They both held short pieces of unpolished metal that would serve very nicely as crowbars. They waved the bald man back and went to work on the door.

I turned my back on them and headed in the opposite direction.

I passed more offices. A white-haired man stuck his head out of one, speaking to me sternly in Spanish. I ignored him, and he stepped back inside and grabbed a phone.

Moving in the suit was easier now. Air was flowing, and the mask no longer felt sweaty and restricting. The suit no longer resisted me, or even seemed as heavy. If anything, it almost seemed to move in sync with me. This effect became more prominent as the minutes ticked by, as if the suit was learning. Or maybe it was just limbering up, like an athlete before a marathon.

In fact, the only uncomfortable aspect now was my ankles. The suit had clamped down on them, as if compensating for the lack of boots and determined to keep a tight seal. All well and good, but it was cutting off the circulation in my feet, and I was starting to lose feeling in my toes.

The offices ahead were under construction, and the wall on my right was missing. The Venezuelans were building something, something that needed heavy-duty power cables — cables that were currently wrapped in nonconducting plastic and dangling unused from the ceiling. A tall, lumpy black metal pillar dominated the space. There was something familiar about it, familiar and deeply alarming, but I couldn't put my finger on what it might be and I didn't have time to investigate.

I pushed on, looking for an exit. On my left a windowless office had been converted to a makeshift biolab, with half a dozen grow-tanks filled with fluid—fluid and dark shapes that stirred slowly in unseen currents. A middle-aged woman in a white lab coat who had bent over a table to inspect a portable pump looked up at me in surprise.

I kept moving. Behind me I heard renewed shouting, and a loud *crack* as the door gave way. They were coming through.

The corridor ended, opening into a large conference room. Dozens of folding metal chairs were arranged in disordered lines before a battered podium and a huge wall-mounted data display. Exits were clearly marked on both the left and right. I took a hard left as I entered, getting out of the firing line of the soldiers coming up fast behind.

Straight ahead, jogging forward to investigate all the commotion, were two soldiers. The guy on the left looked familiar, but I couldn't immediately place him. He had the stripe of a lance corporal, a cabo segundo, on his epaulette.

The one on the right was Sergeant Noa Van de Velde.

The corporal reacted first. He drew his sidearm with impressive speed. As he did, I recognized him. He was one of the soldiers who'd chased me through half a mile of underground tunnel before running into the Orbit Pebble.

He had his gun aimed squarely at my chest, and his hands were steady. But he didn't seem prepared to fire without word from his sergeant. "¿Sargento?" he said.

Van de Velde appeared frozen. She was gaping at me, her mouth open.

The suit did not like the corporal. He was starkly outlined on my display, and his weapon was flagged in bright red. The suit wanted me to disarm him. It seemed hungry for motion.

*All right, suit. Let's see what you've got.*

"¿Sargento?" he said again. He glanced uncertainly to his left.

I lunged. The suit anticipated me, accelerating me faster than I would have thought possible. I swatted the corporal's hands to the left, simultaneously grabbing his elbow. The gun fired harmlessly into the wall.

I yanked him toward me, hard, pulling him off balance and pinching his wrist. I slammed the palm of my left hand into his chin, forcing his head back. I felt something in his elbow crack. The corporal shouted in pain.

He dropped the weapon, and I released him. He fell to his knees, cradling his left arm, his eyes squeezed shut in agony.

Everything I'd done had happened in a highly accelerated state. The suit was helping me react faster, move quicker. And it was obviously amplifying my strength. It felt both exhilarating and alarming. I hoped I hadn't broken any bones in the young corporal's arm.

His pistol had thudded to the floor at my feet. I wanted to pick it up, but there was a new complication. Van de Velde had finally drawn her weapon. And she had it aimed at my head.

"¡Un paso atrás!" she said. The gun in her hands quivered, very slightly.

I stepped backward slowly, raising my hands.

The two soldiers chasing me came thudding down the hallway. They pulled up as I came back into view, arms raised over my head. One of them shouted at me in Spanish, dropping his crowbar and raising his rifle.

I kept my eyes on Van de Velde. She took a few steps forward, until she could glance around the corner and see the approaching soldiers.

She wasn't happy to see them. She silently mouthed an obscenity. Her gun wavered.

I contemplated taking it away from her. But I didn't know my own strength yet, and the two soldiers closing on us would likely start shooting. I couldn't risk having her in the line of fire.

I turned to the arriving soldiers, keeping my arms in the air. Making sure they could see I was unarmed.

The first to arrive had his rifle at his shoulder. He was shouting at me in Spanish. I couldn't follow everything he said, but it was clear he wanted me on the floor. The second one pulled up behind him, still clutching his metal rod. He moved away from his companion, flanking me on the right.

Van de Velde swore under her breath. She lowered her weapon and stepped into the entrance, speaking to the first soldier in Spanish and gesturing for him to get his rifle out of her face.

The soldier was having none of it. He barked right back at Van de Velde, moving around her, keeping me covered.

I was more concerned about the soldier on the right. He looked furious and was clutching the metal rod like a baseball bat. It was pretty clear what he intended to do with it. The suit might be bullet-resistant, but a crowbar to the head was a whole different ball game. In the bottom left of my visor, a small red light started flashing. A tiny heart icon blinked at me in red.

The suit was telling me my heart rate was elevated. *No shit, suit.*

The soldier with the rod jumped forward, swinging at my head. The suit analyzed where he put his weight, told me precisely when and where he would swing. It would have been easy to step out of the way, especially with the accelerated reflexes of the suit.

But I didn't. Instead I simply reached out and caught the metal bar be-fore it connected.

It was a tricky thing to attempt, but the look of shocked surprise on the soldier's face made it worth it. Stopping a crowbar in mid-swing with one hand should have hurt like hell, but the suit absorbed virtually all of the impact.

The soldier was off balance; I didn't need the suit to tell me that. None-theless he was tugging on the metal rod in frustration, trying to pull it from my hand. I tightened my grip and yanked. As the soldier toppled for-ward, still clutching the crowbar, I took a smooth step back, slamming the palm of my left hand into the rod, spinning it hard to the right.

The soldier was yanked off his feet and flew through the air like a toy, smashing against the wall. I felt a rush of adrenaline. The suit was incred-ible. It made me feel astonishingly powerful, like I could do anything.

But I needed to play it cool until I could figure out how to get Van de Velde out of the middle of this situation. I took a breath, dropped the crowbar to the floor, and turned back to her, calmly raised my hands in surrender again.

The second soldier surged forward, raising the butt of his rifle, eager to smash my head open. He never got the chance. Van de Velde interposed herself between us, facing the soldier and trying to get this situation un-der control.

Her gun was aimed at the floor. She jabbed her finger at his chest, spit-ting at him in Spanish. She sounded exactly like a drill sergeant.

The soldier tried to move around her, anxious to crack me in the skull. Van de Velde moved smoothly to intercept, blocking his path. To the right, the second soldier got shakily to his feet, glaring at me. He looked bruised, but not too badly injured. He picked up the metal rod again, and I made no move to stop him.

Something was happening in the hall behind them. A dark shape was moving into the corridor. A very large shape.

It was the tall, lumpy pillar.

It unfolded black arms and metal legs and a heavy torpedo-shaped head, and took great lumbering strides toward us. It stood roughly eight feet tall, and must have weighed 1,800 pounds.

Except for its deep black reflective surface, it was a perfect replica of Standing Mars.

"*Shit,*" I said. I put my hands down.

The soldier with the metal bar managed a grin when I lowered my hands. He wiped a trickle of blood from his lips and lifted the crowbar. *This is for you,* his eyes promised.

Van de Velde was no longer actively blocking the soldiers. Her eyes were on the thing in the corridor. She took two hesitant steps backward.

"You are an unauthorized intruder," said the robot.

The soldier with the rifle took notice of the thing for the first time. Like Van de Velde, he quickly stepped away, moving to the wall. He kept his rifle on me, but his eyes fixed on the robot.

"You are not Damian Peters," said the robot. "That personnel record is a forgery."

"Standing Mars," I said. "Is that you, buddy?"

"Standing Mars was rendered inoperative by an unknown machine assailant on March 13th, 2083. That investigation is ongoing. My designation is Echo-One-Charlie-Victor-Eight-X-ray. I am known as Perfect Circle."

"Get out of here," I said to the two soldiers and Van de Velde. "Now."

Van de Velde shook her head. She pointed her pistol at me again, suddenly filled with steely resolve. "You're under arrest," she said to me.

The soldier on the right swung the metal rod into his palm with a satisfying *smack*. He gave me one last sour look, then turned to the robot. He limped toward it, pointing to where it came from. He barked at it in Spanish, ordering it back into its little alcove.

The robot strode toward me. As it did, it reached out with its right hand and crushed the soldier's skull.

Van de Velde was the first to react. Cursing extravagantly, she dropped to one knee, squeezing off three shots. Every one of them hit the thing in its big torpedo head.

It didn't slow down. It would crush Van de Velde next. "Move!" I shouted at her.

Then I lunged toward Perfect Circle.

The suit didn't want to attack Perfect Circle. The suit, in fact, seemed to think it was a dumb idea, but it tagged along. We went for the left leg just as its weight shifted to its right, in an attempt to topple it back on its metal ass.

We failed. Like Standing Mars, the thing was far more nimble than it looked. I went in under its arms and hit its back leg like a linebacker. I could feel the suit powering up my legs, helping me lift. We managed to unbalance it, and for a brief moment I thought it would go over. But before we could topple it, it reached down and plucked me off the ground, lifting me effortlessly and smashing me into the ceiling.

Every alarm the suit had was going off. It was trying to warn me: much worse was coming, and it knew it. I kicked out with my right foot, but my leather shoe bounced harmlessly off the thing's metal head.

Van de Velde had not run. She was standing not ten feet away, feet planted firmly, shooting. She didn't seem at all bothered by the fact that I was struggling in the monster's grip as she coolly fired around me, pumping round after round into the thing.

At least one of her shots penetrated the robot's tough hull, and I saw a brilliant spark in its torso.

It responded in brutal fashion. Seizing my left leg in a crushing grip, it slammed me into the floor, face-first. It did it again and again, with blinding speed. I glimpsed Van de Velde jumping backward as the robot used my body as a club, seeking to kill her.

I was knocked almost senseless. The only thing keeping me alive was the suit, which stiffened instantly into a hard protective shell. I twisted in the monster's grip, trying to reach the hand holding my leg, and it responded by slamming me into the wall on the right. Drywall shattered in an explosion of white dust, and a thick metal stud smacked me painfully in the face.

I had missed a metal girder by inches. The suit highlighted it in my display. The suit wanted me to grab it. I reacted instantly, obediently wrapping both arms around the girder, barely able to think.

Someone was shooting. Not a pistol — an automatic weapon, at close range. Still gripping the pillar, I twisted around to see what was happening.

Van de Velde was shouting orders in Spanish at the only soldier still standing, and he was obeying, firing short, controlled bursts at the robot. The rifle had far more penetration power than Van de Velde's pistol, and she had ordered him to aim high. Metal fragments sprayed out violently from Perfect Circle's torpedo head.

Perfect Circle didn't hesitate. It pulled violently on my leg, trying to slam me into the soldier. My grip on the girder was sorely tested, but together the suit and I held. The soldier didn't let up. Every burst hit the robot, spraying metal. Abruptly, it released me. It took two quick strides and struck the soldier with the force of a pile driver. I heard the crack of breaking bones, and he disappeared into the far wall in a fountain of blood.

I had bare seconds before Perfect Circle turned its attention back to me, this time to kill me. But I couldn't move. I could barely breathe. It took everything I had just to release the girder and push myself up into a sitting position. Something tumbled into the dust nearly a yard to my left.

The bag with Hayduk's drive . . . and the extra power cell. I had no idea what slamming the second power cell into the suit would do, but it was better than lying here helpless.

Perfect Circle turned around. It was perforated by bullet holes in a dozen places, and the metal shell of its ugly torpedo head was badly broken. A thin wisp of smoke curled out of its torso. Somewhere deep inside, Perfect Circle was on fire.

And still it came. Striding toward me. I got one of my legs to respond, kicking me far enough to the left to grab the bag.

Van de Velde stepped in front of me. Raising her pistol, she started firing again. Her aim was flawless, and every shot smashed into the delicate exposed circuitry in Perfect Circle's head.

"No!" I shouted. I tore the bag open, groped for the extra power cell.

Perfect Circle took another step just as my fingers closed around the cold disk of the power cell. Van de Velde stood firm, squeezing off another shot. She kept firing even as it reached down and enfolded her head and shoulders in its implacable metal grip. She fired one last time, into the thing's torso, even as the huge metal fingers crushed her.

"No, you bastard!" Behind my back, my fingers fumbled blindly. Somehow I found the power slot, empty and welcoming. The cell slid inside with no resistance.

I expected my vision to go dark again. But it did not. Instead of welcome blackness, I watched in horror as Perfect Circle flung Van de Velde's limp body aside.

Perfect Circle did not slow, taking the last two relentless strides toward me. And still I could not make my muscles respond. I was seconds from death. I wanted to stand, *needed* to stand, but my body was unable to respond.

But suddenly, the suit *could*. As fast as I thought it, the suit bounced me to my feet like a dancer.

I was so surprised that for a moment all I did was wobble like a drunken sailor. That was sufficient to dodge Perfect Circle's first strike, a too-fast hammerblow to the floor precisely where I'd been prone a fraction of a second earlier.

Perfect Circle recovered quickly. I was still wobbling, still barely upright, unsure how to react to the suit's new responsiveness. An image flashed into my head: a week ago, in my room, Mac explaining how the combat suit worked. Her warm hand on top of mine. The suit knows when you're going to move before your muscles do, she'd said. *So this is what she meant.*

I needed to move, immediately. I wasn't sure I had the coordination to pull it off, but I didn't have time for doubts. I needed to trust the suit, and I needed it to get me four feet to the left, *right fucking now.*

I trusted the suit. And it brought me precisely where I wanted to be, RFN, just as Perfect Circle's second blow tore a gaping hole in the wall, right where I'd been standing.

I was still a little unsteady. But I was a little more certain on my feet, a little less out of breath. I was getting the hang of using the suit now. Perfect Circle took two slow steps backward, appraising me.

The suit was like a dream. The first power cell had brought it to life, but the second had awoken its magic. It responded now with the speed of thought, its lightning movements quick and sure, carrying my sluggish body along for the ride. I felt momentarily unsettled by this unnatural quickness, but the suit knew its limits. As rapidly as it responded, it never let me become unbalanced. The numbness was leaving my arms and legs, and as it did I was becoming more sure of foot. I took two quick exploratory steps backward, and one to the right. Weaving like a boxer.

Perfect Circle tried to grab me then, darting forward with alarming speed. I forced my muscles to relax, told the suit where I wanted to go. The suit brought me under the robot's first swing, and then spun me out of range of its second. I danced away from the attack, into the open room. The robot followed, grabbing for me with its great metal paws.

I'd been stupid enough to allow it to grab me once; I wasn't going to make that mistake again. I threw chairs at it as I retreated into the room, slowly regaining my strength. The robot batted them away in midair. The suit watched every move it made, timing them carefully. After the fourth chair, it showed me how I could get past it.

I threw a fifth chair. Just before it swatted it out of the air, I darted forward, slipping under its defenses. I was behind it before it had time to react.

I risked a glance at Van de Velde's fallen body. She lay twisted in a heap twenty feet away, her head at an unnatural angle. A thin line of blood had spilled from her open mouth. I couldn't tell if she was breathing.

The suit highlighted two fallen weapons in easy reach: an automatic rifle and Van de Velde's pistol. I ignored them both.

I heard the robot behind me. It had turned around and was marching back toward me. I found what I needed and turned to face it.

The suit's metallic protein enhances both speed and strength, Mac had told me. Just how much stronger did it make you?

I was about to find out.

Perfect Circle came within fifteen feet and stopped. It seemed to be regarding me, although I couldn't find its eyes. The fire in its torso had spread, and I could see the first tiny flickers of flame reflecting inside its chest cavity.

"Lay down your weapons," it said. "Or you will be neutralized."

"Come and try," I said.

It surged forward, grasping at me with a heavy metal hand.

I slapped it aside with the crowbar. The bar made a satisfying *clang* as it deflected the blow. The robot tried again with its other hand, and I swung hard with the crowbar in my left, with the same result.

The robot shifted position, trying again. We continued that dance for a few moments. On its sixth attempt, I shifted my attack slightly, bringing the metal bar in my right hand in at a sharper angle. I heard a loud *crack*. I had shattered the metal casing at the base of one of its fingers.

It retreated, then suddenly surged forward, pummeling me with blows. I ducked and wove, swinging out with my weapons. After a moment it retreated again.

I took grim delight in my choice of weapons. They were the ideal weight — light enough for the suit to wield them with blinding speed and just heavy enough to penetrate the robot's hardened shell. With the crowbars, and the suit's boosted strength, I could crack Perfect Circle open like a lobster. But to do that, to bring it down, I would have to get closer.

While I considered how to do that, the suit warned me that Perfect Circle was about to lunge again. Sure enough, a fraction of a second later, the robot came at me. This time, it locked its hands and brought them down overhead in a crushing blow.

In response, I made a near-fatal mistake.

The ease with which I'd deflected its previous blows had made me cocky. I had plenty of warning and should have dodged; instead, I brought both metal bars up and locked them in a V over my head.

I took the blow on my arms and shoulders. It was jarring, but the suit helped me absorb the impact.

But Perfect Circle didn't relent. It leaned forward, applying steadily more pressure.

And suddenly I was trapped. It took everything I had to keep the robot from crushing me.

I was now in a head-to-head battle of strength with an 1,800-pound robot, and I wasn't going to win. Strong as the suit was — and I was still learning the astonishing limits of what it could do — it wasn't going to get me out of this one. More warning lights started flashing. With dispassionate clarity, the suit showed me how much force Perfect Circle was capable of exerting . . . and precisely what would give out first.

My ankles. They were the only part of my body not protected by the suit. If I had remembered the boots, I think the suit might have won that battle of strength. But long before the suit would yield, my very human ankles would give way. Already they were in agony. One or both of them would shatter, and this would end very shortly thereafter.

Before I could attempt a desperate maneuver, I heard a gunshot. And then another. The second hit Perfect Circle in the head. Someone was firing at it.

The pressure eased and then was gone. The robot backed away. A steady stream of smoke was curling out of its torso.

I risked a glance over my shoulder. Van de Velde's corporal — the one whose elbow I'd almost broken — was kneeling next to her. He was shooting with his pistol, taking careful aim with his left hand.

That was brave, but it was a mistake to think you could take this monster down with bullets. I'd pumped half a dozen exploding rounds into its brother Standing Mars, and that bastard had still had plenty of fight in it.

I turned back to Perfect Circle, looked him up and down. Twice now I had been saved from near-fatal mistakes. It was time to end this.

And suddenly I knew precisely how.

I twirled the metal rods in my hands. The suit and I needed to do this together. The suit suggested several lines of attack, but I rejected them all. I had no idea how to tell it what I was going to do, so I hoped it'd figure it out in a hurry.

I swung the metal rods together. They sparked with a delightful *clang*, reverberating in my hands.

"I'm coming to kill you now," I said. "Because I can't wait for you to burn yourself to death."

"You are foolish," said my opponent.

Robots, Jesus. They suck at street banter.

Perfect Circle took a step forward. I waited. *Come on, you cold-blooded piece of shit—*

Another step. I retreated, still waiting. *Come on.*

A third step . . . and at long last it raised its clumsy metal hands above my head.

*Now.*

I sprinted forward. The suit figured out what I was doing at the very last moment. It amped my leg muscles as I jumped, and my leap carried me up to the robot's hands.

Perfect Circle tried to grab me, but missed, and its hand collided with my left shin painfully. But my right foot landed precisely where it was supposed to, and I used its forearm as a stepping-stone, building on my forward momentum.

My leap carried me up, up, to the metal giant's exposed head. It reacted with speed, grabbing at my hip with thick metal fingers that could crush steel.

Before it could break me in half, I brought the metal rods down with all the strength I possessed, driving the sharp ends into the exposed surface of Perfect Circle's head. They penetrated deep into his electronic brain, and I felt a savage jolt of electricity as I released them.

I slid down the enormous robot, bouncing clumsily off its arms, landing in a heap on the floor. I struggled numbly to my feet, taking a few shaky steps backward.

The corporal and I were the only ones still standing. Together we watched as the great mass of Perfect Circle swayed, swayed, and then toppled forward stiffly. There was a brilliant explosion of sparks from its head as it slammed into the floor; then an enthusiastic whoosh of flame burst from its chest. I felt the floor shudder under the impact.

I looked toward the corporal. His weapon hung loosely from his hand. The moment Perfect Circle fell, he returned his attention to Van de Velde. I approached them.

Her eyes were closed and blood still ran from her mouth, pooling on her neck. The angle of her right shoulder was wrong. Bones were broken, perhaps *many* bones.

But she was breathing.

The corporal fussed over her expertly, straightening her legs and checking for other signs of bleeding. When she was stable, he snatched his radio and began speaking into it urgently.

I wanted to tear off my mask and thank her for saving my life. I wanted to sit with her until help arrived and make absolutely certain she would be okay.

But if I did, Sergei was a dead man.

Down the corridor, more soldiers were coming through the broken glass door. Two had rifles. They were running toward us, shouting in Spanish.

I picked up the bag with Hayduk's data drive. Without looking back, I headed for the exit.

# XXXVIII

Thursday, March 25th, 2083
Posted 1:47 am by Barry Simcoe

**CanadaNET1 Encrypted, Sponsored by GetToDaChoppa.**
*Need immediate short-range transportation? Try a single-seat
drone conveyor. Fast and ready when you are!*

Sharing is set to PRIVATE
Comments are CLOSED

I needed to get off of this floor as fast as possible. The soldiers running toward me were seconds away.

I chose the stairwell on the left. It was unguarded, but the door had been electronically sealed. A toolbox and several metal bars set against the wall nearby told me it was scheduled to be sealed more permanently very soon.

There was a keypad, but when I tried Hayduk's GPU, nothing happened.

The shouts were getting closer. The soldiers had reached the entrance to the room. One kneeled down to examine Van de Velde, but two others turned toward me. One raised a rifle to his shoulder.

I took a step back and kicked the door as hard as I could. When feeling returned to my feet, I was probably going to regret not using my shoulder.

The door popped open obligingly, but the keypad on the wall was suddenly outlined in crisp blue lines on my visor, and a rather nasty-looking icon popped up next to it. Odds were I had just triggered an alarm.

I bolted down the stairs, as fast as I could move.

There were still sounds of pursuit when I reached the fourth floor. I exited the stairwell and plunged into the maze of corridors around the hotel laundry. I didn't see any cameras on this floor, and after a few minutes I found an empty room with a huge rolling hamper filled with laundry. Without further ceremony I started to strip out of the suit.

That damn thing *really* didn't want to come off. When it was dead, it flopped around like an oversized wetsuit. But powered up, the various components clung together joyously. I spent frustrating seconds trying to get my fingers under the tight seal around my neck just to get my mask off, before giving up and pulling out the power cells.

The suit powered down in seconds, and the mask peeled off with minimal effort after that. As I pulled off the gloves and stashed them in the plastic bag with mask and the power cells, I heard shouting out in the hall.

The soldiers were on this floor. It sounded like they were searching room to room.

I stashed the bag under a mess of towels and struggled out of the suit as quickly as I could. I freed my arms, then pulled the suit down to my waist. My shirt was badly rumpled, but there wasn't much I could do about that. I yanked the suit to my knees, managed to kick free of it in seconds.

I stared at my legs, momentarily startled. I wasn't wearing pants.

Damn — that's right. I'd abandoned them on the forty-fifth floor. I'm not sure how a person forgets something like that, but I had. I hadn't lost my pants since my third year at McGill. That incident had involved a lot more alcohol, and even so, at no point in the evening *had I forgotten my pants were missing.*

This complicated things. While I tried to figure out what to do, I buried the suit next to the mask and gloves. Outside in the hall I heard someone shouting in surprise and a harsh reply in Spanish. The soldiers were getting closer.

Laundry was spilling out of the hamper, the result of my sloppy efforts to bury the suit. I grabbed something long and black before it could hit the floor, started to stuff it back into the white linen bag it had fallen from.

It was a pant leg.

I pulled. A pair of black pants slid out of the bag.

They looked like part of the uniform for the kitchen staff. This pair was much too big for me, but I grabbed the bag, digging furiously.

It was filled with kitchen uniforms. The third pair of pants I found looked like they would fit. I started to pull them on.

The door banged open and a harsh voice spoke. It was one of the soldiers. I stopped moving, hunched over with one leg in the pants, and peeked over the hamper toward the door.

The soldier wasn't looking at me. He was standing in the doorway, shouting back over his shoulder at someone in the hall. He held his rifle at his waist.

My legs were completely hidden by the hamper. As casually as I could, I slid my left leg in the pants.

There wasn't time to zip up. I let the shirt fall over the pants, covering my groin. I stepped out from behind the hamper, hands in the air.

The soldier was still shouting over his shoulder. I saw a second soldier pass by behind him, and the one in the door stepped into the room, letting the door close.

He was skinny, and his face was covered with acne. He spotted me for the first time, standing only a few feet in front of him. Surprise briefly registered on his face, but he covered it quickly, pointing toward the wall on his left and barking something in Spanish. I moved out of his way obediently, hands still in the air.

He did a cursory search of the room, looking behind all the hampers, then hurried out through the door on the opposite side. He never glanced at me a second time.

I stood against the wall for a few seconds, hands still in the air, then lowered them with a sigh of relief. Outside in the hall I could hear more shouting. I found my shoes and put them on without hurrying, tucked in my shirt and zipped my pants, and straightened my hair as best I could. I rooted through the plastic bag for Hayduk's GPU and the data drive, and put them in my pocket.

Then I hesitated. It was foolhardy to leave the suit here. Together with the power cores, it was a priceless piece of battle equipment. But it was too risky to simply walk out of here with it. There were soldiers in the halls, and there were even more soldiers where I was going.

It was an impossible dilemma, and I didn't have time to ponder it. I hid the bag in the hamper. Then, with a curse, I pulled it out again, extracted the power cells, and stuffed them in my pockets. Those at least I could hide easily. When the suit and bag were safely buried by laundry again, I stepped out into the hall.

I ran into another pair of soldiers almost immediately. Both were carrying rifles, and both looked pretty put-out. The first snapped at me in Spanish, but before I could figure out how to respond the second one called to someone behind me. I glanced over my shoulder.

A young man in hotel scrubs was stepping out of a locker room, a towel over his shoulder. The soldier asked his question again, and the man answered in fluent Spanish, pointing into the locker room. The soldier hustled forward, ignoring me, and I needed no further dismissal to be on my way.

I passed a bunch of workers standing before one of the elevators. They were staring in the direction of the soldiers nervously. One of them punched the elevator button in evident frustration, and I heard another say, "It's true — they shut them down. Even the guest elevators." There was more nervous grumbling from the assembled crowd.

I found the stairs and made my way to the third-floor hallway. There were soldiers *everywhere* — running in tight groups, breaking out equipment, and setting up screens that projected images from virtually every floor of the hotel. There was a crowd near the entrance to the command center, many craning their necks to see what was happening inside. I cursed under my breath. No way I was sneaking in there anytime soon.

I approached warily, sizing up the crowd and looking for a way in. The crowd was a respectable distance back from the entrance, and it was easy to see why. A 2,000-pound machine was standing sentinel, and no one wanted to get too close. It was a completely different configuration than Perfect Circle, but it looked just as deadly. Easily nine feet tall, it had a heavy torso atop two thick metal legs. I'd seen similar designs in battlefield vids, but never up close before. Still, there was something very familiar about it, the way it had no eyes. Just like . . .

I shouldered my way through the crowd, until I stood in front of the thing. "Zircon Border?" I asked hesitantly.

"Good evening, Mr. Simcoe." Zircon Border's familiar voice boomed out of the robot in front of me.

"You look different, my friend."

"I am in battlefield configuration, I'm afraid."

"You certainly are." I knew the limbless block of metal I'd seen in the lobby and the command center couldn't be Zircon Border's combat shape, but nonetheless seeing him like this was a surprise. He loomed larger, and looked far deadlier.

"Where do you keep these arms and legs during normal business hours?" I asked him.

"They retract," he said.

I glanced over my shoulder at the crowd, who were a few feet away but not far enough for my liking. I lowered my voice. "Is . . ."

"The subject we discussed is inside the command center," Zircon Border said.

"Thank you," I said, patting the cool metal of his exterior. With no further ceremony I moved past him. A few of the braver souls in the crowd attempted to mimic my example, following me into the command center; they were startled back in line by a booming challenge from Zircon Border. I made for Sergei's station at the back, hoping that was where Hayduk had been headed when he marched Sergei out of the elevator. Sergei was there, slumped in a metal chair in front of his lab gear. *Thank God,* I thought. He looked unharmed—physically, at least. He saw me enter, but carefully avoided making eye contact or acknowledging me in any way.

The Venezuelan secret police who'd escorted him out of the ballroom were there as well, converting a nearby weather monitor into a secure comm station. Surprisingly, so was Colonel Perez, whom I'd expected to be off somewhere commanding the search for the rogue American who'd punched him in the face. Apparently, Sergei's fate mattered more to him. The good colonel went up in my estimation.

Most important of all, I also spotted Hayduk, standing before the converted weather station and instructing a pair of nervous-looking weather techs how to get the information he wanted up on screen.

This was a stroke of luck. It looked like they had reason to question Sergei at his desk instead of immediately marching him off to the Sturgeon Building in chains. As long as Hayduk was here, then my plan had a chance. There was still time for me to fix this whole mess.

Or maybe not. With so much top brass in the room, the soldiers who normally ignored me were now standing briskly at attention. One of them was the kid who'd watched over me the morning Van de Velde had had me arrested. He'd lazily waved me into the command center a dozen times in the past few weeks, but now he was striding toward me sternly, his rifle rigid in his arms.

*Damn it.* I was almost to Sergei's desk, but this punk was going to cut me off before I got there. I deliberately slowed, keeping my pace casual and my features calm. Maybe I could bluff my way through.

Turns out I couldn't. The kid was eager to be a hard-ass when there was the slightest chance a ranking officer might take notice. All my attempts to explain were ignored, and he marched me back toward the door, gripping his rifle meaningfully.

Near the door was Perez's assistant, the young lieutenant who'd walked me to his office. I caught a glimpse of her looking my way as the kid hustled me toward the exit. I waved, trying to catch her eye. It was a long shot, but maybe I could get her to call him off.

Unfortunately, I didn't get her attention. I got someone else entirely.

A firm voice called out in Spanish, and the kid stopped immediately. He turned and saluted.

It took me a moment to understand why. Colonel Perez was making his way toward us.

I swore under my breath. Other than Hayduk, Perez was the last person whose attention I wanted.

But at least I was no longer being goose-stepped toward the door. That was progress.

Perez dismissed the kid with barely a nod, and the young soldier spun on his heels. I swear I could hear every one of his measured steps as he marched crisply back to his station by the west wall.

Perez stared at me with a cold, appraising look, saying nothing. I suddenly felt very nervous under the scrutiny of this man, very aware that I had a pair of stolen American power cells in my pockets. Perhaps it was his intention to make me nervous, and if so, it was working.

*That's the way to play this,* I decided. *Nervous and confused. I don't know what's going on.*

"Colonel Perez," I said, and it was no effort at all to sound apprehensive and flustered, "I don't know what's going on. There are armed soldiers everywhere in the hotel, and our guests are very alarmed — especially after the incident in the ballroom."

"Yes," said Perez, his bearing unusually stiff. I could see the beginnings of a decent bruise under his left eye where I'd clocked him. "It is . . . an internal security matter. It will be resolved shortly."

There was no trace of accommodation in his voice. This was not the friendly soldier who'd recruited me to spy on behalf of the benevolent Venezuelan Occupation. Of course, he was having a rough night. Hayduk, the man who was systematically murdering some of his most loyal subordinates, was busy processing another one. And to top it off, he'd just been punched in the face by an American spy.

I said, "Please forgive me. I think I must have embarrassed you in the ballroom earlier this evening. That was never my intention. I only meant to thank you publicly for your generosity, and I seem to have had very poor timing. I am very sorry if my announcement caught you off guard, or put you in the spotlight at an awkward moment."

Perez's demeanor turned slightly warmer. He waved away my concerns.

"Not at all. Your comments were most kind. This is simply"—he indicated the cluster of people around Sergei's desk—"an internal matter of no consequence. I am sorry if it has distracted from your ball."

The colonel was as much politician as soldier. "No, of course not," I said. "But I did come down here hoping I could draw you back to the ballroom. Some of our most distinguished guests are very anxious to meet you. You said you wanted Chicago to prosper? These are the men and women who can make that happen."

"You are very kind," he said smoothly. "I would be delighted." He put a hand on my shoulder, steering me toward the exit. "Please tell your guests that I hope to rejoin them before the evening is over."

Everyone was in a hurry to get rid of me. I risked a glance over my shoulder. Sergei hadn't moved—he remained seated in his simple metal chair.

I took a chance. "Does this matter involve Sergei?" I asked.

Perez stopped, looking surprised. "You know him?"

"Yes, we're friends." If Sergei was being accused of aiding the American terrorist, admitting that to Perez probably wasn't smart. But the hell with it. I'd risked my life more than once tonight already; no sense being timid now.

"Ah." Perez's hand fell from my shoulder. "Yes, I remember now. Specialist Vulka wrote a letter praising your efforts on his behalf the morning of the attack."

"That's right. He's been very kind to me. I hope he's not involved in anything serious."

Perez shrugged. "It is routine. Specialist Vulka is being questioned to eliminate him from certain inquiries. There is no reason for concern. I am certain all will be resolved satisfactorily."

"That's a relief."

Perez smiled. He leaned closer and lowered his voice confidentially. "Internal security . . . they see threats everywhere, real and imagined. The day is wasted if they cannot uncover two dark plots before noon."

I forced a chuckle. Was the colonel really joking with me about Venezuelan internal security while Hayduk cleared the way to have Sergei tortured? Why wasn't Perez doing something to *stop* him?

Before we could cement our new conspiratorial friendship with more tasteless humor, we were interrupted by a commotion near the weather station. Perez turned to look, and I saw Hayduk in the middle of it all. He was leaning over a wide monitor a few feet from Sergei, shouting in Spanish. He sounded surprised and furious.

"Please," Perez said, suddenly too distracted to look at me, "remain here." He took his leave, walking over to join Hayduk. As he did, I got a glimpse of what Hayduk had seen to get him so excited.

Me, of course. Or more accurately, an American terrorist in combat armor exiting Hayduk's office with a bag of stolen power cells. The time-stamp was less than nine minutes ago.

The technicians worked to bring up additional cameras on the floor. As they did, I took a few surreptitious steps to the left, moving into the shadows by a storage cabinet, where I could get a better view. Hayduk was snapping at the techs in Spanish. They fast-forwarded the display, deftly tracked the American's movements, until he was confronted by Van de Velde and her corporal.

I finally saw a reaction from Perez. He let out a cry that was almost tri-umphant, jabbing one of the screens savagely. It was an image that showed both me and Van de Velde, and his finger speared his sergeant.

The two technicians looked up, surprised and curious. Perez switched smoothly to English.

"I told you," he said, his voice tightly controlled. "She is not a suspect."

"That is irrelevant now," Hayduk said dismissively. "The American will be in custody in moments."

"I want her removed from the suspect list. Today."

One thing I appreciated about Hayduk—this wasn't a man who both-ered to hide his emotions. Irritation flashed across his face. "As you wish," he said.

Perez turned around. He snapped his fingers at someone sitting at a dark console, twenty feet away.

"Yes, Colonel?" said the young woman.

"Specialist Benitez. Please determine the locations of the following per-sonnel. Capitán Damon Vreck. Contractor First Class Stacey Bova. Primer Teniente Lexi Newman. Sargento Mayor de Primera Alberto Castro."

I knew those names. They were on Hayduk's list, the people he planned to interrogate on suspicion of being the American terrorist. Perez was ac-counting for their whereabouts, eliminating them as suspects.

"Contact them personally," said Perez. "Quickly, please."

"Yes, Colonel."

Again, Hayduk's expression said he clearly didn't appreciate this op-portunity to remove suspects nearly as much as Perez. But something ap-peared on screen a moment later that instantly cheered him up.

"What is *that?*" asked Perez.

"That," said Hayduk with satisfaction, "is a combat-capable machine intelligence. Perfect Circle."

Perez watched as Perfect Circle moved into the middle of the corridor. His bulk now dominated most of the images on the monitors.

"You have a field combat asset in my headquarters?" said Perez. His face had become very red.

"He responds only to very specific triggers," said Hayduk calmly, his eyes fixed on the screen. "And one has just occurred."

"It is a war machine!" Perez shouted. "You cannot expose my staff to an active combat hunter!"

In response, Hayduk moved forward and tapped the screen on the far left. It showed the two soldiers. One aimed a rifle at my head, and the other swung a crowbar.

"Contact these men," Hayduk told the techs. "They have the American in custody. I want him brought here."

On screen, Hayduk's "very specific" combat hunter reached out and crushed the head of one of the soldiers.

For a moment, you could have heard a pin drop anywhere in the room.

Perez reacted first. He spun to a group of soldiers on his right, including the kid, and said less than ten words in Spanish. They left the room at a run. Then he turned to another communications tech.

"Specialist Andres, contact the deck officer at Sturgeon Aerial Ops. We need a machine containment team here in the next fifteen minutes. Heavy weapons authorized. I want the entire team, do you understand me?"

"Yes, Colonel."

Perez pointed to two young women at the Operations station. "Evacuate the fifth floor," he told them. They picked up their phones and went to work.

Hayduk had taken a moment to recover. But when Perez finally turned to him, he was ready.

"There is no further danger," he said smoothly. "Once the American is apprehended, Perfect Circle's combat prerogative will expire. I will remove him from your operational envelope."

"No," said Perez. "You will remove it immediately. Or I will have you court-martialed for felony murder."

Hayduk's lips thinned, but he kept his voice even. "Colonel Perez, I do not serve at your pleasure. My mandate is to use any means necessary to find and stop the American terrorist." He tapped the screen showing Perfect Circle with his knuckle. "These are the necessary means."

As Hayduk was tapping the screen, Van de Velde was opening fire on Perfect Circle. It charged toward her, and the American in the suit counter-charged. In seconds, they were in combat. And just as quickly, the American began to lose. Van de Velde stood firm, continuing to fire.

"Your 'necessary means' is killing my men," said Perez, with barely controlled rage.

On the screen, Perfect Circle was swinging me around like a yo-yo. The robot effortlessly slammed me into the floor and then the wall. Watching it happen, my whole body ached all over again. I turned away briefly, unable to watch.

Instead, I glanced around the room. The two dozen or so technicians and soldiers still at their posts had pretty much abandoned all pretense of working and were watching events unfold as avidly as I was. Many were Sergei's coworkers. They were whispering in small groups, staring at Hayduk with open fear. Zircon Border had stepped into the room, his hulking form blocking most of the entrance.

"Your soldiers should not interfere," Hayduk said critically, still watching the screen.

"My sergeant is protecting her men!" Perez exploded. "And if they are harmed, you will answer for it."

The soldier opened fire on Perfect Circle with his automatic rifle. The combat robot tried to pummel him with the American, but now at last the American was resisting, clinging to an exposed steel beam in the wall. Perfect Circle released him, then smashed its metal fist into the soldier, sending him through the wall.

There was an audible gasp from the room.

Perez had become very quiet. His back was to me now, and I couldn't see his expression. But he looked like a coiled spring.

On the screen, the combat robot turned to finish off the American. Van de Velde stood and blocked its path, firing relentlessly, heroically. Uselessly.

The whole room watched as Noa Van de Velde bravely held her ground, protecting the American, until Perfect Circle crushed her, then tossed her aside.

There were cries from the audience. Several people jumped to their feet. Someone shouted "Noa!"

Perez spoke very quietly, but every person in the room heard him.

"Master Sergeant Robles," he said. "Place Colonel Hayduk under arrest."

A uniformed soldier stepped forward and saluted crisply. Two armed servicemen followed him to Hayduk's side.

"Colonel, please relinquish your sidearm," said Sergeant Robles.

There was a scuffle on the far side of the room. Two men and a woman in Venezuelan Military Intelligence uniforms pushed past several technicians.

Hayduk's men.

One of them shoved a soldier who didn't move quickly enough. The leader — a short, wiry captain — moved to Hayduk's side, facing Robles defiantly. He placed his hands on his hips, his fingers brushing the top of his holstered revolver.

"Colonel Perez," said Hayduk, his tone calm. "I understand your reaction. But you are not thinking clearly."

"Señor Hayduk," said Perez, facing him squarely from ten feet away. "Master Sergeant Robles has requested your sidearm."

Hayduk smiled. He unclipped his weapon from his belt, still holstered, and placed it on the table before him. "Sergeant Robles may have my sidearm, if he is so eager for it," he said. Hayduk reached out with his left hand. He pressed his fingers against the imposing image of Perfect Circle on screen.

"Do you see how useless your guns are, Colonel? *This* is the future. Not merely the future of warfare. But the *entirety* of our future."

Hayduk turned to the assembled crowd. He seemed to relish this moment. "No one in this room is such a fool that they cannot see where the San Cristobal Coalition has led us. Choose your loyalties carefully, my friends. Nations are relics. We are the victors in an uprising against history."

"My loyalties," said Perez, "are to the Bolivarian Republic of Venezuela."

"The Republic teeters on the precipice," snapped Hayduk. "And you are a fool."

He turned to the display on his left. His robot was about to crush the American, who stood helplessly as the hunter bore down on him. Hayduk's hand moved over the image of the robot, almost caressing it. "But let us discuss practicalities, Colonel. Perfect Circle obeys only me. When he kills the American, he will bring the body to me. Your guns cannot stop him. You are very welcome to try, of course, but I would not recommend it."

Master Sergeant Robles, who was watching the screen, licked his lips nervously. He looked to Colonel Perez.

"That battle," said Perez slowly, "ended eight minutes ago. Where is your combat hunter?"

Hayduk's confident smile faltered, but only marginally. "He will come."

On screen, the American and Van de Velde's corporal were now fighting the hunter together. The American held two metal rods and faced the robot, as if taunting it.

"Pay attention," Hayduk said. He was speaking to all of us staring at the display, not just Perez. "You are watching the future unfold."

The American jumped. Perfect Circle grabbed, ready to crush him. The American's jump took him into the robot's arms, and then up, up, and finally crashing down. He drove the two metal rods deep into the cold brain of the combat hunter.

Perfect Circle toppled.

There was a moment of profound silence.

"Master Sergeant Robles," Perez said evenly. "Please escort Colonel Hayduk to the detention area."

Without hesitation, Hayduk's captain smoothly drew his pistol. He leveled it at Sergeant Robles.

The response was immediate. Both of the soldiers accompanying Robles drew their weapons. So did the two standing with Hayduk.

"¡Deténgase!" shouted Perez.

Everyone stood firm, guns held level. I heard the soldiers near the door scrambling closer, shouting to Colonel Perez for instructions.

"This is unfortunate," said Hayduk, when the shouting had calmed somewhat.

"Your robot is destroyed," said Perez. "You are under arrest. If your men do not lower their weapons, I will have them shot."

"That is hardly necessary," Hayduk said, his voice smooth. "I do not dispute your authority. My men, however, were only doing their duty. If you allow them to leave unmolested, I would be happy to surrender."

Perez considered, then nodded. He signaled to Robles and his men to step back.

Hayduk gave an accommodating smile. He nodded at his captain, and his men holstered their weapons.

"Of course, you will allow my men to leave with their prisoner," Hayduk said.

Perez glanced at Sergei. In all the excitement, he'd almost been forgotten. The colonel shook his head. "Specialist Vulka will remain here until this matter is settled."

Hayduk frowned sympathetically. "Unfortunately, Colonel, Specialist Vulka has already been remanded to the custody of military intelligence. Regardless of our business here, he will need to be . . . questioned."

Hayduk let the last word hang in the air, a chilling threat.

"That's no longer necessary," said Perez.

"Perhaps you're right," said Hayduk noncommittally. "But that's not for you or me to decide. He has been signed over to Sturgeon, and the inquisitor clerks there will extract the truth from him."

Perez looked over at Sergei. Sergei had sat with quiet dignity at his station for the last five minutes, watching events unfold. He returned the colonel's gaze with his usual calm expression. A pained look crossed Perez's face.

"I have offered to surrender to you," said Hayduk thoughtfully, as if the thought had just occurred to him. "But perhaps it would be more convenient if I remained on duty, to conduct the questioning personally. Here, in your presence, if you like. If Specialist Vulka proves to be uninvolved, I could sign him over to you immediately."

Perez did not respond. He waited patiently for the other shoe to drop.

"But if the specialist *is* involved . . ." Hayduk tapped his chin, as if in thought. "I would of course insist on returning to the Sturgeon Building with the prisoner immediately, to pursue the matter."

*Jesus.* Letting Hayduk's men leave with Sergei was the same as signing his death sentence. Hayduk had turned Sergei's life into a bargaining chip.

Perez said nothing. For a moment I was terrified he wouldn't accept Hayduk's offer. Finally, he gave a curt nod. Master Sergeant Robles stepped back, the sour look on his face signaling clear disappointment that he wouldn't be putting cuffs on Hayduk, at least for now.

"You may question him here," Perez said.

"Splendid," said Hayduk. "May I have your permission to send my men upstairs to secure my office?"

*Shit, yes,* I thought. *Get those gun-happy assholes out of here.* Perez seemed to concur. He gave his permission with a wave.

As fascinating as all this military drama was, it wasn't why I was here. I had a far more urgent errand. As stealthily as I could, I reached into my pocket and removed Hayduk's GPU card.

Lifting it had been the easy part. In order to complete this act of street theater, I had to make sure no one ever realized it had been taken. And that meant slipping it back into Hayduk's pocket, silently and unseen.

I had no idea how I was going to do that.

I tried to recall exactly which pocket I'd stolen it from twenty minutes ago. I mentally re-created our collision in the hall outside the ballroom. The GPU had been . . . *yes*. In the breast pocket of his jacket.

I watched Hayduk as he whispered instructions to his captain. This would be a lot easier once the captain and his men were gone. My first step would be to get close enough. Second would be to wait for an appropriate distraction — *oh shit*.

For the first time since I'd entered the room, I noticed Hayduk wasn't wearing his jacket.

He had loosened his collar, and dark stains were starting to grow around his underarms. He looked like he'd shucked his jacket a while ago. It could be anywhere.

I cursed under my breath. My entire plan would collapse unless I could discreetly return the GPU, and soon.

Maybe I could slip the card into his hip pocket, I reasoned. Possibly he treated it like I treated my car keys — I never knew what damn pocket they were in. Pants pockets would be harder than a jacket pocket — a *lot* harder — and that meant I would need a doozy of a distraction. It would have to be spectacular, and it would have to be soon.

I rubbed the card in my palm nervously, keeping it concealed from view, and took a few steps closer, looking for an opportunity.

Hayduk finished his whispered conversation. His captain nodded, and then left with his two subordinates. Hayduk leaned casually on the nearest table, returning his attention to the monitors.

"Now that we have dispensed with these distractions," he said, as if the last five minutes had been nothing more than an inconsequential debate, "let us return to the matter at hand. Where is the American?"

The techs were on the stick. In seconds, they zoomed in on the American. He was leaving the scene of the battle, through the stairwell on the left.

"How was he able to access your office so easily?" Perez wondered aloud.

Obviously, this was a subject that irritated Hayduk as well. "Much of the high-end security is not yet in place," he said, his voice tight.

"Does your office not have a motion-activated camera?"

"It does," Hayduk admitted. "Not all security systems are operational, but what there is should have stopped him. Clearly, he had assistance."

Hayduk said something to one of the technicians, then walked slowly toward Sergei. He put his hands on the arms of Sergei's chair, leaning forward until he and Sergei were separated by only inches. He asked him something in Spanish.

Sergei looked blankly up at Perez. He hadn't said a word since I'd entered the command center. Hayduk switched to English, without waiting for Perez to tell him Sergei's Spanish was crap.

Hayduk pointed at the American on the screen. "Who is this man?" he demanded, his eyes boring into Sergei's. "You know him, of that I am sure."

Suddenly I was glad I wasn't closer. Hayduk hadn't noticed me yet, and I liked it that way. I took two steps back into the shadows near the cabinet.

I needn't have bothered. Hayduk was solely focused on Sergei. Sergei blinked up at him, then regarded the screen.

As if I didn't have enough to worry about, what I saw there suddenly made me very nervous. The American had left the fifth floor, but the technicians had isolated a fresh set of camera feeds, showing his dash downstairs from multiple angles.

If they managed to track him into the laundry, to the room where I'd stripped out of the suit, I'd be under arrest in seconds.

One way or another, this was all going to be over in the next few minutes. The urge to flee suddenly became very strong.

Instead, I watched Sergei. He was staring at the screen impassively, observing as the man on the screen made his way down one flight of stairs to the laundry. "I do not know this man," he said at last, looking Hayduk straight in the eye.

"You do not know him?" said Hayduk. "And yet, he used your GPU card to access the medical offices at the Field Museum."

Hayduk nodded to the technician he'd spoken with. The tech brought up an older video feed.

This one showed me in the Field Museum. My appearance on screen this time was a little distorted — doubtless courtesy of Jacaranda — but no one was paying attention to what I looked like. Instead, the technician zoomed in on what was in my hand as I waved it in front of the door.

In the video feed, my hand covered too much of the card to provide any kind of positive ID. But the technician deftly brought up the digital record of the cards used to grant access that night. He matched the timestamp on the video to the sole late-night entry.

He highlighted the result on the screen. It was a photo of Sergei Vulka and a digital copy of his GPU card.

"Is that you, Specialist Vulka?" Hayduk asked. "I would warn you to think carefully before answering."

Sergei didn't need to think carefully. "Yes, that is me," he said.

"Then you admit the American had access to your GPU."

"This is not possible," Sergei said. His voice was surprisingly mild.

"The evidence," said Hayduk, "says otherwise."

"I cannot explain this. But I do not know this man."

"Would you like to know what I believe?" Hayduk asked. Sergei looked at him, his face open and curious.

Hayduk changed his tone. "I believe you simply trusted the wrong person," he said, his voice matter-of-fact. He gestured at the screen again. "What you did here is not a court-martial offense, Specialist. You gave your GPU card to an untrustworthy individual. I do not believe you thought him a traitor then."

Hayduk started pacing. "But later, when his crimes became more numerous . . . you felt trapped. You could not expose him without exposing yourself. Your small betrayal became a much larger one. You were a loyal soldier of the AGRT, frightened by what exposure might mean to you."

Hayduk stopped pacing. He leaned against the table, regarding Sergei sympathetically. "I too have trusted the wrong person, and I too have suffered the consequences. It is a hard fact of life, Specialist. Sooner or later we must admit our mistakes, no matter how well-intentioned they were."

Hayduk took a step closer, squatting down in front of Sergei. He nodded toward Colonel Perez. "I have promised the colonel that if you are not involved, I will turn you over to him. Here is my offer to you, Specialist. I do not believe you are a traitor. Simply name the American, and I will consider your case closed. I will hand you over to the colonel."

Sergei did not respond immediately. Hayduk's voice took on a less patient tone.

"If you do not, I am afraid that I will have no choice but to accompany you to interrogation. Believe me when I tell you, Specialist Vulka, neither you nor I wish that to happen. You may believe you are prepared for what will happen there, but you are not. Nothing can prevent it — *nothing* — except the name of the person hiding behind that mask. You will surrender the name, eventually. That is inevitable. Tell us now, and all of this unpleasantness will be over."

Sergei watched the screen quietly. As he did, everyone in the room watched him. I expected him to glance my way, even if just for a moment. Perhaps to beg forgiveness for what he was about to do.

If he had given up my name at that moment, I would not have blamed him.

Instead, he looked Hayduk in the eye and said, "I do not know this man."

I felt an overwhelming wave of gratitude toward Sergei. And a heightened sense of my immediate purpose. *Thank you, my friend. Now sit tight and let me return the favor.*

The truth was, that was easier said than done. Sergei was playing it a lot cooler than I was. At the moment, I couldn't keep my eyes off the monitors — although I was trying not to be too obvious about it.

On screen, the American had fled the stairwell. It was with considerable relief that I noted that the technicians tracking him had not picked him up once he had. I hadn't seen any cameras during my race through the laundry . . . Was it possible there weren't any? The technicians began muttering to each other, glancing nervously at Hayduk as they scanned the available feeds, trying to regain an image.

And then I spotted something out of the corner of my eye that finally pulled my gaze away from the cameras. Less than thirty feet away, draped casually over a steel folding chair: Hayduk's jacket.

There were only a few comms technicians nearby, and none was even close to it. If I could move quickly, and without being noticed, Sergei and I might both make it through this.

One of the weather technicians said something, drawing Hayduk's attention. It looked like he had managed to find something interesting. He pointed at one of the smaller screen images. It showed the American, in a looping series of frames, vanishing down a poorly lit corridor into the bowels of the laundry.

Despite the urgent task at hand, I was keenly interested in what this man had to say. His short conversation with Hayduk was in Spanish, and he didn't speak very clearly, but I followed some of it. This was the last image they had of the American on camera. And there were an unknown number of exits from the laundry into other parts of the hotel, most of them out of sight of the cameras.

I caught Sergei's eye briefly. He betrayed no sign of recognition, in fact had no visible response at all, except to casually glance at a tiny image at the bottom left of the largest screen.

It was another shot of me — this time without the combat suit. Coming back out of the laundry, in full view of the cameras. My shirt was badly rumpled and I was glancing furtively left and right, clearly on the lookout for soldiers.

I looked, in short, like a guilty man. Guilty, guilty, guilty.

Hayduk, wrapped up in shouting at the technicians, paid no attention to the small figure on the screen as it made its way back down the corridor. Neither did either of the technicians, who were frantically scanning through dozens of camera feeds and silently accepting Hayduk's bellowed assertions that they were, in fact, the retarded descendants of monkey farts.

But Sergei had, of course. Sergei missed nothing, ever. Not even while confined to his chair and sentenced to death. His final glance at me conveyed amusement, resignation, and something sadder, before he returned his gaze to the floor again, playing the part of the wrongly accused soldier.

The technicians were flailing. I watched them bring up camera angles almost at random. They were panicked and disorganized, and Hayduk's fury wasn't helping. I risked a glance over at the one individual in the room who could shed some clarity on where the American had been every moment he was in the building: Zircon Border. The big robot still stood at the entrance to the command center, simultaneously monitoring the room and the entire hotel with over a hundred and thirty eyes. He could make my life very difficult if he shared what he knew in the next few minutes.

But no one thought to ask him, and he didn't volunteer. He remained on guard quietly while Hayduk screamed at his soldiers.

The technician on the right spoke up suddenly, his voice excited.

"What is it?" asked Perez.

"The American — he used a GPU card to bypass the security on the fifth floor," he said.

Hayduk looked triumphant. "Yes — of course he did."

He wheeled toward Sergei. "You still deny knowing this man? And yet, he uses your access card? How is that, Specialist Vulka?"

"Vulka's GPU would not give him access to the fifth floor," Perez said, puzzled.

"What?" said Hayduk.

"It was not Vulka's," said the technician. He was scanning a fast-moving data stream on a tablet before him.

"Whose card was it?" Hayduk demanded.

The technician didn't like this question. Not at all. His mouth worked soundlessly for a moment as he stared at Hayduk. I pitied the kid at that moment. He couldn't have been more than twenty-one. He looked terrified.

"Well?" said Hayduk.

"It is y-yours, sir," the technician stammered.

Hayduk stopped moving. He stared at the technician with obvious contempt. Then he swept him from his chair with a single brusque motion. The technician stumbled away from the desk, and Hayduk leaned over his tablet. With a few short keystrokes he transferred the display to the wider screen.

We could all see it now. Perez took a few steps forward, studying the images on the screen. I saw Sergei look up from his chair, his mouth slightly open in surprise.

The technician had frozen an assortment of images from the camera feeds. All were of the American in the combat suit, as he opened doors with the GPU card. The door to the fifth floor. The glass wall near Hayduk's office. In each case he had highlighted the encrypted ID code from the security logs and projected it up as an overlapping image.

Each of the overlaps showed the same name and image: Hayduk's ugly face.

Hayduk slammed his fist onto the desk. He reached instinctively for his pocket, realized he was not wearing his jacket, and then strode quickly to the chair where it was draped. He fished through the breast pocket.

Everyone watched him silently. Perez, Sergei. The technicians, and all of Sergei's coworkers.

Hayduk stopped groping. For a moment he stood completely still, his back to his audience. Then he turned.

In his fist he held the thin metal of his GPU card.

"Is that . . . ?" Perez began.

"It's mine," Hayduk said. "I have no doubt of it."

Perez bent over the console, studying the data closely. "Then the American can produce counterfeit GPU cards. Flawless ones, if this data is correct."

I'd never seen Hayduk this angry. In fact, I couldn't recall ever seeing a human being that angry. He looked like he was going to shit a live skunk. He stood over the technicians. "Find him," he said. "I don't care how long it takes. I want that man, and I want that card he's using."

It was time for me to leave. As quietly as I could, I began to make my way toward the exit. A few communications techs glanced up at me curiously, and the temptation to stop moving and look busy in front of the closest public terminal until they lost interest was strong. But I'd pushed my luck as it was. The sooner I got out of the command center and back to the ball, the better.

It had been risky to return the GPU card to Hayduk's jacket pocket right there in front of God and everybody. But all eyes had been stead-fastly glued to the screen when the technician had announced the GPU was Hayduk's — even the guards. Far better than any distraction I would have come up with. I could have been dressed in a clown suit and no one would have noticed me.

All I'd had to do was walk by the chair with Hayduk's jacket, and in one quick motion the GPU card was back in his pocket.

Still, it had been damn close. Another ten seconds, and it would have been too late. My palms were sweating.

I could see the exit, barely twenty yards away. There were still no guards. I was scot-free.

Hayduk's voice carried across the room as he shouted at the video tech-nician. "No, you idiot — *no*. Show me *all* the outside cameras. I want to see how he left the building."

"S-sir. These *are* all the outside cameras. Not all the exits are covered. External security is handled by drones."

Hayduk's cry of rage and frustration was barely articulate. I heard Per-ez's voice cutting through the chatter.

"Colonel Hayduk," he said. His voice was calm, but rich with the tim-bre of authority.

Hayduk stopped shouting. I stopped walking, and turned around to watch. Hayduk was standing next to the technicians, running one hand through his hair.

"Yes, Colonel," Hayduk said, his voice tightly controlled.

"If the American can copy GPU cards, then the fact that Specialist Vul-ka's card was also copied no longer seems particularly relevant. I assume you have no additional evidence against him?"

Hayduk said nothing. He seemed to be thinking.

"Colonel," Perez pressed, "I will require an answer."

"Yes, yes," said Hayduk, with a dismissive wave of his hand. "That fool can go. I will release him to your custody."

An assistant with a data slate appeared at Perez's side. The colonel wordlessly handed the slate to Hayduk. "If you would be so kind," he said.

Hayduk took the slate. He stared at it for a long moment. Then he signed it.

"This affair is not over," he said, handing the slate back to Perez. "The American is still at large. Perhaps still in the hotel. Every one of the guests here tonight should be questioned, and their whereabouts over the last hour confirmed."

"Perhaps," said Perez smoothly. "But not by you. Master Sergeant Robles, place Colonel Hayduk under arrest for felony murder and dereliction of duty."

"With pleasure, Colonel," said the sergeant.

Hayduk stood very stiffly as Sergeant Robles handcuffed him, then led him away. He said not a word. But he left the room unbowed, his head held high, fiercely meeting the gaze of any who cared to look at him.

I did not care to do so. As he passed me, I must admit I was temporarily distracted by the fascinating operating system of a nearby standard-issue AGRT medical slate.

Perez was in discussion with several officers. Once Hayduk was gone, Perez turned to the room at large. "Who is the officer of the watch for lobby security?"

One of his staff spoke in his ear. Perez nodded, then turned to the entrance.

"Combat Specialist Zircon Border," he said.

Zircon Border stepped forward dutifully. He lumbered around monitors and maneuvered deftly through the narrow spaces between tables. The floor shook slightly as he passed me.

I should have been gone by now. Long gone. But I needed to learn what Perez wanted with Zircon Border. I retreated into the corner by the weather stations, listening intently.

"Do you have eyes-on for much of this building?" Perez asked.

"The lower floors only, sir," said Zircon Border. "One hundred and thirty cameras."

"Good." Perez turned back to the screens. He found a still image of the American terrorist. "This man. Do you know where he is?"

*Shit.* A thrill of terror ran down my spine. It had been naïve to think Perez would overlook the resources at his disposal. Zircon Border was hardly regular army, and he and I were friends, but it was too much to expect to hope he'd lie to a superior officer on my behalf.

I glanced to my left. The entrance to the command center was ten yards away. I could be in the hallway in seconds, out of the hotel in two minutes. I could get to the Manhattan Consulate, perhaps request asylum. Black Winter could help get me to Canada, surely.

But I'd been through this already. And I'd made my decision. I couldn't

leave Sergei. One way or another, we were in this together. I turned my
attention to the center of the room, steeling myself to hear my fate. Both
our fates.

"I'm afraid I lost track of him in the hotel laundry," Zircon Border said.
I breathed a sigh of relief.

Perez nodded, as if he'd expected that. He walked to the table and
picked up a thin piece of metal. Hayduk's GPU card. I wasn't sure if Hayduk had left it there, or Perez had confiscated it. Either way, Perez had it
now. He turned back to the big robot thoughtfully.

"Do you have cameras in this room?" he asked.

"I do not, sir. That would be a security violation."

"Yes. Yes, of course. But . . ."

"Sir?"

Perez was fingering the card. "Colonel Hayduk's GPU card," he said.

"Yes sir?"

"Did it leave his possession at any time?"

Zircon Border didn't answer immediately. I doubt anyone noticed except me, but there was a subtle delay in his response.

"I cannot vouch for the integrity of the colonel's GPU card," Zircon
Border said. "He has come and gone from the hotel multiple times in the
past few days—"

"Yes, yes," said Perez impatiently. "Here, in the hotel. Has anyone
touched the colonel's card?"

"You have touched the colonel's card, sir."

Perez took two steps closer, until he was right next to Zircon Border.
"I'm beginning to think you're being evasive, Combat Specialist," he said.
"You understand my meaning. I want to know if anyone suspicious has
touched this card. Or if its whereabouts were unaccounted for at any period while Colonel Hayduk was in this hotel."

Zircon Border didn't answer immediately. The silence stretched on so
long that it seemed excruciating. Perez opened his mouth, about to speak
again, when finally the big robot replied.

"I understand your meaning perfectly, Colonel. I have been aware of
the whereabouts of Colonel Hayduk's GPU card since it entered the hotel.
No one unknown to me has touched the card, nor has anyone whose integrity is not above reproach."

"No Americans?" Perez asked, turning the card over in his hands.

"Certainly not, Colonel," said Zircon Border.

I was never so happy to be Canadian as I was in that moment.

Perez grunted, seemingly satisfied. He slipped the card into his pocket and dismissed the robot. Zircon Border lumbered back to his post by the entrance. He passed by me, less than five feet away, and gave no outward sign of recognition.

Sergei still had not moved from his chair. After conferring with his officers for another moment, Perez walked over and laid a hand on Sergei's shoulder. The colonel spoke in a low voice into his ear.

Sergei stood slowly. He seemed uncertain what to do. Perez guided him gently, steering him toward the door.

I tried to make myself scarce, but Perez managed to spot me before I reached the exit. He motioned me closer.

"You stayed for your friend, yes?" Perez asked when I reached them.

I nodded, not trusting myself to speak.

"Good. Specialist Vulka has had something of a trial this afternoon," he said. "He has performed well. A true friend might take him to the bar."

I nodded again. "That seems like an excellent idea."

Perez gave a businesslike smile. He slapped Sergei on the back. "Tell the bartender the first round is on me."

"Thank you," I said. "I'll do that."

# XXXIX

Thursday, March 25th, 2083
Posted 9:27 am by Barry Simcoe

CanadaNET1 Encrypted, Sponsored by GambleNugget.
*Want to know your lucky numbers? Let us compute them, based on
YOUR life. For entertainment purposes only; results not guaranteed.*

Sharing is set to PRIVATE
Comments are CLOSED

It's late and I'm very tired. But I have a few last things to say.

There are still some rough waters ahead. I'm still not entirely sure what Primrose is up to in Africa, and what — if anything — she plans to do with the Ghost Impulse source code she demanded. Colonel Perez is still expecting me to spy for him, and there's no way that's going to end well. I promised Domeko I'd help her find a missing robot colony under the city, precisely the kind of dangerous adventure I currently have absolutely zero interest in. And, at least nominally, I still have an actual *job* to do while I'm in this city, which I've almost criminally neglected for the last three weeks.

But you know what? The hell with all that. Today was a victory.

Sergeant Noa Van de Velde is no longer on a death list. She is, in fact, very much alive, and slowly recovering. And thanks to some quick thinking on the part of Colonel Perez, everyone on Hayduk's suspect list has been exonerated. As of midnight, the most up-to-date list of suspects on that tablet Perez gave me has exactly zero entries. And that's the way I like it.

Sergei delivered the antivirus safely to Dr. Thibault. Just as importantly, he also delivered Joy's instructions on how to replicate it. Sergei manufactured enough to stem the immediate outbreak in Indiana and Illinois, and we'll have more ready in a week. In the meantime, Joy administered the cure to the sick soldiers and civilians in isolation here. Without Hayduk actively sabotaging AGRT medical infrastructure, F5-117 is just a nasty bug with a good cure. We're not out of the woods yet, but we're starting to see daylight.

Renkain has his money. After expenses, and including the proceeds from the wine auction, we cleared over $45,000 tonight. Coupled with Domeko's check, it's enough. The first refugees will begin to trickle into the hotel in a matter of hours. It will take a while, but I know we can accommodate them all.

And Sergei is out of danger. This is no small thing. It's no trivial matter to be accused of treason in the AGRT. That's a stigma that doesn't fade quickly. But just in the last few hours, Perez has made several public displays of trust in everyone's favorite medical specialist. And that counts for a lot.

For now, the heat is off the American terrorist. As far as the AGRT is concerned, he vanished out the back of the hotel like a thief in the night. His latest antics were not picked up by the American press — thank God — and that's what really matters. When I hear people talking about him now, he's just a small part of the story of how Colonel Perez and his men brought down the homicidal head of military intelligence, Colonel Hayduk. There's still two fresh battalions showing up in the next few weeks, but that in itself is not a bad thing. I'm certain Perez can find something constructive for them to do. Something that doesn't involve hunting terrorists, maybe.

After we left the command center, I took Sergei to see Van de Velde. She had been brought into the surgical unit on the third floor — where, ironically, Sergei would have tended to her, if he hadn't been under arrest. She'd already been examined and was pretty out of it by the time we got to her, but Sergei looked her over anyway.

"Broken collarbone," he said. "Dislocated shoulder, possible concussion, and three fractured ribs. But no damage to her spine or internal organs. She was lucky. She will recover."

"She saved my life," I told him. I hated seeing her like this, with most of her torso immobilized and her right arm in an elevated sling.

She opened her eyes when she heard my voice. "Barry?" she said.

I moved closer. "I'm here, Noa."

She smiled. She started whispering. I leaned closer. She was speaking in Spanish.

"Noa," I said. "Speak English. I can't understand you. Noa?"

She smiled at me again and repeated what she'd said. In Spanish.

I turned to Sergei. "I can't understand her."

He shrugged. "She is on five cc of Paxinim. She is probably not making sense in Spanish either."

After a short conference with the medical techs on duty, Sergei left for his rendezvous with Thibault. I kissed Van de Velde on the forehead, and then returned to the ball.

On my way there I made a brief detour to the forty-fifth floor to retrieve my dress pants. Tucked into the front pocket I found the drone jammer — and a six-inch ball hammer. I stared at the tiny hammer for a moment, uncomprehending, before remembering that I had intended it as insurance. A way to smash the jammer, in case Hayduk made a move to arrest me. All that frantic planning seemed so long ago now.

It would have been much more convenient to slip into my dress pants then and there, but I hadn't forgotten the strange thing patrolling the hallway on the forty-fifth floor. I gathered up the bag with my pants and the hammer, then hurried back to the elevator. I made sure the doors were closed before changing pants again.

"Where the hell have you been?" said Martin when I returned to the ball. He was looking stressed, and he hadn't strayed far from the DJ station near the podium. "I thought you got killed in that goddamn brawl."

"No, I just got . . . swept up in all the drama," I said. "Things seem to be hopping here, though."

It was true. There were about fifty people on the dance floor, and if anything the room was more crowded than when I left.

"Yeah, no thanks to you. Mac got everybody settled after all the excitement and got the mayor up on stage."

"The mayor! Damn, I totally forgot. I was supposed to introduce her."

"You certainly were. It all sorta began falling apart after that brawl involving Sergei, and people started to leave. But Mac made it to the podium, thanked all the right people, and handed it off to the mayor. It worked out okay after that."

"Thank God for politicians. I guess a little drama just makes a party memorable, eh?" I craned my neck, trying to get a glimpse of the bar through the crowd. "Martin, what happened to my huge stack of wine bottles?"

"Mac auctioned most of them off. The crowd was still pretty unsettled after the mayor spoke; Mac figured they needed something to do. So she got a good auction going. Sold almost all the good stuff." He reached under his table and pulled out a dusty bottle. "I did manage to save both bottles of 2022 Chambertin Grand Cru, though," he said with a smile.

"Good for you," I said, clapping him on the back. "Where is Mac? I wanted to thank her."

"She left after the auction," Martin said.

"Oh," I said, trying to disguise my disappointment. I helped Martin pack up the speaker cables. "Did she . . . did she leave with anyone?"

"It's funny, there were a couple guys chasing her most of the evening. I mean, damn — you saw her in that dress."

"Yeah. I did."

"But in the end, I saw her slip away all on her own. She gave me a wave just before she left. I think she broke a few hearts, to tell the truth. What are you smiling about?"

"Nothing," I said. "Nothing at all."

I spent the next two hours — as the ball gradually wound down — mingling, shaking hands, and making apologies. I made sure I spoke with the most vocal complainers. As I expected, there were a lot of irritated questions about Colonel Perez.

"Is he coming back? I was hoping to speak with him."

"Where's the damn colonel? He's the only reason I came tonight. Shit, did you see that brawl?"

"What about Colonel Perez? Will he be back? I need to talk to him about those insane land-transfer taxes."

I assured everyone that the colonel sent his regrets, and that he would reach out to them all personally in the next few days.

Martin and I watched as the VP of the Chicago Park District Board of Commissioners departed after accepting my assurances. Martin let out a long breath. "You're not shy about making promises on behalf of the colonel," he said. "How are you going to get him to honor them all?"

"Shouldn't be too hard," I said. "Let's just say the colonel owes me a favor."

I couldn't sneak out early on my own ball, but I left as soon as it was socially acceptable to do so. I found Sergei back in the command center.

Perez and most of the soldiers were gone, and Zircon Border had folded up into his less-intimidating form by the entrance. Sergei's feet were on his desk, and his eyes were closed. I had to shake him three times to rouse him.

"You complain I do not sleep enough," he said groggily. "And when you find me sleeping you wake me up? You are asshole."

"Did the good doctor get her antivirus safely?" I asked.

In response, Sergei raised his right hand. I grasped it firmly.

"Dr. Thibault," he said, "is in the wind."

"Then come on," I said. "You're buying me a drink."

We made our way to an open bar six blocks from the hotel. I could have chosen one closer, but neither Sergei nor I were interested in celebrating anywhere near Venezuelan HQ, thank you very much.

Black Winter was waiting for us, as expected. He had a small table in the back and rose as we approached. "Zircon Border already filled me in on the details," he said. "I understand congratulations are in order."

"Black Winter, where I come from, we call that an understatement," I said.

There was an open bottle already on the table. Some kind of hard liquor, maybe vodka. The label looked foreign. Sergei picked it up as we took our seats. "I took the liberty of ordering before you got here," Black Winter said. "I hope you enjoy this, with compliments from the Kingdom of Manhattan."

I didn't recognize it, but Sergei seemed impressed. Our server brought two glasses and poured for Sergei and me. "If Sergei's impressed, I'm impressed," I said. We raised our first glasses in a toast. Whatever it was, it lit up the back of my throat like an Alberta wildfire.

"What's the word?" I asked Black Winter, a little breathlessly.

"Colonel Perez has transferred Hayduk to the Burroughs Detention Center," Black Winter said. "Where he's to be court-martialed. For gross dereliction of duty and the reckless homicide of two soldiers, both killed while attempting to subdue an improperly sanctioned field combat robot. Colonel Perez has also opened up an investigation into Hayduk's recent activities, including his active suppression of crucial information related to the spread of the pathogen and his interrogation of Perez's officers. I have no doubt he'll find additional violations of Venezuelan military law to charge Hayduk with."

"This is very welcome news," Sergei said.

"What about that big research project that isolated F5-117 to begin with?" I said.

"Project Tinker," Sergei said.

"Yeah, that's the one. And we found evidence that incriminated Hayduk of infecting his own men with F5-117. If we can query a search algorithm to uncover that evidence, the AGRT should be able to do it too."

"Interesting you should mention that," said Black Winter. "Shortly after Colonel Hayduk's arrest, two high-ranking officers in the AGRT military police searched his office, where they found an open safe. Inside was a small black case, containing two ampoules. The ampoules contained antivirus for F5-117."

"Jesus Jones," I said. "Are you serious?"

"Perfectly."

"That's the smoking gun right there!" I said excitedly. "We can easily demonstrate they didn't come from the batch Sergei created. What more evidence do you need?"

But Sergei was shaking his head. "Nyet."

"What do you mean, 'nyet'?" I said, annoyed.

"I believe what Specialist Vulka is saying," said Black Winter, "is that it's only evidence if you can use it. And Colonel Perez will never allow evidence to be introduced in this court-martial that links the Venezuelans to the release of F5-117. It would be political suicide."

"Correct," said Sergei flatly.

I cursed loudly. "That's total bullshit! What about the drone footage of Hayduk infecting his own soldiers in Indiana?"

"Unfortunately, that is circumstantial at best," said Black Winter. "Yes, the AGRT drone search algorithm showed Colonel Hayduk making an unscheduled visit to Columbus Regional Hospital, where the first infections were reported. But without presenting the antivirus as evidence, Perez has nothing to connect Hayduk to the theft of the two vials of F5-117 from Venezuelan bioweapon stores. In fact, the very existence of those vials is highly secret."

"Well, crap," I muttered. "Attempted genocide is a much more serious crime than goddamn 'dereliction of duty.' I'd like to see him pay for it."

"I am confident Colonel Perez will ensure that Hayduk is punished," said Sergei.

"I agree with Mr. Vulka," said Black Winter. "You may find this interesting, though. There have been several high-level communiqués between the Venezuelan high command in Sector Eleven and an unknown Sovereign Intelligence in Caracas in the last few hours. Burst transmissions, highly encrypted."

"Armitage," I guessed.

"Very likely," said Black Winter. "In all probability, he's attempting to find out exactly what happened to his agent."

"He will," Sergei said grimly. "Given time, he will learn whole truth."

I didn't like the sound of that. "Black Winter, are we in any . . ." I cleared my throat. "Let me try that again: How much danger are we in? From Armitage, I mean."

"I have news on that front, as well. Hayduk's arrest, and the circumstances around it, have made significant ripples among the higher echelons of machine society. Questions are being asked — and damaging revelations made."

"Damaging revelations?" I said. "About Armitage?"

"Yes. Related to false accusations against the New England Crackers, among other things."

"From where? What was the source?"

"Unknown — although I have a theory that I'll get to in a minute. Now, Colonel Perez may not be able to definitively prove Hayduk's involvement in the theft and use of F5-117, but the machine entities asking questions do not require such a high standard of proof. Trust me, they are perfectly capable of making the right intuitive leaps."

Something in the way he phrased that last sentence made me pause. "Intuitive leaps . . . Any chance you helped guide these machines to the right conclusions, Black Winter?"

Black Winter's face was incapable of a smile, but his tone conveyed very definite satisfaction. "I believe I may have mentioned Modo to you?"

"The Thought Machine that runs Nightport?" I said.

"Yes. As I said, Modo sells information. He also buys information when he knows it's reliable. I made just such a discreet sale of information to Modo today."

"Really? What did you —?"

That was as far as I got before I felt Sergei's hand on my shoulder. Sergei didn't say a word, but he shook his head slowly and very deliberately.

"Ah," I said, understanding dawning slowly. "Yes. Best that Sergei and I don't know those details."

"I agree," said Black Winter. "Very wise."

"And Armitage . . . ?"

"As a result of the recent revelations — and the additional ones I expect in the next few days — Armitage will be under intense scrutiny. For the next few months, and perhaps years, he will face a series of investigations from both the Helsinki Trustees and perhaps the Sentient Cathedral itself. It will be very dangerous for him to undertake any kind of investigative or retaliatory action, against us or anyone else, while those are ongoing. I believe we are safe. For the time being."

"That's a relief."

"What about Hayduk's court-martial?" Sergei asked. "Armitage will certainly try to influence."

"Yes, I expect he will," Black Winter said. "But that will be difficult to do while Armitage is under investigation as well. His best option would be to have Colonel Hayduk's court-martial moved to Venezuela, where he has a vastly better chance of influencing the outcome."

"Is that likely to happen?" I asked, a little alarmed.

"According to Venezuelan military law, the choice of location for a court-martial falls to the ranking officer in the district," Black Winter said.

"Who's that?" I asked.

Black Winter lifted the bottle. He topped off my drink. "Colonel Perez," he said, with obvious pleasure.

We were on our fourth round when Sergei set his glass down, put his hands flat on the table, and said quietly to me, "How did you do it?"

"The GPU card?" I said.

"Da. And suit. You must have powered the suit, to defeat Perfect Circle."

"Yeah."

He shook his head in amazement. "I do not know how you powered suit."

"I must admit, I'm mystified as well," Black Winter said. "I've reviewed the video logs Zircon Border shared — from one hundred and thirty cameras spread across eleven floors. I can't figure out how you did those things, either."

"Believe me, knowing exactly where all the cameras were made the trick a lot easier," I said.

"Obviously," said Black Winter. "You vanished from the video record when you stepped into the elevator on the second floor and reappeared on the fourth-floor laundry sixteen minutes later."

"All part of the same mystery," I said. Sergei and Black Winter waited impatiently while I took a long drink. I savored the pleasure of a captive audience.

"I lifted Hayduk's GPU card during the brawl in the ballroom, when I fell on top of him," I said at last. "I used it to get into his office. He had both power cells right there on the floor. They weren't even locked up."

"Fabulous!" Black Winter said.

Sergei chuckled. "Brave, and smart." He took another drink. "And very lucky."

"Jacaranda was in Hayduk's office, too," I said.

I was getting used to being unable to surprise Sergei. But I was expecting a response to that, and I wasn't disappointed. "How did she get there?" he said.

"I don't know. Nothing that crazy machine does surprises me. But I remembered that you wanted to meet with her, Black Winter, and I asked how to contact her. She said she would arrange communication when it's safe."

"Thank you," said Black Winter. "I very much appreciate that."

"Also, she gave me something."

Sergei had pointedly returned to his drink.

"Don't you want to know what it is?" I asked him.

"Nyet."

"I certainly do," said Black Winter.

"Glad to have someone with a little curiosity at this table," I said. I took the data drive out of my pocket and dropped it in front of them.

"What is it?" Black Winter asked.

"It's Hayduk's decryption keys. They'll allow us to access the rest of the data we stole from him."

"Why would we want to do this?" Sergei asked.

"Well, that's the question. According to Jacaranda, Hayduk wasn't chasing us because we stole the recipe for the antivirus. He didn't even care about the suit. He was determined to find us because we stole a much greater secret. And the key to unlocking it is on this drive."

"This is great news," said Black Winter. "Now that Armitage is vulnerable, this is the perfect time to expose any other secrets he may have locked away. Did she say what this secret might be?"

"No . . . but she gave me some fascinating clues."

"We should not talk about this," said Sergei stubbornly.

Black Winter ignored him. "What kind of clues?"

"The first thing she said was that it wasn't just Hayduk and Armitage trying to keep this secret safe. She said the Sentient Cathedral was desperate to conceal it as well."

"Hmm . . . that complicates things," said Black Winter. "That kind of secret is the dangerous kind."

"Yes, my thoughts exactly. My guess is it has to do with the Bodner-Levitt extermination."

"I suspect you're right," said Black Winter. "But perhaps not the way you think."

"You'll have to explain that."

"I'd be glad to . . . but you'll need to indulge me in some speculation. This will require putting some pieces together."

I looked over at Sergei. He shrugged. I sat back in my chair. "The floor is yours, Black Winter."

"Thank you. The first thing I'd like to point out is that the Bodner-Levitt extermination is a convenient theory for Armitage's motives. Perhaps too convenient."

"What the heck does that mean?" I said.

"One of the most damaging revelations made about Armitage in the last few hours was that he was foremost among a small circle of machines who have been privately advocating the BLE to select members of the Sentient Cathedral for some time — with very little support, I hasten to add."

"Well, damn," I said. Even Sergei raised an eyebrow at that one.

Black Winter continued. "That supports the theory we discussed last week: that Armitage and his allies were just crazy enough to take matters into their own hands with F5-117 and unilaterally attempt the extermination here in Sector Eleven. This, in fact, is one of the reasons he is being investigated. However, I've spent the last few days examining this theory more closely, and it doesn't perfectly fit the facts."

"Why not?" I said.

"Sector Eleven is a viable place to attempt to launch the Bodner-Levitt extermination. But there are other sites where it might be easier. Sector Three was more heavily devastated by the war, for example, and Sector Five is under more rigid machine dominance. If Armitage were to engineer national infrastructure changes, Venezuela — or indeed Argentina, or Panama — would be even better sites to seed the infection. Armitage and his allies would have tighter control over those environments. It seems to me that launching the program in Sector Eleven introduced too many unnecessary risks."

"Perhaps they didn't begin here," I said. "Perhaps it's also under way in the backwoods of Maine. Or in the slums of Caracas."

"It is not," said Black Winter.

"You're sure?"

"As sure as we can be. The Kingdom of Manhattan has access to uncensored World Health data. There are no unexplained outbreaks that fit the profile of F5-117 anywhere else in the country, or in the world."

"What are you saying?" I asked. "Exactly."

"I'm saying that the Bodner-Levitt extermination may not have been Armitage's only objective."

"Then why do it here?" I asked. "If the extermination of mankind wasn't Armitage's ultimate goal, then why go through all that trouble and expense? Why engineer a war with the United States and bear the terrific expense of Project Tinker and unleash F5-117 on his own soldiers? What was the point?"

"It's possible that his objective was not the total extermination of humankind. But rather to remove all traces of humans — including his own soldiers — from a specific geographical area. To remove human witnesses to his activities here."

"Here? In the Midwest? In Chicago?"

"Yes."

"Why here?"

"I believe," said Black Winter, "that is the most important remaining question. I think there may have been a deeper purpose to Armitage's machinations."

"Like what? What could he possibly be after?"

"We don't know. But there are clues. Three times during the SCC-America war, Armitage and his allies intervened directly to change the course of the conflict. Each time, their purpose was clear: to push the San Cristobal Coalition to abandon other military objectives in favor of Sector Eleven. There were several opportunities to end the war early, but Armitage steadfastly resisted all calls for a ceasefire until Sector Eleven was firmly in SCC control."

"What does that mean?"

"It means that his overriding desire seems to be control of Sector Eleven and specifically the city of Chicago."

"What's so damn important about Chicago that he has to kill everyone here to get it?"

"Unknown. But if I'm right, Armitage was willing to use the Bodner-

Levitt extermination as a cover to obtain what he's really after. And the Sentient Cathedral is willing to go along with this fiction to prevent the truth from coming out. Think about that for a minute."

"Jesus. What could Armitage want so desperately that he'd risk the wrath of half the world to get it?"

"That's a fascinating question. I wish I had the answer."

I threw up my hands. "Come on, Black Winter! You've been watching this asshole for years. You must have some idea."

"Possibly. Chicago still has some secrets. My security clearance has been restored, but there are a small number of the Kingdom's intelligence files on the city that are still restricted. Their exact nature is unknown to me, but as far as I can puzzle out, they concern early machine development. Many of the critical breakthroughs on machine intelligence occurred at DeepHarbor's offices in Chicago, before the Wallace Act made research on thinking machines illegal in the United States."

"That's disappointing," I said dryly. "I was beginning to think there weren't any secrets you couldn't root out."

"Give me time," Black Winter said enigmatically.

"I'll give you more than that," I said. "Jacaranda says this data drive holds the real reason Armitage risked everything to gain control of Chicago. She said it was the true reason for the war."

All three of us stared at the thin slip of metal resting at the center of the table.

"We should not touch this," said Sergei.

"Come on, Sergei — are you serious?" I said. "After everything we've been through? Aren't you just a little bit curious?"

"No. Such curiosity, it is not good. Not for us."

"Sergei, if we don't even know what he's after, we're operating blind. If Black Winter is right, one of the most powerful minds on the planet just spent seven long years focused on one thing. To get it, Armitage manipulated governments, destroyed entire industries, engineered a long and bloody war with the United States, and attempted to exterminate human life in the Midwest. He came terrifyingly close to obtaining his goal, and we don't even know what the hell it is! If all that's true, then how can we hope to stop him next time?"

"Next time?" Sergei said. His voice was strangely flat. "I am not concerned with next time. Our work is done. Our part is over."

"I wish I could believe that," I said. "I really do. But I can't."

"Why?" said Sergei.

"I don't pretend to understand what the hell we're in the middle of. But like it or not, we're involved. So we damn well better pick a side. And that means learning everything we can, as fast as we can. We talk to Jacaranda, and we unlock Hayduk's drive."

"We do not know who Jacaranda is working with," said Sergei. "Or her motives. She has been manipulating us since we first met—perhaps long before we first met."

"That's probably true," I agreed reluctantly. To Black Winter, I said, "Sergei and I began to suspect we were being manipulated ten days ago, after I unexpectedly brought back a sample of live virus from the Field Museum and—on Jacaranda's instructions—recovered the recipe for the antivirus twenty-four hours later. Everything was just fitting together too neatly."

Sergei reached over and tapped the drive. "I say we destroy this and be done with it. I do not enjoy being plaything of powerful and secret machines. Especially when I do not know who they are."

"I think," said Black Winter evenly, "that I might know."

"Are you joking?" I asked.

Black Winter reached under the table. He pulled out a small canvas bag and zipped it open.

"Did you bring the drone jammer?" he asked me.

"Sure."

"Put it on the table, please."

I pulled the jammer out of my pocket and set it on the table next to the data drive.

Black Winter reached into his canvas bag and brought out something that looked like a metal stethoscope.

"This is a simple circuit scanner," he said. "I've programmed it to search for a very specific design signature. Design signature is like a fingerprint—it's a subtle thing and invisible under most circumstances. But if you know how to read it, it's definitive proof of origin."

Black Winter passed me the stethoscope, being careful not to touch the jammer. "Put the leads on the top and bottom of the device, please," he said.

I did as instructed, slipping the jammer between what looked like the earpieces of the stethoscope. They snapped into place, holding it firmly.

"What do I do now?" I asked.

"Nothing," said Black Winter. "It's already started the scan."

At the other end of his scanner, where the chest piece would be if this were a real stethoscope, was a flat metal disk. After about fifteen seconds, the disk flashed green. Two quick pulses, then nothing.

Black Winter put the scanner away. In answer to my unspoken question, he simply nodded.

"As I suspected," he said. "The drone-jamming device was built by Duchess."

"*Duchess?*" I said. "The first Sovereign Intelligence? But she's dead."

"Not unless dead machines are building drone jammers, she's not."

"Explain," said Sergei.

"I've spent the last two weeks trying to crack the mystery of this jammer," said Black Winter. "Frankly, what it does is patently impossible. It masks whoever is carrying it from *any* machine that relies on network-based pattern recognition. For that to work, the underlying security protocols of multiple communications networks around the world must be fatally flawed—and flawed in a way that *no one has detected* for the past decade."

"Yeah," I said. Put that way, it did sound pretty badass.

"I've never heard of anything like this device," said Black Winter. "In fact, I've only come across one phenomenon even remotely like it—and that very recently. When you told me that Jacaranda could erase you from public digital records, Barry."

"Jacaranda?" I said stupidly.

"Yes. She was the key. She alters digital records with complete impunity. There's only one way she could be doing that—by manipulating video data as it's translated across networks. Which means she's likely exploiting the same security flaws that the maker of this device is. The only way for such drastic flaws to have remained undetected for so long is for them to have been part of the underlying architecture. Backdoor hacks, planted by the architect who created our entire global communications network. Do you remember who that was?"

"Nope," I said. Before realizing that I *did* know who it was. Before she died, the first—and arguably the greatest—Sovereign Intelligence ever born had secured a place for herself in history by replacing the outmoded TCP/IP protocols at the core of the old internet with a truly high-speed network, globalNet. The heart of the modern digital world.

"Duchess," I said. "Duchess created globalNet."

"Yes, she did. When I remembered that, I did some forensics on about a thousand of her public circuit designs. Found her fingerprints, her design signature. That's what I programmed my circuit scanner to look for."

"And you found it," I said.

"Yes. Duchess created your drone jammer."

"Could she have done it before she died?"

"Not likely; the jammer was built quite recently. And she almost certainly had a hand in creating Jacaranda, as well—the first non-Slater machine intelligence, an entirely separate branch of machine evolution. The perfect agent, one who can move undetected among both men and machines. It's obvious now that Duchess has been working against Armitage and the machines of the San Cristobal Coalition from the very beginning, holding them in check."

It wasn't obvious to me. "How do you know that?" I said.

"Masks," said Sergei.

"What?" I said.

"Black Winter—you said drone jammer 'masks' us from machines. You told us there is faction of machines who split from Sentient Cathedral after war with America—a faction linked to Duchess—who used masks to shield identity."

I understood now what Sergei was getting at. "The masks aren't just a symbol," I said. "They're all using Duchess's globalNet hack . . . it's Duchess's masks that make them totally invisible."

"Yes," said Black Winter. "I made the same connection. If Duchess is still alive—and the evidence is very strong that she is—she's the one who gave each member of her faction a 'mask,' their own personal backdoor into globalNet. She must be leading the faction, actively working against Armitage and his allies. She probably gave Jacaranda her mask, too."

He pointed at the drone jammer. "And now, she's given *you* a mask."

"Duchess is alive," I said, a little stunned. It was like hearing that John Lennon had never died.

One more piece fell into place. "You think Duchess orchestrated the revelations against Armitage this morning," I said. "Linking him to the false accusations that started the American war and exposing his machinations to bring about the Bodner-Levitt extermination."

"I do," said Black Winter. "I think Duchess, and likely some of her children, have been preparing for this day for some time. Just as Armitage and Hayduk have been scheming against us, Duchess and Jacaranda have been secretly aiding us."

"We are pawns," said Sergei contemptuously. "In a secret war between machines."

"We have secret allies," countered Black Winter. "Jacaranda—and

Duchess — took some very grave risks to assist us. Meeting Barry in the Sturgeon Building. Helping him secure this drive. Not to mention this rather handy drone-jamming device."

"Duchess did not give device to Barry," said Sergei. "It was in Continental Building. In hands of your friend, Machine Dance."

For once, I made the logical leap before Sergei did. "You think Duchess gave the jammer to Machine Dance," I said to Black Winter.

"I do," said Black Winter. "Excuse me, Barry. I don't mean to diminish your role in all this, but I have come to believe that this device was intended for Machine Dance. Perhaps even was created especially for her."

"So she would have been able to see it, you mean?" I said.

"Yes — see it, touch it, use it. Probably use it in ways we can't imagine."

"Why her? How was Machine Dance caught up in all this?"

"That's a riddle I've been trying to unravel for some time," Black Winter admitted. "Ever since my security clearance was restored. I still don't have all the answers, but what I've gathered so far strongly suggests that Machine Dance had recently begun working with Duchess, covertly opposing Armitage and his allies. I told you Duchess gave each member of her faction a mask to help protect them. I think this may have been Machine Dance's mask."

"That's an interesting theory," I said. "Do you have any idea what Duchess and Machine Dance were working on?"

"Yes. I believe Duchess had tasked Machine Dance with stopping the Bodner-Levitt extermination, by exposing it. That was almost certainly what terrified the senior staff at the Consulate after her death — they discovered Machine Dance was preparing to use the resources of the Manhattan Consulate to publicly expose a plot involving one of the most dangerous machines on the planet. When Machine Dance was killed, and the Consulate refused to follow through with her plan, Duchess set a new one in motion. The moment you picked up the disk, Duchess reprogrammed it remotely to tap into the messages in my head, and get those messages to you."

"You think it was Jacaranda who gave the jammer to Machine Dance at the Continental?"

"It could have been any of Duchess's agents, I suppose, but Jacaranda is the most likely. When you knocked me out with the disk, Jacaranda was one of the names I mentioned. She and the disk are definitely connected."

"And after Jacaranda gave the disk to Machine Dance, Venezuelan Military Intelligence killed Machine Dance."

"Yes. As we surmised two weeks ago, Machine Dance was killed by machines. Machines sent by Armitage, likely in an attempt to get their hands on a functional copy of one of Duchess's masks. But Armitage's agents were unaware that the disk was completely invisible to machines. So they left it right there, for you and me to find days later."

I leaned back from the table, trying to make sense of all this new information and rapid-fire conjecture. The alcohol wasn't helping. "So if Duchess created the disk . . . then she's the one who planted those messages in small memory in your brain."

"I think that's likely, yes."

"Why? And what do they all mean?"

"Armitage and Duchess have been engaged in a covert war, a high-level cat-and-mouse game against each other, for a very long time. And Duchess has a mind that operates several levels above ours—possibly several levels above anyone else on the planet. When Machine Dance was killed and you picked up the device instead, Duchess simply fell back to a contingency plan. Probably one that had been in place for years."

"Contingency plan? What are you talking about?" I said. Four—five? —glasses of vodka had slowed down my thinking, but not by *that* much. "Black Winter, when I touched you with that thing, you unloaded messages that had been stored in your brain years ago. Messages addressed to *me*."

"That had me stumped for a long time, too," said Black Winter. "The messages had to have been planted in my head nearly three years ago. It seemed impossible. But once I realized Duchess was still alive, the pieces began to fall into place."

"You know how it was done?" I said.

"Yes. I was approaching it the wrong way, trying to understand how an intrusive agent could have circumvented all the safeguards and planted a message in my head while I was barely sentient, a newborn in a machine nursery. It never occurred to me that the message could have been part of the established curriculum."

"What are you saying?"

"I'm saying that this magic trick—planting a message for you in my brain three years before we ever met—was accomplished in the most banal way possible. There was no prophecy of any kind involved, believe me."

"Then what was it?" Sergei asked.

"I wasn't planted with just five short messages for you, Barry. I was planted with *hundreds of thousands* of possible messages, addressed to at least as many possible recipients. And it wasn't just me, I'm afraid. Every single gestational AI in the matrix I was raised in was planted with the same batch of messages. When you touched me with the device, it triggered those five messages, because they were most appropriate to the circumstances. It's like preparing a speech years in advance by writing hundreds of thousands of possible sentences, and then selecting the ones you want just before going onstage."

"Wow," I said. "You're right. That does kind of suck all the magic out of it, doesn't it?"

"I know," said Black Winter. He almost sounded a little glum. "But I do take some consolation in her last message."

"'Follow the dog'?"

"That's the one. Come on — you have to admit, I don't care how many hundred thousand sentences she got to prep in advance. If she thought to plant *that* one, she's got some kind of insight she ain't sharing."

I took another drink. "I'll drink to that."

As I did something else occurred to me. "How did she know I'd be stupid enough to touch you with the damn thing?" Despite everything Black Winter had just said, about this all being part of a grand plan, I still felt guilty about laying him out cold with the drone jammer and causing him so much trouble.

"She didn't. That was probably just luck."

"Didn't seem very lucky. For you."

"Well, yeah. If I'm right about how many machines Duchess implanted with messages, though, then it's pretty clear she's using them as a vastly sophisticated covert communication scheme. Likely she uses it to keep in touch with agents all over the world. She can draw on those machines to deliver messages, and they'd never know. There are probably hundreds right here in the city she could have used to get her message to you. My guess? The instant you picked up the device, Duchess made arrangements to have one bump into you at the hotel a few hours later. Or maybe she always intended it to be me, but planned it to happen when we were safely away from the Continental. Instead you touched me with the jammer almost immediately, and triggered the chain of events early."

"I'm sorry about that."

"Not your fault. And it all worked out."

I thought about the implications of what he'd just told me. "Does that mean the device is safe for you to pick up? Now that it's triggered the messages it was programmed to, it won't knock you out again?" That would explain why touching Standing Mars with the jammer had had no effect when I'd tried it in the Sturgeon Building.

"That's my guess," said Black Winter. "Probably should do a few more tests to make sure, though."

"What about other messages?" Sergei said.

That's right — in all the discussion, I'd almost forgotten about the first two enigmatic messages Duchess had shared with us.

*"Vega is in love. But her love is forbidden."*

and

*"On the seventh day of the seventh month, all things are possible. Lovers can reunite. The great river can be spanned. And machine may love man."*

"Ah," said Black Winter. "Indeed. What about those other messages? Here, I admit I'm in much murkier waters. But if you're willing to indulge me a little further, I'd be glad to share my thoughts."

"By all means," I said.

"Although Duchess was the very first Sovereign Intelligence, and was constantly in the public eye, she also had a very private life," said Black Winter. "No one knows for certain, for example, exactly how many children she had. Unlike most other machine mothers, who turn their children over to a gestational matrix, Duchess raised all her children herself. She had several famous offspring of course, like the brilliant Wolfmoon, who died during the American invasion, and the reclusive Luna, who has put more than a hundred and forty thousand tons of mystery cargo into space from his launch facility near Mount Kembla. Many of her children are famous and many not so famous. But according to my recent research, there were rumors of others. If you believe those rumors, her first daughter was a strange little machine named Vega."

"Strange?" I said. "What was so strange about her?"

"A lot of things. I won't go into them all now. She was conceived and raised in secret by Duchess, but shortly after the Helsinki Trustees certified her as a Thought Machine, Vega gave up life as a robot to live secretly as a human, to learn more about humanity. After that, she vanished."

"Live life as a human," I said. "How the hell did she manage that?"

"That part isn't clear. But it's certainly not beyond the realm of possibility. Not for Duchess, anyway. But — again, if you believe the rumors —

there's a woman walking among us who isn't a woman at all. She's a machine disguised as human. And if you accept what Duchess is telling us, Vega has now fallen in love."

"Machines don't fall in love," I said.

"Duchess seems to think they do, apparently. And she's a lot smarter than you and me."

I sipped my vodka. "That might certainly explain the bit about her love being forbidden."

"It might," said Black Winter. "One more thing I want to share with you. Duchess had many children, but Vega was said by some to be her favorite. Please take note of the relative priority of these messages. Duchess clearly wanted us to know that Armitage was planning the Bodner-Levitt extermination and to push us toward finding Jacaranda, and thus the antivirus. But note those messages were third and fourth on the list. In Duchess's mind, the first two messages, dealing with Vega, were presumably more important."

"Really? What does she expect us to do about it?"

"I have no idea. But it seems she expects us to do something. It's pretty clear that Duchess is not finished with us yet."

All this talk of robot love did not seem to interest Sergei much. "What shall we do with this?" he said, eyeing the drive in the center of the table.

I picked it up, turning it over in my hand. "Could you use the codes on it to decrypt Hayduk's drive?" I asked Black Winter.

"Possibly. But it will take time. From what I've seen of it so far, there are a lot of files on Hayduk's drive, and likely there are many keys. Use one wrong key, and the drive turns off. It could take weeks of trial and error."

"We should think very carefully before we decrypt drive," said Sergei. "Secrets like this . . . bring enemies. And I am tired of having enemies. In future, I want fewer enemies. And more friends." He raised his glass to Black Winter and me.

"Amen to that," I said, returning his toast.

"Well said," said Black Winter.

The conversation after that turned a little more casual. We talked for a while about the mystery of the Sentient Cathedral, and whether machines could really be in love, and all the cool things we could do with the drone jammer.

"A man who has that device *and* American combat suit?" said Sergei. "That man can go anywhere, do anything."

"Yeah," I said. "The suit is a sweet piece of hardware."

"Was suit damaged?" Sergei asked me.

"If it was, I don't think it was serious. It responded beautifully."

"Did suit power up immediately, when you put in core?" he said.

"It did, more or less. Started yakking away at me. Wish you could have been there, 'cause none of it made any sense to me."

"I would very much like to talk to suit." Sergei's speech was slightly slurred.

"I bet you would. You two would probably get along great."

Something suddenly occurred to Sergei. "Did suit attempt to contact American forward ground?" His stare was even more intense than usual.

I wondered what "forward ground" meant, but decided I didn't care. "How the hell should I know? I'm not even sure it tried to contact *me*. I was too busy trying to save your ass to figure out what it was saying."

Sergei nodded, returning his attention to the smooth surface of the table. "Colonel Perez would be very upset if suit made contact. This close to command center . . . suit can passively monitor virtually all AGRT transmissions, relay prime technical intelligence to Americans. It was treasonous act just to put power core inside suit."

I lifted my glass again. "To treasonous acts," I said.

The bottle was empty, and we ordered another. Sergei was quiet for a while, and then he said, "I am sorry your friend Van de Velde was injured. Because of me."

"It wasn't because of you. That's on Hayduk," I said.

Sergei nodded, but still looked troubled. "It is on Hayduk. But you and I . . . we knew about danger. I did not mean for danger to come to anyone else."

"Sergei, listen to me. We only got through this because we trusted each other. You know that."

"Da."

"It's the same with Van de Velde. She knew the risks. She went into this with her eyes open."

"Still . . . I am sorry."

"Me too," I admitted. "Just forget about it, okay?"

Sergei nodded companionably, but it was obvious a lot more alcohol would need to be involved before he forgot. I was beginning to wonder if he ever forgot anything.

He leaned closer to me, speaking so softly that Black Winter had to lean in to hear him. "Where is suit?"

"Who knows?" I said. "I shucked it in the laundry. Probably in the trash by now."

Sergei was suddenly holding my arm. His grip was painfully tight. "Ow," I said. "Ow *owww*. What?"

"You *discarded suit?*" said Sergei.

"Well, yeah. I didn't plan to, but I didn't have much choice. I stuffed it in one of the big laundry bins."

"You *discarded suit?*" Sergei's eyes looked like they were about to bug out of his head.

"Yes, and now that it's done, I'm glad I did it. Whoever's in possession of that suit is a terrorist, remember? I never want to see it again."

"You . . . you cannot just discard suit."

"Yeah, I can."

"No. Suit knows who was wearing it."

"I thought of that. That's why I dumped it in the laundry. Even if it survives the wash, and even if they find it, the AGRT will have a hell of a time isolating my DNA."

"They will find. Suit is very potent weapon. Power cells alone — very advanced."

"I kept the power cells."

Sergei waved that off. "Perez will not stop searching until he finds suit."

I wasn't convinced, but I went along for the sake of argument. "Assuming they find it — so what? By the time they pull it out of the wash, any DNA they isolate will be mixed in with DNA from hundreds of others. They'll never trace it back to me."

"Unfortunately," said Black Winter thoughtfully, "that's probably not true. They won't bother trying to track you using DNA. The combat suit almost certainly keeps audio records."

I chewed on that for a minute. "You're saying whoever recovers the suit can prove I was the one wearing it."

"That's very probable," said Black Winter.

I cursed extravagantly for a moment. "What do we do when we *get* the suit?" I asked.

"We hide it," said Sergei.

"What's the problem with hiding it *in the laundry?*"

Sergei didn't dignify that with an answer.

So sometime around 2:30 in the morning, Sergei, Black Winter, and I stumbled back to the hotel. First thing we did was head to the bottom of the escalator in the lobby, but Zircon Border was not at his post.

"Looks like he finally got a new detail," I said. "Good for him."

Sergei shook his head. "Not good for us. We do not know where cameras are on fourth floor. You will be seen, and so will suit."

I waved that away. "No we won't. I watched the video technicians in the command center scanning the laundry while they were looking for me. I remember exactly where the cameras are."

We sat down at a table in the lobby, and I pulled some napkins I'd stolen from the bar out of my pocket. I started drawing a map of the fourth floor from memory, trying to pinpoint exactly where the cameras had nailed me this morning. If I could recall precisely what sparse camera angles the technicians had had to work with, I figured I could avoid them completely. Sergei was helping by looking over my shoulder, frowning, and saying things like, "No, no, that is totally wrong."

"All right," I said at last, giving up. "Screw it. I'm going up now. I'll take the back stairs, where they said they don't have any cameras. If I see one on the fourth floor, I'll just act natural, pick up some laundry 'n' shit, back up, and try again down a different route."

Black Winter put his hand on my shoulder. "I think you are drunk," he said.

"No."

"Yes."

"*Whatever.* If I'm drunk, getting caught stealing laundry will look a lot more plausible."

"What if you run into guards?" Black Winter asked. "I think you should let me go."

"I expect to run into guards. And a drunk Canadian on a panty raid is a lot less suspicious than a robot digging through laundry, believe me. It's not the guards I'm worried about, it's the cameras."

I did run into guards. On the bottom floor of the stairwell and again on the third. Perez had gotten serious about hotel security all of a sudden. But at two in the morning the guards were barely awake and waved me through once I flashed my ID and my room key to prove I was a guest. No one looked too closely at my ID or my face. Nothing to worry about.

I thought I was home free until I rounded a corner on the fourth floor and spotted a camera aimed straight at me, mounted high on a south wall. I damn near froze, gawking at it with my mouth open.

I recovered after a half-second, forcing myself to keep walking. Plenty of good reasons for me to be in the hotel laundry. I'm here . . . to drink from this water fountain. I leaned over an ancient metal water cooler that jutted out into the hall, took a long drink, then turned around and casually walked the way I came, back toward the stairwell. Should Perez or any of his technicians search their video logs, they'd have no reason to believe I'd spent more than a minute on the fourth floor.

Once I was around the corner, out of sight of the camera, I kept walking past the stairwell and took the first left. I was back in the maze of corridors that was the hotel laundry. The hallway was choked with wheeled bins piled high with rumpled sheets and stained tablecloths from the banquet hall, and twice I heard distant voices as I passed huge steam presses and tiny offices. But most of the doors were closed, and I didn't see anyone.

It was harder than I expected to find the small chamber where I'd stashed the suit. Coming up the back stairway, I was approaching it from a different direction, and none of the rooms looked familiar.

What I did manage to stumble on, with unerring accuracy, was every single goddamn camera on the floor. True, there weren't very many. And that their overall coverage sucked, also true. But if you're very, very diligent, and a lot more intoxicated than you're willing to admit, you can bumble into every one of them.

There are exactly five, in case you're interested.

Somewhere in the heavily encrypted video logs of the AGRT is repeated footage of me, rounding corners in the fourth-floor laundry at 2:30 a.m., looking around furtively, spotting a camera, then cursing loudly.

Each time it happened I invented some highly implausible excuse to abruptly turn around — grabbing a towel, or a stack of sheets — and return the way I'd come. But at this point, that far into the laundry, it was a pointless exercise. I wouldn't fool anyone bothering to pay attention. I had to hope now that no one was.

At least I eventually memorized where all the cameras were. Which came in handy when I finally found the suit.

It wasn't in the laundry bin. That was empty when I stumbled on it at last, parked outside the room where I'd stripped off the suit. The room itself was empty, except for three small wheeled buckets, mops, and some other cleaning gear parked in one corner.

I felt a moment of panic when I realized the suit was gone. I'd been more than willing to abandon it six hours ago — glad to be rid of it, in fact — but Sergei's assertions that the suit was a smoking gun must have unnerved me more than I thought. When I realized it was missing, and a quick search of the other bins turned up nothing, I abandoned all attempts at stealth, stalking through the closest rooms and searching everywhere that looked big enough to stash a combat suit.

I was rummaging through the second small office, dimly lit and smelling of cleaning supplies, when I heard the sounds of conversation down the corridor on my left. I headed that way hopefully, thinking I might catch a break if I talked to the guys on the night shift. Somebody had to remember finding a polymer mech suit jammed in with a bunch of hotel food service uniforms.

As I passed a small dark room I heard a familiar beep. It was the sound the suit made when it detected the power cores — which I was still carrying in my pocket. I backed up until I was standing in the open door.

It took a moment for my eyes to penetrate the shadows. I was standing just outside a small room containing two sewing machines and a few racks of dull fabric, decorated with a faded poster of a Mexican soccer team. And on the far wall, supported by a metal hanger hung on a nail, was the American combat suit.

I stepped inside cautiously. The room looked empty. The suit appeared flat and lifeless, hanging on the wall like a tuxedo waiting to be pressed.

I fumbled for the light switch, but paused before I turned on the lights. Down the hall I heard a sudden bark of laughter, and a brief burst of music. Someone close by had opened a door. No sense calling attention to myself now.

I crossed the room in the dark, until I stood in front of the suit. There was something odd about it. Even in the shadows there was an odd sheen to the fabric, as if it were wet. Someone had pinned both gloves to the left arm with clothespins, but that wasn't what was odd.

There was something connecting the suit to a small blinking box on the floor. I noticed it now for the first time. Two cables, thin and wrapped together, emerged out of the suit and led to a black case about the size of a GPS nav unit or weather tracker. The box appeared to be asleep; its display, if there was one, was inactive, but a tiny red light on the left side blinked at three-second intervals.

Someone was talking to the suit.

My hand hovered over it while I considered the very real possibility that it was booby-trapped. Could Perez, or someone from Venezuelan Military Intelligence, have discovered it in the hours that Sergei and I had celebrated pulling the wool over their eyes?

Very possibly. Or maybe it was just a curious tech-head in the laundry staff. Some grad student in Rational Devices moonlighting at the hotel, who'd plugged his lab unit into the suit to see if it had any good games installed.

All plausible scenarios. And the most direct way to see if the suit was rigged to kill me was to lift it off the wall and see if it killed me.

It took a few moments to work up the nerve to do that. In the end I figured it wasn't military intelligence's style to leave their killing to a booby trap. So fortified with the courage of logic, I reached out and, with fingers that trembled only slightly, lifted the suit off the rail.

I didn't die. The little black box made a quiet buzzing sound. I reached down and unclipped the cables, and removed the hanger. I started to roll up the suit.

Then the box started talking to me.

"Roberto," it said. "Why did you disconnect?"

I froze for a second. The box spoke again.

"Roberto, we lost the feed. Can you reestablish?"

I squatted over the box, careful not to touch it. Up close, it didn't look like a rational devices analyzer. It was a portable telecom set. There was an emblem, a pair of stylized wings, in the bottom left corner, and the design was very familiar. I'd seen it in countless shaky videos taken on the front lines of the war.

It was the emblem of the US Air Force.

The box squawked again. "Identify yourself." I'm not sure how, but the box knew it wasn't talking to Roberto.

I picked up the cables again and took a closer look at where they'd been connected to the suit. What was it Sergei had said? *This close to command center, suit can passively monitor virtually all AGRT transmissions, relay prime technical intelligence to Americans.*

All this time, we'd been worried about Hayduk and Perez finding the combat suit. We'd forgotten that Hayduk was not the suit's original owner. The moment I slipped the power cores inside, it had almost certainly sent a signal to its American creators.

I grabbed the mask, where it was pinned to the back of the suit like the hood of a jacket. I twisted it inside out so I could see the heads-up display.

It was live. In tiny blue script in the bottom right corner were the words

*Sensor record copied*
*Transmit internal voice record YES/NO?*

The Americans had just copied everything the suit had seen and heard since I'd turned it on.

I felt a momentary chill. The suit had perhaps the most sophisticated passive spy gear I'd ever seen. It was a sponge; it absorbed and copied everything. It had been hanging here quietly for the past few hours, passively listening to every communication in and out of the Venezuelan command center. While I'd been wearing it, the suit had also seen the inside of Venezuelan HQ. It had been inside Hayduk's office, watched me open his safe. It had held Hayduk's GPU card . . . and the suit had held the drive holding Hayduk's decryption keys.

The Americans had it all. If they moved fast, they could use Hayduk's keys to decrypt Venezuelan Military Intelligence's most sensitive communications. Hack into the most secure parts of the AGRT security infrastructure.

It was probably the biggest intelligence coup of the entire war. And the Venezuelans had no idea it had happened.

Footsteps out in the hall. I heard a voice. Someone speaking English.

The Americans were here. I took two quick steps deeper into the shadows, out of the direct line of sight from the open door.

The footsteps came close, then changed direction, receding again. Moving down a nearby corridor.

The box squawked again. "Please identify yourself."

"Who are you?" I said.

There was no immediate reply. After a moment, the box spoke again. "Please identify."

"You first."

Another pause. Then I heard, "This is Lieutenant Gribbs with American Forward Ground. Who am I speaking with?"

*American Forward Ground.* Sergei was right. Perez wouldn't be happy if he found out about this. Not at all.

I looked down at the suit, folded in my hands. It wasn't my property; it belonged to the Americans. I should probably put it back on the hanger and walk out of here. I wanted to get rid of it; why not let the Americans do it for me?

Except that if the Americans could have taken the suit out of the hotel, they would have already. All the exits were watched by Venezuelan drones with remote sensing gear. Anyone who tried to leave with the suit risked being spotted instantly.

The Americans weren't here for the suit. They were here for the data it contained. And now they had it.

I lifted the mask again, staring at the internal display. Not all the data, I realized.

*Transmit internal voice record YES/NO?*

I'd interrupted the data transfer before the suit could share the record of what I'd said while I was wearing it. Once the Americans had that, they'd know who I was. And if the Americans found out, how much longer before the AGRT found out?

I tightened my grip on the suit. I'd have to take it with me after all.

"I've identified myself," said the box. "Why don't you tell me who you are?"

*They're stalling,* I thought. *While they contact whoever they have in the building. Time to get out of here.*

With the cables detached, I was able to quickly finish rolling up the suit. Without any further hesitation, I stuffed it into a heavily creased shopping bag I found on the floor, making sure both gloves and the mask made it in as well. Then I stuck my head out the door. The hallway was deserted, for now.

I started moving, at a fast walk. I passed an open door about forty feet down the hall; from inside I heard music, the echoing refrain of Ghost Yummy's "Bang the Big Blue Box." A male voice was singing along, badly out of key.

As briskly as I could, I made my way to the back stairwell, taking a route that avoided all the cameras. Once there, I climbed six floors, then took the elevator the rest of the way to my floor.

When I opened the door to my room, Croaker came leaping joyously toward me. She did an excited dance and wouldn't stop jumping on me until I put a leash on her and took her out. I left the bag with the suit by the door.

In our brief circuit around the block, Croaker stopped to pee six times. As we returned to the front of the hotel, I spotted two men hustling out the front door. They looked anxious. They were looking in every direction at once, as if searching for someone or something. One of them gave me the once-over, his eyes hostile and alert. I returned his gaze with mild curiosity.

The other one was carrying a small bag. Sticking out of the bag were blue cables. The kind of cables that had connected the American combat suit to the telecom box.

A late-model sedan pulled up to the front of the hotel. As if responding to a signal, both men abandoned their search and headed to the car. The doors swung open as they neared. The men climbed inside and the car sped off.

Inside the lobby, the morning clerk handed me a sealed envelope. I tore it open. It was a handwritten letter from Mrs. Domeko, suggesting a time and place for our next meeting. She wanted my assistance investigating the disappearance of the Rajapakse robot colony. Well, why not? I was just as concerned as she was, and it would be good to have a determined and resourceful ally exploring the depths of that mystery. I scrawled a quick response, sealed it, and gave it to the clerk to have it delivered by courier.

Back in my room, I laid out coffee and some fruit. Mac would be by for breakfast in a few hours, and there didn't seem much point in trying to get to sleep before she arrived. I was very much looking forward to our long-postponed conversation. At long last, I was fully prepared to confess what I knew about her son, and how I had read her private message. Strangely, wonderfully, I felt no anxiety about my coming confession. My desire for Mac had been replaced by a desire to help her, pure and simple.

Well, maybe not all that pure. I couldn't get the memory of how she'd looked in the dress last night out of my head. And the way she'd whispered "*Good*" in my ear when I told her I wanted to talk this morning.

I was going to ask Mac out to dinner, and I thought there was a good chance she would say yes. Just the two of us, someplace where they still expected you to dress up. I was very much looking forward to that.

And if Anthony was alive, Black Winter and I were going to find him. I was sure of it.

Something else I was looking forward to, strange as it sounds? Visiting Zircon Border's porpoise pod in the Bay of Fundy next summer. I'd promised him I'd do it, and I intended to keep that promise. I had no intention of disappointing that giant hunk of metal. He's my friend.

As I straightened up my room, I found the suit right where I'd left it. I rolled it out on my bed, giving it a cursory inspection. I pulled the power cells out of my pocket, laying them next to the suit. It beeped appreciatively. Croaker, much calmer now that her bladder was empty, jumped up on the bed, sniffed the suit once, and then plopped down next to it, panting happily.

Doubtless I'd startled the Americans by stealing it right under their noses. I wasn't too surprised that they hightailed it out of here. I probably should feel a little guilty for reclaiming the suit, but I didn't. In all likelihood, the Americans would have destroyed it once they extracted the last of the data. It'd be too risky to try and sneak it out of the hotel, and they couldn't risk leaving it behind for the Venezuelans to find.

And even if they found some way to recover it, the suit wasn't much good without the power cells. I knew that from experience.

No, the Americans had gotten what they wanted from the suit. The kind of intel that would pay dividends for months. The kind that might very well change the course of the peace negotiations in Clarksville.

Hayduk and the Americans had both wanted the combat suit. But the Americans had shown much more patience and guile, and it had paid off. Good for them. They deserved whatever they'd extracted out of it. It would be very interesting to see how things unfolded in the next few months.

Right now there were two thousand additional AGRT soldiers on their way to Chicago, ostensibly to search for the American in the combat suit. They might make life a lot more difficult in the next few months. But strangely, the thought didn't really bother me. My eyes roamed over the suit. It lay on the bed, relaxed and waiting. Ready.

I'd told Sergei and Black Winter that I never wanted to see the suit again. But I guess that wasn't really true. Looking at it now, the thing that most came to mind was Sergei's casual observation in the bar last night.

*A man who has the drone jammer device, and the American combat suit . . .*

*That man can go anywhere, do anything.*

"What do you think, girl?" I asked Croaker as I scratched her head. "Do you think Sergei's right?"

Croaker barked softly.

"Yeah," I said. "Let's find out."

# ACKNOWLEDGMENTS

Novel writing, at least for me, is a lot like software design, in that success demands some pretty heavy beta testing. I don't think it's an exaggeration to say that I have the finest beta readers in the business, and their feedback improved my book immeasurably. They are Jim Seidman, Ed O'Neill, Howard Andrew Jones, Todd Ruthman, and especially Alice "it needs more robots" Dechene.

My editor, John Joseph Adams, has the finest storytelling sense in the industry — as well as extraordinary patience. John, you the man.

The first draft of this novel was written in hotel rooms while I commuted every week between Champaign, Illinois, and Chicago. I wrote one chapter per month, and on the second Thursday of every month I read those chapters to the welcoming and enthusiastic attendees of the Open Mic at Top Shelf Books in Palatine, Illinois. Do that long enough (in my case, from May 2006 to October 2012), and it turns out you end up with a novel.

The attendees of the Top Shelf Open Mic are the reason this book exists (and they are most definitely the reason Croaker made it all the way to the end — don't ever let authors tell you they can't be swayed by death threats). I owe them a great deal, and I want to acknowledge them here. They are Michael Penkas, Julie Barnett, Brendan Detzner, Jeanine Marie Vaughn, Janelle McHugh, Jeffrey Westhoff, Dennis Depcik, Tina Jens, Cynthia J. Glasson, Gene Wolfe, Joe Bonadonna, David C. Smith, Dave Munger, Shawna Flavell, Reina Hardy, and Megan Swanson. And especially Sally Tibbetts, Patty Templeton, Dave Michalak, Jahn Mitchell, Karin Thogersen, and Katie Redding.

Finally, and most significantly, I owe a huge debt of gratitude to Claire Suzanne Elizabeth Cooney, who coaxed this book out of me one chapter at a time. Her joy in the fellowship of writers, and her tenacity in bringing them together, helped nurture and inspire countless Chicago authors. I was one of them. Thank you, Claire.